QUEER

FRANK WYNNE is a (queer) literary translator, writer and editor.
He has translated numerous French and Hispanic authors including
Michel Houellebecq, Patrick Modiano, Javier Cercas and Virginie
Despentes. His work has earned him numerous prizes including
the IMPAC Dublin Literary Award, the Scott Moncrieff Prize and the
Premio Valle Inclán. Most recently, his translation of *Animalia* won
the 2020 Republic of Consciousness Prize. He previously edited
the anthology *Found in Translation*, collecting a hundred of
the finest translated stories from around the world.

Also in the anthology series

THE ART OF THE GLIMPSE
100 Irish Short Stories
Chosen by Sinéad Gleeson

**THE BIG BOOK OF CHRISTMAS
MYSTERIES**
100 of the Very Best Yuletide Whodunnits
Chosen by Otto Penzler

DEADLIER
*100 of the Best Crime Stories
Written by Women*
Chosen by Sophie Hannah

DESIRE
100 of Literature's Sexiest Stories
Chosen by Mariella Frostrup
and the *Erotic Review*

FOUND IN TRANSLATION
*100 of the Finest Short Stories
Ever Translated*
Chosen by Frank Wynne

FUNNY HA, HA
80 of the Funniest Stories Ever Written
Chosen by Paul Merton

GHOST
100 Stories to Read With the Lights On
Chosen by Louise Welsh

HOUSE OF SNOW
*An Anthology of the Greatest Writing
About Nepal*
Chosen by Ed Douglas

JACK THE RIPPER
*The Ultimate Compendium of
the Legacy and Legend of History's
Most Notorious Killer*
Chosen by Otto Penzler

LIFE SUPPORT
100 Poems to Reach for on Dark Nights
Chosen by Julia Copus

OF GODS AND MEN
100 Stories from Ancient Greece and Rome
Chosen by Daisy Dunn

QUEER
*A Collection of LGBTQ Writing
from Ancient Times to Yesterday*
Chosen by Frank Wynne

SHERLOCK
*Over 80 Stories Featuring
the Greatest Detective of all Time*
Chosen by Otto Penzler

THAT GLIMPSE OF TRUTH
100 of the Finest Short Stories Ever Written
Chosen by David Miller

THE TIME TRAVELLER'S ALMANAC
100 Stories Brought to You From the Future
Chosen by Jeff and Ann VanderMeer

THE STORY
100 Great Short Stories Written by Women
Chosen by Victoria Hislop

WE, ROBOTS
Artificial Intelligence in 100 Stories
Chosen by Simon Ings

THE WILD ISLES
*An Anthology of the Best of British
and Irish Nature Writing*
Chosen by Patrick Barkham

WILD WOMEN
*and their Amazing Adventures
Over Land, Sea & Air*
Chosen by Mariella Frostrup

QUEER

A Collection
of LGBTQ Writing
from Ancient Times
to Yesterday

CHOSEN BY

**FRANK
WYNNE**

An Apollo Book

First published in the UK in 2021 by Head of Zeus Ltd
This paperback edition published in 2025 by Head of Zeus Ltd,
part of Bloomsbury Publishing Plc

9 7 5 3 1 2 4 6 8

A catalogue record for this book is available from the British Library.

ISBN (PB) 9781035920334
ISBN (E) 9781789542332

Typeset by Adrian McLaughlin

Printed and bound in Great Britain by
CPI Group (UK) Ltd, Croydon CR0 4YY

FSC
www.fsc.org
MIX
Paper | Supporting
responsible forestry
FSC® C013604

Bloomsbury Publishing Plc
50 Bedford Square, London, WC1B 3DP, UK
Bloomsbury Publishing Ireland Limited,
29 Earlsfort Terrace, Dublin 2, D02 AY28, Ireland

HEAD OF ZEUS LTD
5–8 Hardwick Street
London EC1R 4RG

To find out more about our authors and books
visit www.headofzeus.com

For product safety related questions contact productsafety@bloomsbury.com

To Roz and her many avatars.

In memory of Jan Morris, writer, historian, pioneer of light and shade, of inner music.

CONTENTS

Introduction   xi

Homer   *from* The Iliad: *Achilles' Lament*   1

Sappho   *Three poems: Prayer to our Lady of*   4
                                 Paphos / I have not had one word
                                 from her / Afraid of Losing You

The Book of Samuel   *David and Jonathan*   8

Catullus   *Three poems: Sonnets 15, 80 and 99*   11

William Shakespeare   *Three poems: Sonnet 29,*   14
                                 Sonnet 87, Sonnet 126

Aphra Behn   *To the fair Clarinda*   17

Sor Juana Inés de la Cruz   *Inés, dear, with your love I am enraptured*   19

Anne Lister   *from the* Diaries of Anne Lister   21

Walt Whitman   *We Two Boys Together Clinging*   30

Emily Dickinson   *Her Breast is Fit for Pearls*   32

Paul Verlaine   *Sonnet to the Arsehole*   33
  and Arthur Rimbaud

Arthur Rimbaud   *Our Arses Are Not Theirs*   35

Oscar Wilde   *from "De Profundis"*   37

A. E. Houseman   *from* A Shropshire Lad: 43
                                 Look Not In My Eyes

Constantine Cavafy   *One Night*   45

Magnus Hirschfeld   *from* Berlin's Third Sex   46

Amy Lowell   *Three poems: Aubade / Carrefour/*   49
                                 Absence

Renée Vivien	*Three poems: The Latent Night / She Passes / Words to my Love*	52
Radclyffe Hall	*Miss Oglivy Finds Herself*	57
Virginia Woolf	*from* Orlando	77
Katherine Mansfield	*Friendship*	84
Marina Tsvetaeva	*Girlfriend* (Podruga)	86
Wilfred Owen	*Two poems: Music / To Eros*	90
Sylvia Townsend Warner	*Two poems: Since the first toss of gale that blew / Drawing you, heavy with sleep, to lie closer*	93
Federico García Lorca	*The Poet Speaks to his Love on the Telephone*	96
Karin Boye	*Everything Contains You*	98
Langston Hughes	*Blessed Assurance*	100
Valentine Ackland	*The Eyes of the Body*	106
Bruce Nugent	*Smoke, Lilies and Jade*	107
William Burroughs	*Lee and the Boys*	123
Ismat Chughtai	*The Quilt*	129
Jane Bowles	*Everything Is Nice*	139
Carson McCullers	*Like That*	146
Patricia Highsmith	*from* Carol / The Price of Salt	156
Pier Paolo Pasolini	*The Cry of the Excavator*	167
Allen Ginsberg	*Please Master*	186
Thom Gunn	*The Man with Night Sweats*	189
Audre Lorde	*Three poems: Never to Dream of Spiders / Love Poem / Afterlove*	191
Larry Kramer	*from* Faggots	196
Takahashi Mutsuo	*The Chair*	202
Reinaldo Arenas	*The Wedding*	230
Rita Mae Brown	*from* Rubyfruit Jungle	234
Armistead Maupin	*from* Michael Tolliver Lives: Confederacy of Survivors	244

Patrizia Cavalli	*To Simulate the Burning of the Heart*	253
Roz Kaveney	*Three poems (For my Trans Dyke Sisters / Cunt / Me Too)*	255
Hezy Leskly	*Three poems: Isaac / YAKANTALISA / Reuben and I*	259
Alan Hollinghurst	*Highlights*	264
Hervé Guibert	*A Man's Secrets*	280
Murathan Mungan	*Love's Tears, or, Rapunzel and the Drifter*	285
Colm Tóibín	*Three Friends*	305
Neil Bartlett	*Words*	323
Jeanette Winterson	*The Poetics of Sex*	334
Alison Bechdel	*Coming Out Story*	345
Rosie Garland	*You'll Do*	358
A.M. Homes	*A Real Doll*	371
Patrick Gale	*Brown Manilla*	392
Damon Galgut	*Shadows*	408
Philip Hensher	*A Chartist*	418
Tomoyuki Hoshino	*Air*	428
Yau Ching	*Five Poems*	443
A. Revathi	*from* The Truth About Me	451
Hida Viloria	*from* Born Both: *Going Public*	458
Qiu Miaojin	*from* Last Words from Montmartre: *Letter Fourteen*	471
Paul B. Preciado	*Letter from a Trans Man to the Sexual Ancien Régime*	475
Lawrence Schimel	*Handle with Bear*	480
Abdellah Taïa	*The Wounded Man*	494
John Better Armella	*The Brevity of Cigarettes*	502
Nicholas Wong	*Private Parts: Anti-Bodies*	507
Jacek Dehnel	*Fig. 370. Hunchback Due to Tuberculosis of the Spine*	509
Juno Dawson	*from* The Gender Games: *The Penny Drops*	511

Cat Fitzpatrick	*Six Women I'm Not*	521
Sergio Loo	*They Keep Killing Us*	527
Zhang Yueran	*Binary*	533
Keith Jarrett	*A Gay Poem / Emerging from Matter*	542
Kirsty Logan	*Underskirts*	549
Alma Mathijsen	*Forget the Girls*	559
Max Lobe	*The Avenging Whip*	569
Andrew McMillan	*Two poems: Screen / If it Wasn't for the Nights / A Gift*	575
Imogen Binnie	*I Met a Girl Named Bat Who Met Jeffrey Palmer*	579
Niviaq Korneliussen	*from* Crimson	593
Acknowledgements		602
Extended Copyright		604

INTRODUCTION

I began researching this anthology when I was eleven years old, after a fashion. I cannot precisely pinpoint the age at which I knew that I was 'different', that I was 'other', but the first inklings had come when I was seven. I knew-without-knowing that this difference was not something I should talk about openly, or even confide. It was a troubling wrinkle in an otherwise unremarkable childhood in a small village on the west coast of what many people still called Holy Catholic Ireland. In a world where the internet was still a lifetime away, where there were only two television channels, there was only one place I could search for misfits, eccentrics and loners. And so, at the age of eleven, without quite knowing what I was looking for, I began to scour the shelves of my local library for some sense of this otherness. With the hormone rush of later years and my first intimations of sex and sexuality came words to describe the otherness I felt: *bender*, *steamer*, *fairy*, *queer*. I still remember furtively borrowing a copy Mary Renault's *Fire from Heaven* tucked into a stack of literary classics, and I remember the prickle of cold sweat I felt as I stepped into my local bookshop to collect the copy of *A Boy's Own Story* I had dared to order. I was in my teens before I first saw the word 'gay' in print, and twenty when I first managed to say it aloud. By then, the library had tentatively reassured me that, however isolated I felt, I was not alone.

In the fifty years since the brick that triggered the Stonewall Riots was lobbed (according to legend, by the fearless trans activist Marsha P. Johnson, although she always insisted that she did not arrive until later that night), much has changed. The dogged and determined struggle of LGBT activists, writers, poets, politicians, actors and singers (and their friends and allies) has meant that in many countries, LGBT people are now afforded some protection, queer people are now more visible, in twenty-eight countries around the world they can now marry, in the media, gay, lesbian and trans authors can now write without fear of censorship. But even a cursory glance around the world makes it clear that the struggle is far from over: the slow shift towards equality has been met with a backlash: in the United Kingdom, LGBT hate crimes have more than trebled in recent years; in Russia the meagre rights of LGBT citizens have been trampled, in the United States, the rights of trans citizens are being systematically attacked. Meanwhile, in most of Africa and much of Asia, LGBT people still face persecution, criminalisation and, in some countries, even the death penalty. For many, to be queer or trans can still mean insurmountable solitude.

There is hope. In a passage from the luminous acceptance speech given by Pablo Neruda when he was awarded the Nobel Prize for literature:

> There is no insurmountable solitude. All paths lead to the same goal: to convey to others what we are. And we must pass through solitude and difficulty, isolation and silence in order to reach forth to the enchanted place where we can dance our clumsy dance and sing our sorrowful song – but in this dance or in this song there are fulfilled the most ancient rites of our conscience in the awareness of being human...

When I sat down to begin planning this book, I began to measure the scale of the task. The history of queer literature is filled with gaps, with silences. While the poems of Sappho were celebrated in her lifetime, while the great Arab poet Abu Nuwas could openly write poems about same-sex desire, for much of recorded history, queer voices have been smothered and suppressed. Many of those who dared to write did so in private. If this book were to encompass as many countries and cultures, as many eras and languages, as many divergent queer experiences as I hoped, it seemed sensible to include not only poems and short stories, but excerpts from diaries and memoirs, passages from novels and non-fiction – any text that I felt could stand alone and reveal a facet of the author or their character. As I began reading and drawing up an initial list, I also plugged into the hive mind via Twitter, Facebook groups, email and old-fashioned conversations over a pint down the pub, asking for suggestions from editors, writers, translators, poets and readers from every tone and shade of the queer rainbow. I was rewarded with hundreds of names – some of them familiar, but many from countries, even languages I knew only vaguely, if at all.

Every anthology is compiled according to an arbitrary set of rules. I settled on just two: the authors should be queer in the broadest sense. (While I have been powerfully moved by LGBT stories penned by cis/ straight writers, it seemed important that, between these covers at least, we should tell our own stories.) Secondly, I felt that the texts should address some aspect of gender and sexuality. This second rule has meant that, while many of the usual suspects are present and correct, even a casual reader will notice that notable LGBT writers like Somerset Maugham, Katherine Mansfield and Lorraine Hansberry are absent.

There remained the problem of how to decide who – historically – qualifies as *queer*. While representations of gay, lesbian and trans people can be found throughout the history of written literature, from Petronius' *Satyricon* to the hijras in the *Kama Sutra*, the concepts of sexual orientation and of gender identity are relatively recent. Did Catullus think of himself as queer? Was Shakespeare bisexual? Scholars have been wrangling about this for centuries. And what of Emily Dickinson, vituperatively dismissed as a 'scandalous spinster' and a 'virgin recluse'? Since there is no right answer to this question, I decided to be wrong creatively. I have included all of the above – not to mention passages from Homer and the Bible, where the very identity, let alone the sexuality of both authors and characters is at best doubtful. My rules are not hard and fast, but soft and languorous.

I spent considerably more time agonizing over two art forms I decided to exclude from this anthology. From the candid lyrics of Blues legends 'Ma' Rainey and Bessie Smith to the delicate punning of Cole Porter and Noël Coward to the brashness of Bowie and Bronski Beat, popular song arguably did more to champion queer folk than any art form in the twentieth century. Meanwhile, playwrights from Tennessee Williams to Lillian Hellman, Joe Orton to Sarah Daniels with an honorary mention to Mae West for the 1927 play *The Drag* (shut down for being obscene) were in the vanguard in their depiction of LGBT characters. The only excuse I have for excluding them is that they were not intended to be *read*; shorn of singer or actor, the words alone lose something of their power.

The two years I have spent preparing this anthology have been an exhilarating and intoxicating rollercoaster of laughter, tears and passion, of hours spent reading and making lists, of re-reading, whittling and remaking those lists – no doubt I was a source of endless frustration to my patient editors Clare and Christian. This is not an attempt to create a *definitive* collection – what collection can claim to be definitive? It could only ever hope be a selection of writings that were dazzling and different, poignant or pungent, a glimpse into the kaleidoscope of queer literature(s).

This, then, is my patchwork quilt. It ranges from Greece in the eighth century BC to Greenland in the twenty-first century. Although some writers will be familiar, and perhaps too many of the texts were written in English, it manages to span more than thirty countries, bounding across the globe from Israel to Equatorial Guinea, eighteenth-century China to modern Vietnam. In its pages love and loss, desire and lust, rage and grief, and – above all – some glimmer of hope. After a fashion, it is my homage to the writers who helped me survive, a tribute to the poets and the activists who inspired me, a salute to the new voices that every day join this curious polyphony. Above all, it is a celebration to those who have had the courage to follow the dictum of the glorious Harvey Fierstein, 'Never be bullied into silence. Never allow yourself to be made a victim. Accept no one's definition of your life; define yourself.'

FRANK WYNNE
London, 2020

ACHILLES' LAMENT

Homer (*c.*8th century BC)

Perhaps the greatest poet to never exist. While the *Iliad* and the
Odyssey – in countless translations – have had considerable influence
on western literature and poetry, there are no documentary records
of the life of the poet we refer to as Homer before Herodotus, in the
fourth century BC. While Homer never explicity states that the intense
bond between Achilles and Patroclus as sexual, they are described as
lovers by many writers of the Greek classical period. When Alexander
the Great passed through Troy on his Asian campaign, he is said to
have stood with his lover Hephaestion at the sacred tomb of Achilles
and Patroclus in front of the entire army, as a declaration of their
own relationship.

And he himself, mightily in his might, in the dust lay
at length, and took and tore at his hair with his hands, and defiled it.
And the handmaidens Achilleus and Patroklos had taken
captive, stricken at heart cried out aloud, and came running
out of doors about valiant Achilleus, and all of them
beat their breasts with their hands, and the limbs went slack in each
    of them.
On the other side Antilochos mourned with him, letting the tears fall,
and held the hands of Achilleus as he grieved in his proud heart,
fearing Achilleus might cut his throat with the iron. He cried out
terribly, aloud, and the lady his mother heard him
as she sat in the depths of the sea at the side of her aged father,
and she cried shrill in turn, and the goddesses gathered about her,

all who along the depth of the sea were daughters of Nereus.
For Glauke was there, Kymodokē and Thaleia,
Nesaie and Speio and Thoë, and ox-eyed Halia;
Kymothoë was there, Aktaia and Limnoreia,
Melitē and Iaira, Amphithoë and Agauë,
Doto and Proto, Dynamenē and Pherousa,
Dexamenē and Amphinomē and Kallianeira;
Doris and Panopē and glorious Galateia,
Nemertes and Apseudes and Kallianassa;
Klymenē was there, Ianeira and Ianassa,
Maira and Oreithyia and lovely-haired Amatheia,
and the rest who along the depth of the sea were daughters of Nereus.
The silvery cave was filled with these, and together all of them
beat their breasts, and among them Thetis led out the threnody:
"Hear me, Nereïds, my sisters; so you may all know
well all the sorrows that are in my heart, when you hear of them
    from me.
Ah me, my sorrow, the bitterness in this best of child-bearing,
since I gave birth to a son who was without fault and powerful,
conspicuous among heroes; and he shot up like a young tree,
and I nurtured him, like a tree grown in the pride of the orchard.
I sent him away with the curved ships into the land of Ilion
to fight with the Trojans; but I shall never again receive him
won home again to his country and into the house of Peleus.
Yet while I see him live and he looks on the sunlight, he has
sorrows, and though I go to him I can do nothing to help him.
Yet I shall go, to look on my dear son, and to listen
to the sorrow that has come to him as he stays back from the fighting."

    So she spoke, and left the cave, and the others together
went with her in tears, and about them the wave of the water
was broken. Now these, when they came to the generous Troad,
followed each other out on the seashore, where close together

the ships of the Myrmidons were hauled up about swift Achilleus.
There as he sighed heavily the lady his mother stood by him
and cried out shrill and aloud, and took her son's head in her arms, then
sorrowing for him she spoke to him in winged words: "Why then,
child, do you lament? What sorrow has come to your heart now?
Speak out, do not hide it. These things are brought to accomplishment
through Zeus: in the way that you lifted your hands and prayed for,
that all the sons of the Achaians be pinned on their grounded vessels
by reason of your loss, and suffer things that are shameful."

    Then sighing heavily Achilleus of the swift feet answered her:
"My mother, all these things the Olympian brought to accomplishment.
But what pleasure is this to me, since my dear companion has perished,
Patroklos, whom I loved beyond all other companions,
as well as my own life. I have lost him, and Hektor, who killed him,
has stripped away that gigantic armor, a wonder to look on
and splendid, which the gods gave Peleus, a glorious present,
on that day they drove you to the marriage bed of a mortal.
I wish you had gone on living then with the other goddesses
of the sea, and that Peleus had married some mortal woman.
As it is, there must be on your heart a numberless sorrow
for your son's death, since you can never again receive him
won home again to his country; since the spirit within does not drive me
to go on living and be among men, except on condition
that Hektor first be beaten down under my spear, lose his life
and pay the price for stripping Patroklos, the son of Menoitios."

Translated by Richmond Lattimore

SELECTED POEMS
Sappho (*c.*630–*c.*570 BC)

For a poet whose work survives only in a series of fragments, Sappho of Lesbos is now remembered chiefly for giving twin names to female homosexuality – Sapphic and Lesbian. In fact, her poetry followed established conventions of lesbian literature and society. Volcanically popular and prolific in her own time, her poems were neglected or actively suppressed in the Christian era. Only one complete poem survives amongst various fragments. Her lyrics would have originally been sung in public, but they would privately inspire countless future poets.

PRAYER TO OUR LADY OF PAPHOS

Dapple-throned Aphrodite,
eternal daughter of God,
snare-knitter! Don't, I beg you,

cow my heart with grief! Come,
as once when you heard my far-
off cry and, listening, stepped

from your father's house to your
gold car, to yoke the pair whose
beautiful thick-feathered wings

oaring down mid-air from heaven
carried you to light swiftly
on dark earth; then, blissful one,

smiling your immortal smile
you asked, What ailed me now that
me call you again? What

was it that my distracted
heart most wanted? "Whom has
Persuasion to bring round now

"to your love? Who, Sappho, is
unfair to you? For, let her
run, she will soon run after;

"if she won't accept gifts, she
will one day give them; and if
she won't love you—she soon will

"love, although unwillingly..."
If ever—come now! Relieve
this intolerable pain!

What my heart most hopes will
happen, make happen; you yourself join forces on my side!

I HAVE NOT HAD ONE WORD FROM HER

I have not had one word from her

Frankly I wish I were dead.
When she left, she wept

a great deal; she said to
me, "This parting must be
endured, Sappho. I go unwillingly."

I said, "Go, and be happy
but remember (you know
well) whom you leave shackled by love

"If you forget me, think
of our gifts to Aphrodite
and all the loveliness that we shared

"all the violet tiaras,
braided rosebuds, dill and
crocus twined around your young neck

"myrrh poured on your head
and on soft mats girls with
all that they most wished for beside them

"while no voices chanted
choruses without ours,
no woodlot bloomed in spring without song…"

AFRAID OF LOSING YOU

I ran fluttering
like a little girl
after her mother

Translated by Mary Barnard

DAVID AND JONATHAN

The Book of Samuel (*c.*630–540 BC)

One of the most important and influential works ever published in the English language – the *King James Bible*, the work of some sixty translators, expanded on the extraordinary translation by William Tyndale. The text does not explicitly define the nature of the relationship between David and Jonathan, which has been interpreted by some as as one of platonic love and some scholars, writers, and activists as one of romantic love.

1 SAMUEL 18:1–4

1 And it came to pass, when he had made an end of speaking unto Saul, that the soul of Jonathan was knit with the soul of David, and Jonathan loved him as his own soul.

2 And Saul took him that day, and would let him go no more home to his father's house.

3 Then Jonathan and David made a covenant, because he loved him as his own soul.

4 And Jonathan stripped himself of the robe that *was* upon him, and gave it to David, and his garments, even to his sword, and to his bow, and to his girdle.

17 And David lamented with this lamentation over Saul and over Jonathan his son:

18 (Also he bade them teach the children of Judah *the use of* the bow: behold, *it is* written in the book of Jasher.)

19 The beauty of Israel is slain upon thy high places: how are the mighty fallen!

20 Tell *it* not in Gath, publish *it* not in the streets of Askelon; lest the daughters of the Philistines rejoice, lest the daughters of the uncircumcised triumph.

21 Ye mountains of Gilboa, *let there be* no dew, neither *let there be* rain, upon you, nor fields of offerings: for there the shield of the mighty is vilely cast away, the shield of Saul, *as though he had* not *been* anointed with oil.

22 From the blood of the slain, from the fat of the mighty, the bow of Jonathan turned not back, and the sword of Saul returned not empty.

23 Saul and Jonathan *were* lovely and pleasant in their lives, and in their death they were not divided: they were swifter than eagles, they were stronger than lions.

24 Ye daughters of Israel, weep over Saul, who clothed you in scarlet, with *other* delights, who put on ornaments of gold upon your apparel.

25 How are the mighty fallen in the midst of the battle! O Jonathan, *thou wast* slain in thine high places.

26 I am distressed for thee, my brother Jonathan: very pleasant hast thou been unto me: thy love to me was wonderful, passing the love of women.

27 How are the mighty fallen, and the weapons of war perished!

SELECTED POEMS

Catullus (*c*.84–*c*.54 BC)

Many Roman poets celebrated homosexual love, but few more erotically and explicitly than Catullus in his "Odes". This would later pose a problem for Western Christian scholars, who lionised the Roman ideal of masculinity, while censoring descriptions of sexuality. Catullus's poems can be deeply erotic, loving and lyrical, but – typically of his time – he could also threaten opponents with aggressive sexual acts as a sign of masculinity.

15

I'd trust you friend with every love of mine,
for you have standards. Some things you regard
as pure, untouchable. I know it's hard.
But do not touch that boy. He is so fine.

I am not worried random passers-by
will want to fuck him. Too much on their minds.
Your prick though, wanders. Into cute behinds,
often as not. I know you say you're bi,

can take or leave boys. So leave him alone,
make an exception, just for me. For it
is certain that I'll punish you, you shit,
if you betray me. Then you will atone

strung up to be abused by all who pass
with spiny fish and carrots up your arse.

80

Most of the time your lips are ruby red,
Gellius, but then they're sort of flaky white,
a milk moustache when you're out late at night
or if you've spent the afternoon in bed
sharing a nap. There's gossip going round
that you suck lots of dicks. And don't wipe clean,
like a memento of just where you've been
with whom. All the penises you've found
neatly tucked under togas. While at home
poor little Victor is sitting alone
stirring a stockpot with a single bone
you galivant with half the men in Rome.
He strains to come and can't and wants to cry,
poor chap, you broke his balls and sucked them dry.

99

I jumped on you and kissed you—honey kiss—
while you were concentrating on your game.
I made you angry—we've not been the same
since—you were harsh to me. Your anger is

like being crucified. You wiped your lips
as if they had been spat on by some whore,
as if you didn't want me any more
not any scrap or drop. Chased me with whips

as if you were a Fury. Your mouth's taste
on mine changed from the softest sweetness to
the bitterness of aloes, myrhh or rue.
I think we're done, and that is such a waste.

For if my kissing you caused so much pain
I won't hurt you by kissing you again.

Translated by Roz Kaveney

SELECTED POEMS

William Shakespeare (1564–1616)

While his work has become the cornerstone of English literature, details of the private life of William Shakespeare are scant. We know that he married Ann Hathaway, with whom he had three children (and to whom he bequeathed his "second-best bed"). Scholars have relied on the sonnets to tease out information on the "Dark Lady", and of his sexuality, in the 126 sonnets addressed to the "Fair Youth" – the "master-mistress of my passion". While male beauty and passionate friendship were common subjects in the 16th century, there is a playful, punning homoeroticism in certain sonnets that belie a purely aesthetic interest.

SONNET 29

When, in disgrace with fortune and men's eyes,
I all alone beweep my outcast state,
And trouble deaf heaven with my bootless cries,
And look upon myself and curse my fate,
Wishing me like to one more rich in hope,
Featured like him, like him with friends possessed,
Desiring this man's art and that man's scope,
With what I most enjoy contented least;
Yet in these thoughts myself almost despising,
Haply I think on thee, and then my state,
(Like to the lark at break of day arising
From sullen earth) sings hymns at heaven's gate;
  For thy sweet love remembered such wealth brings
  That then I scorn to change my state with kings.

SONNET 87

Farewell! thou art too dear for my possessing,
And like enough thou know'st thy estimate,
The charter of thy worth gives thee releasing;
My bonds in thee are all determinate.
For how do I hold thee but by thy granting?
And for that riches where is my deserving?
The cause of this fair gift in me is wanting,
And so my patent back again is swerving.
Thy self thou gavest, thy own worth then not knowing,
Or me to whom thou gav'st it else mistaking;
So thy great gift, upon misprision growing,
Comes home again, on better judgement making.
    Thus have I had thee, as a dream doth flatter,
    In sleep a king, but waking no such matter.

SONNET 126

O thou, my lovely boy, who in thy power
Dost hold Time's fickle glass, his sickle, hour;
Who hast by waning grown, and therein showest
Thy lovers withering, as thy sweet self growest.
If Nature, sovereign mistress over wrack,
As thou goest onwards still will pluck thee back,
She keeps thee to this purpose, that her skill
May time disgrace and wretched minutes kill.
Yet fear her, O thou minion of her pleasure!
She may detain, but not still keep, her treasure:
Her audit (though delayed) answered must be,
And her quietus is to render thee.

TO THE FAIR CLARINDA

Aphra Behn (1640–1689)

The English playwright, poet and translator began her career working as a spy for the court of Charles II in Antwerp. After a series of unsuccessful and financially ruinous liaisons, Behn devoted herself to literature. Her satirical, sexual works scandalised the very circles where she may have found patronage, but the paying revelled in her carnal humour. Her final work, *Oroonoko: The Royal Slave*, is often credited with inaugurating the modern novel and injecting a seed of anti-slavery sentiment into England's literati.

WHO MADE LOVE TO ME,
IMAGIN'D MORE THAN WOMAN
Fair lovely Maid, or if that Title be
Too weak, too Feminine for Nobler thee,
Permit a Name that more Approaches Truth:
And let me call thee, Lovely Charming Youth.
This last will justifie my soft complainte,
While that may serve to lessen my constraint;
And without Blushes I the Youth persue,
When so much beauteous Woman is in view
Against thy Charms we struggle but in vain
With thy deluding Form thou giv'st us pain,
While the bright Nymph betrays us to the Swain.
In pity to our Sex sure thou wer't sent,
That we might Love, and yet be Innocent:
For sure no Crime with thee we can commit;

Or if we shou'd – thy Form excuses it.
For who, that gathers fairest Flowers believes
A Snake lies hid beneath the Fragrant Leaves.

   Thou beauteous Wonder of a different kind,
Soft *Cloris* with the dear *Alexis* join'd;
When e'er the Manly part of thee, wou'd plead
Thou tempts us with the Image of the Maid,
While we the noblest Passions do extend
The Love to *Hermes*, *Aphrodite* the Friend.

INÉS, DEAR, WITH YOUR LOVE I AM ENRAPTURED

Sor Juana Inés de la Cruz (1648–1695)

The writer, philosopher, composer and poet was born and raised in New Spain (now Mexico). At seventeen she joined The Carmelites Order, where she filled her nun's cell with thousands of books and enjoyed a vibrant, social life and that involved intimate relationships with a number of women. Though a controversial figure in her lifetime, her life and work had considerable influence on Liberation Theology and Latin-American feminism. She remains an icon for many of Mexico's LGBT Catholics.

Inés, dear, with your love I am enraptured
and as object of your love, I am enthralled;
when gazing on your beauty I am captured,
but when I find you jealous, I want to bawl.
I die of jealousy if others you entangle;
I tremble at your grace, your step sublime
because I know, Inés, that you could mangle
the humours of my systematic chime.
When I hold your dainty hand I am aquiver;
in your anger, feel that I must soon expire;
if you venture from your home I am adither,
so I say, Inés, to one thing I aspire:

that your love and my good wine will draw you hither,
and to tumble you to bed I can conspire.

Translated by Margaret Sayers Peden

THE DIARIES OF ANNE LISTER

Anne Lister (1791–1840)

Often called the West's "first modern lesbian" for candidly accepting her attraction to women, Lister was nonetheless persecuted for her sexuality during her lifetime. Known to her lover as "Fred", and to citizens of Halifax as "Gentleman Jack", her literary legacy comprises a long, detailed series of diaries together with many private letters, running to almost a million words – much of it written in code (a combination of algebra and Ancient Greek). The diaries were finally decoded in the 1930s by a relative, John Lister and his friend Arthur Burrell. Although he rejected advice to burn the records.

THURSDAY 11 NOV.
Mrs Barlow allows Anne some success

Breakfast at 9–35. Mrs Barlow came at 10–10, ready to go out shopping immediately. Asked her to sit down for one minute & we sat lovemaking till ten minutes before twelve. Went to a shop in the Rue Neuve St Roch (not far from here) & bought 4 ells each of cambric at 18 francs per ell, Mrs Barlow to hem me 6 handkerchiefs. Got back at 12¾. Found Mme Galvani waiting for me. Spent all the time in conversation. She left me at 2–10. Then immediately came Mrs Barlow to go out again. She jumped on the window seat to see if it rained. I locked the door as usual, then lifted her down and placed her on my knee. By & by she said, 'Is the door fast?' I, forgetting, got up to see, then took her again on my knee

& there she sat till four & threequarters, when Mlle de Sans sent to ask if I could receive. [I] told the maid I was sorry, I could not, I had got so bad a headache. The fact was I was heated & in a state not fit to see anyone. I had kissed & pressed Mrs Barlow on my knee till I had had a complete fit of passion. My knees & thighs shook, my breathing & everything told her what was the matter. She said she did me no good. I said it was a little headache & I should go to sleep. I then leaned on her bosom &, pretending to sleep, kept pottering about & rubbing the surface of her queer. Then made several gentle efforts to put my hand up her petticoats which, however, she prevented. But she so crossed her legs & leaned against me that I put my hand over & grubbled her on the outside of her petticoats till she was evidently a little excited, & it was from this that Mlle de Sans' maid roused us. Mrs Barlow had once whispered, holding her head on my shoulder, a word or two which, I think, were, 'Do you love me?' But I took no notice, still pretending to be asleep. She afterwards said once or twice, 'It is good to pretend to be asleep,' & then once, while I was grubbling pretty strongly, 'You know you pinch me.' From this she never attempted to escape. Before, when rubbing her in front, she had every now & then held my hand but always let me have it back again. After Mlle de Sans' maid roused us, she [drew] her chair close to the bed. I sat on the bed & partly knelt on one knee so as to have her quite close & she began to reproach herself, saying she was a poor, weak creature & what should I think of her. I protested love & respect. Said it was all my fault & I would be miserable if she was too severe to herself. 'Can you not love me one little bit for all the great deal I love you? If you do not love me, I cannot forgive you. You are too cruel thus to sport with the feelings of another – but if you do love me, I am happy.' 'What do you think?' said she. 'Oh,' I replied, 'that you do.' She answered that if she did not love me she could not have done as she did. I kissed her mouth several times when it was a little open & rather warmly. Just before she left she said she was a little tired. I asked why. She answered because her feelings had been excited. She told me she had always kept all others at a great distance. I said I did not doubt it for if she could keep me at a distance under present circumstances, she certainly could others when not so tried. I said she frightened me. She had talked to me before we went out this morning about settling near Southampton with the widow of her husband's oldest brother, General Barlow, who was also her aunt, her mother's sister & about fifty. She had a son & daughter grown up. Dinner at 5½. Saying I had a headache, came upstairs immediately after dinner… Mrs Barlow came at 10¼ &… staid with me till 11¾. She looked a little grave, as if half-ashamed & wondering how I should treat her. I was very respectful tho' affectionate. Said I had fancied I had much to say to her but all seemed gone & I had not a word to say. I was happy, yet could cry like a child if I chose, little as this was ever my custom. She said this would better suit her. I denied this. Asked her to sit on my knee. She refused, saying she did me harm. I still entreated & she yielded on my promise to behave well. I wished she could remain with me. Instead of expressing any objection, she said, 'But as it is impossible, I had better go,' & then went. Now that the ice was a little broken, what will it end in? Has she any hope of attaching me really? She is sufficiently yielding. [On my] saying to Mme Galvani that she was pretty, 'No, not at all,' said she, 'beaucoup plus laide que moi' ['uglier than me'], & that she looked eight & thirty. Her skin & complexion were bad. I thought of all this when kissing her & thought it would not do for always… Said Mrs Barlow [earlier], 'Go to bed early. Do not write tonight.' I answered, 'I have not much to write. No need of it. I can remember today without writing.'

FRIDAY 12 NOV.
Mrs Barlow and Anne understand each other

Dinner at 5–40. Mrs Barlow & I went up together immediately from table into her room where we sat very cozily till 8–35, when (Mrs Barlow not liking to go down) I went by myself & joined the party in the drawing room till 10 & then returned to Mrs Barlow & sat with her till 11–40, when I came up to bed. Loverlike as usual. No recurrence to yesterday that she disliked. She sat cutting out my pocket handkerchief. I said how much happier I was within these few days. I was now assured I was not indifferent to her & that the distance at which she chose to keep me was less the result of inclination than of what she deemed propriety. She did not contradict this. Her manner acknowledged, I maintained, that my very folly was the effect of everything she wished, tho' not itself what she wished. It did not spring from regard so unworthy her acceptance as she imagined. She said she wondered how I could like an old woman as she was. I said if she really thought this, I only hoped it was an argument in favour of what I had just said about my regard. She was not passé, not old, to me – yet, still, it could not be the bloom of youth or beauty that I loved her for. In stooping over her, the waist of my new gown hung off a little. She put her hand down on the left side, almost touching the nipple of the breast, evidently wishing to feel it. She felt the stuffing but made no remark. I let her do it, observing I should hope to do the same. She did not much notice this but with a half no. She said it looked as if ready for anyone. I said for no one but herself, but she might do anything. She said others might who liked. 'No,' said I, 'I do what I like but never permit them to do so.' This seemed to please her. She still fancies Marianna likes me. Tonight [she] insinuated what might have passed [between Anne & Marianna], saying, 'But of course you would never tell me.' I turned this off dexterously as usual & I think, considering Marianna's marriage, she feels unwillingly constrained to believe me. I kissed her neck over her habit-shirt. She said she was all skin & bone now, her pillows were gone. I said she satisfied me. She afterwards drew her shawl close round her saying, as she found me a little empassioned, I did myself harm. She did not like to see me in that state. I kissed her lips & forehead several times & on coming away put my tongue a very little into her mouth. She said, tho' without the least appearance of anger, that I had forgotten myself. I said it was much more difficult to forget myself a little than to remember myself so well, meaning that I had not forgotten myself much – might easily have done more. She begins to stand closer to me. I might easily press queer to queer. Our liking each other is now mutually understood and acknowledged. I asked her this morning how much she thought I liked her. She said as much as contented her & that was not a little. She would not refuse sleeping with me if we could manage it well – & then – & then...

SATURDAY 13 NOV.

Anne explains her sexuality to Mrs Barlow

At 2–20 went down to Mrs Barlow, meaning to go out. She thought it would be too much for her. I therefore sat with her till 4–35. Love-making, vindicating style of conversation respecting myself. A great pickle. 'Scaped my maid & got away among the workpeople. My father was one year in the Militia. When my mother thought I was safe I was running out in an evening. Saw curious scenes, bad women, etc. Then went to the Manor school & became attached to Eliza Raine. Said how it [Anne's preference for, or sexual attraction to, women] was all nature. Had it not been genuine the thing would have been different. [I] said I had thought much, studied anatomy, etc. Could not find it out. Could not understand myself. It was all the effect of the mind. No exterior formation accounted for it. Alluded to their being an internal correspondence or likeness of some of the male or female organs of generation. Alluded to the stones not slipping thro' the ring till after birth, etc. She took all this very well. I said ladies could often hear from a man what they could not from a woman & she could from me what she could not from Mrs Mackenzie. She allowed this, saying it depended on how she loved them. Got on the subject of Saffic [*sic*] regard. [I] said there was artifice in it. It was very different from mine & would be no pleasure to me. I liked to have those I loved near me as possible, etc. Asked if she understood. She said no. [I] told her I knew by her eyes she did & she did not deny it, therefore I know she understands all about the use of a —— [The word is not entered in the journal]. Alluded to self-pollution, how much it was practised. Thought my connection with the ladies more excusable than this. She declared she had never heard of this (I was incredulous at heart). From one thing to another. Got to tell her that the business of Thursday was exhausting beyond measure, as it always was to excite & then disappoint nature. Said if a man loved his wife as he ought, he could say anything to her & indelicacy depended on their own minds. Many things might pass between them without indelicacy that might otherwise be shocking. She agreed, tho' I hinted at things – sometimes having no night-shift at all for a little while. She said if I wore men's clothes she should feel differently. She could not then sit on my knee. If my father had brought me up as a son she would have married me as I am, had I stated my case to her alone, even tho' she had had rank & fortune & been nineteen & at that age she was well worth having. I thanked her. Happening to say I often told my uncle & aunt how I longed to have someone with me, she wondered what they would think of the person. I said my aunt knew nothing about it, nor would my uncle think anything. Then, expressing my wish to have her, she answered, 'But we have had no priest but love. Do you not know the quotation?' I did not yet I said yes. Kissed her repeatedly, rather warmly. We get on gradually. Perhaps I shall have her yet before I go. [I] told her, when speaking of Eliza [Raine], we had once agreed to go off together when of age but my conduct first delayed it & then circumstances luckily put an end to it altogether. Said I had never mentioned this to any human being but herself. At this moment [of writing the journal], I half-fancy I long since told it to Marianna. At 4–35, ran off to the Rue St Honoré for some more flowers. The flower-woman gone, told the porter to get me 2 *very* pretty bouquets, one for Mme de Boyve... the other for Mrs Barlow. Did not dress. Sat down to dinner at 5. Immediately on leaving table went with Mrs Barlow to her room & sat with her from 5–50 to 8. Then dressed. Had the hairdresser after her & paid him 2 francs for making me a terrible grenadier-like looking figure. Mrs Barlow with me here ½ hour & we then went down to the party at 9–10. Perhaps about 70 people. They danced quadrilles (in the drawing room, we all sitting round – 3 card tables in the room next to us & all the gents who were not dancing) & waltzes. Mme de Boyve & sometimes Mlle de Sans playing on the piano, which was all the music they had. The ladies looked by no means all of them first-rate. The gents appeared most the best of the 2. Mrs Williams, of ridiculous notoriety at Bath in 1813 for dancing cotillons with her monkey-faced husband, etc., formerly Mrs Briscoe, wife to the Governor of St Helena of that name – a dashing person risen, I fancy, from nothing – was here tonight & danced, too, at the close of the evening in the same set with her daughter… Tea, bread & butter, & a few sweet cakes. Afterwards, tumbler glasses of common wine & what looked like milk & water. The cakes we had at tea – very indifferent. All the gents held their common round hats in their hands tho' it was professedly a ball – only putting them down while they danced. Mrs Barlow having asked me whether I would have her dance or not, I said no, & she refused, tho' I think with some regrets at doing so &, M. Bellevue, etc., quizzing her, at last I told him it was I would not let her dance. She had a daughter 14. It was time mama gave up dancing. It might do for a Frenchwoman but not for an Englishwoman. She and I left the room at 12–10 & I went into her room & sat with her ½ hour, lovemaking. Kissed her neck. She would have me stay no longer. 'Go,' said she, 'remember the servants. Perhaps they do not love each other as we do.' I rallied her on having said *we*. 'Ah,' said she, 'I hoped you would not notice it.' I perpetually expressed my wish to stay all night with her. She says nothing against it. She said tonight, 'Now sit down & compose yourself. You look poorly,' meaning empassioned. She told me before dinner I had given her a warm look the first morning she had come to call on me & she had remembered it ever since & always liked me.

SUNDAY 14 NOV.
Mrs Barlow realises she has 'gone too far'

Mrs Barlow came to me & staid till 4–50. Sat talking for some time. It did me harm to sit on my knee. It was all for my sake she refused.

At last she consented. Sapphic love was again mentioned. I spoke rather more plainly. It was something Mrs Middleton had said that had made her comprehend what I had said about artifice [the use of a phallus?]. I mentioned the girl at a school in Dublin that had been obliged to have surgical aid to extract the thing. Said boys learnt much vice, too, at school – the practice of Onanism, etc. She said the warm look she had said so struck her the first time she had called on me was directed to her bosom. From little to more. [I] became rather excited. Felt her breasts & queer a little. Tried to put my hand up her petticoat but she prevented. Touched her flesh just above the knee twice. I kissed her warmly & held her strongly. She said what a state I was putting myself into. She got up to go away & went to the door. I followed. Finding she lingered a moment, pressed her closely & again tried to put my hand up her petticoats. Finding that she would not let me do this but still that she was a little excited, I became regularly so myself. I felt her grow warm & she let me grubble & press her tightly with my left hand whilst I held her against the door with the other, all the while putting my tongue into her mouth & kissing her so passionately as to excite her not a little, I am sure. When it was over she put her handkerchief to her eyes &, shedding a few tears, said, 'You are used to these things. I am not.' I remonstrated against this, declaring I was not so bad as one thought me & injustice like this would make me miserable, etc. She blamed herself, saying she was a poor, weak creature. I conjured her not to blame herself. It was all my fault. I loved her with all my heart & would do anything for her. Asked her if she loved me a little bit. 'You know I do,' said she. I still therefore pressed her to let me in tomorrow before she was up, when Mrs Page [Mrs Barlow's servant] was gone with Miss Barlow to school. She would not promise. Asked me what I would do. I said teach her to love me better. Insinuated we had now gone too far to retract & she might as well admit me. In fact, she herself put this into my head by saying I had gone down this morning just before breakfast, when she would not let me in, because I knew Page was away, gone for Miss Barlow. I took the hint. Said I did not like Page's always being there. Said

Mrs Barlow, 'When I am alone it is very well for then she guards me & nobody can say anything against me.' I took no notice but this speech struck me in consequence of all I have heard from Mme de Boyve. On leaving me, her face looked hot, her hair out of curl & herself languid, exactly as if after a connection had taken place... [After dinner] met Mrs Barlow at the door [of Anne's room]... I saw Cordingley smile (but took no notice) when I said she [Mrs Barlow] must come for a few minutes. I said 10, & [she] replied, but my minutes were always so long. However, she came & staid 20 minutes with me – of her own accord sitting on my knee. She looked low & said she was tired. She shed a tear or two & blamed [herself]. I said she would make me miserable & could she do so? 'Oh, no,' said she. 'I wish you were always quiet. I want no more.' I begged to be admitted tomorrow & she spoke as if, tho' she would not promise, she would not refuse. It came out this evening that she liked me for my pride. She used to have much. Now she ought not.

WE TWO BOYS TOGETHER CLINGING

Walt Whitman (1819–1892)

"Do I contradict myself? Very well, then I contradict myself, I am large, I contain multitudes." His poetry is characterised by torrential verse lines, shamanic visions of social utopia and expansive love for American people. For Whitman, homosexuality was one unequivocal manifestation of love – a divine expression of earthly pleasure. His greatest work, the endlessly-revised "Leaves of Grass" was considered scandalous when first published, and the scandal did not abate through its subsequent nine editions. The candid sexuality of the poems and the explicit homoeroticism led academics to label his work "obscene" and "too sensual." When directly asked whether his "Calamus" poems were homosexual, Whitman chose not to respond.

We two boys together clinging,
One the other never leaving,
 Up and down the roads going, North and South excursions making,
  Power enjoying, elbows stretching, fingers clutching,
 Arm'd and fearless, eating, drinking, sleeping, loving.
  No law less than ourselves owning, sailing, soldiering, thieving,
   threatening,

Misers, menials, priests alarming, air breathing,
water drinking, on
    the turf or the sea-beach dancing,
    Cities wrenching, ease scorning, statutes
mocking, feebleness chasing,
    Fulfilling our foray.

WALT WHITMAN (1819–1892)

HER BREAST IS FIT FOR PEARLS

Emily Dickinson (1830–1886)

If Dickinson's sister had respected her dying wishes, almost the entirety of her 765 poems would have been burned and she would be completely unknown. Little is known of her personal life, or her sexuality. Her few relationships were epistolary – notable among them was the one with Susan Gilbert, with whom Dickinson exchanged passionate love letters.

Her breast is fit for pearls,
But I was not a "Diver"—
Her brow is fit for thrones
But I have not a crest.
Her heart is fit for home—
I – a Sparrow – build there
Sweet of twigs and twine
My perennial nest.

SONNET TO THE ARSEHOLE

Paul Verlaine (1844–1896) and Arthur Rimbaud (1854–1891)

A man of contrasts and contradictions, Paul Verlaine was a civil servant who later served in the army of the Third Republic. His delicate, allusive poems belie a tempestuous personal life. He was abusive to his wife out of contempt, and abandoned her and their children for the young poet Arthur Rimbaud, whom he later shot in a jealous rage. In prison, he re-converted to Catholicism. His later years were spent teaching in English grammar schools. He died destitute, but is today widely revered as one of the icons of the Symbolist movement.

Dark and puckered as a puce carnation
It breathes, meekly lurking amid the moss
Still moist with a love trickling into the crevasse
Of pale buttocks and deep into the temptation.

Pale filaments of a milky essence
Have freely flowed, against the fierce wind's fray
Through small clumps here and there of reddish clay
To vanish deep down where that slope beckons.

How oft my Dream has come and kissed this cleft;
My soul, of rightful coitus bereft,
Made it a musky pit of sobs and tears

It is the rapt olive, the tender flute,
Of heavenly praline, the brimming chute,
A feminal Eden rimmed round with smears.

Translated by Frank Wynne and Jeffery Zuckerman

OUR ARSES ARE NOT THEIRS

Arthur Rimbaud (1854–1891)

A poet who has inspired Jim Morrison and Patti Smith, Arthur Rimbaud was the epitome of an artistic rebel. He burst onto the Paris literary scene at the age of sixteen, having already penned the masterpiece "The Drunken Boat" and embarked on a violent and tempestuous relationship with Paul Verlaine. Having written two of the defining works of the 19th century – A *Season in Hell* and *The Illuminations* – he abandoned writing at the age of twenty-one, and spent many years as a mercenary and an arms dealer.

Our arses are not theirs. So often I'd leer
At men unbuttoned behind some bramble,
And, in those shameless baths where youth gambols,
observe the curve and effect of our rear.

Firmer, in men, and often pale, our spheres
are formed of rugged planes, furred and tangled;
in women, only within these spangled
clefts do such bushy silken plaits appear.

A poignant and astounding touch of guile
Only seen in angels of holy pictures
Mimics the dimple fashioned by a smile.
Oh! To be nude, seek out joy and pleasure,

Each turned to face the other's true glory,
Free to murmur and to sob in equal measure?

Translated by Jeffery Zuckerman and Frank Wynne

DE PROFUNDIS
Oscar Wilde (1854–1900)

Saint Oscar's position in the pantheon of gay writers owes as much, if not more to the tragedy of his life as to his writings. A leading figure of the aesthetic movement, Wilde led a dual life – publicly he was a husband and father, the author of a series of dazzling, witty, caustic plays and the darling of London social circles, but he spent his more private moments "feasting with panthers", engaged in tempestuous and passionate relationships with young men. At the height of his career, his love for Bosie (Lord Alfred Douglas) would see him dragged through the courts in three separate trials which culminated in being sentenced to two years hard labour. The ordeal prompted the most passionate public love letter, *De Profundis*. He died in penury in Paris.

Dear Bosie,

After long and fruitless waiting I have determined to write to you myself, as much for your sake as for mine, as I would not like to think that I had passed through two long years of imprisonment without ever having received a single line from you, or any news or message even, except such as gave me pain.

Our ill-fated and most lamentable friendship has ended in ruin and public infamy for me, yet the memory of our ancient affection is often with me, and the thought that loathing, bitterness and contempt should for ever take that place in my heart once held by love is very sad to me: and you yourself will, I think, feel in your heart that to write to me as I lie in the loneliness of prison-life is better than to publish my letters without my permission or to dedicate poems to me unasked, though the world will know nothing of whatever words of grief or passion, of remorse or indifference you may choose to send as your answer or your appeal....

But most of all I blame myself for the entire ethical degradation I allowed you to bring on me. The basis of character is will-power, and my will-power became absolutely subject to yours. It sounds a grotesque thing to say, but it is none the less true. Those incessant scenes that seemed to be almost physically necessary to you, and in which your mind and body grew distorted and you became a thing as terrible to look at as to listen to: that dreadful mania you inherit from your father, the mania for writing revolting and loathsome letters: your entire lack of any control over your emotions as displayed in your long resentful moods of sullen silence, no less than in the sudden fits of almost epileptic rage: all these things in reference to which one of my letters to you, left by you lying about at the Savoy or some other hotel and so produced in Court by your father's Counsel, contained an entreaty not devoid of pathos, had you at that time been able to recognise pathos either in its elements or its expression: – these, I say, were the origin and causes of my fatal yielding to you in your daily increasing demands. You wore one out. It was the triumph of the smaller over the bigger nature. It was the case of that tyranny of the weak over the strong which somewhere in one of my plays I describe as being "the only tyranny that lasts."

And it was inevitable. In every relation of life with others one has to find some moyen de vivre. In your case, one had either to give up to you or to give you up. There was no alternative. Through deep if misplaced affection for you: through great pity for your defects of temper and temperament: through my own proverbial good-nature and Celtic laziness: through an artistic aversion to coarse scenes and ugly words: through that incapacity to bear resentment of any kind which at that time characterised me: through my dislike of seeing life made bitter and uncomely by what to me, with my eyes really fixed on other things, seemed to be mere trifles too petty for more than a moment's thought or interest – through these reasons, simple as they may sound, I gave up to you always. As a natural result, your claims, your efforts at domination, your exactions grew more and more unreasonable. Your meanest motive, your lowest appetite, your most common passion, became to you laws by which the lives of others were to be guided always, and to which, if necessary, they were to be without scruple sacrificed. Knowing that by making a scene you could always have your way, it was but natural that you should proceed, almost unconsciously I have no doubt, to every excess of vulgar violence. At the end you did not know to what goal you were hurrying, or with what aim in view. Having made your own of my genius, my will-power, and my fortune, you required, in the blindness of an inexhaustible greed, my entire existence. You took it. At the one supremely and tragically critical moment of all my life, just before my lamentable step of beginning my absurd action, on the one side there was your father attacking me with hideous card left at my club, on the other side there was you attacking me with no less loathsome letters. The letter I received from you on the morning of the day I let you take me down to the Police Court to apply for the ridiculous warrant for your father's arrest was one of the worst you ever wrote, and for the most shameful reason. Between you both I lost my head. My judgment forsook me. Terror took its place. I saw no possible escape, I may say frankly, from either of you. Blindly I staggered as an ox into the shambles. I had made a gigantic psychological error. I had always thought that my giving up to you in small things meant nothing: that when a great moment arrived I could reassert my will-power in its natural superiority. It was not so. At the great moment my will-power completely failed me. In life there is really no small or great thing. All things are of equal value and of equal size....

You send me a very nice poem, of the undergraduate school of verse, for my approval: I reply by a letter of fantastic literary conceits [reproduced above]: I compare you to Hylas, or Hyacinth, Jonquil or Narcisse, or someone whom the great god of Poetry favoured, and honoured with his love. The letter is like a passage from one of Shakespeare's sonnets, transposed to a minor key. It can only be understood by those who have read the Symposium of Plato, or caught the spirit of a certain grave mood made beautiful for us in Greek marbles. It was, let me say frankly, the sort of letter I would, in a happy if wilful moment, have written to any graceful young man of either University who had sent me a poem of his own making, certain that he would have sufficient wit or culture to interpret rightly its fantastic phrases. Look at the history of that letter! It passes from you into the hands of a loathsome companion: from him to a gang of blackmailers: copies of it are sent about London to my friends, and to the manager of the theatre where my work is being performed: every construction but the right one is put on it: Society is thrilled with the absurd rumours that I have had to pay a huge sum of money for having written an infamous letter to you: this forms the basis of your father's worst attack: I produce the original letter myself in Court to show what it really is: it is denounced by your father's Counsel as a revolting and insidious attempt to corrupt Innocence: ultimately it forms part of a criminal charge: the Crown takes it up: The Judge sums up on it with little learning and much morality: I go to prison for it at last. That is the result of writing you a charming letter....

There is, I know, one answer to all that I have said to you, and that is that you loved me: that all through those two and a half years during which the Fates were weaving into one scarlet pattern the threads of our divided lives you really loved me. Yes: I know you did. No matter what your conduct to me was I always felt that at heart you really did love me. Though I saw quite clearly that my position in the world of Art, the interest my personality had always excited, my money, the luxury in which I lived, the thousand and one things that went to make up a life so charmingly, and so wonderfully improbable as mine was, were, each and all of them, elements that fascinated you and made you cling to me; yet besides all this there was something more, some strange attraction for you: you loved me far better than you loved anybody else. But you, like myself, have had a terrible tragedy in your life, though one of an entirely opposite character to mine. Do you want to learn what it was? It was this. In you Hate was always stronger than Love. Your hatred of your father was of such stature that it entirely outstripped, o'erthrew, and overshadowed your love of me. There was no struggle between them at all, or but little; of such dimensions was your Hatred and of such monstrous growth. You did not realise that there is no room for both passions in the same soul. They cannot live together in that fair carven house. Love is fed by the imagination, by which we become wiser than we know, better than we feel, nobler than we are: by which we can see Life as a whole: by which, and by which alone, we can understand others in their real as in their ideal relations. Only what is fine, and finely conceived, can feed Love. But anything will feed Hate. There was not a glass of champagne you drank, not a rich dish you ate of in all those years, that did not feed your Hate and make it fat. So to gratify it, you gambled with my life, as you gambled with my money, carelessly, recklessly, indifferent to the consequence. If you lost, the loss would not, you fancied, be yours. If you won, yours you knew would be the exultation, and the advantages of victory....

You see that I have to write your life to you, and you have to realise it. We have known each other now for more than four years. Half of the time we have been together: the other half I have had to spend in prison as the result of our friendship. Where you will receive this letter, if indeed it ever reaches you, I don't know. Rome, Naples, Paris, Venice, some beautiful city on sea or river, I have no doubt, holds you. You are surrounded, if not with all the useless luxury you had with me, at any rate with everything that is pleasurable to eye, ear, and taste. Life is quite lovely to you. And yet, if you are wise, and wish to find Life much lovelier still and in a different manner you will let the reading of this terrible letter – for such I know it is – prove to you as important a crisis and turning-point of your life as the writing of it is to me. Your pale face used to flush easily with wine or pleasure. If, as you read what is here written, it from time to time becomes scorched, as though by a furnace-blast, with shame, it will be all the better for you. The supreme vice is shallowness. Whatever is realised is right....

You came to me to learn the Pleasure of Life and the Pleasure of Art.

Perhaps I am chosen to teach you something much more wonderful, the meaning of Sorrow, and its beauty.

Your affectionate friend
    Oscar Wilde

LOOK NOT IN MY EYES

A. E. Houseman (1859–1936)

Born in Worcestershire, Houseman studied classics and wrote extensively about Latin Roman poetry. He is best known for the cycle of poems *A Shropshire Lad*, which adopts a mock-pastoral style, though the homoerotic allusions saw it rejected by publishers, forcing him to fund the first publication of the collection himself. Although it had only moderate success in his lifetime, it proved an inspiration to English musicians and poets before World War I, and has been continuously in print since its first publication.

XV

Look not in my eyes, for fear
   They mirror true the sight I see,
And there you find your face too clear
   And love it and be lost like me.
One the long nights through must lie
   Spent in star-defeated sighs,
But why should you as well as I
   Perish? gaze not in my eyes.

A Grecian lad, as I hear tell,
   One that many loved in vain,
Looked into a forest well
   And never looked away again.
There, when the turf in springtime flowers,

With downward eye and gazes sad,
  Stands amid the glancing showers
    A jonquil, not a Grecian lad.

ONE NIGHT

Constantine Cavafy (1863–1933)

Although recognised today as one of Europe's greatest modern poets,
almost none of Cavafy's poetry was published during his own lifetime.
Born in Egypt, and raised in Alexandria, he earned his living as a civil
servant, he worked on his poems in private, intensively refining his
style and exploring Greek mythology, fatalism, memory and love. His
work is marked by a unique formal beauty and an informal approach
to his weighty and controversial subject matter.

The room was threadbare and tawdry,
hidden above that suspect restaurant.
From the window you could see the alley,
which was filthy and narrow. From below
came the voices of some laborers
who were playing cards and having a carouse.

And there, in that common, vulgar bed
I had the body of love, I had the lips,
sensuous and rose-colored, of drunkenness—
the rose of such a drunkenness, that even now
as I write, after so many years have passed!,
in my solitary house, I am drunk again.

BERLIN'S THIRD SEX

Magnus Hirschfeld (1868–1935)

A German physician and sexologist, later dubbed as "the first advocacy for homosexual and transgender rights", Hirschfeld was born to a Jewish Ashkenazi family. As a physician, he became interested in sexuality when he found that LGBT patients were frequently committing suicide. He elicited intimate and moving accounts of what he called "Berlin's Third Sex" and established the influential Institute of Sexual, which offered free accommodation – visitors included André Gide and Sergei Einstein and Lili Elbe, the trans woman who would later be depicted in *The Danish Girl*.

'Steady relationships' between homosexual men and women, often of significant duration, are extraordinarily common in Berlin.

It is something you have to experience – the numerous unmistakable examples of the tenderness, the bonds that so often unite one with the other, how they care for one another and long for one another, how the lover empathises with the loved one's interests, often so far from his own, the scholar in the affairs of the worker, the artist in those of the sergeant; you have to witness the tortures of body and soul with which these people not infrequently suffer jealousy, and only then does it become apparent that this is not a 'case of unnatural fornication', but rather a part of that great sensation that many believe lends human existence its value, its consecration.

I used to treat an aristocratic lady who had lived with a female friend for a number of years and suffered from a serious nervous complaint.

Neither before nor after in my medical practice have I ever seen such loving devotion of a healthy person toward an invalid as in this case, not between spouses, nor in mothers fretting for their children. The healthy friend was hardly an agreeable individual, there was much that was inconsiderate and obstinate about her, but anyone who witnessed this truly touching love and care, this ceaseless effort day and night, would have credited it to strong, fine sentiment. It was as though the two were joined at the hip. Touch the pained limb of the invalid and the other would flinch reflexively, any discomfort of the patient was reflected in her face, insomnia and poor appetite transferred to the healthy friend. The case was also noteworthy for the fact that the patient's staff, both the nurse and the maid, were unimpeachably uranian.

Not far from this couple lived another, a trainee lawyer and his friend of around 18 years of age, who was a dressmaker. The latter was so feminine that the lawyer once observed that he could just as well have fallen in love with a real woman as this nine-tenths of a woman. His voice, for example, was so womanly that whenever he telephoned and asked to speak to me, my secretary would invariably say, 'a lady wishes to speak with you'. The two lived in perfect harmony, each went to his own work every day, the one to the court, the other to the dressmakers'. When the lawyer left Berlin, he took his friend with him. When his father, a simple Berlin labourer, asked him to explain, he – as he related with shame – had to dim the light in the room. It came as no surprise to the father, who had long suspected something of the sort, and he declared himself in agreement with the situation.

The little dressmaker had a colleague, no less girlish than he. Their profession is more apt to attract the uranian element than any other in Berlin. This colleague fell in love with the lawyers brother, an engineer, who shortly before had undertaken a serious attempt at suicide following an unhappy affair with a male student. As he lay seriously injured in hospital, he and his similarly oriented brother revealed all, neither having previously suspected the other. Gradually a second love pact developed between the engineer and the other dressmaker, and there was no little drollery when the two handsome, well-built brothers strolled through the Grunewald of a Sunday with their two little dressmaker boys Willi and Hans, just like the others parading with their milliner sweethearts.

In Berlin it is far from unheard of for parents to come to an accommodation with the uranian natures, even the homosexual lives, of their children.

Recently I attended the burial of an old doctor in a cemetery on the outskirts of Berlin. At the open grave stood the only son of the deceased, to the right the aged mother, on the other side the 20-year-old friend, all three in deepest mourning. The father was over 70 years old when he became aware of his sons uranian nature and, close to despair, he sought out several alienists who could offer advice but no assistance. Then he immersed himself in literature on the topic and increasingly came to recognise that his son, whom he loved more than anything, had been homosexual from birth. At his residence, he had no objection to the son taking in his friend, indeed the good parents transferred all their love to the young man, who came from the most humble background. They exerted an obvious positive influence on each other; while each would have had difficulty getting ahead on his own, as a pair they managed splendidly, because the wisdom and kindness of the one found its complement in the energy and thrift of the other.

On his deathbed the old doctor bade farewell to his wife and his 'two lads', and the sight of these three individuals, united in tears and mourning to the sound of Mendelssohns 'It Is Surely God's Will', made a much deeper impression on the soul than the eulogy of the shrill young priest, praising the deeds of the deceased to whom he was a complete stranger.

Translated by James J. Conway

SELECTED POEMS
Amy Lowell (1874–1925)

Born into a wealthy and important Boston family, Amy Lowell did not attend university since her family deemed it "improper" for a woman, but compensated as an avid reader. She travelled widely and, at twenty-eight, began to write poetry. Throughout her life she suffered from crippling self-esteem and she was cruelly mocked by some contemporaries, but championed by others – including Heywood Broun who wrote that, outwardly, she was "a New Englander and a spinster. But inside everything was molten like the core of the earth" Her love poems, which mix traditional metres with free verse, are the surviving testament to her relationship with Ada Dwyer Russell, after letters were destroyed according to Lowell's will. She was posthumously awarded the Pulitzer Prize in 1926.

AUBADE

As I would free the white almond from the green husk
So I would strip your trappings off,
Beloved.
And fingering the smooth and polished kernel
I should see that in my hands glittered a gem beyond counting.

CARREFOUR

O You,
Who came upon me once
Stretched under apple-trees just after bathing,
Why did you not strangle me before speaking
Rather than fill me with the wild white honey of your words
And then leave me to the mercy
Of the forest bees.

ABSENCE

My cup is empty to-night,
Cold and dry are its sides,
Chilled by the wind from the open window.
Empty and void, it sparkles white in the moonlight.
The room is filled with the strange scent
Of wistaria blossoms.
They sway in the moon's radiance
And tap against the wall.
But the cup of my heart is still,
And cold, and empty.

When you come, it brims
Red and trembling with blood,
Heart's blood for your drinking;
To fill your mouth with love
And the bitter-sweet taste of a soul.

SELECTED POEMS

Renée Vivien (1877–1909)

Born to a wealthy British family, Pauline Mary Tarn was educated in Paris, where she remained for much of her life. As Renée Vivien, she wrote wrote exclusively in French. She idolised Sappho, and adopted the formal Parnassian mode. A prolific poet, she was known as the "Muse of the Violets", and was celebrated for her sensuous, autobiographical poems. Though outwardly spirited and confident, she was plagued by depression and anorexia. Her passionate affairs with women were tempestuous and volatile. When abandoned by her great love, Baroness Hélène van Zuylen in 1907, she spiralled into a suicidal depression and died at thirty-seven. A public square in the Marais in Paris is named after her.

THE LATENT NIGHT

The dusk, a gentle shepherd, sings
Its rustic solo tune...
I chew a sprig of heliotrope
Like Fra Diavolo, and soon
The smoke-fumes of the latent night
Spark, a dark Vesuvius alight,
With kiln-smoke veiling all the white
Bright aureole of the moon.

I am the fervent follower
Of the dusk and of the sea.

Lust, unique and multiple,
In my mirror looks at me…
I'm sorry for my clown-like face.
I seek your corpse, your resting-place,
A haven, calm and full of grace,
my lovely Misery!

Ah! the cold of hand in hand
Beneath the marble, here with you,
Beneath the heavy earth anointed
With the tree-sap and the dew!
My soul, which agony exalts,
Approaches, languishing, to halt
Before these columns of basalt
With all their viaduct-blue.

When analysis explores
The gaping chasm of the night,
In my revolt convulses, spasms,
A giant's fury and his might.
And, weary of fair, false renown,
Of joy in which the spirit drowns,
turn away and I bow down
Before your void so glossy-bright.

SHE PASSES

The sky encases her like relic-ashes,
And centuries could go by without a sight
Of her. She is the miracle of night.
The holy moment glows and chimes. She passes...

I have come here with the leprous throng,
Before the dawn, and knowing I'll be healed.
They gaze on her, as on the truth revealed,
Weeping low. I weep along with them.

In the air, a ray of bright hope flashes,
For her bare feet have sanctified the path.
A lily-flower's fallen from her hand...
The sobs go still. She passes.

She's made her saints of all who wept, abashed,
And now among us no one is afraid.
She will not come again along this way,
But I no longer suffer, since I saw her pass.

WORDS TO MY LOVE

You understand me: I am mediocre,
Not good, not very bad, calm, a little sly.
I hate strong perfumes and the voice raised high,
And gray is more to me than red or ochre.

I love the dying day extinguished gradually,
The fire, the cloistered closeness of a chamber
Where lampshades, veiling their transparent amber,
Blush red the bronze and blue the pottery.

My eyes upon the rug more worn than sand,
I lazily evoke the gold-grained shore,
The glimmers of the drifting tides of yore...
And nonetheless, I bear a guilty brand.

You see: I'm at the age the virgin yields her hand
To the man her weakness seeks and fears,
And I have no companion for my years,
Since you appeared just at the pathway's bend.

The hyacinth was bleeding on the scarlet glen,
You dreamt, while Love went walking by your side...
Women have no right to beauty. I'd
Been banished to the ugliness of men.

And I had the terrible audacity to yearn
For sister-love, of bright, white, pure light,
The gentle voice uniting with the night,
The furtive step that doesn't break the fern.

Your eyes, your hair had been forbidden me,
Because your hair is long and full of fragrant scents,
Because your eyes have fires so intense
They cloud themselves, like the rebellious sea.

They pointed fingers in their rage at me,
Because my eyes looked for your gentle eyes...
No one, to see us pass, would recognize
That I had chosen you in all simplicity.

Think on the vile law that I transgress,
And judge my love, which knows no evil will,
As honest, as essential, and as fatal still
As any man's desire for his mistress.

They did not read the brightness in my gaze
Upon the path whereto my fortune led...
"Who is that damned woman" (so they said)
"Toward whom the flames of Hell so deafly blaze?"

Let's leave them to their impure moralities,
For dawn is gold as honey and as bright,
And unembittered days, and better nights
Will come, the friends who put our minds at ease

Let's watch the brightness of the stars above...
What matters it, to us, man's judgment from afar?
And what have we to fear, knowing that we are
Pure in this life and knowing that we love...?

Translated by Samantha Pious

MISS OGILVY FINDS HERSELF
Radclyffe Hall (1880–1943)

Born in Hampshire to a wealthy, dysfunctional family, Radclyffe Hall experienced an epiphany at the age of twenty-seven when she fell in love with the singer Mabel Batten. She accepted her sexuality, and described herself as a "congenital invert". Her most famous novel, *The Well of Loneliness*, the first overt lesbian novel was greeted by a storm of controversy. In the Sunday Express, the editor James Douglas opined, "I would rather give a healthy boy or a healthy girl a phial of prussic acid than this novel." Although not remotely risqué, let alone explicit, in 1928 the publisher was prosecuted under the Obscene Publications Act and the magistrate ordered that copies of the book be burned.

1

Miss Ogilvy stood on the quay at Calais and surveyed the disbanding of her Unit, the Unit that together with the coming of war had completely altered the complexion of her life, at all events for three years.

Miss Ogilvy's thin, pale lips were set sternly and her forehead was puckered in an effort of attention, in an effort to memorize every small detail of every old war-weary battered motor on whose side still appeared the merciful emblem that had set Miss Ogilvy free.

Miss Ogilvy's mind was jerking a little, trying to regain its accustomed balance, trying to readjust itself quickly to this sudden and paralysing change. Her tall, awkward body with its queer look of strength, its broad, flat bosom and thick legs and ankles, as though in response to her jerking mind, moved uneasily, rocking backwards and forwards. She had this trick of rocking on her feet in moments of controlled agitation. As usual, her hands were thrust deep into her pockets, they seldom seemed to come out of her pockets unless it were to light a cigarette, and as though she were still standing firm under fire while the wounded were placed in her ambulances, she suddenly straddled her legs very slightly and lifted her head and listened. She was standing firm under fire at that moment, the fire of a desperate regret.

Some girls came towards her, young, tired-looking creatures whose eyes were too bright from long strain and excitement. They had all been members of that glorious Unit, and they still wore the queer little forage-caps and the short, clumsy tunics of the French Militaire. They still slouched in walking and smoked Caporals in emulation of the Poilus. Like their founder and leader these girls were all English, but like her they had chosen to serve England's ally, fearlessly thrusting right up to the trenches in search of the wounded and dying. They had seen some fine things in the course of three years, not the least fine of which was the cold, hard-faced woman who commanding, domineering, even hectoring at times, had yet been possessed of so dauntless a courage and of so insistent a vitality that it vitalized the whole Unit.

'It's rotten!' Miss Ogilvy heard someone saying. 'It's rotten, this breaking up of our Unit!' And the high, rather childish voice of the speaker sounded perilously near to tears.

Miss Ogilvy looked at the girl almost gently, and it seemed, for a moment, as though some deep feeling were about to find expression in words. But Miss Ogilvy's feelings had been held in abeyance so long that they seldom dared become vocal, so she merely said 'Oh?' on a rising inflection – her method of checking emotion.

They were swinging the ambulance cars in mid-air, those of them that were destined to go back to England, swinging them up like sacks of potatoes, then lowering them with much clanging of chains to the deck of the waiting steamer. The porters were shoving and shouting and quarrelling, pausing now and again to make meaningless gestures; while a pompous official was becoming quite angry as he pointed at Miss Ogilvy's own special car – it annoyed him, it was bulky and difficult to move.

'Bon Dieu! Mais dépêchez-vous donc!' he bawled, as though he were bullying the motor.

Then Miss Ogilvy's heart gave a sudden, thick thud to see this undig-nified, pitiful ending; and she turned and patted the gallant old car as though she were patting a well-beloved horse, as though she would say: 'Yes, I know how it feels – never mind, we'll go down together.'

2

Miss Ogilvy sat in the railway carriage on her way from Dover to London. The soft English landscape sped smoothly past: small homesteads, small churches, small pastures, small lanes, with small hedges; all small like England itself, all small like Miss Ogilvy's future. And sitting there still arrayed in her tunic, with her forage-cap resting on her knees, she was conscious of a sense of complete frustration; thinking less of those glorious years at the Front and of all that had gone to the making of her, than of all that had gone to the marring of her from the days of her earliest childhood.

She saw herself as a queer little girl, aggressive and awkward because of her shyness: a queer little girl who loathed sisters and dolls, prefer-ring the stable-boys as companions, preferring to play with footballs and tops, and occasional catapults. She saw herself climbing the tallest beech trees, arrayed in old breeches illicitly come by. She remembered insisting with tears and some temper that her real name was William and not Wilhelmina. All these childish pretences and illusions she remembered, and the bitterness that came after. For Miss Ogilvy had found as her life went on that in this world it is better to be one with the herd, that the world has no wish to understand those who cannot conform to its stereotyped pattern. True enough in her youth she had gloried in her strength, lifting weights, swinging clubs and developing muscles, but presently this had grown irksome to her; it had seemed to lead nowhere, she being a woman, and then as her mother had often protested: muscles looked so appalling in evening dress – a young girl ought not to have muscles.

Miss Ogilvy's relation to the opposite sex was unusual and at that time added much to her worries, for no less than three men had wished to propose, to the genuine amazement of the world and her mother. Miss Ogilvy's instinct made her like and trust men for whom she had a pronounced fellow-feeling; she would always have chosen them as her friends and companions in preference to girls or women; she would dearly have loved to share in their sports, their business, their ideals and their wide-flung interests. But men had not wanted her, except the three who had found in her strangeness a definite attraction, and those would-be suitors she had actually feared, regarding them with aversion. Towards young girls and women she was shy and respectful, apologetic and sometimes admiring. But their fads and their foibles, none of which she could share, while amusing her very often in secret, set her outside the sphere of their intimate lives, so that in the end she must blaze a lone trail through the difficulties of her nature.

'I can't understand you,' her mother had said, 'you're a very odd creature – now when I was your age…'

And her daughter had nodded, feeling sympathetic. There were two younger girls who also gave trouble, though in their case the trouble was fighting for husbands who were scarce enough even in those days. It was finally decided, at Miss Ogilvy's request, to allow her to leave the field clear for her sisters. She would remain in the country with her father when the others went up for the Season.

Followed long, uneventful years spent in sport, while Sarah and Fanny toiled, sweated and gambled in the matrimonial market. Neither ever succeeded in netting a husband, and when the Squire died leaving very little money, Miss Ogilvy found to her great surprise that they looked upon her as a brother. They had so often jibed at her in the past, that at first she could scarcely believe her senses, but before very long it became all too real: she it was who must straighten out endless muddles, who must make the dreary arrangements for the move, who must find a cheap but genteel house in London and, once there, who must cope with the family accounts which she only, it seemed, could balance.

It would be: 'You might see to that, Wilhelmina; you write, you've got such a good head for business.' Or: 'I wish you'd go down and explain to that man that we really can't pay his account till next quarter.' Or: 'This money for the grocer is five shillings short. Do run over my sum, Wilhelmina.'

Her mother, grown feeble, discovered in this daughter a staff upon which she could lean with safety. Miss Ogilvy genuinely loved her mother, and was therefore quite prepared to be leaned on; but when Sarah and Fanny began to lean too with the full weight of endless neurotic symptoms incubated in resentful virginity, Miss Ogilvy found herself staggering a little. For Sarah and Fanny were grown hard to bear, with their mania for telling their symptoms to doctors, with their unstable nerves and their acrid tongues and the secret dislike they now felt for their mother. Indeed, when old Mrs. Ogilvy died, she was unmourned except by her eldest daughter who actually felt a void in her life – the unforeseen void that the ailing and weak will not infrequently leave behind them.

At about this time an aunt also died, bequeathing her fortune to her niece Wilhelmina who, however, was too weary to gird up her loins and set forth in search of exciting adventure – all she did was to move her protesting sisters to a little estate she had purchased in Surrey. This experiment was only a partial success, for Miss Ogilvy failed to make friends of her neighbours; thus at fifty-five she had grown rather dour, as is often the way with shy, lonely people.

When the war came she had just begun settling down – people do settle down in their fifty-sixth year – she was feeling quite glad that her hair was grey, that the garden took up so much of her time, that, in fact, the beat of her blood was slowing. But all this was changed when war was declared; on that day Miss Ogilvy's pulses throbbed wildly.

'My God! If only I were a man!' she burst out, as she glared at Sarah and Fanny, 'if only I had been born a man!' Something in her was feeling deeply defrauded.

Sarah and Fanny were soon knitting socks and mittens and mufflers and Jaeger trench-helmets. Other ladies were busily working at depots, making swabs at the Squire's, or splints at the Parson's; but Miss Ogilvy scowled and did none of these things – she was not at all like other ladies.

For nearly twelve months she worried officials with a view to getting a job out in France – not in their way but in hers, and that was the trouble. She wished to go up to the front-line trenches, she wished to be actually under fire, she informed the harassed officials.

To all her inquiries she received the same answer: 'We regret that we cannot accept your offer.' But once thoroughly roused she was hard to subdue, for her shyness had left her as though by magic.

Sarah and Fanny shrugged angular shoulders: 'There's plenty of work here at home,' they remarked, 'though of course it's not quite so melodramatic!'

'Oh...?' queried their sister on a rising note of impatience – and she promptly cut off her hair: 'That'll jar them!' she thought with satisfaction.

Then she went up to London, formed her admirable unit and finally got it accepted by the French, despite renewed opposition.

In London she had found herself quite at her ease, for many another of her kind was in London doing excellent work for the nation. It was really surprising how many cropped heads had suddenly appeared as it were out of space; how many Miss Ogilvies, losing their shyness, had come forward asserting their right to serve, asserting their claim to attention.

There followed those turbulent years at the front, full of courage and hardship and high endeavour, and during those years Miss Ogilvy forgot the bad joke that Nature seemed to have played her. She was given the rank of a French lieutenant and she lived in a kind of blissful illusion; appalling reality lay on all sides and yet she managed to live in illusion.

She was competent, fearless, devoted and untiring. What then? Could any man hope to do better? She was nearly fifty-eight, yet she walked with a stride, and at times she even swaggered a little.

Poor Miss Ogilvy sitting so glumly in the train with her manly trench-boots and her forage-cap! Poor all the Miss Ogilvies back from the war with their tunics, their trench-boots, and their childish illusions! Wars come and wars go but the world does not change: it will always forget an indebtedness which it thinks it expedient not to remember.

3

When Miss Ogilvy returned to her home in Surrey it was only to find that her sisters were ailing from the usual imaginary causes, and this to a woman who had seen the real thing was intolerable, so that she looked with distaste at Sarah and then at Fanny. Fanny was certainly not prepossessing, she was suffering from a spurious attack of hay fever.

'Stop sneezing!' commanded Miss Ogilvy, in the voice that had so much impressed the Unit. But as Fanny was not in the least impressed, she naturally went on sneezing.

Miss Ogilvy's desk was piled mountain-high with endless tiresome letters and papers: circulars, bills, months-old correspondence, the gardener's accounts, an agent's report on some fields that required land-draining. She seated herself before this collection; then she sighed, it all seemed so absurdly trivial.

'Will you let your hair grow again?' Fanny inquired... she and Sarah had followed her into the study. 'I'm certain the Vicar would be glad if you did."

'Oh?' murmured Miss Ogilvy, rather too blandly.

'Wilhelmina!'

'Yes?'

'You will do it, won't you?'

'Do what?'

'Let your hair grow; we all wish you would.'

'Why should I?'

'Oh, well, it will look less odd, especially now that the war is over – in a small place like this people notice such things.'

'I entirely agree with Fanny,' announced Sarah.

Sarah had become very self-assertive, no doubt through having mismanaged the estate during the years of her sister's absence. They had quite a heated dispute one morning over the south herbaceous border.

'Whose garden is this?' Miss Ogilvy asked sharply. 'I insist on auricula-eyed sweet-williams! I even took the trouble to write from France, but it seems that my letter has been ignored.'

'Don't shout,' rebuked Sarah, 'you're not in France now!'

Miss Ogilvy could gladly have boxed her ears: 'I only wish to God I were,' she muttered.

Another dispute followed close on its heels, and this time it happened to be over the dinner. Sarah and Fanny were living on weeds – at least that was the way Miss Ogilvy put it.

'We've become vegetarians,' Sarah said grandly.

'You've become two damn tiresome cranks!' snapped their sister.

Now it never had been Miss Ogilvy's way to indulge in acid recriminations, but somehow, these days, she forgot to say 'Oh?' quite so often as expediency demanded. It may have been Fanny's perpetual sneezing that had got on her nerves; or it may have been Sarah, or the gardener, or the Vicar, or even the canary; though it really did not matter very much what it was just so long as she found a convenient peg upon which to hang her growing irritation.

'This won't do at all,' Miss Ogilvy thought sternly, 'life's not worth so much fuss, I must pull myself together.' But it seemed this was easier said than done; not a day passed without her losing her temper and that over some trifle: 'No, this won't do at all – it just mustn't be,' she thought sternly.

Everyone pitied Sarah and Fanny: 'Such a dreadful, violent old thing,' said the neighbours.

But Sarah and Fanny had their revenge: 'Poor darling, it's shell-shock, you know,' they murmured.

Thus Miss Ogilvy's prowess was whittled away until she herself was beginning to doubt it. Had she ever been that courageous person who had faced death in France with such perfect composure? Had she ever stood tranquilly under fire, without turning a hair, while she issued her orders? Had she ever been treated with marked respect? She herself was beginning to doubt it.

Sometimes she would see an old member of the Unit, a girl who, more faithful to her than the others, would take the trouble to run down to Surrey. These visits, however, were seldom enlivening.

'Oh, well... here we are...' Miss Ogilvy would mutter.

But one day the girl smiled and shook her blonde head: 'I'm not – I'm going to be married.'

Strange thoughts had come to Miss Ogilvy, unbidden, thoughts that had stayed for many an hour after the girl's departure. Alone in her study she had suddenly shivered, feeling a sense of complete desolation. With cold hands she had lighted a cigarette.

'I must be ill or something,' she had mused, as she stared at her trembling fingers.

After this she would sometimes cry out in her sleep, living over in dreams God knows what emotions; returning, maybe, to the battlefields of France. Her hair turned snow-white; it was not unbecoming yet she fretted about it.

'I'm growing very old,' she would sigh as she brushed her thick mop before the glass; and then she would peer at her wrinkles.

For now that it had happened she hated being old; it no longer appeared such an easy solution of those difficulties that had always beset her. And this she resented most bitterly, so that she became the prey of self-pity, and of other undesirable states in which the body will torment the mind, and the mind, in its turn, the body. Then Miss Ogilvy straightened her ageing back, in spite of the fact that of late it had ached with muscular rheumatism, and she faced herself squarely and came to a resolve.

'I'm off!' she announced abruptly one day; and that evening she packed her kit-bag.

4

Near the south coast of Devon there exists a small island that is still very little known to the world, but which, nevertheless, can boast an hotel; the only building upon it. Miss Ogilvy had chosen this place quite at random, it was marked on her map by scarcely more than a dot, but somehow she had liked the look of that dot and had set forth alone to explore it.

She found herself standing on the mainland one morning looking at a vague blur of green through the mist, a vague blur of green that rose out of the Channel like a tidal wave suddenly suspended. Miss Ogilvy was filled with a sense of adventure; she had not felt like this since the ending of the war.

'I was right to come here, very right indeed. I'm going to shake off all my troubles,' she decided.

A fisherman's boat was parting the mist, and before it was properly beached, in she bundled.

'I hope they're expecting me?' she said gaily.

'They du be expecting you,' the man answered.

The sea, which is generally rough off that coast, was indulging itself in an oily ground-swell; the broad, glossy swells struck the side of the boat, then broke and sprayed over Miss Ogilvy's ankles.

The fisherman grinned: 'Feeling all right?' he queried. 'It du be tiresome most times about these parts.' But the mist had suddenly drifted away and Miss Ogilvy was staring wide-eyed at the island.

She saw a long shoal of jagged black rocks, and between them the curve of a small sloping beach, and above that the lift of the island itself, and above that again, blue heaven. Near the beach stood the little two-storied hotel which was thatched, and built entirely of timber; for the rest she could make out no signs of life apart from a host of white seagulls.

Then Miss Ogilvy said a curious thing. She said: 'On the south-west side of that place there was once a cave – a very large cave. I remember that it was some way from the sea.'

'There du be a cave still,' the fisherman told her, 'but it's just above highwater level.'

'A-ah,' murmured Miss Ogilvy thoughtfully, as though to herself; then she looked embarrassed.

The little hotel proved both comfortable and clean, the hostess both pleasant and comely. Miss Ogilvy started unpacking her bag, changed her mind and went for a stroll round the island. The island was covered with turf and thistles and traversed by narrow green paths thick with daisies. It had four rock-bound coves of which the southwestern was by far the most difficult of access. For just here the island descended abruptly as though it were hurtling down to the water; and just here the shale was most treacherous and the tide-swept rocks most aggressively pointed. Here it was that the seagulls, grown fearless of man by reason of his absurd limitations, built their nests on the ledges and reared countless young who multiplied, in their turn, every season. Yes, and here it was that Miss Ogilvy, greatly marvelling, stood and stared across at a cave; much too near the crumbling edge for her safety, but by now completely indifferent to caution.

'I remember... I remember...' she kept repeating. Then: 'That's all very well, but what do I remember?'

She was conscious of somehow remembering all wrong, of her memory being distorted and coloured – perhaps by the endless things she had seen since her eyes had last rested upon that cave. This worried her sorely, far more than the fact that she should be remembering the cave at all, she who had never set foot on the island before that actual morning. Indeed, except for the sense of wrongness when she struggled to piece her memories together, she was steeped in a very profound contentment which surged over her spirit, wave upon wave.

'It's extremely odd', pondered Miss Ogilvy. Then she laughed, so pleased did she feel with its oddness.

5

That night after supper she talked to her hostess who was only too glad, it seemed, to be questioned. She owned the whole island and was proud of the fact, as she very well might be, decided her boarder. Some curious things had been found on the island, according to comely Mrs. Nanceskivel: bronze arrow-heads, pieces of ancient stone celts; and once they had dug up a man's skull and thigh-bone – this had happened while they were sinking a well. Would Miss Ogilvy care to have a look at the bones? They were kept in a cupboard in the scullery.

Miss Ogilvy nodded.

'Then I'll fetch him this moment,' said Mrs. Nanceskivel, briskly.

In less than two minutes she was back with the box that contained those poor remnants of a man, and Miss Ogilvy, who had risen from her chair, was gazing down at those remnants. As she did so her mouth was sternly compressed, but her face and her neck flushed darkly.

Mrs. Nanceskivel was pointing to the skull; 'Look, miss, he was killed,' she remarked rather proudly, 'and they tell me that the axe that killed him was bronze. He's thousands and thousands of years old, they tell me. Our local doctor knows a lot about such things and he wants me to send these bones to an expert: they ought to belong to the Nation, he says. But I know what would happen, they'd come digging up my island, and I won't have people digging up my island, I've got enough worry with the rabbits as it is.' But Miss Ogilvy could no longer hear the words for the pounding of the blood in her temples.

She was filled with a sudden, inexplicable fury against the innocent Mrs. Nanceskivel: 'You… *you*…' she began, then checked herself, fearful of what she might say to the woman.

For her sense of outrage was overwhelming as she stared at those bones that were kept in the scullery; moreover, she knew how such men had been buried, which made the outrage seem all the more shameful. They had buried such men in deep, well-dug pits surmounted by four stout stones at their corners – four stout stones there had been and a covering stone. And all this Miss Ogilvy knew as by instinct, having no concrete knowledge on which to draw. But she knew it right down in the depths of her soul, and she hated Mrs. Nanceskivel.

And now she was swept by another emotion that was even more strange and more devastating: such a grief as she had not conceived could exist; a terrible unassuageable grief, without hope, without respite, without palliation, so that with something akin to despair she touched the long gash in the skull. Then her eyes, that had never wept since her childhood, filled slowly with large, hot, difficult tears. She must blink very hard, then close her eyelids, turn away from the lamp and say rather loudly:

'Thanks, Mrs. Nanceskivel. It's past eleven – I think I'll be going upstairs.'

6

Miss Ogilvy closed the door of her bedroom, after which she stood quite still to consider: 'Is it shell-shock?' she muttered incredulously. 'I wonder, can it be shell-shock?'

She began to pace slowly about the room, smoking a Caporal. As usual her hands were deep in her pockets; she could feel small, familiar things in those pockets and she gripped them, glad of their presence. Then all of a sudden she was terribly tired, so tired that she flung herself down on the bed, unable to stand any longer.

She thought that she lay there struggling to reason, that her eyes were closed in the painful effort, and that as she closed them she continued to puff the inevitable cigarette. At least that was what she thought at one moment – the next, she was out in a sunset evening, and a large red sun was sinking slowly to the rim of a distant sea.

Miss Ogilvy knew that she was herself, that is to say she was conscious of her being, and yet she was not Miss Ogilvy at all, nor had she a memory of her. All that she now saw was very familiar, all that she now did was what she should do, and all that she now was seemed perfectly natural.

Indeed, she did not think of these things; there seemed no reason for thinking about them.

She was walking with bare feet on turf that felt springy and was greatly enjoying the sensation; she had always enjoyed it, ever since as an infant she had learned to crawl on this turf. On either hand stretched rolling green uplands, while at her back she knew that there were forests; but in front, far away, lay the gleam of the sea towards which the big sun was sinking. The air was cool and intensely still, with never so much as a ripple or bird-song. It was wonderfully pure – one might almost say young – but Miss Ogilvy thought of it merely as air. Having always breathed it she took it for granted, as she took the soft turf and the uplands.

She pictured herself as immensely tall; she was feeling immensely tall at that moment. As a matter of fact she was five feet eight which, however, was quite a considerable height when compared to that of her fellow-tribesmen. She was wearing a single garment of pelts which came to her knees and left her arms sleeveless. Her arms and her legs, which were closely tattooed with blue zig-zag lines, were extremely hairy. From a leathern thong twisted about her waist there hung a clumsily made stone weapon, a celt, which in spite of its clumsiness was strongly hafted and useful for killing.

Miss Ogilvy wanted to shout aloud from a glorious sense of physical well-being, but instead she picked up a heavy, round stone which she hurled with great force at some distant rocks.

'Good! Strong!' she exclaimed. 'See how far it goes!'

'Yes, strong. There is no one so strong as you. You are surely the strongest man in our tribe,' replied her little companion.

Miss Ogilvy glanced at this little companion and rejoiced that they two were alone together. The girl at her side had a smooth brownish skin, oblique black eyes and short, sturdy limbs. Miss Ogilvy marvelled because of her beauty. She also was wearing a single garment of pelts, new pelts, she had made it that morning. She had stitched at it diligently for hours with short lengths of gut and her best bone needle. A strand of black hair hung over her bosom, and this she was constantly stroking and fondling; then she lifted the strand and examined her hair.

'Pretty,' she remarked with childish complacence.

'Pretty,' echoed the young man at her side.

'For you,' she told him, 'all of me is for you and none other. For you this body has ripened.'

He shook back his own coarse hair from his eyes; he had sad brown eyes like those of a monkey. For the rest he was lean and steel-strong of loin, broad of chest, and with features not too uncomely. His prominent cheekbones were set rather high, his nose was blunt, his jaw somewhat bestial; but his mouth, though full-lipped, contradicted his jaw, being very gentle and sweet in expression. And now he smiled, showing big, square, white teeth.

'You... woman,' he murmured contentedly, and the sound seemed to come from the depths of his being.

His speech was slow and lacking in words when it came to expressing a vital emotion, so one word must suffice and this he now spoke, and the word that he spoke had a number of meanings. It meant: 'Little spring of exceedingly pure water.' It meant: 'Hut of peace for a man after battle.' It meant: 'Ripe red berry sweet to the taste.' It meant: 'Happy small home of future generations.' All these things he must try to express by a word, and because of their loving she understood him.

They paused, and lifting her up he kissed her. Then he rubbed his large shaggy head on her shoulder; and when he released her she knelt at his feet.

'My master; blood of my body,' she whispered. For with her it was different, love had taught her love's speech, so that she might turn her heart into sounds that her primitive tongue could utter.

After she had pressed her lips to his hands, and her cheek to his hairy and powerful forearm, she stood up and they gazed at the setting sun, but with bowed heads, gazing under their lids, because this was very sacred.

A couple of mating bears padded towards them from a thicket, and the female rose to her haunches. But the man drew his celt and menaced the beast, so that she dropped down noiselessly and fled, and her mate also fled, for here was the power that few dared to withstand by day or by night, on the uplands or in the forests. And now from across to the left where a river would presently lose itself in the marshes, came a rhythmical thudding, as a herd of red deer with wide nostrils and starting eyes thundered past, disturbed in their drinking by the bears.

After this the evening returned to its silence, and the spell of its silence descended on the lovers, so that each felt very much alone, yet withal more closely united to the other. But the man became restless under that spell, and he suddenly laughed; then grasping the woman he tossed her above his head and caught her. This he did many times for his own amusement and because he knew that his strength gave her joy. In this manner they played together for a while, he with his strength and she with her weakness. And they cried out, and made many guttural sounds which were meaningless save only to themselves. And the tunic of pelts slipped down from her breasts, and her two little breasts were pear-shaped.

Presently, he grew tired of their playing, and he pointed towards a cluster of huts and earthworks that lay to the eastward. The smoke from these huts rose in thick straight lines, bending neither to right nor left in its rising, and the thought of sweet burning rushes and brushwood touched his consciousness, making him feel sentimental.

'Smoke,' he said.

And she answered: 'Blue smoke.'

He nodded: 'Yes, blue smoke – home.'

Then she said: 'I have ground much corn since the full moon. My stones are too smooth. You make me new stones.'

'All you have need of, I make,' he told her.

She stole close to him, taking his hand: 'My father is still a black cloud full of thunder. He thinks that you wish to be head of our tribe in his place, because he is now very old. He must not hear of these meetings of ours, if he did I think he would beat me!'

So he asked her: 'Are you unhappy, small berry?'

But at this she smiled: 'What is being unhappy? I do not know what that means any more.'

'I do not either,' he answered.

Then as though some invisible force had drawn him, his body swung round and he stared at the forests where they lay and darkened, fold upon fold; and his eyes dilated with wonder and terror, and he moved his head quickly from side to side as a wild thing will do that is held between bars and whose mind is pitifully bewildered.

'Water!' he cried hoarsely, 'great water – look, look! Over there. This land is surrounded by water!'

'What water?' she questioned.

He answered: 'The sea.' And he covered his face with his hands.

'Not so,' she consoled, 'big forests, good hunting. Big forests in which you hunt boar and aurochs. No sea over there but only the trees.'

He took his trembling hands from his face: 'You are right... only trees,' he said dully.

But now his face had grown heavy and brooding and he started to speak of a tiling that oppressed him: 'The Round-headed-ones, they are devils,' he growled, while his bushy black brows met over his eyes, and when this happened it changed his expression which became a little sub-human.

'No matter,' she protested, for she saw that he forgot her and she wished him to think and talk only of love. 'No matter. My father laughs at your fears. Are we not friends with the Roundheaded-ones? We are friends, so why should we fear them?'

'Our forts, very old, very weak,' he went on, 'and the Roundheaded-ones have terrible weapons. Their weapons are not made of good stone like ours, but of some dark, devilish substance.'

'What of that?' she said lightly. 'They would fight on our side, so why need we trouble about their weapons?'

But he looked away, not appearing to hear her. 'We must barter all, all for their celts and arrows and spears, and then we must learn their secret.

They lust after our women, they lust after our lands. We must barter all, all for their sly brown celts.'

'Me… bartered?' she queried, very sure of his answer otherwise she had not dared to say this.

'The Roundheaded-ones may destroy my tribe and yet I will not part with you,' he told her. Then he spoke very gravely: 'But I think they desire to slay us, and me they will try to slay first because they well know how much I mistrust them – they have seen my eyes fixed many times on their camps.'

She cried: 'I will bite out the throats of these people if they so much as scratch your skin!'

And at this his mood changed and he roared with amusement: 'You… woman!' he roared. 'Little foolish white teeth. Your teeth were made for nibbling wild cherries, not for tearing the throats of the Roundheaded-ones!'

'Thoughts of war always make me afraid,' she whimpered, still wishing him to talk about love.

He turned his sorrowful eyes upon her, the eyes that were sad even when he was merry, and although his mind was often obtuse, yet he clearly perceived how it was with her then. And his blood caught fire from the flame in her blood, so that he strained her against his body.

'You… mine…' he stammered.

'Love,' she said, trembling, 'this is love.'

And he answered: 'Love.'

Then their faces grew melancholy for a moment, because dimly, very dimly in their dawning souls, they were conscious of a longing for something more vast than this earthly passion could compass.

Presently, he lifted her like a child and carried her quickly southward and westward till they came to a place where a gentle descent led down to a marshy valley. Far away, at the line where the marshes ended, they discerned the misty line of the sea; but the sea and the marshes were become as one substance, merging, blending, folding together; and since they were lovers they also would be one, even as the sea and the marshes.

And now they had reached the mouth of a cave that was set in the quiet hillside. There was bright green verdure beside the cave, and a number of small, pink, thick-stemmed flowers that when they were crushed smelt of spices. And within the cave there was bracken newly gathered and heaped together for a bed; while beyond, from some rocks, came a low liquid sound as a spring dripped out through a crevice. Abruptly, he set the girl on her feet, and she knew that the days of her innocence were over. And she thought of the anxious virgin soil that was rent and sown to bring forth fruit in season, and she gave a quick little gasp of fear:

'No… no…' she gasped. For, divining his need, she was weak with the longing to be possessed, yet the terror of love lay heavy upon her. 'No… no…' she gasped.

But he caught her wrist and she felt the great strength of his rough, gnarled fingers, the great strength of the urge that leapt in his loins, and again she must give that quick gasp of fear, the while she clung close to him lest he should spare her.

The twilight was engulfed and possessed by darkness, which in turn was transfigured by the moonrise, which in turn was fulfilled and consumed by dawn. A mighty eagle soared up from his eyrie, cleaving the air with his masterful wings, and beneath him from the rushes that harboured their nests, rose other great birds, crying loudly. Then the heavy-horned elks appeared on the uplands, bending their burdened heads to the sod; while beyond in the forests the fierce wild aurochs stamped as they bellowed their love songs.

But within the dim cave the lord of these creatures had put by his weapon and his instinct for slaying. And he lay there defenceless with tenderness, thinking no longer of death but of life as he murmured the word that had so many meanings. That meant: 'Little spring of exceedingly pure water.' That meant: 'Hut of peace for a man after battle.' That meant: 'Ripe red berry sweet to the taste.' That meant: 'Happy small home of future generations.'

*

7

They found Miss Ogilvy the next morning; the fisherman saw her and climbed to the ledge. She was sitting at the mouth of the cave. She was dead, with her hands thrust deep into her pockets.

ORLANDO

Virginia Woolf (1882–1941)

Considered a founder of Modernist prose and a godmother of twentieth-century feminism, Woolf may be the most influential novelist of all time. Raised in a prominent London family, she joined the liberal Bloomsbury Group in her twenties, where homosexuality was relatively uncontroversial. Her six-year relationship with Vita Sackville-West is credited with a relief of her mental health problems and a creative high-point in her career.

At length, with a gesture of extraordinary majesty and grace, first bowing profoundly, then raising himself proudly erect, Orlando took the golden circlet of strawberry leaves and placed it, with a gesture which none that saw it ever forgot, upon his brows. It was at this point that the first disturbance began. Either the people had expected a miracle—some say a shower of gold was prophesied to fall from the skies—which did not happen, or this was the signal chosen for the attack to begin; nobody seems to know; but as the coronet settled on Orlando's brows a great uproar rose. Bells began ringing; the harsh cries of the prophets were heard above the shouts of the people; many Turks fell flat to the ground and touched the earth with their foreheads. A door burst open. The natives pressed into the banqueting rooms. Women shrieked. A certain lady, who was said to be dying for love of Orlando, seized a candelabra and dashed it to the ground. What might not have happened, had it not been for the presence of Sir Adrian Scrope and a squad of British bluejackets, nobody can say. But the Admiral ordered the bugles to be sounded; a hundred bluejackets stood instantly at attention; the disorder was quelled, and quiet, at least for the time being, fell upon the scene.

So far, we are on the firm, if rather narrow, ground of ascertained truth. But nobody has ever known exactly what took place later that night. The testimony of the sentries and others seems, however, to prove that the Embassy was empty of company, and shut up for the night in the usual way by two A.M. The Ambassador was seen to go to his room, still wearing the insignia of his rank, and shut the door. Some say he locked it, which was against his custom. Others maintain that they heard music of a rustic kind, such as shepherds play, later that night in the courtyard under the Ambassador's window. A washer-woman, who was kept awake by toothache, said that she saw a man's figure, wrapped in a cloak or dressing gown, come out upon the balcony. Then, she said, a woman, much muffled, but apparently of the peasant class, was drawn up by means of a rope which the man let down to her on to the balcony. There, the washer-woman said, they embraced passionately 'like lovers', and went into the room together, drawing the curtains so that no more could be seen.

Next morning, the Duke, as we must now call him, was found by his secretaries sunk in profound slumber amid bed clothes that were much tumbled. The room was in some disorder, his coronet having rolled on the floor, and his cloak and garter being flung all of a heap on a chair. The table was littered with papers. No suspicion was felt at first, as the fatigues of the night had been great. But when afternoon came and he still slept, a doctor was summoned. He applied remedies which had been used on the previous occasion, plasters, nettles, emetics, etc., but without success. Orlando slept on. His secretaries then thought it their duty to examine the papers on the table. Many were scribbled over with poetry, in which frequent mention was made of an oak tree. There were also various state papers and others of a private nature concerning the management of his estates in England. But at length they came upon a document of far greater significance. It was nothing less, indeed, than a deed of marriage, drawn up, signed, and witnessed between his Lordship,

Orlando, Knight of the Garter, etc., etc., etc., and Rosina Pepita, a dancer, father unknown, but reputed a gipsy, mother also unknown but reputed a seller of old iron in the market-place over against the Galata Bridge. The secretaries looked at each other in dismay. And still Orlando slept. Morning and evening they watched him, but, save that his breathing was regular and his cheeks still flushed their habitual deep rose, he gave no sign of life. Whatever science or ingenuity could do to waken him they did. But still he slept.

On the seventh day of his trance (Thursday, May the 10th) the first shot was fired of that terrible and bloody insurrection of which Lieutenant Brigge had detected the first symptoms. The Turks rose against the Sultan, set fire to the town, and put every foreigner they could find, either to the sword or to the bastinado. A few English managed to escape; but, as might have been expected, the gentlemen of the British Embassy preferred to die in defence of their red boxes, or, in extreme cases, to swallow bunches of keys rather than let them fall into the hands of the Infidel. The rioters broke into Orlando's room, but seeing him stretched to all appearances dead they left him untouched, and only robbed him of his coronet and the robes of the Garter.

And now again obscurity descends, and would indeed that it were deeper! Would, we almost have it in our hearts to exclaim, that it were so deep that we could see nothing whatever through its opacity! Would that we might here take the pen and write Finis to our work! Would that we might spare the reader what is to come and say to him in so many words, Orlando died and was buried. But here, alas, Truth, Candour, and Honesty, the austere Gods who keep watch and ward by the inkpot of the biographer, cry No! Putting their silver trumpets to their lips they demand in one blast, Truth! And again they cry Truth! and sounding yet a third time in concert they peal forth, The Truth and nothing but the Truth!

At which—Heaven be praised! for it affords us a breathing space— the doors gently open, as if a breath of the gentlest and holiest zephyr had wafted them apart, and three figures enter. First, comes our Lady of

Purity; whose brows are bound with fillets of the whitest lamb's wool; whose hair is as an avalanche of the driven snow; and in whose hand reposes the white quill of a virgin goose. Following her, but with a statelier step, comes our Lady of Chastity; on whose brow is set like a turret of burning but unwasting fire a diadem of icicles; her eyes are pure stars, and her fingers, if they touch you, freeze you to the bone. Close behind her, sheltering indeed in the shadow of her more stately sisters, comes our Lady of Modesty, frailest and fairest of the three; whose face is only shown as the young moon shows when it is thin and sickle shaped and half hidden among clouds. Each advances towards the centre of the room where Orlando still lies sleeping; and with gestures at once appealing and commanding, OUR LADY OF PURITY speaks first:

'I am the guardian of the sleeping fawn; the snow is dear to me; and the moon rising; and the silver sea. With my robes I cover the speckled hen's eggs and the brindled sea shell; I cover vice and poverty. On all things frail or dark or doubtful, my veil descends. Wherefore, speak not, reveal not. Spare, O spare!'

Here the trumpets peal forth.

'Purity Avaunt! Begone Purity!'

Then OUR LADY OF CHASTITY speaks:

'I am she whose touch freezes and whose glance turns to stone. I have stayed the star in its dancing, and the wave as it falls. The highest Alps are my dwelling place; and when I walk, the lightnings flash in my hair; where my eyes fall, they kill. Rather than let Orlando wake, I will freeze him to the bone. Spare, O spare!'

Here the trumpets peal forth.

'Chastity Avaunt! Begone Chastity!'

Then OUR LADY OF MODESTY speaks, so low that one can hardly hear:

'I am she that men call Modesty. Virgin I am and ever shall be. Not for me the fruitful fields and the fertile vineyard. Increase is odious to me; and when the apples burgeon or the flocks breed, I run, I run; I let my mantle fall. My hair covers my eyes. I do not see. Spare, O spare!'

Again the trumpets peal forth:

'Modesty Avaunt! Begone Modesty!'

With gestures of grief and lamentation the three sisters now join hands and dance slowly, tossing their veils and singing as they go:

'Truth come not out from your horrid den. Hide deeper, fearful Truth. For you flaunt in the brutal gaze of the sun things that were better unknown and undone; you unveil the shameful; the dark you make clear, Hide! Hide! Hide!'

Here they make as if to cover Orlando with their draperies. The trumpets, meanwhile, still blare forth,

'The Truth and nothing but the Truth.'

At this the Sisters try to cast their veils over the mouths of the trumpets so as to muffle them, but in vain, for now all the trumpets blare forth together,

'Horrid Sisters, go!'

The sisters become distracted and wail in unison, still circling and flinging their veils up and down.

'It has not always been so! But men want us no longer; the women detest us. We go; we go. I (PURITY SAYS THIS) to the hen roost. I (CHASTITY SAYS THIS) to the still unravished heights of Surrey. I (MODESTY SAYS THIS) to any cosy nook where there are ivy and curtains in plenty.'

'For there, not here (all speak together joining hands and making gestures of farewell and despair towards the bed where Orlando lies sleeping) dwell still in nest and boudoir, office and lawcourt those who love us; those who honour us, virgins and city men; lawyers and doctors; those who prohibit; those who deny; those who reverence without knowing why; those who praise without understanding; the still very numerous (Heaven be praised) tribe of the respectable; who prefer to see not; desire to know not; love the darkness; those still worship us, and with reason; for we have given them Wealth, Prosperity, Comfort, Ease. To them we go, you we leave. Come, Sisters, come! This is no place for us here.'

They retire in haste, waving their draperies over their heads, as if to shut out something that they dare not look upon and close the door behind them.

We are, therefore, now left entirely alone in the room with the sleeping Orlando and the trumpeters. The trumpeters, ranging themselves side by side in order, blow one terrific blast:— 'THE TRUTH! at which Orlando woke. He stretched himself. He rose. He stood upright in complete nakedness before us, and while the trumpets pealed Truth! Truth! Truth! we have no choice left but confess—he was a woman.

The sound of the trumpets died away and Orlando stood stark naked. No human being, since the world began, has ever looked more ravishing. His form combined in one the strength of a man and a woman's grace. As he stood there, the silver trumpets prolonged their note, as if reluctant to leave the lovely sight which their blast had called forth; and Chastity, Purity, and Modesty, inspired, no doubt, by Curiosity, peeped in at the door and threw a garment like a towel at the naked form which, unfortunately, fell short by several inches. Orlando looked himself up and down in a long looking-glass, without showing any signs of discomposure, and went, presumably, to his bath.

We may take advantage of this pause in the narrative to make certain statements. Orlando had become a woman—there is no denying it. But in every other respect, Orlando remained precisely as he had been. The change of sex, though it altered their future, did nothing whatever to alter their identity. Their faces remained, as their portraits prove, practically the same. His memory—but in future we must, for convention's sake, say 'her' for 'his,' and 'she' for 'he'—her memory then, went back through all the events of her past life without encountering any obstacle. Some slight haziness there may have been, as if a few dark drops had fallen into the clear pool of memory; certain things had become a little dimmed; but that was all. The change seemed to have been accomplished painlessly and completely and in such a way that Orlando herself showed no surprise at it. Many people, taking this into account, and holding that such a change of sex is against nature, have been at great pains to prove (1) that Orlando had always been a woman, (2) that Orlando is at this moment a man. Let biologists and psychologists determine. It is enough for us to state the simple fact; Orlando was a man till the age of thirty; when he became a woman and has remained so ever since.

FRIENDSHIP

Katherine Mansfield (1888–1923)

Born and educated in New Zealand Mansfield arrived in England
at the age of nineteen and reimagined the European short story.
She developed a stark, naturalistic style, touching only lightly on
emotions. Her symbolical domestic settings dramatized new ideas
advanced by psychoanalysis. Although she admired the Decadents and
socialised with the Bloomsbury Group, she was from a conservative
New Zealand background and expressed romantic joy in her diary
only. She died aged thirty-four.

When we were charming Backfisch
With curls and velvet bows
We shared a charming kitten
With tiny velvet toes.

It was so gay and playful;
It flew like a woolly ball
From my lap to your shoulder
And, oh, it was so small,

So warm – and so obedient
If we cried: 'That's enough!'
It lay and slept between us,
A purring ball of fluff.

But now that I am thirty
And she is thirty one,

I shudder to discover
How wild our cat has run.

It's bigger than a Tiger,
Its eyes are jets of flame,
Its claws are gleaming daggers,
Could it once have been tame?

Take it away, I'm frightened!
But she, with placid brow,
Cries: 'This is our Kitty-witty!
Why don't you love her now?'

GIRLFRIEND (*PODRUGA*)

Marina Tsvetaeva (1892–1941)

Widely considered the finest 20th-century poet in the Russian language, Tsvetaeva was born to a wealthy artistic family in Moscow and educated in Lausanne and Paris. At eighteen, she met and married Sergei Efron and at about the same time, began an affair with the poet Sophia Parnok to whom she wrote numerous poems. In 1922, she and her husband fled the Soviet Union and eventually settled in Paris, but returned in the late 1930s. In 1941, her husband and her daughter Alya were arrested and charged with espionage, her husband was executed. Tsvetaeva committed suicide in 1941.

1

Are you happy? You wouldn't say!
And for the better—let it be!
To me, it seems you've kissed too many,
There lies your grief.

All the Shakespearean tragic heroines,
I see in you.
But you, a young and tragic lady
No one has saved!

You've grown so worn,
Repeating that erotic
Chatter. How eloquent,
That iron band around your bloodless hand.

I love you—sin hangs above you
Like a storm cloud!
Because you're venomous, you sting,
You're better than the rest,

Because we are, our lives are different
In this darkness,
Because—your passionate seductions,
And your dark fate,

Because with you, my steep-browed demon
There's no future,
And even if I burst above your grave,
You can't be saved!

Because I'm trembling, because can it be true?
Is this a dream?
Because of the delightful irony
That you—are not a he.

—*October 16, 1914*

2

Beneath caresses of a soft plaid throw,
I summon yesterday... a dream?
What was it? Who's the victor?
Who, the overthrown?

Rethinking all of it anew,
I'm tormenting myself again.
And that, for which I have no words,
Was... love? But can it...?

Who was the hunter? Who—the prey?
Oh devil, all of it, it's upside down!
And the Siberian cat,
What did he grasp amidst his drawling, purring sounds?

And in this battle of the wills,
Who ended up whose tool?
Whose heart was it, yours or mine,
That flew?

And yet, what was it?
What do I long for? What is it that I so regret?
I'm still uncertain, did I win?
Or was I had?

—October 23, 1914

3

Today melted today
I spent it standing at the window.
My gaze had sobered, my chest felt freer,
I was pacified again.

I don't know why, it must be simply
That my soul had tired
But somehow,
I didn't want to touch that pencil... it rebelled.

And so, I stood there—in the fog—
So far from any good or evil,
Drumming lightly with my finger
Against the softly ringing glass.

My soul no better, and no worse
Than any passerby—take that one.
Than those opaline puddles
Where the horizon splattered,

A soaring bird,
That unbothered dog running by,
Even the singing beggar
Didn't draw tears from my eyes.

Oblivion, oh what a darling art,
The soul has long accustomed to it.
And some big feeling
Was melting in my soul today.

—October 24, 1914

Translated by Masha Udensiva-Brenner

SELECTED POEMS

Wilfred Owen (1893–1918)

Regarded by many as the defining poet of the First World War, Owen is said to have discovered his poetic vocation at the age of eleven. His work is marked by the war itself and by his life in the trenches. His poems are also marked by his gradual discovery of his sexuality – although, long after his death Owen's family and his early biographers sought to suppress his homosexuality and the truth was only finally "revealed" in 1987, in a polemical article by Jonathan Cutbill entitled "The Truth Untold". While a significant number of Owen's letters were destroyed at his request on his death, his friend, Siegfried Sassoon published his posthumous *Poems* in 1920.

MUSIC

I have been urged by earnest violins
And drunk their mellow sorrows to the slake
Of all my sorrows and my thirsting sins.
My heart has beaten for a brave drum's sake.
Huge chords have wrought me mighty: I have hurled
Thuds of gods' thunder. And with old winds pondered
Over the curse of this chaotic world,-
With low lost winds that maundered as they wandered.

I have been gay with trivial fifes that laugh;
And songs more sweet than possible things are sweet;

And gongs, and oboes. Yet I guessed not half
Life's symphony till I had made hearts beat,
And touched Love's body into trembling cries,
And blown my love's lips into laughs and sighs.

TO EROS

In that I loved you, Love, I worshipped you,
In that I worshipped well, I sacrificed
All of most worth. I bound and burnt and slew
Old peaceful lives; frail flowers; firm friends; and Christ.

I slew all falser loves; I slew all true,
That I might nothing love but your truth, Boy.
Fair fame I cast away as bridegrooms do
Their wedding garments in their haste of joy.

But when I fell upon your sandalled feet,
You laughed; you loosed away my lips; you rose.
I heard the singing of your wing's retreat;
Far-flown, I watched you flush the Olympian snows
Beyond my hoping. Starkly I returned
To stare upon the ash of all I burned.

SELECTED POEMS

Sylvia Townsend Warner (1893–1978)

Sylvia Townsend Warner is remembered as an English novelist and poet whose "accidental career" began with a gift of paper with a "particularly tempting surface." She met Valentine Ackland in 1930, and they immediately fell in love. They lived together until Ackland's death in 1969.

When they met, Warner was already an established writer, while Ackland was finding it difficult to get published. In 1934, they wrote a cycle of erotic love poems, *Whether a Dove or a Seagull*. The collection was dedicated to Robert Frost, who rather primly wrote to the editor to request that he 'not... connect me with the book any more than you have to.' Warner and Ackland are buried together at St Nicholas, Chaldon Herring, Dorset.

'SINCE THE FIRST TOSS OF GALE THAT BLEW'

Since the first toss of gale that blew
Me in to you
The wind that our still love awakened
Has never slackened,
But watchful with nightfall keeps pace
With each embrace.
If we love out the winter, my dear,
This will be a year
That babes now lulled on arm will quote
With rusty throat.

For long meeting of our lips
Shall be breaking of ships,
For breath drawn quicker men drowned
And trees downed.
Throe shall fell roof-tree, pulse's knock
Undermine rock,
A cry hurl seas against the land,
A raiding hand,
Scattering lightning along thighs
Lightning from skies
Wrench, and fierce sudden snows clamp deep
On earth our sleep.
Yet who would guess our coming together
Should breed wild weather
Who saw us now? – with looks as sure
As the demure
Flame of our candle, no more plied
By tempest outside
Than those deep ocean weeds unrecking
What winds, what wrecking.
What wrath of wild our dangerous peace
Waits to release.

'DRAWING YOU, HEAVY WITH SLEEP'

Drawing you, heavy with sleep to lie closer,
Staying your poppy head upon my shoulder,
It was as though I pulled the glide
Of a full river to my side.

Heavy with sleep and with sleep pliable
You rolled at a touch towards me. Your arm fell
Across me as a river throws
An arm of flood across meadows.

And as the careless water its mirroring sanction
Grants to him at the river's brim long stationed,
Long drowned in thought, that yet he lives
Since in that mirroring tide he moves,

Your body lying by mine to mine responded:
Your hair stirred on my mouth, my image was dandled
Deep in your sleep that flowed unstained
On from the image entertained.

THE POET SPEAKS TO HIS LOVE ON THE TELEPHONE

Federico García Lorca (1898–1936)

A founding member of the Generation of '27 poets, Lorca was introduced to surrealism through his friendships with Luis Buñuel and Salvador Dalí (with whom he had a passionate platonic friendship). Lorca drew dramatic intensity from the frightening metaphors and unconscious passions of surrealism, his sensual, tragic, often brutal works were also inspired by gypsy culture, flamenco and local folklore. Although Lorca accepted his sexuality, it caused him considerable anguish since he felt forced to conceal his identity. His legacy was further complicated by efforts by his family and by the Franco regime to expunge any reference to his sexuality from even his most overt works.

    In its sweet housing of wood
your voice watered the sand-dune of my heart.
To the south of my feet it was Spring,
north of my brow bracken in flower.

    Down tight space a pine tree of light
sang without dawn or seedbed.
and for the first time my lament
strung crowns of hope across the roof.

Sweet distant voice poured for me.
Sweet distant voice savoured by me.
Sweet distant voice, dying away.

Distant as a dark wounded doe.
Sweet as a sob in snow.
Sweet and distant, in the very marrow!

Translated by Martin Sorrell

EVERYTHING CONTAINS YOU

Karin Boye (1900–1941)

A pioneer of Swedish modernism, Boye's poetry remains highly popular in her native country, but she is more famous elsewhere for her novels, particularly the dystopian novel *Kallocain* which won her international renown. In 1931, she co-founded the poetry magazine *Spektrum*, and translated many of T.S. Eliot's works into Swedish. Although Boye contracted a "lavender marriage", she and her husband divorced in 1932. In the same year she met Margot Hanel, with whom she lived for the remainder of her life.

Everything contains you, more than a deadly
  toll.
You are light and darkness in a double bowl.

How one shimmers naked and cool.
Air of mother-of-pearl over water of pale opal.
Seeing, seen,
dressed for the day
dawn slowly opens its oyster shell.

But the other broods quiet and dusky,
also an oyster, but down deep where the sea is
  still.

Unopened,
since the end of creation
defending the secret room of a mother's
    slumber.

Everything is you, the whole of my essence's
    goal.
You are the day and night in a double bowl.

Translated by Jenny Nunn

BLESSED ASSURANCE

Langston Hughes (1902–1967)

A crucial figure of the Harlem Renaissance, Langston Hughes was a poet, social activist, novelist and playwright. Though born in Kentucky, his parents were political activists. Although Hughes' poetry and shorts stories are marked by veiled references to sexuality and some biographers believe he was asexual, others point to a cache of unpublished poems written to a male lover. In later years, Hughes was a leading figure in the civil rights movement.

Unfortunately (and to John's distrust of God) it seemed his son was turning out to be a queer. He was a brilliant queer, on the Honor Roll in high school, and likely to be graduated in the spring at the head of the class. But the boy was colored. Since colored parents always like to put their best foot forward, John was more disturbed about his son's transition than if they had been white. Negroes have enough crosses to bear.

Delmar was his only son, Arletta, the younger child, being a girl. Perhaps John should not have permitted his son to be named Delmar—Delly for short—but the mother had insisted on it. Delmar was *her* father's name.

"And he is *my* son as well as yours," his wife informed John.

Did the queer strain come from *her* side? Maternal grandpa had seemed normal enough. He was known to have had several affairs with women outside his home—mostly sisters of Tried Stone Church, of which he was a pillar.

God forbid! John, Delly's father thought, could he himself have had any deviate ancestors? None who had acted even remotely effeminate could John recall as being a part of his family. Anyhow, why didn't he name the boy at birth *John, Jr.*, after himself? But his wife said, "Don't saddle him with Junior." Yet she had saddled him with Delmar.

If only Delly were not such a sweet boy—no juvenile delinquency, no stealing cars, no smoking reefers ever. He did the chores without complaint. He washed dishes too easily, with no argument, when he might have left them to Arletta. He seldom, even when at the teasing stage, pulled his sister's hair. They played together, Delly with dolls almost as long as Arletta did. Yet he was good at marbles, once fair at baseball, and a real whiz at tennis. He could have made the track team had he not preferred the French Club, the Dramatic Club, and the Glee Club. Football, his father's game in high school, Delly didn't like. He couldn't keep his eye on the ball in scrimmage. At seventeen he had to have glasses. The style of rather exaggerated rims he chose made him look like a girl rather than a boy.

"At least he didn't get rhinestone rims," thought John halfthought didn't think felt faint and aloud said nothing. That spring he asked, "Delmar, do you have to wear *white* Bermuda shorts to school? Most of the other boys wear Levi's or just plain pants, don't they? And why wash them out yourself every night, all that ironing? I want you to be clean, son, but not *that* clean."

Another time, "Delmar, those school togs of yours don't have to match so perfectly, do they? Colors *blended*, as you say, and all like that. This school you're going to's no fashion school—at least, it wasn't when I went there. The boys'll think you're sissy."

Once again desperately, "If you're going to smoke, Delmar, hold your cigarette between your *first* two fingers, not between your thumb and finger—like a woman."

Then his son cried.

John remembered how it was before the boy's mother packed up and left their house to live with another man who made more money than any Negro in their church. He kept an apartment in South Philly and another in Harlem. Owned a Cadillac. Racket connections—politely called *poli-*

tics. A shame for his children, for the church, and for him, John! His wife gone with an uncouth rascal!

But although Arletta loathed him, Delly liked his not-yet-legal step-father. Delly's mother and her burly lover had at least had the decency to leave Germantown and change their religious affiliations. They no longer attended John's family church where Delmar sang in the Junior Choir.

Delly had a sweet high tenor with overtones of Sam Cooke. The women at Tried Stone loved him. Although Tried Stone was a Baptist church, it tended toward the sedate—Northern Baptist in tone, not down-home. Yet it did have a Gospel Choir, scarlet-robed, since a certain untutored segment of the membership demanded lively music. It had a Senior Choir, too, black-robed, that specialized in anthems, sang "Jesu, Joy of Man's Desiring," the Bach cantatas, and once a year presented the *Messiah*. The white-robed Junior Choir, however, even went so far as to want to render a jazz recessional—Delly's idea—which was vetoed. This while he was trying to grow a beard like the beatniks he had seen when the Junior Choir sang in New York and the Minister of Music had taken Delly on a trip to the Village.

"God, don't let him put an earring in his ear like some," John prayed. He wondered vaguely with a sick feeling in his stomach should he think it through then then think it through right then through should he try then and think it through should without blacking through think blacking out then and there think it through?

John didn't. But one night he remembered his son had once told his mother that after he graduated from high school he would like to study at the Sorbonne. The Sorbonne in Paris! John had studied at Morgan in Baltimore. In possession of a diploma from that *fine* (in his mind) Negro institute, he took pride. Normally John would have wanted his boy to go there, yet the day after the Spring Concert he asked Delmar, "Son, do you still want to study in France? If you do, maybe—er—I guess I could next fall—Sorbonne. Say, how much is a ticket to Paris?"

In October it would be John's turn to host his fraternity brothers at his house. Maybe by then Delmar would—is the Sorbonne like Morgan?

Does it have dormitories, a campus? In Paris he had heard they didn't care about such things. Care about such what things didn't care about what? At least no color lines.

Well, anyhow, what happened at the concert a good six months before October came was, well—think it through clearly now, get it right. Especially for that Spring Concert, Tried Stone's Minister of Music, Dr. Manley Jaxon, had written an original anthem, words and score his own, based on the story of Ruth:

Entreat me not to leave thee,
Neither to go far from thee.
Whither thou goeth, I will go.
Always will I be near thee...

The work was dedicated to Delmar, who received the first handwritten manuscript copy as a tribute from Dr. Jaxon. In spite of its dedication, one might have thought that in performance the solo lead—Ruth's part— would be assigned to a woman. Perversely enough, the composer allotted it to Delmar. Dr. Jaxon's explanation was, "No one else can do it justice." The Minister of Music declared, "The girls in the ensemble really have *no* projection."

So without respect for gender, on the Sunday afternoon of the program, Delmar sang the female lead. Dr. Jaxon, saffron-robed, was at the organ. Until Delmar's father attended the concert that day, he had no inkling as to the casting of the anthem. But when his son's solo began, all John could say was, "I'll be damned!"

John had hardly gotten the words out of his mouth when words became of no further value. The "Papa, what's happening?" of his daughter in the pew beside him made hot saliva rise in his throat—for what suddenly had happened was that as the organ wept and Delmar's voice soared above the choir with all the sweetness of Sam Cooke's tessitura, back- wards off the organ stool in a dead faint fell Dr. Manley Jaxon. Not only did Dr. Jaxon fall from the stool, but he rolled limply down the steps from the organ loft like a bag of meal and tumbled prone onto the rostrum, robes and all.

Amens and Hallelujahs drowned in the throats of various elderly sisters who were on the verge of shouting. Swooning teenage maidens suddenly sat up in their pews to see the excitement. Springing from his chair on the rostrum, the pastor's mind deserted the pending collection to try to think what to say under the unusual circumstances.

"One down, one to go," was all that came to mind. After a series of pastorates in numerous sophisticated cities where Negroes did everything whites do, the Reverend Dr. Greene had seen other choir directors take the count in various ways with equal drama, though perhaps less physical immediacy.

When the organ went silent, the choir died, too—but Delmar never stopped singing. Over the limp figure of Dr. Jaxon lying on the rostrum, the "Entreat me not to leave thee" of his solo flooded the church as if it were on hi-fi.

The members of the congregation sat riveted in their pews as the deacons rushed to the rostrum to lift the Minister of Music to his feet. Several large ladies of the Altar Guild fanned him vigorously while others sprinkled him with water. But it was not until the church's nurse-in-uniform applied smelling salts to Dr. Jaxon's dark nostrils, did he lift his head. Finally, two ushers led him off to an anteroom while Delmar's voice soared to a high C such as Tried Stone Baptist Church had never heard.

"Bless God! Amen!" cried Reverend Greene. "Dr. Jaxon has only fainted, friends. We will continue our services by taking up collection directly after the anthem."

"Daddy, why did Dr. Jaxon have to faint just when brother started singing?" whispered John's daughter.

"I don't know," John said.

"Some of the girls say that when Delmar sings, they want to scream, they're so overcome," whispered Arletta. "But Dr. Jaxon didn't scream. He just fainted."

"Shut up," John said, staring straight ahead at the choir loft. "Oh,

God! Delmar, *shut up*!" John's hands gripped the back of the seat in front of him. "Shut up, son! *Shut up*," he cried. "Shut up!"

Silence...

"We will now lift the offering," announced the minister. "Ushers, get the baskets." Reverend Greene stepped forward. "Deacons, raise a hymn. Bear us up, sisters, bear us up!"

His voice boomed:

Blessed assurance!

He clapped his hands once.

Jesus is mine!

"Yes! Yes! Yes!" he cried.

Oh, what a fortress
Of glory divine!

The congregation swung gently into song:

Heir of salvation,
Purchase of God!

"Hallelujah! Amen! Halle! Halle!"

Born of the Spirit

"God damn it!" John cried. "God *damn* it!"

Washed in His blood...

THE EYES OF THE BODY

Valentine Ackland (1906–1969)

Unlike her lover Sylvia Townsend Warner, Valentine Ackland was a poet whose career has been all but forgotten. The two met in 1930 and immediately fell in love and lived together until Ackland's death in 1969.

The eyes of the body, being blindfold by night,
Refer to the eyes of mind – at brain's command
Study imagination's map, then order out a hand
To journey forth as deputy for sight.

Thus and by these ordered ways
I come at you – Hand deft and delicate
To trace the suavely laid and intricate
Route of your body's maze.

My hand, being deft and delicate, displays
Unerring judgment; cleaves between your thighs
Clean, as a ray-directed airplane flies.

Thus I, within these strictly ordered ways,
Although blindfolded, seize with more than sight
Your moonlit meadows and your shadowed night.

SMOKE, LILIES AND JADE

Bruce Nugent (1906–1987)

Bruce Nugent was a queer writer and artist of the Harlem Renaissance
– which, though widely associated with black empowerment, also
embraced drag balls, cabarets and queer blues concerts. He was a
member of a group of gay Harlem artists, but while most remained
closeted, at least on the national stage, Nugent was defiantly out. During the 1960s, Nugent was one of the co-founders of the Harlem
Cultural Council. Much of his writing was forgotten, and resurfaced
during the 1980s, when it proved an inspiration for the Black gay
movement.

He wanted to do something... to write or draw... or something...
but it was so comfortable just to lie there on the bed... his shoes
off... and think... think of everything... short disconnected
thoughts... to wonder... to remember... to think and smoke... why
wasn't he worried that he had no money... he *had* had five cents... but he
had been hungry... he *was* hungry and still... all he wanted to do was...
lie there comfortably smoking... think... wishing he were writing...
or drawing... or something... something about the things he felt and
thought... but what did he think... he remembered how his mother had
awakened him one night... ages ago... six years ago... Alex... he had
always wondered at the strangeness of it... she had seemed so... so... so
just the same... Alex... I think your father is dead... and it hadn't seemed
so strange... yet... one's mother didn't say that... didn't wake one at
midnight every night to say... feel him... put your hand on his head...
then whisper with a catch in her voice... I'm afraid... ssh don't wake
Lam... yet it hadn't seemed as it should have seemed... even when he

had felt his father's cool wet forehead... it hadn't been tragic... the light had been turned very low... and flickered... yet it hadn't been tragic... or weird... not at all as one should feel when one's father died... even his reply of... yes he is dead... had been commonplace... hadn't been dramatic... there had been no tears... no sobs... not even a sorrow... and yet he must have realized that one's father couldn't smile... or sing anymore... after he had died... everyone remembered his father's voice... it had been a lush voice... a promise... then that dressing together... his mother and himself... in the bathroom... why was the bathroom always the warmest room in the winter... as they had put on their clothes... his mother had been telling him what he must do... and cried softly... and that had made him cry too but you mustn't cry Alex... remember you have to be a little man now... and that was all... didn't other wives and sons cry more for their dead than that... anyway people never cried for beautiful sunsets... or music... and those were the things that hurt... the things to sympathize with... then out into the snow and dark of the morning... first to the undertaker's... no first to Uncle Frank's... why did Aunt Lula have to act like that... to ask again and again... but when did he die... when did he die... I just can't believe it... poor Minerva... then out into the snow and dark again... how had his mother expected him to know where to find the night bell at the undertaker's... he was the most sensible of them all though... all he had said was... what... Harry Francis... too bad... tell mamma I'll be there first thing in the morning... then down the deserted streets again... to grandmother's... it was growing light now... it must be terrible to die in daylight... grandpa had been sweeping the snow off the yard... he had been glad of that because... well he could tell him better than grandma... grandpa... father's dead... and he hadn't acted strange either... books lied... he had just looked at Alex a moment then continued sweeping... all he said was... what time did he die... she'll want to know... then passing through the lonesome street toward home... Mrs. Mamie Grant was closing a window and spied him... hallow Alex... an' how's your father this mornin'... dead... get out... tch tch tch an' I was just around there with a cup a' custard yesterday... Alex puffed contentedly on his cigarette... he was hungry and comfortable... and he had an ivory holder inlaid with red jade and green... funny how the smoke seemed to climb up that ray of sunlight... went up the slant just like imagination... was imagination blue... or was it because he had spent his last five cents and couldn't worry... anyway it was nice to lie there and wonder... and remember... why was he so different from other people... the only things he remembered of his father's funeral were the crowded church and the ride in the hack... so many people there in the church... and ladies with tears in their eyes... and on their cheeks... and some men too... why did people cry... vanity that was all... yet they weren't exactly hypocrites... but why... it had made him furious... all these people crying... it wasn't *their* father... and he wasn't crying... couldn't cry for sorrow although he had loved his father more than... than... it had made him so angry that tears had come to his eyes... and he had been ashamed of his mother... crying into a handkerchief... so ashamed that tears had run down his cheeks and he had frowned... and someone... a woman... had said... look at that poor little dear... Alex is just like his father... and the tears had run fast... because he *wasn't* like his father... he couldn't sing... he didn't want to sing... he didn't want to sing... Alex blew a cloud of smoke... blue smoke... when they had taken his father from the vault three weeks later... he had grown beautiful... his nose had become perfect and clear... his hair had turned jet black and glossy and silky... and his skin was a transparent green... like the sea only not so deep... and where it was drawn over the cheek bones a pale beautiful red appeared... like a blush... why hadn't his father looked like that always... but no... to have sung would have broken the wondrous repose of his lips and maybe that was his beauty... maybe it was wrong to think thoughts like these... but they were nice and pleasant and comfortable... when one was smoking a cigarette through an ivory holder... inlaid with red jade and green..........

he wondered why he couldn't find work... a job... when he had first come to New York he had... and he had only been fourteen then... was it because he was nineteen now that he felt so idle... and contented...

or because he was an artist... but was he an artist... was one an artist until one became known... of course he was an artist... and strangely enough so were all his friends... he should be ashamed that he didn't work... but... was it five years in New York... or the fact that he was an artist... when his mother said she couldn't understand him... why did he vaguely pity her instead of being ashamed... he should be... his mother and all his relatives said so... his brother was three years younger than he and yet he had already been away from home a year... on the stage... making thirty-five dollars a week... had three suits and many clothes and was going to help mother... while he... Alex... was content to lay and smoke and meet friends at night... to argue and read Wilde... Freud... Boccacio and Schnitzler... to attend Gurdjieff meetings and know things... Why did they scoff at him for knowing such people as Carl... Mencken... Toomer... Hughes... Cullen... Wood... Cabell... oh the whole lot of them... was it because it seemed incongruous that he... who was so little known... should call by first names people they would like to know... were they jealous... no mothers aren't jealous of their sons... they are proud of them... why then... when these friends accepted and liked him... no matter how he dressed... why did mother ask... and you went looking like that... Langston was a fine fellow... he knew there was something in Alex... and so did Rene and Borgia... and Zora and Clement and Miguel... and... and... and all of them... if he went to see mother she would ask... how do you feel Alex with nothing in your pockets... I don't see how you can be satisfied... Really you're a mystery to me... and who you take after... I'm sure I don't know... none of my brothers were lazy and shiftless... I can never remember the time when they weren't sending money home and when your father was your age he was supporting a family... where you get your nerve I don't know... just because you've tried to write one or two little poems and stories that no one understands... you seem to think the world owes you a living... you should see by now how much is thought of them... you can't sell anything... and you won't do anything to make money... wake up Alex... I don't know what will become of you........

it was hard to believe in one's self after that... did Wilde's parents or Shelley's or Goya's talk to them like that... but it was depressing to think in that vein... Alex stretched and yawned... Max had died... Margaret had died... so had Sonia... Cynthia... Juan-Jose and Harry... all people he had loved... loved one by one and together... and all had died... he never loved a person long before they died... in truth he was tragic... that was a lovely appellation... The Tragic Genius... think... to go through life known as The Tragic Genius... romantic... but it was more or less true... Alex turned over and blew another cloud of smoke... was all life like that... smoke... blue smoke from an ivory holder... he wished he were in New Bedford... New Bedford was a nice place... snug little houses set complacently behind protecting lawns... half-open windows showing prim interiors from behind waving cool curtains... inviting... like precise courtesans winking from behind lace fans... and trees... many trees... casting lacy patterns of shade on the sun-dipped sidewalks... small stores... naively proud of their pseudo grandeur... banks... called institutions for saving... all naive... that was it... New Bedford was naive... after the sophistication of New York it would fan one like a refreshing breeze... and yet he had returned to New York... and sophistication... was he sophisticated... no because he was seldom bored... seldom bored by anything... and weren't the sophisticated continually suffering from ennui... on the contrary... he was amused... amused by the artificiality of naiveté and sophistication alike... but maybe that in itself was the essence of sophistication or... was it cynicism... or were the two identical... he blew a cloud of smoke... it was growing dark now... and the smoke no longer had a ladder to climb... but soon the moon would rise and then he would clothe the silver moon in blue smoke garments... truly smoke was like imagination.........

Alex sat up... pulled on his shoes and went out... it was a beautiful night... and so large... the dusky blue hung like a curtain in an immense arched doorway... fastened with silver tacks... to wander in the night was wonderful... myriads of inquisitive lights... curiously prying into the dark... and fading unsatisfied... he passed a woman... she was not beautiful... and he was sad because she did not weep that she would never be beautiful... was it Wilde who had said... a cigarette is the most perfect pleasure because it leaves one unsatisfied... the breeze gave to him a perfume stolen from some wandering lady of the evening... it pleased him... why was it that men wouldn't use perfumes... they should... each and every one of them liked perfumes... the man who denied that was a liar... or a coward... but if ever he were to voice that thought... express it... he would be misunderstood... a fine feeling that... to be misunderstood... it made him feel tragic and great... but maybe it would be nicer to be understood... but no... no great artist is... then again neither were fools... they were strangely akin these two... Alex thought of a sketch he would make... a personality sketch of Fania... straight classic features tinted proud purple... sensuous fine lips... gilded for truth... eyes... half opened and lids colored mysterious green... hair black and straight... drawn sternly mocking back from the false puritanical forehead... maybe he would make Edith too... skin a blue... infinite like night... and eyes... slant and gray... very complacent like a cat's... Mona Lisa lips... red and seductive as... as pomegranate juice... in truth it was fine to be young and hungry and an artist... to blow blue smoke from an ivory holder............

here was the cafeteria... it was almost as though it had journeyed to meet him... the night was so blue... how does blue feel... or red or gold or any other color... if colors could be heard he could paint most wondrous tunes... symphonious... think... the dulcet clear tone of a blue like night... of a red like pomegranate juice... like Edith's lips... of the fairy tones to be heard in a sunset... like rubies shaken in a crystal cup... of the symphony of Fania... and silver... and gold... he had heard the sound of gold... but they weren't the sounds he wanted to catch... no... they must be liquid... not so staccato but flowing variations of the same caliber... there was no one in the cafe as yet... he sat and waited... that was a clever idea he had had about color music... but after all he was a monstrous clever fellow... Jurgen had said that... funny how characters in books said the things one wanted to say... he would like to know

Jurgen… how does one go about getting an introduction to a fiction character… go up to the brown cover of the book and knock gently… and say hello… then timidly… is Duke Jurgen there… or… no because if one entered the book in the beginning Jurgen would only be a pawnbroker… and one didn't enter a book in the center… but what foolishness… Alex lit a cigarette… but Cabell was a master to have written Jurgen… and an artist… and a poet… Alex blew a cloud of smoke… a few lines of one of Langston's poems came to describe Jurgen.....

Somewhat like Ariel
Somewhat like Puck
Somewhat like a gutter boy
Who loves to play in muck.
Somewhat like Bacchus
Somewhat like Pan
And a way with women
Like a sailor man........

Langston must have known Jurgen… suppose Jurgen had met Tonio Kroeger… what a vagrant thought… Kroeger… Kroeger… Kroeger… why here was Rene… Alex had almost gone to sleep… Alex blew a cone of smoke as he took Rene's hand… it was nice to have friends like Rene… so comfortable… Rene was speaking… Borgia joined them… and de Diego Padro… their talk veered to… James Branch Cabell… beautiful… marvelous… Rene had an enchanting accent… said sank for thank and souse for south… but they couldn't know Cabell's greatness… Alex searched the smoke for expression… he… he… well he has created a fantasy mire… that's it… from clear rich imagery… life and silver sands… that's nice… and silver sands… imagine lilies growing in such a mire… when they close at night their gilded underside would protect… but that's not it at all… his thoughts just carried and mingled like… like odors… suggested but never definite… Rene was leaving… they all were leaving… Alex sauntered slowly back… the houses all looked sleepy…

funny… made him feel like writing poetry… and about death too… an elevated crashed by overhead scattering all his thoughts with its noise… making them spread… in circles… then larger circles… just like a splash in a calm pool… what had he been thinking… of… a poem about death… but he no longer felt that urge… just walk and think and wonder… think and remember and smoke… blow smoke that mixed with his thoughts and the night… he would like to live in a large white palace… to wear a long black cape… very full and lined with vermilion… to have many cushions and to lie there among them… talking to his friends… lie there in a yellow silk shirt and black velvet trousers… like music-review artists talking and pouring strange liquors from curiously beautiful bottles… bottles with long slender necks… he climbed the noisy stair of the odorous tenement… smelled of fish… of stale fried fish and dirty milk bottles… he rather liked it… he liked the acrid smell of horse manure too… strong… thoughts… yes to lie back among strangely fashioned cushions and sip eastern wines and talk… Alex threw himself on the bed… removed his shoes… stretched and relaxed… yes and have music waft softly into the darkened and incensed room… he blew a cloud of smoke… oh the joy of being an artist and of blowing blue smoke through an ivory holder inlaid with red jade and green…

the street was so long and narrow… so long and narrow… and blue… in the distance it reached the stars… and if he walked long enough… far enough… he could reach the stars too… the narrow blue was so empty… quiet… Alex walked music… it was nice to walk in the blue after a party… Zora had shone again… her stories… she always shone… and Monty was glad… everyone was glad when Zora shone… he was glad he had gone to Monty's party… Monty had a nice place in the village… nice lights… and friends and wine… mother would be scandalized that he could think of going to a party… without a copper to his name… but then mother had never been to Monty's… and mother had never seen the street seem long and narrow and blue… Alex walked music… the click of his heels kept time with a tune in his mind… he glanced into a lighted cafe window… inside were people sipping coffee… men… why did they sit there in the loud light… didn't they know that outside the street… the narrow blue street met the stars… that if they walked long enough… far enough… Alex walked and the click of his heels sounded… and had an echo… sound being tossed back and forth… back and forth… someone was approaching… and their echoes mingled… and gave the sound of castanets… Alex liked the sound of the approaching man's footsteps… he walked music also… he knew the beauty of the narrow blue… Alex knew that by the way their echoes mingled… he wished he would speak… but strangers don't speak at four o'clock in the morning… at least if they did he couldn't imagine what would be said… maybe pardon me but are you walking toward the stars… yes, sir, and if you walk long enough… then may I walk with you… I want to reach the stars too… perdone me señor tiene usted fósforo… Alex was glad he had been addressed in Spanish… to have been asked for a match in English… or to have been addressed in English at all… would have been blasphemy just then… Alex handed him a match… he glanced at his companion apprehensively in the match glow… he was afraid that his appearance would shatter the blue thoughts… and stars… ah… his face was a perfect compliment to his voice… and the echo of their steps mingled… they walked in silence… the castanets of their heels clicking accompaniment… the stranger inhaled deeply and with a nod of content and a smile… blew a cloud of smoke… Alex felt like singing… the stranger knew the magic of blue smoke also… they continued in silence… the castanets of their heels clicking rhythmically… Alex turned in his doorway… up the stairs and the stranger waited for him to light the room… no need for words… they had always known each other………

as they undressed by the blue dawn… Alex knew he had never seen a more perfect being… his body was all symmetry and music… and Alex called him Beauty… long they lay… blowing smoke and exchanging thoughts… and Alex swallowed with difficulty… he felt a glow of tremor… and they talked and… slept…

Alex wondered more and more why he liked Adrian so... he liked many people... Wallie... Zora... Clement... Gloria... Langston... John... Gwenny... oh many people... and they were friends... but Beauty... it was different... once Alex had admired Beauty's strength... and Beauty's eyes had grown soft and he had said... I like you more than anyone Dulce... Adrian always called him Dulce... and Alex had become confused... was it that he was so susceptible to beauty that Alex liked Adrian so much... but no... he knew other people who were beautiful... Fania and Gloria... Monty and Bunny... but he was never confused before them... while Beauty... Beauty could make him believe in Buddha... or imps... and no one else could do that... that is no one but Melva... but then he was in love with Melva... and that explained that... he would like Beauty to know Melva... they were both so perfect... such compliments... yes he would like Beauty to know Melva because he loved them both... there... he had thought it... actually dared to think it... but Beauty must never know... Beauty couldn't understand... indeed Alex couldn't understand... and it pained him... almost physically... and tired his mind... Beauty... Beauty was in the air... the smoke... Beauty... Melva... Beauty... Melva... Alex slept... and dreamed.....

he was in a field... a field of blue smoke and black poppies and red calla lilies... he was searching... on his hands and knees... searching... among black poppies and red calla lilies... he was searching and pushed aside poppy stems... and saw two strong white legs... dancer's legs... the contours pleased him... his eyes wandered... on past the muscular hocks to the firm white thighs... the rounded buttocks... then the lithe narrow waist... strong torso and broad deep chest... the heavy shoulders... the graceful muscled neck... squared chin and quizzical lips... Grecian nose with its temperamental nostrils... the brown eyes looking at him... like... Monty looked at Zora... his hair curly and black and all tousled... and it was Beauty... and Beauty smiled and looked at him and smiled... said... I'll wait Alex... and Alex became confused and continued his search... on his hands and knees... pushing aside poppy stems and lily stems... a poppy... a black poppy... a lily... a red lily... and when he looked back he could no longer see Beauty... Alex continued his search... through poppies... lilies... poppies and red calla lilies... and suddenly he saw... two small feet olive-ivory... two well-turned legs curving gracefully from slender ankles... and the contours soothed him... he followed them... past the narrow rounded hips to the tiny waist... the fragile firm breasts... the graceful slender throat... the soft rounded chin... slightly parting lips and straight little nose with its slightly flaring nostrils... the black eyes with lights in them... looking at him... the forehead and straight cut black hair... and it was Melva... and she looked at him and smiled and said... I'll wait Alex... and Alex became confused and kissed her... became confused and continued his search... on his hands and knees... pushed aside a poppy stem... a black-poppy stem... pushed aside a lily stem... a red-lily stem... a poppy... a poppy... a lily... and suddenly he stood erect... exultant... and in his hand he held... an ivory holder... inlaid with red jade... and green............

and Alex awoke... Beauty's hair tickled his nose... Beauty was smiling in his sleep... half his face stained flush color by the sun... the other half in shadow... blue shadow... his eyelashes casting cobwebby blue shadows on his cheek... his lips were so beautiful... quizzical... Alex wondered why he always thought of that passage from Wilde's Salome... when he looked at Beauty's lips... I would kiss your lips... he *would* like to kiss Beauty's lips... Alex flushed warm... with shame... or was it shame... he reached across Beauty for a cigarette... Beauty's cheek felt cool to his arm... his hair felt soft... Alex lay smoking... such a dream... red calla lilies... red calla lilies... and... what could it all mean... did dreams have meanings... Fania said... and black poppies... thousands... millions... Beauty stirred... Alex put out his cigarette... closed his eyes... he mustn't see Beauty yet... speak to him... his lips were too hot... dry... the palms of his hands too cool and moist... through his half-closed eyes he could see Beauty... propped... cheek in hand... on one elbow... looking at him... lips smiling quizzically... he wished Beauty wouldn't look so hard... Alex was finding it difficult to breathe... breathe normally... why *must* Beauty look so long... and smile *that way*... his face seemed nearer... it was... Alex could feel Beauty's hair on his forehead... breathe normally... breathe normally... could feel Beauty's breath on his nostrils and lips... and it was clean and faintly colored with tobacco... breathe normally Alex... Beauty's lips were nearer... Alex closed his eyes... how did one act... his pulse was hammering... from wrist to finger tip... wrist to finger tip... Beauty's lips touched his... his temples throbbed... throbbed... his pulse hammered from wrist to finger tip... Beauty's breath came short now... softly staccato... breathe normally Alex... you are asleep... Beauty's lips touched his... breathe normally... and pressed... pressed hard... cool... his body trembled... breathe normally Alex... Beauty's lips pressed cool... cool and hard... how much pressure does it take to waken one... Alex sighed... moved softly... how does one act... Beauty's hair barely touched him now... his breath was faint on... Alex's nostrils and lips... Alex stretched and opened his eyes... Beauty was looking at him... propped on one elbow... cheek in his palm... Beauty spoke... scratch my head please Duke... Alex was breathing normally now... propped against the bed head... Beauty's head in his lap... Beauty spoke... I wonder why I like to look at some things Duke... things like smoke and cats... and you... Alex's pulse no longer hammered from... wrist to finger tip... wrist to finger tip... the rose dusk had become blue night... and soon... soon they would go out into the blue.......

the little church was crowded... warm... the rows of benches were brown and sticky... Harold was there... and Constance and Langston and Bruce and John... there was Mr. Robeson... how are you Paul... a young man was singing... Caver... Caver was a very self-assured young man... such a dream... poppies... black poppies... they were applauding... Constance and John were exchanging notes... the benches were sticky... a young lady was playing the piano... fair... and red calla lilies... who had ever heard of red calla lilies... they were applauding... a young man was playing the viola... what could it all mean... so many poppies... and Beauty looking at him like... like Monty looked at Zora... another young man was playing a violin... he was the first real artist to perform... he had a touch of soul... or was it only feeling... they were hard to differentiate on the violin... and Melva standing in the poppies and lilies... Mr. Phillips was singing... Mr. Phillips was billed as a basso... and he had kissed her... they were applauding... the first young man was singing again... Langston's spiritual... Fy-ah-fy-ah-Lawd... fy-ah's gonna burn ma soul... Beauty's hair was so black and curly... they were applauding... encore... Fy-ah Lawd had been a success... Langston bowed... Langston had written the words... Hall bowed... Hall had written the music... the young man was singing it again... Beauty's lips had pressed hard... cool... cool... fy-ah Lawd... his breath had trembled... fy-ah's gonna burn ma soul... they were all leaving... first to the roof dance... fy-ah Lawd... there was Catherine... she was beautiful tonight... she always was at night... Beauty's lips... fy-ah Lawd... hello Dot... why don't you take a boat that sails... when are you leaving again... and there's Estelle... everyone was there... fy-ah Lawd... Beauty's body had pressed close... close... fy-ah's gonna burn my soul... let's leave... have to meet some people at the New World... then to Augusta's party... Harold... John... Bruce... Connie... Langston... ready... down one hundred thirty- fifth street... fy-ah... meet these people and leave... fy-ah Lawd... now to Augusta's party... fy-ah's gonna burn ma soul... they were at Augusta's... Alex half lay... half sat on the floor... sipping a cocktail... such a dream... red calla lilies... Alex left... down the narrow streets... fy-ah... up the long noisy stairs... fy-ahs gonna bu'n ma soul... his head felt swollen... expanding... contracting... expanding... contracting... he had never been like this before... expanding... contracting... it was that... fy-ah... fy-ah Lawd... and the cocktails... and Beauty... he felt two cool strong hands on his shoulders... it was Beauty... lie down Dulce... Alex lay down... Beauty... Alex stopped... no no... don't say it... Beauty mustn't know... Beauty couldn't understand... are you going to lie down too Beauty... the light went out expanding... contracting... he felt the bed sink as Beauty lay beside him... his lips were dry... hot... the palms of his hands so moist and cool... Alex partly closed his eyes... from beneath his lashes he could see Beauty's face over his... nearer... nearer... Beauty's hair touched his forehead now... he could feel his breath on his nostrils and lips... Beauty's breath came short... breathe normally Beauty... breathe normally... Beauty's lips touched his... pressed hard... cool... opened slightly... Alex opened his eyes... into Beauty's... parted his lips... Dulce... Beauty's breath was hot and short... Alex ran his hand through Beauty's hair... Beauty's lips pressed hard against his teeth... Alex trembled... could feel Beauty's body... close against his... hot... tense... white... and soft... soft... soft........

they were at Forno's... everyone came to Forno's once... maybe only once... but they came... see that big fat woman Beauty... Alex pointed to an overly stout and bejeweled lady making her way through the maze of chairs... that's Maria Guerrero... Beauty looked to see a lady guiding almost the whole opera company to an immense table... really Dulce... for one who appreciates beauty you do use the most abominable English... Alex lit a cigarette... and that florid man with white hair... that's Carl... Beauty smiled... The Blind Bow-Boy... he asked... Alex wondered... everything seemed so... so just the same... here they were laughing and joking about people... there's Rene... Rene this is my friend Adrian... after that night... and he felt so unembarrassed... Rene and Adrian were talking... there was Lucrecia Bori... she was bowing at their table... oh her cousin was with them... and Peggy Joyce... everyone came to Forno's... Alex looked toward the door... there was Melva... Alex beckoned... Melva this is Adrian... Beauty held her hand... they talked... smoked... Alex loved Melva... in Forno's... everyone came there sooner or later... maybe only once... but.........

up... up... slow... jerk up... up... not fast... not glorious... but slow... up... up into the sun... slow... sure like fate... poise on the brim... the brim of life... two shining rails straight down... Melva's head was on his shoulder... his arm was around her... poised... the down... gasping... straight down... straight like sin... down... the curving shiny rail rushed up to meet them... hit the bottom then... shoot up... fast... glorious... up into the sun... Melva gasped... Alex's arm tightened... all goes up... then down... straight like hell... all breath squeezed out of them... Melva's head on his shoulder... up... up... Alex kissed her... down... they stepped out of the car... walking music... now over to the Ferris Wheel... out and up... Melva's hand was soft in his... out and up... over mortals... mortals drinking nectar... five cents a glass... her cheek was soft on his... up... up... till the world seemed small... tiny... the ocean seemed tiny and blue... up... up and out... over the sun... the tiny red sun... Alex kissed her... up... up... their tongues touched... up... seventh heaven... the sea had swallowed the sun... up and out... her breath was perfumed... Alex kissed her... drift down... soft... soft... the sun had left the sky flushed... drift down... soft down... back to earth... visit the mortals sipping nectar at five cents a glass... Melva's lips brushed his... then out among the mortals... and the sun had left a flush on Melva's cheeks... they walked hand in hand... and the moon came out... they walked in silence on the silver strip... and the sea sang for them... they walked toward the moon... we'll hang our hats on the crook of the moon Melva... softly on the silver strip... his hands molded her features and her cheeks were soft and warm to his touch... where is Adrian... Alex... Melva trod silver... Alex trod sand... Alex trod sand... the sea *sang* for her... Beauty... her hand felt cold in his... Beauty... the sea *dinned*... Beauty... he led the way to the train... and the train dinned... Beauty... dinned... dinned... her cheek *had* been soft... Beauty... Beauty... her breath *had* been perfumed... Beauty... Beauty... the sands *had* been silver... Beauty... Beauty... they left the train... Melva walked music... Melva said... don't make me blush again... and kissed him... Alex stood on the steps after she left him... and the night was black... down long streets to... Alex lit a cigarette... and his heels clicked... Beauty... Melva... Beauty... Melva... and the smoke made the night blue...

Melva had said... don't make me blush again... and kissed him... and the street had been blue… one *can* love two at the same time… Melva had kissed him… one *can*… and the street had been blue… one *can*… and the room was clouded with blue smoke… drifting vapors of smoke and thoughts… Beauty's hair was so black… and soft… blue smoke from an ivory holder… was that why he loved Beauty… one *can*… or because his body was beautiful… and white and warm… or because his eyes… one *can* love……..

… To Be Continued…

LEE AND THE BOYS

William Burroughs (1914–1997)

Born in 1914 to a wealthy family in St Louis Missouri, Burroughs spent a lifetime subverting the bourgeois morality inculcated in him. His time at Harvard was marked by weekend jaunts to the gay bars of Greenwich Village. He later moved to pre-war Weimar Germany. One of the crucial figures of the Beat Generation, Burroughs' early writings, *Queer* and *Junkie* offered only a glimpse of his dazzling, visceral postmodern novels. The seminal *Naked Lunch* – with its cut-up techniques and explicit sexuality – triggered the last major US censorship case. His work has influenced artists as diverse as David Bowie, J. G. Ballard and Kurt Cobain.

The sun spotlights the inner thigh of a boy sitting in shorts on a doorstep, his legs swinging open, and you fall in spasms—sperm spurting in orgasm after orgasm, grinding against the stone street, neck and back break… now lying dead, eyes rolled back, showing slits of white that redden slowly, as blood tears form and run down the face—

Or the sudden clean smell of salt air, piano down a city street, a dusty poplar tree shaking in the hot afternoon wind, pictures explode in the brain like skyrockets, smells, tastes, sounds shake the body, nostalgia becomes unendurable, aching pain, the brain is an overloaded switchboard sending insane messages and countermessages to the viscera. Finally the body gives up, cowering like a neurotic cat, blood pressure drops, body fluids leak through stretched, flaccid veins, shock passes to coma and death.

Somebody rapped on the outside shutter. Lee opened the shutter and looked out. An Arab boy of fourteen or so—they always look younger than they are—was standing there, smiling in a way that could only mean one thing. He said something in Spanish that Lee did not catch. Lee shook his head and started to close the shutter. The boy, still smiling, held the shutter open. Lee gave a jerk and slammed the shutter closed. He could feel the rough wood catch and tear the boy's hand. The boy turned without a word and walked away, his shoulders drooping, holding his hand. At the corner the small figure caught a patch of light.

I didn't mean to hurt him, Lee thought. He wished he had given the boy some money, a smile at least. He felt crude and detestable.

Years ago he had been riding in a hotel station wagon in the West Indies. The station wagon slowed down for a series of bumps, and a little black girl ran up smiling and threw a bouquet of flowers into the car through the rear window. A round-faced, heavyset American in a brown gabardine suit gathered up the flowers and said, "No want," and tossed them at the little girl. The flowers fell in the dusty road, and the little girl turned around crying and ran away.

Lee closed the shutter slowly.

In the Rio Grande valley of South Texas, he had killed a rattlesnake with a golf club. The impact of metal on the live flesh of the snake sent an electric shiver through him.

In New York, when he was rolling lushes on the subway with Roy, at the end of the line in Brooklyn a drunk grabbed Roy and started yelling for the law. Lee hit the drunk in the face and knocked him to his knees, then kicked him in the side. A rib snapped. Lee felt a shudder of nausea.

Next day he told Roy he was through as a lush worker. Roy looked at him with his impersonal brown eyes that caught points of light, like an opal. There was a masculine gentleness in Roy's voice, a gentleness that only the strong have: "You feel bad about kicking that mooch, don't you? You're not cut out for this sort of thing, Bill. I'll find someone else to work with." Roy put on his hat and started to leave. He stopped with the doorknob in his hand and turned around.

"It's none of my business, Bill. But you have enough money to get by. Why don't you just quit?" He walked out without waiting for Lee to answer.

Lee did not feel like finishing the letter. He put on his coat and stepped out into the narrow, sunless street.

The druggist saw Lee standing in the doorway of the store. The store was about eight feet wide, with bottles and packages packed around three walls. The druggist smiled and held up a finger.

"One?" he said in English.

Lee nodded, looking around at the bottles and packages. The clerk handed the box of ampules to Lee without wrapping it. Lee said, "Thank you."

He walked away through a street lined on both sides with bazaars. Merchandise overflowed into the street, and he dodged crockery and washtubs and trays of combs and pencils and soap dishes. A train of burros loaded with charcoal blocked his way. He passed a woman with no nose, a black slit in her face, her body wrapped in grimy, padded pink cotton. Lee walked fast, twisting his body sideways, squeezing past people. He reached the sunny alleys of the outer Medina.

Walking in Tangier was like falling, plunging down dark shafts of streets, catching at corners, doorways. He passed a blind man sitting in the sun in a doorway. The man was young, with a fringe of blond beard. He sat there with one hand out, his shirt open, showing the smooth, patient flesh, the slight, immobile folds in the stomach. He sat there all day, every day.

Lee turned into his street, and a cool wind from the sea chilled the sweat on his thin body. He hooked the key into the lock and pushed the door open with his shoulder.

He tied up for the shot, and slid the needle in through a festered scab. Blood swirled up into the hypo—he was using a regular hypo these days. He pressed the plunger down with his forefinger. A passing caress of pleasure flushed through his veins. He glanced at the cheap alarm clock on the table by the bed: four o'clock. He was meeting his boy at eight. Time enough for the Eukodal to get out of his system.

Lee walked about the room. "I have to quit," he said over and over, feeling the gravity pull of junk in his cells. He experienced a moment of panic. A cry of despair wrenched his body: "I have to get *out* of here. I have to make a break."

As he said the words, he remembered whose words they were: the Mad Dog Esposito Brothers, arrested at the scene of a multiple-slaying holdup, separated from the electric chair by a little time and a few formalities, whispered these words into a police microphone planted by their beds in the detention ward.

He sat down at the typewriter, yawned, and made some notes on a separate piece of paper. Lee often spent hours on a letter. He dropped the pencil and stared at the wall, his face blank and dreamy, reflecting on the heartwarming picture of William Lee—

He was sure the reviewers in those queer magazines like *One* would greet Willy Lee as heartwarming, except when he gets—squirming uneasily—well, you know, a bit out of line, somehow.

"Oh, that's just boyishness—after all, you know a boy's will is the wind's will, and the thoughts of youth are long, long thoughts."

"Yes I know, but... the purple-assed baboons..."

"That's gangrened innocence."

"Why didn't I think of *that* myself. And the piles?"

"All kids are like hung up on something."

"So they are... and the prolapsed assholes feeling around, looking for a peter, like blind worms?"

"Schoolboy smut."

"Understand, I'm not trying to *belittle* Lee—"

"You'd better not. He's a one-hundred-percent wistful boy, listening to train whistles across the winter stubble and frozen red clay of Georgia."

—yes, there was something a trifle disquieting in the fact that the heartwarming picture of William Lee should be drawn by William Lee himself. He thought of the ultimate development in stooges, a telepathic stooge who tunes in on your psyche and says just what you want to hear: "Boss, you is heartwarming. You is a latter-assed purple-day saint."

Lee put down the pencil and yawned. He looked at the bed.

I'm sleepy, he decided. He took off his pants and shoes and lay down on the bed, covering himself with a cotton blanket. *They don't scratch.* He closed his eyes. Pictures streamed by, the magic lantern of junk. There is a feeling of too much junk that corresponds to the bed spinning around when you are very drunk, a feeling of gray, dead horror. The pictures in the brain are out of control, black and white, without emotion, the deadness of junk lying in the body like a viscous, thick medium.

A child came up to Lee and held up to him a bleeding hand.

"Who did this?" Lee asked. "I'll kill him. Who did it?"

The child beckoned Lee into a dark room. He pointed at Lee with the bleeding stub of a finger. Lee woke up crying "No! No!"

Lee looked at the clock. It was almost eight. His boy was due anytime. Lee rummaged in a drawer of the bed table and found a stick of tea. He lit it and lay back to wait for KiKi. There was a bitter, green taste in his mouth from the weed. He could feel a warm tingle spread over his body. He put his hands behind his head, stretching his ribs and arching his stomach.

Lee was forty, but he had the lean body of an adolescent. He looked down at the stomach, which curved in flat from the chest. Junk had sculpted his body down to bone and muscle. He could feel the wall of his stomach right under the skin. His skin smooth and white, he looked almost transparent, like a tropical fish, with blue veins where the hipbones protruded.

KiKi stepped in. He switched on the light.

"Sleeping?" he asked.

"No, just resting." Lee got up and put his arms around KiKi, holding him in a long, tight embrace.

"What's the matter, Meester William?" KiKi said, laughing.

"Nothing."

They sat down on the edge of the bed. KiKi ran his hands absently over Lee's back. He turned and looked at Lee.

"Very thin," he said. "You should eat more."

Lee pulled in his stomach so it almost touched the backbone. KiKi laughed and ran his hands down Lee's ribs to the stomach. He put his thumbs on Lee's backbone and tried to encircle Lee's stomach with his hands. He got up and took off his clothes and sat down beside Lee, caressing him with casual affection.

Like many Spanish boys, KiKi did not feel love for women. To him a woman was only for sex. He had known Lee for some months, and felt a genuine fondness for him, in an offhand way. Lee was considerate and generous and did not ask KiKi to do things he didn't want to do, leaving the lovemaking on an adolescent basis. KiKi was well pleased with the arrangement.

And Lee was well pleased with KiKi. He did not like the process of looking for boys. He did not lose interest in a boy after a few contacts, not being subject to compulsive promiscuity. In Mexico he had slept with the same boy twice a week for over a year. The boy had looked enough like KiKi to be his brother. Both had very straight black hair, an Oriental look, and lean, slight bodies. Both exuded the same quality of sweet masculine innocence. Lee met the same people wherever he went.

THE QUILT
Ismat Chughtai (1915–1991)

Born in Uttar Pradesh, the ninth of ten children, Ismat Chugtai faced fierce resistance from her family when she chose to study at the Aligarh Muslim University. It was here she became associated with the Progressive Writers' Movement. Her novels and stories explore female sexuality and femininity, middle-class gentility, and class conflict. Intimations of lesbianism in the story, *The Quilt* led to Chughtai being charged with obscenity by the Lahore High Court. She was exonerated. She went on to write a dozen novels and many screenplays.

In winter, when I put a quilt over myself, its shadows on the wall seem to sway like an elephant. That sends my mind racing into the labyrinth of times past. Memories come crowding in.

Sorry. I'm not going to regale you with a romantic tale about my quilt. It's hardly a subject for romance. It seems to me that the blanket, though less comfortable, does not cast shadows as terrifying as the quilt dancing on the wall.

I was then a small girl and fought all day with my brothers and their friends. Often I wondered why the hell I was so aggressive. At my age, my other sisters were busy drawing admirers, while I fought with any boy or girl I ran into.

That was why, when my mother went to Agra for about a week, she left me with an adopted sister of hers. She knew that there was no one in that house, not even a mouse, with whom I could get into a fight. It was a severe punishment for me! Amma left me with Begum Jaan, the same lady whose quilt is etched in my memory like the scar left by a blacksmith's brand. Her poor parents had agreed to marry her off to the nawab who was of 'ripe years' because he was very virtuous. No one had ever seen a nautch girl or prostitute in his house. He had performed hajj and helped several others undertake the holy pilgrimage.

He, however, had a strange hobby. Some people are crazy enough to cultivate interests like breeding pigeons or watching cockfights. Nawab Saheb had only contempt for such disgusting sports. He kept an open house for students – young, fair, slender-waisted boys whose expenses were borne by him.

Having married Begum Jaan, he tucked her away in the house with his other possessions and promptly forgot her. The frail, beautiful Begum wasted away in anguished loneliness.

One did not know when Begum Jaan's life began – whether it was when she committed the mistake of being born or when she came to the nawab's house as his bride, climbed the four-poster bed and started counting her days. Or was it when she watched through the drawing-room door the increasing number of firm-calved, supple-waisted boys and the delicacies that were sent for them from the kitchen! Begum Jaan would have glimpses of them in their perfumed, flimsy shirts and feel as though she was being hauled over burning embers!

Or did it start when she gave up on amulets, talismans, black magic and other ways of retaining the love of her straying husband? She arranged for night-long readings from the Quran, but in vain. One cannot draw blood from a stone. The nawab didn't budge an inch. Begum Jaan was heartbroken and turned to books. But she found no relief. Romantic novels and sentimental verse depressed her even more. She began to spend sleepless nights, yearning for a love that had never been.

She felt like throwing all her clothes into the fire. One dressed up to impress people. But the nawab didn't have a moment to spare for her. He was too busy chasing the gossamer shirts. Nor did he allow her to go out. Relatives, however, would come for visits and stay on for months while she remained a prisoner in the house. These relatives, freeloaders all, made her blood boil. They helped themselves to rich food and got warm clothes made for themselves while she stiffened with cold despite the new cotton stuffed in her quilt. As she tossed and turned, her quilt made newer shapes on the wall, but none of them held any promise of life for her. Then why must one live? Particularly, such a life as hers... But then, Begum Jaan started living, and lived her life to the full.

It was Rabbu who rescued her from the fall.

Soon her thin body began to fill out. Her cheeks began to glow, and she blossomed. It was a special oil massage that brought life back to the half-dead Begum Jaan. Sorry, you won't find the recipe for this oil even in the most exclusive magazines.

When I first saw Begum Jaan, she was around forty. Reclining on the couch, she looked a picture of grandeur. Rabbu sat behind her, massaging her waist. A purple shawl covered her feet as she sat in regal splendour, a veritable maharani. I was fascinated by her looks and felt like sitting by her for hours, just adoring her. Her complexion was marble white, without a speck of ruddiness. Her hair was black and always bathed in oil. I had never seen the parting of her hair crooked, nor a single hair out of place. Her eyes were black and the elegantly plucked eyebrows seemed like two bows spread over the demure eyes. Her eyelids were heavy and her eyelashes dense. The most fascinating feature of her face, however, was her lips – usually coloured with lipstick and with a mere trace of down on her upper lip. Long hair covered her temples. Sometimes her face seemed to change shape under my gaze and looked as though it were the face of a young boy...

Her skin was white and smooth, as though it had been stitched tightly over her body. When she stretched her legs for the massage, I stole a glance, enraptured by their sheen. She was very tall and the ample flesh on her body made her look stately and magnificent. Her hands were large and smooth, her waist exquisitely formed. Rabbu used to massage her back for hours together. It was as though the massage was one of the basic necessities of life. Rather, more important than life's necessities.

Rabbu had no other household duties. Perched on the couch she was always massaging some part or the other of Begum Jaan's body. At times I could hardly bear it – the sight of Rabbu massaging or rubbing at all hours. Speaking for myself, if anyone were to touch my body so often, I would certainly rot to death.

But even this daily massage wasn't enough. On the days when Begum Jaan took a bath, Rabbu would massage her body with a variety of oils and pastes for two hours. And she would massage with such vigour that even imagining it made me sick. The doors would be closed, the braziers would be lit, and then the session would begin. Usually Rabbu was the only person allowed to remain inside on such occasions. Other maids handed over the necessary things at the door, muttering disapproval.

In fact, Begum Jaan was afflicted with a persistent itch. Despite the oils and balms, the stubborn itch remained. Doctors and hakeems pronounced that nothing was wrong, the skin was unblemished. It could be an infection under the skin. 'These doctors are crazy… There's nothing wrong with you,' Rabbu would say, smiling while she gazed at Begum Jaan dreamily.

Rabbu. She was as dark as Begum Jaan was fair, as purple as the other was white. She seemed to glow like heated iron. Her face was scarred by smallpox. She was short, stocky and had a small paunch. Her hands were small but agile, and her large, swollen lips were always wet. A strange sickening stench exuded from her body. And her tiny, puffy hands moved dexterously over Begum Jaan's body – now at her waist, now at her thighs, and now dashing to her ankles. Whenever I sat by Begum Jaan, my eyes would remain glued to those roving hands.

All through the year Begum Jaan wore white and billowing Hydera-badi jaali karga kurtas and brightly coloured pyjamas. And even when it was warm and the fan was on, she would cover herself with a light shawl. She loved winter. I too liked to be in her house in that season. She rarely moved out. Lying on the carpet she would munch dry fruits as Rabbu rubbed her back. The other maids were jealous of Rabbu. The witch! She ate, sat and even slept with Begum Jaan! Rabbu and Begum Jaan were the subject of their gossip during leisure hours. Someone would mention their names, and the whole group would burst into loud guffaws. What juicy stories they made up about them! Begum Jaan was oblivious to all this, cut off as she was from the world outside. Her existence was centred on herself and her itch.

I have already mentioned that I was very young at that time and was in love with Begum Jaan. She, too, was fond of me. When Amma decided to go to Agra, she left me with Begum Jaan for a week. She knew that if left alone at home I would fight with my brothers or roam around. The arrangement pleased both Begum Jaan and me. After all, she was Amma's adopted sister. Now the question was… where would I sleep? In Begum Jaan's room, naturally. A small bed was placed alongside hers. Till ten or eleven at night, we chatted and played 'Chance'. Then I went to bed. Rabbu was still rubbing her back as I fell asleep. 'Ugly woman!' I thought to myself.

I woke up at night and was scared. It was pitch dark and Begum Jaan's quilt was shaking vigorously, as though an elephant was struggling inside.

'Begum Jaan…' I could barely form the words out of fear. The elephant stopped shaking, and the quilt came down.

'What is it? Get back to sleep.' Begum Jaan's voice seemed to come from somewhere else.

'I'm scared,' I whimpered.

'Get back to sleep. What's there to be scared of? Recite the Ayatul Kursi.'

'All right…' I began to recite the prayer, but each time I reached 'ya lamu ma bain…' I forgot the lines though I knew the entire Ayat by heart.

'May I come to you, Begum Jaan?'

'No, child… Get back to sleep.' Her tone was rather abrupt. Then I heard two people whispering. Oh God, who was this other person? I was really afraid.

'Begum Jaan… I think a thief has entered the room.'

'Go back to sleep, child… There's no thief.'

This was Rabbu's voice. I drew the quilt over my face and fell asleep.

By morning I had totally forgotten the terrifying scene enacted at night. I have always been superstitious – night fears, sleepwalking and talking in my sleep were daily occurrences in my childhood. Everyone used to say that I was possessed by evil spirits. So the incident slipped from my memory. The quilt looked perfectly innocent in the morning.

But the following night I woke up again and heard Begum Jaan and Rabbu arguing in subdued tones. I could not hear what the upshot of the tiff was, but I heard Rabbu crying. Then came the slurping sound of a cat licking a plate… I was scared and went back to sleep.

The next day Rabbu went to see her son, an irascible young man. Begum Jaan had done a lot to help him out – bought him a shop, got him a job in the village. But nothing really pleased him. He stayed with Nawab Saheb for some time. The nawab got him new clothes and other gifts, but he ran away for no good reason and never came back, even to see Rabbu…

Rabbu had gone to a relative's house to see her son. Begum Jaan was reluctant to let her go but realized that Rabbu was helpless. So she didn't prevent her from going.

All through the day Begum Jaan was out of sorts. Every joint ached, but she couldn't bear anyone's touch. She didn't eat anything and moped in bed all day.

'Shall I rub your back, Begum Jaan…?' I asked zestfully as I shuffled the deck of cards. She peered at me.

'Shall I, really?' I put away the cards and began to rub her back while Begum Jaan lay there quietly.

Rabbu was due to return the next day… but she didn't. Begum Jaan grew more and more irritable. She drank cup after cup of tea, and her head began to ache.

I resumed rubbing her back, which was smooth as the top of a table. I rubbed gently and was happy to be of some use to her.

'A little harder… open the straps,' Begum Jaan said.

'Here… a little below the shoulder… that's right… Ah! What pleasure…' She expressed her satisfaction between sensuous breaths.

'A little further...' Begum Jaan instructed though her hands could easily reach that spot. But she wanted me to stroke it. How proud I felt! 'Here... oh, oh, you're tickling me... Ah!' She smiled. I chatted away as I continued to massage her.

'I'll send you to the market tomorrow... What do you want?... A doll that sleeps and wakes up at your will?'

'No, Begum Jaan... I don't want dolls... Do you think I'm still a child?'

'So, you're an old woman, then,' she laughed. 'If not a doll, I'll get you a babua... Dress it up yourself. I'll give you a lot of old clothes. Okay?'

'Okay,' I answered.

'Here.' She would take my hand and place it where it itched and I, lost in the thought of the babua, kept scratching her listlessly while she talked.

'Listen... you need some more frocks. I'll send for the tailor tomorrow and ask him to make new ones for you. Your mother has left some dress material.'

'I don't want that red material... It looks so cheap.' I was chattering, oblivious of where my hands travelled. Begum Jaan lay still... Oh God! I jerked my hand away.

'Hey girl, watch where your hands are... You hurt my ribs.' Begum Jaan smiled mischievously. I was embarrassed.

'Come here and lie down beside me...' She made me lie down with my head on her arm. 'How skinny you are... your ribs are showing.' She began counting my ribs.

I tried to protest.

'Come on, I'm not going to eat you up. How tight this sweater is! And you don't have a warm vest on.' I felt very uncomfortable.

'How many ribs does one have?' She changed the topic.

'Nine on one side, ten on the other.' I blurted out what I'd learnt in school, rather incoherently.

'Take away your hand... Let's see... one, two, three...'

I wanted to run away, but she held me tightly. I tried to wriggle away, and Begum Jaan began to laugh loudly. To this day, whenever I am reminded of her face at that moment, I feel jittery. Her eyelids had drooped, her upper lip showed a black shadow and tiny beads of sweat sparkled on her lips and nose despite the cold. Her hands were as cold as ice but clammy as though the skin had been stripped off. She wore a shawl, and in the fine karga kurta, her body shone like a ball of dough. The heavy gold buttons of the kurta were undone.

It was evening, and the room was getting enveloped in darkness. A strange fear overcame me. Begum Jaan's deep-set eyes focused on me and I felt like crying. She was pressing me as though I were a clay doll and the odour of her warm body made me want to throw up. But she was like a person possessed. I could neither scream nor cry.

After some time she stopped and lay back exhausted. She was breathing heavily, and her face looked pale and dull. I thought she was going to die and rushed out of the room...

Thank God Rabbu returned that night. Scared, I went to bed rather early and pulled the quilt over me. But sleep evaded me for hours.

Amma was taking so long to return from Agra! I was so terrified of Begum Jaan that I spent the whole day in the company of the maids. I felt too nervous to step into her room. What could I have said to anyone? That I was afraid of Begum Jaan? Begum Jaan who was so attached to me?

That day, Rabbu and Begum Jaan had another tiff. This did not augur well for me because Begum Jaan's thoughts were immediately directed towards me. She realized that I was wandering outdoors in the cold and might die of pneumonia. 'Child, do you want to put me to shame in public? If something happened to you, it would be a disaster.' She made me sit beside her as she washed her face and hands in the basin. Tea was set on a tripod next to her.

'Make tea, please... and give me a cup,' she said as she wiped her face with a towel. 'I'll change in the meantime.'

I drank tea while she dressed. During her body massage she sent for me repeatedly. I went in, keeping my face turned away, and ran out after doing the errand. When she changed her dress I began to feel jittery. Turning my face away from her I sipped my tea.

My heart yearned in anguish for Amma. This punishment was much more severe than I deserved for fighting with my brothers. Amma always disliked my playing with boys. Now tell me, were they man-eaters that they would eat up her darling? And who were the boys? My own brothers and their puny little friends! She was a believer in strict segregation for women. But Begum Jaan here was more terrifying than all the loafers of the world. Left to myself, I would have run out into the street – even further away! But I was helpless and had to stay there much against my wish.

Begum Jaan had decked herself up elaborately and perfumed herself with the warm scent of attar. Then she began to shower me with affection. 'I want to go home,' was my answer to all her suggestions. Then I started crying.

'There, there... come near me... I'll take you to the market today. Okay?'

But I kept up the refrain of wanting to go home. All the toys and sweets of the world held no interest for me.

'Your brothers will bash you up, you witch.' She tapped me affectionately on my cheek.

'Let them.'

'Raw mangoes are sour to the taste, Begum Jaan,' hissed Rabbu, burning with jealousy.

Then, Begum Jaan had a fit. The gold necklace she had offered me moments ago was flung to the ground. The muslin net dupatta was torn to shreds. And her hair-parting, which was never crooked, became a tangled mess.

'Oh! Oh! Oh!' she screamed between spasms. I ran out.

Begum Jaan regained her senses after a great deal of fuss and ministrations. When I peered into the room on tiptoe, I saw Rabbu rubbing her body, nestling against her waist.

'Take off your shoes,' Rabbu said while stroking Begum Jaan's ribs. Mouse-like, I snuggled into my quilt.

There was that peculiar noise again. In the dark Begum Jaan's quilt was once again swaying like an elephant. 'Allah! Ah!...' I moaned in a feeble voice. The elephant inside the quilt heaved up and then sat down. I was mute. The elephant started to sway again. I was scared stiff. But I had resolved to switch on the light that night, come what may. The elephant started shaking once again, and it seemed as though it was trying to squat. There was the sound of someone smacking her lips, as though savouring a tasty pickle. Now I understood! Begum Jaan had not eaten anything the whole day. And Rabbu, the witch, was a notorious glutton. She must be polishing off some goodies. Flaring my nostrils I inhaled deeply. There was only the scent of attar, sandalwood and henna, nothing else.

Once again the quilt started swinging. I tried to lie still, but the quilt began to assume such grotesque shapes that I was shaken. It seemed as though a large frog was inflating itself noisily and was about to leap on to me.

'Aa... Ammi...' I whimpered. No one paid any heed. The quilt crept into my brain and began to grow larger. I stretched my leg nervously to the other side of the bed, groped for the switch and turned the light on. The elephant somersaulted inside the quilt which deflated immediately. During the somersault, a corner of the quilt rose by almost a foot...

Good God! I gasped and sank deeper into my bed.

Translated by M. Asaduddin

EVERYTHING IS NICE

Jane Bowles (1917–1973)

Born into a Jewish family in New York City, Jane Sydney Auer developed a passion for literature while still at school. In 1937, she met the writer and composer Paul Bowles. The following year, they married. Both were openly bisexual and explored numerous other relationships. Her only novel, *Two Serious Ladies*, a modernist cult classic, deftly skewers conventional notions of womanhood – as one of its protagonists proclaims: "I have gone to pieces, which is a thing I've wanted to do for years."

The highest street in the blue Moslem town skirted the edge of a cliff. She walked over to the thick protecting wall and looked down. The tide was out, and the flat dirty rocks below were swarming with skinny boys. A Moslem woman came up to the blue wall and stood next to her, grazing her hip with the basket she was carrying. She pretended not to notice her, and kept her eyes fixed on a white dog that had just slipped down the side of a rock and plunged into a crater of sea water. The sound of its bark was earsplitting. Then the woman jabbed the basket firmly into her ribs, and she looked up.

"That one is a porcupine," said the woman, pointing a henna-stained finger into the basket.

This was true. A large dead porcupine lay there, with a pair of new yellow socks folded on top of it.

She looked again at the woman. She was dressed in a haik, and the white cloth covering the lower half of her face was loose, about to fall down.

"I am Zodelia," she announced in a high voice. "And you are Betsoul's friend." The loose cloth slipped below her chin and hung there like a bib. She did not pull it up.

"You sit in her house and you sleep in her house and you eat in her house," the woman went on, and she nodded in agreement. "Your name is Jeanie and you live in a hotel with other Nazarenes. How much does the hotel cost you?"

A loaf of bread shaped like a disc flopped on to the ground from inside the folds of the woman's haik, and she did not have to answer her question. With some difficulty the woman picked the loaf up and stuffed it in between the quills of the porcupine and the basket handle. Then she set the basket down on the top of the blue wall and turned to her with bright eyes.

"I am the people in the hotel," she said. "Watch me."

She was pleased because she knew that the woman who called herself Zodelia was about to present her with a little skit. It would be delightful to watch, since all the people of the town spoke and gesticulated as though they had studied at the *Comédie Française*.

"The people in the hotel," Zodelia announced, formally beginning her skit. "I am the people in the hotel."

"'Good-bye, Jeanie, good-bye. Where are you going?'

"'I am going to a Moslem house to visit my Moslem friends, Betsoul and her family. I will sit in a Moslem room and eat Moslem food and sleep on a Moslem bed.'

"'Jeanie, Jeanie, when will you come back to us in the hotel and sleep in your own room?'

"'I will come back to you in three days. I will come back and sit in a Nazarene room and eat Nazarene food and sleep on a Nazarene bed. I will spend half the week with Moslem friends and half with Nazarenes.'"

The woman's voice had a triumphant ring as she finished her sentence; then, without announcing the end of the sketch, she walked over to the wall and put one arm around her basket.

Down below, just at the edge of the cliff's shadow, a Moslem woman was seated on a rock, washing her legs in one of the holes filled with sea water. Her haik was piled on her lap and she was huddled over it, examining her feet.

"She is looking at the ocean," said Zodelia.

She was not looking at the ocean; with her head down and the mass of cloth in her lap she could not possibly have seen it; she would have had to straighten up and turn around.

"She is *not* looking at the ocean," she said.

"She is looking at the ocean," Zodelia repeated, as if she had not spoken.

She decided to change the subject. "Why do you have a porcupine with you?" she asked her, although she knew that some of the Moslems, particularly the country people, enjoyed eating them.

"It is a present for my aunt. Do you like it?"

"Yes," she said. "I like porcupines. I like big porcupines and little ones, too."

Zodelia seemed bewildered, and then bored, and she decided she had somehow ruined the conversation by mentioning small porcupines.

"Where is your mother?" Zodelia said at length.

"My mother is in her country in her own house," she said automatically; she had answered the question a hundred times.

"Why don't you write her a letter and tell her to come here? You can take her on a promenade and show her the ocean. After that she can go back to her own country and sit in her house." She picked up her basket and adjusted the strip of cloth over her mouth. "Would you like to go to a wedding?" she asked her.

She said she would love to go to a wedding, and they started off down the crooked blue street, heading into the wind. As they passed a small shop Zodelia stopped. "Stand here," she said. "I want to buy something."

After studying the display for a minute or two Zodelia poked her and pointed to some cakes inside a square box with glass sides. "Nice?" she asked her. "Or not nice?"

The cakes were dusty and coated with a thin, ugly-colored icing. They were called *Galletas Ortiz*.

"They are very nice," she replied, and bought her a dozen of them.

Zodelia thanked her briefly and they walked on. Presently they turned off the street into a narrow alley and started downhill. Soon Zodelia stopped at a door on the right, and lifted the heavy brass knocker in the form of a fist.

"The wedding is here?" she said to her.

Zodelia shook her head and looked grave. "There is no wedding here," she said.

A child opened the door and quickly hid behind it, covering her face. She followed Zodelia across the black and white tile floor of the closed patio. The walls were washed in blue, and a cold light shone through the broken panes of glass far above their heads. There was a door on each side of the patio. Outside one of them, barring the threshold, was a row of pointed slippers. Zodelia stepped out of her own shoes and set them down near the others.

She stood behind Zodelia and began to take off her own shoes. It took her a long time because there was a knot in one of her laces. When she was ready, Zodelia took her hand and pulled her along with her into a dimly lit room, where she led her over to a mattress which lay against the wall.

"Sit," she told her, and she obeyed. Then, without further comment she walked off, heading for the far end of the room. Because her eyes had not grown used to the dimness, she had the impression of a figure disappearing down a long corridor. Then she began to see the brass bars of a bed, glowing weakly in the darkness.

Only a few feet away, in the middle of the carpet, sat an old lady in a dress made of green and purple curtain fabric. Through the many rents in the material she could see the printed cotton dress and the tan sweater underneath. Across the room several women sat along another mattress, and further along the mattress three babies were sleeping in a row, each one close against the wall with its head resting on a fancy cushion.

"Is it nice here?" It was Zodelia, who had returned without her haik. Her black crepe European dress hung unbelted down to her ankles, almost grazing her bare feet. The hem was lopsided. "Is it nice here?" she asked again, crouching on her haunches in front of her and pointing at the old woman. "That one is Tetum," she said. The old lady plunged both hands into a bowl of raw chopped meat and began shaping the stuff into little balls.

"Tetum," echoed the ladies on the mattress.

"This Nazarene," said Zodelia, gesturing in her direction, "spends half her time in a Moslem house with Moslem friends and the other half in a Nazarene hotel with other Nazarenes."

"That's nice," said the women opposite. "Half with Moslem friends and half with Nazarenes."

The old lady looked very stern. She noticed that her bony cheeks were tattooed with tiny blue crosses.

"Why?" asked the old lady abruptly in a deep voice. "*Why* does she spend half her time with Moslem friends and half with Nazarenes?" She fixed her eye on Zodelia, never ceasing to shape the meat with her swift fingers. Now she saw that her knuckles were also tattooed with blue crosses.

Zodelia stared back at her stupidly. "I don't know why," she said, shrugging one fat shoulder. It was clear that the picture she had been painting for them had suddenly lost all its charm for her.

"Is she crazy?" the old lady asked.

"No," Zodelia answered listlessly. "She is not crazy." There were shrieks of laughter from the mattress.

The old lady fastened her sharp eyes on the visitor, and she saw that they were heavily outlined in black. "Where is your husband?" she demanded.

"He's traveling in the desert."

"Selling things," Zodelia put in. This was the popular explanation for her husband's trips; she did not try to contradict it.

"Where is your mother?" the old lady asked.

"My mother is in our country in her own house."

"Why don't you go and sit with your mother in her own house?" she scolded. "The hotel costs a lot of money."

"In the city where I was born," she began, "there are many, many automobiles and many, many trucks."

The women on the mattress were smiling pleasantly. "Is that true?" remarked the one in the center in a tone of polite interest.

"I hate trucks," she told the woman with feeling.

The old lady lifted the bowl of meat off her lap and set it down on the carpet. "Trucks are nice," she said severely.

"That's true," the women agreed, after only a moment's hesitation. "Trucks are very nice."

"Do *you* like trucks?" she asked Zodelia, thinking that because of their relatively greater intimacy she might perhaps agree with her.

"Yes," she said. "They are nice. Trucks are very nice." She seemed lost in meditation, but only for an instant. "Everything is nice," she announced, with a look of triumph.

"It's the truth," the women said from their mattress. "Everything is nice."

They all looked happy, but the old lady was still frowning. "Aicha!" she yelled, twisting her neck so that her voice could be heard in the patio. "Bring the tea!"

Several little girls came into the room carrying the tea things and a low round table.

"Pass the cakes to the Nazarene," she told the smallest child, who was carrying a cut-glass dish piled with cakes. She saw that they were the ones she had bought for Zodelia; she did not want any of them. She wanted to go home.

"Eat!" the women called out from their mattress. "Eat the cakes."

The child pushed the glass dish forward.

"The dinner at the hotel is ready," she said, standing up.

"Drink tea," said the old woman scornfully. "Later you will sit with the other Nazarenes and eat their food."

"The Nazarenes will be angry if I'm late." She realized that she was lying stupidly, but she could not stop. "They will hit me!" She tried to look wild and frightened.

"Drink tea. They will not hit you," the old woman told her. "Sit down and drink tea."

The child was still offering her the glass dish as she backed away toward the door. Outside she sat down on the black and white tiles to lace her shoes. Only Zodelia followed her into the patio.

"Come back," the others were calling. "Come back into the room."

Then she noticed the porcupine basket standing nearby against the wall. "Is that old lady in the room your aunt? Is she the one you were bringing the porcupine to?" she asked her.

"No. She is not my aunt."

"Where *is* your aunt?"

"My aunt is in her own house."

"When will you take the porcupine to her?" She wanted to keep talking, so that Zodelia would be distracted and forget to fuss about her departure.

"The porcupine sits here," she said firmly. "In my own house."

She decided not to ask her again about the wedding.

When they reached the door Zodelia opened it just enough to let her through. "Good-bye," she said behind her. "I shall see you tomorrow, if Allah wills it."

"When?"

"Four o'clock." It was obvious that she had chosen the first figure that had come into her head. Before closing the door she reached out and pressed two of the dry Spanish cakes into her hand. "Eat them," she said graciously. "Eat them at the hotel with the other Nazarenes."

She started up the steep alley, headed once again for the walk along the cliff. The houses on either side of her were so close that she could smell the dampness of the walls and feel it on her cheeks like a thicker air.

When she reached the place where she had met Zodelia she went over to the wall and leaned on it. Although the sun had sunk behind the houses, the sky was still luminous and the blue of the wall had deepened. She rubbed her fingers along it: the wash was fresh and a little of the powdery stuff came off. And she remembered how once she had reached out to touch the face of a clown because it had awakened some longing. It had happened at a little circus, but not when she was a child.

LIKE THAT

Carson McCullers (1917–1967)

McCullers' marriage became strained when her career surpassed her husband's, whose work remained obscure. She divorced and moved to Paris, where she became known for her audacious pursuits and unrequited infatuations with preeminent women. Her novels explore loneliness, rejection, awkwardness, insecurity and ageing in the expanses of America's Deep South, where she was raised. Her work may be considered Southern Gothic.

Even if Sis is five years older than me and eighteen we used always to be closer and have more fun together than most sisters. It was about the same with us and our brother Dan, too. In the summer we'd all go swimming together. At nights in the wintertime maybe we'd sit around the fire in the living room and play three-handed bridge or Michigan, with everybody putting up a nickel or a dime to the winner. The three of us could have more fun by ourselves than any family I know. That's the way it always was before this.

Not that Sis was playing down to me, either. She's smart as she can be and has read more books than anybody I ever knew – even school teachers. But in High School she never did like to priss up flirty and ride around in cars with girls and pick up the boys and park at the drugstore and all that sort of thing. When she wasn't reading she'd just like to play around with me and Dan. She wasn't too grown up to fuss over a chocolate bar in the refrigerator or to stay awake most of Christmas Eve night either, say, with excitement. In some ways it was like I was heaps older than her. Even when Tuck started coming around last summer I'd sometimes have to tell her she shouldn't wear ankle socks because they might go down town or she ought to pluck out her eyebrows above her nose like the other girls do.

In one more year, next June, Tuck'll be graduated from college. He's a lanky boy with an eager look to his face. At college he's so smart he has a free scholarship. He started coming to see Sis the last summer before this one, riding in his family's car when he could get it, wearing crispy white linen suits. He came a lot last year but this summer he came even more often – before he left he was coming around for Sis every night. Tuck's O.K.

It began getting different between Sis and me a while back, I guess, although I didn't notice it at the time. It was only after a certain night this summer that I had the idea that things maybe were bound to end like they are now.

It was late when I woke up that night. When I opened my eyes I thought for a minute it must be about dawn and I was scared when I saw Sis wasn't on her side of the bed. But it was only the moonlight that shone cool looking and white outside the window and made the oak leaves hanging down over the front yard pitch black and separate seeming. It was around the first of September, but I didn't feel hot looking at the moonlight. I pulled the sheet over me and let my eyes roam around the black shapes of the furniture in our room.

I'd waked up lots of times in the night this summer. You see Sis and I have always had this room together and when she would come in and turn on the light to find her nightgown or something it woke me. I liked it. In the summer when school was out I didn't have to get up early in the morning. We would lie and talk sometimes for a good while. I'd like to hear about the places she and Tuck had been or to laugh over different things. Lots of times before that night she had talked to me privately about Tuck just like I was her age – asking me if I thought she should have said this or that when he called and giving me a hug, maybe, after. Sis was really crazy about Tuck. Once she said to me: "He's so lovely – I never in the world thought I'd know anyone like him—"

We would talk about our brother too. Dan's seventeen years old and was planning to take the co-op course at Tech in the fall. Dan had gotten older by this summer. One night he came in at four o'clock and he'd been drinking. Dad sure had it in for him the next week. So he hiked out to the country and camped with some boys for a few days. He used to talk to me and Sis about diesel motors and going away to South America and all that, but by this summer he was quiet and not saying much to anybody in the family. Dan's real tall and thin as a rail. He has bumps on his face now and is clumsy and not very good looking. At nights sometimes I know he wanders all around by himself, maybe going out beyond the city limits sign into the pine woods.

Thinking about such things I lay in bed wondering what time it was and when Sis would be in. That night after Sis and Dan had left I had gone down to the corner with some of the kids in the neighborhood to chunk rocks at the street light and try to kill a bat up there. At first I had the shivers and imagined it was a smallish bat like the kind in Dracula. When I saw it looked just like a moth I didn't care if they killed it or not. I was just sitting there on the curb drawing with a stick on the dusty street when Sis and Tuck rode by slowly in his car. She was sitting over very close to him. They weren't talking or smiling – just riding slowly down the street, sitting close, looking ahead. When they passed and I saw who it was I hollered to them. "Hey, Sis!" I yelled.

The car just went on slowly and nobody hollered back. I just stood there in the middle of the street feeling sort of silly with all the other kids standing around.

That hateful little old Bubber from down on the other block came up to me. "That your sister?" he asked.

I said yes.

"She sure was sitting up close to her beau," he said.

I was mad all over like I get sometimes. I hauled off and chunked all the rocks in my hand right at him. He's three years younger than me and it wasn't nice, but I couldn't stand him in the first place and he thought he was being so cute about Sis. He started holding his neck and bellering and I walked off and left them and went home and got ready to go to bed.

When I woke up I finally began to think of that too and old Bubber Davis was still in my mind when I heard the sound of a car coming up the block. Our room faces the street with only a short front yard between. You can see and hear everything from the sidewalk and the street. The car was creeping down in front of our walk and the light went slow and white along the walls of the room. It stopped on Sis's writing desk, showed up the books there plainly and half a pack of chewing gum. Then the room was dark and there was only the moonlight outside.

The door of the car didn't open but I could hear them talking. Him, that is. His voice was low and I couldn't catch any words but it was like he was explaining something over and over again. I never heard Sis say a word.

I was still awake when I heard the car door open. I heard her say, "Don't come out." And then the door slammed and there was the sound of her heels clopping up the walk, fast and light like she was running.

Mama met Sis in the hall outside our room. She had heard the front door close. She always listens out for Sis and Dan and never goes to sleep when they're still out. I sometimes wonder how she can just lie there in the dark for hours without going to sleep.

"It's one-thirty, Marian," she said. "You ought to get in before this."

Sis didn't say anything.

"Did you have a nice time?"

That's the way Mama is. I could imagine her standing there with her nightgown blowing out fat around her and her dead white legs and the blue veins showing, looking all messed up. Mama's nicer when she's dressed to go out.

"Yes, we had a grand time," Sis said. Her voice was funny – sort of like a piano in the gym at school, high and sharp on your ear. Funny.

Mama was asking more questions. Where did they go? Did they see anybody they knew? All that sort of stuff. That's the way she is.

"Goodnight," said Sis in that out of tune voice.

She opened the door of our room real quick and closed it. I started to let her know I was awake but changed my mind. Her breathing was quick and loud in the dark and she did not move at all. After a few minutes she felt in the closet for her nightgown and got in the bed. I could hear her crying.

"Did you and Tuck have a fuss?" I asked.

"No," she answered. Then she seemed to change her mind. "Yeah, it was a fuss."

There's one thing that gives me the creeps sure enough – and that's to hear somebody cry. "I wouldn't let it bother me. You'll be making up tomorrow."

The moon was coming in the window and I could see her moving her jaw from one side to the other and staring up at the ceiling. I watched her for a long time. The moonlight was cool looking and there was a wettish wind coming cool from the window. I moved over like I sometimes do to snug up with her, thinking maybe that would stop her from moving her jaw like that and crying.

She was trembling all over. When I got close to her she jumped like I'd pinched her and pushed me over quick and kicked my legs over. "Don't," she said. "Don't."

Maybe Sis had suddenly gone batty, I was thinking. She was crying in a slower and sharper way. I was a little scared and I got up to go to the bathroom a minute. While I was in there I looked out the window, down toward the corner where the street light is. I saw something then that I knew Sis would want to know about.

"You know what?" I asked when I was back in the bed.

She was lying over close to the edge as she could get, stiff. She didn't answer.

"Tuck's car is parked down by the street light. Just drawn up to the curb. I could tell because of the box and the two tires on the back. I could see it from the bathroom window."

She didn't even move.

"He must be just sitting out there. What ails you and him?"

She didn't say anything at all.

"I couldn't see him but he's probably just sitting there in the car under the street light. Just sitting there."

It was like she didn't care or had known it all along. She was as far over the edge of the bed as she could get, her legs stretched out stiff and her hands holding tight to the edge and her face on one arm.

She used always to sleep all sprawled over on my side so I'd have to push at her when it was hot and sometimes turn on the light and draw the line down the middle and show her how she really was on my side. I wouldn't have to draw any line that night, I was thinking. I felt bad. I looked out at the moonlight a long time before I could get to sleep again.

The next day was Sunday and Mama and Dad went in the morning to church because it was the anniversary of the day my aunt died. Sis said she didn't feel well and stayed in bed. Dan was out and I was there by myself so naturally I went into our room where Sis was. Her face was white as the pillow and there were circles under her eyes. There was a muscle jumping on one side of her jaw like she was chewing. She hadn't combed her hair and it flopped over the pillow, glinty red and messy and pretty. She was reading with a book held up close to her face. Her eyes didn't move when I came in. I don't think they even moved across the page.

It was roasting hot that morning. The sun made everything blazing outside so that it hurt your eyes to look. Our room was so hot that you could almost touch the air with your finger. But Sis had the sheet pulled up clear to her shoulders.

"Is Tuck coming today?" I asked. I was trying to say something that would make her look more cheerful.

"Gosh! Can't a person have *any* peace in this house?"

She never did used to say mean things like that out of a clear sky. Mean things, maybe, but not grouchy ones.

"Sure," I said. "Nobody's going to notice you."

I sat down and pretended to read. When footsteps passed on the street Sis would hold onto the book tighter and I knew she was listening hard as she could. I can tell between footsteps easy. I can even tell without looking if the person who passes is colored or not. Colored people mostly make a slurry sound between the steps. When the steps would pass Sis would loosen the hold on the book and bite at her mouth. It was the same way with passing cars.

I felt sorry for Sis. I decided then and there that I never would let any fuss with any boy make me feel or look like that. But I wanted Sis and me to get back like we'd always been. Sunday mornings are bad enough without having any other trouble.

"We fuss lots less than most sisters do," I said. "And when we do it's all over quick, isn't it?"

She mumbled and kept staring at the same spot on the book. "That's one good thing," I said.

She was moving her head slightly from side to side – over and over again, with her face not changing. "We never do have any real long fusses like Bubber Davis's two sisters have—"

"No." She answered like she wasn't thinking about what I'd said.

"Not one real one like that since I can remember."

In a minute she looked up the first time. "I remember one," she said suddenly.

"When?"

Her eyes looked green in the blackness under them and like they were nailing themselves into what they saw. "You had to stay in every afternoon for a week. It was a long time ago."

All of a sudden I remembered. I'd forgotten it for a long time. I hadn't wanted to remember. When she said that it came back to me all complete.

It was really a long time ago – when Sis was about thirteen. If I remember right I was mean and even more hardboiled than I am now. My aunt who I'd liked better than all my other aunts put together had had a dead baby and she had died. After the funeral Mama had told Sis and me about it. Always the things I've learned new and didn't like have made me mad – mad clean through and scared.

That wasn't what Sis was talking about, though. It was a few mornings after that when Sis started with what every big girl has each month, and of course I found out and was scared to death. Mama then explained to me about it and what she had to wear. I felt then like I'd felt about my aunt, only ten times worse. I felt different toward Sis, too, and was so mad I wanted to pitch into people and hit.

I never will forget it. Sis was standing in our room before the dresser mirror. When I remembered her face it was white like Sis's there on the pillow and with the circles under her eyes and the glinty hair to her shoulders – it was only younger.

I was sitting on the bed, biting hard at my knee. "It shows," I said. "It does too!"

She had on a sweater and a blue pleated skirt and she was so skinny all over that it did show a little.

"Anybody can tell. Right off the bat. Just to look at you anybody can tell."

Her face was white in the mirror and did not move.

"It looks terrible. I wouldn't ever ever be like that. It shows and everything."

She started crying then and told Mother and said she wasn't going back to school and such. She cried a long time. That's how ugly and hard-boiled I used to be and am still sometimes. That's why I had to stay in the house every afternoon for a week a long time ago…

Tuck came by in his car that Sunday morning before dinner time. Sis got up and dressed in a hurry and didn't even put on any lipstick. She said they were going out to dinner. Nearly every Sunday all of us in the family stay together all day, so that was a little funny. They didn't get home until almost dark. The rest of us were sitting on the front porch drinking ice tea because of the heat when the car drove up again. After they got out of the car Dad, who had been in a very good mood all day, insisted Tuck stay for a glass of tea.

Tuck sat on the swing with Sis and he didn't lean back and his heels didn't rest on the floor – as though he was all ready to get up again. He kept changing the glass from one hand to the other and starting new conversations. He and Sis didn't look at each other except on the sly, and then it wasn't at all like they were crazy about each other. It was a funny look. Almost like they were afraid of something. Tuck left soon.

"Come sit by your Dad a minute, Puss," Dad said. Puss is a nickname he calls Sis when he feels in a specially good mood. He still likes to pet us.

She went and sat on the arm of his chair. She sat stiff like Tuck had, holding herself off a little so Dad's arm hardly went around her waist. Dad smoked his cigar and looked out on the front yard and the trees that were beginning to melt into the early dark.

"How's my big girl getting along these days?" Dad still likes to hug us up when he feels good and treat us, even Sis, like kids.

"O.K.," she said. She twisted a little bit like she wanted to get up and didn't know how to without hurting his feelings.

"You and Tuck have had a nice time together this summer, haven't you, Puss?"

"Yeah," she said. She had begun to see-saw her lower jaw again. I wanted to say something but couldn't think of anything.

Dad said: "He ought to be getting back to Tech about now, oughtn't he? When's he leaving?"

"Less than a week," she said. She got up so quick that she knocked Dad's cigar out of his fingers. She didn't even pick it up but flounced on through the front door. I could hear her half running to our room and the sound the door made when she shut it. I knew she was going to cry.

It was hotter than ever. The lawn was beginning to grow dark and the locusts were droning out so shrill and steady that you wouldn't notice them unless you thought to. The sky was bluish grey and the trees in the vacant lot across the street were dark. I kept on sitting on the front porch with Mama and Papa and hearing their low talk without listening to the words. I wanted to go in our room with Sis but I was afraid to. I wanted to ask her what was really the matter. Was hers and Tuck's fuss so bad as that or was it that she was so crazy about him that she was sad because he was leaving? For a minute I didn't think it was either one of those things. I wanted to know but I was scared to ask. I just sat there with the grown people. I never have been so lonesome as I was that night. If ever

I think about being sad I just remember how it was then – sitting there looking at the long bluish shadows across the lawn and feeling like I was the only child left in the family and that Sis and Dan were dead or gone for good.

It's October now and the sun shines bright and a little cool and the sky is the color of my turquoise ring. Dan's gone to Tech. So has Tuck gone. It's not at all like it was last fall, though. I come in from High School (I go there now) and Sis maybe is just sitting by the window reading or writing to Tuck or just looking out. Sis is thinner and sometimes to me she looks in the face like a grown person. Or like, in a way, something has suddenly hurt her hard. We don't do any of the things we used to. It's good weather for fudge or for doing so many things. But no she just sits around or goes for long walks in the chilly late afternoon by herself. Sometimes she'll smile in a way that really gripes – like I was such a kid and all. Sometimes I want to cry or to hit her.

But I'm hardboiled as the next person. I can get along by myself if Sis or anybody else wants to. I'm glad I'm thirteen and still wear socks and can do what I please. I don't want to be any older if I'd get like Sis has. But I wouldn't. I wouldn't like any boy in the world as much as she does Tuck. I'd never let any boy or any thing make me act like she does. I'm not going to waste my time and try to make Sis be like she used to be. I get lonesome – sure – but I don't care. I know there's no way I can make myself stay thirteen all my life, but I know I'd never let anything really change me at all – no matter what it is.

I skate and ride my bike and go to the school football games every Friday. But when one afternoon the kids all got quiet in the gym basement and then started telling certain things – about being married and all – I got up quick so I wouldn't hear and went up and played basketball. And when some of the kids said they were going to start wearing lipstick and stockings I said I wouldn't for a hundred dollars.

You see I'd never be like Sis is now. I wouldn't. Anybody could know that if they knew me. I just wouldn't, that's all. I don't want to grow up – if it's like that.

CAROL

Patricia Highsmith (1921–1995)

Born in Texas, Highsmith moved with her family to New York as a child. One of the defining twentieth-century writers of crime fiction, she wrote twenty-two novels in the course of her career including the Tom Ripley novels, that would become her lasting legacy. Her novel *The Price of Salt* (later renamed *Carol*), originally written under a pseudonym, was "the first lesbian novel with a happy ending".

Carol walked barefoot with little short steps to the shower room in the corner, groaning at the cold. She had red polish on her toenails, and her blue pyjamas were too big for her.

'It's your fault for opening the window so high,' Therese said.

Carol pulled the curtain across, and Therese heard the shower come on with a rush. 'Ah, divinely hot!' Carol said. 'Better than last night.'

It was a luxurious tourist cabin, with a thick carpet and wood-panelled walls and everything from cellophane-sealed shoe rags to television.

Therese sat on her bed in her robe, looking at a road map, spanning it with her hand. A span and a half was about a day's driving, theoretically, though they probably would not do it. 'We might get all the way across Ohio today,' Therese said.

'Ohio. Noted for rivers, rubber, and certain railroads. On our left the famous Chillicothe drawbridge, where twenty-eight Hurons once massacred a hundred – morons.'

Therese laughed.

'And where Lewis and Clark once camped,' Carol added. 'I think I'll wear my slacks today. Want to see if they're in that suitcase? If not, I'll have to get into the car. Not the light ones, the navy blue gaberdines.'

Therese went to Carol's big suitcase at the foot of the bed. It was full of sweaters and underwear and shoes, but no slacks. She saw a nickel-plated tube sticking out of a folded sweater. She lifted the sweater out. It was heavy. She unwrapped it, and started so she almost dropped it. It was a gun with a white handle.

'No?' Carol asked.

'No.' Therese wrapped the gun up again and put it back as she had found it.

'Darling, I forgot my towel. I think it's on a chair.'

Therese got it and took it to her, and in her nervousness as she put the towel into Carol's outstretched hand her eyes dropped from Carol's face to her bare breasts and down, and she saw the quick surprise in Carol's glance as she turned around. Therese closed her eyes tight and walked slowly towards the bed, seeing before her closed lids the image of Carol's naked body.

Therese took a shower, and when she came out, Carol was standing at the mirror, almost dressed.

'What's the matter?' Carol asked.

'Nothing.'

Carol turned to her, combing her hair that was darkened a little by the wet of the shower. Her lips were bright with fresh lipstick, a cigarette between them. 'Do you realize how many times a day you make me ask you that?' she said. 'Don't you think it's a little inconsiderate?'

During breakfast, Therese said, 'Why did you bring that gun along, Carol?'

'Oh. So that's what's bothering you. It's Harge's gun, something else he forgot.' Carol's voice was casual. 'I thought it'd be better to take it than to leave it.'

'Is it loaded?'

'Yes, it's loaded. Harge got a permit, because we had a burglar at the house once.'

'Can you use it?'

Carol smiled at her. 'I'm no Annie Oakley. I can use it. I think it worries you, doesn't it? I don't expect to use it.'

Therese said nothing more about it. But it disturbed her whenever she thought of it. She thought of it the next night, when a bellhop set the suitcase down heavily on the sidewalk. She wondered if a gun could ever go off from a jolt like that.

They had taken some snapshots in Ohio, and because they could get them developed early the next morning, they spent a long evening and the night in a town called Defiance. All evening they walked around the streets, looking in store windows, walking through silent residential streets where lights showed in front parlours, and homes looked as comfortable and safe as birds' nests. Therese had been afraid Carol would be bored by aimless walks, but Carol was the one who suggested going one block further, walking all the way up the hill to see what was on the other side. Carol talked about herself and Harge. Therese tried to sum up in one word what had separated Carol and Harge, but she rejected the words almost at once – boredom, resentment, indifference. Carol told her of one time that Harge had taken Rindy away on a fishing trip and not communicated for days. That was a retaliation for Carol's refusing to spend Harge's vacation with him at his family's summer house in Massachusetts. It was a mutual thing. And the incidents were not the start.

Carol put two of the snapshots in her billfold, one of Rindy in jodhpurs and a derby that had been on the first part of the roll, and one of Therese, with a cigarette in her mouth and her hair blowing back in the wind. There was one unflattering picture of Carol standing huddled in her coat that Carol said she was going to send to Abby because it was so bad.

They got to Chicago late one afternoon, crept into its grey, sprawling disorder behind a great truck of a meat-distributing company. Therese sat up close to the windshield. She couldn't remember anything about the city from the trip with her father. Carol seemed to know Chicago as well as she knew Manhattan. Carol showed her the famous Loop, and they stopped for a while to watch the trains and the homeward rush of five-thirty in the afternoon. It couldn't compare to the madhouse of New York at five-thirty.

At the main post office, Therese found a post-card from Dannie, nothing from Phil, and a letter from Richard. Therese glanced at the letter and saw it began and ended affectionately. She had expected just that, Richard's getting the general delivery address from Phil and writing her an affectionate letter. She put the letter in her pocket before she went back to Carol.

'Anything?' Carol said.

'Just a post-card. From Dannie. He's finished his exams.'

Carol drove to the Drake Hotel. It had a black and white checked floor, a fountain in the lobby, and Therese thought it magnificent. In their room, Carol took off her coat and flung herself down on one of the twin beds.

'I know a few people here,' she said sleepily. 'Shall we look somebody up?'

But Carol fell asleep before they quite decided.

Therese looked out the window at the light-bordered lake and at the irregular, unfamiliar line of tall buildings against the still greyish sky. It looked fuzzy and monotonous, like a Pissarro painting. A comparison Carol wouldn't appreciate, she thought. She leaned on the sill, staring at the city, watching a distant car's lights chopped into dots and dashes as it passed behind trees. She was happy.

'Why don't you ring for some cocktails?' Carol's voice said behind her.

'What kind would you like?'

'What kind would you?'

'Martinis.'

Carol whistled. 'Double Gibsons,' Carol interrupted her as she was telephoning. 'And a plate of canapés. Might as well get four Martinis.'

Therese read Richard's letter while Carol was in the shower. The whole letter was affectionate. You are not like any of the other girls, he wrote.

He had waited and he would keep on waiting, because he was absolutely confident that they could be happy together. He wanted her to write to him every day, send at least a post-card. He told her how he had sat one evening rereading the three letters she had sent him when he had been in Kingston, New York, last summer. There was a sentimentality in the letter that was not like Richard at all, and Therese's first thought was that he was pretending. Perhaps in order to strike at her later. Her second reaction was aversion. She came back to the old decision, that not to write him, not to say anything more, was the shortest way to end it.

The cocktails arrived, and Therese paid for them instead of signing. She could never pay a bill except behind Carol's back.

'Will you wear your black suit?' Therese asked when Carol came in.

Carol gave her a look. 'Go all the way to the bottom of that suitcase?' she said, going to the suitcase. 'Drag it out, brush it off, steam the wrinkles out of it for half an hour?'

'We'll be a half-hour drinking these.'

'Your powers of persuasion are irresistible.' Carol took the suit into the bathroom and turned the water on in the tub.

It was the suit she had worn the day they had had the first lunch together.

'Do you realize this is the only drink I've had since we left New York?' Carol said. 'Of course you don't. Do you know why? I'm happy.'

'You're beautiful,' Therese said.

And Carol gave her the derogatory smile that Therese loved, and walked to the dressing table. She flung a yellow silk scarf around her neck and tied it loosely, and began to comb her hair. The lamp's light framed her figure like a picture, and Therese had a feeling all this had happened before. She remembered suddenly: the woman in the window brushing up her long hair, remembered the very bricks in the wall, the texture of the misty rain that morning.

'How about some perfume?' Carol asked, moving towards her with the bottle. She touched Therese's forehead with her fingers, at the hair-line where she had kissed her that day.

'You remind me of the woman I once saw,' Therese said, 'somewhere off Lexington. Not you but the light. She was combing her hair up.' Therese stopped, but Carol waited for her to go on. Carol always waited, and she could never say exactly what she wanted to say. 'Early one morning when I was on the way to work, and I remember it was starting to rain,' she floundered on. 'I saw her in a window.' She really could not go on, about standing there for perhaps three or four minutes, wishing with an intensity that drained her strength that she knew the woman, that she might be welcome if she went to the house and knocked on the door, wishing she could do that instead of going on to her job at the Pelican Press.

'My little orphan,' Carol said.

Therese smiled. There was nothing dismal, no sting in the word when Carol said it.

'What does your mother look like?'

'She had black hair,' Therese said quickly. 'She didn't look anything like me.' Therese always found herself talking about her mother in the past tense, though she was alive this minute, somewhere in Connecticut.

'You really don't think she'll ever want to see you again?' Carol was standing at the mirror.

'I don't think so.'

'What about your father's family? Didn't you say he had a brother?'

'I never met him. He was a kind of geologist, working for an oil company. I don't know where he is.' It was easier talking about the uncle she had never met.

'What's your mother's name now?'

'Esther – Mrs Nicolas Strully.' The name meant as little to her as one she might see in a telephone book. She looked at Carol, suddenly sorry she had said the name. Carol might some day – A shock of loss, of helplessness, came over her. She knew so little about Carol after all.

Carol glanced at her. 'I'll never mention it,' she said, 'never mention it again. If that second drink's going to make you blue, don't drink it. I don't want you to be blue tonight.'

The restaurant where they dined overlooked the lake, too. They had a banquet of a dinner with champagne and brandy afterwards. It was the first time in her life that Therese had been a little drunk, in fact much drunker than she wanted Carol to see. Her impression of Lakeshore Drive was always to be of a broad avenue studded with mansions all resembling the White House in Washington. In the memory there would be Carol's voice, telling her about a house here and there where she had been before, and the disquieting awareness that for a while this had been Carol's world, as Rapallo, Paris, and other places Therese did not know had for a while been the frame of everything Carol did.

That night, Carol sat on the edge of her bed, smoking a cigarette before they turned the light on. Therese lay in her own bed, sleepily watching her, trying to read the meaning of the restless, puzzled look in Carol's eyes that would stare at something in the room for a moment and then move on. Was it of her she thought, or of Harge, or of Rindy? Carol had asked to be called at seven tomorrow, in order to telephone Rindy before she went to school. Therese remembered their telephone conversation in Defiance. Rindy had had a fight with some other little girl, and Carol had spent fifteen minutes going over it, and trying to persuade Rindy she should take the first step and apologize. Therese still felt the effects of what she had drunk, the tingling of the champagne that drew her painfully close to Carol. If she simply asked, she thought, Carol would let her sleep tonight in the same bed with her. She wanted more than that, to kiss her, to feel their bodies next to each other's. Therese thought of the two girls she had seen in the Palermo bar. They did that, she knew, and more. And would Carol suddenly thrust her away in disgust, if she merely wanted to hold her in her arms? And would whatever affection Carol now had for her vanish in that instant? A vision of Carol's cold rebuff swept her courage clean away. It crept back humbly in the question, couldn't she ask simply to sleep in the same bed with her?

'Carol, would you mind—'

'Tomorrow we'll go to the stockyards,' Carol said at the same time, and Therese burst out laughing. 'What's so damned funny about that?' Carol asked, putting out her cigarette, but she was smiling, too.

'It just is. It's terribly funny,' Therese said, still laughing, laughing away all the longing and the intention of the night.

'You're giggly on champagne,' Carol said as she pulled the light out.

Late the next afternoon they left Chicago and drove in the direction of Rockford. Carol said she might have a letter from Abby there, but probably not, because Abby was a bad correspondent. Therese went to a shoe-repair shop to get a moccasin stitched, and when she came back, Carol was reading the letter in the car.

'What road do we take out?' Carol's face looked happier.

'Twenty, going west.'

Carol turned on the radio and worked the dial until she found some music. 'What's a good town for tonight on the way to Minneapolis?'

'Dubuque,' Therese said, looking at the map. 'Or Waterloo looks fairly big, but it's about two hundred miles away.'

'We might make it.'

They took Highway 20 towards Freeport and Galena, which was starred on the map as the home of Ulysses S. Grant.

'What did Abby say?'

'Nothing much. Just a very nice letter.'

Carol said little to her in the car, or even in the café where they stopped later for coffee. Carol went over and stood in front of a juke box, dropping nickels slowly.

'You wish Abby'd come along, don't you?' Therese said.

'No,' Carol said.

'You're so different since you got the letter from her.'

Carol looked at her across the table. 'Darling, it's just a silly letter. You can even read it if you want to.' Carol reached for her handbag, but she did not get the letter out.

Some time that evening, Therese fell asleep in the car and woke up with the lights of a city on her face. Carol was resting both arms tiredly on the top of the wheel. They had stopped for a red light.

'Here's where we stay the night,' Carol said.

Therese's sleep still clung to her as she walked across the hotel lobby. She rode up in an elevator and she was acutely conscious of Carol beside her, as if she dreamed a dream in which Carol was the subject and the only figure. In the room, she lifted her suitcase from the floor to a chair, unlatched it and left it, and stood by the writing table, watching Carol. As if her emotions had been in abeyance all the past hours, or days, they flooded her now as she watched Carol opening her suitcase, taking out, as she always did first, the leather kit that contained her toilet articles, dropping it on to the bed. She looked at Carol's hands, at the lock of hair that fell over the scarf tied around her head, at the scratch she had gotten days ago across the toe of her moccasin.

'What're you standing there for?' Carol asked. 'Get to bed, sleepy-head.'

'Carol, I love you.'

Carol straightened up. Therese stared at her with intense, sleepy eyes. Then Carol finished taking her pyjamas from the suitcase and pulled the lid down. She came to Therese and put her hands on her shoulders. She squeezed her shoulders hard, as if she were exacting a promise from her, or perhaps searching her to see if what she had said were real. Then she kissed Therese on the lips, as if they had kissed a thousand times before.

'Don't you know I love you?' Carol said.

Carol took her pyjamas into the bathroom, and stood for a moment, looking down at the basin.

'I'm going out,' Carol said. 'But I'll be back right away.'

Therese waited by the table while Carol was gone, while time passed indefinitely or maybe not at all, until the door opened and Carol came in again. She set a paper bag on the table, and Therese knew she had only gone to get a container of milk, as Carol or she herself did very often at night.

'Can I sleep with you?' Therese asked.

'Did you see the bed?'

PATRICIA HIGHSMITH (1921–1995)

It was a double bed. They sat up in their pyjamas, drinking milk and sharing an orange that Carol was too sleepy to finish. Then Therese set the container of milk on the floor and looked at Carol who was sleeping already, on her stomach, with one arm flung up as she always went to sleep. Therese pulled out the light. Then Carol slipped her arm under her neck, and all the length of their bodies touched, fitting as if something had prearranged it. Happiness was like a green vine spreading through her, stretching fine tendrils, bearing flowers through her flesh. She had a vision of a pale white flower, shimmering as if seen in darkness, or through water. Why did people talk of heaven, she wondered.

'Go to sleep,' Carol said.

Therese hoped she would not. But when she felt Carol's hand move on her shoulder, she knew she had been asleep. It was dawn now. Carol's fingers tightened in her hair, Carol kissed her on the lips, and pleasure leaped in Therese again as if it were only a continuation of the moment when Carol had slipped her arm under her neck last night. I love you, Therese wanted to say again, and then the words were erased by the tingling and terrifying pleasure that spread in waves from Carol's lips over her neck, her shoulders, that rushed suddenly the length of her body. Her arms were tight around Carol, and she was conscious of Carol and nothing else, of Carol's hand that slid along her ribs, Carol's hair that brushed her bare breasts, and then her body too seemed to vanish in widening circles that leaped further and further, beyond where thought could follow. While a thousand memories and moments, words, the first darling, the second time Carol had met her at the store, a thousand memories of Carol's face, her voice, moments of anger and laughter flashed like the tail of a comet across her brain. And now it was pale blue distance and space, an expanding space in which she took flight suddenly like a long arrow. The arrow seemed to cross an impossibly wide abyss with ease, seemed to arc on and on in space, and not quite to stop. Then she realized that she still clung to Carol, that she trembled violently, and the arrow was herself. She saw Carol's pale hair across her eyes, and now Carol's head was close against hers. And she did not have to ask if this was right, no one had to tell her, because this could not have been more right or perfect. She held Carol tighter against her, and felt Carol's mouth on her own smiling mouth. Therese lay still, looking at her, at Carol's face only inches away from her, the grey eyes calm as she had never seen them, as if they retained some of the space she had just emerged from. And it seemed strange that it was still Carol's face, with the freckles, the bending blonde eyebrow that she knew, the mouth now as calm as her eyes, as Therese had seen it many times before.

'My angel,' Carol said. 'Flung out of space.'

Therese looked up at the corners of the room, that were much brighter now, at the bureau with the bulging front and the shield-shaped drawer pulls, at the frameless mirror with the bevelled edge, at the green-patterned curtains that hung straight at the windows, and the two grey tips of buildings that showed just above the sill. She would remember every detail of this room for ever.

'What town is this?' she asked.

Carol laughed. 'This? This is Waterloo.' She reached for a cigarette. 'Isn't that awful.'

Smiling, Therese raised up on her elbow. Carol put a cigarette between her lips. 'There's a couple of Waterloos in every state,' Therese said.

THE CRY OF THE EXCAVATOR

Pier Paolo Pasolini (1922–1975)

Born in Bologna, Pasolini was one of the most important – and controversial – figures of 20th century Italian culture – as film director, poet and writer. His work explored the hardships of poverty, corruption, religion and fascism and sexuality. More than thirty lawsuits were brought against him for obscenity, contempt of the state and public outrage. He was brutally murdered at the age of fifty-three in circumstances that remain mysterious.

I

Only loving, only knowing matter.
Not the fact of having loved, or
having known. We become only sadder

living out a love that's over.
The soul can no longer grow.
And now in the enchanted night, hot

and full, as countless lives still echo
here between the river's bends
and sleepy visions of a city aglow

with scattered lights, a disaffection,
mystery, and sensual misery
turn me against these reflections

of the world, even though just yesterday
they were my reason for living.
Bored and tired, I head home, making my way

through dark market squares and gloomy streets
around the river's port, past shacks thrown
together with warehouses in the midst

of the country's last fields. Here
a deathly silence reigns, but farther down,
on Viale Marconi, or at Trastevere

Station, the evening still looks sweet.
Smiling, unwashed—in overalls or work trousers,
but spurred on by a festive heat—

the young return to their quarters,
their slums, on small motorbikes, friends
seated behind. Here and there,

standing at tables in cafes still bright
but half empty, the evening's last clients
loudly converse in the night.

Stunning, wretched city,
you've taught me what men learn
as children, lighthearted and fierce,

the small things that let one discover
life's greatness in peace, how
to step hard and ready into the fray

of the streets, to go up to another man
without trembling, how without shame
to examine the change handed lazily back

by the bus's sweaty ticketman,
as behind him the façades stream by
with the unending colors of summer;

how to defend myself, how to offend,
how to keep the world before my eyes
and not just in my heart; how to realize

that few people know the passions
I have lived—and while they may
not treat me in brotherly fashion

they are my brothers simply because
they have human passions
and, lighthearted, unknowing, and whole,

they thrive on experiences
unknown to me. Stunning, wretched
city, you've let me experience

this unknown life—and in the end
let me discover what is
the world in every one of us.

The moon fades in silence, giving life
to the stillness, shining white amid violent
glimmers that dazzle without shedding light

upon an earth in a hush with its fine
avenues, its narrow old streets, as a few
warm banks of cloud on the skyline

cast reflections all over the world.
It's the most beautiful night of the summer.
Amid a smell of the straw of old stables

and taverns emptied of clientele,
Trastevere is not yet asleep:
the dark corners, placid walls

still echo with magical sounds.
Men and boys are coming home
—under garlands of lights now alone—

to narrow streets choked with darkness
and garbage, walking with the same
soft steps that used to fill my soul

when I truly loved, when
I truly wanted to understand. And they
disappear singing, as they did back then.

II

Poor as a cat in the Colosseum,
I lived in a suburban slum all whitelime
and dust clouds, far from the city,

far from the country, crammed each day
into a wheezing city bus;
and every ride, whether on the way

to work or back, was a nightmare of sweat
and anguish. Long walks in the warm haze,
long twilights in front of papers

piled on my desk, between muddy roads,
low walls, and whitewashed little houses
with no window frames, and curtains for doors...

The olive man and ragman would come
from some other outlying slum
bearing dusty goods that looked as though

stolen, wearing the cruel expression
of youngsters who'd grown old as the vice-
ridden children of a hard, hungry mother.

Renewed by this new world,
and free—a flame, a breath
I can't explain gave a sense of untroubled

holiness to a reality teeming
humble and dirty, vast and confused
on the city's southern periphery.

A soul inside me, not only my own,
a little soul was growing in that boundless
world, nourished by the joy of one

who loved, though unrequited.
And all was lit up by this love
—still a boy's love, perhaps, and heroic,

yet seasoned by the experience
coming to life at history's feet.
I was at the center of the world,

in a world of sad, bedouin suburbs,
yellow grasslands lashed
by a wind forever restless

either blowing from the warm sea waters
of Fiumicino or from the *agro*, where
the city disappeared amid the shanties—

in a world over which only
the Penitentiary—square yellow
specter in the yellowy haze,

pierced by a thousand identical
windows with bars—could preside,
between ancient fields and sleepy hamlets.

The waste paper and dust cast about
here and there by the breeze,
the meager, echoless voices

of little women come down from
Sabine hills and Adriatic seas,
and now encamped here, with swarms

of withered, tough little children
screaming in their ragged T-shirts
and their drab, faded shorts,

the African sun, the violent downpours
that turned the streets into rivers
of mud, the city buses foundering

in their corners at the terminus,
between the last strip of white grass
and some acrid, burning garbage heap...

This was the center of the world, just
as my love for it was at the center
of history; and in this ripeness

—which, being newborn,
was still love—everything was
about to become clear—it *was*

clear! This suburb naked to the wind,
not Roman, not Southern,
not working-class, was life

in its most current light:
life, and life's light, complete
in a chaos not yet proletarian,

as the crude newssheet
of the local cell, the latest
offset flyer, would have it: backbone

of daily existence,
pure in being all too
near, absolute in being

all too wretchedly human.

III

And now I head home, enriched by times
still so fresh I should never have guessed
I would see them grow old in a soul

now as far from them as from all the past.
I walk up the Janiculum's avenues, stop
at an Art Nouveau junction, in a piazza

with trees, at a remnant of wall, by now
at the edge of the city, on the plain
rolling down to the sea. And in my soul,

dark and inert as the night giving in
to its fragrance, a seed now too old
to bear fruit germinates again

in the accumulated mass of a life
long since turned weary and bitter...
Here's Villa Pamphili and, in the light

that quietly makes the new walls glitter,
the street that I live on.
Near my home, on a bit of grass little

more than a dingy froth,
a trickle over chasms freshly
dug out of the tufa—the wrath

of destruction now silent—there rises lifeless
against sundry buildings and shreds of sky,
an excavator...

What is this sorrow that fills me, at the sight
of these tools strewn about here and there
in the mud, and that scrap of red cloth

hung from a trestle in a corner
where the night seems grimmest?
Why, seeing that faded, bloody color,

does my conscience so blindly resist
and take cover, as if distressed
to its core by some wild remorse?

Why do I have the same presentiment
inside, of days forever unfulfilled,
as I sense in the dead firmament

over that sun-whitened excavator?

I undress in one of countless rooms
in Via Fontenaia where people sleep.
Time, you may cut deep into everything—

hopes, passions—but not into these pure
forms of life... They become one
with man himself, when experience

and faith in the world are at their height.
Oh, the days of Rebibbia,
which I had thought lost in a light

of necessity, and which I now know were so free!

Like my heart, which through the difficult
straits that had thrown it off
the path to a human destiny

gained through fervor a clarity
denied, and through naïvety
an unlikely balance—my mind,

too, those days, attained clarity
and balance. And thus blind
regret, the mark of all my

struggles with the world, was kept
at bay by adult but untried ideologies…
The world was becoming a subject

no longer of mystery but of history.
The joy of knowing it—with the humble
knowledge that every man has—

increased a thousandfold.
Marx and Gobetti, Gramsci and Croce
were alive in the experience of life.

The stuff of ten years of obscure
vocation changed, when I strove to bring
to light what seemed like the ideal figure

for an ideal generation;
every page, every line I wrote
during my exile in Rebibbia

displayed this eagerness, this presumption,
this gratitude. I was new
to my new situation

of old labor and old poverty,
and the few friends who called on me
on forgotten mornings and evenings

up by the Penitentiary,
saw me in a brilliant light:
a gentle, violent revolutionary

in heart and language. A man in bloom.

IV

He holds me close to his aging fleece,
which smells of the woods, and places his snout,
with its boarlike tusks or the teeth

of a stray bear with breath like roses,
over my mouth—and the room around me
turns into a glade, and the blanket, corroded

by the last sweats of youth, dances
like a cloud of pollen... Actually
I'm walking down a road that advances

through the first fields of spring
as they vanish in heavenly light...
Carried away by the waves of my footsteps,

what I'm leaving behind me, wretched,
lighthearted, is not Rome's periphery: everywhere
I see *"Viva Mexico!"* written in whitewash, or etched

into the ruined temples and decrepit
walls, airy as bones, at the crossroads
and the edges of a burning, shudderless sky.

There, atop a hill, between clouds
and the undulant contours
of an ancient ridge of Apennines,

lies the town, half empty even at this hour
of the morning, when the women go
shopping—or in evening's golden glow

when children run to their mothers
from the courtyards of the schools.
The streets fill with deep silence,

the slightly disconnected cobbles blur,
old as time, gray as time,
and two long, stone walkways,

shiny, lifeless, flank the streets.
Someone, in the silence, is moving:
an old woman, a little boy

lost in play, who sees perhaps
a charming Cinquecento portal
open gently, or a small well

with little creatures carved along the rim
resting on the meager grass
at some forgotten crossroads or corner.

At the top of the hill, the town's main square
lies deserted, and between the houses,
behind a low wall and the green

of a great chestnut, you can see the space
of the valley below, but not the valley.
A space that shimmers pale blue

or slightly ashen... But the Corso continues
beyond the familiar piazzetta
suspended in the Apennine sky,

makes its way through huddled houses
and halfway down the slope: farther down
—as the small baroque houses thin out—

one sees, at last, the valley—and the wild.
Take a few more steps toward the bend,
where the road already runs through stark

little meadows, scrubby and steep,
and on the left, against the hillside,
as if a church had collapsed there,

stands an apse full of frescoes
blue and red, scrolls shattered
all along the eroded scars

of the collapse—which only it,
an enormous shell, has survived
to gape against the sky.

And here a wind begins to blow
from the wild beyond the valley, light,
desperate, burning the skin with sweetness...

It's like those smells of just-
watered fields or riverbanks
that blow over the city on the first

days of fair weather, and you
don't know what it is but, almost
mad with regret, you wonder

if it's from a fire burning over the frost
or from grapes or medlars forgotten
in some barn loft now warming

in the sun of that stupendous morning.
I cry out for joy, so much does it hurt,
deep in my lungs, to breathe the air

like warmth or light
as I gaze upon the valley
....

V

A little peace is all one needs to see
the anguish within the heart,
limpid as the bottom of the sea

on a sunny day. You recognize,
but do not feel, the evil there
in your bed, with chest, thighs

and feet exposed in air
as on a crucifix—or like the drunken
Noah dreaming, naïvely unaware

of his mirthful sons, who,
strong and pure, make light over him...
The day now looms over you,

like a sleeping lion in your room.

By what roads will the heart gain
fulfilment and perfection, even
in this mix of bliss and pain?

A little peace... And in you war,
and God, are reawakened. No sooner are
the passions quelled, a fresh wound healed,

than at once you deplete your soul
—which had seemed already depleted—
in feats of dream that don't yield

anything... When, for example, kindled
by hope—as Khrushchev, old lion
stinking of vodka, makes vows to the world

from his offended Soviet Union—
you suddenly realize you are dreaming.
It's as if your every passion,

your every inner torment, all
your naïve shame at not being
present, in your heart, at the renewal

of the world, were burning
in the happy peace of August.
In fact the new wind blowing

drives you backwards, to where
there's no wind at all; and there, like
a tumor reforming, you repair

to love's ancient cauldron,
sensation, terror, joy.
And in that same oblivion

is light... in that unconsciousness
of infants, beasts, or naïve libertines
is purity... in that flight

the most heroic frenzies, the most divine
emotions—in a lowly human act
performed in the sleep of a morning.

VI

In the blaze of the morning
sun's abandon—now glancing
hot over the construction sites,

warming the fixtures—frantic
tremors scrape at the silence,
which smells hopelessly of old milk,

empty squares, and innocence.
The jolts have been growing with the sun
since at least seven o'clock. Present

are a dozen scraggly aging workers,
their rags and T-shirts burning
with sweat. Their scattered voices

and their struggles with the sliding dirt
and clods of mud strewn about
seem to be undone by all the shaking.

But between the stubborn bursts
of the backhoe, as it blindly shatters,
blindly shovels, blindly scoops

as if to no purpose, a sudden,
human cry rings out,
then repeats itself at intervals,

so wild with sorrow that at once
it seems no longer human, but
only a lifeless screech. Then it slowly

starts anew, in the violent sun,
between the blinded buildings, same
as before, a cry that only someone

in the last moments before death might emit
in the cruel rays still shining down
and softened, now, by a light sea breeze...

What's wailing, wracked by months
and years of early morning sweat
in the company of its mute

throng of stonecutters, is
the old excavator; but it's
also the fresh-ravaged earth,

or the whole district in the confines
of the modern skyline... It's
the city, bathed in a festive light

—it's the world. What cries is all that ends
and begins again. What used to be
a stretch of grass, an open expanse,

and is now a courtyard white as snow
enclosed within walls of resentment,
what used to be a kind of sideshow

of fresh plaster façades askew in the sun
and is now a new city block, bustling
with an order made of dull misfortune.

What cries is whatever changes, even
for the better. The light of the future
never stops wounding us, not even

for an instant: it's right here, burning
in our every daily gesture,
tormenting even the confidence

that gives us life, the passion of Gobetti
for these workers as they hoist,
in this street on the other front of humanity,

their red tatter of hope.

1956

Translated by Stephen Sartarelli

PLEASE MASTER

Allen Ginsberg (1926–1997)

Born in New Jersey, Ginsberg studied at Columbia University, where he met and befriended Jack Kerouac and William Burroughs. One of the defining voices of the Beat Generation, he was also a passionate social activist. His poem *Howl* was the subject of one of the last obscenity trials. The judge dismissed the charges. From 1954 until his death, he lived with his partner Peter Orlovsky in what they called a "marriage sealed by vows."

Please master can I touch your cheek
please master can I kneel at your feet
please master can I loosen your blue pants
please master can I gaze at your golden haired belly
please master can I gently take down your shorts
please master can I have your thighs bare to my eyes
please master can I take off my clothes below your chair
please master can I kiss your ankles and soul
please master can I touch lips to your hard muscle hairless thigh
please master can I lay my ear pressed to your stomach
please master can I wrap my arms around your white ass
please master can I lick your groin curled with blonde soft fur
please master can I touch my tongue to your rosy asshole
please master may I pass my face to your balls,
please master, please look into my eyes,
please master order me down on the floor,
please master tell me to lick your thick shaft

please master put your rough hands on my bald hairy skull

please master press my mouth to your prick-heart

please master press my face into your belly, pull me slowly strong
      thumbed

till your dumb hardness fills my throat to the base

till I swallow & taste your delicate flesh-hot prick barrel veined
      Please

Master push my shoulders away and stare in my eye, & make me
      bend over the table

please master grab my thighs and lift my ass to your waist

please master your hand's rough stroke on my neck your palm
      down my backside

please master push me up, my feel on chairs, till my hole feels the
      breath of your spit and your thumb stroke

please master make me say Please Master Fuck me now Please

Master grease my balls and hairmouth with sweet vaselines

please master stroke your shaft with white creams

please master touch your cock head to my wrinkled self-hole

please master push it in gently, your elbows enwrapped round my
      breast

your arms passing down to my belly, my penis you touch w/ your
      fingers

please master shove it in me a little, a little, a little,

please master sink your droor thing down my behind

& please master make me wiggle my rear to eat up the prick
      trunk

till my asshalfs cuddle your thighs, my back bent over,

till I'm alone sticking out, your sword stuck throbbing in me

please master pull out and slowly roll into the bottom

please master lunge it again, and withdraw to the tip

please please master fuck me again with your self, please fuck me
      Please

Master drive down till it hurts me the softness the

Softness please master make love to my ass, give body to center,
    & fuck me for good like a girl,
tenderly clasp me please master I take me to thee,
& drive in my belly your selfsame sweet heat-rood
you fingered in solitude Denver or Brooklyn or fucked in a maiden
    in Paris carlots
please master drive me thy vehicle, body of love dops, sweat fuck
body of tenderness, Give me your dog fuck faster
please master make me go moan on the table
Go moan O please master do fuck me like that
in your rhythm thrill-plunge & pull-back bounce & push down
till I loosen my asshole a dog on the table yelping with terror
    delight to be loved
Please master call me a dog, an ass beast, a wet asshole,
& fuck me more violent, my eyes hid with your palms round my
    skull
& plunge down in a brutal hard lash thru soft drip-fish
& throb thru five seconds to spurt out your semen heat
over & over, bamming it in while I cry out your name I do love
    you
please Master.

May 1968

THE MAN WITH NIGHT SWEATS

Thom Gunn (1929–2004)

Born in Kent and educated at Cambridge, Thom Gunn published *Fighting Terms*, his acclaimed first collection of poetry in 1954. He later moved to the USA, and from the 1960s lived in San Francisco, where he felt free to explore his sexuality, and where his work blossomed to use bold poetic forms. His collection of AIDS elegies, *The Man with Night Sweats* won him the Lenore Marshall Poetry Prize in 1993.

I wake up cold, I who
Prospered through dreams of heat
Wake to their residue,
Sweat, and a clinging sheet.

My flesh was its own shield:
Where it was gashed, it healed.

I grew as I explored
The body I could trust
Even while I adored
The risk that made robust,

A world of wonders in
Each challenge to the skin.

I cannot but be sorry
The given shield was cracked,
My mind reduced to hurry,
My flesh reduced and wrecked.

I have to change the bed,
But catch myself instead

Stopped upright where I am
Hugging my body to me
As if to shield it from
The pains that will go through me,

As if hands were enough
To hold an avalanche off.

SELECTED POEMS
Audre Lorde (1934–1992)

There is no better description of Lorde than her own: "black, lesbian, mother, warrior, poet". Born in New York in 1934 to Caribbean immigrant parents, she struggled to communicate as a child, and would often reply to a question by reciting a poem. She published her first poem while in high school. A writer, feminist and civil rights activist, she devoted her extraordinary talent to giving voice to "those outside this society's definition of acceptable women."

NEVER TO DREAM OF SPIDERS

Time collapses between the lips of strangers
my days collapse into a hollow tube
soon implodes against now
like an iron wall
my eyes are blocked with rubble
a smear of perspectives
blurring each horizon
in the breathless precision of silence
one word is made.

Once the renegade flesh was gone
fall air lay against my face
sharp and blue as a needle
but the rain fell through October

and death lay   a condemnation
within my blood.

The smell of your neck in August
a fine gold wire bejeweling war
all the rest lies
illusive as a farmhouse
on the other side of a valley
vanishing in the afternoon.

Day three   day four   day ten
the seventh step
a veiled door leading to my golden anniversary
flameproofed free-paper shredded
in the teeth of a pillaging dog
never to dream of spiders
and when they turned the hoses upon me
a burst of light.

LOVE POEM

Speak earth and bless me with what is richest
make sky flow honey out of my hips
rigis mountains
spread over a valley
carved out by the mouth of rain.

And I knew when I entered her I was
high wind in her forests hollow
fingers whispering sound
honey flowed
from the split cup
impaled on a lance of tongues
on the tips of her breasts on her navel
and my breath
howling into her entrances
through lungs of pain.

Greedy as herring-gulls
or a child
I swing out over the earth
over and over
again.

AFTERLOVE

In what had been a pathway
inbetween
our bed and a shared bathroom
broken hours lap at my heels
reaching my toothbrush
finally
I see
wide valleys filled with water
folding into myself
alone
I cross them into the shower the
tiles right themselves
in retreat
my skin thrills
bruised and battered
as thunderspray splatters
plasma on my horizons
when no more rain comes
I cast me out lightly
returning
on tiptoe
shifting and lurching
against my eyes
plastic curtains
I hung
last December
watching the sun flee
through patterns
spinning
always and never
returning

I spiced my armpits
courting the solstice
and never once did I abandon
believing
I would contrive
to make my world
whole again.

FAGGOTS

Larry Kramer (1935–2020)

Kramer, an Academy Award-nominated screenwriter, wrote his first novel, *Faggots*, to a divided reception. His observations of drug addiction, self-hatred and emotionally unrewarding promiscuity in New York were admonished by many gay critics at a time when groups were promoting an image of stable, gay, American men. In 1982, Kramer founded the Gay Men's Health Crisis, which remains a leading AIDS service organisation.

There are 2,556,596 faggots in the New York City area.

The largest number, 983,919, live in Manhattan. 186,991 live in Queens, or just across the river. 181,236 live in Brooklyn and 180,009 live in the Bronx. 2,469 live on Staten Island, substantiating that old theory that faggots don't like to travel or don't like to live on small islands, depending on which old theory you've heard and/or want substantiated.

Westchester and Dutchess Counties, together with that part of New Jersey which is really suburban New York, hold approximately 297,852, though this figure may be a bit low.

Long Island, or that which is beyond Queens, at last count numbered 211,910. (This goes all the way to Montauk, remember.)

Suburban Connecticut (not primarily of concern here, nor for that matter are suburban New Jersey or suburban New York—but you might as well have the advantage of all the statistics, since they were exhaustively collected), which includes the heavily infested Danbury triangle area, has 211,910 also, which makes it a sister statistic to Long Island, which is as it should be since the two share a common Sound.

There are now more faggots in the New York City area than Jews. There are now more faggots in the entire United States than all the yids and kikes put together. (This is subsidiary data, not overtly relevant, but ipso facto nevertheless.)

The straight and narrow, so beloved of our founding fathers and all fathers thereafter, is now obviously and irrevocably bent. What is God trying to tell us…?

There will be seven disco openings this holiday weekend. Though the premier palais de dance, Billy Boner's Capriccio, is closing tonight for the season so that Billy can open The Ice Palace at Cherry Grove, its closest competitor, Balalaika, run by the inseparable Patty, Maxine, and Laverne, will remain open, to cater to the hot-weather crowd on those weekends they don't make it to Fire Island.

Everyone wonders which of the newcomers will be the first to go under, because, ignorant of the above vital statistics, the fear is there's not enough business to go round.

On Saturday evening opens The Toilet Bowl. But that's meant to be more than a disco.

Later, it would be recollected as the False Summer. Everything had bloomed too quickly. Fire Island, this Memorial Day, would be like the Fourth of July. Too much too soon. Everyone was caught in the never-never land of City? Capriccio? The Tubs? Balalaika? The Pits? The Toilet Bowl? Fire Island? All cups runneth over. The weather was no help either—

the glorious summer sun now obviously out to stay—and thus useless in defining and dictating destinations and activities, as it usually did when cold meant dancing and very cold meant television, joints, and bed.

And here it was only May.

… Is there indeed a God who would understand such as:

"Baby, I want you to piss all over me!"

Fred Lemish had never urinated on anything before, except perhaps some country grass late at night when he was drunk and no one was looking.

"Or let me piss on you!"

This Fred Lemish had never allowed.

Fred stood there helplessly. Why was he inert in a moment requiring action? The guy wasn't bad-looking. Should Fred enter, or walk away?

"Or fuck my friend and I'll suck your come out of his asshole."

This suggestion Fred recognized as "felching." Was he interested in joining a felcher?

"Or I could tie you up. Or you could tie us up. Or either one of us. Or anything else your cock desires!"

The man certainly offered a range of choices. Should Fred? Shouldn't Fred?

"Are you into shit?"

Fred shouldn't.

Why was he even hesitating, Fred asked himself, instead of just walking on? Because he was horny, that's why, and this guy looked better than anybody else, there not being many here this afternoon anyway, and he wanted to get it over with and leave. That's why. And he had not seen Dinky Adams in three weeks, six days, and, checking his Rolex Submariner, which he never took off, sixteen hours. That's why, too. OK, he thought, what does this man want of me? Or since the man had offered the plethora of suggestions, what would Fred be capable of doing with this man? Piss and shit he wasn't up to, though the former intrigued him, God strike him dead. It would, however, not be difficult, Fred decided, stepping in ever so casually, no commitment, only a look, to fuck the friend, who had an attractive and perfectly rounded set of white buttocks, lying just right down there, staring up at him, saying Hello.

But then Fred became unsettled—for he now looked closer at the first chap, the chunky one who had propositioned him into the cubbyhole of a space, and noted that chunky was more akin to fat and that what had at three feet appeared to be well-formed pecs (so important), at two feet were revealed as sagging tits, a definite turnoff, mini-udders, no doubt from years of being chewed and tugged. This man was also now mumbling, almost as a litany, "… my friend's a good slave, he's a good slave…," an additional turnoff, Fred not, at this moment, drawn toward bondage either, and our Hero, rendered further into indecision by third thoughts, and fourth and fifth ones too, began to wonder if he might be sick if Master did as advertised, polished everything off by protruding his tongue into Slave's rectum to felch.

Yet here Fred was, viewing the Slave on the bed. He wondered, too, what it was like to be a Slave.

The Slave remained prone and silent, up-ended, as any good slave must obviously remain.

"What do you usually do on a Friday?" the Master asked, massaging Fred's cock.

"Huh? Unh, go dancing later. Capriccio's closing party tonight."

"Good-looking fellow like you… nice-sized dick… bet everybody's after you. Bet you'll still be here."

"Nah."

"Dancing, eh? I'll bet you're a wonderful dancer. Greatlooking legs you've got." The Master massaged Fred's great-looking legs. "I call dancing fairy sports. Fairy sports is our athletics."

This made Fred laugh.

"No, seriously. Dancing is sports for faggots. We're the best at it. And there's no win or lose. No competition. No being last guy chosen in gym." He began to suck Fred's cock.

Fred figured he might as well stay. As long as he was here.

The Everhard Baths on West 19th Street was owned by a syndicate of businessmen and not by the Firemen's Benevolent Athletic League, as rumored—a rumor obviously and happily encouraged by management so that the boys would feel safe. The building, not dissimilar to bath houses the world over, of whatever persuasion, was large and ugly, barrel-vaulted beneath and corridored above. It contained what no one boasted was the first heated swimming pool in New York, or anywhere else, at this moment a little too fetid for everyday use, as were the entire premises, though Murray, the night manager, in response to inquiries why the place was always dirty, claimed, with facts and figures rushing round above his head, that attendance fell off after a thorough cleaning.

Diamond Drew Everard (the "h" was added for business reasons when the place went obviously gay in the Swinging Sixties), had been a beer baron who needed a congenial place to soak out for the last half of the last century, so he bought this old church and converted. "Congenial" came to mean more than that along around 1920 (then as now a three-star, "worthy of a detour," national shrine in the faggot Michelin), though undoubtedly itineraries were a bit more covert in 1920 than they are today. The genealogy found the premises passed along over the years to Tammanys, Piping Rock sportsmen taking a flyer, several members of the cloth (both ecclesiastical and judicial), even a madam and her girls, all looking for a quiet turn on their investment. Up at bat now was this syndicate, one William Boner in the saddle, which evidently kept the policemen on the beat most happy with regular contributions to the Church of the Most Precious Blood, since many plaques attested to same and no harassment, which is no small feat for a business netting six million dollars cash on the barrel for providing like with like, statutorily illegal in this city and this country and this time—but there you have it, ipso facto again.

While he fucked the Slave, hoping all the while that Master would watch only and not give vent, Fred attempted to remember his decisions:

Had he not decided to write about a Voyage of Discovery into this World in which he lived? This Faggot World.

Had he not—just three months ago, as they both sat perched and observing from the edge of Capriccio's dance floor, watching the passing throngs—quoted to his good friend Gatsby (Tall, Blond, Handsome, Fred's Trinity, Fred's Robert Redford, intelligent, witty, and wise, another trinity, yes, everything Fred always wanted in a lover, though Gatsby was not interested) from the *Penguin Companion to Literature, European:* "'The Stendhalian hero refuses any form of authority that would impinge on his personal liberty, and in defiance of both good sense and history, sets out to remake the universe in his own image.'"

THE CHAIR

Takahashi Mutsuo (1937–)

Born in Kyushu, Takahashi spent his early years living in rural Japan. He moved to Tokyo at the age of twenty-five and published his first anthology of poetry *Rose Tree, Fake Lovers* in 1964. While best known as a poet, he has written many novels, Nō and Kyōgen plays, reworkings of ancient Greek dramas and epic poetry.

1

This is the chair in which I sat until just a few moments ago. A few moments ago – but no, I may be mistaken in that. Speaking in the customary way, perhaps I ought to say "until yesterday." At any rate, the May sunlight, neither too strong nor too weak, was encroaching on the chair in just the same way as always; and, in just the same way, a breeze too gentle to be called a wind passed through the leaves of the trees in the garden from time to time, and brushed against my bare throat, worn by illness, and against the back of my hand, which was gripping one arm of the chair.

Suddenly, I could no longer feel the warmth of the sunlight or the softness of the breeze. I was, as always, sitting in the chair. I…or, perhaps better, my body. The I-who-felt was separated from the body of the I-in-the-chair and, from somewhere obliquely above, was looking down at the body that had, until just now, constituted the whole of the flesh belonging to me, a forty-five-year-old invalid. There was a withered right hand. This thin, blackened, monkey-like right hand, which protruded from a slightly yellowed hempen kimono sleeve, continued to grasp, as always, the rattan arm-rest of the chair, but all power was gone from its bony knuckles and joints. There was a left hand. The left hand hung down outside the left armrest and swung there slowly, due to its weight. And there was a face. Both cheeks of the face, which was supported by the back of the chair, were leaden gray and emaciated. White-speckled whiskers grew sparsely on the upper lip and around the mouth. Wrinkles surrounded the eye-cavities, which gaped wide, and the cloudy objects that filled those cavities were directed toward the precise space where the I-who-felt was. Yet I could tell from the lack of any light in those cloudy things that they were seeing nothing.

The shoji paper screens that separated the veranda where the chair was from the inner room opened, and his clean-looking, short-cropped head peered out, dazzled by the sunlight. At once he noticed the change in the invalid seated in the chair, let out a small gasp of surprise, and went back into the room. When he emerged after a moment, his face, with its thick eyebrows drawn together and tightly compressed lips, showed decisiveness as he approached the chair. He held the invalid's shoulders in his arms and raised him from the chair. But the dead-weight of the nearly six-feet tall invalid, though wasted by illness, was too much for the fifteen-year-old boy's strength. In the course of the two or three steps it took to get from the chair to the opened shoji, both the supporting boy and the supported invalid stumbled several times.

The I-who-felt stayed outside the shoji, now closed again. In the distance, beyond the shoji and several doors, I could hear the sound of a telephone being dialed. The telephone had not been dialed for several years. Fine dust must now lightly cover the numbers from 1 to 0 inside the ten little holes into which his fingertip had to be inserted. The dust would dirty his slightly moist fingertip.

Finally, the telephone began to ring intermittently, and soon I could hear people's voices. It had been years since the sound of voices was heard in this house. Gradually there were sounds of more people talking, and even of occasional laughter. To the sky beyond the trees in the garden a beautiful twilight came: the twilight's crimson changed to purple, and the purple slowly gave way to the deep blue of night. How strange it felt to be there in the midst of shifting time, sensing from a certain distance the noise of the funeral for the decaying substance that had been myself. The sound of voices went on through the night and began to seem like merry-making.

How much time had passed? The deep blue of night shifted back to purple, and the purple to crimson; and then the chair was in the midst of the morning and its dew. Right below the veranda where the chair sat began an irregular stone pathway leading to the garden, and on top of the largest, flattest stone were my garden clogs, sitting a bit awry, as I had left them. The indigo of the clog thongs had faded in the repeated dews of night and dawn, staining the area around the holes through which the thongs passed. The morning sunlight shone through the cherry trees just opposite and bathed the clogs in a radiance faintly smelling of blood.

The morning sun. The morning sun shone directly onto the veranda. I amused myself by calling it "my veranda facing the sun." For I had sat in this chair on this veranda for many months, even at night, facing in the direction of the morning sun. When I needed to pass water, I stamped my foot lightly on the floor. Though he ought to have been sound asleep, the boy would look out from the shoji wearing denims and a shirt, not looking especially sleepy, and give me the chamber pot. It was our custom.

Beyond the dark trees in the garden was a dark road. The dark road sloped downward, and at the bottom there was a dark town, and far beyond the dark rows of houses, was the dark horizon. Below the line of the horizon, there was without doubt the morning, ascending moment by moment. The sensations in my hands, forehead, and bare, thin chest had by now grown very weak, yet I could still feel to some degree the deep night chill upon them as I waited. The unmoving deep night chill began, after a long period of time that seemed itself almost immobile, subtly to move. I felt it on my deadened skin. The dawn chill that had just begun to move was more intense than the night's had been, but it was easier to bear because it did move.

At last the first light came. That first light, which arrived after shooting through the leaves of the cherry trees, was an awl that broke the skin of morning, and at the same time it was the blood that poured from the broken skin. I clearly recognized that raw smell: I, who had almost completely lost all sensation. "Ah, it was to experience this raw smell of blood that I kept on waiting," I realized anew each morning.

I am no longer in the chair, and in a real sense, I no longer have any sensations. But the memory of me being in the chair before and of my sensations there do remain, and I can trace the outlines of my mixed feelings of pain and peace of mind in the morning and the sensation of the raw smell of blood in the morning sun. Ants have started to crawl around the slight depressions in the garden clogs that my toes had made. The little birds are noisy. The whole space seems to be filled with twittering.

There are the sounds of guests who, tired from talking through the night, had drowsed off, and now were awakening. And once again there are loud voices and laughter. But the talk sounds diffused, quite unlike what it had been in the darkness – no doubt because light had entered and come between the guests. As usual, no one opened the paper screens beyond which was the veranda, bathed in sunlight.

May cicadas (the ones called "mugiurashi") began to emit their irritated cries from the pine tree that stood beside the entranceway, invisible from this angle. When one began, another began as well. The third cry may have from the Himalayan cedar near the house across the road, beyond the entranceway and our front gate. Then a much louder voice joined in – a sutra for the dead was being recited.

…Nii jii, Oushaa Daijou, uu ichi taishi, myou Aajaasee.
Zuijun Joudatsu aku-uu shii kyou, shuu shuu buuou Binbaashaaraa,
Yuu hei chii ou shichijuu shitsunai, sei shougunshin, ippuu toku ou…

[At that time there was in the great city of Rajagriha a prince named Ajatasatru. Following the advice of a wicked friend named Devadatta, he arrested his father, King Bimbisara, and held him in a cell behind seven-fold walls, not allowing any officials or noblemen access to him.]

What I could not clearly hear, my memory supplied. Naturally, since it was my favorite sutra, *The Sutra of Meditation on the Buddha of Infinite Life*. Of the three Pure Land sutras, I especially like this one because it centers on the feelings of a son, Prince Ajatasatru, toward his father, King Bimbisara. As the sutra progresses, however, the figures of both Ajatasatru and Bimbisara fade, giving way to the figure of the mother, Queen Vaidehi, and to Sakyamuni Buddha, who gives her his teachings, and to the words of wisdom that emerge from the Buddha's mouth. It was because of her sorrow at the bad relations between her son and her husband that Queen Vaidehi asked the Buddha to visit her, and the tragedy of father and son form a constant backdrop to Sakyamuni's radiant words.

Even so, why am I so drawn to the Meditation Sutra rather than others? I have no strong religious faith, and I am certainly not a member of one of the Pure Land sects. I really do like this sutra, but I've never said so to anyone. And of course, not to him as well. After all, I've hardly spoken with him for over a year now. I imagine he found the Meditation Sutra open along with various specialist texts on the desk in my study there inside the shoji, and thought of using it at my funeral service.

The recitation has come to the section on the contemplation of water, of which I am particularly fond.

...Shii saa sui sou. Ken sui choushou, yaku ryou myouryou, mu bu san i. Kii ken sui i, tou kii hyou sou. Ken pyouyou tetsu, saa ruurii sou...

[Next, perform the water visualization. See the water as pure and clean. See it clearly, and do not allow your mind to wander. When you have perfectly visualized the water, see it as ice. When you have seen the ice as brilliantly shining throughout, visualize it as lapis lazuli.]

The white radiance of this astronomical theory of elementary particles, which far surpasses human imagination… Am I now within a globe of water, of ice, of lapis lazuli, both inwardly and outwardly transparent? Or am I in one of ten million pavilions that sit upon a calyx of light projected into space from those globes? I am, at any rate, now in the light and intensely pure space that I used to love imagining most; and from there, I am gazing at the heavy, easily defiled place where I formerly was.

In time the sutra recitation ended, and the area in front of the entranceway grow noisy. There was the sound of a crowd of people stepping down into the entranceway, which had been left open. Car horns blare. The hearse must have come to a stop in the narrow road in front of the house, blocking traffic. People stand in line in front of the entranceway, and someone is extending greetings to them. Finally, the hearse started to move away, and the sound of car horns ceased. The sound of people's voices also gradually grew fainter.

I was left alone. As before, I felt around me the warmth of sunlight and a soft breeze. I am ruminating over and over on the time from then until now. "Am ruminating…?" Am I really here? And if I am, what is that thing that was once myself, then was nailed into a coffin, and is now being shaken about in the hearse as it moves through the afternoon streets? In ten minutes, the hearse will arrive at the crematorium outside town, and that thing, in which the process of putrefaction is already well under way, will be burned up, giving off sounds like fresh wood as it burns. I can see that as clearly as if I were gazing through a globe of crystal.

I am at peace.

2

Rain is falling.

When did it begin? Several days ago? Several weeks? My consciousness remembers the garden bathed in May sunlight very recently, yet this gloomy rain seems to have been falling on the garden continuously, from beyond an eternity of time. In fact, in the rain, the green of the garden has deepened; and this green, so deep it looks almost black, seems to hint at a kind of "perpetuity of green."

There are the shoji screens, the veranda, and the chair. The chair shows no signs of having been moved since then. As far as non-movement goes, the position of the garden clogs sitting on the steppingstone outside the veranda is also just as it was. The steppingstone and the garden clogs were both wet from the steady drizzle. A still finer spray had fallen into the rain shutters' wooden grooves, dry and slightly splintered, since they had not been used for over a year.

The indigo from the clogs' thongs had seeped into the area around the three thong-holes on each clog many times, and the fresh spray from the rain made the blue color brighter on the section of the thong that passed over the instep. The sight of this made the soles of my feet feel itchy – absurdly, since how could I any longer have soles? I even felt the cold indigo of the clog-thongs dying the white, moist skin between my big toe and the next. I remember that.

Exactly one year ago, a fine drizzle was falling, the same as now. I was standing on the wooden floor and feeling the strength of my lower body leave through the soles of my feet. I gazed blankly at the leaves of the cherry trees in the drizzling rain, and at the purple of the hydrangeas, seemingly blurred by the rain. As I looked at the many clusters of hydrangeas trembling slightly under the pressure of the rain, a chill passed over my feverish eyes, and I felt again the coldness of the wooden floor under the soles of my feet.

Simultaneously, I felt a cold heaviness in one hand. Oh, yes – I was holding a pair of scissors. I had come out onto the veranda, planning to go down into the garden and cut some hydrangeas. As I traced the progress of this seemingly simple action, my abstracted state of mind seemed like a bottomless swamp, and I felt a helplessness hard to express.

But I went down into the garden. I stepped onto the garden clogs. They were not only cold but sodden, and when the thongs passed between my toes, water dyed indigo from them oozed out. I started to move toward the hydrangeas, stepping from stone to stone.

Just then, I felt as if the very core of my lower body had been pulled straight down out of me from the center of the sole of my raised foot, and I reeled. The next moment, my face lay in the mud of garden earth mixed with rainwater. I felt no pain. I tried to move my legs in order to stand up, but there was no strength in them. Nor did I have the power to use my hands to rise. By slowly, slowly shifting my head, I managed to turn it to one side. The nearest things in my line of vision were the clumps of mud sticking to my eyelashes. A bit further on was the side surface of a steppingstone. It was wet with rainwater, and had become a cloudy mirror.

My face as reflected in this mirror of stone was no more than a vague mask of light and darkness. Yet I was able to restore that light/dark mask to a proper face. It had been ten days earlier. I had made my way to the bathroom, grabbing onto the walls and doors, and was on my way back, stopping at the washbasin to wash my hands. When, clinging to the tile rim of the basin, I raised my head, I saw an open window there before me, and from the space formed by the window frame, a dead man was peering at me. So I thought.

There was another surprise waiting for me in the next instant: the dead man's face was my own. And the space formed by the window frame was a mirror. I had almost forgotten that there were mirrors in the world. I hate mirrors. And particularly since that operation half a year ago, I had removed mirrors from any place where I might see them. To think that that mirror was placed by the washbasin just in front of the bathroom, along that most everyday of routes! Had he placed it there so that he could get a good look at his face, adolescent that he was? Or was it because he wanted to let me know something...?

I gazed long and hard at my face in the mirror, seen now for the first time in half a year. Half a year.... Yet it seemed like several decades had passed.

The eyes were sunk deep in their orbits, the edges of which clearly showed the lines of the skull, to which leaden, wrinkled skin clung. In front of the two empty-looking eyes were two lifeless eyebrows, like dirty wads of hemp. The bridge of the nose between the two eyebrows and eyes was sharp and thin as a knife-blade. An utterly decrepit face. The face of an old man of forty-five. I covered my face with my hands. As I did so, I peered through my fingers and saw that my hands were as shriveled as mummified chickens' feet....

In the depths of that stone mirror's blurred image, there was unquestionably the face of that decrepit old man. Lying on my side in the mud, facing the stone mirror, I thought of what had happened the week before my operation. An empty examination room in the prefectural hospital, a little past four in the afternoon, just after the New Year's holidays. Beyond the frosted glass window a wintry rain was falling on the bushes. Water was boiling on top of a heating-stove placed between the slightly overweight, ruddy-faced doctor who had once been my colleague and myself, thin, with a sickly gray complexion. From beyond the stove, his face even redder from the heat, the doctor gazed at me, his eyes like narrow threads inside his rimless glasses.

"Well anyway, let's take it out. Then we can see how things are over the next half year."

He must have known there was no point in trying to hide things from me, who had studied at medical school at one point. My former colleague, now a well-known surgeon, nodded without putting on a smile. The seriousness of the situation was clear. But I wasn't in the least worried. On the contrary, the very gravity of it gave me a certain feeling of peace.

For the next half year, I sat on the inside of the veranda screens, blankly confronting my work, "The Inter-relationship between Oral Stage Sexual Desire and Riddles." I had been working on it for well over ten years without any real progress. When tired, I would open the screens and go out onto the veranda, where I spent many hours in my chair.

It was as if time had vanished from around me. Or, to put it more exactly, I had intentionally distanced time from myself. If my essay had made no progress, it was because I wouldn't allow it to. One could say that I had caused time to lose all meaning, and thus tried to prolong the feeling of peace that I had experienced in that hospital examination room. That's why the sudden appearance of the mirror had been such a shock to me.

In comparison with that shock, I felt at peace when I looked at the stone mirror as I lay on my side in the mud. The difference in the intensity of my experiences on those two occasions corresponded somewhat to the difference between a clear glass mirror and a dull stone one. It was pleasant, rather, as I lay there, to be able still to feel the sensation of the wet mud with one half of my body and the sensation of the fine drizzle of rain with the other half.

I raised my voice and tried to call him. I could open my mouth wide, but the inside of the mouth was strangely dry, and my tongue just moved convulsively, without making any sound. And yet I came at some point to even take pleasure in this self that could not speak. I opened my mouth many times and moved my tongue convulsively many times; I batted my eyelashes, wet with drizzle, and smiled a little.

How long did I continue this slightly desperate, childish game, I wonder.

When, suddenly sensing something, I shifted my gaze, I found him standing atop the stone mirror, the steppingstone, looking down at me. Perhaps because I was gazing up at him from a low vantage point, lying in the mud, he looked strangely tall as he stood on that stone, his bare feet slightly apart. With the sunlit shoji at his back, he seemed a dazzling, unapproachable figure.

But that unapproachable figure came down into the mud and bent forward gracefully. My body was lifted from the mud into the air. I felt his moist young breath on my neck's withered skin. His eyes were open wide, but there was no trace of emotion in them.

I was placed in the chair. Then he left the veranda and appeared again with a change of clothes under his arm. As with an infant, my dirty clothes were taken off me, and I was dressed in the new, clean ones.

When he left with the dirty clothes under one arm, the same way he had come in moments before, I happened to look at his head. It almost touched the top of the doorframe. It had not been only my low vantage point that had made him seem so strangely and dazzlingly tall there in the garden. While I had been avoiding him, and he me, he had matured to an amazing degree. I saw as if before my very eyes that tired old face in the mirror from ten days before. The steepness of the slope that was the half year when I had been distancing myself from everything had been doubled by my remarkable decline and his amazing maturation. He went in, behind the shoji, and I was left alone.

I continued to sit in the wicker chair there outside the shoji. Meals, sleep, relieving myself – all happened there. There had been no conversation between him and me for a long time now, so I signaled to him by lightly stamping on the veranda floor. There was, however, no need for that. Wordlessly, he understood my biological rhythms: at the right time he brought me my food-tray, or gave me the chamber pot or hand-urinal, or covered me with a blanket. At night he slept in the study so as to be able to respond immediately to my signal.

I no longer called for the doctor. I had closed my eyes to time for half a year, but now I was determined not to avert my eyes from even its minutest part.

For example, the subtle waves in the atmosphere at the instant when gloomy afternoon passes into evening. Or the tremulous details of the sky in the east changing moment by moment when the long painful night transforms into dawn.

I was as far removed from life as I was from death. Life was, for instance, the hydrangeas that I had been approaching, holding the scissors. Sitting there embraced by the back and arms of the chair, I spent my days gazing at the hydrangeas, wetted by rain and changing their color day by day, as I muttered a pair of phrases that were like a magic spell: "the distance to life," "the distance to death."

Even more distant from me than the hydrangeas in the rain was his manner, as he approached me only to move away again at once.

*

3.

In time, the hydrangeas, which had changed color from green to white and from white to purple, ended. Sickly yellowish leaves appeared here and there among the now darker mass of foliage. The cherry trees' leaves also grew steadily darker, making me feel the weakening of life in the very midst of high summer. And that weakening had nothing of appeasement about it.

The cicadas were noisy. Different kinds of cicada came to the garden, but it was the so-called "oil cicadas" that cried from early morning on. Their name suggests the kind of sound they make, like oil hissing in the bottom of a hot metal pan. There was nothing at all refreshing about the sound. Here and there in the garden I could hear grasshoppers chirping and stopping, chirping and stopping.

There was an irritating stench of dog excrement rising from the steamy grass. The garden's back gate had collapsed during a typhoon at the close of the rainy season, allowing stray dogs to make their way in. But what could there be for them to eat in such a wild, overgrown garden? They would spend a long time sniffing around the garden, which was nothing but weeds by now, then deposit their turds, and leave. The whole business filled me with an irritating sense of futility.

"Sense," did I say? Can I in fact "feel" or "sense" now? Do I still exist as an entity that feels? When I still had that heavy thing we call a "body," it often occurred to me that the very fact of having something as unclear as a sensation was itself the best proof that I did not exist. So, what about now that this illusory heaviness is gone. Having been freed from the flesh, do I now exist, in a real sense? If so, then what does it mean that sensations seem to remain to me, even if only in the form of memories?

Having returned from school unexpectedly one day, he was standing between the steppingstone and the hydrangeas. He must have come in by the back gate, as the stray dogs did, rather than by the front entranceway. He seemed to have just finished some intense exertion, since both his forehead and the tip of his nose were sweaty, as were the training pants and polo shirt that clung tightly to his skin. He tossed his satchel onto the veranda and peered into the hydrangea bushes. Ah yes, there was a water tap there. When the garden was still well tended, there had been a flowerbed surrounding the cherry tree where different flowers bloomed during all four seasons. The water tap had functioned as a spring providing the flowers with water. In time, tall grass grew up in the flowerbed, and the water tap was completely hidden by the encroaching hydrangea bushes.

He seemed to have found the tap, and began pushing the bushes aside. Hidden by them was a rusty water pipe with a tap on top. The faucet must have been hard to turn: he twisted it with his right hand, his eyebrows tensely drawn together. As the faucet gave, the pent-up force of the water made it spurt straight down. Leaving the rushing water as it was, he ran out of my field of vision.

When he came back, he had in hand a dark blue plastic hose. He turned the water off and placed one end of the hose over the faucet's opening. When it was well in place, he turned the faucet on again. The pressure of the water made the hose suddenly leap up and then strike the ground, snake-like; the water spurting from the hose's free end struck the side of the steppingstone and then sprayed onto the geta on top of it, wetting them thoroughly.

He rushed to pick up the hose and then roughly wriggled his feet out of his sneakers. His toes, looking somehow more adult than his years would warrant, emerged comfortably into the open air from the dark, humid enclosure of his shoes. He directed the spray of water onto his feet, wanting to cool them off.

The hand that held the hose, however, stretched straight up, and from that height turned the end of the hose downward. The water struck against his short cropped head and cascaded down his face, immediately soaking his polo shirt and training pants. He didn't care, but kept the water streaming, now turning the end of the hose toward the chest, stomach, and back areas of his polo shirt, and the front and the seat of his training pants. In a minute's time, he was as wet as a drowned rat.

He threw the hose, which was continuing to spout water, down onto the wet earth. Then, opening his eyes wide and looking up at the sky, he rolled his polo shirt up to his neck and pulled it off, tossing it onto the foliage of the hydrangea bushes. His belly, like a starved young beast's; his chest, which, though it had begun to show some suggestion of brawn, had still not quite emerged from boyish flat-chestedness (yet his two dark nipples were a sign that he had in fact become a man); his shoulders, at once boney and softly rounded; his arms, so elegantly graceful that they seemed perhaps a bit too long for his torso – they seemed all the more vital for being dripping wet.

Next he pulled his training pants down toward his knees and took them off. His shins and thighs, too, were long, and his kneecaps had the oval shape peculiar to youths who exercise. He pulled down the white shorts that covered those long thighs and stood there naked.

Surrounded by the dark green of high summer, unseen by anyone, his naked body was now sufficient to itself. Suddenly his hand grasped the hose, which lay on the ground energetically spewing water, and directed its spray toward the portion of his groin that was covered with a dark thicket. The water spurting from the hose, which he held with both hands, kept beating at that part until it began to show a quiet but increasingly rapid change. Soon, his hands tossed aside the hose, grasped the flesh within the thicket, and began slowly to make it move. Gradually the hand movements grew faster. Planting his feet on the ground, jutting his head back, he gazed at the bright blue summer sky, with a kind of pain. Suddenly, a thick fluid burst from inside him, and above and below the oval-shaped knees, the two long thighs and two long shins twitched convulsively. And can I really claim that, at that moment, I did not stretch out my arms so as to embrace him from behind, place my hands over his, and assist him in his fall?

It had all happened three years before, when I shortened by one day my stay at a major academic conference. Though I had never acted on impulse this way before, I decided that day not to enter the house from the front entrance, but to go through the back gate and then around to the veranda through the garden. Passing between the plants and bushes,

I came to the side of my study and peeked at the veranda: there he was, stark naked. He was seated on the edge of the veranda with his legs hanging down and his hands touching his groin: he was right in the act of indulging in that lonely pleasure. Beside him were a notebook and textbooks, a pencil case and his undershorts. I assumed that he had been doing his summer vacation homework, gotten tired, and suddenly started in. I was supposed to be coming home the next day, and he hadn't seemed to notice the presence of an unwelcome visitor. He must have felt completely safe playing with himself there.

Then, unexpectedly, he noticed me and became flustered; but there was no way he could hide his nakedness, exposed to the bright light of the midsummer's day. With his hands still at his groin, he lowered his head, and his face turned bright red. I stepped up onto the veranda and sat so as to embrace the naked boy from behind. My legs hung down alongside his legs, and I placed my hands on top of his. He never looked me in the face; and yet, with my cooperation, he climbed, panting, to the heights, and then collapsed.

At the time, I told myself that there had been no other way to save him from feelings of shame, but had that really been all there was to it? Rather, had I not engaged in that strange behavior to save *myself*, who had discovered him in the act, from a sense of shame? Or, to press the matter further, perhaps shame had been part of the very relationship between him and me.

He had slipped down into the garden almost as if making an escape from between my thighs, and then went through the garden in the direction of the bath. From beyond several layers of shoji and wooden doors, the sound of the shower went on and on. I stayed sitting on the edge of the veranda, my thighs spread wide, as they had been when I held him, naked, between them.

The flesh of my thighs still felt the warmth of his body with a raw intensity, but he was no longer there. The sun went down, and still I sat there.

After that happened, he began to avoid me in a very obvious way.

Not only that – he stopped coming to my study and the veranda beyond it, which he had often entered before. Clearly, he was trying to avoid the memory of that day.

And I? I, on the contrary, often vacantly immersed myself in that memory. Many a time I found myself sitting with thighs spread wide, as they had been when I held his nakedness between them on the veranda that day. Of course, he wasn't there. But, in going over that event again and again in my mind, was I not violating him anew each time?

As I went on violating him in my thoughts, I felt a fearful regret. Not over my violating him. It was, rather, an irritated regret resulting from the consciousness of my old age in contrast with his youth, a youthfulness that overflowed in him unavoidably, even though he was avoiding me. In actuality, I was only forty-two; but the fact that I had not yet entered what the world regards as old age made my sense of being old even more irritating.

The longing and desire that were part of his adolescence and, as precisely the other side of the same coin, the sense of loss and regret in my old age.

By violating again and again the youthfulness within him, was I not descending deeper and deeper into the madness of old age? It's not inconceivable that the hurried onset of my illness and my premature ageing were the result of that....

He must have left the clothes he'd cast aside there among the hydrangeas when he went to the bath. The rubber hose still moved on the ground, spouting water. On top of the mud that was drinking in the water, the cloudy white substance he had emitted lay scattered about, already giving off a sour odor. Flies, drawn to that odor, buzzed nosily.

How could I not be counted as one of those flies? How could I not be counted as one of the hungry ghosts that extend their long tongues toward the fresh excreta of the living, in the medieval Buddhist painting-scrolls?

Only, what I am extending my tongue toward to lick is not dead excreta but his living liquid, and my own sense of regret and loss that lies beneath its sour taste.

That I seem able to be here even now, feeling this – could this not be merely my sense of regret and loss that have remained behind, making it seem as if I myself were feeling this?

It is the season of Urabon, when offerings are made to hungry ghosts.

It is the fearful season of regret and loss.

4

The snow that began to fall in the darkness of night continues to fall even now, close to noon, covering the withered trees in the garden in the forms of trunks, the forms of branches. The ground and stones in the garden too are hidden by the snow; and the geta sitting atop the stepping-stone near the veranda are buried in snow, but still retain their forms as geta, rising a little higher than the stepping-stone itself. In the grooves of the veranda's rain shutters, left open as always, the snowflakes look like miniscule rice-crackers, blown there by the wind. Those that make it further into the veranda melt away at once on the wooden floor. But the whole house is completely enveloped in snow.

Everything is enveloped in snow. There is not a sound to be heard anywhere, as if all the sounds in the air have been sucked inside the globules of falling snow, enfolded within them. What might seem to be the sound of snow falling is, in fact, the sound of silence, falling incessantly and piling up.

Snow. Cocoons of chill whiteness ceaselessly falling from a dark rent in the sky above. Am I enclosed in one lone cocoon that has escaped the ranks of those whose fall is so regular? As usual, I am in some invisible spot, seeing through the present and the distant times of this garden and its veranda.

When one sees through the falling of snow each winter, its falling for the past ten some years, all the time in those years seems filled with a ceaseless procession of snow. That day, too, is was snowing. I made my way up the snowy slope with difficulty and at last arrived home, and then entered my study. The heater was going full blast, and next to it was a basket heaped with children's clothes. I had completely forgotten that, having been told that his foster-mother would be bringing him back to me that day, I had sent her the key to the house. I stretched my hands out over the heater and wondered how I should engage with the boy whom I had not seen for three years. When I had put him into foster-care, he was so small he couldn't even see. It would be a reencounter for me, but to this three-year-old it would be, in effect, our first meeting.

I heard a voice, and, looking at the shoji bright with the snow's reflected light, I saw the shadowy movements of a human form. A child's hesitant-sounding voice asked "Okay now?" And a woman answered, in a still more childish-sounding voice, "It's okay!" He was playing hide-and-seek with his foster mother there in the snow.

Opening the shoji a crack, I peeked out. Framed by that long thin opening in the midst of the falling snow, I saw him, wearing the duffle coat and boots I had sent him at some point, walking with his woolen-gloved hands stretched out in front. I knew from the letters I'd received from time to time that he had grown, but I felt very moved by the actual sight of him.

He was looking for the "It" in the game of hide-and-seek there in the snow. Where had that simple woman hidden herself, playing the "It," I wondered. But opening the shoji a little wider, I could see the woman's sturdy back covered in splash-patterned cotton stuff. She was helping him look for the "It"! So then, who was he looking for?

The idea that it was me they were looking for suddenly flashed through my mind, and I became agitated without knowing why. The woman must have been aware that I'd come back when I entered the front entrance hall; she then took the boy into the garden and started a game of hide-and-seek with me as "It," thinking to please me. She'd known all along that I was peeking out at them and just pretended not to notice.

Suddenly he opened his little mouth. I stared at it. The little mouth opened once more: "Mama!"

I could hardly believe my ears. How could he know anything about his "mama"? But I soon understood the situation, because the woman joined him in calling "Mama! Mama!" That insensitive peasant woman had defiled his sweetly ignorant, snow-white little heart with the idea of "mother." Yes, I was sure of it!

No sooner had I opened the shoji than I jumped down into the garden. The woman reacted by picking up the child and standing as if on guard. Her white hairs, mingled with the black; her small eyes that looked both stupid and cunning; her shoulders, tensely raised beneath her cheap kimono; her fat, dirty fingers gripping the child – I hated them all. The fact that the child was staring at me with the same animalistic gaze as the woman multiplied my hatred of her. I grabbed the child from her and pushed the woman down onto the snow.

She left then, sobbing loudly like some damn fool. The child and I were alone in the snowy garden. He had been crying since the moment I grabbed him from her arms. I put him down on the cold veranda and went back inside, behind the shoji.

His broken sobs were sucked into the cocoons of snow, and each time the silence deepened. Rising and falling like waves, his sobs gradually grew weaker. At last the sobs were reduced to occasional hiccups, and it was clear that his tantrum would soon be over. Then he would become aware that the skin under his eyes, now red and rough from his tears, was in fact his own skin. Until then, it would be a relief to him to keep on crying.

From that day on, I was rushed off my feet with caring for him, who had returned to me. Through the long snowy days he stayed silent, and I began to fear he would become autistic. I went into town and bought him far too many toys and picture books; eventually, he showed an interest in some of the latter.

Among the picture books he seemed to like best was a book of riddles. He was comfortable enough with me by then to climb onto my lap, after a reassuring glance at the expression on my face; and he would bring the "Riddles" book along and have me repeat them. I would read. He would remain silent. I would read the next page. He would still remain silent.

Then one day it occurred to me to read the same riddle-question on the same page over and over again, and encourage him to answer. His large eyes peered into mine and then began to mist over, and soon the liquid overflowed into teardrops. His little lips trembled and at last opened: "Mama!"

"No, that's not it!" I said almost imploringly. But he just kept on saying "Mama! Mama!" through his sob-like hiccups. I was forced to change the question. Yet no matter what question from what page I chose, all he did was stubbornly repeat "Mama!" through his hiccups. When I realized that my plea to this young child, made virtually on my knees, was being so coldly rejected, an unreasoning anger welled up inside me. I set the boy, who was clinging to me as he cried, on his feet and put him outside the shoji, on the snowy veranda, as I had that first day.

From inside the shoji, I listened to the sound of him crying, but my anger gradually passed. My by now calm and collected mind could see into the depths of his childish one. He had been carefully trained by his foster-mother to search ceaselessly for his real mother. All of his forms of play were variations on hide-and-seek for the mother. That was why, for him, at the dead-end of every labyrinthine riddle was his mother. It was my duty, then, to help him in his quest for his mother.

As I sat listening to his by now intermittent crying outside the shoji, I decided on my lecture-topic for the next autumn's academic conference: "The Inter-relationship between Oral Stage Sexual Desire and Riddles." This plan, however, had first occurred to me soon after his mother's death.

Perusing the great, late-Edo literary collection, the *Gunsho ruiju*, in the university library one day, I happened on a text several tens of pages long entitled "Riddles Chosen by the Retired Emperor Gonara." Later investigation revealed that its formal title was "Nazodate" (Posing Riddles), and that it was an anthology of riddles that were popular among the courtiers and aristocrats of the Muromachi Period (c. 15th through 16th centuries). As the title indicates, it was compiled at the age of twenty-one by Imperial Prince Tomohito, who later became the Retired Emperor Gonara. The criteria for inclusion were not only their interest as riddles but also especially the beauty of their imagery and the refinement of their diction. So the Imperial Prince must have chosen the riddles by the same standards with which the Retired Emperor Gotoba chose the poems in the *Shin Kokinshuu* (The New Collection of Poems, Ancient and Modern).

The over seven hundred riddles in the "Nazodate" are all beautiful. As I rolled the sounds over my tongue riddle by riddle and noted the solution to each, I came across a very strange one. The "Nazodate" says: "Twice I meet with mother, but with father, never." The answer given is: "The lips." I couldn't figure out why the text gave this solution, no matter how I tried; but to leave the problem unsolved would not do: The images and sounds of the riddle stayed with me. So, with the book open to that very page, I went to see a librarian of my acquaintance and asked him about it.

Now this librarian is a specialist in the history of the Japanese language, and the point of his explanation was as follows: Until the middle of the Muromachi Period, when Japanese pronounced the word for "mother," they did not say "haha," as at present, but rather "fafa." "H" is a guttural sound, so it is pronounced with the upper and lower lips open, but "f" is a plosive, so one must bring the upper and lower lips together and then open them. Since there are two "f's" in "fafa," the upper and lower lips meet twice. In the case of "chichi" for "father," however, they never meet. Hence, "Twice I meet with mother, but with father, never."

Ah yes, I nodded, at this clear, logical explanation. And yet I thought there must be something more to it. Isn't it likely that the gentle beauty of this riddle has its deepest roots in the tragic relationship between father and son? Humans encounter their mothers, in the strongest possible way, twice, at the times of birth and of death. (Isn't it often reported that young soldiers dying on the battlefield cry out "Mother!" rather than, say, "Long live His Majesty the Emperor!") But they never truly encounter their fathers.

It is the "lips," those purest and at the same time most easily defiled of things, that are the meeting point between a child and its mother. During what Freud calls the oral stage, the child of course experiences the resilience of its mother's nipples through its own lips. And at the time of death, a man once again returns to the oral stage and experiences his mother in the form of the word itself. If so, then the words of a language are repeatedly uttered in order to confirm the perfect image of the mother in the oral stage, after that stage has passed. And they must also be repeatedly uttered in order to capture, it is hoped, the father whom one has never encountered. The hesitant repetitions of riddle-games arise from the very nature of language, which is, in fact, the search for the father and mother. This is the point I wished to argue in my phantasmal doctoral thesis, which I was unable ever to complete, much less in time for the upcoming academic conference.

Was that period not, however, perhaps the happiest in my life? The period when I held him in my arms in front of the heater on those snowy days and, as I opened the book of riddles before him, pursued in my thoughts my chosen theme. When I gaze at the snow falling just as it did in those bygone days, I feel as though I still held the three-year-old child in my arms and went on repeating together with him that riddle of the search for the father and mother.

Right now the heater is roaring away inside the shoji, and he seems to be reading some book or other. In contrast to those snowy days of long ago, it is now I who am crying outside the shoji. In an earthly sense, I don't exist, and the sound of my crying never takes the form of an actual voice…

5

May has come round again.

Only the calyxes, visible after the flower petals had fallen from the cherry trees, remained here and there, their withered stamens leaving a dingy impression. Then at some point the calyxes too all fell as the strong, vital leaves of the cherry trees appeared luxuriantly, their color a dark, blackish green. No doubt it was the life of those leaves, pushing up through the dark paths within the twigs, that made the remains of the blossoms fall, after they had served their purpose and were now reduced to calyxes. The patterns of generation present such sad scenes to our eyes.

The remains of the fallen blossoms were a bit too heavy to be borne away by the breezes of late spring. They fell onto the young flowering hydrangeas just beneath the trees, and hung suspended among the spider webs that covered the hydrangea leaves like silk floss. The calyxes' pale green stamens had turned yellowish.

I remember. There were the same luxuriantly leafing cherry trees during the same late spring season sixteen years before. The leaves looked all the heavier, all the darker, seen through frosted glass windows. On this side of the frosted windows was a wooden bed, on which lay a pregnant woman. I was sitting on a chair next to the bed, peering down at the pregnant woman. The antiseptic smell of disinfectant made the atmosphere in the room heavier than usual. We were on the second floor of the local maternity clinic.

A sour-faced nurse of around forty was bustling about.

Shadowed by the dark green light that came through the frosted window, the pregnant woman's face was very pale. Her pale forehead and eyelids were covered with small drops of perspiration and kept twitching nervously. She suddenly opened her eyes and met my gaze with her own weaker one. Her dry lips moved and she murmured "Open the window…"

I stood up, went around the foot of the bed where the pregnant woman lay, and pushed against the window, which opened on rusted, creaking hinges to left and right. A heavy green flood seemed to sweep into the sickroom. The woman closed her eyes, and drew her eyebrows together tensely: "So gloomy, so depressing…"

I wonder if that complaint, emerging through her painful breathing, was not a reference to my own gloominess. Wishing to escape from my heavy, "green" presence standing there, blocking her, she probably had no way out apart from addiction to sleeping pills. Her constant reliance on sleeping pills and her close to bi-monthly massive overdoses, clearly suicide-attempts, had never ceased since our marriage.

She was obviously punishing herself by weakening her body through this bad habit; and was she not also trying to take revenge on me, on the side? And if so, were my makeshift attempts to prevent her from indulging in her bad habit and thus to put off for a time her physical collapse anything more than futile attempts at expiation, for her sake and my own? Feeling me to be a heavy, painful burden, it was no wonder that she fell more and more deeply into hopeless addiction.

She was twenty-five at the time; and it was not me she really loved, but her younger brother. And I too was in love with him, not her. The family had been reduced to the twenty-five-year-old sister and the fifteen-year-old brother when I came to live with them as her fiancée in an arranged marriage. I had just turned thirty. The year before, my mother, whose family-home we had been living in, had died, and I had no family left; so there was no obstacle to my moving in with my future bride. I commuted from there to my school in a nearby city.

When I married the orphaned elder sister, her younger brother would naturally become my younger brother as well. But I was in love, not with the sister, but with the younger brother. When I arrived with my meager possessions, the shy adolescent helped me with them while his proud elder sister stayed aloof. Soon, we two became intensely close. The fifteen-year-old boy responded to this thirty-year-old man's somewhat insistent invitations like a tender young plant; and we loved each other within the fictive relationship of future older and younger brothers.

The site where our warm relations found expression was this very veranda. My late father-in-law's study inside the veranda shoji became my territory after I arrived, and even my future wife could not invade it whenever she liked. Now, there was a very full stand of trees in the garden, just opposite the veranda, and beyond those trees was a stone wall, which formed one side of the sloping road that ran past. The veranda, then, was a place where we could make love without being bothered by anyone.

It was in May. We, the fictive older and younger brothers, had just ended an embrace and sat up on the sun-filled veranda. The shoji that separated the veranda from the study were open a bit. When I pushed back the shoji and went into the study, I could see that the door ahead of me had been left open to the inside corridor. We had been watched.

I was in too much of a hurry even to scuff into the slippers that were placed in the corridor, and just ran to my fiancée's room. Her door was locked from the inside. When, over half an hour later, I managed to force the lock and enter, I found my fiancée more dead than alive. An empty box of sleeping pills had fallen under the bed. My fifteen-year-old lad gave a quiet cry and left the room.

Around the time the brightness of the morning sun began to peek through the gaps in the curtain beyond my fiancée's bed, she at last began to revive.

I left her and went to my study for a short nap. The shoji there were open, and on the veranda, now cool from the morning chill, the boy lay lifeless. On the nearby steppingstone sat an empty box of sleeping pills, just like my fiancée's, wet with morning dew. The stand of cherry-trees cut off the rays of the sun, which had just begun to rise, leaving the veranda in darkness.

The day of his funeral was so hot it seemed like midsummer. As I sat in formal fashion on the tatami, listening to the songs of the great reed warblers and the voice of the priest reciting the sutras, my neck was covered with sweat. My fiancée, looking even more pale than usual due to the black mourning kimono she wore, whispered in my ear, urging that we marry as soon as possible. I had neither reason nor the energy to refuse, and so, immediately after the forty-nine days of mourning were ended, we were married in a private ceremony at the local Shinto shrine.

This marriage – a form of revenge for her, a means of expiation for me – was a dark, depressing relationship from the start. And the pregnancy that resulted only made things more complicated. She must have wanted to eliminate her own body before giving birth to this mistaken fruit of vengeance. But I prevented that. I was to her truly like the foliage of the cherry trees that covered her window in darkness. And her dead younger brother was the young, fragile flower of the rose-sakura, and that of the simplest, five-petal sort...

In her hospital room, shut off by the leaves of the cherry-tree, the pregnant woman started to experience birth pangs around three in the afternoon. I went outside, and when I came back an hour later, the room was filled with the cries of the newborn baby. Its mother was dead. As I looked at her face in death, peaceful now, so different from what it had been a while ago, I couldn't help thinking about the difficult future that awaited this infant and me.

Before my very eyes, the face of the baby came to resemble that of the dead boy who had been mine. I named the infant after him.

That veranda. That stepping stone. That stand of trees. Those shoji, opening which, he emerged. Ahh, that boy I loved – how greatly he had come to resemble the dead youth, who was to him an uncle. He squinted briefly, as if dazzled by the reflected light from the cherry-tree leaves just in front of him, then looked at the chair and nodded. He lifted the chair above his head in fun and put it on like some gigantic hat; and then, rather than using the steppingstone, he jumped down directly onto the ground. His bare feet emerged from below his pale-yellow chinos, and the contact with the sun-warmed earth seemed to give the soles of his feet sensations at once ticklish and pleasant.

After having made two or three light jumps, still wearing the wicker chair like a hat, he bent way forward, letting the chair's legs touch the ground, and removed his head from the chair. Four marks from the chair's legs could be clearly seen on the section of the veranda where it had been set.

He brought his feet together and jumped right up onto the veranda, enjoying his fun; then he made a run for the corridor, leaving the shoji wide open. When he reemerged, he had in his right hand a stack of writing-paper and in his left, a small box of matches. He jumped down into the garden again. He overturned the chair. Crouching in front of it, he rolled many sheets of writing-paper into balls – the beginnings of my thesis on "The Inter-Relationship between Oral Stage Sexuality and Riddle Games" must have been among them – and stuffed them here and there into the chair. He struck a match. At first the fire was a bluish, flickering flame, which then became a steady red flame as it passed along the matchstick, moving slowly toward the fingertips that held the end of the match. Those fingertips transferred the flame to a wad of writing-paper, as if by magic.

The flame that was transferred moved to the next wad of paper. Soon all the wads were aflame, blazing away. Among the flames was surely the sentence "We meet twice with mother, but with father, never." It would have been scorched to pieces in the flames. Thus, for example, "with mother" and "we meet twice" would be in two pieces, while "with father" and "never" would also be in two. "We meet twice" might encounter "with father," and for an instant form the sentence "We meet twice with father." In the flames beautifully blazing there, I certainly saw a fantasy of such a composite sentence.

At last the flames leapt to the wicker that formed the surface of the chair. The dry sound of the tongues of flame licking at the wicker was explosive. The four legs, the two arms, the back – the whole chair was burning while still keeping its shape: It had become a chair of flames. That chair now wrapped in intense flames was the same chair I had been sitting in before. As I watched, it seemed I was still sitting in that same chair now, opening my arms wide to hold tight him who sat facing me... that was how I felt. The fantasy image of the boy I was embracing burned and split open with raw, horrid sounds. Thus, existence itself burns furiously, is burnt up, and reduced to ashes. It seems, however, that when they have been burnt and become cool ashes, an encounter between one existence and another becomes possible for the first time; their embrace becomes possible.

Crouching beside the fiercely burning fantasy-image, the boy knows nothing of it. He stretches out his hands to the flames, squints, and whistles a childish tune.

My consciousness gradually becomes transparent, like shimmer climbing up from a flame. Mingling with the boy's whistling and the explosive sounds of the flames, those now-distant passages from the sutra come to the ears of my consciousness, which is almost identical with the atmosphere:

Ichi ichi houmen. Hyappou shojou. Ichi ichi koumyou.. Hachiman shisen shoku. Ei ruri chi. Nyo okusen nichi. Fuka guken. Ruri chijou... Ichi ichi houchuu. Yuu gohyaku shikikou...

I now feel myself to be inexpressibly light, inexpressibly spacious. Will the flames burn the chair, burn my deep-rooted delusions, and release me into Great Emptiness? I have now become infinitely light, infinitely spacious, and am virtually one with Great Emptiness. I am embracing him who crouches in the garden, burning the chair. "Him"? No, I should not speak of "him." I shall call him "son." O my son!

Now, my son is forgiving me. And that boy who would have been my son's uncle is forgiving me, too. Unreasonable though it may be to say so, I too will forgive my son, and the boy. One year has passed, and now is the time of forgiveness.

Fading away. Fading away. My sense of self grows weaker and weaker. I know that it will fade away and become one with Great Emptiness.

Now my son is stretching out a hand to grasp the garden geta on the stepping-stone, and now he has thrown them into the flames.

Translated by Paul McCarthy

THE WEDDING

Reinaldo Arenas (1943–1990)

As a teenager, Arenas abandoned Castro's mountain rebels to pursue a university education. While working at the National Library, he began writing beguiling modernist satires, many of which were smuggled abroad. After a period of unsteady government support, he was jailed for his counterrevolutionary values and open homosexuality. As a refugee in America, suffering from AIDS and unable to write, he took his own life in 1990.

Near my aunt's house there was an empty room in one of the abandoned homes. Whoever had once lived there had died years ago; no one was there now. I requested it through UNEAC, but Bienvenido Suárez, a crook who could at times be charming, told me that the room could only be given to a married couple. What Bienvenido Suárez was evidently trying to tell me was that the Revolution was not going to give the room to a homosexual for him to bring men there. I had to find a woman, get married, and submit a formal request for the room to Mrs. Noelia Fonseca, the district director.

Ingrávida Félix was a talented actress who had given an extraordinary performance in *La noche de los asesinos* (The Night of the Murderers), a theater piece written by José Triana and directed by Vicente Revuelta. She was also featured in one of the most famous Cuban movies of the time, *Lucía*, by Humberto Solás. Ingrávida liked men, she was certainly not a lesbian; she was divorced, and her private life could not be considered immoral just for having a lover now and then. However, Castro's puritanism also looked askance at single women who had a rather free sex life. For these reasons, Ingrávida was parameterized and fired from her job, in spite of her enormous acting talent. This parameterization even caught up with the famous singer Alba Marina because she had a lover twenty or thirty years her junior.

During that time, there were notorious arrests of women at trysting hotels. These hotels had been created by the Revolution so that hetero-sexuals could rent a room for a few hours to make love. The police, however, would raid them to find out which women were committing adultery, especially if any happened to be the wife of some Communist Party stalwart. The women were punished and even fired from their jobs, and their husbands were immediately informed in a public assembly.

The Castro regime, in other words, regarded women, along with homo-sexuals, as inferior beings. "Macho" men could have several women and it was seen as a sign of virility. This situation brought women and homo-sexuals together, at least for protection, and especially if the woman, like Ingrávida Felix, had suffered persecution for the same weakness: because she liked men. So when I spoke with Ingrávida about my predicament, she agreed to marry me, and I could then submit an application for that room. She had two kids and had to figure out a way to support them and herself; I helped her with my UNEAC salary. Virgilio Piñera also organized collections so that she and her children would not starve. With the purchase permits given in Cuba to people about to be married, we bought some clothes, and then got married.

The best man at the wedding was Miguel Figueroa, who wanted to go to bed with Ingrávida that same night, provided I did the same with Olga. Poor Miguel, always looking for gays to go to bed with his wife. I refused because I was eager to go to the beach. Another extraordinary privilege for newlyweds was that they could rent a house at the beach for four or five days.

Ingrávida finally agreed to go to a hotel with Miguel, or perhaps to the house where he lived with Olga, and she would meet me at the beach the following day. There was a group of young guys next to the beach house, and while I was waiting for Ingrávida I developed a relationship with one of them. I told him I was waiting for my wife and that I had just gotten married; this seemed to get him even more excited. We had a memorable encounter, although perhaps because I was the man who had just married, he decided to play the passive part. He was, all the same, really virile and this was quite unexpected.

When Ingrávida arrived, I already had a lover who began acting jealous because my wife was so beautiful; Ingrávida was then an extremely beautiful woman. She came with her kids, who had never had a chance to play at the beach. There was a park with a playground nearby, and we spent the whole day pushing the kids on the swings, always under the jealous eyes of my young lover.

At the beach we wrote the letter to Noelia Silva Fonseca requesting the room. The gossip of the town was that this woman was Celia Sánchez's lover. The text of the letter was pretty pathetic, making an appeal to Noelia's womanhood and to her Revolutionary spirit. But that room, like all our plans, was never to be anything else: just a plan.

The woman did not even bother to answer us. I had to stay in the maid's room at my aunt's house, with my aunt always threatening to throw me out into the street or send me to jail. To top it all, Ingrávida became pregnant, not even knowing herself by whom; she had no idea whether the baby she was expecting would be black, brown, or have Asian features. Her financial situation became desperate, and since we were married, I would be legally bound to take care of that baby.

I felt besieged and with good reason. Sometimes while I was writing, the patrol car came by and was parked under my window for hours; it was like a warning or a way of further intimidating me. Now Miguel Figueroa, Jorge Dávila, and I met only on the beach, where there would be no police to listen in on us. Olga had gone to Paris again, and Miguel had asked her to bring swim fins and diving equipment so he could escape, even if it meant he would have to swim out and, once on the open sea, hope that some ship would pick him up and take him no matter where.

At Lezama's home I heard the story of a woman who jumped into the water at the Malecón in the hope of swimming out to a Greek ship that was leaving port. The Greeks helped her aboard, and then called the Cuban police and turned her over to them. Those Greeks were a distant cry from the classic Greeks who fought in the battle of Troy.

At times people were arrested with no clear proof that they had intended to leave the country. They were arrested just because of some suspicious comment or plan they had made. This happened, for example, to Julián Portales, who had told some friends that he wanted to seek asylum in a Latin American embassy. His friends were State Security informers, and they encouraged him to go to the Argentine embassy. He was arrested before he had even made it to the embassy side of the street.

This was one of the most vicious acts perpetrated by Castroism: to break the bonds of friendship. To make us mistrust our best friends because the system was turning them into informers, into undercover agents, I already mistrusted many of my friends.

The most dramatic aspect of this situation was that such people were victims of blackmail as well as of the system itself, and they were on the point of becoming dehumanized.

Ingrávida finally gave birth to a white boy with sort of bluish eyes. Whose child could he be? Ingrávida said René de la Nuez was the father, but he was enraged and forced her to officially state in a letter that he was not the father of her son. This man was a member of the Communist Party, and worked as a cartoonist for *Granma*; he did not want to be involved with a woman of ill repute.

Translated by Dolores M. Koch

RUBYFRUIT JUNGLE
Rita Mae Brown (1944–)

A fearless feminist writer, novelist and civil rights campaigner, Brown is best known for debut novel *Rubyfruit Jungle*, hailed by Gloria Steinem as "The rare work of fiction that has changed real life." Notorious in its day for its honest, funny, whip-smart account of Molly Bolt's coming out, it has become one of the classics of LGBT fiction. Brown is also an Emmy-nominated screenwriter and a poet.

Senior year was a victory. Connie and I never had to go to class if we didn't want to. Mr Beers wrote us blue freedom slips at a moment's notice. The only class we condescended to attend was Advanced English with Mrs Godfrey. She was such a great teacher that we didn't mind learning Middle English to read Chaucer. Carolyn was in the class also. The three of us sat in the front row and fought it out between us for the highest grade.

Carolyn was captain of the cheerleaders and she usually showed up in the lunchroom in her uniform with blue tassels on her white boots. Connie and I scoffed at such a thing as cheerleading, but Carolyn was the social leader of the school because of it. The three of us also dated three boys who were close friends. Whenever we were seen with our respective boyfriends, we paid the usual fondling attention to him demanded by rigid high-school society but in truth, none of the three of us gave a damn about any of them. They were a convenience, something you had to wear when you went to school functions, like a bra. Carolyn was becoming tighter than a violin string because Larry kept pushing her to sleep with him. Connie and I told her to go ahead and get it over with because we were sick of hearing her bitch about Larry grabbing her boob at 12:20 A.M. every Saturday night. Besides Connie and I were both doing it with our boyfriends with no harmful side effects. No one was supposed to know of course, but everyone did in that behind-the-hand manner. All this overt heterosexuality amused me. If they only knew. Our boyfriends thought they were God's gift because we were sleeping with them but they were so tragically transparent that we forgave them their arrogance.

Carolyn decided, again with her relentless logic, that if we won the football game against Stranahan, she'd do it with Larry. We creamed them. Carolyn's face walking off the field of honor was not the usual bright cherry red from screaming her lungs out but an ashen and drawn white. Connie and I went over to her to bolster her. Then the three of us went back to the locker room to wait for our dates—all Princeton haircuts, Weejun shoes, and Gold Cup socks. Clark came out with a gash on his cheek and wanted sympathy. I told him he was a football hero, which he was, having made two touchdowns. Connie's Douglas lumbered out (right tackles tend to grow large) and she told him he was a football hero. Larry stumbled coming out of the door he was in such a rush to see Carolyn. She didn't have time to tell him he was a football hero because he gave her a bonecrushing kiss which was a rerun of an Errol Flynn movie and picked her up bodily, placing her in his Sting Ray convertible. Carolyn nervously waved good-bye and we all waved back. Then the four of us climbed into Doug's car and headed for Wolfie's for endless talk about this missed tackle and that fine block interspersed with bananas and hot fudge sundaes.

The next morning the phone rang around 9:00 A.M. It was Carolyn. 'I have to talk to you right now. Are you awake?'

'I guess I am if I answered the phone.'

'I'm coming over and we can have breakfast at the Forum, okay?'

'Okay.'

Fifteen minutes later Carolyn arrived looking paler than usual. As I slid in the front seat of the car I asked, 'How is Ft. Lauderdale High's newest harlot?'

She grimaced. 'I'm all right, but I have to ask you some questions so I know I did it right.'

Over eggs that looked as though the chickens rejected them, she began, 'Is it always such a mess? You know, when I stood up all this stuff ran down my leg. Larry said it was sperm. It was so disgusting I nearly barfed.'

'You get used to it.'

'Yech. And another thing—what am I supposed to do during all this, lie there? I mean, what do you really do? There they are on top of you sweating and grunting and it's not at all like I thought.'

'Like I said, you get used to it. It isn't very mystical if that's what you're waiting for. I'm not an expert or anything, but different people are different. Larry may not be the hottest lay in the world, so don't base your judgment on his one performance. Anyway, they're supposed to get technically better as they grow older. We hit them at that awkward age, I guess.'

'That's not what the medical book says. It says they reach their prime at eighteen and we reach ours at thirty-five. How's that for timing? It's all so ridiculous. You and Connie must think I'm a real spastic.'

'No, you take it too seriously, that's all.'

'Well, it is serious.'

'No, it isn't. It's a big dumb game and it doesn't mean anything at all unless you get pregnant, of course. Then it means you're screwed.'

'I'll try. Hey, you want to go drinking Friday?'

'Sure. What about Connie?'

'She has to go to some journalism conference in Miami for the week-end.'

'Okay, so it will be the two of us.'

Friday night we went to the children's playground at Holiday Park. No one came there late at night, and the police patrols were too busy beating the bushes and their own meat to harass the playground. I didn't really like drinking so I took a few swings to make it look good, but Carolyn got blasted. She slid down the fireman's pole, played on the swings and discarded various pieces of her clothing at each go round. When she got down to her underwear, she made a beeline for the grounded blue jet and crawled in the open tail to the fuselage. She stayed in there making airplane sounds and showed no sign of giving up her piloting. I crawled in after her. It was a tiny, narrow space so I had to lie down next to her.

'Carolyn, maybe you should join the Air Force when you graduate. You've got the sound effects down pat.'

'Whoosh.' Then she leaned up on one elbow and asked in a coy voice, 'How does Clark kiss you?'

'On the lips, where else? What do you mean how does he kiss me? What a dumb question.'

'Want me to show you how Larry kisses?'

Without waiting for my sober answer she grabbed me and laid the biggest kiss on my face since Leota B. Bisland.

'I doubt he kisses that way.' She laughed and kissed me again. 'Carolyn, do you know what you're doing?'

'Yes, I'm giving you kissing lessons.'

'I'm very grateful but we'd better stop. We'd better stop because one more kiss and you're going to get more than you bargained for, lady. Or maybe that's what you are bargaining for?'

'Ha.' She dropped another one on me this time with her entire body pressed against mine. That did it. I ran my hands along her side, up to her breast, and returned her kiss with a vengeance. She encouraged this action and added a few novelties of her own like nibbling my sensitive ears. By this time I began to worry about being in the tail end of an old blue jet in the middle of the children's playground in Holiday Park. Carolyn had no such worries and threw off what was left of her clothing. Then she started taking off mine and tossed them up in the cockpit. If I was worried, I got over it. All I could think about was making love with Carolyn Simpson, head cheerleader and second-year chaplain of

Ft. Lauderdale High School—and a cinch for prom queen. We were in that plane half the night coming in the wild blue yonder. I know we broke the sound barrier. Eventually, the sky began to lighten and the air became chilly. I thought it was time to go. 'Let's get out of here.'

'I don't want to get out, I want to stay in here for ten years and play with your breasts.'

'Come on.' I reached up and got her underwear and my clothes. Then I backed out of the plane and collected her dew-covered bermuda shorts, Villager blouse, and white, worn-out sneakers. Shivering, we ran to the car.

'Are you hungry?' I asked.

'For you.'

'Carolyn, you are so goddamned corny. Let's go to the "Egg and You" and get something good.'

I ordered two breakfasts for all the energy I burned up, and Carolyn had bacon and eggs.

'Molly, you won't tell will you? I mean we could really get in trouble.'

'No, I'm not telling but I hate lying. It seems pretty impossible that anyone would ask such a thing, so the coast is clear.'

'I hate to lie too, but people will say we're lesbians.'

'Aren't we?'

'No, we just love each other, that's all. Lesbians look like men and are ugly. We're not like that.'

'We don't look like men, but when women make love it's commonly labeled lesbianism so you'd better learn not to cringe when you hear the word.'

'Have you ever done that before?'

'When I was in sixth grade but that was about seven centuries ago. Did you?'

'At camp this summer. I thought I'd die from the fright but she was so terrific, this other counselor. I never thought of her as a lesbian, you know. We spent all our time together and one night she kissed me, and we did it. I didn't stop to think about it at the time, it felt too good.'

'Do you write her?'

'Sure. We'll try to go to the same college. Molly, do you think you can love more than one person at a time? I mean, I love you and I love Susan.'

'I guess so. I'm not jealous, if that's what you're after.'

'Kinda. You want to know something else? It's a lot better than doing it with Larry. I mean there's no comparison, you know?'

'That I know.' We laughed and ordered two hot fudge sundaes at 6:00 in the morning.

Carolyn started waiting for me in the lunchroom and paying all kinds of attention to me. She forgot to pay attention to Larry or Connie. Larry didn't mind as long as he got his weekend fuck, but Connie was more sensitive. Because of it, I tried to spend more time with Connie, which made Carolyn mad. The times the three of us were together became more and more strained until I began to feel like a bone between two dogs. We were the witches for the English class's production of *Macbeth* and during rehearsal I tried to explain to Carolyn what I thought was happening and that she should cool it. She burst out with, 'Are you sleeping with Connie?'

Connie who was sitting on the other side of a cardboard rock popped her head over the top and said, 'What?!'

This is it. Now what do I do? 'Carolyn, that's a stupid thing to say. No, I am not sleeping with Connie, but I do love her. She's my best friend and you'd better get used to it.' Carolyn began to cry.

Connie looked at me in amazement, and I shrugged my shoulders. 'Molly, why would she think we're sleeping together? What's going on?'

'Connie.' Pause. What the flying fuck do I say now? 'Connie, there's no use trying to lie about it. Carolyn and I have been sleeping together. End of sentence. She got jealous I guess. I don't know.' I turned to Carolyn, 'Anyway, what the hell are you jealous about, you're the one with Susan, not me. It makes no sense.'

Carolyn started to offer an answer through a sniffle but Connie, recovering from shock, beat her to it. 'I want to make certain I've got this right. You make love with Carolyn?'

'Yes, I make love with Carolyn. Carolyn makes love with me. I make love with Clark and Carolyn makes love with Larry. All we need is a circular bed and we can have a gang bang. Christ.'

'Do the boys know?'

'Of course not. Nobody knows but you. You know what would happen if it leaked out.'

'Yeah, everybody would call you queer, which you are, I suppose.'

'Connie!' Carolyn shrieked. 'We are not queer. How can you say that? I'm very feminine, how can you call me a queer? Maybe Molly, after all she plays tennis and can throw a football as far as Clark, but not me.'

Carolyn was dropping her beads, all right. I tried to pretend I didn't know she'd run a number like that when cornered, but I knew it inside. A delicate whiff of hate curled round my nostrils. I'd like to bust her feminine head.

'What does Molly's tennis have to do with it?' Connie was becoming increasingly confused.

'You know, lesbians are boyish and athletic. I mean Molly's pretty and all that but she's a better athlete than most of the boys that go to this school, and besides she doesn't act like a girl, you know? I'm not like that at all. I just love Molly. That doesn't make me queer.'

Quiet anger was in Connie's voice as she faced Carolyn. 'Well, I'm about fifteen pounds overweight, hefty is what I believe it's called, plus I don't remember that I've ever cooed and giggled in true female fashion, so why don't you come right out and call me a dyke too if that's how your mind is misfunctioning?'

Carolyn was genuinely stunned. 'Oh, I never meant that about you. You're just straightforward. Anyway, you're lazy, that's why you're fat. The last thing you are is athletic. You're the career-woman type.'

'Carolyn, you make me sick.' I threw off my witch's tatters and headed for the auditorium door.

'Molly!' Carolyn screamed.

Connie took off her costume and came out after me. 'Where are you going?'

'I don't know, mostly I want to get away from Miss Teenage America in there.'

'I've got the car, let's go to the park.'

We drove over to Holiday Park and positioned ourselves in the cockpit of the blue jet. I didn't bother to tell Connie about my last time in the jet.

'Do you think you're a queer?'

'Oh great, you too. So now I wear this label "Queer" emblazoned across my chest. Or I could always carve a scarlet "L" on my forehead. Why does everyone have to put you in a box and nail the lid on it? I don't know what I am—polymorphous and perverse. Shit. I don't even know if I'm white. I'm me. That's all I am and all I want to be. Do I have to be something?' Connie looked down at her hands and her eyebrows wrinkled over her eyes. 'Come on, Connie, what's on your mind?'

'No, you don't have to be anything. I'm sorry I asked you if you were a queer. But this is a big jolt. Things your mother didn't tell you and all that. I guess I'm square, or maybe I'm scared. I don't think you or anyone else should wear a label and I don't understand why who you sleep with is so Goddamned important and I don't understand why I'm all strung out over this. All this time I thought I was this progressive thinker, this budding intellectual among the sandspurs, now I find out I'm as shot through with prejudice as the next asshole. I cover them up with layers of polysyllables.' She inhaled and continued, 'It wrecked me when you said you were sleeping with Carolyn—*me*, Miss Sarcasm of Ft. Lauderdale High, Miss Fake Sophisticate.' I started to say something, but she kept on. 'I'm not through, Molly, I don't know if I can be your friend anymore. I'll think about it every time I see you. I'll be nervous and wonder if you're going to rape me or something.'

Now it was my turn to be shocked. 'That's crazy. What do you think I do, run around panting at every female I see? I'm not going to leap on you like a hyperthyroid ape. Goddammit!'

'I know that. I *know* that, but it's in my head. It's me, not you. I'm sorry. I really am sorry.' She swung her leg over and climbed down from the cockpit. 'Come on, I'll take you home.'

'No. It's not far. I want to walk it.'

She didn't look up. 'Okay.'

That night Carolyn called and filled my ear with four thousand sugary apologies. I told her to shut up and I didn't give a shit what she thought. She could take her prom queen tiara and shove it up her ass.

School was buzzing with the breakup of the gleesome threesome, but none of us spoke so the gossips had to concoct their own stories. One widely accepted was Missy Barton's theory that Connie wanted to sleep with Clark and I wouldn't stand for it. She explained Carolyn's behavior by saying she was torn between the two of us. When I regained my sense of humor, I thought it was pretty funny but it also made me green around the edges, people are so stupid. Sell them shit in a red cellophane package and they'd buy it.

I was becoming more and more isolated in the splendor of my office. It was a tiring little game once the glamor of being student council president wore off. I longed to return to the potato patch and raise hell with kids who didn't know the difference between Weejuns and Old Maine trotters. But those kids grew up and wore tons of eye-makeup, iridescent pink fingernail polish and scratched each other's eyes out over the boy with the metalflake, candy apple red '55 Chevy with four on the floor. There was no place to go back to. No place to go to. College was going to be like high school, only worse. But I gotta go. I don't get that degree and I'm another secretary. No thanks. I got to get it and head for a big city. Got to hang on. That's what Carl told me once, you got to hang on. It would be nice to talk to Carl. God, it would be nice to talk to someone who wasn't fucked up.

One week before graduation a colorful event rocked the school. Someone had snuck into the girls' shower room before first period gym and unscrewed the shower heads, putting in powdered dyes. Sixty girls had first period gym and the first twenty or so in the showers came out red, yellow, green or blue. The stuff didn't wash off either. That Saturday night as diplomas were handed out it gave me a certain degree of pleasure to notice that Carolyn resembled a consumptive movie-set Indian and Connie looked definitely blue.

When I was handed my diploma, I received a standing ovation from my constituency and a hug from Mr Beers. When the noise ebbed, he said in the humming microphone, 'There's our governor in twenty years.' Everyone cheered again and I thought Mr Beers was as silly or maybe as kind as Carl, who used to tell everyone at work the same thing.

CONFEDERACY OF SURVIVORS

Armistead Maupin (1944–)

Maupin was one of many émigré authors inspired by San Francisco life in the late 1970s. As his career continued through the decades, he observed many changes in queer culture, and became particularly adept at analysing sexuality through the lens of generational difference. Maupin is currently overseeing the third TV adaptation of *Tales of the City*, his famous cycle of novels.

Not long ago, down on Castro Street, a stranger in a Giants parka gave me a loaded glance as we passed each other in front of Cliff's Hardware. He was close to my age, I guess, not *that* far past fifty—and not bad-looking either, in a beat-up, Bruce Willis-y sort of way—so I waited a moment before turning to see if he would go for a second look. He knew this old do-si-do as well as I did, and hit his mark perfectly.

"Hey," he called, "you're supposed to be dead."

I gave him an off-kilter smile. "Guess I didn't get the memo."

His face grew redder as he approached. "Sorry, I just meant... it's been a really long time and... sometimes you just *assume*... you know..."

I did know. Here in our beloved Gayberry you can barely turn around without gazing into the strangely familiar features of someone long believed dead. Having lost track of him in darker days, you had all but composed his obituary and scattered his ashes at sea, when he shows up in the housewares aisle at Cala Foods to tell you he's been growing roses in Petaluma for the past decade. This happens to me a lot, these odd little supermarket resurrections, so I figured it could just as easily happen to someone else.

But who the hell *was* he?

"You're looking good," he said pleasantly.

"Thanks. You too." His face had trenches like mine—the usual wasting from the meds. A fellow cigar store Indian.

"You *are* Mike Tolliver, right?"

"Michael. Yeah. But I can't quite—"

"Oh… sorry." He thrust out his hand. "Ed Lyons. We met at Joe Dimitri's after the second Gay Games."

That was no help at all, and it must have shown.

"You know," the guy offered gamely. "The big house up on Collingwood?"

Still nothing.

"The circle jerk?"

"Ah."

"We went back to my place afterward."

"On Potrero Hill!"

"You remember!"

What I remembered—*all* I remembered after nineteen years—was his dick. I remembered how its less-than-average length was made irrelevant by its girth. It was one of the thickest I'd ever seen, with a head that flared like a caveman's club. Remembering *him* was a good deal harder. Nineteen years is too long a time to remember a face.

"We had fun," I said, hoping that a friendly leer would make up for my phallocentric memory.

"You had something to do with plants, didn't you?"

"Still do." I showed him my dirty cuticles. "I had a nursery back then, but now I garden full time."

That seemed to excite him, because he tugged on the strap of my overalls and uttered a guttural "woof." If he was angling for a nooner, I wasn't up for it. The green-collar job that had stoked his furnace had left me with some nasty twinges in my rotator cuffs, and I still had podocarps to prune in Glen Park. All I really wanted was an easy evening with Ben and the hot tub and a rare bacon cheeseburger from Burgermeister.

Somehow he seemed to pick up on that. "You married these days?"

"Yeah… pretty much."

"*Married* married or just… regular?"

"You mean… did we go down to City Hall?"

"Yeah."

I told him we did.

"Must've been amazing," he said.

"Well, it was a mob scene, but… you know… pretty cool." I wasn't especially forthcoming, but I had told the story once too often and had usually failed to convey the oddball magic of that day: all those separate dreams coming true in a gilded, high-domed palace straight out of *Beauty and the Beast*. You had to have *witnessed* that long line of middle-aged people standing in the rain, some of them with kids in tow, waiting to affirm what they'd already known for years. And the mayor himself, so young and handsome and… *neat*… that he actually *looked* like the man on top of a wedding cake.

"Well," said Ed Lyons, stranger no more, now that I'd put a name to the penis. "I'm heading down to the bagel shop. How 'bout you?"

I told him I was headed for my truck.

"Woof!" he exclaimed, aroused by the mere mention of my vehicle.

I must've rolled my eyes just a little.

"What?" he asked.

"It's not that butch a truck," I told him.

He laughed and charged off. As I watched his broad shoulders navigate the stream of pedestrians, I wondered if I would find Ed's job—whatever it might be—as sexy as he found mine. *Oh, yeah, buddy, that's right, make me want it, make me buy that two-bedroom condo! That Century 21 blazer is so fucking hot!*

I headed for my truck (a light-blue Tacoma, if you must know), buzzing on a sort of homegrown euphoria that sweeps over me from time to time. After thirty years in the city, it's nice to be reminded that I'm still glad to be here, still glad to belong to this sweet confederacy of survivors, where men meet in front of the hardware store and talk of love and death and circle jerks as if they're discussing the weather.

It helps that I have Ben; I know that. Some years back, when I was still single, the charm of the city was wearing thin for me. All those imperial dot-commers in their SUVs and Hummers barreling down the middle of Noe Street as if leading an assault on a Third World nation. And those freshly minted queens down at Badlands, wreathed in cigarette smoke and attitude, who seemed to believe that political activism meant a subscription to *Out* magazine and regular attendance at *Queer as Folk* night. Not to mention the traffic snarls and the fuck-you-all maître d's and the small-town queers who brought their small-town fears to the Castro and tried to bar the door against The Outsiders. I remember one in particular, petitions in hand, who cornered me on the sidewalk to alert me that the F streetcar—the one bearing straight tourists from Fisherman's Wharf—was scheduling a new stop at Castro and Market. "They just can't do this," he cried. "This is the center of our spirituality!" We were standing in front of a window displaying make-your-own dildos and dick-on-a-rope soap. I told him my spirituality would survive.

The dot-commers have been humbled, of course, but house prices are still rising like gangbusters, with no end in sight. I'm glad I staked a claim here seventeen years ago, when it was still possible for a nurseryman and a nonprofit preservationist to buy a house in the heart of the city. The place hadn't seemed special at the time, just another starter cottage that needed serious attention. But once my partner, Thack, and I had stripped away its ugly green asbestos shingles, the historic bones of the house revealed themselves. Our little fixer-upper was actually a grouping of three "earthquake shacks," refugee housing built in the parks after the 1906 disaster, then hauled away on drays for use as permanent dwellings. They were just crude boxes, featureless and cobbled together at odd angles, but we exposed some of the interior planking and loved telling visitors about our home's colorful catastrophic origins. What could have been more appropriate? We were knee-deep in catastrophe ourselves—the last Big One of the century—and bracing for the worst.

But then I didn't die. The new drug cocktails came along, and I got better, and Thack worked up the nerve to tell me he wanted out. When he left for a job in Chicago in the mid-nineties, the house became mine alone. It was a tomb at first, filled with too many ghosts, but I exorcised them with paint and fabric and furniture. Over the next eight years, almost without noticing, I arrived at a quiet revelation: You *could* make a home by yourself. You could fill that home with friends and friendly strangers without someone sleeping next to you. You could tend your garden and cook your meals and find predictable pleasure in your own autonomy.

In other words, I was ready for Ben.

I met him on the Internet. Well, not exactly; I saw him on the Internet, and met him on the street in North Beach. But I would never have known who he was, or rather what he was looking for, had my friend Barney not modeled for a website catering to older gay men. Barney is forty-eight, a successful mortgage broker, and something of a muscle daddy. He's a wee bit vain, too. He could barely contain himself when he stopped me on Market Street one day to tell me that his big white marble ass was now available to World Wide Wankers for only $21.95 a month, credit card or online check.

Once upon a time, this would have struck me as sleazy, but the Internet has somehow persuaded half the world to get naked for the enjoyment of the other half. Barney is a fairly sexy guy, but I squirmed a little when I checked out his photos on the site. Maybe I've just known him too long, but there was something incestuous and unsettling about it, like watching your Aunt Gladys flashing titty for the troops.

At any rate, there was a personals section on the website, so once I'd fled the sight of Barney's winking sphincter, I checked out the guys who were looking for Sex, Friendship, or Long Term Relationships. There were lots of geezers there—by which I mean anyone my age or older— regular Joes from Lodi or Tulsa, smiling bravely by their vintage vehicles, or dressed for some formal event. Most of them offered separate close-ups of their erections, artfully shot from below, so that doubtful browsers could find their way past the snow on the roof to the still-raging fire in the furnace.

What surprised me, though, was the number of young guys on the site. Guys in their twenties or thirties specifically looking for partners over forty-five. The one who caught my attention, and held it—CLEAN-CUTLAD4U—was a sandy blond with a brush cut and shining brown eyes. His actual name was not provided, but his profile identified him as thirty-three and Versatile, a resident of the Bay Area. He was lying against a headboard, smiling sleepily, a white sheet pulled down to the first suggestion of pubic hair. For reasons I still can't name, he came across like someone from another century, a stalwart captured on daguerreo-type, casually masculine and tender of heart.

So how did this work? Did I have to submit a profile or could I just email him directly? He'd want to see a photo, wouldn't he? Would I have to get naked? The young can keep a little mystery, it seems to me, but the old have to show you their stuff. Which, of course, is easier said than done. Sure, the right dick can distract from a falling ass, and some people actually get off on a nice round stomach, but who has any use for that no-man's-land between them, that troublesome *lower* stomach of sloppy skin?

Maybe I could pose in my dirty work clothes with just my dick hang-ing out? (I could call myself NICENDIRTY4U.) But who would take the picture? Barney was the logical choice, but I had a sudden gruesome flash of him directing my debut and thought better of it. Who was I kidding, anyway? CleanCutLad probably got hundreds of offers a week.

It was wiser to stick to my monthly night at the Steamworks, where the goods were always on the table, and rejection, when it came, was instant and clean.

And that's the way I left it, aside from printing out the guy's webpage and posting it above my potting shed. It stayed there for ages, curling at the edges, a pinup boy for a war that would never be waged. I might not have met him at all if my friend Anna Madrigal hadn't called to invite me for dinner at the Caffe Sport.

The Caffe Sport is on Green Street, way across town in North Beach, a gaudy Sicilian cavern that dishes up huge creamy mounds of seafood and pasta. Anna had been going there for over thirty years and often used its peasanty charms as a way of luring me out of my complacent nest in the Castro. At eighty-five, she was convinced I was growing too set in my ways. I needed some excitement, she said, and she was the gal to provide it.

So there we sat, awash in colors and aromas, when the impossible happened. Anna was adjusting her turban at the time, consulting the mirror behind my back as she fussed with wisps of snowy hair. Yet somehow she *still* caught the look on my face.

"What is it, dear?"

"I'm not sure," I said.

"Well, you must have an idea."

A cluster of departing diners had moved toward the door, obscuring my view. "I think I saw someone."

"Someone you know?"

"No... not exactly."

"Mmm... someone you *want* to know." She shooed me with a large gloved hand. "Go on, then. Catch up with him."

"I don't know..."

"Yes you do. Get the hell out of here. I'll be here with my wine."

So I sprang to my feet and shimmied through the tightly packed crowd. By the time I reached the door he was nowhere in sight. I looked to the right, toward the fog-cushioned neon of Columbus, then left, toward

Grant Avenue. He was almost at the end of the block and picking up speed. I had no choice but to make myself ridiculous.

"Excuse me," I yelled, hurrying after him.

No response at all. He didn't even stop walking.

"Excuse me! In the blue jacket!"

He stopped, then turned. "Yeah?"

"Sorry, but... I was in the restaurant and—"

"Oh, shit." He reached reflexively for his back pocket. "Did I leave my wallet?"

"No," I replied. "Just *me*."

I had hoped that this would prove to be an ice-breaker, but it landed with a dull thud, missing the ice completely. The guy just blinked at me in confusion.

"I think I saw you on a website," I explained.

Another blink.

"CLEANCUTLAD4U?"

Finally he smiled. There was a fetching gap between his two front teeth, which only enhanced the fuckable Norman Rockwell image.

"I could've sent you my profile," I told him, "but I figured it was easier just to chase you down the street."

He laughed and stuck out his hand. "I'm Ben McKenna."

"Michael Tolliver."

"I saw you inside with that lady." He had held my hand a little longer than actually required. "Was that your mother?"

I chuckled. Anna would love to hear that. "Not exactly," I said.

"She looks interesting,"

"She *is*, believe me." We were rapidly veering off the subject, so I decided to take the bullock by the horns. "I have to get her home, as a matter of fact. Would you mind giving me your phone number? Or I could give you mine."

He looked almost surprised. "Either way," he said with a shrug.

We went back into the restaurant for pencil and paper. As Ben scribbled away by the cash register I looked across the room and saw that Anna was watching this transaction with a look of smug accomplishment on her face. And I knew this would not be the end of it; something this juicy could amuse her for weeks.

"My, my," she said as soon as I returned. "I hope you carded him."

"He's thirty-three. Cut me some slack."

"You *asked* him his age?"

"I read it online."

"O Brave New World," she intoned melodramatically. "Shall we head down to the park, dear? Before we call it a night?"

"Thought you'd never ask," I said.

So I walked her down to Washington Square, where we sat in the cool foggy dark and shared a quick doobie before bedtime.

TO SIMULATE THE BURNING OF THE HEART

Patrizia Cavalli (1947–)

Born in Todi, Perugia, Cavalli has published several collections of poetry in her native Italian. *My Poems Won't Change the World: Selected Poems* offers an excellent introduction to her work in English. Cavalli is a translator in her own right, and has translated plays by Shakespeare and Molière.

To simulate the burning of the heart, the humiliation
of the viscera, to flee cursed
and cursing, to horde chastity
and to cry for it, to keep my mouth
from the dangerous taste of other mouths
and push it unfulfilled to fulfill itself with the poisons of food,
in the apotheosis of dinners when the already
swollen belly continues to swell;
to touch unreachable solitude and there
at the foot of a bed, a chair
or the stairs to recite a goodbye,
so that I can expel you from my fantasy
and cover you with ordinary clouds
so that your light will not fade my path,
will not muddle my circle from which
I send you, you unintentional star,
unexpected passage who reminds me of death.

For all this I asked you for a kiss
and you, kind and innocent accomplice, didn't give it to me.

Translated by Judith Baumel

SELECTED POEMS

Roz Kaveney (1949–)

Poet, novelist, translator, trans activist, feminist, sci-fi buff and acknowledged expert on *Buffy the Vampire Slayer*, Roz Kaveney is a force of nature. She was a core member of the Midnight Rose collective. Her novel *Tiny Pieces of Skull* won a 2016 Lambda Literary Award. Her translations of the poems of Catullus were published in 2018. Her four-volume fantasy cycle *Rhapsody of Blood* – a story of death, love and the end of worlds – is published by Plus One Press.

FOR MY TRANS DYKE SISTERS

Perhaps excessive neatness, or a scar
that spirals round the hood. You press your lips
against it, and she squirms up with her hips
and you lose track a moment. We all are

so prone to giggles of astonished joy
that what was hard won was a total gain.
Fingers force inner scars, a little pain
but worth it. She is wet. Let's not be coy

Some of us love our sisters. On a date
saves time, we can avoid the big reveal.
They told us we were sick. Here's how we heal,
here's how those storms of self-contempt abate.

We bite and lick and groan in sweet surprise
then check our lip gloss in each other's eyes

CUNT

The surgeons left me with a patchwork cunt
stitch-marks and scars, and smooth skin flayed from thigh.
I bled. I oozed. With speculums, I'd try
to burn new keloids off. I'd grope and hunt

for small hard bits I'd missed. That now are smooth.
Things levelled out. You'd never know the sore
torn places that were there. For an old whore
it's sweet and neat and innocent as truth.

I paid in blood and pus. Here's what I got.
Not some mere hole, but tenderness. A maze
of flesh love's fingers have explored for days
and found its spring, gushing and furnace hot.

I dared not hope. Yet my reward was this—
to hang in ecstasy on sweet girl kiss.

ME TOO

Soho was where I hung out with my friends
The seedy grubbiness of streets by day
Dust on cheap turned off neon tubes. The gray
Of unslept faces unbrushed hair split ends
Chipped varnish nails. There's something oddly real
When glamour's in its twentysecond hour
And fading but it still retains some power
For cynic aesthetes. Somehow it can steal
Upon you as it cannot in the night
All sequin and pretend that you belong
You've seen it lounge in a half torn sarong
It's not your home yet but one day it might
Let you. Dizzy on newly woman no control
Thinking I knew things I had yet to learn
Unschooled by pain. Still pretty. Green as fern
And fragile stagger innocent as foal
As thin longlegged and so he knew me prey
Managed three clubs and knew that I was trans
Six foot plus stylish boots and quite large hands
And was it seems his choice to fuck that day
A shoulder tap. A large suit seized my wrist
Aftershave muscles. Sudden through a door
I'd never noticed. Upstairs second floor
Office. Desk. Sofa. Photos. You could list
Celebrities he had upon his wall
Perhaps he knew. Walked over. Touched my hair
Stroked chin for stubble. Strutted to his chair
Black leather streaked in places. Trousers fall
Quite unselfconcious. And no underwear.
Knew what to do and did. Small soft and pink
And slightly bitter. Faster than you'd think

No threat except the large suit standing there
Watching and waiting. 'We've seen you around
Head in a book. We don't like our girls read.
Want job? Don't need time off. You queens don't bleed.
Good workers. What I've nearly always found.
No?' pulled his trousers up and we were done
Face blank as paint. A tissue. Did my lips.
And left. Met Maz. Had shepherd pie and chips
Took taste away. Soho no longer any fun
But just some streets. This pretty butch I knew
Seven years later crying over tea.
Turned out same guy same stuff the same as me
Sighed sisterguilt that I'd not warned. 'Me too.'

SELECTED POEMS

Hezy Leskly (1952–1994)

A child of Czech Holocaust survivors, Leskly left Israel to study art and dance in the Netherlands. When he returned, he established himself as an innovative choreographer, sculptor and installation artist. His poetry, which involves rapidly shifting imagery and disjointed syntax, shows clear traces of his avant-garde visual back ground. His provocative phrasing dissects gender, family roles, Hebrew scripture and the AIDS crisis.

ISAAC

Years back
Izik
was
my soulmate.
He died of AIDS.
Peter died of AIDS (boots, dancing)
Hans died of AIDS (opera)
Diogenes died of AIDS (Japan)
Ulysses died of AIDS (private collection)

Shulamit
was strangled by a cabbie from Suriname
(telephone cord)
I think Suriname's the place, I'm not sure
about this.
They were all real people.

Years back
my friend Benny (Bernhard) and I used to hang around
one of Amsterdam's canals
(Oh admirable canals!)
and I said to him: I have a feeling
that the plane that bombed Hiroshima
flew by and wiped out
Amsterdam's
gay population.

Suddenly a thought struck,
yes, like lightning:
the name of the plane—or was it the bomb?—I can't
remember exactly, plane
or bomb;
every
where
the name:
Enola Gay
(Oh admirable canals!)

YAKANTALISA

Bent is the smell of Yakantalisa
as bent as its stalk and its bent
philosophy.
Bent are those who speak fondly of
Yakantalisa's scent.
Yakantalisa flowering
in the clear yellow marshes
in the dark yellow marshes
of rotten kingdoms
over drowsy kings
on truck seats laden with lyrical,
scent bent, appalling Yakantalisas.

Ah deviant kings—
—Truck drivers crowned in vain!
O kings of piss
grabbing gay men made from the flesh of crooked Yakantalisa,
Yakantalisa of love!

Kings of the nothing that clangs like a thousand
bells. Kings of nothing crushing my body
on summer nights.
Kings of instant coffee *ding
dong*.

REUBEN AND I

Boredom breeds beauty like
an onion breeds
a bad smell.

When I'm bored
I lick
that thin margin
between two words.

One time I licked the thin margin
between "where" and "you"
and lo my tongue came across a house
with a family inside.
The house was a yawn for the house for yawning
and the family was a sect of gossips with a muddled
and tangled tongue. Tangled up in the curtains and table legs,
tangled up in the dog's tail and dinner songs,
tangled up in the washbasins and the matriarch's jewelry.
Zvika said: "Where's the salt?" and "the meat is bland"
Noa said: "The lemon is like sour milk"
And Reuben said: "I love you. I will never leave your side."

Boredom breeds a bad smell
like onion breeds a clipped beauty.
Reuben is bored,
eats an onion and loves
me only.
Boredom and I breed
Reuben
and teach him how to yawn and stink.
When he yawns, we say to him:

This is the house where you will live and dance
with Reuben.

Translated from the Hebrew by Adriana X. Jacobs

HIGHLIGHTS

Alan Hollinghurst (1954–)

Although better known today as novelist, Alan Hollinghurst started his career as a poet, winning the Newdigate Prize for poetry in 1974. He studied at Magdalen College, Oxford, and worked at the Times Literary Supplement before publishing his first novel, *The Swimming Pool Library*, which proved an unexpected success in the claustrophobic world of Thatcher's Britain. His novel *The Line of Beauty* won the Booker Prize in 2004, prompting the predictably homophobic headline "Gay Sex Wins Booker". Hollinghurst responded "… if only it was that easy."

'Surely we're not going to Rome for discos.'

1

They were at Gatwick, Colin and Archie, waiting to check in, and Colin refusing to think about whether it was a good idea. Already Archie was talking to the young Italian ahead of them in the queue, who had the new kind of iPod he wanted. Colin knelt down by his suitcase to get out his copy of *I promessi sposi*, which he was still working his way through in Italian. He wasn't wholly pleased to find Archie could speak Italian too, albeit only in the present tense; he didn't want him running off speaking Italian all over Rome. Now Archie was sending the young man his mobile number, and asking him something about a *discoteca*. Oh, God, thought Colin. Surely we're not going to Rome for discos. Though with a tiny part of himself he thought it might be rather thrilling to come back having gone to one.

Colin Cardew was fifty-two, and worked for Latimer, publishers of the well-known cultural guides. He lived alone, drank a bit too much, and was thought to be duller and older than he was by people who met him at book parties. He had been to Rome twenty years before, with a friend who had later died, and a sense of awkwardness and regret had kept him away from the place ever since. Archie was told nothing of this, and in a way his ignorance was the beauty of the plan. He had asked to be taken there, asked to be shown something new. Colin glanced discreetly at his small, neat form, the fashionable inches of underwear white above low-waisted jeans. There hadn't been sex, or anything close, since the previous May. Archie would wriggle away or say, 'Goodness, I'm hungry!' and they would go to the local trattoria. He had made himself, touchingly but frustratingly, into a friend: Colin still paid, but for dinner rather than fifty minutes in bed. Well, he knew you could never spell these things out, but he felt fairly sure that by accepting a free weekend in Rome his young companion had agreed to something more.

On the plane Archie insisted on the aisle seat, claiming a tendency to claustrophobia. As soon as everyone was belted in and the doors were closed the first officer announced a delay of eighty minutes. Archie showed great forbearance for the first one and a half of these minutes, but after that he said, 'I knew we should have flown BA.'

Colin went over one paragraph in *I promessi sposi* several times, stung by the criticism of his arrangements, and unable to see why BA should be any less subject to delays on the tarmac than Alitalia. Well, it was a useful reminder: that Archie, though he liked to be paid for, didn't care to be planned for. He could fret if he wasn't in charge of arrangements, and treats and surprises didn't always go down well with him. Sometimes, if he got wind of a plan, he took it over himself and changed it, so that it turned into a surprise for Colin instead.

Colin said, 'Well, at least you can start getting in the Italian mood,' and passed him the *Latimer Cultural Guide to Rome*. Archie said, 'Right…' with a worried frown; and then laughed and rested his head on Colin's shoulder in a gesture of trust and affection, child-like as much as lover-like. 'I just want to get to Italy,' he said.

'I know,' said Colin, suddenly encouraged. 'So do I.'

'I'm very lucky to have you to show it to me.'

'Yes, you are,' said Colin; and then, thinking it was probably time for their first lesson, 'So, who are the two great architects of baroque Rome?'

Archie detached himself and leaned out to gaze down the aisle at a retreating steward.

'You haven't answered the question,' said Colin.

'Um...' Archie smiled dimly and sent his eyes from side to side in a mime of thought. 'Yes... now... who are they?' he said.

'Well, they're very easy to remember. There's Bernini and there's Borromini: the two Bs.'

'Oh!... right. So it's Bernini—and... what was it again?'

'Borromini.'

'*Bernini*,' said Archie. 'And *Borromini*.'

'And there's also a third one, called Pietro da Cortona, but I'm not going to bother you with him till we get there and can actually visit a church by him.'

It wasn't clear that Archie had imagined their actually visiting churches. 'Okay...' he said; and then, 'No, the two Bs are probably quite enough for my little brain.'

'I thought,' said Colin.

'Look at this guy's biceps,' said Archie, as the steward, colossal in his short-sleeved shirt, sauntered back down the aisle. Archie grinned at him, and got a sly raised eyebrow in return.

'You'll see much finer examples of that in Rome,' said Colin gamely, reopening *I promessi sposi* and reading the faintly familiar paragraph for the fourth time.

2

The lift at the hotel was very small, but then it was a small hotel, family-run, in a historic building, and close to the Forum... Colin hoped these advantages were evident to Archie as he edged into the space between him and the porter and their two cases. Despite the awkward comedy of the lift, he had a sense of ritual, in being taken upstairs, with a handsome young man, to the bedroom he knew already from the website, with its view of the Forum, its cable TV, and its 'matrimonial bed'. That matrimonial bed was a bold decision, but the smiling porter seemed to solemnize it. He wasn't really a porter, he was.Silvio, the son of the owner. As the lift door closed they all started speaking in Italian at the same time, so that Colin missed what Silvio was saying, quickly and humorously, to Archie – it was something to do with the telephone. Archie frowned and shook his head as if to close the subject, and shifted to give Colin a wide close-up smile. It was a smile that seemed full of shared expectancy. Colin blushed and looked down, abashed by the presence of Silvio, who was laughing contentedly.

At the end of a narrow landing Silvio unlocked a door and went ahead of them into a room of which all Colin saw at first was a ward-robe and a shuttered window and the high coving of the ceiling. Archie strolled in after him, with a quick scanning glance, and Colin, his smile in the mirror looking almost sarcastic with tension, came last. 'Ah...' he said, as Silvio brandished the TV control and then crossed to open the bathroom door. 'Um...!' – for a minute Colin's Italian failed him; while Archie was saying, '*Perfetto!*' and pressing an absurdly large tip into Silvio's hand. 'Um... yes,' said Colin, scrambling to repossess himself and looking round, as the door closed and they were left alone, at the wardrobe, and the bowl of fruit, and the two high bolstered single beds.

3

They had breakfast next morning on the rooftop terrace, which did, strictly speaking, have a view of the Forum. A distant wedge of ruined wall could be glimpsed between the neighbouring house and the awnings on the roof terrace of the much grander hotel in front of them. Their own roof terrace had a bar with a coffee machine, half a dozen tables with paper cloths clipped against the breeze, and pots of geraniums wired to its wrought-iron railings. Colin said, 'You can just see the top of the dome of S. Luca and S. Martina; which is indeed two churches, S. Luca on top and S. Martina beneath. It's rather fascinating.'

It seemed unlikely, from Archie's look, as he spread some red jam on a white roll, that anything had ever fascinated him less. He leaned back to signal to the waitress for more coffee. 'It's by Pietro da Cortona,' Colin went on.

'Right...' said Archie.

'Well, you'll see,' said Colin. 'I hope it will be open. Last time I was here it was closed for restoration.'

Archie brightened a little at this. 'You are going to take me shopping, aren't you?' he said.

'Well, what do you want?'

'I don't know yet, I want to see what there is. And we've got to get you sorted out, too: get you some nice jeans, something a bit more casual, Colin. That's my task for this weekend.'

Colin drank his little glass of concentrated orange juice. 'We'll want to do some sightseeing first,' he said. 'You haven't forgotten about the two Bs?'

To his relief this seemed to be a game Archie was prepared to play. His smile was happy, and confusingly like smiles he'd given Colin in the past. 'Ah yes, now... who are they?' he said.

'You can't have forgotten,' said Colin, still excited by the remembered smiles.

'They're B... B...'

'Bernini,' Colin murmured.

'Bernini! Yes, they're Bernini and... B...'

'Borromini,' said Colin.

'Exactly!' said Archie.

It wasn't clear who'd won the game, once they'd played it. Archie sipped his hot coffee and sank back into a vaguely critical silence. Though the silence itself, the untuned and rhythmless hum and squeal and nearby clatter of the city, had for a minute or two past been eaten into by the strident electronic bleeps of a reversing vehicle. Only their recurrence, after nine or ten seconds of peace, made Colin start to picture the van, some narrow negotiation in the street below.

'God, I can't stand that noise,' he said.

'Forget about it. It'll stop in a minute,' said Archie, who tended to meet impatience with patience, and vice versa.

Colin got up and leaned over the railing, but he couldn't see where the noise was coming from. 'I wonder if a single injury has ever been prevented by those bloody things,' he said.

'Well, we'll never know, will we?' said Archie. 'I mean, you can't count things that don't happen.'

Colin sat down again, frowning madly, wondering if Archie would let him make a joke about the things that hadn't happened the night before. 'How very true,' he said.

Archie was cool and practical. 'We need to get going,' he said. 'We haven't got much time here, you know.' But just then there was a different bleep: Archie had a text message, in fact two text messages. He sat there thumbing and chuckling to himself for the next ten minutes.

4

As soon as they were in the street they saw where the noise was coming from. Behind the hotel a large building had been demolished, and they looked down into the excavation where two mechanical diggers were shifting and levelling the rubble. Forward they rushed, from different sides, clanking and jolting, to scoop up dirt and twisted metal and broken Roman bricks; they seemed to bow to each other with their scoops. Then almost together came the bleeps, and the trundling erratic reverse. No one else was on the site, but the warning was sounded. It was piercing and implacable, with an echo that came back dead off the buildings like a knock. Colin laughed thinly at his continuing bad luck.

He marched Archie up the hill, to the high open-sided piazza on the Quirinal, where they had their first view across the whole city, with the dome of St Peter's in the distance and the wide brown jumble of roofs below. Archie seemed to like that, and the twenty-foot-high naked statues of Castor and Pollux. Size was in general a mark of authenticity, for Archie. They pondered the colossal fig leaves of the two young gods, colossal absolutely, but proportionally on the small side, and Colin made a joke about 'Pollux's bollocks', which Archie seemed to enjoy more than anything since they'd left London. Colin wished it was the sort of remark that came to him more easily. Harnessing the mood of childish hilarity, he hurried them along to the pair of neighbouring churches, where Archie would have his first taste of the two Bs.

His own first feeling, as the door of S. Andrea thumped softly shut behind them, muting the roar of the traffic, was, It's still here. The mild light on grey marble, the cherubs and the gilding, the candle trays and parish notices, the one woman praying: it was all as it had been twenty years ago. The notices referred to a new famine and a new pope, but the mood was the same, the mid-morning vacancy of a church in Italy, with the rumble of lorries and whine of Vespas in the long hot street outside. He walked slowly around, tipped his head back to look up at the elliptical dome, with a dull protest from his neck. He smiled to encourage Archie, and also, in a way, himself. It wasn't quite working for him, great though it was. He felt that if Archie would say something, smile, make even a tiny gesture of surrender, it probably would work: his own long-ago sense of discovery would revive.

He went over to Archie, who was still standing near the door, with his hands on his hips. Colin kept smiling purposefully, but Archie's half-smile was that of someone not easily taken in.

'Isn't it wonderful?' said Colin.

Archie glanced around. 'It's quite small, isn't it?' he said.

'I know,' said Colin, and nodded enthusiastically.

A twinkle came into Archie's eye. 'I was just looking at you there, Mr Cardew. You're getting quite a pot on you. We're going to have to get you down to the gym when we get back; do some work on those abs before it's too late.'

'Oh, it already is too late, for that,' said Colin.

'Never too late,' said Archie, with charm, and the way he had of seeming to allude to Colin's fantasies, and play on them. He reached out and squeezed his shoulder. 'Let's get on,' he said, as if Colin had been dawdling intolerably. 'We haven't got long here, you know.'

Out in the street, Colin said, 'We'll just have a quick look in S. Carlo alle Quattro Fontane, shall we?'

'S. Carlo alle Quattro Fontane,' said Archie, with a certain stoniness under his mimicry. They bustled along the narrow pavement, Colin fiddling with his top shirt button, as he did when he was nervous and responsible. It was hard to talk because of the roar of buses and taxis. 'God, this city's polluted,' said Archie.

'I suppose it is,' said Colin.

'I can hardly breathe,' said Archie.

As they drew close to the church, on its busy crossroads, Colin said, 'We ought to cross over to see the facade properly. It is rather amazing.' But Archie had already dropped behind, and when Colin turned round he was standing with his mouth pulled down and his fist rubbing at his left eye. 'Are you all right?' said Colin.

Archie was somewhat abstruse. He said it was his allergies, and also that he had a bit of grit in his eye.

'Let me look at it,' said Colin, and after a minute of blinking and squeezing, Archie let him look, with the child-like submission and bravery that anyone will show when they have something in their eye. 'I can't see anything,' said Colin, keeping Archie's head steady with one hand while he held his eye open with the thumb and forefinger of the other. It didn't escape him that this was their most intimate moment in over a year.

After Colin let him go Archie carried on frowning and rolling his eyes.

He was breathing noisily, as he did in his sleep. 'I've got to have a drink of water,' he said. 'I'm so dry.'

'Well, all right,' said Colin, with a smirk that showed he wasn't easily taken in either. They set off in search of a cafe, leaving the church unvisited.

'Rome is so beautiful,' said Archie airily, taking Colin's arm for a moment. 'What's that over there?'

'It's the back of the post office,' said Colin.

5

In the afternoon, Colin tried a different tack, and took Archie to the Baths of Caracalla. 'I think you'll like this,' he said, as they got into a taxi. 'It's both old and large.'

'Great,' said Archie, sleepy but mischievous after two martinis and a bottle of Corvo. 'You know, it's all new to me,' he said, with a yawn.

'It's where Shelley wrote *Prometheus Unbound*,' said Colin, as if that might focus it for him.

At the entrance to the site there was a little kiosk, where they bought plastic bottles of water. Colin took his jacket off, and led Archie through the deserted grassy precincts towards the great broken vaults of the baths. It was splendid, but perhaps a little dull. It required some patient reimagining, which on a hot April afternoon seemed somehow beyond them both.

'They are quite large,' Archie conceded.

'I think Shelley somehow got right on the top,' said Colin, looking in the *Latimer Cultural Guide*. 'He talks about the "mountainous ruins" and "immense platforms".'

'Mountainous,' said Archie. 'Immense.' He hopped up a low mound, and sat down against a ruined wall, facing the sun. Colin scrambled up beside him with some difficulty in his leather-soled shoes. 'I've been thinking,' said Archie.

'Oh yes,' said Colin.

'We need to get your hair sorted out, get you a new look, something a bit younger. Have you ever thought of having some tints?'

'What, a blue rinse you mean, I suppose.'

Archie laughed happily at this. 'No, not yet,' he said. 'No, just some highlights, a few little blond streaks. You know, just as if you'd been in the sun. It would take years off you.'

'I doubt it,' said Colin. 'Anyway, I'm happy the way I am.'

'Are you?' said Archie, with a devilish grin.

His own hair colour had changed several times since Colin had known him. When he'd first had him round it had been straw blond; now it was a reddish brown, which was probably nearer the natural tint.

'You forget that I'm twenty years older than you, or is it twenty-four years older? You must let me know when you stop being twenty-eight.'

'Colin,' said Archie reproachfully, undoing three buttons and then pulling his shirt over his head. 'Well, I'm going to get some sun.'

'Hmm… good idea,' said Colin, though he waited till Archie was napping before he took off his own shirt and then his shoes. He lay uncomfortably on the stony grass, looking at Archie's pale body.

6

Colin's mood of anxiety, going up to Nino's salon, was heightened by the large framed photos of women that lined the staircase, and by a stifling smell that he associated with his mother, and her formidable perms. Staunchly unfeminized, Colin had the feeling, as he was greeted and gowned, of seeing something he wasn't meant to, like a glimpse into the ladies' lavatory at a theatre. Sunday, too. In his Rome you couldn't have done this, but new European Rome seemed perpetually open for business. Archie had looked into it: now he was talking confidentially with Nino, and responding to the dapper old man's remarks with Italianate gestures of his own.

'It's *my hair*,' said Colin firmly into the mirror, 'and I'm just having it trimmed a bit. I'm *not* having any highlights—' and here his voice jumped, so that he wondered if he was about to make a scene.

In a minute Archie went away, like a prudent parent, leaving Colin to brave it out. What was Archie going to do, unsupervised, Colin wondered—he seemed to disappear with a sense of purpose. Nino approached, smiling remotely, and fingered Colin's bushy grey hair, which was, in truth, a bit longer than usual because he'd thought Archie might find it more romantic; though what he meant by romantic was as vague as it was ineradicable. Nino, like any professional, wanted to flatter him but also to suggest there was serious work to be done and paid for. He pursed his lips and pushed Colin's hair around, then nodded competently before sending him off to be washed.

Half an hour later, Colin was sitting with a large art book in his lap and numerous twists of silver foil in his hair. Nino, it turned out, was a member of a special Borromini society devoted to restoring the master's works, each one of which was the subject of a beautiful scholarly book. He brought out several of these from his office to keep Colin distracted as the colouring took hold; Colin said how much he liked the buildings, and found himself wanting to impress Nino, who, he saw now, was a rather distinguished old man. He spoke to him as though what was happening on top of his head was not a pathetic surrender, to Archie's will and to some tiny speculative vanity of his own; as if it was normal and indeed benign. After all, who would say no and mean it when offered the chance of growing ten years younger, which was Nino's casual prediction? They would just be highlights, very subtle, very natural, as if the signore had been in the sun. Then the signore was left alone with a cup of coffee, hardly daring to look at the freak in the mirror. Behind him, in the white salon, women were reading under driers or chatting candidly with the stylists. He wondered, with sudden horror, what the people at work would say. From time to time Nino drifted back, peeped cautiously inside a silver tress, then wrapped it up tight for a further baking.

When Colin was back in the street, it was nearly lunchtime. He went hurriedly towards the hotel, knowing everyone was looking at him. The whole treatment had cost 190 euros, to which, in complex embarrassment, he had added a handsome tip. He couldn't quite look at what had been done to him, but now, as he glanced in a dark shop window, he saw the effect, architectural as much as painterly, that Nino had produced with his scissors and heaters and silver foil. Still, he managed a tense grin for Archie, who was hurrying the other way, perhaps to meet him, and who walked straight past without recognizing him.

7

In the restaurant, after a quickly dispatched martini, Colin said, 'Please don't keep looking at it.'

'Looking at what?' said Archie.

Colin signalled to the waiter for another drink. He could tell that Nino had gone a bit further than Archie had expected. Archie had wanted him to make Colin less embarrassing, but it seemed he had ended up making him more so. This was an irony in which Colin himself could take only a limited satisfaction. The whole thing was a botch, and it would need a visit to another Nino to redress it.

'Your hair, you mean,' said Archie. 'It looks great... amazing!'

'You think I look a fool,' said Colin.

'Really, Colin, no one will notice,' said Archie.

'Well, make your mind up,' said Colin.

Archie gave him the wounded look of the well-meaning meddler. 'Well, I think—' he said, but then his phone bleeped, and he had a text message to deal with. The second martinis came, and Colin sipped at his, feeling the alcohol sharpen his resentment of Archie's mobile, and of these friends whose mere illiterate texts were apparently so amusing. Well, you could hardly call them texts. He watched Archie press Send, and put the phone down beside his glass, ready perhaps for a reply. 'That was Aldo,' he said.

'And who might Aldo be?' said Colin. 'Someone you met this morning?'

'Aldo – we met him when we were checking in. With the little goatee? We're going to a club with him tonight.'

'Are we?' said Colin, and found his martini had gone already.

'Well, you may have to wear a hat,' said Archie. 'Joke! Joke!'

They drank a bottle of wine with their main course, and when Archie said, 'Shall we have another?' Colin said, 'Why not?' He saw the day could sensibly be disposed of this way; and when they were drunk together the blur of a chance of fun seemed to shine through the misery, the expensive folly. Colin could take his drink, but he was wandering a bit as he went to the lavatory. He heard his name, looked round stupidly for three seconds, and there at a corner table were the Gortons.

'We didn't like to interrupt,' said George suavely.

'He looks rather super,' said Emma. 'Good for you!'

'Oh… yes,' said Colin, with a little gasp.

They eyed each other, jovially but warily. 'You're looking well,' said Emma. 'You've done something to your hair.'

'Oh… gosh,' said Colin, who had actually forgotten this fact as he approached their table. Now, he ran his hand through it. It felt silky but stiff.

'Very dashing,' said George.

'Very bold,' said Emma. And since Colin just stood there: 'Well, lovely to see you. Don't let us keep you from your friend. We haven't exactly been spying on you, but we can see you're having a marvellous time!'

8

Really very drunk, in the street, barging each other as they went along. Colin put his arm round Archie's shoulders. It seemed absurd, but then again perhaps only prudent, to have another drink. 'I suppose we should go to St Peter's,' he said.

'Umm…' said Archie, distracted by the window, the interestingly priced Armani suits. 'Shall we go in here?'

Colin was saying, '... of course we could just go back to the hotel and have some fun.'

Archie, abstracted for a moment, staring across the crowded square... 'Yes!' he said.

'Great!' said Colin, of course it was all going to be all right.

'Yes! I know what we must do,' said Archie. 'We must go for a ride in a carriage. I cannot go back to London without first having had a ride in a carriage.' Pulling at Colin's arm.

'Don't be ridiculous,' Colin said.

'Oh, please,' said Archie. 'Please, please, please.'

'I'm not going for a ride in a carriage, and that's that,' said Colin.

'It'll be something to remember,' said Archie. Stumbling him towards the rank, with three or four carriages waiting. Crocheted cushions, plastic flowers.

'It's a total tourist trap,' said Colin, smelling the horse dung.

'They're a total rip-off.'

'I'll pay!' said Archie.

'You haven't got any money,' said Colin.

'I can make some! I'll pay you back.'

They were almost scuffling, Colin heaving him away; Archie had started talking to the driver, he was being handed up the listing step of the vehicle, agreeing to the mad first price that was mentioned. Colin said, 'No, no, no, that's fifty quid as near as dammit,' reaching up, tugging hard on Archie's arm – anyway, they went in the carriage, Archie on the mobile to Aldo and making Colin speak to him too. Colin slid down on the plastic cushions, dreading being seen by the Gortons.

9

He woke at 6.25, and lay for a while measuring the violence of his headache and the sundered intimacy of their two beds. The digital clock cast a faint green light across the table between them and drew Archie's face very dimly out of the blackness. He was sleeping steadily, open-mouthed, eyebrows raised, as if phrasing a question.

Colin felt the horrible tightening under his ribs and pure instinct hurried him out of bed, patting and stumbling in the near-darkness – the blaze of the bathroom lights was like the spasm of his own body, swallowing wildly to gain the two seconds he needed to reach the bowl and double up.

In the shivering frailty afterwards, tears blurring his eyes, the tiny unaccountable prickle of pride… He rinsed his mouth out and cautiously drank a glass of water, leaning against the edge of the basin. In the mirror he saw the bony moppet, ghastly with age, grey-jawed, its grey-and-gold hairdo squashed tall by sweat and sleep. The vein in his temple twitched with its pain, and behind it, slipping in one against the other, the disordered images of the night, the shared taxis, the insane new friends, the cash machines, the immense walk home, and somewhere, in the second club, an image seen only from the corner of the eye, Archie signalling to Aldo that Colin was blind drunk and that this was their moment. A moment that had seemed a long weekend to Colin, gripped by his own simple but absurd idea.

He got his nail scissors out of his sponge bag and, tilting his head forward in the mirror, started hacking at his gold highlights, which came away in small jagged tufts, mixed up with the adjacent grey. He kept moving his scissors in the wrong direction, snipping at the air, poking at his scalp. This showed he was still very drunk. He piled the rough clippings on the glass shelf beside his toothpaste and the cologne he had bought for Archie at Gatwick. A whorish cologne, he'd felt at the time, though that was the one thing he could never say to his young friend, companion, whatever the hell he was.

'What are you doing?' said Archie, sounding bored, barely awake.

'I've just been violently sick,' said Colin.

'Hmm,' said Archie.

'I hate this hair,' said Colin.

Archie looked at him in the mirror, and what might have been guilt, or maybe some harder impersonal sense of comedy, twitched for a moment under his sleepy frown. Colin put down the scissors.

'What's the matter?' said Archie amicably, but as if he had limited time for the answer.

Colin looked at the little offering of his own hair. 'What's the matter?' he said. 'Um… yes, what… is… the matter…'

His heart was pounding at the scale of the opportunity; he held the edge of the basin and looked into it with a pant of panic. He saw that if he started to answer, if he opened that padded and studded door a chink, he would be answering all day, all the way to the airport, and on the flight, and in the long anticlimax of the train to Victoria.

He managed to sleep again, with his fist against his forehead, to equalize the pain. Archie was sleeping too. At eight the piercing bleeps of the diggers began. It was Monday morning, it was that time already, they had started and they weren't going to stop. Archie pulled the covers over his head, and Colin lay across from him, looking at the shrouded hump he had become. There were the brief intermittences, distant rumbling and clanking; and then the bleep again, the bleep of a thousand busy reversals.

A MAN'S SECRETS

Hervé Guibert (1955–1991)

One of the originators of the French genre "autofiction", Hervé Guibert's writings combined diary, memoir, and fiction, penned with often startling frankness. In 1991, in his autobiographical novel *To the Friend Who Did Not Save My Life*, he publicly announced that he was living with HIV, and in the following years did much to change public attitudes to the disease. In all, he published twenty-five books before his death at the age of thirty-six.

When it came to trepanning, the specialist said: I could never touch this brain, it would be a crime, I would feel like I was attacking a work of art, or hacking at perfection, or burning a masterpiece, or flooding a landscape that needed to stay dry, or throwing a grenade into an exquisitely structured termite mound, scratching a polished diamond, ruining beauty, sterilizing fertility, tying off the canals of all creation, every cut of the blade would be an assault upon intelligence, thrusting iron into this divine mass would be an auto-da-fé for this genius; only a barbarian, an illiterate, an enemy would commit such a crime! The enemy existed. Sarcastically, examining the three lesions spreading across the scanner's images, he says: how could such brilliance be left to rot? We have to open this. This intelligence had pierced him, personally, not by name, but by condemning all the deceit in his system, in several books. The man of the mind had castigated the man of law: the doctor, the judge; the philosopher had ultimately accused his ancient predecessors of abuse of thoughts; in their texts, he tried to find the exact moment when the thread was lost, imperceptibly but insidiously, when the right words, drawn from the right thoughts, slipped ever so slightly, were recovered maladroitly, and turned into wrong words, oppressive words. The surgeon took pride in assailing such a fortress, especially considering how he called his prestige groundless; a man's head, he said to his assistants, is nothing more than a bit of flab, of cured meat. But when the orb was opened, he was astonished by the powerful beauty that matter exuded; his disdain was as mute as his tongue, and his stylet fell from his hands; all he could do, now that he had been converted, was contemplate. The brain was no longer a simple, tender walnut with manifold, indecipherable convolutions, but a luminescent, teeming terrain as yet uncongealed by anesthesia, and every fiefdom was busy working, gathering, connecting, charting, drifting, damming, rerouting, refining; three strongholds had collapsed, that was easy to see, but all around the moat kept golden thoughts and laughter flowing. The most noticeable veins carried along all sorts of nasty old ruined things, prison turrets, torture vises; but the whips seemed to gleam royally like scepters, and the gags were woven like finery. Exposed discourses glittered on the surface, opened up to derision; their reek of arrogance was absolved by their aroma. Digging just a little revealed corridors full of savings, reserves, secrets, childhood memories, and unpublished theories. The childhood memories were buried deepest of all, in order not to clash against idiotic interpretations or poorly woven veils that were meant to be enlightening but which instead shrouded the work. Two or three images were buried in his vessels' depths like vile dioramas. The first one showed the young philosopher led by his father, himself a surgeon, through a Poitiers hospital room where a man's leg had been amputated, that's how the boy's manliness gets shaped. The second revealed a typical backyard the little philosopher was walking past, which was aquiver with the recent news: right there, on a straw mattress, in this sort of garage, was where the woman all the papers were calling the Poitiers Prisoner had lived for dozens of years. The third retold the beginning of a story, wax figures coming to life through the machinery hidden beneath their clothes: in high school, the little philosopher, who had been the top of his class, was threatened by the sudden and seemingly inexplicable invasion of an arrogant band of little Parisians who were sure to be more talented than the rest. The ousted philosopher-child came to hate them, insult them, hurl all sorts of curses upon them: the refugee Jewish children in the area did disappear by being deported to the camps. These secrets would have sunk in the Atlantis ever so slowly, ever so sumptuously chiseled, suddenly shattered by lighting, had a vow of friendship not raised the vague and uncertain possibility of their being passed on...

Each of these strongholds were threatened, one by one: the cache of proper names emptied. Then it was personal memories that were very nearly ruined: he fought to keep the scourge from winning out. Even the existence of his books vanished: what had he written? had he even written? Sometimes he wasn't sure at all. The books there, in his hands, could have borne witness. But the books weren't himself, he had once written that and he remembered it still: that the book wasn't the man, that between the book and the man was the labor that had dissociated the two, and sometimes drove them apart like two enemies. But was that actually what he had written? He hesitated to return to the text itself, he was afraid to find himself locked out as an idiot. So he wrote and rewrote his name on a piece of paper, and underneath he drew rows of squares, circles, and triangles, a ritual he had taught himself to verify his mental integrity. When people came into his room, he hid the paper.

He had to finish his books, this book he had written and rewritten, destroyed, renounced, destroyed once more, imagined once more, created once more, shortened and stretched out for ten years, this infinite book, of doubt, rebirth, modest grandiosity. He was inclined to destroy it forever, to offer his enemies their stupid victory, so they could go around clamoring that he was no longer able to write a book, that his mind had been dead for ages, that his silence was just proof of his failure.

He burned or destroyed all the drafts, all the evidence of his work, all he left on his table were two manuscripts, side by side, he instructed a friend that this abolition was to continue. He had three abscesses in his brain but he went to the library every day to check his notes.

His death was stolen from him, who wished to be master of his own death, and even the truth of his death was stolen from him, who wished to be master of the truth. Above all the name of the plague was not to be spoken, it was to be disguised in the death records, false reports were given to the media. Although he wasn't dead yet, the family he had always been ostracized from took in his body. The doctors spoke abjectly of blood relatives. His friends could no longer see him, unless they broke and entered: he saw a few of them, unrecognizable behind their plastic-bag-covered hair, masked faces, swaddled feet, torsos covered in jackets, gloved hands reeking of alcohol he had been forbidden to drink himself.

All the strongholds had collapsed, except for the one protecting love: it left an unchangeable smile on his lips when exhaustion closed his eyes. If he only kept a single image, it would be the one of their last walk in the Alhambra gardens, or just his face. Love kept on thrusting its tongue in his mouth despite the plague. And as for his death it was he who negotiated with his family: he exchanged his name on the death announcement for being able to choose his death shroud. For his carcass he chose a cloth in which they had made love, which came from his mother's trousseau. The intertwined initials in the embroidery could bear other messages.

As the body was collected in the morgue's rear courtyard, masses of flowers lay all around the coffin: in wreaths, in rows, from editors, from the institute where he had taught, from foreign universities. On the coffin itself stood a small pyramid of roses among which a band of mauve taffeta revealed and concealed the letters of three names. The bier traveled the whole day, from the capital to the rural village, from the hospital to the church and from the church to the cemetery, it passed from hand to hand, but the pyramid of roses, which the florist had not stapled or taped to the wood, was never knocked off the structure. Several hands tried to move it. Either those hands were immediately caught in a moment's hesitation after which they reconsidered, or other hands reached out to stop them. An occult, imperious order bound the pyramid of roses with its three names to the coffin. When the coffin was gently set in the pit, the mother was asked what should be done with this spray of flowers, and she gestured, she who was not crying, to leave them on the coffin. Nobody got rid of the letter that someone had left when the body was collected, or worried about whether it contained love or hurt, the cut flowers buried it. A tall young man with bare shoulders, in a leather jacket, sunglasses, stood in the distance, accompanied by an old crooked man who seemed to be his father, or servant, or driver; from the capital to the village, from the morgue to the church, from the church to the cemetery they had traveled in an elegant sports car. I had never seen this young man and when he threw flowers into the ditch after me with his sunglasses still on, I suddenly recognized him and I went up to him, I said: are you Martin?, he said: hello, Hervé. I said: he always wanted us to meet, and now we have. We kissed each other and perhaps we kissed him at the same time over the grave.

Translated by Jeffrey Zuckerman

LOVE'S TEARS, OR, RAPUNZEL AND THE DRIFTER

Murathan Mungan (1955–)

Turkey legalised homosexuality more than a century before most Western countries, but the region remained, socially, extremely conservative. Mungan was one of very few openly gay figures during the particularly hostile decade of the 1980s. He wrote radical transgender narratives, playing with the linguistic ambiguity of pronouns in the Turkish language. His realistic prose is punctuated with perplexing images and is, at its best, transcendent.

Never run dry, you tears of love.

Even a glance at the hurriedly snapped photo on his driver's license gives away the swarthy gloom of Efkar's manhood. Working since age fifteen driving the Aydınlık-to-Çankaya taxi-bus route, he's something of a rogue-beauty, toughing it out around these slums. Driving with a steady hand, looking after the vehicle like it was a young lady. You can hear the horn from his taxi three neighborhoods down, lit up from within flashing red and purple, pumping out all the latest and newest heartbreak songs. Only the latest and greatest. Efkar's gotten himself into hundreds of brawls, and then back out of them all, too. On his street, and in the neighborhoods around, he's known as a red-blooded lad, trustworthy. Lies and hypocrisy never cross his lips, and you'll never find him looking sideways at anyone else's honor. He'll go fingering through those prayer beads on his left wrist two-hundred times a minute, and his mouth doesn't turn quick to vulgarity. But if you provoke him, and he starts cursing, no one can shut him down. He'll get out two hundred fifty curses in one breath, one after the other—a literature of profanities. We mentioned that he is a brave lad, but don't think he has the face of a tough trouble-maker. No, his face is more the face of a girl, his heart the heart of a child, and he's one heck of a young man. Change his clothes, and you'd take him for one of those silver-spoon types from up in Çankaya. With a laugh, he'll toss his head way up in the air, blushing, dimming his eyes, breaking off your gaze. Before you know it, his face will be all but buried up in that air. He's aloof of all the adolescent hearts beating inside of so many teenage girls, in love with him from afar. His headstrong, merciless look, ever at odds with that soft inside, where he's delicate, nearly timid actually. Who knows, maybe that's what all the fights are for, to beat off the timidity, to go on offense till he sees the light. Back in the Ottoman days, he'd have been one of those fire brigadiers, for sure. You'd love him if you saw him, believe me. Ümit loved him at once, loved him without letting on, riding back and forth, back and forth in Efkar's taxi-bus on the Aydınlık-Çankaya line, sitting with a bowed head, eyes cast to the ground, meek, resigned.

When he'd gotten back from the army, Efkar's father'd bought him a taxi, announcing: "It'll win you your bread." Efkar gave the vehicle the name Warship and, before his first quest out, the neighborhood gathered around it to celebrate, throwing buckets and buckets of water behind him, as the vehicle set off. They weren't thinking all that hard about what their joy was about, or about the tears in their eyes—just chalking it all up to the pride of the slums on this one particular day. The taxi-bus was decked out like a bride's limousine—a warship putting to sea, descending from the hills of the outskirt slums into the city center, into the guts of it, those terrestrial canals of asphalt.

That night Efkar's father—whether out of grief or elation is unclear—got drunker than he'd ever been in his life.

A flashy, glittery car, Warship was always parked crossways on the sidewalk, its hood sticking straight into the wall as if waiting, jacket swung over shoulder, for its owner to show up again. As for that owner, he usually takes a break in the beerhall as soon as he gets done with work, soothing himself with drink as best he might. Whoever you ask will say, "He drinks too much." If you ask him, he'll say he drinks "in the evenings" and "knows what he can handle." What would he be doing anyway, if not drinking? Just please don't say to him, for example, "So, what's troubling you? Why do you drink this much?" He'd just say "Things, in general." What does *general* mean? What kind of *general*? Efkar's heart, you see, is just betrothed to the underlying sorrows and dilemmas of the world—to doom, to how situations turn out, to the basic farce of our lives. "That's life," he'll say. What do you mean, *life*? He just shrugs his shoulders, "You know, stuff." He'll say, "Nothing, one big nothing.…" Put simply, he's been tossed off life too early, like every other young man who started life too early. Around his heart, a foggy mountain range you'll never get past… Nothing gets past.

His is just one of the hundreds of taxis we get in every day. His eyes always set off in the distance, stuck out there for good. No way to approach him. He'd run off to get one of those old folk-tale lithographs from the sidewalk markets at Hacıbayram, or to the hundreds of tiny stores buried in prayer beads, rose attar perfumes, musky smelling salts, prayer rugs, kilim carpets, old books, green and white skullcaps, and old hand-written manuscripts that smell like ancestors. He could feel these tales from the depth of his heart. As if they would never be lived again, not once…. They've left us behind forever. Love has abandoned us, it seemed. All of what we feel has lost its power. The desert between us and Mejnun, the mountain we have to dig our way through to get to Ferhat, nothing's left of them. Love has abandoned us. From now on, no one will love another, till death part them. Till death…. Love is an impossible thing on the Aydınlık-Çankaya taxi line, and on all the other lines of this world. This is what love's tears are about now—for this alone. All the old loves have been replaced by mere excursions and one-night stands, fickle affairs, and all the casual ease that comes with them. All the magic of love, all its illusions, they've flown off, escaped from our lives. Romance is a lost paradise. No one will toil again for the beloved.

Leyla and Mejnun, Ferhat and Shirin, Kerem and Aslı, Arzu and Kamber are all crammed in together, among the day's newspapers and the cigarette packets, on the visor over the dashboard. Sometimes he reads a few pages of them when parked at a stop. He buries these pages deep in his heart, and waits. Waits for what? Waits for whom? He doesn't know. Maybe he's sentenced to wait his whole life, for something he knows full well will never come.

Sometimes he thinks about one of those romantic movies from his father's childhood, *The Tears of Love*. Some drunken nights, he makes his father tell the story from that movie.

He wakes early, takes the first passengers of the morning—the students and civil servants—to wherever it is they're going. Wherever he is going doesn't exist. Nowhere. How many times he goes back and forth, back and forth on the same road; he'll spend all his life coming and going on this one road, he thinks. It's as if there's no difference between lolling back and forth across Ankara from one end to the other and lolling across his life from one end to the other. At night, when he parks the car, he goes over to *Obsession,* where all the boys in the neighborhood spend out their lives hanging around. He joins in the crowds of men wiping the beer foam from their thick, black mustaches with the back of their hands, stretching their emptied glass toward the bartender, saying "Pull me another beer."

He is struck dumb by this one passenger who jumps in and sits next to him every morning at the last stop, with giant blue eyes, auburn hair full of gold, bangs falling down into those eyelashes, and a copper blaze of skin. In the sad timidity and destitute innocence of the passenger, he sees his own adolescence, the days when his own youth was still intact. "Could you stop hereabouts, wherever convenient?" are always the passenger's words, each time beginning with a clearing of the throat, taking pains so that the words should come out clear and smooth, though always escaping his gaze. In a warm and soft voice…. And so he stops at a convenient place indeed. Thick eyelashes casting shadow down onto cheeks, a depth, a privacy, a culpability shaped this face. This one doesn't fit in here, doesn't fit in here at all, isn't from here. YOU AREN'T FIT FOR THIS NEIGHBORHOOD. Now Efkar just stops at the intended convenient place, without any words exchanged. And then he turns and gazes back after the passenger. As if wanting to say, I have learned where you get in and where you get out. Sometimes while driving or changing gears, their knees or arms would touch, and it was like an electric shock each time for them both. Both unaware of the other's emotional electricity. Both living in their distance to one another. Only much later did he learn the passenger's name, Ümit. It took him a long time to confess to himself that he was crushed out on a sixteen-year old. (Love can only be experienced when it's confessable, when it's confessed.) Every time, the passenger from that last stop came straight up to where he sits, sat next to him. In the first few days, Ümit was just one among many passengers for him. A few times, they drove right by the convenient spot. Thinking that they were going to someplace different, Efkar didn't say a thing, but soon after, Ümit got out of the taxi in a rush. Once, when he said "You were going to get off here, right?" Ümit just said "Yes, yes, I must have not been paying attention." (So it was absent-mindedness.) For some reason, a few times, Ümit got in and just sat in the back row, which aggravated Efkar, who kept checking Ümit out from the rear-view mirror. In such moments, Ümit always avoided meeting his eyes and Efkar intentionally looked right back into those same eyes. (As if they were punishing each other.) As if they were party to a private, deep, and obvious guilt. There was some kind of distemper between them that never spilled over into words, like two trapeze artists walking across a high-voltage line, regarding one another as they somersaulted into the emptiness. Efkar now knew this wasn't just some ordinary passenger for him. Each night, dressed to impress at the gloomy beerhalls, he'd think of Ümit, and realize he couldn't brush this vision out of his eyes. He'd catch himself often, thinking of that deep face, the secret eyes, and each time he felt a profound guilt. This was a fact he couldn't hide any longer, even from himself. By then, every morning when he started up the taxi-bus, his heart shuddered, and he understood why he couldn't sleep nights, and why so many tiny and tense troubles had started to come out in his life lately. He was in love, there was no way around confessing that he was deep in love.

So that Ümit would see, so that Ümit would read and feel them, he cut out the most beautiful love proverbs, written on stickers or in publications, and stuck them all over the inside of the vehicle. Hot-blooded love proverbs... all of them endless and immortal. About longing, and loving, and forgetting, and betrayal, and separation. On top of his rearview mirror, he stuck a blood-filled heart, shot through with an arrow. All these endless, undying ah's and oh's from the hands of love. But did Ümit see them? Think about them? Feel them? Know that they were all meant especially for... NOW A VIOLENT WIND OF LOVE BLEW THROUGH HIS HEART, THROUGH ALL THE LEAVES WAITING THERE WITHIN IT.

He was just a driver love-struck by his passenger now.

Whom he would always drive around.

Everywhere.

At the wheel with his steel-blue eyes, thick mustache, black scarf, leather jacket thrown over his shoulders, he was now thinking about Ümit incessantly. "Maybe thinking is loving," he said.

In the evenings, he rubbed shoulders in the crowds of melancholic, wistful, insolent men. He used to feel more confident here, now the ground beneath him shudders. Later I'll forget, he thinks. Later I'll settle down. In all of the quavering passions he saw in the videos and in the break-up movies, he sees himself, his desolation. Where do people who were created for grand loves, grand lives, stow their hearts when they can't live grandly? In what sort of lives? In which miracles? Hearts stowed in small lives: what kind of hopelessness befalls them? Now, he was one of those lonely men who live with a grand heart and a deep remorse.

One day, Ümit didn't come to the stop. Didn't come running to jump in the vehicle.

The same the next day.

The one after too.

And the days after.

Efkar spent these days on the threshold of mania. It was as if he was losing something, losing infinitely. Losing it right at the moment he found it. Without even holding it in his hand, it slipped from his palms and faded into the endless distance. He thought he'd lost something that he would never be able to experience again. Didn't know its name, address, identity; he was love-struck with someone he didn't know a single thing about. And yet loved desperately. Maybe this was the only way love could be true. Loving at a distance without knowing what, without knowing how. Loving that distance. Ümit was a dove with white wings that flew up and behind Mount Kaf. The Warship was going to drive up that mountain. Before his eyes, the wall panels depicting Fatih's conquest of Istanbul came alive, all the walls of the coffeehouses came alive too. And destroyed him. He had lost. There was nothing else left for him than to tie his hopes to the prospect of a chance encounter, one day some-place. As it was, he didn't know anyone he might ask about Ümit, find out something. Unspeakable things came to mind. Leaving the country, dying, going somewhere else.

From now on, he thought, he would never be able to forget Ümit, till death. Even if they never saw each other again, at least once a day he would remember, and his inside would go dry. He would remember, with a wide, stark vacancy.

If only it had been one of those unforgettable street loves, a chance meeting of eyes, a sigh. As the years pass, the sheer beauty of this one moment would continue to grow. In our memory, it would have been that endless, unforgettable love.

But that's not how it happened.

*

He's drinking more than he used to.

More than before, he drinks.

Every morning he arrives at the last stop with the same wish—sometimes he comes early and sits waiting, then the next day he comes a little bit later, and waits, waits, waits.

And one morning he saw Ümit at the stop.

The waiting had ended.

He was crazy in joy, he couldn't keep his heart in his chest. As soon as Ümit was sitting beside him, he stepped on the gas. All the other commuters were just left waiting at the curb.

"Where've you been all this time?" he said.

"I was sick."

There was something in his voice that seemed to be scolding Ümit for bad behavior, but Ümit didn't understand why, didn't understand the reasons for his questions, just responded to them.

Empty, the taxi-bus rushed by the stops, right by lines of people waiting, right by the crowds. They all cursed after the taxi-bus as it sped off, hurled swear words at them.

"You'd think you'd let me know or something, no?"

Ümit couldn't conceal being surprised, and looked at him with timid eyes. Let whom know? For what? Why?

So…

This was when Ümit knew, and felt beloved.

And couldn't believe this miracle. Abruptly, right out of the middle of our hum-drum lives, a miracle falls. Out of the most brittle earth of our lives, a sudden sprig sprouts. WE AREN'T ALONE ANYMORE. NOW WE ARE NOT ALONE ON THIS EARTH. Love begins its magic—one after another, the stops left behind—oh the grand illusion of love. So, this taxi-bus driver I am madly in love with loves me too, he has worried about and agonized over me, and feels other feelings… Ümit cannot believe it. had always thought that love was never mutual, had always thought that way. Always believed this. The movies, the novels, the stories, and fairy tales—these would never happen in real life. Life was otherwise, entirely otherwise. All of them were just a game, a sleight of hand, a mirage, a spell. Love was impossible.

"All these days I went mad, I couldn't sleep until morning, I was thinking about you every second. I was always with you. Every night I drank through the pain, until I choked and drooled. I thought you were dead. I thought you had left. I thought you had abandoned me and the Warship. How many days has it been now that no one has sat beside me...."

"I was sick, I was bedridden," said Ümit, just repeating the same words over and over, voice trembling, almost tearing up. So this was what they called love. Trembling all the way through one's life, that was love. Something that we experience only in tiny fragments of time and cannot extend into infinity, that was the thing we called love. In our episodic lives and our episodic selves, this thing that we can only experience on and off. Our feelings, our passions had already withered away. Our integrity sliced to pieces, our passions shrunken, our beliefs and values vanished. We would never again love as we had before. Never again. Now everything is forgotten, time patches it back up. All the casual tasks and tangles of life shrink, retreat, and fade out in a sweltering confusion, love along with it. We were living in a dry season, hostages of our small lives.

But now, Ümit's voice was trembling, unable to endure this much delight and joy. Being loved brought on the trembling. In fact, in the years after, happiness would never become any more digestible. There was always something in happiness that made Ümit unhappy.

"Where are we going?" said Ümit.

"To the end of the line," said Efkar, looking both at Ümit and the road, gauging both of them—at the road for Ümit's sake, at Ümit for the sake of the road.

"If it's true you love me back, we'll go to the end of the line," he said. Love's magic bound their eyes. All the past years added up to nothing.

"OK, in that case, till death," said Ümit.

"Till death," said Efkar.

They put their hands in each other's. Tears wetted Ümit's cheeks, who wasn't even aware that tears were falling.

"What is this?" asked Efkar.

"These are the tears of love," said Ümit.

They passed by all the stops, looked out at all the people standing in line. No one would understand them. No one would believe this passion. They would be left alone, totally alone. Ümit knew this the best.

The Warship climbed up the slopes of Çankaya, there was a little beveled hill at the top, they climbed that, and then the slope ended. Having climbed the highest hills, now a wide ocean captivated their gaze. An immense, blue-black sea, all of love's illusions; all of the murmurs of the sun, the light, the salt, and the water, the phosphorescence, other climates, other feelings. Warship slowly descended to this sea. Into the ocean. They were alone, totally alone. In happy lunacy.

Had love really broken away and left our lives behind? Or was this just something returning from the distant past? Was it so for all people? Ümit thought about his mother, Mrs. Güzide. His brother Ömer had had a brief crush, it lasted three years. Just as they were about to get married, Güzide, the mother, came between them and separated them. I never thought they would separate. They never thought they would either. My mother didn't know the girl's family. She thought their family was some good-for-nothing family. In her eyes, a bride whose family one didn't know, whose past one wasn't clear about, was the source of all evils. She was one of those women who made their own lives by running the lives of others, especially their children's. And she had been looking for a girl for her son for a long time. In fact, there was this girl named Sevil who came around at one point; she was from the same town as herself. My brother Ömer resisted for a long time. He wasn't having any of it. He loved this girl very much, he wrote her love poems, he shed tears for her, he got drunk on her. If this all wasn't real, then what was it for? What was real in our lives? Afterward they ran away together to Adana. My mother Mrs. Güzide ran after them, and separated her son from the girl. She stormed in with all of the rights of a mother: "don't forget all the milk I have fed you"s, "all of my slaving for you"s, "was all that toiling in vain"s, and separating her son from the girl and brought him back. They came down into Ankara in the dark of dawn; throughout the trip on the bus they didn't say a word to each other. When they came into the house, my mother bore the air of a victorious commandant, back from the war. Like she had saved her son from the edge of the abyss and had carried out her parental offices successfully, had once again demonstrated her motherhood. Her face tired, self-deprecating, worn, and happy. I've never hated my mother more than I did on that morning. The girl had surrendered to him there in Adana. My brother was never to come to terms with this, I think. That she submitted to him there, that they didn't wait for the wedding. Obviously eloping had said it all for the girl. Whereas for my brother… he was still Mrs. Güzide's son.

"She was a virgin," said my brother. "I saw the blood on the sheets." "She was playing a game with you," said my mother. "She wiped the blood on the sheets herself." For days, the topic of conversation was whether the virgin was a virgin or not. They talked about this question for days. My brother was ambivalent. My mother: "If she was a virgin, they would have called in the authorities. They would have charged you." They didn't call in the authorities. They didn't charge him with anything. This bolstered my mother's and my brother's doubts. But the girl must have sensed that she had lost something much more important than her virginity. My brother and my mother never understood this. With all the fights about whether she was a virgin or not, their fugitive love in Adana became polluted and stayed that way in the bleak dinner hours we spent in our rooms, darkened by thick curtains and cracking white-washed walls. My brother's defence got weaker in time, maybe he also believed in the end that the girl was not a virgin, or maybe he was secretly expecting her to sue. Not another word was heard from the girl. For a while she was never mentioned, I was the only one who didn't forget her, just me. Then my brother married Sevil. They have three children. He comes and goes from the company he works at, briefcase in hand, ironed slacks, polished shoes, the same expression on his face, always. The love poems he wrote, the tears he shed, the running away together, being madly in love, where are they now? My mother just says, "He's matured now." "He's concerned with his children and family." On holidays they come to kiss the elders' hands, and I just watch it all from afar. All of their behaviors, all of their styles seem to have something untrue about them. They're interested in nothing but their kids, how's business, daily questions and such. They spend their lives shuttling between all these details. Is my brother happy? I don't know. I can't read anything from his face anymore. The bright expression his face used to have, the rebel eyes, they've lost something. His face and gaze have flattened. No passion, no joy, no happiness, no rage. As if all the noble feelings, all the passions have been expelled from his heart. His is a smooth, empty face. Now he's just someone, anyone for me. Before, love had beautified him, just as rage beautified him. He was exuberant, sharp, enchanting and very young. Love had made him something new. Did he love Sevil? What did they share with each other? What did they talk about at night? My mother Mrs. Güzide was happy, her son had married the girl of her wishes. There were grandchildren, young bucks, and she knew the bride's family, knew the father and mother-in-law, knew their past. Her son was happy too, apparently—may God not spoil the sweetness of their mouths. There is nothing wayward about them, someday they will witness their own children make happy marriages. This is how life goes. But how much I had loved that other girl. Even though I didn't know her, know anything about her, oh how I loved her. Love for me always took the form of a rebellion, I only understood this many years later. Way back then, in Ömer and that girl's love affair, and how that love infuriated my mother and father, disturbed everything in our midst, I saw all of the meanings of life, all of the light of a new world. The world was in our hands; it would be made anew. Then my brother left the girl behind. My mother went and had a spell cast on them, or that's what my older sister said. That's what it's about, those spells, my sister kept insisting. For her, the whole world, the things whose meanings she could not understand, the secrets she could not interpret, all of it was a spell. My brother ditched the girl. If I leave you, I won't be able to live, I'll die, he had said. And then they parted. Then he was forced to get engaged. And he lived. Then he was forced to get married. He didn't die. I can't go back on my mother's word, he said. And he didn't go back on it. My brother ditched that girl. He got engaged, got married. I could never make peace with that. A few years later, when he was in a car accident and I went to see him I understood that I would never make peace with it. I didn't pity him, he was just a stranger to me, I was even unsure whether I loved him anymore. My brother had taken away my capacity for empathy. I thought about all this while sitting watching him at his sick bed, helpless. He had betrayed his love, love in general, life, his life. He had hacked it all to pieces, not rebelled. Which meant love was merely a phase, or a problem of conformity. In this, the mothers and fathers in Turkish films were right. Love stings for a few months, or perhaps for a few years at the most, and then ceases. This one would also pass. Everything passed. Especially now, especially now. Love, quite simply, went out of circulation. The grand loves, the noble loves, the irremediable catastrophes, they only live on in songs. Where you live, where you work, your circle of friends are all bound to the values that envelop you, the boundaries of your life. (In my brother's change of heart, I experienced the rage of seeing my own future, and the future of love in general.) According to all of this, love only consisted of choosing someone and living with them. Now no one climbs mountains for love's sake, swims rivers, travels from land to land. Mejnun depleted all the deserts, no deserts are left for us in the world. The mirages are gone, and the oases dried up with them. If not this, then the other thing, if not that then this, if not that, then that other thing. IT DOESN'T MATTER. IT DOESN'T MATTER. No one but that. Only that. That to the end. You. You. You. You. No one says these anymore.

No one is anyone's You anymore.

Not anymore.

*

Coincidences usually determine everything. Small lives, little feelings, we roam to and fro on the narrow acreage of small hearts. We submitted to petty sensitivities, one-night stands, to marriages of convenience, fake loves, struggles to live what we learn from films and novels, the forged love adventures, the summer loves, the dark street meetings, we have lowered our life and expectations. We trample upon our noble instincts, our merits, our passions, our deep pains, our capacities, our selves.

Back then I didn't know this.

After my brother, my mother married off my other older brother Halil. As soon as he came back from the compulsory military service, they found a girl for him. And when Halil saw the girl, he liked her, then loved her, then they got along well, then they married. That's all there was. Chaste, presentable, knows how to sew, diligent in household chores, what else could you ask of Allah? As soon as he was back from the army they got engaged. Having too much time between the engagement and the wedding wasn't a good idea, they said, so they were married, and there was lemonade, biscuits, and an accordion at the wedding. Everything was glum, pathetic, and affected. (There's something glum about any wedding though.) They rented my brother a black tux, and the bridal gown was rented, as was the wedding salon, their house, and their life and even themselves. But they didn't notice these at all. Life was enough for them, so what was my problem? Especially back in those years, when I was so young. Why did it matter to me? They bought furniture sets for the dining room, bedroom, and living room, and put them on layaway. This is how they would live, on layaway. We all lived our lives like that. With the interest collecting. Military service on layaway, wedding on layaway, fatherhood on layaway, grandfatherhood on layaway, that's how Halil would live and die. Everyone's hair was quaffed, the children were constantly pacing around on the dancefloor; a fifth-class singer brandishing her blond hair, wagging her thighs in her slitted dress as she sang, mumbling a few things here and there, offering the newlyweds her best wishes for their happiness. The wedding director rolled out all the old drab wisecracks from the last wedding, trying to get a laugh with a few dated jokes, which was successful in the end. The sisters-in-law and bridesmaids in a line behind the bride, cheering her to step on the groom's foot, the brothers-in-law cheering for the groom, trying to overpower them. All the same jests and drolls from the last wedding, always received with the same gushing attention. After which, a folk dance, some cheery Gypsy tune. Widowed sisters-in-law and girl cousins who still lived at home were asked to dance by the handsome boy cousins, and then some distant relative's child, who used to be called Girl Jemil, does an oriental dance, and everyone applauds with a mix of melancholy, toleration, and admiration. The brothers-in-law and uncles who do not wish to sacrifice their masculinity to the fashionable dances of the day or the flirty dances do the Ankara Greeting or the Harmandalı instead, taking whatever opportunity they have to let their manly plumes convulse and shake… My mother was having one of the happiest nights of her life. She ran back and forth, shedding tears at seeing her children all grown and getting married; she greeted the guests, showed them to their seats, demonstrated she was a good host. Bracelets, rings, and broaches were pinned on the bride. I hate everyone and everything, I am forever in a fog of nausea. These sham lives had something in them that destroyed humanity, that depleted it, extinguished it, but how happy everyone was, how could they be so full of belief? Where does this credence come from, this faith in what they were experiencing? Now Halil is happy. His wife is pregnant with their second child, his father-in-law made him a partner in his business. Were they really happy? Or was this the happiness of unawareness? Do they think these tiny, sheltered lives were happiness? Yes, they all do. They all do think so. They believe in all this. Their whole life is assuming. They find consolation in what happens to other people on the dramas on television at night, nourishing themselves by nibbling on the adventures of others, they think they themselves are the special beloved that all the songs tell of. The aunties telling each other about what's going on in the magazines and newspapers, about the artists' lives, their latest scandals, their ignominious deeds, their exhibits, their latest clothes, their latest cars, they nibble on their latest fate. And then their children's ailments, the radiator that doesn't work. The only thing in their cheap lives that's expensive is "the cost of living." On the weekend, visits from the neighbors, the blouse bought at the discount store, and the skirt, the summers, the winters, the seasons, all of what life was. And then they become like my mother. Like their mothers. Is Halil happy? Is this everything he wanted from life? What did he say to himself when he got back from military service: "My ideal is a pretty girl, some kids, a good job, living and getting done with it..." Why don't I believe it? What was it about this life that makes me not believe it? As soon as they married, he became a family guy, he goes to the cafes in the neighborhood with his friends, he got fat, greasy, ugly, he became just another man. Wasn't there anything Halil experienced that shocked him? His heart remained whole. He didn't suffer. People only live as much as their hearts do, there isn't one life for all people. My revolt is shouldering all the hearts. Maybe this is what I never knew, never learned. People who never go to the cliff at the edge of the heart infuriate me. Maybe if they had another way of living, maybe if social relations were reorganized, people could really feel all the acreage of the heart, and could live according to it. Maybe someday, maybe in another period of time, people will really be free.

Afterwards, they sent my big sister Pervin (who had stayed at home and become a spinster) to Sweden to get married. She came back a month later. Her husband apparently was having a relationship with the dog they were looking after. They all had slept in the same bed: bride, groom, dog. My sister had gone mad when she came back from Sweden. The Turks there had become heartless and cruel, she reported. (But the groom's family was from the same town with ours, and they had wanted an honorable, presentable girl from Turkey to marry.) After this my sister never married again. She couldn't marry, she resented all men, all people, all countries, all dogs, all mothers and fathers. She spent bilious days in front of her window. She knitted sweaters, shawls, pullovers, and booties forever. She spent her whole life shuffling between the cigarettes she smoked hidden from my mother, hiccupping coughs, and broken laughter.

Then I got stuck on Efkar. Stuck like crazy.

That day, when the Warship went down toward the ocean, I was carrying with me all the loves in the world. All the existing and nonexisting loves that I had witnessed.

I stayed alive, taking stock of others' lives.

Efkar is drinking again. Ümit can't get him to stop.

Ümit understood by then that there was nothing on earth that Efkar loved more than drinking, a lot. The only thing that he wouldn't be able to give up was drinking. He and Ümit understood this together somehow. All the little resentments, the spells of enraged jealousy, the short-lived stints of detachment, the grand and fond moments of reunion, the tears and little laughs, the mutually solicited contritions, the questions of love and vanity, the salt and pepper of any love, any relationship, the variations, the sweet sleeps, the tides—they lived all of it. The people in line at the taxi-bus never forgave them.

They had been together for three years.

One day at the end of three years—they had reached the end of the ocean, they had been picaroons for three years—Efkar said:

"Ümit, do you love me?

This astounded Ümit, who gave a bitter smile and a shoulder shrug. For three years now they'd been talking back and forth about all their experiences. They ought to know each other by now.

"If you love me there is one thing I'm going to want from you. Just one thing."

"Men always want just one thing, their whole life long," said Ümit. "Everything."

This time it was Efkar who smiled bitterly and shrugged.

"Look, I've been with you for three years," he said. "I've worshiped you like Allah, you know that. We've had our sweet days, our bitter days. We've loved each other. A great deal. Every time we've made love, there's been just one thing I've wanted you to keep from me. These three years,

I've resisted with all my might the pressure of the society, my family, my friends. I've protected you, I've protected our love. OUR LOVE IS A SIN. I never let anyone say a bad word about you. Did I? While everyone else thought this was a casual thing, I loved you all the more. But now I have no more strength to resist, to defend you with. Everyone has started looking at me suspiciously. They all must be thinking my skin is starting to look like yours. Now I have something to ask of you. If you love me, if you really love me, take away the thing that you always keep from me when we make love."

"Meaning what?" said Ümit.

"Meaning get the surgery already," said Efkar. "Cut that off, become a woman."

Ümit didn't say anything. Didn't say anything for a long time, eyes just filling with rueful clouds. "Exactly three years," said Ümit. Easier said than done. "After three years, Efkar?"

"We're at a crossroads, Ümit," said Efkar. "You know society, you know the world we live in. We've suffered a lot. We're two people, they're a mob. They hold the world in their hands. Even if we are enough for each other, even if we can rely on each other, how could we ever fight back? The only solution is to be like them," he said.

"You mean, like a painted bird," said Ümit.

"Yes, a painted bird," said Efkar. "Since the painted bird is painted, its peers want to kill it by plucking out its feathers. I can't keep protecting you, I couldn't protect you, forgive me, forgive... This is as far as my strength goes. Now we have to look like them. We have to be like them. We have to take their colors, take society's colors. They're in the majority, we're the minority. Everything gets down to this, we're stuck in a dead-end here," he said. "If you love me, you'll do this, you'll do it for me."

"I love you, but are you aware you are asking to remove myself from me?" said Ümit.

"How much more can we take of this, my love? But if you become a woman, we'll get married. At least we will be married, don't we love each other anyway? Won't we grow old together? Won't we die together?

If you're a woman or a man, what does it matter? If we marry, no one will have anything more to say. We can even leave here if you want, to somewhere else, to other countries. Places we will never be able to return from."

Ümit agonized for days.

Ümit was at the limits of Ümit's body.

Efkar now waits for Ümit to decide—elusive, keeping back. He's cold and as far away as can be. Like he'll walk away, walk away any minute, as if he can walk away. Like he'll never return.

"So you don't love me," says Efkar. "If you loved me you wouldn't hurt me. You don't love me. Or at least it seems so."

One day.... one morning....

"So," said Ümit. "If I get it cut off, if I get the operation, if I become a woman, are you going to believe that I love you?"

"I will believe it," said Efkar. "I'll believe it until I die."

"Until death," said Efkar.

Friends would now call her Golden Scissors. She laid down under the knife, and bid farewell to her manhood as it left her body. She had breasts made, got shots, started getting epilation, cleaned all the hair off her body. Her hair grew and thickened, her thighs and hips widened. The day she was to be discharged from the hospital, she had her long, long hair combed for a long, long time. She was Rapunzel letting her long hair out of the tall castle window for Efkar to hold onto.... And when she left the hospital she ran to Efkar.

"What is my name going to be?" she said to Efkar. "Give me a name, like my mother did, like my father did, as if you gave birth to me anew, created me anew. Give me a name," she said.

"Ümit is fine," said Efkar.

"Can it stay like that?" she said.

And then, not even nine months into her womanhood, Efkar left Ümit.

"I'm sorry," he said. "This isn't going to work. Won't work this way either. I'm not sure why, believe me I don't know, but we have to break up. I just can't. I can't. Can't. Can't."

The ocean finished, they had reached the end or the beginning of the road. They were on the shore from which all seas had retreated. Ümit got out of the Warship. The people waiting in line started to pile in. Without looking back Ümit walked to the end of the road, then heard the taxi bus rolling away. "I'll give myself a name," she said. "From now on, my name is Yudum. Yudum, a mouthful of ocean."

Now Efkar is back spending his evenings at the beerhouses—mixing his vodka, raki, and who knows what. As if nothing had happened, nothing had ever changed, as if he hadn't gone through any of this. IS IT POSSIBLE? IS IT POSSIBLE? Now he's quite a bit sadder than he used to be, quite a bit more Efkar-like. He just drinks, drinks, drinks constantly. The only thing that never changes in his life is the drink. He got a belly, got all oily, his cheeks started to sag, his eyes hang down like empty bags, his gaze lost and bloody, his face matt and heavy.

"Not sure whom or what I love, but I love madly, brother," he says. "I love madly." (Is he going to Hacıbayram again? Is he reading the old folk tales again?)

Yudum is now a nightclub hostess. Mourning after that one man all the time, she distributes herself to all the men, to all the loves, all the lives. Each time around, the love's forever. Thinking about Efkar fills Yudum's heart with a feeling that's like nothingness. Not anger, not rage, not loving, not hatred, just nothing. Nothing. Nothing. Nothing. Now Efkar only has an unnamed ache in his heart, without a name to put on it. Golden Scissors Feride says "Maybe without even knowing it, he killed in you the thing he loved. He didn't know. He couldn't know."

Ümit loves all the men like crazy now, with the same endless love, crying the tears of love every night, tears for the death of love.

March 1984

Translated by David Gramling

THREE FRIENDS

Colm Tóibín (1955–)

Tóibín's fiction is spare and melancholy as well as lucid and frank. He probes the most damaging and degrading aspects of life in the Republic of Ireland. Travel and immigration often expose habits of thought learnt at home, though he espouses movement as a human right. Tóibín is also a gay historian specialising in cultures of concealment. He is Chancellor of the University of Liverpool.

On the Monday, when the others had gone to the hotel for lunch, Fergus stayed alone with his mother's body in the funeral parlour. She would, he knew, have so far enjoyed her own funeral. The hush of conversation with old friends, the conjuring up of memories, the arrival of people she would not have seen for years, all of this would have put a gleam into her eyes. But she would not, he thought, have enjoyed being alone now in the shadowy candlelight with her son, all the life gone out of her. She was not enjoying herself now, he thought.

He was tempted to whisper to her some words of comfort, to say that she would be all right, that she was at peace. He stood up and looked at her. Her dead face had none of her live face's softness. He hoped some day he would be able to forget what she looked like as she lay inert in her coffin, with faint traces of an old distress behind the mask of stillness and peace and immobility. The undertakers or the nurses who had laid her out had made her chin seem firmer and more settled, almost pointed at the end with strange creases. If she spoke now, he knew, her old chin would come back, her old voice, her old smile. But that was all gone now; anyone seeing her for the first time would never know her. She was beyond knowing, he thought, and suddenly realized that he was going to cry.

When he heard the noise of feet outside, a man's heavy shoes against the concrete, he felt almost surprised that someone should come now to break his vigil with her. He had been sitting there as though the door were closed and he could not be disturbed.

The man who appeared was middle-aged and tall; he walked with a slight stoop. He had a mild, modest look; Fergus was sure that he had never seen him before. He paid no attention to Fergus as he moved towards the coffin with a stiff reverence, blessing himself, and then reaching down gently to touch the dead woman's forehead. He had the look of someone from the town, not a neighbour, Fergus felt, but some-one she must have known years earlier. Being on display like this, being touched by anyone who came, would, he knew, have horrified his mother, but she had only a few more hours of it before the coffin would be closed and taken to the cathedral.

The man sat down beside him, still watching his mother's face, gazing at it as though waiting for it to do something in the flickering candle-light. Fergus almost smiled to himself at the idea of telling the man that there was no point in looking at her so intensely, she was dead. The man turned to him as he blessed himself again and offered his large hand and his open-faced sympathy.

'I'm very sorry for your trouble.'

'Thank you,' Fergus replied. 'It was very good of you to come.'

'She's very peaceful,' the man said.

'She is,' Fergus replied.

'She was a great lady,' the man said.

Fergus nodded. He knew that the man would now have to wait for at least ten minutes before he could decently go. He wished that he would introduce himself or give some clue about his identity. They sat in silence looking at the coffin.

As the time elapsed, it seemed odd to Fergus that no one else came. The others surely would have finished at the hotel; his mother's friends had come all morning, and some relatives. It made no sense that all of them had left this gap for Fergus and a stranger to sit so uneasily beside each other for so long. This stretch of time appeared to Fergus to belong to a dark dream which took them out of all familiar elements into a place of dim, shimmering lights, uncomfortable silence, the unending, dull and neutral realm of the dead. As the man cleared his throat, Fergus glanced at him and saw in his dry skin and his pale face further evidence that these minutes did not belong to ordinary time, that they both had been dragged away by his mother's spirit into a place of shadows.

'You were never a hurler,' the man said quietly. His tone was friendly.

'That's right,' Fergus said.

'Conor was the hurler of the family,' the man said.

'He was good in his day all right,' Fergus said.

'Are you the brainy one?'

'No,' Fergus smiled. 'That's Fiach. He's the youngest.'

'Your father,' the man began and hesitated. Fergus looked at him sharply. 'Your father taught me in school.'

'Is that right?'

'I was in the same class as George Mahon. Do you see that dove on the wall there? George drew that.'

He pointed to the back wall of the funeral parlour.

'He was to make a big painting when the place opened. That was just the drawing for it, a kind of preparation. He had to fill in the colours still.'

Fergus looked at the faint outlines in pencil on the wall behind the coffin, he could make out a dove, a few figures and perhaps a hill or a mountain in the distance.

'Why did he not finish it?' Fergus asked.

'Matt's wife,' the man said, 'died suddenly a few weeks before he was ready to open this place and he had to decide whether to coffin her himself or give her to the main competition. So he did it himself, even though this place wasn't finished. It was fine, there was no problem with it, but the painting hadn't been done. And once Matt's wife had been laid out here, George Mahon said he wouldn't come back. He'd be too frightened, he said. The space was all ruined. Or so he said. He couldn't work. You'd never know what'd come up behind you, he said, when you'd be painting here.'

The man spoke in a monotone, staring at the coffin all the time. When Fergus looked away from him, he tried to picture his face, but he could not; his features appeared to fade as soon as Fergus turned. He would, Fergus realized, be hard to describe; tall, but not especially so; thin, but not very thin; his hair brown or sandy-coloured; the face was unremarkable and the voice disembodied. In the silence of the funeral parlour when the man had stopped talking, if someone were to whisper that this man had come to take away his mother's spirit, it would not have seemed strange. It was, for a few seconds, the most likely possibility that this visitor had suspended time to utter banalities and tell stories while he was working to take Fergus's mother away so that all that was left of her to be buried was her spent and useless body.

Soon, however, when the man had left and the others come back, and some neighbours called, the spell was broken and the man's visit seemed ordinary, what was to be expected in a small town, not worth describing to the others, even though it had left its mark.

The next day, as they followed the coffin down the centre aisle of the cathedral towards the waiting hearse, Fergus kept his head down. He listened to the music, the last hymn to be sung for his mother, and tried not to think of the people congregated on each side of the aisle, standing now, studying him and his sisters and brothers and his aunt as they walked slowly towards the main door. When he came to the last few rows, however, he looked around him and was surprised to see three friends from Dublin, from his life at the weekend and from a recent trip to Amsterdam, standing sombre-faced, as though they were ashamed of something, catching his eye now, but not smiling or even nodding at him in recognition. He had never seen them serious before; this must be how they had looked in school when they were in trouble, or during job interviews or when questioned at airports or stopped by the cops. He was tempted to whisper to them, ask laughingly if they had any drugs, but by the time he thought of this he was out in the open.

In the graveyard, his father's gravestone looked like history now, the carved dates already fading. The priest had set up a microphone and a stand at the other side of it. The early September sunshine made the day warm. There was no wind, but nonetheless the whole place seemed oddly windswept. He wondered why they did not grow trees in this graveyard, even evergreens. As the priest began to intone the prayers, Fergus noticed George Mahon the painter and decorator standing close to a gravestone in the distance. He was the only figure in the graveyard who did not come close, who did not huddle in the crowd standing close to the grave. He was over six feet tall and was resting his hands on the headstone. Fergus could feel the power of his gaze, and could sense that George Mahon had drawn an invisible line in the graveyard which he would not cross. He was, as the man who had come to the funeral parlour explained, afraid of the dead. He had known Fergus's mother all of his life so he could not have easily stayed away, but his not coming near the grave, his keen study of the scene around the priest and the hearse and the coffin, the fierce independence of his stance, made Fergus shiver as the coffin was moved towards the open grave.

Afterwards, Fergus stood and shook hands with anyone who came, thanking them and trying to smile. He noticed that one of his sisters was crying. At the end of the line, shyly, stood Mick, Alan and Conal.

'The three musketeers,' he said.

'I'm sorry for your trouble, Fergus,' Mick said and shook his hand. He was wearing a jacket and tie. The other two approached and embraced him softly.

'I'm really sorry,' Alan said.

Conal held his hand and shook his head sadly.

'Will you come to the hotel for a bite?' Fergus asked.

'We'd love to, but we have to go,' Mick smiled. 'When are you heading back to Dublin?'

'Thursday, I think,' Fergus said.

'Will you come around Thursday night, or give us a ring on the mobile?'

'OK, thanks, I'll do that.'

On the night after the funeral, he and his siblings and his brother-in-law drank until four in the morning. Most of them stayed over the next night, promising each other that they would go to bed early, but over dinner they began to drink wine and then went on to beer and whiskey until there was nothing left but more wine which Fergus and his sisters and brothers drank until the dawn had long appeared. He did not wake until the early afternoon. It was Thursday now and time to leave. He had planned all along to stop at the graveyard on the way out of the town and stand by his mother's grave and offer to her, or receive from her, some comfort, but he was tired and drained. All night they had laughed until there were no more funny stories left. He felt a gnawing guilt at her death as he drove past the graveyard, as though he were implicated in its cause. Rather than move closer to her, he needed to get away from her house, her grave, the days of her funeral. He drove directly to his house in Stoneybatter, dreaming that he would never go out again, but would sleep once darkness was down and do this night after night.

As he was preparing for bed, the phone rang. It was Mick.

'It doesn't matter about tonight,' he said. 'It matters about tomorrow night. We have something special for you. The lads are coming. It's a beach rave.'

'No,' Fergus said. 'I'm not coming.'

'You have to come,' Mick said.

'I'm too old for techno,' Fergus said. 'Actually, I take that back. Techno is too boring for me. And I hate beaches.'

'This is special. I said it was special. Bring two warm pullovers and a big towel.'

'No.'

'Nine o'clock at my place. I'm driving. If it's boring I'll leave with you. But please come.'

'Nine?' Fergus asked and laughed for a moment.

'Nine sharp,' Mick replied.

'And we can stay for half an hour?'

'It'll be nine in the morning and you won't want to leave,' Mick said.

They set out from the city when night had fallen. It was warm as they drove north; they kept the windows open until Alan lit a joint and then they closed them so they could enjoy wallowing in the smoke. Already, in Mick's flat, they had each snorted a line of cocaine, which had made Fergus feel sharp and nervous, and oddly lucid. He pulled on the joint with all his energy, taking too much smoke in, and then concentrating on holding it, relishing the taste and the power as he closed his eyes; he felt almost faint. He put his head back as a thrill of weakness coursed through him. He was ready to sleep, but it was a readiness which came with darting thoughts which led nowhere. He tried to relax in the back of the car, taking pleasure in the battle going on between the golden lethargy which the dope brought and the sweet electric shock of the cocaine.

'You know something?' Alan said. 'I felt so bad after your old lady's funeral that I decided I was neglecting mine. So I bought her flowers and went out to see her.'

'A small step for mankind,' Conal said.

'I should have phoned her first,' Alan said, 'but she's no good on the phone, she treats it like it was a poisonous snake.'

'How long was it since you'd seen her?' Mick asked.

'June. And the time before that was February and she kept nagging at me about it and I said: "Well, I'm here now," as though that would make up for everything. And she nearly bit me. She kept saying: "That's all very well." She gets very narked very easily.'

'Is that where you get it from?' Mick asked.

'So I turn up with the flowers and there's no one there and Miss Bitch next door appears in her apron and shouts at me that I'm not getting the key. "And your mother's in Italy," she says. And on a beach, if you don't mind, one of the trendy places, with oul' Mrs Kingston, buying up property the two of them, or new earrings.'

'What did you do with the flowers?' Mick asked.

'I fucked them into the bin beside the bus stop.'

'Jesus,' Conal said. 'Maybe we shouldn't be talking like this in front of Fergus. Are you all right, Fergus?'

'I'm fine,' Fergus said. He had his head back and his eyes closed.

'There'll be more white powder when we get there,' Mick said. 'Don't worry.'

'I'm ready for bed,' Fergus said. 'When I was a kid I used to love staying in the car while the rest of them went down to the strand.'

'Well, you've grown up now,' Mick said.

Mick drove slowly, once he was off the main road. Fergus guessed that they were somewhere between Drogheda and Dundalk but heading directly towards the coast, or driving parallel to it. He noticed that Mick had difficulty seeing in front of him because of patches of thick fog which appeared at intervals. He stopped several times and switched on the dim overhead light so he could consult a page of elaborate directions.

'We're very near now, but I have instructions not to ask for directions from anyone or behave suspiciously,' Mick said. 'I'm looking for a second bungalow on the right and then I have to turn down a narrow, sandy lane.'

'Are you sure someone isn't making a complete eejit out of you?' Alan asked.

'Yeah, I am. It's the same crowd who did the last one. They're sound.'

He stopped at the second bungalow and got out of the car to check in the fog that there was a lane to the right.

'We're here,' he said. 'Down this lane and we're there.'

Briars and brambles hit against the body of the car as they drove along the narrow lane, so rutted that a few times something seemed to cut through the underbelly of the car and Mick was almost forced to stop. They were silent as though frightened as the car rocked from side to side more than it appeared to move forward. When the lane ended, Mick opened the window and they could hear the roar of the sea. He parked the car close to a number of others. Once they opened the doors and stood out in the night the sound of electronic music came clearly towards them from the distance. Fergus noticed that there was a mild, warm wind coming in from the sea, like a summer wind, even though the summer just ended had offered nothing but low skies and constant rain.

'We should have a snort here in the car so the wind won't blow it away,' Mick said.

They sat back into the car, closing the doors and the windows, and Mick laid out the lines neatly on the surface of a CD cover. Having waited his turn to snort the cocaine, using a fifty-euro note which Mick recommended, Fergus relished the sour taste of the powder as it made its way towards the back of his throat. He swallowed hard so that he could taste it better and then, since he was the last, he put his finger on the CD cover to absorb any stray grains of white powder and rubbed them into his gums.

In a holdall, they carried pullovers and towels, bottles of water and cans of beer, and a bottle of tequila. They stood watching as a set of head-lights appeared and a car approached and parked and six or seven dazed figures emerged from it. Mick lit a joint and passed it around.

'We're not too early and we're not too late,' he said.

With the help of a torch, he guided them along a headland towards the music, which came from a sheltered cove, down a set of steep stone steps from a field which they had crossed.

'The music is boring,' Fergus whispered to Mick.

Mick handed him the joint again. He pulled on it twice and then handed it back.

'I want you to close your eyes and open your mouth,' Mick said. He shone the torch into Fergus's face as Alan and Conal stood by laughing. Fergus saw Mick biting a tablet in two; as he closed his eyes, Mick put one half on his tongue.

'Swallow that,' he said. 'It's what doctors recommend for boredom.'

The organizers must have been working all day, Fergus thought, as soon as he saw the lights and the generators and the powerful speakers and decks. They had set up an elaborate, instant disco in the cove, with throbbing lights and loud techno, but far away enough from the nearest house or road that if they were lucky they would remain undisturbed all through the night. It was still early, he knew, and even though the Ecstasy tablet had not begun to affect him, the cocaine, the dope and the fresh sea air made him feel exhilarated, ready for a night which would not end, as nights in the city invariably ended, with bouncers shouting and places closing too early and no taxis in the city centre and nowhere to go save home.

As they joined the crowd, leaving their belongings in a safe place in the darkness, about thirty people were dancing. Some of them looked like friends who had travelled together, or maybe they had just become friends, Fergus thought, as they coordinated their movements while also remaining tightly apart from each other.

He stood at the edge of the dancers sipping from a can of beer which Mick had handed him, aware that he was being watched by a tall, skinny, black-haired guy who was dancing to a beat of his own invention, pointing at the sky and then pointing at Fergus and smiling. He was glad that he had spent enough time among straight people to know that the dancer had taken Ecstasy; he was happy and was smiling to show this. It was not a come-on, even though it could seem like one; there was no sexual content in what he was doing. He was like a child. Fergus pointed his finger at him to the stark dull rhythm of the music and smiled back.

He noticed that his nose and chin were tingling with pins and needles as the Ecstasy made its way through his body with its message of support. He began to dance, with Mick and Alan and Conal dancing close by. He was pleased that they were beside him, but he felt no need to look at them or speak to them, or even smile at them. Whatever was happening now with the drugs and the night and the tinny piercing sounds as the tempo rose and the volume was turned up meant that he was wholly connected to them, a part of the group they had formed. He needed only to feel that connection and a rush of warmth would go through him and he hoped that he might stay like that until the dawn and maybe after the dawn into the next day.

When he and Mick had shared another tablet and drunk some water and smoked a joint together, the music, in all its apparent monotony, and then its almost imperceptible variations, began to interest Fergus, pull him towards it with a greater force than the faces or the bodies around him. He listened out for changes in tone and beat, following the track of the music with the cool energy which the night, as it wore on, offered him. He kept close to the others and they to him. They pushed against each other sometimes in mock aggression, dancing in strange and suddenly invented harmonies, smiling at each other, or touching each other in reassurance, before stepping easily away, each of them dancing alone in the surging crowd.

Mick was in control, deciding when joints would be lit, more pills taken, beer sipped, water swigged, or when all four of them should retreat from the crowd, lie on their towels on the sand smoking, laughing, barely talking, knowing that there would be much more time to dance, and that this was a small respite which Mick thought they would need from the shifting beauty of the music and the dancers.

*

All night they moved around each other, as though they were guarding something deeply playful and wonderful that would disappear if they ceased to remain close. Fergus could feel the sand in his hair and embedded in the sweat down his back and in his trainers. Sometimes he felt tired, and then it seemed that the tiredness itself was impelling him, allowing him to sway with the music, and smile and close his eyes and hope that time was passing slowly, that this cocoon of energy had been left alone for the moment and could enclose him and keep him safe against the night.

It seemed hours later when Mick took him aside and made him move away from the lights and showed him the first stirrings of the dawn in the horizon over the sea. It resembled grey and white smoke in the distance, no redness or real sign of the sun. It looked more like fading light than the break of day. They joined the dancers again for the last stretch under the frantically flickering lights.

As the first rays of sun hit the strand, the light remained grey and uneasy as though it were building up for a day of low clouds and rain. Shivering, they walked over to where they had left the pullovers and towels and began to swig from the tequila bottle. At first it tasted like poison.

'This is rich in toxic energy,' Fergus said. Alan fell down on the soft sand in laughter.

'You sound like God the father, or Einstein,' Conal said.

Mick was putting the towels into the holdall, and checking to make sure that they had left no litter.

'I've got bad news,' he said. 'We're going for a swim.'

'Ah, Jesus!' Alan said.

'I'm on for it,' Conal said, standing up and stretching. 'Come on, Alan, it'll make a man of you.'

He helped Alan to his feet.

'I've no togs,' Alan said.

'And no clean underpants either, I bet.'

Mick handed Fergus the bottle of tequila, which they drank from as they walked away from the last ravers to a point at the far end of the cove, where there was nobody. Mick left down the holdall, took out a towel which he left on the sand and began to undress. He handed an Ecstasy tablet to Alan and Conal.

'This will warm you up,' he said.

He bit on another and handed half of it to Fergus, who was suddenly aware of Mick's saliva on the jagged edge of the pill he put into his mouth, and sharply alert to the afterglow of the long hours when they had been sharing and touching and staying close. He stood on the strand watching Mick until he was fully undressed, realizing with a gasp that he was going naked into the water.

'Last in is Charlie Haughey,' Mick shouted as he neared the edge of the sea.

In the strange, inhospitable half-light, his body seemed oddly and powerfully awkward, his skin blotchy and white. Soon, Alan followed him, also naked, skinnier, shivering, dancing up and down to keep the cold at bay. Conal wore his underpants as he moved gingerly towards the water. Fergus slowly undressed, shivering too, watching as the others shrieked at the cold water, jumping to avoid each wave, until the look of them there began to interest him. Mick and Conal chose the same moment to dive under an incoming wave.

As soon as his feet touched the water, Fergus stepped back. He watched the other three cavorting further out, swimming with energy and abandon, letting themselves be pulled inwards by the waves, and then diving under as though the water itself were a refuge from the cold. This, he thought, as he wrapped his arms around his body to keep warm, and allowed his teeth to chatter, was going to be an ordeal, but he could not return to the strand and dress himself now; he would have to be brave and join the others, who showed no sign of coming back to dry land as they beckoned him not to be a baby.

He made himself think for a moment that he was nobody and nothing, that he had no feelings, that nothing could hurt him as he waded into the water. He crashed into a wave as it came towards him and then dived under it and did a breast stroke out towards his friends. His mother, he remembered, had always been so brave in the water, never hesitating at the edge for a single second, always marching determinedly into the cold sea. She would not have been proud of him now, he thought, as he battled with the idea that he had wet himself enough and could run back quickly to the strand and dry himself. He dismissed the thought, tried to stay under the water and move blindly, thrashing about as much as he could to keep warm. When he reached his friends, they laughed and put their arms around him and then began an elaborate horseplay in the water which made him forget about the cold.

When Alan and Conal waded in towards the shore, Mick stayed behind with Fergus, who was oblivious enough now to the cold that he could spread his arms out and float, staring up at the sky growing lighter. Mick did not venture far from him, but after a while urged him to swim out further to a sandbank where the waves made no difference and it was easy to float and stand and float again. As they swam out they kept close and hit against each other casually a few times, but when they found the bank Fergus felt Mick touching him deliberately, putting his hand on him and keeping it there. Fergus felt his own cock stiffen. When Mick moved away he floated on his back, too happy in the water to care if Mick saw his erection, being certain that Mick would swim back towards him before long.

He did not even open his eyes when Mick swam in between his legs and, surfacing, held his cock, putting the other hand under him. When he tried to stand, he realized that Mick was holding him, trying to enter him with the index finger of his right hand, pushing and probing until he was deep inside. Fergus winced and put his arms around Mick's neck, moving his mouth towards Mick's until Mick began to kiss him fiercely, biting his tongue and lips as he stood on the sandbank. When Fergus reached down, he could feel Mick's cock, hard and rubbery in the water. He smiled, almost laughed, at the thought of how difficult it would be to suck a cock under water.

'I have sort of wanted to do this,' Mick said, 'but just once. Is that all right?'

Fergus laughed and kissed him again. As Mick worked on his cock with his hand, he tried to ease a second finger into him and Fergus cried out but did not pull away. He spread his legs as wide as he could, letting the second finger into him slowly, breathing deeply so that he could open himself more. He held his two arms around Mick's neck and put his head back, closing his eyes against the pain and the thrill it gave. In the half-light of morning he began to touch Mick's face, feeling the bones, sensing the skull behind the skin and the flesh, the eye sockets, the cheekbones, the jawbone, the forehead, the inert solidity of teeth, the tongue that would dry up and rot so easily, the dead hair.

Mick was not masturbating him now, but putting all his concentration into his two fingers, moving them in and out roughly. Fergus touched Mick's cock, his hips, his back, his balls; then he began to direct his energy, all of it, all of his drug-lined grief and pure excitement, into taking Mick's tongue in his mouth, holding it there, offering his tongue in return, tasting his friend's saliva, his breath, his feral self. He realized that neither of them wanted to ejaculate; it would, somehow, be a defeat, the end of something, but neither could they decide to stop, even though both of them were shivering with the cold. Fergus became slowly aware that Alan and Conal were standing on the strand watching them. When finally the water became too cold for them and they began to wade in towards the shore, the other two turned away nonchalantly.

By the time they were all dressed and ready to walk back towards the car, the day had dawned. They passed the organizers taking the machinery of the previous night asunder, working with speed and efficiency.

'How do they make their money?' Alan asked.

'They make it on other nights,' Mick said, 'but they do this out of love.'

Mick had to reverse the car without any passengers so that the wheels would not get stuck in the sand. When he had the car turned, Fergus sat in the front passenger seat and the two others in the back. They rocked silently along the lane, the brambles on each side laden with blackberries. Fergus remembered some road out of his town, empty of traffic with tall trees in the distance, and each of them, his brothers and sisters and his mother, with a colander or an old saucepan gathering blackberries from the bushes in the ditches, his mother the most assiduous, the busiest, filling colander after colander into the red bucket in the back seat of the old Morris Minor.

As they made their way from a side road towards the main Dublin road, Fergus realized that he could not face the day alone. He was not sleepy, although he was tired; he was, more than anything, restless and excited. The taste from Mick's mouth, the weight of him in the water, the feel of his skin, the sense of his excitement, had allied themselves now with the remnants of the drugs and the tequila to make him want Mick again, want him alone in a bedroom, with clean sheets and a closed door. He regretted that he had not come off in the sea, and was sorry too that he had not made Mick come off with him. Their sperm mingling with the salt water and the slime and the sand would have put an end to his yearnings, for a time at least. He knew that his house was the first stop as they entered the city; he wished he could turn to Mick, without the two in the back overhearing, and ask him to stay with him for a while.

When Alan asked Mick to stop the car, announcing that he was going to be sick, and Mick pulled in on the hard shoulder of the dual carriageway, they watched him without comment as he heaved and vomited, listening calmly to the retching sounds. Fergus thought then that it might be a good moment to mention to Mick that he could not go home alone.

'Conal, why don't you go and help him?' he asked.

'He always pukes,' Conal said. 'It's genetic, he says. There's nothing I can do for him. He's a wimp. His father and mother were wimps too. Or so he says, anyway.'

'Did they go to raves?' Mick asked.

'Whatever it was in their day,' Conal replied. 'Dances, I suppose, or hops.'

Alan, much chastened and very pale, got back into the car. Since there was no traffic, Fergus knew that he would be home in half an hour. He would have no chance now to tell Mick what he wanted. He could try later on the phone, but this would be a day when Mick might not answer the phone. His own desperate need might have abated by then in any case, become dull sadness and disappointment.

His small house, when he came in the door, seemed to have been hollowed out from something, the air inside it felt trapped, specially filtered to a sort of thinness. The sun was shining through the front window so he went immediately to close the curtains, creating the pretence that it was still the early morning. He thought of putting music on the CD player, but no music would please him now, just as alcohol would not help and sleep would not come. He felt then that he could walk a hundred miles if he had somewhere to go, some clear destination. He was afraid of nothing now save that this feeling would never fade. His heart was beating in immense dissatisfaction at how life was; the echo of the music in his ears and the aftershine of the flashing lights in his eyes were still with him. He felt as though he had been brushed by the wings of some sharp knowledge, some exquisite and mysterious emotion almost equal to the events of the past week. He lay on the sofa, dazed and beaten by his failure to grasp what had been offered to him, and fell into a stupor rather than a sleep.

He did not know how much time had passed when someone banged the knocker on the front door. His bones ached as he went automatically to answer it. He had forgotten what he had wanted so badly in the car, but as soon as he saw Mick, who looked as though he had gone home and showered and changed his clothes, he remembered. Mick had a bag of groceries in his hand.

'I'm not coming in unless you promise that you'll wash all that sand out of every orifice,' Mick said.

'I promise,' Fergus said.

'Immediately,' Mick insisted.

'OK.'

'I'll make breakfast,' Mick said.

Fergus deliberately turned the hot-water tap on too high to see if this could restore him to the state of excitement he had been in. He washed and shaved and found fresh clothes. Quickly, he changed the sheets and the duvet on his bed. When he came downstairs the table was set; there was steaming tea and scrambled eggs and toast and orange juice. They ate and drank ravenously, without speaking.

'I would have bought the morning papers,' Mick said, 'except I can barely see.'

Fergus wondered how quickly he could move Mick to the bedroom once breakfast was finished. He smiled at him and nodded in the direction of upstairs.

'Are you ready so?' he asked.

'I am, I suppose, but I haven't been converted or anything. Just once, OK?'

'You said that before.'

'I was drugged. I mean it this time.'

Mick took out a small plastic bag from his pocket and pushed back the tablecloth to the bare wood of the table. With his credit card he began to make two long orderly lines of cocaine. He took a fifty-euro note from his pocket.

'Which of us goes first?' he asked and grinned.

WORDS

Neil Bartlett (1958–)

A theatre director by trade, Bartlett is also known as a translator, performer and novelist. His work shows an interest in the footprint of history on modern life and the pervasive influence of literature and tradition. He is an expert in queer history and has written about his perspectives on the AIDS crisis from within the theatre world of 1980s London.

Mere words! Was anything so real as words!

I have no words for how I love you.

The letter L section of the *New English Dictionary*, the first self-proclaimed "complete" English Dictionary, and which was later to be the *Oxford English Dictionary*, was written from 1901 to 1903. This is the recognized authority on the words from which Wilde and the others contrived their language. It is the guide I am supposed to turn to. It devotes three and a half pages to the definition of the word love. This is a dictionary without peer, and so I read it carefully when it tells me that Love is *that feeling of attachment which is based upon difference of sex; the affection which subsists between lover and sweetheart and is the normal basis of marriage.* Love: *used specifically with reference to love between the sexes.* Love: *to have a passionate attachment to a person of the opposite sex.* I have no place in these pages, although I wonder if the editor knew what he was doing when he cited a quotation from A. E. Housman (*A Shropshire Lad XVIII*, 1896) as one of his authorities on the subject: *Oh when I was in love with you, then I was clean and brave.* At the end of the nineteenth century we had no name, even if we had the daring to speak. Under "H" (written between 1897–99) there is no entry for **Homosexual** (although one was included in the 1972 Supplement); there are entries for **Effeminate** (1888–93), **Invert** (1899–1901) and **Pervert** (1904–09), but I looked them up and none of them refer to us. We do appear at considerable length as **Sodomites** and **Buggers**, but these words are used of us, not by us.

According to the *Dictionary*, we had no voice of our own. Don't you believe it. In a different part of the city, our language was spoken, if not recorded. Our history is not a gallery of mute faces. We were using then the words we are using now, the words…

Oh! The shame of it, the shame of it. To tell it is to live through it all again. Actions are the first tragedy in life, words are the second. Words are perhaps the worst. Words are merciless… Oh!

The Dictionary is not a record of speech. Its tone is studiously academic. Among all the books of the library, the most precious and the hardest to find are those which record a man speaking for himself.

I met them in Soho Square. He took his hat off respectfully. "Go ahead, and I'll follow," said I… (We) crossed Oxford Street, to a long street, out of which turning up a paved court, he opened with a latch key a door, and up we all went to a first floor over a shop, and into a well-furnished sitting-room, and a bedroom.

"Are you fond of a bit of brown"—he asked—I did not understand and he explained.—"We always say a bit of brown among ourselves"— he questioned me—had I been up a man. "No"—There was no pleasure like it.—"Shall I suck it?" "You?"—"Yes?"—"Do you do so?"—"Lord yes, I have had it so thick in my mouth, that I've had to pick it out of my mouth with a toothpick." … "Do let me sod you" said he all at once quite affectionately; "I should so like to do it to you and take your virginity."

A pick-up in the 1870s; from My Secret Life, Volume 6 pp 131–4.

A text such as this is moving, one hundred years on, not because of anything that is said, but because of the language that is used to say it. I suddenly realize that I recognize the words, that words I use have been used by others. I wasn't the first to talk like this, or to be attracted to someone because they do. Even if my phrasing sometimes seems forced, tentative, there is always this language, these ridiculous and lovable and necessary words that for a hundred years have been springing from the mouths of those men, the others. I recognize the voice because it is *ours*. In the enforced silence of the library, which is no more a still or quiet silence than the frantic rustling of a busy cottage, there is a moment of intimacy. I understand what this Soho queen of the 1870s is saying. This fragment of her voice, small as it is, tells me that there was a different world (how sweet is that *among ourselves*), a different experience of sex (of course being fucked is a pleasure) and, best of all, a different language (*I did not understand*—the tables are turned for once, it is he who is baffled by our words).

When we speak in our own language, we destroy the notion that talking about a gay experience is even worse than doing it. The best thing about talking dirty is that it makes both the act and the description clean; expressible, visible, imaginable. This technique of deliberate utterance becomes even more powerful when transferred from sex to other areas of our lives. To speak of sex is an abomination so widely acknowledged and broken as to be only a token taboo; *sod* was a common word then, and *fuck* is a common word now. But what if the Soho queen had talked of love? Imagine whispering to another man: *I want you to take care of me.*

Even these whisperings have a history. In the years between Wilde's London and mine the silences of the *Dictionary* were gradually filled in, by more or less hostile languages, languages that spoke of us, named us: medical, legal, "scientific", journalistic languages. Meanwhile, we were speaking for and of ourselves. We were speaking in the first person, rather than being talked about. The voices of confession and allusion, the documentary voice of the case study or the witness stand were not the only voices we used. It is not true that we were speechless or nameless. Our declarations of love were not always as tongue-tied as Basil Hallward's for Dorian Gray, or as Wilde's for Bosie (*You are the divine thing I want... but I don't know how to do it*). We talked among ourselves.

> *The position of a young man so tormented is really that of a man buried alive and conscious, but deprived of speech.*
>
> Edmund Gosse to J. A. Symonds, 5 March 1890.

The need to talk among ourselves has made our language elaborate. Not for us the literary "realism" and simplicity of expression that is meant to characterize a confession or autobiography. At times we have talked in languages that no one else could understand. Wilde delighted in the language of imported poets and novelists—the strange ones—Mallarmé, the Flaubert of *St Antoine*, Verlaine, Baudelaire, Huysmans—those in whose hands words again became obscure, precious, horrid with new meanings. His delight was not just "literary". On the worst evening of Dorian Gray's life, the evening when he must dispose of the body of a man he has murdered (since such handsome, bloody evidence will surely give away his terrible secret, reveal him for what he really is), on that very evening Wilde has Gray elegantly pick up his copy of the 1881 Charpentier-Jacquemart edition of the poems of Théophile Gautier. He knows that a few obscure words in a foreign language have the power to transport him to another country, another city. He is safe again. Dorian, like his creator, understands the real Importance of Speaking Differently. Only a hundred pages into the novel, we recognize this devotion to *that curious jewelled style, vivid and obscure at once, full of argot and archaisms, of technical expressions and of elaborate phrases*. He could be describing Symbolist literature, or gay street talk, or talking dirty. The obscurity (*Keep your horrible secrets to yourself*) allows the man who writes or talks like this to distance himself from polite language. He can speak more or less in code, create areas of meaning that are open only to the initiate. He can speak to those he wishes to address. In Wilde's exotic, allusive vocabulary, high literature aspires to the status of slang.

This style was to bear its deadliest fruit in the works of Genet, where the thief (the connoisseur) was to litter his texts with *expressions banales, vidés, creusés, invisibles* (banal, empty, worn-out, unnoticed). A true queen, he too hoarded words that no one else fancied, words that no one else loved or could understand, just as Dorian furnished his house with what others would find revolting or incomprehensible. Genet's Divine Divine chooses to frock herself in other, uncherished colours on the day when the whole of France wears the red, white and blue; I hoard all these ridiculous words, the ones my straight friends don't understand, and I write them here. Genet created his style (in a prison cell, just like Wilde) because, he said, he was "*reprenant ma vie*", keeping hold of his own life, talking to and for himself, keeping hold of his own experience, refusing to let it be taken over, spoken, rephrased in the language of the majority. I remember reading Genet for the first time, when I was a boy in a small town and had no one else to tell me stories, barely understanding a word (since I had no idea that the city was a real place, that one day my friends would be queens, that I too would walk home at dawn in the tatters of my drag, singing and drunk and in love), but sensing that these words were somehow meant for our ears only. And I remember that there are passages in Dorian Gray's story that sound as though they should only be whispered, late at night, by one man to another.

The *Dictionary* does not record a comprehensive gay slang in use in the nineteenth century. But the fragments I've been able to re-collect can be strung together; we had invented at least the idea of another, a different language. Remnants, single words, remain in our contemporary speech. Later, in the forties and fifties, our city was decorated with a gay slang of which whole sentences survive. *Polari* epitomizes the pleasures of being incomprehensible. It was designed to be used, if necessary, within earshot of the naffs; a true code. Now we use it only for pleasure; its expressions, however gorgeous, are now archaic, because we sense that speaking or living entirely in code is no longer a historical necessity. We are in the luxurious position of being able, sometimes and if we choose, to speak plainly for ourselves. We don't have to speak apart from the world. But the words are still there, however, should we need or want them, lying like spare jewellery in the bottom of the drawer. Some of them are replace-able—*hair*, *face*, *look*, *man* and *woman* will do for *riah*, *eek*, *varda*, *omi* and *polone*—if you don't mind the rest of the bus understanding you when you shriek your disapproval of an especially unfortunate haircut. Some are still used from necessity, because there is no precise equivalent. There is no word as accurate as *bona*, unless you are comfortable with the American *hot* as a commendation of an especially striking stranger; *cruise* doesn't capture the tackiness of *troll*; and anyway, who wants to *discuss* rather than *dish* a friend? Mostly the words are dusted off and brought out when we wish to *zhoosh* up the conversation, to announce a particular delight in our queenly style. This style is sometimes talked of as if it was extinct, an anthropologist's relic from *those days*. The *omi-polones* who created the language have changed into other crea-tures, but our past is not silenced. Gay men whose attitudes and self image are unrestrained by debts to the past can still use the words when they choose; one of the distinctive pleasures of our society is that our past is still with us, the words and the styles of the 1890s, or 1950s, are still being reused and rephrased, played with. Consider the pages of our dictionary again. Do you recognize any of the words there from your own lexicon of gossip, seduction or obscenity? Perhaps you also use the words *queen*, *trade* or *drag*. Does it follow that you would then be able to talk to, understand, even flirt with those men from ninety years ago, if on some extraordinary drugged evening we could all meet? It would be like costume night at the pub; such strangely different styles and voices, but no one a stranger. Since so much of our verbal finery is handed down, we would recognize some of the words and phrases. Would they still describe the same experiences? Would there be enough for us all to talk to one another?

The city changes. As we no longer speak only in private, or only in slang, or only in books, how do we, now, a hundred years on, talk about our lives? Our style must still always be various, chameleon, our speech adaptable, since we speak in such different locations, public and private (the bus, the bar, the bedroom, the living room); it must also accommodate itself to the fact that not everyone speaks the same language at the same time. East still meets West End; a butch queen can't be butch all the time; and a sixteen-year-old must talk to a sixty-year-old. A particular sentence must have a different meaning for a man who is still waiting to come out, a man who is rarely in a room filled with other gay men, and for a man who goes to a gay pub at least three times a week, who has a lover and has been on the scene for six years. A pub in Soho does not speak the same language as a pub in Wimbledon. An opera queen may want to confess to the crudest desire.

And our speech must constantly acknowledge and play with the fact that there is and cannot be a language that is ours alone. Our words are not entirely under our own control. The city of 1895 which I'd set out to explore only rarely had places that belonged entirely to us (the bedrooms, as always; some cruising grounds that were relatively undisturbed; some private houses). We think of our city as different, as having a relative wealth of spaces that are ours. But the language we use is still partly the language of the city that surrounds us. We use the same words. I would defend the right of any queen to go looking for a "real man"; but hidden in that phrase are straight ideas and straight desires waiting to surprise even those of us who really thought we knew what we were doing. Even those books which are for our eyes only (gay porn) continually phrase themselves in terms of a masculinity, a maleness which is hardly under our control. *Teleny*, published in 1893 and London's first gay porn novel, is full of gay characters and incidents, and certainly included gay men among its authors. It seems to relate our story, in our language, because it seems that this text—hidden for so long and part of our dark, private world, speaking a pornographic language which seems hardly to have changed at all—this text speaks of how close to our history I am, of how we created our own lives and own desires even then. But just at the moment when my reading of it becomes tense, and excited, the text will, without pausing for breath, without changing its identity, lapse into vitriolically misogynist, heterosexual phrasings when it wants to eulogize the sole object of its devotion, a man's cock. The idea that this is in any sense a "gay language" evaporates. There is no separate stream of language, a gutter of arcane gossip, that we can claim as ours. Our language has always been part of the other languages which the *Dictionary* assembles. We should not be misled by the fact that a new word, "homosexual", had to be invented to describe us. All the other words we use to articulate our lives come to us loaded with existing meanings, and as we try to use them in new, appropriate ways we must be careful. We must remember that even the simplest words, the word "man" for instance, have a history. They have a life of their own.

All the time, I needed to find our own words, even if I spoke the same language as other men. I knew from experience that this speech would be marred and decorated by resistance and confusion. We have very different things to express. This requires the invention of different mannerisms and inflections to alter the meaning of our city's language. I listened to my peers, to the continuous gay chatter of the past hundred years, and I learnt how to do it.

Our first experience of talking *as* gay men (which is always different from talking *of* gay men) is the experience of lying. I overhear lies again and again in the London of a hundred years ago. How else could Oscar Wilde have possibly spoken to Constance, what would have made any sense to her at all, since a married woman living in Chelsea could never have learnt the language of Lisle Street, or Leicester Square, or the

Alhambra. We all still grow up as liars. At a certain point we become expert in describing our experiences falsely, as in "I am going to London for the weekend." Certain words become especially false: "I went out with a *friend*" (although a lover or a man you've just slept with is not a friend) or "I went to the pub" (a gay pub is not just the pub). Wilde was familiar with this mode, the testing of lies. When he tried to explain to Bosie's mother what had happened, he said, *I went as far as I could possibly go.* He took a deep breath and calmly said that he had first met Bosie when he was in *very serious trouble of a very particular character.* One of his characters notes that: *A short primer,* When to Lie and How, *if brought out in an attractive and not too expensive a form, would no doubt command a large sale.* Wilde himself later completed such a text, but it is not short, and is entitled *The Complete Works of Oscar Wilde.*

After this education, we have our revenge. Forced to deny the real meaning of some words, we invest others with senses that the other world would rather keep them pure of. Our revenge on the myth that we are without family, that we lead lives of thoughtless promiscuity, is to redistribute the conventional endearments of family, love and marriage with gay abandon: on our lips, *dear, darling, sister, daddy, boy, baby, mother, girl* are all free to fly from friend to lover to colleague to stranger. Striking even deeper, we describe one another, and those who listen to and watch us as *him* or *her* exactly as and when it suits us. The small phrase *look at her,* as applied to a straight man by a queen holding court with her sisters, redraws the perspectives of the city. It undermines the authority of the dictionary in its function of guide book to our culture's sights and monuments.

Creative abuse, now as then, is not enough. It makes our descriptions of the world seem forever provisional (perhaps that is their, and our, greatest strength). Consider our descriptions of our relationships. Our life is not the life of August 1894, but I always enjoy asking a friend, in all drunken seriousness, *how's the wife?* We both know that there is no useful comparison between heterosexual marriage and the relationship being referred to. But in using the word, I recall the house at

46 Fitzroy Street, WC1, where on 12 August 1894 Alfred Taylor and Charles Mason were arrested with sixteen other men, including one Arthur Marling, taken away in a frock of black and gold lace. Was it in that house that Taylor "married" Mason? What did they wear? If there was a ceremony, at least a gathering of other gay men, then it may have been staged as serious or riotous; but whatever the tone of the evening, it announced their participation in a tradition of gay London (and Paris; remember the Princess Salomé) which reaches back at least to the early eighteenth century. Then queens in frocks were called *mollies;* they refered to sex as *marriage,* to the private room in the pub where they met as the *chapel,* and they staged their own frocked-up ceremonies, behind closed doors, in their own world, on their own terms. They insolently affirmed the status of a gay relationship by dressing it up in full finery; and their parody expressed all the real and lovely bitterness we feel that our loves are not solemnized or publicly celebrated. Oscar wrote to Alfred and Charles to wish them well in their marriage, and in *The Portrait of Mr W.H.* in 1889 he wished that Shakespeare might have pleaded with his boy, *This great friendship of ours is indeed a marriage.* And so we are right still to use the word (the word still fits) because we have been using it for so long, because in using it we invite those men from Fitzroy Street to be our witnesses, because the word acknowledges how precious and how ludicrous such love truly is. Of course we continue to use the word; how could we not? We grew up knowing that "love", "security", "sex" and "property" should all find their home within "marriage", and we know that our desire for (some of) these things is as real as anyone else's. Of course the word is fragile; its complexities of meaning must be handled deftly. The joke can wear thin; I would despair if anyone were actually to treat me as his wife, make me stand behind his shoulder.

And often I wish that I had a word for the kind of couple we are. I still wish sometimes that I could leave London, that there was a new language for us, another dictionary entirely. The existing words can become inadequate, painful. And *I love you* still seems much harder to say than, *I want you to fuck me.* We know that declarations of love between men are different, the words cannot have (we do not wish them to have) the same weight or meanings that they had for our parents. That is why I hunt through the *fin-de-siècle* queen's vocabulary for inspiration and reassurance; that is why I listen carefully when an older man dusts off the phrases of forty years ago. That is why we love to chatter, to bitch, to talk in slang, to talk dirty, to learn the different languages peculiar to our version of the city, to rephrase ourselves continually. We want the pleasure of saying what we mean.

Can you say what you mean to him (not just *him,* but any chosen man, anyone to whom you are giving or from whom you are taking any of the pleasures we choose to describe as love)? That is, do you have words for your love, a hundred years after we dared not speak our name, a hundred years after Oscar was speechless with love? (I could hardly continue reading the letters the night I read, *I have no words for how I love you,* in the same letter of July 1894 as he wrote, *I can't live without you.* That he should say that, the man who spent his whole life talking, writing words, the man who everybody said could talk so brilliantly, that he of all men could be silent, at a loss for words.) I've tried calling him *darling.* I've described him as my lover, my boyfriend (but only in joke), my friend, mate, fuck, trick, man (*That's my man*). He is master, husband, wife, affair, love, himself (*Where's himself tonight*), the other half, the number one. Words fail me.

THE POETICS OF SEX

Jeanette Winterson (1959–)

Winterson's adoptive parents raised her to become a Pentecostal Christian missionary. The only non-religious book in her home was Thomas Malory's *Le Morte d'Arthur*. Her novels, both for children and adults, are imbued with myth and religion and wield an assertive, ominous narratorial style. Her topics are as far-reaching as Brexit, artificial intelligence, Shakespeare and time-travel. She finds the term "lesbian literature" isolating.

WHY DO YOU SLEEP WITH GIRLS?

My lover Picasso is going through her Blue Period. In the past her periods have always been red. Radish red, bull red, red like rose hips bursting seed. Lava red when she was called Pompeii and in her Destructive Period. The stench of her, the brack of her, the rolling splitting cunt of her. Squat like a Sumo, ham thighs, loins of pork, beefy upper cuts and breasts of lamb. I can steal her heart like a bird's egg.

She rushes for me bull-subtle, butching at the gate as if she's come to stud. She bellows at the window, bloods the pavement with desire. She says, 'You don't need to be Rapunzel to let down your hair.' I know the game. I know enough to flick my hind-quarters and skip away. I'm not a flirt. She can smell the dirt on me and that makes her swell. That's what makes my lithe lover bulrush-thin fat me. How she fats me. She plumps me, pats me, squeezes and feeds me. Feeds me up with lust till I'm as fat as she is. We're fat for each other we sapling girls. We neat clean branching girls get thick with sex. You are wide enough for my hips like roses, I will cover you with my petals, cover you with the scent of me. Cover girl wide for the weight of my cargo. My bull-lover makes a matador out of me. She circles me and in her rough-made ring I am complete. I like the dressing up, the little jackets, the silk tights, I like her shiny hide, the deep tanned leather of her. It is she who gives me the power of the sword. I used it once but when I cut at her it was my close fit flesh that frilled into a hem of blood. She lay beside me slender as a horn. Her little jacket and silk tights impeccable. I sweated muck and couldn't speak in my broken ring. We are quick change artists we girls.

WHICH ONE OF YOU IS THE MAN?

Picasso's veins are Kingfisher blue and Kingfisher shy. The first time I slept with her I couldn't see through the marble columns of her legs or beyond the opaque density of each arm. A sculptor by trade, Picasso is her own model.

The blue that runs through her is sanguine. One stroke of the knife and she changes colour. Every month and she changes colour. Deep pools of blue silk drop from her. I know her by the lakes she leaves on the way to the bedroom. Her braces cascade over the stair-rail, she wears earrings of lapis lazuli which I have caught cup-handed, chasing her deshabillée.

When she sheds she sheds it all. Her skin comes away with her clothes. On those days I have been able to see the blood-depot of her heart. On those days it was possible to record the patience of her digestive juices and the relentlessness of her lungs. Her breath is blue in the cold air. She breathes into the blue winter like a Madonna of the Frost. I think it right to kneel and the view is good.

She does perform miracles but they are of the physical kind and ordered by her Rule of Thumb to the lower regions. She goes among the poor with every kind of salve unmindful of reward. She dresses in blue she tells me so that they will know she is a saint and it is saintly to taste the waters of so many untried wells.

I have been jealous of course. I have punished her good deeds with some alms-giving of my own. It's not the answer, I can't catch her by copying her, I can't draw her with a borrowed stencil. She is all the things a lover should be and quite a few a lover should not. Pin her down? She's not a butterfly. I'm not a wrestler. She's not a target. I'm not a gun. Tell you what she is? She's not Lot no. 27 and I'm not one to brag.

We were by the sea yesterday and the sea was heavy with salt so that our hair was braided with it. There was salt on our hands and in our wounds where we'd been fighting. 'Don't hurt me' I said and I unbuttoned my shirt so that she could look at my breasts if she wanted to. 'I'm no saint' she said and that was true, true too that our feet are the same size. The rocks were reptile blue and the sky that balanced on the top of the cliffs was sheer blue. Picasso made me put on her jersey and drink dark tea from a 50s flask.

'It's winter' she said. 'Let's go.'

We did go, leaving the summer behind, leaving a trail of footprints two by two in identical four. I don't know that anyone behind could have told you which was which and if they had there would have been no trace by morning.

WHAT DO LESBIANS DO IN BED?

Under cover of the sheets the tabloid world of lust and vice is useful only in so much as Picasso can wipe her brushes on it. Beneath the sheets we practise Montparnasse, that is Picasso offers to paint me but we have sex instead.

We met at Art School on a shiny corridor. She came towards me so swiftly that the linoleum dissolved under her feet. I thought, 'A woman who can do that to an oil cloth can certainly do something for me.' I made the first move. I took her by her pony tail the way a hero grabs a runaway horse. She was taken aback. When she turned round I kissed her ruby mouth and took a sample of her sea blue eyes. She was salty, well preserved, well made and curved like a wave. I thought, 'This is the place to go surfing.'

We went back to her studio, where naturally enough, there was a small easel and a big bed. 'My work comes first,' she said. 'Would you mind?' and not waiting for an answer she mixed an ochre wash before taking me like a dog my breasts hanging over the pillow.

Not so fast Picasso, I too can rumple you like a farm hand, roll you like good tobacco leaf against my thighs. I can take that arrogant throat and cut it with desire. I can make you dumb with longing, tease you like a doxy on a date.

Slowly now Picasso, where the falling light hits the floor. Lie with me in the bruised light that leaves dark patches on your chest. You look tubercular, so thin and mottled, quiescent now. I picked you up and carried you to the bed dusty with ill-use. I found a newspaper under the sheets advertising rationing.

The girl on the canvas was sulky. She hadn't come to be painted. I'd heard all about you my tear-away tiger, so fierce, so unruly. But the truth is other as truth always is. What holds the small space between my legs is not your artistic tongue nor any of the other parts you play at will but the universe beneath the sheets that we make together.

We are in our igloo and it couldn't be snugger. White on white on white on white. Sheet Picasso me sheet. Who's on top depends on where you're standing but as we're lying down it doesn't matter. What an Eskimo I am, breaking her seductive ice and putting in my hand for fish. How she wriggles, slithers, twists to resist me but I can bait her and I do. A fine catch, one in each hand and one in my mouth. Impressive for a winter afternoon and the stove gone out and the rent to pay. We are warm and rich and white. I have so much enjoyed my visit.

'Come again?' she asked. Yes tomorrow, under the sodium street lights, under the tick of the clock. Under my obligations, my history, my fears, this now. This fizzy, giddy all consuming now. I will not let time lie to me. I will not listen to dead voices or unborn pain. 'What if?' has no power against 'What if not?' The not of you is unbearable. I must have you. Let them prate, those scorn-eyed anti-romantics. Love is not the oil and I am not the machine. Love is you and here I am. Now.

WERE YOU BORN A LESBIAN?

Picasso is an unlikely mother but I owe myself to her. We are honour-bound, love-bound, bound by cords too robust for those healthy hospital scissors. She baptised me from her own font and said, 'I name thee Sappho.' People often ask if we are mother and child.

I could say yes, I could say no, both statements would be true, the way that lesbians are true, at least to one another if not to the world. I am no stranger to the truth but very uncomfortable about the lies that have dogged me since my birth. It is no surprise that we do not always remember our name.

I am proud to be Picasso's lover in spite of the queer looks we get when holding hands on busy streets. 'Mummy, why is that man staring at us?' I said when only one month old. 'Don't worry dear, he can't help it, he's got something wrong with his eyes.'

We need more Labradors. The world is full of blind people. They don't see Picasso and me dignified in our love. They see perverts, inverts, tribades, homosexuals. They see circus freaks and Satan worshippers, girl-catchers and porno turn-ons. Picasso says they don't know how to look at pictures either.

WERE YOU BORN A LESBIAN?

A fairy in a pink tutu came to Picasso and said, 'I bring you tidings of great joy. All by yourself with no one to help you you will give birth to a sex toy who has a way with words. You will call her Sappho and she will be a pain in the ass to all men.'

'Can't you see I've got a picture to finish?' said Picasso.

'Take a break' said the fairy. 'There's more to life than Art.'

'Where?' said Picasso, whose first name wasn't Mary.

'Between your legs' said Gabriel.

'Forget it. Don't you know I paint with my clit?'

'Here, try a brush,' said the fairy offering her a fat one.

'I've had all the brushes I need,' said Picasso.

'Too Late' said the fairy. 'Here she comes.'

Picasso slammed the door on her studio and ran across to the Art College where she had to give a class. She was angry so that her breath burnt the air. She was angry so that her feet dissolved the thin lino tiles already scuffed to ruin by generations of brogues. There was no one in the corridor or if there was she was no one. Picasso didn't recognise her, she had her eyes on the door and the door looked away. Picasso, running down the clean corridor, was suddenly trip-wired, badly thrown, her hair came away from her glorious head. She was being scalped. She was being mugged. She was detonated on a long fuse of sex. Her body was half way out of the third floor window and there was a demon against her mouth. A poker-red pushing babe crying, 'Feed me, Feed me now.'

Picasso took her home, what else could she do? She took her home to straighten her out and had her kinky side up. She mated with this creature she had borne and began to feel that maybe the Greek gods knew a thing or two. Flesh of her flesh she fucked her.

They were quiet then because Sappho hadn't learned a language. She was still two greedy hands and an open mouth. She throbbed like an outboard motor, she was as sophisticated as a ham sandwich. She had nothing to offer but herself, and Picasso, who thought she had seen it all before, smiled like a child and fell in love.

WHY DO YOU HATE MEN?

Here comes Sappho, scorching the history books with tongues of flame. Never mind the poetry feel the erection. Oh yes, women get erect, today my body is stiff with sex. When I see a word held hostage to manhood I have to rescue it. Sweet trembling word, locked in a tower, tired of your Prince coming and coming. I will scale you and discover that size is no object especially when we're talking inches.

I like to be a hero, like to come back to my island full of girls carrying a net of words forbidden them. Poor girls, they are locked outside their words just as the words are locked into meaning. Such a lot of locking up goes on on the Mainland but here the doors are always open.

Stay inside, don't walk the streets, bar the windows, keep your mouth shut, keep your legs together, strap your purse around your neck, don't wear valuables, don't look up, don't talk to strangers, don't risk it, don't try it. He means she except when it means Men. This is a Private Club.

That's all right boys, so is this. This delicious unacknowledged island where we are naked with each other. The boat that brings us here will crack beneath your weight. This is territory you cannot invade. We lay on the bed, Picasso and I, listening to the terrible bawling of Salami. Salami is a male artist who wants to be a Lesbian.

'I'll pay you twice the rent' he cries, fingering his greasy wallet.

'I'll paint you for posterity. I love women, don't you know? Oh God I wish I was a woman, wafer-thin like you, I could circle you with one hand.' He belches.

Picasso is unimpressed. She says, 'The world is full of heterosexuals, go and find one, half a dozen, swallow them like oysters, but get out.'

'Oh whip me' says Salami getting moist.

We know the pattern. In half an hour he'll be violent and when he's threatened us enough, he'll go to the sleeze pit and watch two girls for the price of a steak.

As soon as he left we forgot about him. Making love we made a dictionary of forbidden words. We are words, sentences, stories, books. You are my New Testament. We are a gospel to each other, I am your annunciation, revelation. You are my St Mark, winged lion at your feet. I'll have you, and the lion too, buck under you till you learn how to saddle me. Don't dig those spurs too deep. It's not so simple this lexographic love.

When you have sunk me to the pit I'll mine you in return and we shall be husbands to each other as well as wives.

I'll tell you something Salami, a woman can get hard and keep it there all night and when she's not required to stand she knows how to roll. She can do it any way up and her lover always comes. There are no frigid lesbians, think of that.

On this island where we live, keeping what we do not tell, we have found the infinite variety of Woman. On the Mainland, Woman is largely extinct in all but a couple of obvious forms. She is still cultivated as a cash crop but is nowhere to be found growing wild.

Salami hates to hear us fuck. He bangs on the wall like a zealot at an orgy. 'Go home,' we say, but he doesn't. He'd rather lie against the skirting board complaining that we stop him painting. The real trouble is that we have rescued a word not allowed to our kind.

He hears it pounding through the wall day and night. He smells it on our clothes and sees it smeared on our faces. We are happy Picasso and I. Happy.

DON'T YOU FIND THERE'S SOMETHING MISSING?

I thought I had lost Picasso. I thought the bright form that shapes my days had left me. I was loose at the edges, liquid with uncertainty. The taut lines of love slackened. I felt myself unravelling backwards, away from her. Would the thinning thread snap?

For seven years she and I had been in love. Love between lovers, love between mother and child. Love between man and wife. Love between friends. I had been all of those things to her and she had been all of those things to me. What we were we were in equal parts, and twin souls to one another. We like to play roles but we know who we are. You are beauty to me Picasso. Not only sensuous beauty that pleases the eye but artistic beauty that challenges it. Sometimes you are ugly in your beauty, magnificently ugly and you frighten me for all the right reasons.

I did not tell you this yesterday or the day before. Habit had silenced me the way habit does. So used to a thing no need to speak it, so well known the action no need to describe it. But I know that speech is freedom which is not the same as freedom of speech. I have no right to say what I please when I please but I have the gift of words with which to bless you. Bless you Picasso. Bless you for your straight body like a spire. You are the landmark that leads me through the streets of the everyday. You take me past the little houses towards the church where we worship. I do worship you because you are worthy of praise. Bless you Picasso for your able hands that carry the paint to the unbirthed canvas. Your fingers were red when you fucked me and my body striped with joy. I miss the weals of our passion just as I miss the daily tenderness of choosing you. Choosing you above all others, my pearl of great price.

My feelings for you are Biblical; that is they are intense, reckless, arrogant, risky and unconcerned with the way of the world. I flaunt my bleeding wounds, madden with my certainty. The Kingdom of Heaven is within you Picasso. Bless you.

There is something missing and that is you. Your clothes were gone yesterday, your easel was packed flat and silent against the wall. When I got up and left our unmade bed there was the smell of coffee in the house but not the smell of you. I looked in the mirror and I knew who was to blame. Why take the perfect thing and smash it? Some goods are smashed that cannot be replaced.

It has been difficult this last year. Love is difficult. Love gets harder which is not the same as to say that it gets harder to love. You are not hard to love. You are hard to love well. Your standards are high, you won't settle for the quick way out which is why you made for the door. If I am honest I will admit that I have always wanted to avoid love. Yes give me romance, give me sex, give me fights, give me all the parts of love but not the simple single word which is so complex and demands the best of me this hour this minute this forever.

Picasso won't paint the same picture twice. She says develop or die. She won't let yesterday's love suffice for today. She makes it new, she remixes her colours and stretches her canvas until it sighs. My mother was glad when she heard we'd split up. She said 'Now you can come back to the Mainland. I'll send Phaeon to pick you up.' Phaeon runs a little business called LESBIAN TOURS. He drives his motor-boat round and round the island, just outside the one mile exclusion zone. He points out famous lesbians to sight-seers who always say, 'But she's so attractive!' or 'She's so ugly!'

'Yeah,' says Phaeon, 'and you know what? They're all in love with me.' One sight-seer shakes his head like a collecting box for a good cause. 'Can't you just ask one of 'em?' he says. 'I can ask them anything' says Phaeon who never waits to hear the answer.

WHY DO YOU SLEEP WITH GIRLS?

Picasso has loved me for fifty years and she loves me still. We got through the charcoal tunnel where the sun stopped rising. We no longer dress in grey.

On that day I told you about I took my coat and followed her footprints across the ice. As she walked the world froze up behind her. There was nothing for me to return to, if I failed, I failed alone. Despair made it too dark to see, I had to travel by radar, tracking her warmth in front of me. It's fashionable now to say that any mistake is made by both of you. That's not always true. One person can easily kill another.

Hang on me my darling like rubies round my neck. Slip onto my finger like a ring. Give me your rose for my buttonhole. Let me leaf through you before I read you out loud.

Picasso warms my freezing heart on the furnace of her belly. Her belly is stoked to blazing with love of me. I have learned to feed her every day, to feed her full of fuel that I gladly find. I have unlocked the storehouses of love. On the Mainland they teach you to save for a rainy day. The truth is that love needs no saving. It is fresh or not at all. We are fresh and plentiful. She is my harvest and I am hers. She seeds me and reaps me, we fall into one another's laps. Her seas are thick with fish for my rod. I have rodded her through and through.

She is painting today. The room is orange with effort. She is painting today and I have written this.

COMING OUT STORY

Alison Bechdel (1960–)

Bechdel, an American cartoonist, gave her name to the Bechdel Test, which measures gender representation in works of fiction. For a piece to pass the test, two female characters must, at some point, talk about something other than a man (around half of all films fail). She is known for the comic strip *Dykes to Watch Out For* and her graphic novel memoirs.

I HAD JUST BEEN BROWSING AT THE CAMPUS BOOK-STORE, SOMETHING I DID A LOT OF IN THOSE DAYS.

I WAS LONELY, A NEW TRANSFER STUDENT. BEING ENTIRELY ASEXUAL, APOLITICAL, AND ASOCIAL, I HADN'T MADE MANY FRIENDS YET.

WHEN I WASN'T IN CLASS OR AT THE BOOKSTORE, I WAS GETTING HIGH AND GOING TO MOVIES.

MY CINEMATIC EDUCATION WOULD HAVE BEEN EXCELLENT IF I COULD REMEMBER ANY OF IT.

THE DRUGS, THE ENDLESS MOVIEGOING, THE HOURS OF BROWSING THROUGH BOOKS... I WAS TRYING DESPERATELY TO DISTRACT MYSELF FROM A TRUTH THAT WAS SLOWLY BUT SURELY STRUGGLING TO THE SURFACE OF MY SOLITARY, SEX-STARVED SOUL.

ONE OF THE BOOKS I CHANCED TO FLIP THROUGH THAT PARTICULAR GRAY AFTERNOON WAS "ABOUT HOMOSEXUALS," AS I LATER NOTED IN MY JOURNAL.

VARIOUS PEOPLE WERE INTERVIEWED ABOUT HOW THEY HAD COME TO REALIZE THEY WERE GAY, AND WHAT THEIR LIVES WERE LIKE.

I READ FOR A WHILE, THEN AT MY USUAL TIME I LEFT THE BOOKSTORE AND HEADED BACK TO MY DORM.

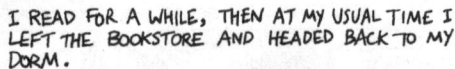

MY ROUTE LAY ACROSS A LARGE, SQUARE PARK. I WAS NEAR THE MIDDLE WHEN IT HAPPENED.

IT WAS AS IF I'D CROSSED SOME INVISIBLE BOUNDARY.

ON THE OTHER SIDE, THINGS WOULD NEVER BE THE SAME.

SLOW-MOTION TECHNIQUE

I'M REMINDED OF THE MYTH OF ATHENA'S BIRTH. YOU KNOW THE STORY. SHE SPRINGS, FULLY GROWN AND IN COMPLETE ARMOR, FROM ZEUS'S **HEAD.**

MY **OWN** FESTERING BRAIN, AFTER YEARS OF IGNORANCE AND DENIAL, HAD FINALLY **ERUPTED!**

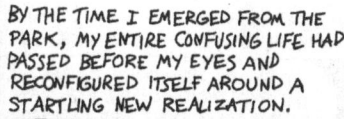

BY THE TIME I EMERGED FROM THE PARK, MY ENTIRE CONFUSING LIFE HAD PASSED BEFORE MY EYES AND RECONFIGURED ITSELF AROUND A STARTLING NEW REALIZATION.

JEEZ, THIS EXPLAINS EVERYTHING.

SCREEE!

I'M A LESBIAN.

YES, MY BURST OF INSIGHT IN THE SQUARE WAS A BIG STEP. BUT IT WAS ONLY THE **FIRST** OF A LONG, HARD JOURNEY.

IN A CRUEL TWIST OF FATE, I FOUND MYSELF FENDING OFF **NERDBOYS** WHILE MY WILDLY POPULAR AND HIP HETEROSEXUAL ROOMMATE HAD DISCOVERED **REAL LIVE LESBIANS!**

SHE SEEMED TO HAVE ACCESS TO A WORLD I DIDN'T EVEN KNOW EXISTED... AND SHE SPOKE SO CARELESSLY OF MY DEEPEST HOPES AND FEARS!

DESPAIR BECKONED... WHAT WAS "PRO-CHOICE?" IT SOUNDED LIKE SOME **FRINGE** POLITICAL GROUP! AND MEETINGS AT THE **WOMEN'S CENTER?** THIS STUFF WAS WAY OUT OF MY LEAGUE!

BUT I PERSEVERED, IN MY OWN QUIET WAY. THE BOOKSTORE YIELDED ANOTHER HELPFUL VOLUME.

TOO NERVOUS TO READ SOMETHING SO BLATANT IN PUBLIC, I **BOUGHT** IT.

PULSE WELL ABOVE MAXIMUM RECOMMENDED RATE.

I READ THE WHOLE BOOK VORACIOUSLY. IT WAS VERY ENCOURAGING. WHEN I WAS DONE, I TORE THE COVER OFF, STUFFED THE REST OF IT IN A BROWN PAPER BAG, AND HID IT UNDER MY MATTRESS.

NEXT, I TOOK TO READING THE LESBIAN CHAPTER OF MY ROOMMATE'S **HITE REPORT** WHILE SHE WAS OUT.

HI!

HI... UH... I WAS JUST LOOKING FOR YOUR DICTIONARY.

ONE THING LED TO ANOTHER, AND BEFORE THE SEMESTER WAS OVER I HAD DEVOURED **DESERT OF THE HEART, RUBYFRUIT JUNGLE,** AND **THE WELL OF LONELINESS.**

WHERE'S TH' SEXY PARTS?

FLIP

THE WALL OF LONELINESS RADCLYFFE HALL

CHRISTMAS BREAK WAS INTERMINABLE. MY PARENTS FAILED TO NOTICE THAT I HAD BECOME A THREAT TO THE NUCLEAR FAMILY.

A CHENILLE ROBE! THANKS.

AT LAST I WAS BACK AT SCHOOL. I WAS ENROLLED IN AN INTENSIVE COURSE ON JAMES JOYCE'S **ULYSSES.** I SKIMMED IT...

768 PAGES...

... MY FULL ACADEMIC PASSION WAS RESERVED FOR A **DIFFERENT** ODYSSEY... THE QUEST FOR MY **PEOPLE**.

WHAT A LITTLE BOOKWORM! I HAD AN INSATIABLE HUNGER FOR KNOWLEDGE.

YEAH, AMONG OTHER THINGS. DON'T FORGET TO MENTION THE LONG HOURS YOU SPENT **WHACKING OFF**.

HUMP HUMP

WELL, YES... OF COURSE THERE WAS A DEGREE OF SEXUAL FRUSTRATION INVOLVED.

KOFF.

AFTER ALL, I STILL HADN'T MET ANY LESBIANS. AND IF I **DID**, WOULD THEY FIND ME AS ATTRACTIVE AS THE **NERDBOYS** SEEMED TO?

I WAS DYING TO HAVE SEX WITH A WOMAN. DYING.

I'M DYING.

ALSO SWIPED FROM ROOMMATE

I PRAYED FOR A KINDLY, EXPERI-ENCED LESBIAN TO COME RESCUE ME FROM MY LONELY AGONIES.

YES?

NOK NOK

BUT ALL I GOT WAS ANOTHER BOY.

HI. I MET YOU AT THE LIBRARY, REMEMBER? CARE TO SMOKE A STOGIE?

WHY NOT?

THIS ONE WAS DIFFERENT, THOUGH. WE REALLY HIT IT OFF AND ENDED UP TALKING ALL NIGHT IN HIS ROOM.

YOU DRAW? COULD I SEE YOUR SKETCH-BOOKS SOMETIME?

YEAH, SURE.

INSTEAD OF FEELING REPULSED WHEN HE MADE HIS MOVE AT 4 A.M., I JUST FELT SAD.

WELL, I FEEL LIKE IT'S ABOUT TIME TO LIGHT A CANDLE AND LIE DOWN.

OH.

I RETURNED, NUN-LIKE, TO MY CELL.

WELL, I'D BETTER BE GOING THEN. I HAD A LOVELY EVENING.

HE SHOWED UP AT MY DOOR THE NEXT DAY AT NOON.

I COULDN'T SLEEP. I'VE BEEN WALKING ALL OVER... I WROTE YOU THIS POEM.

IT WASN'T HALF-BAD, EITHER.

WE HAD A LONG, HALTING DISCUSSION ABOUT WHY I'D LEFT HIS ROOM SO ABRUPTLY. FINALLY, HE SAID SOMETHING SO REMARKABLE THAT I ANSWERED WITHOUT THINKING.

...I DON'T UNDERSTAND. I MEAN, IF YOU WERE MORE ATTRACTED TO **WOMEN**...

THAT'S EXACTLY IT!

IT WAS AS IF A **THUNDERBOLT** HAD SPLIT THE AIR! MY SECRET WAS **REVEALED!** I HAD COME OUT TO ANOTHER PERSON!

INTOXICATED WITH RELIEF, I POURED MY HEART AND SOUL OUT TO THAT UNFORTUNATE YOUNG MAN. HE WAS QUITE DECENT ABOUT IT.

FROM EARLIEST CHILDHOOD, I KNEW I WAS DIFFERENT FROM OTHER GIRLS...

BUT AFTERWARDS, I PANICKED.

WHAT HAVE I DONE?! DO I ACTUALLY THINK I HAVE THE **NERVE** TO BE A LESBIAN? I DON'T EVEN **KNOW** ANY WOMEN! WHAT MAKES ME THINK I'M **ATTRACTED** TO THEM?!

GODDAMN FUCKING BOOKS!

OW.

GAY FOOD

I REALIZED I WAS GOING TO HAVE TO TAKE A MORE ACTIVE ROLE IN MY QUEST. I STARTED LOOKING AT WOMEN.

I LEARNED THAT THERE WAS A GAY ORGANIZATION ON CAMPUS!

235 GAY UNION

MEETING? TUESDAY?

ANITA BRYANT SUCKS ORANGES

I KNEW I HAD TO GO. I SPENT ALL TUESDAY AFTERNOON PSYCHING MYSELF UP.

AS I ENTERED THE STUDENT UNION BUILDING THAT NIGHT, I FELT SURE EVERYONE KNEW WHERE I WAS HEADED.

LESBO

WALKING INTO THAT MEETING WAS PROBABLY THE BRAVEST THING I'VE EVER DONE.

I HAVE NO IDEA WHAT THE GROUP TALKED ABOUT. I SAT IN A CORNER, OVERWHELMED WITH THE SYMBOLIC WEIGHT OF SIMPLY BEING THERE, AMONG OTHERS. MY PEOPLE! I HAD FOUND THEM!

BUT **NOW** WHAT?

WELCOME! WE USUALLY GO DOWNSTAIRS FOR A BEER AFTER MEETINGS. WANNA COME?

UM... NO THANKS

THE FIRST LESBIAN I EVER MET. ♥

I COULDN'T TAKE ANY MORE STIMULATION. I NEEDED TO BE ALONE. AS I LEFT THE BUILDING, I HOPED EVERYONE COULD TELL WHERE I'D BEEN.

I WENT BACK TO THE GAY UNION DURING OFFICE HOURS. THEY HAD A TREASURE TROVE OF MAGAZINES AND BOOKS I HADN'T SEEN BEFORE.

NEXT WEEK, I WENT OUT AFTER THE MEETING WITH THE "UNION" CROWD. I WAS A LITTLE NERVOUS ABOUT BEING SEEN IN PUBLIC WITH THEM.

THEY WERE EAGER TO INSTRUCT A NOVICE, BUT I COULDN'T REALLY RELATE TO THEM. I WAS PLAGUED WITH DOUBT.

I KEPT GOING TO MEETINGS, THOUGH, AND GRADUALLY WE HIT ON SOME COMMON BONDS.

SLOWLY, I GAINED CONFIDENCE. I CAME OUT TO MY ROOMMATE.

I DISCOVERED THE EXHILARATION OF SPEAKING OUT AGAINST PREJUDICE.

I DISCOVERED ALCOHOL.

BUT I STILL HADN'T DISCOVERED **SEX**. THAT FINAL FRONTIER LOOMED AHEAD, TAUNTING ME, MOCKING MY PRIM, CEREBRAL PROGRESS THUS FAR.

FINALLY, AFTER A NIGHT OF DRUNKEN REVELRY, I BROUGHT TWO OF MY NEW FRIENDS BACK TO MY ROOM TO GET HIGH. I REMEMBER THE PIPE I RIGGED UP OUT OF AN EMPTY TOILET PAPER TUBE, BUT I DON'T REMEMBER WHAT WE TALKED ABOUT.

I DON'T REMEMBER BECKY LEAVING, BUT I DO REMEMBER THAT JOAN STAYED.

MIND IF I CRASH HERE? IT'S SO LATE.

I TURNED OFF THE LIGHT. WE REMOVED OUR JEANS AND GOT INTO MY SINGLE BED. STILL IN MY BRA AND WOOL SWEATER, I WAS PROFOUNDLY UNCOMFORTABLE.

AS WE LAY THERE, I BEGAN TO **SHIVER** UNCONTROLLABLY.

JEEZ, THIS IS WEIRD. MUST BE THAT GRAIN ALCOHOL..

THE WHOLE BED BEGAN TO SHAKE, BANGING AGAINST THE WALL.

WHAT'S WRONG?

CHATTER

THUMPA THUMP!

JOAN TRIED TO SOOTHE ME, BUT WHEREVER SHE TOUCHED ME, I WAS UNBEARABLY **TICKLISH**.

WHA HA HA!

EVENTUALLY, I RELAXED A BIT AND WE KISSED.

SHE SEEMED TO KNOW WHAT SHE WAS DOING, AND GOT US BOTH UNDRESSED.

UNH.

SNAP!

TO BE PERFECTLY HONEST, I REMEMBER VERY LITTLE OF WHAT FOLLOWED, EXCEPT THAT SHE WENT DOWN ON ME...

I'M DYING!

...AND THAT I HAD ABSOLUTELY NO IDEA HOW TO TOUCH HER.

JEEZ, WHAT'S THIS RUBBERY PART?

SHE SLEPT, BUT I LAY AWAKE ALL NIGHT, PINNED BETWEEN HER AND THE WALL. AT 9 O'CLOCK, SHE GOT UP AND LEFT AFTER A BRIEF CHAT.

SO, D'YOU WANNA COME TO BRUNCH?

UM... NO THANKS

UNFAMILIAR WITH THE PROTOCOL OF SUCH SITUATIONS, I DIDN'T REALIZE HOW CHURLISH MY REFUSAL WAS. (IN SPITE OF THIS, JOAN AND I EVEN-TUALLY BECAME LOVERS.)

THAT MORNING I WANTED TO BE ALONE TO SAVOR MY EXQUISITELY JARRING SENSATIONS. I FELT DEBAUCHED AND EXULTANT, MELANCHOLY AND HOPEFUL.

GUESS I'M REALLY A LESBIAN NOW.

I WISH I HAD A MORE ROMANTIC, LESS DRUG-INDUCED **FIRST TIME** FOR YOU.

BUT I'VE TOLD THE TRUE STORY.

MY OWN HUMBLE CONTRIBUTION TO THAT EPIC TALE OF COLLECTIVE SELF-REVELATION THAT MY SISTERS AND BROTHERS HAVE BEEN TELLING FOR GENERATIONS.

IT'S AN HONOR, IT REALLY IS.

THANKS FOR DROPPING BY.

COME OUT AGAIN.

CIAO.

YOU'LL DO

Rosie Garland (1960–)

Garland is a singer and performer with an extravagant career in punk rock and cabaret. Over the last ten years, she has published a huge amount of eclectic written work – novels, short stories, essays and five volumes of poetry. Gothic aesthetics decorate plotlines of sexual transience and points of social concern. Grim historical settings and nefarious communities often extract truths about individual characters.

I'm driving with my girlfriend through town after fuckwit town. Just to get away, but that's another story. We've left all that behind us now. She's driving, I'm riding. She doesn't mind, which is good, because I don't drive. Can't drive. Just never got to learn. I'm the only person I know who doesn't drive, apart from my old girlfriend Janet, and she was weird in other ways too. Lives in Maine now. There you go. Weird. We couldn't hold it together. Both of us stationary. Lack of transportation got the better of us, I guess. That was a long time ago, before all of this.

I look over at Nancy. She doesn't complain. She's driving in that detached way that feels comfortable to me now. I know she's not blanking off from me; she's just a little drawn into the road out in front. It's like a meditation, a restful state for her. And I don't disturb it. Drink it in myself. I've found her calmness increasingly calming, now I've gotten over resisting it. She was patient with me in those early days, more than I deserved, I used to say. She'd say right back that just showed I had low self-esteem and we'd laugh.

The light catches the silky hair on her forearm, resting on the wheel. Blond, fine like baby hair, but long. Sometimes when we're lying down I search her arm and find these hairs two, maybe three inches long on her arm, like mutants. She laughs, won't let me pull them out. She doesn't complain. She knows it's not criticism. I just love to explore her body. I love the difference in all women's bodies. From the start I've always been drawn to bodies like mine, yet so unlike when you get down to it. Yeah, you've worked it out, we're two girls together. You can say it: dykes. That's OK. I've been called as bad and survived worse. I sleep with women. Fuck them too. And if you're a man reading this, I guess there's a four in five chance you go for girls as well. So hey, that makes for some common ground, right? Anyway, it's not important for this story. This isn't some heart-rending tale of unrequited lesbian love in a car across one of the more tedious of this great nation's states. No pussy scenes, guys. You can check out here if that's all that got you this far.

So we're driving.

The land is flat and nearly featureless. Far away to my right there's a line of grey hills running parallel to the road; pale rock, no vegetation. More miles away than I care to imagine, probably. One of those tricks of the light. Because they're damn near the only thing to look at they seem closer than they are. I think about how long it would take to walk to them and my head goes into movie mode; what Nancy calls my fertile imagination. I see myself trudging over the pebbly ground, staggering a little maybe, looking up at the sun which burns down out of a big silver sky, raise my circular canteen to my lips, but it's empty, so I throw it away, just like in those old black-and-white movies I'd watch on a Saturday afternoon as a kid. I never understood why the guy threw away the canteen. What if he found some water? What would he put it in? It happened in every movie and I thought it was real stupid every time.

I pop open a soda for Nancy and one for me. Who says there's no such thing as association? Nancy gives me a real nice smile.

"Watching movies?" she says.

"Yeah." I smile back. "Those hills made me think of *Treasure of The*

Sierra Madre, and all those ones I can't even remember their names: used to watch them on TV."

"Yeah. And the hero always threw away his canteen, didn't he?"

There's a twinkle in her eye, like she knows what I was thinking all along. These days I'm not surprised, more sheepish that I could forget how well she knows me. She reaches over with her free hand and runs her fingers through my hair where it flops over my forehead. The car doesn't swerve. She keeps us on course. After a while she puts her hand back on the wheel.

"I want to stop soon and get some rest," she says. "Sleep rest."

The first motel we come to is just before we enter the town. It's advertising bar-be-q special midweek for $9.95. It looks like a dump.

"Yeah, well, I'm not that tired," says Nancy, barely slowing the car. "Let's see what's in town."

Town is one of those descriptives you realise fast is an overstatement. It's a mile-long stretch of ugly tarmac, with two intersections where traffic lights sway over damn-near deserted roads. We pass one diner fronted by a parking lot with a handful of trucks and cars scattered across it. It looks like it's going to be our only choice for food later on. Oh great.

"Not what you'd call crowded," I moan.

"At least it has a few customers, so it can't be poisoning folks."

"Unless it's killing them off with the tuna special and selling their cars as a sideline."

"Where did that come from?"

"Just my great sense of humour, honey." I give Nancy a cheesy grin.

By now we've passed through and are out the far side of town. The buildings dwindle to a trickle, then nothing. There's one large, low building on the left and we slide up to it. It's a motel, and looks even less exciting than the first. We pull up.

"Christ, this one doesn't even have bar-be-q for ten bucks. Let's go back to the other one. Or do you want to drive on, honey?" I look over at Nancy. She suddenly looks real tired, lets out a long breath, crumples a little before my eyes. I realise just how long she's been driving, remember just how much we've driven away from. She scratches the back of her hand with a nervous gesture I've not seen for so long I'd almost forgotten it. I reach over and cup my hand round her cheek.

"Hey sweetheart." I smile at her and she looks at me. "We don't have to stay here, but you're exhausted. So we stop here if you want. As long as it's got a shower and a bed, that's fine. I'll go and fetch us some food."

She leans into my hand. "I had no idea I was this tired until we stopped," she sighs. "I guess it's not a surprise. But yeah, the other place looks better than this. I'll drive us back. I'd rather."

She shifts the car into reverse and backs into the driveway to turn, and the car cuts out. She turns the key. Nothing. Cars are a mystery to me. They start, they don't start. One is as mysterious as the other to my way of thinking. And this one is refusing to start. Mystery or not, it's a pain in the ass.

Nancy is starting to get frustrated. She jiggles the key around a few more times without success, heaves out a long breath, turns to me and says *sorry*, head bowed. This surprises me more than the car dying on us. I can't remember when was the last time I heard Nancy apologise for something that wasn't her fault. She's fair. If she's out of line she says so. But not this.

"Hey, it's OK, it's a machine. You don't need to say sorry for a heap of metal."

"Yeah, you're right." She lifts her head. "I'm tired, I guess. Well, it looks like we might be staying here after all." She pauses. "They can tell us where the nearest car mechanic is. I cannot be bothered getting under that hood, however simple the problem."

She's back to her decisive self again. Good.

We get out the car and walk across the empty lot towards the office. It's part of a large, one-storey building with a flat roof. The motel cabins are over the other side of the parking lot. Low, flat roofed again. At least they look clean. But the place is so empty. I go into movie mode and imagine tumbleweeds rolling around, the squeak of the motel sign as it sways in the wind, the whine of Ennio Morricone music playing in the background. But there's no air moving here.

I expect the door of the office to creak as I push it open, but it's noiseless on oiled hinges. There are some deep horizontal scratches in the plastic woodgrain like something heavy's been dragged past. But neatly painted over. Well, they're houseproud, which I hope is a good sign. I think back to some of the places I've stayed with Nancy, and not just in the good ol' U. S. of A. Some people don't like two women staying either because they figure we'll be hauling back carloads of guys and beer and having an orgy, or they figure we're dykes and just hate us anyway.

The office is dim and cool after the direct sun outside. I look for a bell on the counter, but a door in the wall behind it opens and a small woman steps through. I get a glimpse of a kitchen area behind. Her features look as if they were arranged in a hurry by someone whose work wasn't checked carefully enough. She pushes her lips together in what I guess is a smile, but is more nondescript. She stands there and blinks at us.

"We'd like a room," says Nancy.

"A room! Right, ladies." It's like someone's switched her on. She broadens what is passing for a smile into what she must think is a grin and reaches under the counter, dragging out a large book.

"If you'll just sign in here." Her voice has a sing-song quality, as if she's learnt this spiel by rote and says the same thing to all comers, substituting *gentlemen* where appropriate. And I guess that is exactly what she and countless other motel owners do across the country. Tiring quickly of finding new things to say to the faceless people who pass through.

Nancy's finished scratching in the book, so I take my turn. The woman takes it back off me and contemplates our scribblings for a moment, squinting up her eyes. I prepare to say we're sisters, but she's not interested and slides the register back where it came from. She looks back at us and moves those features around into what I'd swear is meant to be sincere apology.

"I'm afraid I'll have to ask you ladies to pay in advance..." She lets her words hang in the air.

"That's no problem," smiles Nancy, showing her how a genuine smile really can be done. "We'd really appreciate it if you could tell us where the nearest garage is. Our car cut out in the driveway back there."

Nancy tilts her head back in the direction of the car and the woman follows the movement with large glassy eyes as if she can see it, which of course she can't as there's a wall in the way.

"Well, I'm sorry to hear that." Her face has switched into concern now. I could watch it for hours. "My brother's an auto mechanic. He'll be back in a half hour."

Nancy isn't the kind to demur, and certainly not as exhausted as she is right now.

"Just see it as part of the service we offer. And of course, I don't expect you to pay in advance without seeing your room. There are the cabins over the far side of the parking lot," she says, "and we also have a new development of more luxurious hotel-style rooms in this area." She really does sound like a glossy brochure now. "We're rather proud of them. Each room has ensuite luxury bathroom with bath. Direct from Europe."

She just said the magic word. A bath. What wouldn't I give just to stretch out in a tub. Fuck the expense. I want to dance around and shout, *Yes we'll take it!* Then run on in, turn on both taps full, tear my clothes off and jump in. Instead I restrict myself to a small smile.

"That sounds just great," I say.

The proprietor smiles back. Hey, she's getting better at it too. Maybe she just needed the practice.

"If you'll follow me, ladies."

She swings up half the counter top and comes through, walking over to a door in the wall I hadn't noticed when we came in. She's wearing neatly pressed chinos which surprises me a little. I had her down as a skirt type. Closer to, her face looks less haphazard. Maybe it's the kind that grows on you. Her jaw seems firmer. In fact, it dawns on me that she looks rather dykey. And she did mention a brother rather than a husband. Well, well. Baths from Europe and now a lesbian motel owner.

I try to catch Nancy's eye to see if she's guessed too, and fail. We step through the door and I realise I'm beginning to enjoy myself.

We're in a corridor that's pleasantly cool and has four, five doors off it, each spaced a long way from the other. The rooms must be pretty big. Maybe they need to be to fit that bath in. I see myself lounging, surrounded by bubbles in a tub the size of Nevada. We troop in the first door on the right and are steered straight for the holy of holies.

"So, the bathroom!"

Our guide clasps her hands over her breasts, breathing excitedly. They really have gone to town on it. The tub is massive; gold taps, fancy tiling, mirrors that look foreign and expensive. And the carpet, I swear I could sleep in it, it's so deep and soft. I'm in heaven, grinning like a kid. The owner looks at me and smiles right back. She seems much more, well, real now. Like she just needed to warm up some.

"It's fantastic," I hear myself saying.

Out of the corner of my eye I see Nancy's head flick in my direction, so I turn to her. Usually she's good at veiling her face in the presence of others, but I catch a powerful if unspoken shot of *what the hell are you on about?* She's looking at the room like there's roaches crawling on the bathmat. I question her with my eyes and she fixes me with a look that could fell a horse. I'm thrown. Two minutes ago she was all sweetness and smiles.

The motel owner places her palms together in something that's halfway between prayer and subservience. She's too much.

"I'll leave you two ladies alone to decide. I'll be right outside." She slides out of the room.

I whisper, "What's up Nancy?" but she shrugs me off like I'm poison. She's shaking. It dawns on me she's angry, which throws me even more. Then I'm angry too, out of nowhere. This is more than tiredness.

"Look at me, will you?" I hiss. "We get here, the rooms are great, the motel's clean, the owner looks like a dyke and her brother's going to fix the car for chrissakes. What the hell more do you want?"

Nancy swings her head around and fixes me with her eyes. "What I want…" she says, her voice trembling with something that's nearly tears, "is for you to stop the fuck making eyes at this fucking woman. She looks like *Jackie*, for god's sake."

"What?" The breath goes out of me. Jackie? A name, maybe *the* name out of all the names we're driving to leave behind. I know Nancy's got to be worn down after these past few days, weeks, we've been through, but what *is* this? The proprietor may look like a lesbian, but there's no way on god's earth she looks anything like Jackie. The edge of my delight has gone. Nancy and I are brewing for a huge fight, which I know is going to erupt the minute we're left alone. And I have no goddam idea where it's coming from at all.

All this happens in seconds. Then the woman in question is standing in the door frame. She looks at Nancy, then me, then back at Nancy again, with that fixed half-smile of hers. C'mon lady, I think. If you're a lesbian, you've seen this a million times. But her smile is blank, non-judgemental. She raises her arm and gestures us out of the room. She really does not look like Jackie. And I am not, repeat not, making eyes at her.

"So?"

"It's fine. We'll take it," I say flatly. I know all the enthusiasm I felt a few minutes back has drained from my voice and I feel a twinge of guilt. The bathroom is clearly this woman's pride and joy and here I am, sounding like I've been offered a can of past-the-sell-by-date beans. What the hell. It's not my problem.

"Well, if we go back to the office we can settle up."

If she's noticed my lack of spirit, she doesn't indicate it. I feel absurdly grateful. We trudge down the corridor. She pauses and glances at us again. For a moment, I feel like an ant in a jar.

"Let's cut through the kitchen." She sounds almost conspiratorial. "It's quicker to the office and I'd like to show you our refit. I can tell you ladies appreciated the bathroom."

What the hell planet does this woman come from? She wants us to look at her new kitchen? OK, the bathroom was nice, but I don't want a house tour. I want to be alone with Nancy. I open my mouth and close it again. It feels like far, far too much effort to argue. Nancy's not saying a word. I look over at her but her head's tilted away from me so I can't see her expression. She looks like her stuffing's leaked out. I want to put my arms around her, say *sorry, let's just work this out, honey*. But I don't. Instead I follow our hostess up the passageway.

She opens the kitchen door, strides in and swings round to face us. Her eyes are shining and there's a pink flush rising from her neck. I half-expect her to raise her arms and shout, "Ta-daa!" like a ringmaster announcing the big act, she's so worked up. Hell, if she is a dyke, she can't have much of a sex life to get so excited about a goddam kitchen. She can barely contain herself.

"It's real nice." I feel I have to say something. It is big, I'll give her that. Must take up the whole of one side of the building. The walls are lined with cabinets and appliances. Everything gleams. I turn round to check on Nancy and she's just behind me, looking over to the far side of the room. I follow her gaze to where there's a kid sitting, dwarfed by a huge table.

Though he's perched on a high chair, his shoulders barely clear the top of it. There's an empty plate in front of him and I can't tell whether he's just cleared it or is waiting for it to be filled. He's very still and is surveying us intently. The motel owner has also followed our eyes and sweeps over the shining floor to the boy.

"And this is Dean," she beams. The flush is creeping over her cheeks now. "My brother's boy. My brother just loves kids. Say hello now, Dean."

Dean declines the invitation and continues to stare at us. He has the same sort of blank, faraway look as his aunt. Must be some kind of family trait. Or maybe it's just living out here. How many people do they actually get staying? Presumably enough to finance this fancy refit. Or maybe this rather dowdy dyke is a cocaine dealer for some Colombian cartel. Oh, yeah, right. More likely her brother's loaded. Christ, listen to me. Why am I bothering to waste my time thinking about this shit? I'm so tired I could cry. I've no idea what the hell is wrong with Nancy. It's making me frantic. And here I am wondering where they get their fucking money from. Jesus.

Dean decides to concentrate his attention on me. His aunt's gazing at him like she's besotted. Then she follows his line of vision and rests her eyes on me.

"So, you'll stay?"

For a second I think she means just me. As in, "you" in the singular. I push the idea away.

"Yes," I say.

"No," Nancy splutters simultaneously. I turn around.

"Nancy?"

She looks like she's fighting to hold down a tornado of rage, and gradually losing her grip. Her mouth is twitching. I've never seen her this mad. I've never seen *anyone* this mad, period. She doesn't trust herself to answer me. Suddenly I want to scream, *what in Christ's name is up with you? We have no car, this is embarrassing, stop it, let's get a room and sort this out.* But I squeeze out, "Nancy, honey?" and pray she gets the message.

"I am not staying here," she says very slowly, picking each word carefully.

I guess, more than any other moment, that's when everything changes. I turn away from her and back to the motel owner.

"So, you'll stay?"

It's like she hasn't heard, or is ignoring Nancy. Then I realise that she is talking to me, just me. And I know that, yes, I am going to stay. So I say simply, "yes".

She holds me with eyes which are now warm and animated. I feel something like relief wash through me. There's this voice somewhere in my head saying, *you're home, you know.*

"Unless, of course, you want to go with your girlfriend."

There's the tiniest edge of sarcasm in the last word.

I turn back to Nancy, who is swaying slightly in front of me. Must be my eyes. I don't really know why I'm doing this.

"No," I say.

Nancy gives me a look of pure unadulterated hate, which kind of swims over me now.

"You lousy fuck." It's like all the contempt she's ever felt is concentrated into those words. But I don't cry. I don't feel much of anything. I'm floating above all of this. The little voice is still there, saying, *hey, Nancy's lost it. She's nuts. You're seeing what she's really like, deep down. You don't need her. Let her go.* I'm finding it so easy to listen to that voice.

Nancy walks away. Or maybe I move a few steps closer to the motel owner, I don't know. What I do know, as I look at her, is that I am going to stay. More than just the night. Something's happening here. I know with a certainty that if she asks, I'm going to follow this woman for the rest of my life. And I have no idea why.

She raises her arms lazily and holds them out to me. Now, I think, she will touch me and I will understand. I wait, my eyes half-closed. Her fingers reach my shoulders and I wait for her to pull me to her, but she doesn't.

"You'll do," she says quietly.

Her hands slide up quickly and fix lightly round my throat. Instinct makes my eyes spring open and my own hands fly up to my neck. She's not letting go. She's still smiling at me as she starts to swell. Her face is now scarlet to the roots of her hair, which is growing as I watch, fanning out around her like it's charged with static.

She's filling up, expanding. Her hands grow larger round my neck, and though they seem to be just resting there, I can't loosen them. I claw at them furiously. I feel one of my hands grow slick, and look at it. I've ripped off two of my nails and my hand's covered in blood. My blood. I'm not leaving a scratch on her. I flail at her face frantically, but can't reach her now. Her head's like a red balloon, features stretched out, distended. And that blank smile is stretched right across her face like some obscene cartoon. The rest of her body is growing too, and I feel my feet lift off the ground as she expands up towards the ceiling. I kick desperately, trying to keep my toes in contact with the floor.

I cast around wildly, searching for Nancy, but all I can see is the child Dean, sitting silently behind his empty plate. He's picked up his knife and fork, and is watching me die with detachment. As my eyesight starts to fade it occurs to me he's a lot older than he looks. Older than me. Older than all of us. It makes me want to laugh. A rattle rises from my constricted throat and I feel water run out of my eyes. I'm laughing, I'm crying. My face is wet with snot.

Then I feel another pair of hands on me. I twist my head round as far as I can and see Nancy. She's shrieking at whatever's got hold of me to let go, scratching, hitting, screaming, and like me not leaving a mark. We lock eyes for an instant and in that second I want her to know that I understand now how we've been set up. Right from when the car cut out. Most of all I want to say sorry. Then it's over. Nancy catapults away from me as Dean grabs the hair on top of her head and drags her back. He has grown too, is now the size of a man, but still with the proportions of a child. He wraps his arms around her and hugs her to him, like he's keeping a favourite toy to himself. He looks down at her with curiosity while she's struggling, then reaches out to the table, picks up his empty plate and slowly begins to push it into Nancy's mouth. Her screaming becomes a high-pitched squeal coming from the back of her throat. The plate's too wide to fit, but he keeps pushing. Her whine gets higher, crazier, as the sides of her mouth start to split open under the pressure. He keeps forcing the plate in. Blankeyed. He's not even focused on her. She isn't going to get away.

The last thing I see is my killer's face. Her distended head is brushing the ceiling and she's hauling me up towards her face. Her mouth is pursing into a kiss, one that can swallow me whole. Somewhere below and behind me I hear a retching sound and a wet slap as Nancy vomits onto the floor. Those clean, clean tiles. Oh, Nancy.

I think of the last time we were ever alone, in the car back out there in the driveway. How tired she looked, how I cupped my hand round her cheek. How much I was in love with her. How much I do love her. I want to hold onto that.

Things are ebbing away. My arms have fallen to my sides. They're starting to twitch and I can't stop them. My bowels loosen and I sense liquid seeping down my legs. All that's left of me is retreating into my head. I try to hold onto Nancy in there. I want Nancy to be the last thing on my mind. But I'm losing her. Pushing her aside are questions: how many people stop here, how many ever get to use that bath, what these people, if that's what they are, will use to bait the next trap. Most of all, I wonder what this is all for. I never get any answers. Finally, what fills my head is the memory of those scratches I saw on the door of the office when we came in. The long horizontal marks as if something heavy had been dragged past. Deep, animal scratches.

Then it all goes black.

A REAL DOLL

A.M. Homes (1961–)

Born in Washington D.C., Holmes was adopted as a baby and raised in Maryland. Although she wrote her first novel *Jack* at the age of nineteen, it was not published until almost a decade later. Her first collection of stories, *The Safety of Objects*, showcased her unusual, unsettling style and subsequent novels have been greeted with acclaim and some controversy. Her novel *May We Be Forgiven* won the Women's Prize for Fiction.

I'm dating Barbie. Three afternoons a week, while my sister is at dance class, I take Barbie away from Ken. I'm practicing for the future.

At first I sat in my sister's room watching Barbie, who lived with Ken, on a doily, on top of the dresser.

I was looking at her but not really looking. I was looking, and all of the sudden realized she was staring at me.

She was sitting next to Ken, his khaki-covered thigh absently rubbing her bare leg. He was rubbing her, but she was staring at me.

"Hi," she said.

"Hello," I said.

"I'm Barbie," she said, and Ken stopped rubbing her leg.

"I know."

"You're Jenny's brother."

I nodded. My head was bobbing up and down like a puppet on a weight.

"I really like your sister. She's sweet," Barbie said. "Such a good little girl. Especially lately, she makes herself so pretty, and she's started doing her nails."

I wondered if Barbie noticed that Miss Wonderful bit her nails and that when she smiled her front teeth were covered with little flecks of purple nail polish. I wondered if she knew Jennifer colored in the chipped chewed spots with purple magic marker, and then sometimes sucked on her fingers so that not only did she have purple flecks of polish on her teeth, but her tongue was the strangest shade of violet.

"So listen," I said. "Would you like to go out for a while? Grab some fresh air, maybe take a spin around the backyard?"

"Sure," she said.

I picked her up by her feet. It sounds unusual but I was too petrified to take her by the waist. I grabbed her by the ankles and carried her off like a Popsicle stick.

As soon as we were out back, sitting on the porch of what I used to call my fort, but which my sister and parents referred to as the playhouse, I started freaking. I was suddenly and incredibly aware that I was out with Barbie. I didn't know what to say.

"So, what kind of a Barbie are you?" I asked.

"Excuse me?"

"Well, from listening to Jennifer I know there's Day to Night Barbie, Magic Moves Barbie, Gift-Giving Barbie, Tropical Barbie, My First Barbie, and more."

"I'm Tropical," she said. I'm Tropical, she said, the same way a person might say I'm Catholic or I'm Jewish. "I came with a one-piece bathing suit, a brush, and a ruffle you can wear so many ways," Barbie squeaked.

She actually squeaked. It turned out that squeaking was Barbie's birth defect. I pretended I didn't hear it.

We were quiet for a minute. A leaf larger than Barbie fell from the maple tree above us and I caught it just before it would have hit her. I half expected her to squeak, "You saved my life. I'm yours, forever." Instead she said, in a perfectly normal voice, "Wow, big leaf."

I looked at her. Barbie's eyes were sparkling blue like the ocean on a good day. I looked and in a moment noticed she had the whole world, the cosmos, drawn in makeup above and below her eyes. An entire galaxy, clouds, stars, a sun, the sea, painted onto her face. Yellow, blue, pink, and a million silver sparkles.

We sat looking at each other, looking and talking and then not talking and looking again. It was a stop-and-start thing with both of us constantly saying the wrong thing, saying anything, and then immediately regretting having said it.

It was obvious Barbie didn't trust me. I asked her if she wanted something to drink.

"Diet Coke," she said. And I wondered why I'd asked.

I went into the house, upstairs into my parents' bathroom, opened the medicine cabinet, and got a couple of Valiums. I immediately swallowed one. I figured if I could be calm and collected, she'd realize I wasn't going to hurt her. I broke another Valium into a million small pieces, dropped some slivers into Barbie's Diet Coke, and swished it around so it'd blend. I figured if we could be calm and collected together, she'd be able to trust me even sooner. I was falling in love in a way that had nothing to do with love.

"So, what's the deal with you and Ken?" I asked later after we'd loosened up, after she'd drunk two Diet Cokes, and I'd made another trip to the medicine cabinet.

She giggled. "Oh, we're just really good friends."

"What's the deal with him really, you can tell me, I mean, is he or isn't he?"

"Ish she or ishn' she," Barbie said, in a slow slurred way, like she was so intoxicated that if they made a Breathalizer for Valium, she'd melt it.

I regretted having fixed her a third Coke. I mean if she o.d.'ed and died Jennifer would tell my mom and dad for sure.

"Is he a faggot or what?"

Barbie laughed and I almost slapped her. She looked me straight in the eye.

"He lusts after me," she said. "I come home at night and he's standing there, waiting. He doesn't wear underwear, you know. I mean, isn't that strange, Ken doesn't own any underwear. I heard Jennifer tell her friend that they don't even make any for him. Anyway, he's always there waiting, and I'm like, Ken we're friends, okay, that's it. I mean, have you ever noticed, he has molded plastic hair. His head and his hair are all one piece. I can't go out with a guy like that. Besides, I don't think he'd be up for it if you know what I mean. Ken is not what you'd call well endowed…. All he's got is a little plastic bump, more of a hump, really, and what the hell are you supposed to do with that?"

She was telling me things I didn't think I should hear and all the same, I was leaning into her, like if I moved closer she'd tell me more. I was taking every word and holding it for a minute, holding groups of words in my head like I didn't understand English. She went on and on, but I wasn't listening.

The sun sank behind the playhouse, Barbie shivered, excused herself, and ran around back to throw up. I asked her if she felt okay. She said she was fine, just a little tired, that maybe she was coming down with the flu or something. I gave her a piece of a piece of gum to chew and took her inside.

On the way back to Jennifer's room I did something Barbie almost didn't forgive me for. I did something which not only shattered the moment, but nearly wrecked the possibility of our having a future together.

In the hallway between the stairs and Jennifer's room, I popped Barbie's head into my mouth, like lion and tamer, God and Godzilla.

I popped her whole head into my mouth, and Barbie's hair separated into single strands like Christmas tinsel and caught in my throat nearly choking me. I could taste layer on layer of makeup, Revlon, Max Factor, and Maybelline. I closed my mouth around Barbie and could feel her breath in mine. I could hear her screams in my throat. Her teeth, white, Pearl Drops, Pepsodent, and the whole Osmond family, bit my tongue and the inside of my cheek like I might accidently bite myself. I closed my mouth around her neck and held her suspended, her feet uselessly kicking the air in front of my face.

Before pulling her out, I pressed my teeth lightly into her neck, leaving marks Barbie described as scars of her assault, but which I imagined as a New Age necklace of love.

"I have never, ever in my life been treated with such utter disregard," she said as soon as I let her out.

She was lying. I knew Jennifer sometimes did things with Barbie. I didn't mention that once I'd seen Barbie hanging from Jennifer's ceiling fan, spinning around in great wide circles, like some imitation Superman.

"I'm sorry if I scared you."

"Scared me!" she squeaked.

She went on squeaking, a cross between the squeal when you let the air out of a balloon and a smoke alarm with weak batteries. While she was squeaking, the phrase *a head in the mouth is worth two in the bush* started running through my head. I knew it had come from somewhere, started as something else, but I couldn't get it right. *A head in the mouth is worth two in the bush,* again and again, like the punch line to some dirty joke.

"Scared me. Scared me. Scared me!" Barbie squeaked louder and louder until finally she had my attention again. "Have you ever been held captive in the dark cavern of someone's body?"

I shook my head. It sounded wonderful.

"Typical," she said. "So incredibly, typically male."

For a moment I was proud.

"Why do you have to do things you know you shouldn't, and worse, you do them with a light in your eye, like you're getting some weird pleasure that only another boy would understand. You're all the same," she said. "You're all Jack Nicholson."

I refused to put her back in Jennifer's room until she forgave me, until she understood that I'd done what I did with only the truest of feeling, no harm intended.

I heard Jennifer's feet clomping up the stairs. I was running out of time.

"You know I'm really interested in you," I said to Barbie.

"Me too," she said, and for a minute I wasn't sure if she meant she was interested in herself or me.

"We should do this again," I said. She nodded.

I leaned down to kiss Barbie. I could have brought her up to my lips, but somehow it felt wrong. I leaned down to kiss her and the first thing I got was her nose in my mouth. I felt like a St. Bernard saying hello.

No matter how graceful I tried to be, I was forever licking her face. It wasn't a question of putting my tongue in her ear or down her throat, it was simply literally trying not to suffocate her. I kissed Barbie with my back to Ken and then turned around and put her on the doily right next to him. I was tempted to drop her down on Ken, to mash her into him, but I managed to restrain myself.

"That was fun," Barbie said. I heard Jennifer in the hall.

"Later," I said.

Jennifer came into the room and looked at me.

"What?" I said.

"It's my room," she said.

"There was a bee in it. I was killing it for you."

"A bee. I'm allergic to bees. Mom, Mom," she screamed. "There's a bee."

"Mom's not home. I killed it."

"But there might be another one."

"So call me and I'll kill it."

"But if it stings me I might die." I shrugged and walked out. I could feel Barbie watching me leave.

I took a Valium about twenty minutes before I picked her up the next Friday. By the time I went into Jennifer's room, everything was getting easier.

"Hey," I said when I got up to the dresser.

She was there on the doily with Ken, they were back to back, resting against each other, legs stretched out in front of them.

Ken didn't look at me. I didn't care.

"You ready to go?" I asked. Barbie nodded. "I thought you might be thirsty." I handed her the Diet Coke I'd made for her.

I'd figured Barbie could take a little less than an eighth of a Valium without getting totally senile. Basically, I had to give her Valium crumbs since there was no way to cut one that small.

She took the Coke and drank it right in front of Ken. I kept waiting for him to give me one of those I-know-what-you're-up-to-and-I-don't-like-it looks, the kind my father gives me when he walks into my room without knocking and I automatically jump twenty feet in the air.

Ken acted like he didn't even know I was there. I hated him.

"I can't do a lot of walking this afternoon," Barbie said.

I nodded. I figured no big deal since mostly I seemed to be carrying her around anyway.

"My feet are killing me," she said.

I was thinking about Ken.

"Don't you have other shoes?"

My family was very into shoes. No matter what seemed to be wrong my father always suggested it could be cured by wearing a different pair of shoes. He believed that shoes, like tires, should be rotated.

"It's not the shoes," she said. "It's my toes."

"Did you drop something on them?" My Valium wasn't working. I was having trouble making small talk. I needed another one.

"Jennifer's been chewing on them."

"What?"

"She chews on my toes."

"You let her chew your footies?"

I couldn't make sense out of what she was saying. I was thinking about not being able to talk, needing another or maybe two more Valiums, yellow adult-strength Pez.

"Do you enjoy it?" I asked.

"She literally bites down on them, like I'm flank steak or something," Barbie said. "I wish she'd just bite them off and have it over with.

This is taking forever. She's chewing and chewing, more like gnawing at me."

"I'll make her stop. I'll buy her some gum, some tobacco or something, a pencil to chew on."

"Please don't say anything. I wouldn't have told you except..." Barbie said.

"But she's hurting you."

"It's between Jennifer and me."

"Where's it going to stop?" I asked.

"At the arch, I hope. There's a bone there, and once she realizes she's bitten the soft part off, she'll stop."

"How will you walk?"

"I have very long feet."

I sat on the edge of my sister's bed, my head in my hands. My sister was biting Barbie's feet off and Barbie didn't seem to care. She didn't hold it against her and in a way I liked her for that. I liked the fact she understood how we all have little secret habits that seem normal enough to us, but which we know better than to mention out loud. I started imagining things I might be able to get away with.

"Get me out of here," Barbie said. I slipped Barbie's shoes off. Sure enough, someone had been gnawing at her. On her left foot the toes were dangling and on the right, half had been completely taken off. There were tooth marks up to her ankles. "Let's not dwell on this," Barbie said.

I picked Barbie up. Ken fell over backwards and Barbie made me straighten him up before we left. "Just because you know he only has a bump doesn't give you permission to treat him badly," Barbie whispered.

I fixed Ken and carried Barbie down the hall to my room. I held Barbie above me, tilted my head back, and lowered her feet into my mouth. I felt like a young sword swallower practicing for my debut. I lowered Barbie's feet and legs into my mouth and then began sucking on them. They smelled like Jennifer and dirt and plastic. I sucked on her stubs and she told me it felt nice.

"You're better than a hot soak," Barbie said. I left her resting on my pillow and went downstairs to get us each a drink.

We were lying on my bed, curled into and out of each other. Barbie was on a pillow next to me and I was on my side facing her. She was talking about men, and as she talked I tried to be everything she said. She was saying she didn't like men who were afraid of themselves. I tried to be brave, to look courageous and secure. I held my head a certain way and it seemed to work. She said she didn't like men who were afraid of femininity, and I got confused.

"Guys always have to prove how boy they really are," Barbie said.

I thought of Jennifer trying to be a girl, wearing dresses, doing her nails, putting makeup on, wearing a bra even though she wouldn't need one for about fifty years.

"You make fun of Ken because he lets himself be everything he is. He doesn't hide anything."

"He doesn't have anything to hide," I said. "He has tan molded plastic hair, and a bump for a dick."

"I never should have told you about the bump."

I lay back on the bed. Barbie rolled over, off the pillow, and rested on my chest. Her body stretched from my nipple to my belly button. Her hands pressed against me, tickling me.

"Barbie," I said.

"Umm Humm."

"How do you feel about me?"

She didn't say anything for a minute. "Don't worry about it," she said, and slipped her hand into my shirt through the space between the buttons.

Her fingers were like the ends of toothpicks performing some subtle ancient torture, a dance of boy death across my chest. Barbie crawled all over me like an insect who'd run into one too many cans of Raid.

Underneath my clothes, under my skin, I was going crazy. First off, I'd been kidnapped by my underwear with no way to manually adjust without attracting unnecessary attention.

With Barbie caught in my shirt I slowly rolled over, like in some space shuttle docking maneuver. I rolled onto my stomach, trapping her under me. As slowly and unobtrusively as possible, I ground myself against the bed, at first hoping it would fix things and then again and again, caught by a pleasure/pain principle.

"Is this a water bed?" Barbie asked.

My hand was on her breasts, only it wasn't really my hand, but more like my index finger. I touched Barbie and she made a little gasp, a squeak in reverse. She squeaked backwards, then stopped, and I was stuck there with my hand on her, thinking about how I was forever crossing a line between the haves and the have-nots, between good guys and bad, between men and animals, and there was absolutely nothing I could do to stop myself.

Barbie was sitting on my crotch, her legs flipped back behind her in a position that wasn't human.

At a certain point I had to free myself. If my dick was blue, it was only because it had suffocated. I did the honors and Richard popped out like an escape from maximum security.

"I've never seen anything so big," Barbie said. It was the sentence I dreamed of, but given the people Barbie normally hung out with, namely the bump boy himself, it didn't come as a big surprise.

She stood at the base of my dick, her bare feet buried in my pubic hair. I was almost as tall as she was. Okay, not almost as tall, but clearly we could be related. She and Richard even had the same vaguely surprised look on their faces.

She was on me and I couldn't help wanting to get inside her. I turned Barbie over and was on top of her, not caring if I killed her. Her hands pressed so hard into my stomach that it felt like she was performing an appendectomy.

I was on top, trying to get between her legs, almost breaking her in half. But there was nothing there, nothing to fuck except a small thin line that was supposed to be her ass crack.

I rubbed the thin line, the back of her legs and the space between her legs. I turned Barbie's back to me so I could do it without having to look at her face.

Very quickly, I came. I came all over Barbie, all over her and a little bit in her hair. I came on Barbie and it was the most horrifying experience I ever had. It didn't stay on her. It doesn't stick to plastic. I was finished. I was holding a come-covered Barbie in my hand like I didn't know where she came from.

Barbie said, "Don't stop," or maybe I just think she said that because I read it somewhere. I don't know anymore. I couldn't listen to her. I couldn't even look at her. I wiped myself off with a sock, pulled my clothes on, and then took Barbie into the bathroom.

At dinner I noticed Jennifer chewing her cuticles between bites of tuna-noodle casserole. I asked her if she was teething. She coughed and then started choking to death on either a little piece of fingernail, a crushed potato chip from the casserole, or maybe even a little bit of Barbie footie that'd stuck in her teeth. My mother asked her if she was okay.

"I swallowed something sharp," she said between coughs that were clearly influenced by the acting class she'd taken over the summer.

"Do you have a problem?" I asked her.

"Leave your sister alone," my mother said.

"If there are any questions to ask we'll do the asking," my father said.

"Is everything all right?" my mother asked Jennifer. She nodded. "I think you could use some new jeans," my mother said. "You don't seem to have many play clothes anymore."

"Not to change the subject," I said, trying to think of a way to stop Jennifer from eating Barbie alive.

"I don't wear pants," Jennifer said. "Boys wear pants."

"Your grandma wears pants," my father said.

"She's not a girl."

My father chuckled. He actually fucking chuckled. He's the only person I ever met who could actually fucking chuckle.

"Don't tell her that," he said, chuckling.

"It's not funny," I said.

"Grandma's are pull-ons anyway," Jennifer said. "They don't have a fly. You have to have a penis to have a fly."

"Jennifer," my mother said. "That's enough of that."

I decided to buy Barbie a present. I was at that strange point where I would have done anything for her. I took two buses and walked more than a mile to get to Toys R Us.

Barbie row was aisle 14C. I was a wreck. I imagined a million Barbies and having to have them all. I pictured fucking one, discarding it, immediately grabbing a fresh one, doing it, and then throwing it onto a growing pile in the corner of my room. An unending chore. I saw myself becoming a slave to Barbie. I wondered how many Tropical Barbies were made each year. I felt faint.

There were rows and rows of Kens, Barbies, and Skippers. Funtime Barbie, Jewel Secrets Ken, Barbie Rocker with "Hot Rockin' Fun and Real Dancin' Action." I noticed Magic Moves Barbie, and found myself looking at her carefully, flirtatiously, wondering if her legs were spreadable. "Push the switch and she moves," her box said. She winked at me while I was reading.

The only Tropical I saw was a black Tropical Ken. From just looking at him you wouldn't have known he was black. I mean, he wasn't black like anyone would be black. Black Tropical Ken was the color of a raisin, a raisin all spread out and unwrinkled. He had a short afro that looked like a wig had been dropped down and fixed on his head, a protective helmet. I wondered if black Ken was really white Ken sprayed over with a thick coating of ironed raisin plastic.

I spread eight black Kens out in a line across the front of a row. Through the plastic window of his box he told me he was hoping to go to dental school. All eight black Kens talked at once. Luckily, they all said the same thing at the same time. They said he really liked teeth. Black Ken smiled. He had the same white Pearl Drops, Pepsodent, Osmond family teeth that Barbie and white Ken had. I thought the entire Mattel family must take really good care of themselves. I figured they might be the only people left in America who actually brushed after every meal and then again before going to sleep.

I didn't know what to get Barbie. Black Ken said I should go for clothing, maybe a fur coat. I wanted something really special. I imagined a wonderful present that would draw us somehow closer.

There was a tropical pool and patio set, but I decided it might make her homesick. There was a complete winter holiday, with an A-frame house, fireplace, snowmobile, and sled. I imagined her inviting Ken away for a weekend without me. The six o'clock news set was nice, but because of her squeak, Barbie's future as an anchorwoman seemed limited. A workout center, a sofa bed and coffee table, a bubbling spa, a bedroom play set. I settled on the grand piano. It was $13.00. I'd always made it a point to never spend more than ten dollars on anyone. This time I figured, what the hell, you don't buy a grand piano every day.

"Wrap it up, would ya," I said at the checkout desk.

From my bedroom window I could see Jennifer in the backyard, wearing her tutu and leaping all over the place. It was dangerous as hell to sneak in and get Barbie, but I couldn't keep a grand piano in my closet without telling someone.

"You must really like me," Barbie said when she finally had the piano unwrapped.

I nodded. She was wearing a ski suit and skis. It was the end of August and eighty degrees out. Immediately, she sat down and played "Chopsticks."

I looked out at Jennifer. She was running down the length of the deck, jumping onto the railing and then leaping off, posing like one of those red flying horses you see on old Mobil gas signs. I watched her do it once and then the second time, her foot caught on the railing, and she went over the edge the hard way. A minute later she came around the edge of the house, limping, her tutu dented and dirty, pink tights ripped at both knees. I grabbed Barbie from the piano bench and raced her into Jennifer's room.

"I was just getting warmed up," she said. "I can play better than that, really."

I could hear Jennifer crying as she walked up the stairs.

"Jennifer's coming," I said. I put her down on the dresser and realized Ken was missing.

"Where's Ken?" I asked quickly.

"Out with Jennifer," Barbie said.

I met Jennifer at her door. "Are you okay?" I asked. She cried harder. "I saw you fall."

"Why didn't you stop me?" she said.

"From falling?"

She nodded and showed me her knees.

"Once you start to fall no one can stop you." I noticed Ken was tucked into the waistband of her tutu.

"They catch you," Jennifer said.

I started to tell her it was dangerous to go leaping around with a Ken stuck in your waistband, but you don't tell someone who's already crying that they did something bad.

I walked her into the bathroom, and took out the hydrogen peroxide. I was a first aid expert. I was the kind of guy who walked around, waiting for someone to have a heart attack just so I could practice my CPR technique.

"Sit down," I said.

Jennifer sat down on the toilet without putting the lid down. Ken was stabbing her all over the place and instead of pulling him out, she squirmed around trying to get comfortable like she didn't know what else to do. I took him out for her. She watched as though I was performing surgery or something.

"He's mine," she said.

"Take off your tights," I said.

"No," she said.

"They're ruined," I said. "Take them off."

Jennifer took off her ballet slippers and peeled off her tights. She was wearing my old Underoos with superheroes on them, Spiderman and Superman and Batman all poking out from under a dirty dented tutu. I decided not to say anything, but it looked funny as hell to see a flat crotch in boys' underwear. I had the feeling they didn't bother making underwear for Ken because they knew it looked too weird on him.

I poured peroxide onto her bloody knees. Jennifer screamed into my ear. She bent down and examined herself, poking her purple fingers into the torn skin; her tutu bunched up and rubbed against her face, scraping it. I worked on her knees, removing little pebbles and pieces of grass from the area.

She started crying again.

"You're okay," I said. "You're not dying." She didn't care. "Do you want anything?" I asked, trying to be nice.

"Barbie," she said.

It was the first time I'd handled Barbie in public. I picked her up like she was a complete stranger and handed her to Jennifer, who grabbed her by the hair. I started to tell her to ease up, but couldn't. Barbie looked at me and I shrugged. I went downstairs and made Jennifer one of my special Diet Cokes.

"Drink this," I said, handing it to her. She took four giant gulps and immediately I felt guilty about having used a whole Valium.

"Why don't you give a little to your Barbie," I said. "I'm sure she's thirsty too."

Barbie winked at me and I could have killed her, first off for doing it in front of Jennifer, and second because she didn't know what the hell she was winking about.

I went into my room and put the piano away. I figured as long as I kept it in the original box I'd be safe. If anyone found it, I'd say it was a present for Jennifer.

*

Wednesday Ken and Barbie had their heads switched. I went to get Barbie, and there on top of the dresser were Barbie and Ken, sort of. Barbie's head was on Ken's body and Ken's head was on Barbie. At first I thought it was just me.

"Hi," Barbie's head said.

I couldn't respond. She was on Ken's body and I was looking at Ken in a whole new way.

I picked up the Barbie head/Ken and immediately Barbie's head rolled off. It rolled across the dresser, across the white doily past Jennifer's collection of miniature ceramic cats, and *boom* it fell to the floor. I saw Barbie's head rolling and about to fall, and then falling, but there was nothing I could do to stop it. I was frozen, paralyzed with Ken's headless body in my left hand.

Barbie's head was on the floor, her hair spread out underneath it like angel wings in the snow, and I expected to see blood, a wide rich pool of blood, or at least a little bit coming out of her ear, her nose, or her mouth. I looked at her head on the floor and saw nothing but Barbie with eyes like the cosmos looking up at me. I thought she was dead.

"Christ, that hurt," she said. "And I already had a headache from these earrings."

There were little red dot/ball earrings jutting out of Barbie's ears.

"They go right through my head, you know. I guess it takes getting used to," Barbie said.

I noticed my mother's pin cushion on the dresser next to the other Barbie/Ken, the Barbie body, Ken head. The pin cushion was filled with hundreds of pins, pins with flat silver ends and pins with red, yellow, and blue dot/ball ends.

"You have pins in your head," I said to the Barbie head on the floor.

"Is that supposed to be a compliment?"

I was starting to hate her. I was being perfectly clear and she didn't understand me.

I looked at Ken. He was in my left hand, my fist wrapped around his waist. I looked at him and realized my thumb was on his bump. My thumb was pressed against Ken's crotch and as soon as I noticed I got an automatic hard-on, the kind you don't know you're getting, it's just there. I started rubbing Ken's bump and watching my thumb like it was a large-screen projection of a porno movie.

"What are you doing?" Barbie's head said. "Get me up. Help me." I was rubbing Ken's bump/hump with my finger inside his bathing suit. I was standing in the middle of my sister's room, with my pants pulled down.

"Aren't you going to help me?" Barbie kept asking. "Aren't you going to help me?"

In the second before I came, I held Ken's head hole in front of me. I held Ken upside down above my dick and came inside of Ken like I never could in Barbie.

I came into Ken's body and as soon as I was done I wanted to do it again. I wanted to fill Ken and put his head back on, like a perfume bottle. I wanted Ken to be the vessel for my secret supply. I came in Ken and then I remembered he wasn't mine. He didn't belong to me. I took him into the bathroom and soaked him in warm water and Ivory liquid. I brushed his insides with Jennifer's toothbrush and left him alone in a cold-water rinse.

"Aren't you going to help me, aren't you?" Barbie kept asking.

I started thinking she'd been brain damaged by the accident. I picked her head up from the floor.

"What took you so long?" she asked.

"I had to take care of Ken."

"Is he okay?"

"He'll be fine. He's soaking in the bathroom." I held Barbie's head in my hand.

"What are you going to do?"

"What do you mean?" I said.

Did my little incident, my moment with Ken, mean that right then and there some decision about my future life as queerbait had to be made?

"This afternoon. Where are we going? What are we doing? I miss you when I don't see you," Barbie said.

"You see me every day," I said.

"I don't really see you. I sit on top of the dresser and if you pass by, I see you. Take me to your room."

"I have to bring Ken's body back."

I went into the bathroom, rinsed out Ken, blew him dry with my mother's blow dryer, then played with him again. It was a boy thing, we were boys together. I thought sometime I might play ball with him, I might take him out instead of Barbie.

"Everything takes you so long," Barbie said when I got back into the room.

I put Ken back up on the dresser, picked up Barbie's body, knocked Ken's head off, and smashed Barbie's head back down on her own damn neck.

"I don't want to fight with you," Barbie said as I carried her into my room. "We don't have enough time together to fight. Fuck me," she said.

I didn't feel like it. I was thinking about fucking Ken and Ken being a boy. I was thinking about Barbie and Barbie being a girl. I was thinking about Jennifer, switching Barbie and Ken's heads, chewing Barbie's feet off, hanging Barbie from the ceiling fan, and who knows what else.

"Fuck me," Barbie said again.

I ripped Barbie's clothing off. Between Barbie's legs Jennifer had drawn pubic hair in reverse. She'd drawn it upside down so it looked like a fountain spewing up and out in great wide arcs. I spit directly onto Barbie and with my thumb and first finger rubbed the ink lines, erasing them. Barbie moaned.

"Why do you let her do this to you?"

"Jennifer owns me," Barbie moaned.

Jennifer owns me, she said, so easily and with pleasure. I was totally jealous. Jennifer owned Barbie and it made me crazy. Obviously it was one of those relationships that could only exist between women. Jennifer could own her because it didn't matter that Jennifer owned her. Jennifer didn't want Barbie, she had her.

"You're perfect," I said.

"I'm getting fat," Barbie said.

Barbie was crawling all over me, and I wondered if Jennifer knew she was a nymphomaniac. I wondered if Jennifer knew what a nympho-maniac was.

"You don't belong with little girls," I said.

Barbie ignored me.

There were scratches on Barbie's chest and stomach. She didn't say anything about them and so at first I pretended not to notice. As I was touching her, I could feel they were deep, like slices. The edges were rough; my finger caught on them and I couldn't help but wonder.

"Jennifer?" I said, massaging the cuts with my tongue, as though my tongue, like sandpaper, would erase them. Barbie nodded.

In fact, I thought of using sandpaper, but didn't know how I would explain it to Barbie: *you have to lie still and let me rub it really hard with this stuff that's like terry-cloth dipped in cement.* I thought she might even like it if I made it into an S&M kind of thing and handcuffed her first.

I ran my tongue back and forth over the slivers, back and forth over the words "copyright 1966 Mattel Inc., Malaysia" tattooed on her back. Tonguing the tattoo drove Barbie crazy. She said it had something to do with scar tissue being extremely sensitive.

Barbie pushed herself hard against me, I could feel her slices rubbing my skin. I was thinking that Jennifer might kill Barbie. Without meaning to she might just go over the line and I wondered if Barbie would know what was happening or if she'd try to stop her.

We fucked, that's what I called it, fucking. In the beginning Barbie said she hated the word, which made me like it even more. She hated it because it was so strong and hard, and she said we weren't fucking, we were making love. I told her she had to be kidding.

"Fuck me," she said that afternoon and I knew the end was coming soon. "Fuck me," she said. I didn't like the sound of the word.

Friday when I went into Jennifer's room, there was something in the air. The place smelled like a science lab, a fire, a failed experiment.

Barbie was wearing a strapless yellow evening dress. Her hair was wrapped into a high bun, more like a wedding cake than something Betty Crocker would whip up. There seemed to be layers and layers of angel's hair spinning in a circle above her head. She had yellow pins through her ears and gold fuck-me shoes that matched the belt around her waist. For a second I thought of the belt and imagined tying her up, but more than restraining her arms or legs, I thought of wrapping the belt around her face, tying it across her mouth.

I looked at Barbie and saw something dark and thick like a scar rising up and over the edge of her dress. I grabbed her and pulled the front of the dress down.

"Hey big boy," Barbie said. "Don't I even get a hello?"

Barbie's breasts had been sawed at with a knife. There were a hundred marks from a blade that might have had five rows of teeth like shark jaws. And as if that wasn't enough, she'd been dissolved by fire, blue and yellow flames had been pressed against her and held there until she melted and eventually became the fire that burned herself. All of it had been somehow stirred with the lead of a pencil, the point of a pen, and left to cool. Molten Barbie flesh had been left to harden, black and pink plastic swirled together, in the crater Jennifer had dug out of her breasts.

I examined her in detail like a scientist, a pathologist, a fucking medical examiner. I studied the burns, the gouged-out area, as if by looking closely I'd find something, an explanation, a way out.

A disgusting taste came up into my mouth, like I'd been sucking on batteries. It came up, then sank back down into my stomach, leaving my mouth puckered with the bitter metallic flavor of sour saliva. I coughed and spit onto my shirt sleeve, then rolled the sleeve over to cover the wet spot.

With my index finger I touched the edge of the burn as lightly as I could. The round rim of her scar broke off under my finger. I almost dropped her.

"It's just a reduction," Barbie said. "Jennifer and I are even now."

Barbie was smiling. She had the same expression on her face as when

I first saw her and fell in love. She had the same expression she always had and I couldn't stand it. She was smiling, and she was burned. She was smiling, and she was ruined. I pulled her dress back up, above the scarline. I put her down carefully on the doily on top of the dresser and started to walk away.

"Hey," Barbie said, "aren't we going to play?"

BROWN MANILLA

Patrick Gale (1962–)

Gale was raised on the Isle of Wight. His father was a prison governor and his mother suffered psychological problems following a car crash. He began writing in the mid-1980s, when the UK was socially conservative and the prime minister enacted homophobic laws. His novels feature mannerly, reserved characters who have peculiar thoughts, habits or occupations. His brilliant takes on subjectivity produce subtly broad illuminations.

Pregnancy suited Sylvia. Other women puffed and sweated through it, complaining incessantly, but all five of her pregnancies had seen her attain a state of charged wellbeing like nothing she had experienced in what she came to think of as her *empty* periods. Far from being a time of distortion, pregnancy seemed to her an all too brief perfecting, a sculptor's rounding-off.

Throughout her youth she had been restless, goaded by a sense of entitlement as indignant as it was directionless. She had worried that to achieve whatever it was that would finally satisfy her would take more money than her family possessed or more education than her father was prepared to purchase. When Richard found her at the regimental dance she had only attended to please a bossy friend, and proceeded to court her with quiet assurance, she decided it was marriage she had been craving.

And it did bring her satisfaction: the handsome guard of honour, the conferring of family jewels and silver, the charming of his widowed father and the muffling of her name in Richard's felt as flattering to her femininity as his borrowed greatcoat over night-chilled shoulders. And yet it was only with the sensation of a second life quickening within her that she felt at last a deep, calm fulfilment come upon her.

She adored each baby, marvelled at her cleverness in producing such perfection, wondered at the ordinary miracle that each should grow so alike and yet so distinct from its siblings, and she relished the small work-shop of the nursery – its nappies, its bottles, its carefully selected toys and well-made clothes – and his acknowledgment of her expertise within it. She knew, however, that this child, warm and heavy beneath her pinny, must be her last. They had agreed to stop at four, with a tidy two of each, because, although he had made brigadier while still in his forties, they were comfortable rather than rich and Richard had a quaint horror of their being taken for Catholics.

He was not a passionate man and did not find self-restraint a challenge. She gathered from other regimental wives she should be grateful for this. Some men were beasts. When the need arose, he used condoms he bought from his barber, mysterious things she never actually touched or saw, for which he fumbled in his sock drawer and of which all trace had gone come morning. This fifth pregnancy, arising after a four-year interval, had taken them both by surprise.

She had been on the point of giving away the pretty cot and the Silver Cross pram outgrown by their four-year-old, and had long since converted all the nappies to dusters and floor cloths.

"It's utterly inconceivable," he exclaimed when she broke the news, then laughed at the unwitting witticism, which they had both repeated so often since it would surely enter family lore.

Without it being discussed, it seemed they had agreed to treat the fifth baby as a sort of blessing. No further condoms had been called for – in a moment of extreme boldness she had looked in his sock drawer that morning and found nothing but socks and loose change – and she detected him withdrawing from her as though fearing that, God-like, he could impregnate her by the bestowal of a glance or passing caress. The oldest children were of an age to be noisily excited at the prospect of a baby. The youngest was wary and unconvinced and cast grim looks at the bulge where her waistline had been, as though to blight whatever rival lurked there. But neither toddler's curse nor husband's withdrawal could wound her, cushioned as she was by the potent combination of birth hormones and profound satisfaction.

Her mind was not so bliss-fogged that she couldn't see the timing was dreadful: the baby was due in two weeks but in four they were due to move house. The regiment, together with attendant wives and families, was moving to Germany. They were to exchange a plain Georgian officer's house in a Berkshire garrison town for a bungalow in a featureless army camp in a country where they had no friends and no language. It was a reversal of fortune but one she found could not trouble her. It was as though she were in shock.

As usual, her mother would come to stay a few days before the birth to supervise the others and keep house, the difference this time being that she would take the children away to stay with her in Ascot until after the move to Germany. Although Sylvia knew the pregnancy was not her fault, she had taken on herself the burden of preparing for the upheaval in the spirit of a penance. Her mother was apt to find fault and to treat Richard as a victim of wifely neglect. Sylvia was thus determined that, well before she went into labour, every wardrobe and chest of drawers, every over-burdened bookshelf, bursting toy cupboard and chaotic kitchen drawer should have been tidied and its contents winnowed so as to be ready for the packers. Any adult clothes beyond repair or redemption, any children's ones too tired to be worn by yet another child, had been bundled and tied for the rag-and-bone man. Bag after bag had been filled with rubbish they seemed to have been hoarding: incomplete jigsaws, knives with wonky handles, dolls that had lost their legs and balls that had lost their bounce.

She enjoyed herself. It was a task that called for a ruthless decisiveness that came easily to her. She worked at it in the mornings, while the toddler was at playgroup, and aimed to purge one room a day. She kept herself clean with a pinny and tied up her hair in a cheerily spotty cotton scarf. She tuned the radio to dance music and felt like an illustration in *Good Housekeeping*.

She had tackled their bedroom (which was how she finally knew the contents of his sock drawer). Today it was the turn of his study. Their quarters in Germany were a fraction of the size and certainly lacked either nursery or study. The study was tiny but it was attractive and an established child-free territory, and they would miss it keenly. The desk was a distinguished bureau bookcase inherited from his grandfather. The glass-fronted bookcase was still filled with grandfatherly books – Kipling, Dickens, Scott and Thackeray. Apart from the *Just So Stories*, *Thy Servant a Dog* and *The Rose and the Ring*, which she had read to the first two children and would read to the rest in turn, nobody had disturbed them but she had pledged to start reading them to herself once the children were more grown up.

The bureau below had two large drawers and, above them, two identical but artificial drawer fronts which together folded down to reveal the desk section with its blotter and array of tiny drawers and compartments. She knew her way around the desk and used it more than Richard did, as he had an office elsewhere and she was a keen letter writer. She wrote to her mother and brother on alternate Monday mornings. It was easily readied for packing – the pens and pencils zipped into a pencil case, writing paper, envelopes and postcards tucked into a Three Candlesticks box. She made a note to remind herself to order stationery with their German address on from the local printers before they left, then she sat with the wastepaper basket close beside her and tossed in an empty ink bottle, an ancient sheet of blotting paper and a cache of the better Christmas cards she had hoarded with the thrifty intention of converting them to present labels or bookmarks. In the little drawers, she found an assortment of small things inexplicably retained – a stick of sealing wax, a farthing, a suspender clip complete with ragged scrap of flesh-pink ribbon – and tossed them into the bin.

It wasn't enough, however. Perhaps it was an effect of all the books but the room felt little emptier than when she had started. Standing with effort, she pulled her chair back a little then tugged open the first of the big drawers. She knew exactly what was in here: every reply dutifully written by her mother and brother to every letter she had dutifully penned. Why on earth had she kept them? In the dim hope they would acquire with age a piquancy they had not displayed on receipt? Or as evidence of virtue against some future inspection?

Humming along to the stupid Frank Sinatra song that had come on the radio, she fetched a big cardboard bag from Dickins & Jones she had been saving and began to fill it in a kind of fever, surprised that she felt so little temptation to reopen any of the envelopes. She filled the bag almost to overflowing, tipped the contents directly into the dustbin, then returned to the drawer and almost filled it again, astonished that there were so many letters to dispose of.

Tucked away at the drawer's back, she came across a large manilla envelope, its original address heavily scribbled out. She snatched it up and was about to toss it after the rest but checked herself when she felt it wasn't empty. She tipped the contents onto what the baby had left of her lap.

It was a clutch of letters and postcards. She knew at once they weren't hers because her habit had always been to store letters in their envelopes because they were tidier that way and the postmarks were a speedy guide to a letter's date and origin. She flattened out the first to come to hand. The paper was good quality, thick, pre-war stock, but unheaded. The handwriting was distinctive, italic, the ink a smoky blue. She liked to think she could tell a man's writing from a woman's but in this case she was quite uncertain. Then she started to read.

Dear Richard. This separation is a perfect agony. I work and walk and drive about and take commands. I go through the motions so well I doubt anyone notices anything out of the usual about me but all I think about is last weekend and you…

The date was 1944, reassuringly before he had first asked Sylvia to dance. He had mentioned no old girlfriends – the only past loves he had spoken of were dogs – and, uncharitably, she had always assumed this was because he had none. Now she saw he had simply been showing a well-bred respect for her feelings. Touched and obscurely flattered, she flicked the page over to glance at the letter's end and saw only. *All my love, your E.* Then, shamed into emulating his rectitude, she refolded the letter and tucked it back inside the brown manilla envelope with the others and returned them to the drawer, which otherwise was now quite empty.

She fetched herself a cup of coffee and a rock bun, trying to put it out of her mind, then tackled the drawer below. This turned out to be a graveyard of old bills he had pointlessly stashed there and stacks of the little yellow folders in which her photographs were returned from the developer's. Any pictures that came out well, she stuck in carefully annotated albums soon after they arrived (it was the nearest she had to a hobby). All the folders contained now were negatives and the photographs she had never stuck in. However funny or evocative, they were all more or less hopeless so she tossed packet after packet in the rubbish bag after briskly checking the contents of each. She sang along to the radio but all the time she was thinking about the stash of letters in the other drawer.

Honesty was always the best policy. When he came home for lunch, she would find a discreet moment in which to tell him, honestly, she had stumbled on the letters while tidying the drawer, and see if he told her anything in return. But what if he simply threw them in the dustbin and told her nothing more? It would be unbearable not to know. Who was the girl, this mysterious E? An Evelyn or an Enid? Was she an older woman, even, or married? What did she look like? Perhaps if she looked more closely into the package she would find a photograph, an inscribed one. A pretty face, smiling bravely in a WAF uniform or a nurse's one. Or a smoky vamp with a flirtatious half-veil. But vamps, she sensed, would never have been his type. Perhaps there was a tragedy? Had E gone off with some handsome American once the separation she wrote of proved longer than her heart could bear? Or had she stayed true but been killed in an air raid? The letter Sylvia had glimpsed had been maddeningly – purposely – denuded of clues. Not even a town or house name. Merely that reassuring date.

By the time she needed to tidy herself up and fetch the youngest from playgroup and set soup and rolls to heat for lunch, there was nothing left in the bottom drawers but files of bank statements, a shoebox full of precious school reports and, bomb-like in its insignificant brown housing, the testimony to Richard's romantic past.

She always made an effort at weekday lunchtimes because they were the only time, apart from sleepy late evenings, when she could be sure of having him to herself for a little precious adult conversation. The four-year-old was always grouchily ravenous after a long morning of play-group so she would feed her the moment they got home then settle her down for an afternoon nap while she enjoyed lunch alone with him, hair brushed, a little lipstick on, a dab of scent and with her pinny firmly left in the kitchen. It was quite possible he was unaware of these details but she felt they mattered and was sure he would notice their absence.

Sometimes he was barely home for half an hour before he had to hurry out again but it was still half an hour in which they could speak quietly and calmly without the happy hubbub of childish demands and arguments coming between them. That day was one of the brutally curtailed lunch breaks. Even as he came in he was apologizing for having to rush. Some bigwig from the MOD was visiting unexpectedly in the afternoon and Richard was not convinced the barracks were ready for him. "I'm sorry, darling," he said. "We'll have to talk tonight instead."

He called her darling all the time now, she had noticed. When they were first married he called her by her name or by her nickname, Billy, short for Silly Billy. She tried not to dwell on it but sometimes she felt it sounded as though he were speaking from a script and encouraging her to do the same, as though they were Kenneth More and Kay Kendall and not themselves at all. *Dear Richard* was all the letter had said, not *Darling* or even *My dear.*

"That's quite all right," she told him. "Is everything bloody?"

"It is a bit."

"More soup?"

"Thank you, no. It's delicious but I must get on. How's the beastie?" He grinned as he gestured towards the ceiling, meaning the four-year old, whom she suspected was his favourite.

"Oh. A bit teary. She'll be fine in the end. Nobody likes being an ex-baby. Mummy will probably spoil her rotten when she comes. That might help, actually. Don't you want pudding, even? Apple and cheese?"

He was on his feet again already. "No time. Anyway, the Minister will expect fruit cake with his tea so I shan't starve. Was that oxtail?"

"Mulligatawny."

"Very good. Bye, darling."

She washed up the lunch things then checked on the four-year-old, who was still fast asleep, still clutching the pink rabbit she would never let Sylvia wash, still frowning. She was such a thundery, passionate child. Sylvia hoped she would grow out of it. Thunder and passion rarely made for happiness or easy friendships. She woke her slowly by quietly drawing her curtains then tiptoed out and returned, without a moment's hesitation, to the study and the drawer and the brown manilla envelope.

There was no fighting it. She had to know everything.

She opened the desk again and tipped the letters and postcards out over the blotter. Resisting the urge to read immediately, she made herself sort them by date then began at the beginning and worked through to the end. She was dimly aware of time passing, of her daughter getting up and beginning to play by herself, talking to her rabbit then squeaking terrible, formless tunes to it on the descant recorder she had stolen from her oldest sister, but her conscious mind was on the pages before her and the vivid scenes they evoked.

At first it was a struggle to understand. The pair had clearly known each other a long time, known each other's families even, but something had changed all their former easiness in the course of a weekend where E had initiated a risky conversation. The first letter was written in a state of suspense. She had clearly said things to Richard in the conversation she could never take back, confessed her feelings for him, presumably, before they had been interrupted by her mother and sister and Richard was left no space in which to answer. The next letter made it clear Richard's response had been encouraging. Then the pair had met for a country walk. They had kissed in a barn.

Sylvia felt a spasm of jealousy at that. Richard had always seemed uncomfortable, even disapproving, at public displays of affection. He had certainly never been moved to kiss her in the day-lit open air, even when unobserved. Reading E's rapturous response to it she began to feel something like anger.

When you held me in your arms and kissed me like that, it felt like an un-expected homecoming. I know we can never speak of it, that for any hint to get out would be a catastrophe, but I'm afraid you've left me so excited and happy I want to shout it from the rooftops. I don't understand how people can say the things they do, disapprove as they do, when loving like this feels so entirely right, so meant!

So that was it! E was a married woman. Small wonder Richard had never mentioned her. Sylvia wondered more than ever who she could have been. If the families were friends, then there was every likelihood she had met her by now at a wedding or a funeral. Perhaps she had even been there when Sylvia married the man E loved?

She read on through the little pile, tossing aside a snapshot of some army friend of Richard's that had come among the letters by mistake. She read a postcard from Tenby which said only:

All day, all night (especially the latter) I think of you, your face, your hands. Your E, and another, of an elegant youth by Ramsay, which said, *I think that was an experiment best left unrepeated. Don't you?*

There was a letter largely taken up with memories of an adored older brother just lost in action. Another, inspired by an idyllic weekend the pair had just snatched in some friend's borrowed cottage, was full of a future life together. *Somewhere safe, where we can be unremarkable, unjudged. Can there be such a place?*

There was something odd, however. The letters were circumspect, of course, as all wartime letters had to be. Nobody was mentioned by name. Places, even, were rarely specified. And yet there seemed to be an extra caution at work, as though they were not just lovers but spies or criminals, as though not just reputations but lives were at stake. E's descriptions of her war work were especially opaque because she edited so much out with inky scribble and tended to refer to everyone simply by letters of the alphabet.

> *Yesterday was particularly hard to take. All morning I had to listen, and yes, join in as X was sounding off to Y about how all p------s should be sniffed out like rats and shot or sent to a camp somewhere to avoid infecting the ranks and depleting morale. I almost ruined everything when Y suggested there should be camps on Anglesey and the Isle of Wight (just imagine, darling!) and I got the giggles amongst my files and had to pretend to be choking on a biscuit crumb. I'm sure they suspect nothing, I know they don't, but still...*

The tone had grown less effusive by now. There was a sense, not of the affair petering out, but of its having achieved an equilibrium. Or resigned impasse. Presumably because leaving E's husband and family (if she had one) was out of the question. For the first time, Sylvia found herself wondering why he had kept these letters. Had he done it unthinkingly, the way he did his bills, simply amassing them as they came in the post but never rereading them? Or was this a cherished cache he returned to repeatedly? Most of the pages felt barely creased or handled. They certainly hadn't been kept under pillows or wept over.

There were just two letters left. As she unfolded the penultimate one, her name flared out at her from the page and it took considerable presence of mind to read from the beginning and not dart down to that line.

What can I say? Sylvia is lovely. Idealistic. Innocent. If you insist on marry-
ing then I dare say she is perfect for you. I hope you will be happy. I know
you long for fatherhood but... Oh Robert. Perhaps I was naive? I had
thought you were more courageous than this. I dared to think that when
this bloody war was finally over we could go somewhere. Paris, maybe, or
Tangiers. Somewhere we're not known and could build a life. But I know
you. I know your unswerving moral compass. Sylvia represents the Right
Thing and I've no doubt you expect and trust me to re-embrace respectable
normality in my turn, as though what we have shared was nothing more
than an adolescent adventure. And I dare say you will succeed in shaming
me into compliant orthodoxy. But I know I will never entirely surrender.
I know that marriage, whatever its blessings, whatever the relief of escap-
ing from this constant subterfuge, will seem like a bare, grey room after the
garden we've been walking in...

She had the letters out of order. This was the sad, quiet *adieu* – the next
letter came from a few weeks before and was far less interesting. The
phrase was so insignificant Sylvia almost read past it without noticing.
Blah blah blah, she read (E's style was frankly rather undistinguished
and a bit novelettish). *Blah blah blah, the other men, blah blah blah.*
She had read to the bottom of the page and was turning before its
meaning snagged her attention and her eyes flicked back to reread it.
Z had suggested he spend the afternoon going over the plans with me
and the other men.
The four-year-old had made her way downstairs and chose that
moment to say, "Mummy" suddenly from the doorway. Sylvia jumped
and, nonsensically stacking the letters out of harm's way before attending
to her, brushed the small photograph onto the carpet.
"Coming, poppet." Leaning to pick it up, she found it had landed
face down. *To R from E*, she read. No grotesque love or kisses. Nothing
untoward. A friendly gift from one soldier to another. But the handwriting was unmistakable.
"Mummy!"

Trained that the room was territory forbidden to her, the child came no further in for all her anxiety.

"Oh darling, I'm coming!" Sylvia said, more sharply than she had intended and the child began to cry in the over-dramatic, attention-seeking way she did when thwarted. Sadly, she was beyond the age of being left to cry herself out in a pram at the bottom of the garden. "I'm sorry, I'm sorry." Sylvia left the desk and, ambushed by emotion, scooped her up, kissed her and danced her around the hall in her arms, face pressed into her golden curls until the child was laughing hysterically and it was the mother who, for a few jagged breaths, was weeping out loud. "I know," she sniffed. "Let's play with the buttons."

"Yes."

"You want that?"

"Yes."

The child had a thing about the button box, perhaps because she had been forbidden to touch it unsupervised lest she swallow a button or suck one into her little windpipe. As they jigged to the sitting room, Sylvia drew a few moments of intense comfort from being able to hold her close.

"My precious," she said.

"Buttons," the child replied then shouted, "Buttons!" so loudly it hurt at close range.

Sylvia set her down on the rug by the fireplace, fetched the button box – an old Turkish delight tin – and, after teasing her a moment ("Ready?" "Yes." "Are you sure?" "Yes!") tipped its glittering, clattering contents onto the floor before her. She stretched past her to the shelf where, only yesterday, when she had been a kind of unknowing doll, she had tidied the photograph albums and arranged them by age.

The oldest and thinnest was his mother's – a haphazard assemblage of snaps from the twenties and thirties, mostly frustratingly small and unascribed. The next oldest, not much larger, was Richard's. He had been given a Box Brownie for his twelfth birthday but had taken so few photographs with it that the evidence of his entire life between then and his meeting Sylvia occupied less than two-thirds of its length. At that point, it became obvious that his young wife, much the keener and abler photographer, had taken up the duties of household chronicler.

There were lopsided pictures of his parents and dog (several of the dog) and of an unfeasibly large cat and a few pictures of boys at his prep school, uniformed or in cricket whites. Then there was a whole page of pictures of a strikingly handsome boy, fourteen or fifteen, grinning awkwardly in a cloister somewhere (a cathedral or their school). *Tim Endersly*, the still-childish hand announced, *came to stay all summer*. The answering page showed an array of adults and children in holiday mode, the boy among them. *Assorted Enderslys*, it said, *came to fetch him back*. Thereafter Endersly appeared almost to the exclusion of anyone else in a way she (Fool. Fool!) had always thought a touching proof of a deep and lasting friendship, evidence that, however undemonstrative, her husband was a man of enduring loyalty. Endersly was pictured on other holidays, up at Cambridge and then, before the blank pages ensued, in September 1939 as a member of a well-wrapped student reading party in the Lake District. There were young men and women in the picture, many of them obviously paired up for the camera. Endersly was standing noticeably alone, the only one not smiling as he met the camera's eye. Her husband's eye.

Of course she had met him. A smartly suited civilian, introduced as Richard's best and oldest friend which, naturally, he was – Richard never lied about anything – he had been best man at their wedding and delivered a short and extremely witty speech. Two years later, within the space of six months, he had been a godfather at their firstborn's christening and boasted Richard as best man at his wedding in turn. She recalled a faintly hysterical occasion in the bride's home village in Hampshire, dominated by assorted Enderslys. The bride had been weepy and rather drunk and Richard, Sylvia remembered now, noticeably short-tempered. Since then, the wife had been fulfilling all the godfatherly duties, sending clumsily unsuitable presents with cards signed by her in her husband's name or not at all, and had missed the last birthday entirely.

"Sad," was Richard's only comment on the omission, which their son had accepted with a version of his father's stoicism. "She drinks, I gather."

Suddenly it was time to fetch the others from school. She tidied the remaining buttons away, stowed the four-year-old on the back seat and drove into town and back, feeling like a drunk herself, alarmingly detached and out of control as she negotiated turnings, zebra crossings and roundabouts with her precious brood noisy about her.

They washed their hands and sat around the kitchen table and she gave them glasses of milk and banana-and-honey sandwiches and heard from one then another about their day, stories of miniature endurance or injustice so crucial to them, so completely unimportant to her just now. When she could bear it no longer she lurched to her feet and left them to crumble hastily delivered slices of fruit cake.

The pile of letters was where she had left it. She seized it off the desk, scrabbled up the little photograph too and took them all to the sitting room fireplace where she tossed them into the grate and put a match to them. She waited, staring, until the pile had flared and was turning to curling ash. Then she stabbed it a few times with the poker before returning, heart racing, to the kitchen where the children had already abandoned a crumby chaos of tea things and school bags to race upstairs to watch *Children's Hour* in the nursery.

She would not tell him. Where, how could she begin? He had been a criminal repeatedly – if she had interpreted the letters correctly – committing acts that would see him thrown out of the army and into prison, if brought to light. This morning all was well. She cleared the tea things and made a start on supper. A few hours ago she knew nothing of this and all was well. When he came home she flinched instinctively but found he was the same man she had calmly loved and accepted at breakfast. She had changed, however, as surely as if his secret was something she had eaten that had stained her tongue and poisoned her.

If he should ever happen to ask what became of the letters, she decided, then they would have the conversation. Otherwise she would take the matter to her grave, as many a wife must have done before her.

As she laid the table and opened a tin of pineapple rings, as she arranged gammon steaks under the grill and oversaw the youngest's bath, she fantasized as she often did about scenes in their future life. The German army base might be better than she imagined, with trees and a park and a library. She might make a new friend among the wives there, a soulmate of the kind she had not enjoyed since school. The children would grow up and she would have to endure the regular trauma of enrolling each in turn in boarding school. Richard and she would make the perfectly normal, even expected, shift to having twin beds. They would survive.

And yet, once she had them all gathered about the table again, the youngest and oldest on either side of her and he, so distinguished and reserved at the other end, so serious in his calm interrogation of the middle two beside him, she knew this was a secret she would have to share. Sooner or later it would bubble out of her or be drawn from her by some accidental imprudence. As they ate and talked, drank and argued, she looked at each child in turn and imagined the moment when she burdened it with the odd, unthinkable truth. The oldest boy and girl were so earnest, so correct, she could imagine them blaming her: either insisting she was mistaken or that the whole thing had been somehow her fault. She could not imagine them offering her consolation or relief. The youngest girl adored him entirely too much and would never forgive Sylvia for the perceived calumny. The youngest boy, her guilty favourite and licensed clown, would refuse to take it seriously and make her feel that her years of secrecy had been a wasted, delusional effort.

She eased herself back in her chair and briefly met Richard's gaze as she dropped a hand to her belly. Which is when she knew it was her unborn child's birthright, born past the period of its mother's innocence, to be the only one of them to know her utterly. It might not hear the full truth for fifteen or sixteen years but, boy or girl, for better or worse, she would make it hers, bind it to her with secrets and prepare it for life as she feared she could never prepare the others, with vaccinations of the bitterest truth.

"Everything all right, darling?" he asked her, and something in his tone caused the children to fall silent and turn to her with small questions on their faces.

"I'm fine," she said, abashed, and instinctively reached out to touch the youngest one's cheek to reassure it. "Just a bit of indigestion, that's all. Now. Who's for pudding?"

SHADOWS

Damon Galgut (1963–)

Born in Pretoria, South Africa, Galgut first began to write stories as a child to engage his brain during a long, bedbound recovery from cancer. He published his first novel aged seventeen. His novels *The Good Doctor* (2003) and *In a Strange Room* (2010) have been shortlisted for the Booker Prize. He has written a number of stage plays. He lives in Cape Town.

The two of us are pedalling down the road. The light of the moon makes shadows under the trees, through which we pass, going fast. Robert is a little ahead of me, standing up in his seat. On either side of his bike the dogs are running, Ben and Sheba, I can never tell the difference between them.

It's lovely to be like this; him and me, with the warm air going over us like hands.

'Oh,' I say. 'Oh, oh, oh...'

He turns, looking at me over his shoulder. 'What?' he calls.

I shake my head at him. He turns away.

As we ride, I can see the round shape of the moon as it appears between the trees. With the angle of the road it's off to the right, above the line of the slope. The sky around it is pale, as if it's been scrubbed too long. It hurts to look up.

It's that moon we're riding out to see. For two weeks now people have talked about nothing else. 'The eclipse,' they say. 'Are you going to watch the eclipse?' I didn't understand at first, but my father explained it to me. 'The shadow of the earth,' he says, 'thrown across the moon.'

It's awesome to think of that, of the size of some shadows. When people ask me after this, I tell them, 'Yes,' I tell them. 'I'm going to watch the eclipse.'

But this is Robert's idea. A week ago he said to me, 'D'you want to go down to the lake on Saturday night? We can watch the eclipse from there.'

'Yes,' I said. 'We can do that.'

So we ride down towards the lake under the moon. On either side the dogs are running, making no sound in the heavy dust, their tongues trailing wetly from the corners of their mouths.

The road is beginning to slope down now as we come near to the lake. The ground on either side becomes higher, so that we're cycling down between two shoulders of land. The forest is on either side, not moving in the quiet air. It gives off a smell: thick and green. I breathe deeply, and my lungs are full of the raw, hairy scent of the jungle.

We're moving quite fast on the downhill, so we don't have to pedal anymore. Ahead of me, I see Robert break from the cut in the road and emerge again into the flat path that runs across the floor of the forest. A moment later I do so too, whizzing into the heavy layers of shadows as if they are solid. The momentum is wonderful, full of danger, as if we're close to breaking free of gravity. But it only lasts a moment. Then we're slowing again, dragged back by the even surface of the road and the sand on the wheels.

The turnoff is here. I catch up with Robert and we turn off side by side, pedalling again to keep moving. Ahead of us the surface of the lake is between the trees, stretched out greenly in the dark. The trees thin out, there's a bare strip along the edge of the water.

We stop here. The path we were riding on goes, straight and even, into the water. That's because it used to lead somewhere before they flooded the valley to make the lake. They say that under the water there are houses and gardens, standing empty and silent in the currents below. I think of them and shiver. It's always night down there at the bottom of the lake; the moon never shines.

But we've stopped far from where the path disappears. We're still side by side, straddling the bikes, looking out. The dogs have also stopped, stock-still, as if they can smell something in the air. There's a faint wind coming in off the water, more of a breeze really. On the far side of the lake we can see the lights of houses. Far off to the right, at the furthest corner of the water, are the lights of my house. I glance towards it and try to imagine them: my father and mother, sitting out on the front veranda, looking across the water to us. But there are no lights where we are.

'There,' says Robert.

He's pointing. I follow his finger and I also see it: the moon, clear of the trees on the other side. It really is huge tonight, as if it's been swollen with water. If you stare at it for long enough you can make out the craters on its surface, faint and blue, like shadows. Its light comes down softly like rain and I see I was wrong – it makes the water silver, not green.

'We've got a view of it,' I say.

But Robert is moving away already. 'Come,' he says. 'Let's make a fire.'

We leave the bikes leaning together against the trunk of a tree and set out to look for firewood. We separate and walk out by ourselves into the forest. But I can still see Robert a little distance away as he wanders around, bending now and then to pick up bits of wood. The dogs are with him. It isn't dense or overgrown down here. The floor of the forest is smooth. Apart from the sound of our feet and the lapping of the lake, it's quiet here.

There isn't much dead wood around. I pick up a few branches, some chunks of log. I carry them down to where the bikes are. Robert has already made one trip here, I see from a small pile of twigs. I don't much feel like this hunting in the dark, so I delay a while, wiping my hands on my pants. I look out over the water again. I feel so calm and happy as I stand, as if the rest of my life will be made up of evenings like this. I hear Robert's whistling coming down to me out of the dark behind. It's a tune I almost recognise. I start to hum along.

As I do I can see Robert in my mind's eye, the way he must be. When he whistles, small creases appear round his lips. He has a look of severe concentration on his face. The image of him comes often to me in this way, even when I'm alone. Sometimes late at night as I lie trying to sleep, a shadow cast in from outside will move against the wall and then he breaks through me in a pang, quick and deep. We've been friends for years now, since I started high school. It's often as if I have no other friends. *He* has, though. I see him sometimes with other boys from the school, riding past my house in a swirling khaki pack down to the lake. It hurts me when this happens. I don't know what they speak about, whether they talk of things that I could understand. I wonder sometimes if they mention me. I wonder if they mock me when I'm not there and if Robert laughs at me with the rest of them.

He comes down now, carrying a load of wood in his arms. 'Is that all?' he says, looking at what I collected. 'What's the matter with you?'

'Nothing,' I say, and smile.

He drops his wood along with the rest and turns. He's grinning at me: a big skew grin, little bits of bark stuck to his hair and the front of his shirt.

'Do we need any more?'

'No,' he says. 'That should do fine.'

We build a fire. Rather – he builds the fire and I sit against a tree to watch. It always seems to be this way: him doing the work, me watching. But it's a comfortable arrangement, he doesn't mind. I like the way he moves. He's a skinny boy, Robert, his clothes are always slightly loose on him. Now as I watch, my eye is on his hands as they reach for the wood and stack it. His hands are slender and brown. He's brought a wad of newspaper on his bike. He twists rolls of paper into the openings between the logs.

Like me, the dogs are sitting still and watching. They stare at him with quiet attention, obedient and dumb.

He lights the fire. He holds the burning match and I'm looking for a moment at this white-haired boy with flame in his hand. Then he leans and touches it to the paper. Smoke. He shakes out the match.

The fire burns, the flames go up. In a minute or two there's a nice blaze going. We're making our own light to send across the water. I think of my parents on the wooden veranda, looking across to the spark that's started up in the darkness. They point. 'There,' they say. 'That's where they are.' I smile. The fire burns. The flames go up. The heat wraps over my face like a second skin. The dogs get up and move away, back into the dark where they shift restlessly, mewing like kittens.

In a little time the fire burns down to a heap of coals. They glow and pulse, sending up tiny spurts of flame. We only have to throw on a stick now and then. Sitting and staring into the ring of heat, it would be easy to be quiet, but we talk, though our voices are soft.

'We should camp out here sometime,' he says. 'It's so still.'

'Yes,' I say. 'We should do that.'

'It's great to be away,' he says. 'From them.'

He's speaking of his family; his home. He often speaks of them this way. I don't know what he means by this: they all seem nice enough. They live in a huge, two-storeyed house made out of wood, about half an hour's ride from us. They're further up the valley, though, out of sight of the lake. There are five of them: Robert, his parents, his two brothers. I'm alone in my home, I have no brothers. Perhaps it's this that makes their house a beautiful place to me. Perhaps there really is something ugly in it that I haven't seen. Either way, we don't spend much time there. It's to my home that Robert likes to come in the afternoons when school is done. He's familiar to us all. He comes straight up to my room, I know the way he knocks on my door. Bang-bang, thud.

My mother has spoken to me about him. At least twice that I can remember she's sat on my bed, smiling at me and playing with her hands.

'But what's wrong with it?' I say. 'Everyone has friends.'

'But lots,' she says. 'Lots of friends. You do nothing else, you see no one else...'

'There's nothing else to do,' I say. 'Other people bore me.'

'There's sport,' she says. 'I've seen them at the school, every afternoon. Why don't you play sport like other boys? You're becoming thinner and thinner.'

It's true. I am. When I look at myself in the mirror I'm surprised at how thin I am. But I'm not unhealthy, my skin is dark, I'm fit. We ride for miles together, Robert and me, along the dust roads that go around the lake.

'It's him,' I say. 'Isn't it? It's him you don't like.'

'No,' she says. 'It isn't that. I like him well enough. It's you, you that's the matter.'

I don't want to upset them, my parents. I want to be a good son to them. But I don't know any way to be fatter than I am, to please them. I do my best.

'I'll try,' I say. 'I'll try to see less of him.'

But it doesn't help. Most afternoons I hear his knock at my door and I'm glad at the sound. We go out on our bikes. This happens at night too, from time to time. As now – when we find ourselves at the edge of the lake, staring at the moon.

'D'you want a smoke?' he says.

I don't answer. But he takes one out of the box anyway, leaning forward to light it in the fire. He puffs. Then he hands it to me. I take a drag, trying to be casual. But I've never felt as easy about it as Robert seems to. The smoke is rough in my throat, it makes my tongue go sour. I don't enjoy it. But for the sake of Robert I allow this exchange to take place, this word-less passing back and forth, this puffing in the dark. I touch his hand as I give it back to him.

'Are you bored?' he asks. 'Why're you so quiet?'

'No,' I say. 'I'm fine.' I think for a while, then ask, 'Are you?'

'No,' he says.

But I wonder if he is. In sudden alarm I think of the places he might rather be, the people he might rather be with. To confirm my fear, he mutters just then:

'Emma Brown—'

'Why are you thinking about Emma Brown?' I say. 'What made you think of her now?'

He's looking at me, surprised. He takes the cigarette out of his mouth. 'I was just wondering,' he says. 'I was just wondering where she is.'

'Why?' I say.

'I just wondered if she was also watching the moon.'

'Oh,' I say, and smile bitterly into the fire. I don't know what's going through his head, but mine is full of thoughts of her: of silly little Emma Brown, just a bit plump, with her brown hair and short white socks. I remember a few times lately that I've seen her talking to Robert; I remember him smiling at her as she came late to class.

'I was just thinking,' he says, and shrugs.

I finish the cigarette. I throw the butt into the fire. We don't talk for a long time after that. I can hear the dogs licking each other, the rasping noise of their tongues. I begin to feel sad. I think of my anger and something in me slides, as if my heart is displaced.

He reaches out a hand and grazes my arm. It's just a brief touch, a tingle of fingers, but it goes into me like a coal. 'Hey,' he says. 'What's the matter?'

'Nothing,' I say. 'Nothing.' I want to say more, but I don't like to lie. Instead I say again, 'Nothing.' I feel stupid.

The fire burns down to a red smear on the ground. Across the water the lights have started to go out. Only a few are left. I look off to the right: the lights in my house are still on. My parents keep watch.

When I look back, Robert is on his feet. His head is thrown back. I don't stand, but I gaze over his shoulder at what he's watching: the white disc of the moon, from which a piece has been broken. While we were talking, the great shadow of the earth has started to cover the moon. If you look hard enough, the dark piece can still be seen, but only in outline, as if it's been sketched with chalk.

We stare for a long time. As we do, the shadow creeps on perceptibly. You can actually see it move.

'Wow,' he says.

Sensing something, one of the dogs throws back its head in imitation of us and begins to howl. The noise goes up, wobbling on the air like smoke.

'Sheba,' says Robert. 'Be quiet.'

We watch the moon as it sinks slowly out of sight. Its light is still coming down, but more faintly than before. On the whole valley, lit weirdly in the strange blue glow, a kind of quiet has fallen. There is nothing to say. I lower my eyes and look out over the water. Robert sits down next to me on his heels, hugging his knees. 'You know,' he says, 'there's times when everything feels… feels…'

He doesn't finish.

'I know,' I say.

We sit and watch. Time goes by. The trees are behind us, black and big. I look across to my home again and see that the lights have gone out. All along the far shore there is dark. We're alone.

'It's taking a long time,' he says. 'Don't you think?'

'Yes,' I say. 'It is.'

It's hot. The dogs are panting like cattle in the gloom. I feel him along my arm. A warmth. I spring up, away. 'I'm going to swim,' I say, unbuttoning my shirt.

I take off my clothes, and drop them on the sand. The dogs are standing, staring at me. Robert also watches, still crouched on his heels, biting his arm. When I'm naked I turn my back on him and walk into the lake. I stop when the water reaches my knees and stand, arms folded across my chest, hands clinging to my ribs as if they don't belong to me. It isn't cold, but my skin goes tight as if it is. One of the dogs lets out a bark. I walk on, hands at my sides now, while the water gets higher and higher. When it reaches my hips I dive. It covers my head like a blanket. I come up, spluttering. 'It's warm,' I say, 'as blood.'

'Hold on,' he calls. 'I'm—'

As I turn he's already running. I catch a glimpse of his body, long and bright as a blade, before he also dives. When he comes up, next to me, the air is suddenly full of noise: the barking of the dogs as they run along the edge of the lake, the splashing of water, the shouts of our voices. It is our voices I hear, I'm surprised at the sound. I'm laughing. I'm calling out.

'Don't you,' I say, 'don't you *try*—'

We're pushing at each other, and pulling. Water flies. The bottom of the lake is slippery to my feet, I feel stones turn. I have hold of Robert's shoulder. I have a hand in his hair. I'm trying to push him under, wrenching at him while he does the same to me. He laughs.

Nothing like this has taken place between us before. I feel his skin against me, I feel the shape of his bones as we wrestle and lunge. We're touching each other. Then I slide, the water hits my face. I go under, pulling him with me, and for a moment we're tangled below the surface, leg to leg, neck to neck, furry with bubbles, as if we'll never pull free.

We come up together into quiet. The laughter has been doused. We still clutch to each other, but his fingers are hurting me. We stand, face to face. While we were below, the last sliver of moon has been blotted out. A total dark has fallen on the valley, so that the trees are invisible against the sky. The moon is a faint red outline overhead. I can't see Robert's face, though I can feel his breath against my nose. We gasp for air. The only sound to be heard is the howling of the dogs that drifts in from the shore: an awful noise, bereaved and bestial.

I let go. And he lets go of me. Finger by finger, joint by joint, we release one another till we are standing, separate and safe, apart. I rub my arm where he hurt it.

'Sorry,' he mutters.

'It's okay,' I say. 'It doesn't matter.'

After that we make our way to shore. I wade with heavy steps, as if through sand. By the time I reach the edge and am standing, dripping, beside my clothes, the moon has begun to emerge from shadow and a little light is falling. The dogs stop howling. I don't look up as I dress. I put my clothes on just so, over my wet body. They stick to me like mud.

I wait for him to finish dressing. As he ties his shoelaces I say, not even looking at him, 'What d'you think will happen?'

'What d'you mean?' he says.

'To us,' I say. 'D'you think in ten years from now we're even going to know each other?'

'I don't know what you mean,' he says.

He sounds irritated as he says this, as if I say a lot of things he doesn't understand. Maybe I do. I turn away and start to walk back to the bikes.

'Hey,' he calls. 'What you... don'tcha want another smoke or some-thin' before we go?'

'No,' I say. 'Not me.'

I wait for him at the tree where the bikes are leaning. He takes his time. I watch him scoop water over the coals. They make a hissing noise, like an engine beneath the ground. Then he walks up towards me along the bank, hands in his pockets. The sight of him this way, sulking and slow, rings in me long after we've mounted our bikes and started back up the path.

By the time we rejoin the dust road a little way on, the soreness in me is smaller than it was. One of the dogs runs into his way and he swears. At this I even manage to laugh. I look off and up to the left, at the moon which is becoming rounder by the minute. Its light comes down in soft white flakes, settling on us coldly as we ride.

A CHARTIST

Philip Hensher (1965–)

After graduating from Oxford and Cambridge University, Hensher worked as a clerk at the House of Commons, where he was sacked for an interview he gave to a gay magazine. His debut novel, *Other Lulus*, was published when he was twenty-nine. Since then, he has published eleven novels, including *The Northern Clemency* which was shortlisted for the 2008 Man Booker Prize, and *Scenes from Early Life*, which won the 2013 Ondaatje Prize. He collaborated with composer Thomas Adès, writing the libretto for the opera *Powder her Face*. He has edited both *The Penguin Book of the British Short Story* and *The Penguin Book of the Contemporary British Short Story*.

There was no one upstairs at all. I went up three times in an hour, in case they had all knocked off for a tea break, which seemed unlikely, but there were just a lot of men with their shirts off wandering up and down. It was three in the morning in a club in Brixton.

You felt the lack of the dealers. The club was full of men dancing in a rather hopeful sort of way, bopping in a sixth form manner rather than the usual, hips-out strut, there were occasional little pockets, islands of men who had obviously planned ahead and brought their own gear, men flailing and grinning, their jaws working. They seemed odd among the cheerily unsorted crowd.

The third time I went up there I bumped into Sean.

'What's up?' I said.

'Nothing,' he said. 'What are you after?'

'Some gear,' I said. 'There's nothing going on.'

'No,' he said. 'I was talking to the barman. He said they've been raided and they all got carried off by half eleven. No chance. Who are you with?'

'Some people I was at dinner with,' I said. 'They sent me up here to get them enough E for five.'

'No chance.'

Sean was a friend of mine. I'd known him on and off for a year, I'd never been to his house and he'd never been to mine. I saw him in the same two places: in clubs, and at the first nights in galleries. Once or twice I'd been out for a drink with him. He'd never be much more than a half-friend I sometimes had a drink with. He was quite a glamorous artist – the sort people talk about, though not the sort people buy, since his works were too absurd to even contemplate setting up. One man in North London *had* set one up, had bought a room-sized piece for a sum of money which, Sean said, had kept him going for a year and a half. There had been a gratifying stream of press coverage – some of which I'd written – and afterwards a complete lack of any further commissions. Though a fair amount of interest from which anything might come, and a little bit of fame.

The joke of Sean was that I always pretended to be passionately obsessed with him. Friends of mine always referred to him as 'your lover' since he was very good-looking and I liked him. 'Saw your lover the other day.' It wasn't true – I wasn't obsessed with him, though he was a nice man and at his best with his shirt off. He was famous for being monoga-mous, or almost so; though, as someone once remarked to me, sometimes it was hard to believe when you saw him in a club at five in the morning. I knew what I thought, and didn't say anything to anyone about it.

'Where's Joe?' I said. Joe was his partner.

'No idea,' he said. 'Haven't seen him for a week.'

'Is he away?' I said. I shouted a bit over the noise and the thump as the first swathe of the number dissolved into accelerating beats, before the dance music cut back in.

'No,' he said. 'I don't think so. He moved out.'

'He moved out?'

'Yeah,' he said. 'It's a bummer.'

'Come on,' I said. 'Let's go and talk about it.'

The club has a room slightly insulated from the dancing floor, so that the music comes out as a dull thud rather than the speakered shout that makes your ribs thud. People go there, it is said, to chill out; I never heard anyone use the expression, except in the same ironic way that they might say, 'Had some well dodgy gear Sat'day'. So Sean and I went into this room without a proper name. There were three bespectacled drag queens practising their low-level bitchery in a corner; one man who had overdone it was lying on his back on the floor, quite ignored, quite unaware that he had lost a shoe.

'I don't know what happened,' he said. 'It was my fault.'

'I'm sure it wasn't,' I said. 'Come on, tell me.'

We'd never slept with anyone else, Sean said. You know he was the first man I ever slept with. And he was late coming to terms with it, and he'd only ever had one other man before he met me, in York. Joe was a really shy man. He didn't look it; he was. He liked going to clubs, and to bars, but he would do anything to get out of going to a party. He hated going to dinner parties, he hated giving dinner parties. When he changed his job, he lost a lot of sleep just thinking about how he was going to get on with the people he was going to work with.

It was mad. He wasn't the most confident person in the world. No one would have thought he was. But he was easy to like. It was the combination of a man who went out all the time and one who was self-deprecating, shy, easily embarrassed by small difficulties. No one found him intimidating, or hard, or anything; everyone saw the little problems he had, and didn't talk about. People liked him.

The thing was, what people didn't see, was that he'd turned his shyness into a kind of virtue. He didn't see any reason to try and get rid of it, though he'd rather not have been shy. He just thought that was the way things were and there was no altering any of it. That was really where the monogamy thing came into it. We'd decided that we weren't going to sleep with anyone else, we weren't going to pick up a boy at a club and say to each other, well, see you tomorrow. There's nothing wrong with that, I don't think. It used to be the way things were.

But he wasn't doing it because he thought it was a good idea. We decided that we wouldn't sleep with anyone else because he didn't believe he could pick someone else up. It was all because he wasn't confident enough. Of course he could have done. People used to come on to him here, when he was dancing, or whatever. Whenever I went off somewhere, when I came back there was always some really gorgeous boy grinding his arse against Joe's crotch, and him with this apologetic look on his face, as if he couldn't help it.

You'd think that would have persuaded someone that they could score as easily as anything. But it didn't. When I said this to Joe – I only ever said it to cheer him up, to make him think that he wasn't as hopeless as he thought he was, I never said it to persuade him to go ahead and sleep around – he'd only ever say, 'Oh, the thing about this place is people are always playing weird games with each other. It doesn't mean anything.' He seemed to believe it. He really seemed to think that if he'd said to one of these boys who was coming on to him like that, 'All right then, come home with me,' they'd have laughed at him for taking it seriously.

And it was the same everywhere. Once there was this guy who was coming on to him to this unbelievable extent at some dinner party – not just flirting, but, by the end of the evening, asking him for his phone number, and not believing him when he said, 'I don't think that would be a good idea.' When we got home, he said to me, 'Oh, he was just saying that,' as if the man wasn't serious. I really had to persuade him that it was a bit more than that. Crazy. That was where the monogamy came from, not from wanting only me, or thinking not having every man on a dance floor wasn't, in itself, a good idea. What really scared him was this idea that if we started saying, like everyone else, 'Oh, well, we can have it off with some Spaniard now and again without worrying about whether it's going to mess up our relationship,' then we'd set off and I'd score and he wouldn't be able to.

The weird thing was that I didn't particularly want to tap off with anyone else. I was just mad about Joe. I know it sounds completely unbelievable, but still after seven years, he'd take his shirt off and I'd be struck with lust. I just wanted to fuck him the whole time. Even when he was being a complete pain in the arse, I still wanted to fuck him. I fancied other people, of course I did, but I never wanted to get off with them particularly. And I never thought of myself as being particularly faithful. It was like monogamy had been forced on us by something outside, something outside our control. For him it was just the fear that there was no one else for him; for me it was this lust I couldn't control, just for him. We'd both rather have been without it. But there was nothing we could change, and it looked like such a good idea from outside, we never really talked about it, we never really complained about it. Maybe there was nothing to complain about. Probably there wasn't. You never know what holds people together, what that glue is.

About a year ago, I met this man. He was all right. He wasn't mad, or anything. I saw him around and we always talked. He was funny, and everything; a nice man. It wasn't that I ever missed him if he wasn't at a party, or down here, but when I saw him, I thought, oh, right, he's here, good, I'll talk to him in a bit. Joe met him and he thought about the same of him that I did, nice man, nice-looking, let's have him round to dinner some time. And that was it. Of course, we never did have him round to dinner, just carried on bumping into him. You think the same thing about probably twenty people at any time in your life; you think, oh, must get him round, but there's no particular reason to.

Last November I was down here and bumped into him – I remember when it was, it was when there was that big storm. I'd been here since midnight, and when I came out at six, I'd no idea anything had happened. There were all these trees just lying all over the place, and I remember coming out and just looking. There was a car outside with its windscreen shattered – a roof tile had just gone straight through it. I'd met this man that night. It stuck in my mind.

'Do you mind if I talk to you?' a boy said to Sean and me. He had just come up.

'We're just talking to each other,' Sean said.

'Oh, I'm just looking for someone to share a cab to Trade,' the boy said. 'Are you going there?'

'I don't think so,' I said. The boy was too skinny to be nice to.

'Only I've just come up for the night,' he said. 'I've never been here before. I was looking to see if I could get any E but there doesn't seem to be any about.'

'No,' I said. 'No one takes drugs here.'

'Get away,' he said. 'I know better than that.'

'Well, I've no idea where to get any,' Sean said. Then he leaned forward and put his face right against the boy's. 'I'll tell you a secret. We're not clubbers. We're not queers, either. We're plainclothes policemen, and we're looking for poofs who take drugs.'

'Get away,' the boy said. He turned from us and went out of the room, looking for someone to share his taxi with. Sean rolled his eyes, and went on with what he was saying.

He was someone I sort of knew, this man I met. I used to meet him most weeks down here. Anyway, we danced a bit together, then I said, I'm knackered, come and have a sit down. We were both off our faces, and you know how everyone seems then. So we were sitting here – Joe was away, I think – anyway, he certainly wasn't there. And I don't know why, but this man started telling me about what seemed like his main hobby.

'I like to know who's had who,' he said. I didn't know what he meant. 'I like to know who's slept with who.' I didn't understand why anyone would want to know something like that. Well, I could, I suppose. It's quite interesting when you hear that two people you know have just started sleeping together, or when you hear that two people you know used to sleep together ten years ago and now just bump into each other at parties and are just friendly with each other. So I can see that's quite interesting. But this man had taken it a stage further than that. He'd actually drawn up a chart of who'd slept with who.

'Why are you telling me all this?' I said.

'Wait,' Sean said. 'There's more.'

He didn't have the chart with him, Sean went on, but he drew a little example of what it looked like, and explained how you got on to the chart. A name would be connected to another name by a line, which would lead on to someone else. The aim was to establish how many fucks you were from anyone else, anyone you hadn't actually fucked or would want to. He was quite proud of the fact that he was only three fucks away from Leonard Bernstein in one direction, and seven from Prince Charles in another.

Then he explained how you got on to the chart. He had a word for people who had got on to the chart. He called them chartists. It was a joke – at least he thought it was funny. I did, too. I'm talking as though I despised it from the start, but I definitely didn't. I thought it was a funny thing to do. I thought it sounded as if it was full of these kind of scandalous glamorous people. I sort of wanted to be one.

I didn't stand a chance, though. You didn't get on it by fucking just one person. You had to be connected to two people. And I'd only ever fucked Joe in my life, so that was that. And he wouldn't get on the chart because he'd only ever fucked me and this man in York. So I laughed and said I'd like to see the chart some time and forgot about it.

About a week later I was in Soho and saw this man in a bar. I went up and said hi again to him. Like you do. And there was something the next day, something or other I thought he'd be going to. I asked him if he was going, and he said yes, and let's have a beer afterwards. And then I said, hey, bring your chart along, I'd like to see it. He looked at me in this weird way. 'I didn't know I'd told you,' he said. 'Well, you did,' I said. 'Last week. I remember even if you don't.' He came along the next night and afterwards we went out for a beer. I didn't think he'd have brought it, but he had.

I don't know really why I was interested. Most of the people I'd never heard of, apart from a few people we both knew, and a few people every-one's heard of, like Cary Grant or whoever. It was like this huge piece of paper – I remember being in the Café Pelican and everybody obviously thinking we were completely off our heads with this piece of paper twice the size of the tablecloth, and laughing like hyenas. We'd been laughing about who'd fucked who for about half an hour when I noticed this name. 'Who's that?' I said. 'Oh, it's just some bloke in York this friend of mine fucked and then told some friend of his who went up and fucked him too. It was about a year ago. He's quite a useful link.' 'I'll say,' I said. The thing was, this bloke in York was Joe's ex-boyfriend.

It wasn't much of a coincidence, and it didn't mean anything. But anyway, I said Joe had gone out with this man, and things started getting interesting. 'We could get Joe on to it,' he said. 'If he's fucked him and you. But you're not on it.' 'No,' I said. 'I've never slept with anyone else.' 'You're joking,' he said. I wasn't. 'Is that true?' he said. 'I thought that was just your line. You've never had anyone else?' 'No,' I said. 'Not that I wouldn't mind.'

Till I said that I didn't know I thought it. It really annoyed me, in a way, that I couldn't be on the chart because I'd never slept with anyone. It doesn't sound now like much of a reason to shag someone else, because you want your name on a piece of paper. Maybe I always wanted that, to have my name on a piece of paper, to get noticed. To be history. Now I am history. That's funny. It isn't much of a reason. But you only need one.

'Just never had the opportunity?' he said. 'No,' I said.

That was the opportunity. The opportunity I needed to fuck up my life for good, get rid of someone I loved and who loved me for no reason at all. Well, you know the rest, or you can guess it. I went back with the man and fucked him. No, I didn't even go back with the man; I never went to his place, and he never came to mine. We fucked in the alley behind a bar in Covent Garden. You know the one. Yes, you do.

Two days later, this packet came through the post. I opened it. It was a new chart, it was exactly the same as the old one, except now it had two new names on it, a new series of lines, drawing connexions.

I opened the chart at breakfast. Joe wanted to see it.

He moved out about a fortnight later.

Sean stopped talking. He closed his eyes. The room seemed terribly small; the music thudding too close to me. I didn't know what to say.

'Why have you told me this?' I said.

'Because you didn't know it,' he said.

'Yes I did,' I said. It was almost true. 'I knew that I'd told you about the chart, and I remember having it off with you. It was only three months ago.'

'You didn't know what happened.'

I didn't know what to say. I could hardly bear to listen to him telling me a story about myself, I could hardly bear to listen to my own actions, and their consequences.

'I'm sorry,' I said. It was just a joke, the chart; it was an idle amusement, and it had never occurred to me that having a name on it, that having recorded someone's bland liaison could in any way affect anyone else's life. For a bizarre moment, I stopped thinking about Sean, and Joe. I wondered about the other two hundred names on the chart, the two hundred chartists. I wondered what had happened in their lives because of what I had written on a piece of paper, and I wondered what that piece of paper had caused. 'I'd never have done it,' I said.

'You didn't do it,' he said. 'It was me really.'

'What's the time?' I said.

'Four,' he said. 'It's going on late tonight.'

I took his hand in mine.

'I can't do anything to make it up,' I said. Perhaps I was sincere. 'I would do anything to change things for you, but I can't.'

'No,' he said. 'The thing is, that this was always planted in things from the beginning. The way me and Joe would end was there from the start, because he wanted faithfulness for the wrong reasons, and I wanted faithfulness for the wrong reasons, I suppose. Maybe not.'

'I think fancying someone is a good reason for faithfulness,' I said. 'It's the only one – it's the only free one.'

'I'm thinking about going,' he said. 'Have you got money for a cab?'

I got out my wallet. I looked in it for twenty quid among the usual detritus of receipts and bills and notes of phone numbers. In there, among all this, was a little snap-fastened plastic sachet. I fished it out.

'Look,' I said. 'I'd forgotten about it.'

'What is it?'

There were two pills in the sachet. I had bought them last week; I hadn't got round to taking them. I had forgotten about them. They might be the only two pills left in the club; in the world. They would do for me; one now, one in two hours' time. They would.

'Do you want one?'

'Go on then.'

So things were different. I took him in my arms. We danced till dawn. All that.

AIR

Tomoyuki Hoshino (1965–)

Born in Los Angeles, Hoshino and his family moved back to Japan before he was three. He spent his late twenties living in Mexico before returning to Japan. He published his first novel in 1997, and his second novel *The Mermaid Sings Wake Up* won the Yukio Mishima Prize. His work reached the English-speaking world through the queer journal *Chroma*, and has led to growing fame in the West.

The flute played the quiet with its hoarse-throated cry. It was a song like wind allowing a flute to sculpt its contours, a Tōru Takemitsu composition called "Air." My chest tightened as its birdsong phrase repeated. It felt like Tsubame had flown into my room and was whispering in my ear.

With "Air" playing on a loop in the background, I spread tissues across the floor beneath my desk chair, dropped my pants, and rubbed myself erect. Then I took the alcoholwiped blade of my X-Acto knife and pressed it carefully against my penis, gently pulling it along the skin. The cold came first, followed closely by sharp pain, and a light flow of blood began running toward the root. I wrapped the shaft in tissue paper. With my spit-wet finger I caressed the mouth of the wound. An involuntary cry of pain escaped me. The stopper that had blocked my throat like the pit of a plum worked itself free at last, and sadness surged up all at once. My tears and cries seemed to have no end.

I don't do it because it feels good. I do it because if I didn't, I would lose any sense I was still alive. It was a variation on the theme of the wrist cut, the penis cut. I have no desire to approach death, so I avoid my wrists.

I want to approach a deeper, more fundamental loss, so I cut my penis. I can get as close as possible to the loss of Tsubame this way.

I say I lost him, but he didn't die, we didn't even have a falling out. Tsubame simply went along with his diplomat lover, Dr. Hiroda (as everyone called her), when she was transferred to Mexico. At the farewell party the two of them held at their home, Tsubame had told me lightheartedly, "Come visit us! We'll have three spare rooms, you can stay for as long as you like. Any one of them is bigger than your entire apartment, Tsubasa!" But I had already reached my limit. I couldn't stand this one-sided affair any longer. It was just that I couldn't bring myself to end things when he was near. When he told me he was going to Mexico, I realized my chance had come. Seeing that I could no longer stand the situation I'd found myself in, destiny had lent its helping hand.

So I vowed never to go to Mexico, never to see Tsubame again as long as I lived. And with this feeling filling me, I sang him a farewell song at his farewell party. It was "La Golondrina," a song sung in Mexico at times of parting, which I'd memorized phonetically for the occasion.

Are you leaving, where are you going, *golondrina*?

If you hurry so, you'll tire,
Lose your way in the wind,
Have nowhere to rest your wings.

I'll make you a nest near my bed,
You can weather the cold months there.

I am lost here too.
O Heaven! I cannot fly like you, *golondrina*.

Oh, my lovely *golondrina*, I hear your song,
And think of home, and weep.

I'd also recorded myself playing the flute, and I sang with the recording as accompaniment. As I sang, the thought that the words were a direct expression of my heart overwhelmed me, and I started to cry. And once I started, I couldn't stop. No one knew of my decision. Tsubame remained ignorant of the confession I was singing to him as I mouthed the Spanish syllables of "La Golondrina." So my song was received with a vague sort of generalized pensiveness, punctuated by a few women bursting into tears in sympathy with mine.

Tsubame praised my flute playing. He knew how hard I'd practiced to make the instrument my own.

The first time we ever did anything alone together was when I went with him to a memorial concert for Tōru Takemitsu. Dr. Hiroda, who was originally supposed to have gone with him, had had something come up, so he asked me to go in her stead. I'd never heard the name "Tōru Takemitsu" before, and I found contemporary classical music so boring that I was fighting to stave off sleep throughout the show. I even abstained from the wine offered during the intermission. Still, Tsubame saw through all my efforts, of course.

The concert ended with Takemitsu's posthumous work "Air," then the house lights came up. Tsubame hurriedly wiped tears from his eyes, saying softly, "I want that piece played at my funeral. It makes me feel like I wouldn't mind no longer being human."

Was the piece really that great? Spurred by this thought, I ran out and bought it on CD. Patrick Gallois was the flutist on the recording. Even though I didn't understand what made it so great, I listened to it over and over. And as I did, the Takemitsu-borne wind that Gallois played began to penetrate my flesh, to blow through my body. It was music, yet it wasn't. It fell somewhere between a natural breeze and a man-made breath. I felt as if by opening my body to this wind, I, too, could tran- scend my own humanity.

This must have been what Tsubame had meant, and I was filled with joy at my realization, and ran to tell him. And wouldn't you know, he ended up giving me a flute of my own as a present.

"It doesn't matter if you're bad at it. You understand the feeling, so I want you to play the wind," he told me, rather affectedly. Artists have a tendency to say pretentious things without a hint of irony. Tsubame was an unsuccessful artist who painted all sorts of bric-a-brac in colorful abstractions, and who Dr. Hiroda, the daughter of a gallery owner and fifteen years his senior, discovered and later made her lover. To cut a long story short, I ended up meeting Tsubame because a close friend from middle school had a sister who was an editor for an art magazine, and we were introduced at a party at her house.

Truth be told, the flute he gave me was somewhat of a burden. But I gave it my all because I knew it pleased him. I took lessons whenever I had a day off, and even during normal workdays I'd practice for an hour in the park early in the morning. I'd initially planned on mastering the phrase from "Air" that I liked so much, but this turned out to be much too distant a goal, seeing how I found myself occupied entirely with just "La Golondrina."

Listening to "Air" again now, I caressed the wounds cut into my penis, and as I blew on them, the pain seeping into my flesh, I felt the air rush through me. The wind blowing through my hollow core seemed to produce a hoarse-throated sound. I became a flute as the wind passed through me, and I played my own version of "Air." I thought of Tsubame, who'd crossed the sky and left me. He'd shown me the difference between him and me, flightless wing that I am, and yet he also made me feel what it was to be alive. I resisted the urge to cut myself again.

Layers of scars adorned my penis like the patterns carved by waves. When Misaki was about to go down on me the first time, she noticed them and pulled back. "What's that? Some kind of disease?" she asked. "Well, of a sort," I replied ruefully, "A disease of the heart."

"I didn't know you were into that kind of thing. You like it rough? I must not be enough for you!"

"You are more than enough for me. It's just when I'm alone, I end up hurting myself."

I told her the truth. I told her all about Tsubame, save for my pathetic feelings for him. But the explanation didn't ring true even to myself. I'd never fallen in love with a man, my seduction success rate with women averaged about sixty percent, and things with Misaki were going perfectly well, so I hadn't known what to make of my quickening heartbeat when I'd first met Tsubame. Did I simply respect a man so able to live life on his own terms? Was I just drawn to someone whose talents exceeded my own?

Tsubame was popular. With his svelte physique, his gentle voice and way of speaking, his meltingly sweet disposition, his guileless way of approaching things that fell outside his ken, he possessed an openness that put everyone at ease while concealing the sharpness of his true insights. These elements blended miraculously to produce a sultry allure that wafted from him almost palpably. Yet he was devoted to Dr. Hiroda exclusively. All others who crowded around remained firmly in their places as dear friends, nothing more. Myself included.

Yet I had the feeling that in his heart of hearts, I stuck out at least a little from the rest of these "dear friends." And regardless, I simply wanted to be near him. It didn't matter if it was just the two of us or not. It was happiness itself just to hear his voice speak his words, to have him laugh or be moved or get excited by mine. Our moods would melt into each other and become inextricably mixed. And then I would decide not to think about these feelings any further. I would shed my clothes and satisfy myself with Misaki.

But even so… At long last, I confessed my secret feelings to Misaki. Her response was unexpected, or maybe I should say, old-fashioned. In short, she became a ball of fire ignited by jealousy and trust betrayed.

"What is this load of crap? The truth is you like your junk slapped around by some dominatrix, don't you? You get off when it hurts, right? So why don't I try biting you? I'll chew you up and spit you out, you animal, you monkey who walks like a man!"

As she said this, she actually tried to bite me. Naturally, we soon split up. The truth was, I was playing at being something I wasn't even more than Misaki guessed, so my fault in the matter was hardly trifling. But even so, I made use of Misaki's convenient misunderstanding.

My cuts scab over and the scars they leave after I peel them off overlap and build on each other, deforming my penis until it looks like it's ringed with rubber washers. I was running out of places for my blade to slice.

I wanted proof that I was alive. I wanted to remake myself into a form I could point to and say, "*That* is Tsubasa Tsutsui." I imagined myself with a vagina, tracing the line coarsely referred to as the "ant trail" that runs from behind my balls to my anus with the point of the blade.

I felt as if I already had a vagina. What other explanation could there be for the sweet pain that overcomes me? It was simply buried beneath this thick wall of flesh. My body was hiding my vagina deep within itself. A vagina concealed a hollowness. I was a flute, I was hollow too, wind rushing through my empty core. If I could just split my flesh open, my hollowness could be exposed. I could just turn my flesh back on itself and voila! A vagina would appear! Just as Takemitsu sculpted the air by caressing its contours to make wind into music, I could make myself into an instrument just by cutting through the hymen obstructing my flute! And then I would be my true self at last, and living my life would regain its meaning.

Excited by these thoughts, I drove the blade hard into my perineum. Pain incomparable to any penis cut shot through me from my spine to the crown of my skull. This was my penis's root. It was more resilient that I'd imagined, and more sensitive. But to cut into it was to make the vagina cut. If I couldn't stand to do it, I'd never become my true self. The extent of the sacrifice gave value to the act's completion.

I pictured myself penetrating my own hole, exploring it with my fingers. Just imagining it, my body was gripped with agony. If I really did it, I suppose I'd pass out, ascend to heaven. Ascend. I'd rise like Tsubame up into the sky. We'd ride the wind and dance up there, together in the air.

Today it happened in a crowded train. A penis appeared at my crotch. It was so sudden it hurt. It pressed up against someone's thigh. I supposed there were a lot of men who did this, who molested their neighbors with an innocent look on their faces. I supposed that now I knew what it felt like to be one of them, however involuntarily.

Though no one else could tell that my penis was there. My penis wasn't real. It was invisible. I was just your run-of-the-mill woman, my body as feminine as anyone else's, except from time to time I felt a penis sprout from my crotch. It was only the feeling that sprouted, though, my physical body didn't change at all. I called it my air penis.

I don't really remember when it first appeared, but I do recall that sometime before I was old enough to go to school, I wet my pants trying to pee off the edge of a river-bank while standing up, even though no one had ever told me that was possible, and I ended up getting scolded by my parents. My parents had thought I'd simply lost control. I tried to explain that the pee hadn't come out the hole I expected it to, but they didn't understand.

I was afflicted off and on with this illusory feeling ever since, and I began to worry about why this was happening to me as I neared puberty. I didn't otherwise feel like a boy, and I wasn't attracted to other girls. If only for this one little problem, I'd be able to wax lyrical about my girl-hood like any other woman. My air penis held a certain sort of innocent sex appeal for me, and it began to interfere with my sexual development as a woman. This was because my hallucinatory penis was maturing right along with the rest of me.

It was about a year after I first started to get my period that one morning I awoke to the feeling that my lower body was swelled to its very limit. Thinking I just had to pee, I went into the bathroom. I'd already sat down on the toilet before I realized that it was really just the feeling of my air penis growing harder than it ever had before.

I'd already experienced the occasional erection before then. I found that if I just ignored them, they'd dissipate before too long, taking the air penis itself along with them. But this time it hurt, like a stake was being driven into my crotch. The pain was sweet, though. I put my hand on my air penis. A tingling kind of ache washed over me, making me dizzy. Before I knew it, I'd rubbed my air penis until I came. Of course, no sperm spurted out.

After much painful consideration, I finally came to a conclusion on the matter I could live with. Say you were to lose your right arm for some reason. Even though there's no arm there any more, a phantom arm may sprout and replace it, and it can grab things just as before, or you can feel like you're writing with it, or biting its nails, or stroking your lover's skin; the phantom arm can itch or hurt or even feel pleasure. Even after years have passed and you've become accustomed to everyday life with one arm, you may still be bothered by this sort of phantom arm sprouting up from time to time.

This air penis of mine was surely the same sort of thing. It was the remainder of something that used to be there but was removed. Maybe in a past life, a man driven by a desire to become something else cut off his own penis and, at that moment, gave birth to me.

Since reaching this conclusion, I became much more relaxed. Because my origins were different, it no longer mattered that I was developing differently than the other girls around me. I didn't know if I was really a man, or, since I may have been driven to cut off my own penis when I was a man, I was really a woman, or if I was really neither one. I felt like a real woman most of the time, but when I started to think deeply about which gender I might truly be, I sometimes felt like a "counterfeit woman, hiding from the world." Counterfeit yet real. But nevertheless, a woman.

With my relaxation came my first boyfriend. I could even have sex normally. One morning, I opened my eyes and then took off my clothes, asking him,

"Can you see my wee-wee?"

I'd woken up with an erection. Though it had almost nothing to do with sexual excitement, my air penis was hard.

"I see it, I see it," Masakazu replied, and he reached out and fondled my clitoris. Oh, for the—well, what could I do? What I really wanted was for him to feel my penis the way I did, to touch it and suck it and put it up his ass, but this would have to suffice.

It was my personal idol. I couldn't see it, but I knew my air penis was real. It was like a ghost, something that was removed and should have disappeared yet didn't, as if it had unfinished business. What compelled it to appear, what excited its interest? I became increasingly intrigued by the shrouded origins and mysterious desires of my air penis.

The temperature had risen to nearly 40°C. It was the hottest it'd been all summer. It seemed to me that the humidity in the staging area was making the heat twice as intense. Even so, the drag queens waiting for their turn to go, the people dressed like speed skaters covered in arabesque patterns, the bodybuilders displaying their bulked-up chests, the bearded men wrapped in leather and dripping with chains, the people made up to look like who knows what, the couples with their smiles so broad they seemed close to bursting, all their energy seemed inexplicably high. The only one who seemed to give off any negative energy was me, my bashful, retiring bearing paradoxically making me feel all the more conspicuous and anxious.

I was attending the Tokyo Gay and Lesbian Pride Parade. I'd found out about this festival for sexual minorities on the Internet after making a cursory search to see if I was alone in having an air penis. If I hadn't possessed such a thing, if I were just your average girl, I likely would have never encountered even the term "sexual minority" my whole life. I also found out for the first time that "heterosexual" was the term for those who weren't "homosexual." Of course, homosexuals weren't the only "sexual minorities" out there. There were those who liked both boys and girls, as well as countless other, more complex conjunctions of love and identity. And since that was true, it seemed natural that a girl with an air penis could find a place among these folks. At the very least, I figured I'd meet others who shared some of the realities of my existence, so I found myself wandering out to watch the parade.

A vehicle approached, covered with pink and white and rainbow-colored balloons and blaring club music loudly into the air. Beautiful men danced atop the stage it carried, showing off their toned bodies. A welcoming cry welled up from the crowd that lined the street, and a crowd of musclebound men stripped to the waist flooded the street in the vehicle's wake. There was another vehicle covered with women wearing golden dresses like royalty, followed by a group of lesbians and then a group of serious-faced men and women brandishing placards and shouting slogans. All the participants exuded an aggressive, "I'm so-and-so and such-and-such, here I am!" sort of pride, and it was a bit much for me to take. I felt humiliated. "I have an air penis! I have genitals made of nothing! It might just be a hallucination! It's not even as real as a dildo! Never mind me, I'll leave now!"

Yet, as my loneliness increased, so did my desire to assert my presence, and before long I'd darted into the street and mixed into the lively crowd of men and women who trailed after the tail end of the parade with little self-consciousness. There seemed to be plenty of others who'd gotten wrapped up in the festivities and left the sidewalk to join in even though they'd not officially registered as participants, so it seemed unlikely I'd be reprimanded for doing the same. And in fact, another young man jumped in and joined the group right after I had.

This young man seemed as uncomfortable as I was, walking along with his body hunched and his eyes fixed on the ground. It looked as if he'd come alone and was unsure whether he really belonged, so he'd watched from the sidelines until the urge to join in the parade became overwhelming and he found himself following me when I darted into the fray.

We seemed to be the only ones walking lonely and unaccompanied within the group. Telling myself that this was a festival, that the sky was clear and cloudless, I approached the young man and said, "You didn't come with your boyfriend?" The man looked shocked and gave me a hateful look, shooting back combatively, "And what about you? Your girlfriend dump you?" I was unsure how to respond for a moment, but then concluded that though I was there to assert my existence and pride, the worst thing to do would be to pretend to be a lesbian, and so I said, "My boyfriend doesn't share my opinion on these issues." The man's face twisted, and he snorted a laugh. Perhaps thinking that this was too rude a response, he added, "So, you joined the parade out of a sense of justice, because you oppose discrimination?" He was looking at my wrist as he spoke. There was a rainbow-colored bracelet hanging from it. In an attempt to get into the spirit of things, I'd bought it from one of the booths that lined the parade route. I didn't really understand what the English words ACT AGAINST HOMOPHOBIA written on it meant exactly, but I figured I'd fit in better with these colors on my body somewhere.

"You saw me run into the street from the sidewalk, didn't you?"

He nodded, muttering his assent. He seemed to realize that he'd followed my lead because he'd sensed a discomfort in my actions that resembled his own.

"Well, we all have our reasons. I guess we all came here because no one understands us, no one sympathizes with our situations. I wouldn't say I've found a place to call home, but it did seem like I might not feel so ashamed if I came here," he explained with sudden gentleness.

A list of possible "reasons" scrolled across the back of my mind, but it occurred to me that it might be precisely because his fit none of them that he found himself in search of "a place to call home." His sense of shame once he got here might be due to his not being gay exactly.

"I'm sorry for earlier, saying 'boyfriend' without thinking."

This at last brought a smile to his face, though a dark one, and he said, "That's okay. After all, he was never really my boyfriend."

His words sounded a chord within me, played a beautiful melody. My air penis appeared. I suddenly got the feeling that maybe this was someone who would actually be able to see it. My whole body finally became suffused with a heat appropriate to my surroundings. Energy began to pulse outward from inside me, igniting my flesh. Turning my newly heated gaze on him once more, he appeared translucent. It seemed as though if my inner furnace got any hotter, he might start to shimmer and eventually disappear altogether. He seemed like a man whose body was bound to the earth solely by the density of his emotions, whose borders were only vaguely defined. I found myself on the verge of reaching out and touching his uncertain skin. I wanted to embrace him, even if it meant embracing a cloud. Suppressing this urge, instead I said, "There seems to be an afterparty. Do you want to go with me?"

At the gay club in Shinjuku Ni-chōme where the afterparty took place, we gave ourselves over to the movement of our bodies and danced all night. Tsubasa seemed unused to this kind of place, his native uncertainty becoming even more pronounced, but nonetheless he seemed to make the best of it as he put his body through its paces.

I'd figured that the afterparty was to go all night, so it didn't surprise me much when at around four in the morning, this woman who said her name was Hina told me with flushed cheeks that she was exhausted and then said, "My house is close, do you want to come over?" All I really wanted was to talk with her somewhere intimate, just the two of us, so I didn't really care whether we went to her house or somewhere else, but in order to capitalize on the heat we'd unearthed during our conversation in the parade, it seemed like now, with our emotions and endurance peaking, it was the right time for liftoff.

As soon as we entered her fifth-floor apartment, Hina opened the windows. The air that had been trapped in the room started to exchange with the comparatively cool air from outside. The summer sky was already starting to brighten with the coming dawn, and we could hear song-birds singing noisily. "I don't have an air conditioner, sorry," she said, turning on a fan instead. We crouched together in front of it. "It's so ho—ot," said Hina, and she took her clothes off quickly, soon becoming completely naked. Taken aback, I just looked at her, and then she asked, "Do you see it?" while spreading her legs. She didn't seem to be propositioning me, but rather seemed to be actually pointing at something. All I saw there was what I'd been imagining as I made my vagina cuts, just a set of normal female genitals. But I intuited that telling her that would disappoint her, so instead I just looked into her eyes.

"So you don't see it either?"

Hina muttered this to herself, her voice and expression deeply disheartened, as if her very existence had just been refuted. A certain note of self-deprecation also sounded in her words, and I felt myself stirred by a tender sort of pity. "Can I touch it?" I asked, reaching my hand out. Hina nodded absently.

Not knowing quite what it was I was supposed to be touching, I started aimlessly caressing the area around her vagina. And then I suddenly withdrew my hand. What was that?

My body responded to his touch like a plucked string. He really touched it! I grabbed Tsubasa's hand and made him touch it again. His hand was fearful, pulling back against me fairly forcefully, but his fingers were curious. They slowly traced the contours of the air penis. Experiencing the touch of another for the first time, it unfurled like time-elapse footage of a sprouting plant, erecting quickly to quivering stiffness. Startled once more, Tsubasa withdrew his hand. This time I made him grip it with his whole hand. As I did, my body convulsed with a pleasure I'd never known before. I moaned involuntarily. I communicated my desire to him with my eyes.

But I didn't respond to her right away. After all, there were things I wanted her to know about me, too. Impatiently stripping off my clothes, I exposed my crotch to her, asking as I pulled my bothersome penis out of the way, "Can you see it?"

There were countless scars there. Some places were swollen like welts, while others were covered with raw, red scabs that looked about to spurt with blood if peeled loose. Tsubasa was obviously not showing me these. He wanted me to see something invisible. Not see it exactly, but know it was there. I tentatively brought my fingers close. And then, in the area where the wounds seemed most concentrated, I touched him. Tsubasa, like me, responded convulsively. In a tense, high-pitched voice, he said, "That's where I open up. Do you see?" I nodded. I lay on my stomach and licked him there. Just as Masakazu did to me, I caressed the tip of Tsubasa's real penis as if it were a clitoris. Tsuabasa cried out hoarsely. The place I was licking soon became wet with something other than just saliva. Tsubasa's vagina opened its red flesh walls to me and I pushed my tongue farther in. The smell grew thicker. Tears ran freely from Tsubasa's eyes.

Unable to control my passion, I opened my body as my emotions over-flowed. Hina breathed into my invisible vagina. Her breath blew through my hollow core and past all the other holes opening up all over my body, etching musical scales into the air. My music began to play.

And as it did, I put Hina's invisible penis, which I had been gripping the whole time, into my mouth. She made a sound like the song of a rare tropical bird.

Her penis was like a rod of mochi skewered on a chopstick. It filled my mouth and made me start to choke, so I pulled my mouth away. I decided to nibble its side instead. Like playing a flute. I was playing Hina. I put the head in my mouth and worked my tongue and teeth like it was the reed of a clarinet. My eyes shed sparks in response to his touch, and I sang out, "Oh, oh, no, oh, no!" I raised my body up and made Tsubasa lay face up. Hina looked down at me from above. Her eyes saw me as I really was. Not as some person shaped approximately like any other man, but as I was, a body that produced sound when wind blew through it, an existence so faint it seemed about to disappear, yet still persists: she caressed the real Tsubasa Tsutsui. Tsubasa, who held me as I was, who needed no terms or labels, not gay or lesbian, not man or woman, not any of the myriad other ways I could be categorized: Tsubasa held me, accepted the air penis that made me unlike anyone else, as if I was just another person, just like everyone else. Tsubame had entered my heart and together we'd taken flight, yet alone I'd crashed back down, I couldn't fly alone, but now I'd found Hina, who understood my vagina's wish to be opened, who made my spirit soar, and tenderness for this Hina gushed up from within me like oil from a well as our bodies of air fit together, melded, saturating me with happiness, and sadness too.

Tsubasa was getting wetter and wetter, and so, as I gazed into his eyes, I plunged my air penis into his air vagina.

Hina's still-swelling air penis continued to grow, and Tsubasa's newly opened vagina was still quite narrow, so they came quickly, releasing cries like rushes of wind from their mouths. Hina's voice sounded to Tsubasa like the cry of a raptor at the moment it fixes on its prey. Tsubasa's voice burned into Hina's ear like the squeal of a flute blown suddenly and too hard. As her air penis drove further and further into his air vagina, Tsubasa heard an unearthly wind blow through the conjoined hollow-ness they formed as the circuit between them closed, and his chest swelled with simple joy at the thought that the duet this wind carried might travel all the way to reach Tsubame's ears. As the air vagina engulfed the air penis, the heat melted their doubled flutes into each other and produced a dazzling brightness. Tsubasa grew completely transparent as Hina looked at him through the nearly blinding light, and to Tsubasa, Hina's entire body was transforming into one huge invisible penis.

As the two winds sounded their unbearably highpitched notes in unison, their melting, liquid bodies vaporized completely, billowing out the window into the boundless sky outside to evaporate into thin air. A breeze blew through the empty room, ruffling the curtains as it passed. The first golden rays of the morning sun fell across the tatami-matted floor. Even now, the intermingled sounds of the dual wind continue to play their hoarse-throated "Air."   *2006*

Translated by Brian Bergstrom

FIVE POEMS

Yau Ching (1966–)

Born and raised in Hong Kong, Yau Ching is a writer, poet, filmmaker and installation artist. While best known in the English speaking world for her films and installations, she is also the author of many books of poetry. Translations of her poems have appeared in *World Literature Today*, *Asymptote*, and other literary reviews. Yau Ching is a parrionate educator, and co-founded an educational organization for sexual minorities in Hong Kong, and the Asian Lesbian Film Festival in Taiwan, among other initiatives.

APRÈS GENET

As I sit here in this stately country manor, my thoughts reach out to you. I write: The world is filled with all these things I do not want, whereas I am filled with you. In *The Thief's Journal*, Genet says, I had a simple elegance, the easy bearing of the hopeless. My courage consisted in destroying all the usual reasons for living and unearthing whole new ones. The discovery came slowly. Like Genet, I too have labored to find a reason for living, but in contrast to what so many believe I found mine not in love but in what love cannot accomplish. A longing laced with sweat and tears that spills across the tree tops and scatters on the plains to become fodder for the birds. The sheer waste and hopelessness of love. And yet this very hopelessness forces me to confront my life. It forces me to live. At times like this, when things begin to fall apart— the final rallying call at Waterloo, Hitler in his Führerbunker beneath the Reich Chancellery, the long-awaited hour when the glory and the grandeur that were Germany and England and France crumble into dust—one must feel a certain joyful release and lightness of being in which death itself seems ethereal as down. Xiang Yu, the hegemon-king whose strength could pull down mountains, turns to bid farewell to his beloved concubine and is felled by the knowledge that love cannot conquer all, that life and death and love and hatred are neither glorious nor grand. It is only at such moments that I can love even in the face of what love cannot accomplish; if the former makes me feel alive, the latter gives me reason for living.

A BEAUTIFUL CRISIS

I am my mom's
exemplar of a beautiful life
this fills me with suspicion of myself   and the world
that represents me   I quickly scoot sideways around and past
   a series
of rectangular objects
and lug back a basket of small round Japanese
angel apples

they are crunchy and gone in five minutes
sometimes I remember to look up and trim the dead branches
when I got back from holiday the bougainvillea had half withered
it committed suicide by leaping off the balcony when the branch
   broke
                                                during the typhoon
the cats fight every day one is obese one is excessively thin
   because
one keeps stealing the other one's food and the other one lets it
   keep eating
                                                until it throws up
and the cats never mop the floor
how can anyone maintain a semblance of so-called
peace and quiet in this kind of life never mind the content
a beautiful life is humanly impossible
all afternoon I'm stuck in a meeting to discuss fifteen new classes
   for
                                                the associate degree
financial fitness surgical enhancement the cerebrum and
   cerebellum of
                                                the employee

crisis management I'd like to enroll in a school like this the
parents I rely on to keep me alive moment by moment to keep my
sense of crisis alive how beautiful
how can I tell my mom your mom the world's moms that
I indeed am
the exemplar of a beautiful life
unsure if this is the fall of the beautiful or of the exemplary

I AM A FOOT

I have to turn in a one-line biography
which forces my presbyopic middle-aged eyes to take a hard
   look at
what Yau Ching is
I am always over-acting the part
some things some tasks some likes and dislikes
on limited repeat
unlike wind flowers   cats or even grass
I am not therefore I have no limits
a foot cannot step twice into the same river
before it steps out   it has already become a different foot
how is it possible to become this foot
how is it possible to bear each stepping in and out   in each
   moment
the river is different
every inch of the foot
has already become the river

THE TEMPTATIONS OF EDEN

We are orphans
we don't belong in Asia
we've never had neighbors friends or brothers
all our lives we've been chased by monsters
we're chronically oxygen deprived
we can't even take a deep breath
when the past became now
when the lost was found
the angels filled in the holes
threw us onto the rubble of the city's ruins and locked the gate
so we'd slaughter each other
so we'd despise each other and cling to each other
blast ourselves into the void
at the speed of the fastest maglev
past endless mountains and rivers waiting
to be taken over
yet again by neighboring regions
this is Eden

ISLAND COUNTRY

There's this island
that used to have many languages now they've become
one called English
another called Chinese
you're not allowed to ever use
your own language
if your name is not an English name
the island will give you one

There's this island
that keeps imagining it's a country
keeps shouting about its honor and dignity! dignity! dignity!
shouting only makes it that much sadder and streaks its face with
                                        enough tears
to drown five thousand years of grievances
the island makes a stack
of TV channels its howls quake the Great Wall

There's this island
that only has walls no doors
no one can leave so it's decided
it's a multinational corporation so it shouts about being
    international!
                                international! international!
to leave the island you must be extra patriotic: shout
go north! go north! go north! then shout
national shame! shame! shame! The more it yells the more hate it
    has
it rues being born in times like these it bemoans its wasted talent
resents the rich despises the poor and banishes all the beautiful
    people

it can't poison itself fast enough with the MSG it puts in roast
   duck

There's this island that
is hurrying to build a wall
to barricade itself
no exit no entry
except on a private jet
because the people on the island
have long since stopped believing
this island (or two) exists

*"Après Genet" is translated by Steve Bradbury and the remaining poems
by Chenxin Jiang.*

THE TRUTH ABOUT ME

A. Revathi (1968–)

Born to a peasant family in Tamil Nadu, Revathi suffered violence and rejection at school and at home for her 'feminine' ways. As a teenager, ran away to Delhi so that she could be true to her gender identity. There, she lived with the Hijra – a third gender community that traces its roots back to the Kama Sutra. Her autobiography, *The Truth about Me* caused a sensation when published in 2011. She is a staunch activist working for the rights of sexual minorities.

Mumbai Dadar, Chennai Central—the things I saw at these places filled me with sorrow. Men and even women stared at us and laughed, and heckled us. I realized what a burden a hijra's daily life is. Do people harass those who are men and women when they go out with their families? Why, a crippled person, a blind person—even they attract pity and people help them. If someone has experienced physical hurt, they are cared for both by the family and by outsiders who come to know of it. But we—we are not considered human.

After we got off at Dadar, in order to get out of the station, we had to climb a flight of stairs and walk across the bridge that connects the many platforms. The looks I got then and the things I heard hurt me more than my wound. I wondered too, if I had not actually asked for this. Maybe I would have been better off as a blind man or woman, an invalid of either sex, than what I was now. I found myself asking the same questions again and again: Why did God give me these feelings? Why must we be tortured by people's looks? If we, my gurubai chela and I, had not met the four hijras at Chennai Central, we would not have reached Mumbai alive. In fact, I am convinced we would not have made it.

We reached my nani's house in Ghatkopar and were welcomed with burning camphor stuck on a coconut and an *arthi*. Nani said, 'Enter, you women!' The four hijras who had seen us home safely were likewise welcomed, and with great respect. My kaalaguru prepared warm water for us to bathe, and everyone crowded around us, enquiring about our health and well-being.

When we narrated all that we had undergone at the hospital and after-wards, to our nani and kaalaguru, nani responded, 'Well, it's not easy, becoming a woman.' She added, 'You say you were in great pain, but what if you'd had to undergo a thayamma operation?'

Our kaalaguru then helped each of us bathe in turn. She cleaned the wound and dusted boric powder on it, and expressed her opinion that the operation had been done with great skill. Later, the hijras who had accompanied us were seen off ceremoniously.

Whether a hijra undergoes a surgery or a thayamma nirvaanam, she has to abide by certain rules for forty days thereafter. We have to abstain from having milk and fruit. We were told it was good for us to eat chap-patis and bitter gourd. Mutton soup and the head of lamb were good as well, we found out. We could not bring ourselves to eat bitter gourd, but nani stood watch over us, stick in hand, until we had eaten it all up.

We had to sleep with our legs apart. If not, the hole through which we had to urinate could close up. We continued to drink copious amounts of black tea in order to be able to pee with some ease. We were told not to look into a mirror, to see men or to comb our hair. We had to refrain from doing paampaduthi to elders.

We bathed in warm water, after which we applied medication on the wound. This usually caused the wound to ooze. We would then use cotton to wipe ourselves clean. Once again, we would wash with soap and keep the area dry with a clean cotton cloth. At the end of all this, we dusted boric powder. Every day, for fifteen days, we saw a local doctor who gave us penicillin injections. Our kaalaguru helped us through this period of healing. May she live a hundred years, wherever she is! She did not mind that I was much younger to her, and she even washed my blood-stained clothes.

On the twelfth and twentieth days, hijras in the neighbourhood are invited to come and pour water over our heads. On those days, the elders at home, as well as our peers, rubbed turmeric all over our bodies, performed arthi for us and filled our mouths with sugar. Hijras who came to see us brought gifts of wheat, sugar, ghee and sometimes even tea. Apparently, it is good for us to drink black tea with a dollop of ghee. By the twentieth day, the day of the second ritual bath, the wound is mostly healed. A scar remains though. And once our wounds had healed, we were asked to help around the house, as before.

As the fortieth day approached, we noticed that we seemed feminine, especially in certain parts—the face, the legs and the arms. We longed for the fortieth day to dawn, feeling trapped at home, unable to move about freely. It was only after the *haldi-mehndi* ritual, followed by a puja to Mata and another ritual similar to the puberty rites done after the first menses to declare the girl free from pollution, that we could leave the house.

The fortieth-day ceremony was held at nani's house in Bhandup, which was devoted to sex work, not at her Ghatkopar house. And nani did not participate in the ritual. I came to know about this only on the day of the ceremony.

Hijras in rich, colourful saris, older and younger hijras, and a few sex workers came to take part in the ceremony. We were seated in a separate room and did not know what was happening outside. But we heard a number of people come and go, and heard happy, jolly music and the sound of dancing feet. There also seemed to be a lot of cooking happening that day.

Some of the visitors came into the room to see us. They ribbed us in a comradely manner, 'So, where is the ceremony and where are these women?' All of them stayed to eat—we too were served food in our room. At around 2 o'clock in the morning, they made us both wear skirts, which we tied high on the chest. They sat us down, and we were anointed with mehndi and turmeric. Meanwhile others were preparing for puja, cleaning and decorating Mata's image.

The custom was that the guru gifts her chelas who had undergone nirvaanam with a *jok*. The jok comprises a green sari, a blouse and an inner skirt, and a nose-ring, anklets and toe-rings. Our hijra friends bathed us, braided our hair, decorated the braids with flowers and then made us wear the jok. They pulled the ends of our saris over our heads to cover our faces. Clad thus, we were led up to the image of Mata. The smell of incense and camphor merged with the sounds of voices singing Mata's praise. A coconut was broken and a puja performed. *Jani Jai Santhoshi Mata* sang the hijras, full of emotion, as they placed garlands on us and tied small bundles of betel-leaves and areca nuts into the folds of the green sari. We remained there, waiting for Mata to descend on us, while the others whirled around, praying and dancing. We too were asked to chant her name, which we did.

It must have been around 4 o'clock in the morning. The hour, the fragrance of burning camphor, the hijras all around us clapping their hands and calling out to Mata—I was profoundly affected by the experience, I felt my body beginning to sway to the rhythm. As if they had been waiting all along for that instant, the hijras took up the Mata chorus even more loudly, and chanting, they lifted a pot of milk and placed it on my head. Two hijras stood behind me to help me balance the pot. The same was done for my gurubai chela. Attended by other hijras, the two of us were taken to the nearest well, balancing milk-pots on our head. We were asked to pour the milk into the well, but without taking the pot off. We had to bend our heads to do this. Then we were asked to fill our pots with water and pour it back into the well. This happened about two times, after which we filled our pots with water, balanced them on our heads and retraced our steps.

Back in front of Mata's image, we were asked to uncover our faces and look at her glorious image. We were asked to recite: 'Take me away and give yourself to me.' She looked gorgeous and her face glowed, as if it were made of gold. As I whispered, 'Take my form away and bless me with yours,' I felt tears sting my eyes. A moment later, I was asked to bend low and offer obeisance to the image. A mirror was then thrust into my hands—I had to look at myself, and I had not looked into a mirror for forty days. The mirror was of such a size that I could view my face and Mata's face. Beguiled by her rich beauty, I could not recognize myself. My face had changed! I felt like a flower that had just blossomed. It seemed to me that my earlier male form had disappeared and in its place was a woman. I felt exultant.

'All right, all right, you pottais now have to eat what you like best,' said a hijra, pointing to the heap of offerings in front of Mata. There were nine kinds of fruit, fried snacks, sweets, broken coconuts... On both sides of the image were mounds of rava kesari, with 'Om' inscribed on them. We stared, wondering what we should to eat, while the others waited eagerly. Several were waiting to eat the offerings, but we had to eat first. Unsure as to what I ought to eat first, I reached out for one of the kesari mounds, broke off a small bit and put it into my mouth. At once, all the hijras present started shouting, 'Seesaa! Seesaa!' My gurubai chela took an apple and bit into it and was rewarded with the same shouts of approbation. After this, everyone attacked the food heaps, searching for their favourite titbit.

Hijras believe that our future would be as the food we chose to eat. For those who chose sweets and fruit, life would be pleasant. No one tells you about this before though and so many of us don't know what to eat first. If I had witnessed this ritual before, perhaps my choice would have been informed. The first ritual I participated in was my own! After the ritual was completed we were asked to say paampaduthi to everyone present. We also fell at the feet of our elders. Each blessed us in her own way.

'Be well, beta. From now on, your guru's parivar is your own and you must make your guru's name proud. Listen to what your guru says.

Remember you've had nirvaanam done to you. So, no lifting your skirts in public! You have to respect and abide by the codes that hijras live by. You're a woman now and so must learn to act like one. Cutting your hair, running away to your home—none of this is allowed. And don't spoil your life by taking on a husband.' We were subject to hundreds of such homilies. The older women in the Bhandup house called us 'pinjus', implying we were still tender and young. Some of the younger girls however called us 'amma'. We realized that in these places, the women followed the culture of hijras.

After we had received blessings from all present, my gurubai chela and I, still in our jok garb, left for nani's Ghatkopar house. We had to take her blessings. As soon as we entered nani's Ghatkopar home, she exclaimed, 'So here you are, women!' We rushed in and fell at her feet, and said 'Paampaduthi nani.' To which she replied, 'Paampaduthi daadi! Jiyo beta, be well.' She also said, 'Beta, now that you've undergone nirvaanam, you must not think you can behave badly just because you don't have a thing dangling between your legs. You must not lift your skirt and exhibit yourself, whether you are fighting with other pottais or with a shop-keeper who hasn't given you money! No arrogance to be displayed! We do all this because we want to live like women. Not because we want to flaunt it in front of the world and shame ourselves thereby. So be careful.'

Nani then gave us each another sari to wear, 'Now take off your green sari, and the blouse and skirt. You can wear the jok only today. Tomorrow you should give it off to those *akuva pottais*. I'll buy you another jok.'

Nani had in fact booked our joks out to various akuva pottais, that is, those who are yet to undergo nirvaanam. They believe that if you wear the jok of those who've had it done, Mata would descend on them as well. My jok was given away to one of my younger gurubais, who lived in a sex worker's home in Kamatipura. My gurubai chela gave hers away to her gurubai who lived Bhandup.

'A person might be able to afford nirvaanam and plan for it. Ultimately, the time has to be right—the hour has to beckon you. If the moment is not ours, then we won't be able to do it, and will encounter all sorts of obstacles. Mata has to descend on us, otherwise it never happens. Look how you've had it done, just like that. You've been here only for six months, but in that time you've become a woman. Some of us have been here for three years and yet we haven't been able to attain that nirvaanam stage. Your nani has not seen it fit to send us, but she chose you. Your gurubai chela has been here two years and she was chosen only now. It all depends on Mata's grace—when one gets to have the thing done. Because her grace favoured you, you had it done early.' So spoke my kaalaguru. Hearing her fervent words, I understood her faith and was moved by her devotion.

As far as I am concerned, I feel that while there is much to be said for faith of this kind, there is also the fact that I had been a good chela. I did all that nani asked of me. I was respectful and nani approved of my behaviour and attitude. I felt therefore that for these reasons too nani might have sent me for my nirvaanam.

Soon my gurubai chela left for her guru's house in Bhandup. But nani kept me with her and, as before, I started helping around the house and going to the shops.

Translated by V. Geetha

GOING PUBLIC

Hida Viloria (1968–)

Viloria is one of the world's foremost intersex authors and activists. S/he campaigns against medically unnecessary genital surgeries and non-consensual hormone treatments being conducted on infants and minors. He/r landmark memoir *Being Both*, while addressing the cruelty of intersex genital mutilation (IGM), also explores life as an intersex adult – sexuality, love, community and self-fulfilment.

San Francisco, California
January 2001

"Hi, Hida," a voice on my answering machine says. "My name is Alice, and I'm a producer for the ABC News program *20/20*. Were doing a segment on intersex and I'm wondering if I could talk to you about possibly being in it."

I'd grown up watching *20/20* almost every Friday once I was old enough to stay up till eleven. Although I stopped watching TV almost entirely once I left home, it's still a popular and respected show. Also, my mom watches it.

"Geez, *20/20*—that's the big-time!" Beth says when I tell her.

I'm hanging at her place, as I often do on the weekends.

"How'd they find you?" she asks.

"From some article in a New Orleans newspaper, apparently, which is interesting because I haven't done any interviews in New Orleans, but I forgot to ask them for details…"

"Did I hear you say *20/20?*" Marina asks, walking into the room.

"Yeah," I answer. "Kind of crazy, right?"

"Yeah, a lot of people watch that show. Are you sure you're ready for that kind of exposure?" she asks.

"Yeah, I bet your mom still watches that," Beth adds.

"She does. Not religiously or anything, but often."

This means I'll have to tell her about it. It wouldn't be fair to her for it to be a surprise, or for a coworker who recognizes my name to see it and ask her about it. Telling her that I'm an intersex activist and that I'm going to out myself on a major television show is not something I have any desire to do, given what a hard time she has dealing with the fact that I'm openly gay. But I guess I'll have to because being on *20/20* is too important for intersex visibility to pass up.

Fortunately, the *20/20* production team is meticulous in their preparation, and filming won't take place for months, which gives me time to mentally prepare myself. Also, I learn that Barbara Walters will not be the one interviewing me, which is a relief. As much as I respect her, she's known for asking those blunt, difficult, and somewhat invasive questions that can sometimes make people cry. Just speaking about being intersex so publicly is revealing and stressful enough for me. Also, the fact that I do respect her and have been watching her for years would only make me more nervous.

"Everyone says navy blue is a good choice for these kinds of things," Diana says.

We've been hanging out a lot since Burning Man, which is fantastic. I've also decided to go shopping way in advance of the interview so I don't freak out at the last minute about what I'm going to wear on camera.

"Good to know," I say. "I want to be myself, but not my super-freaky self, because I'm trying to appeal to conservative parents who might be thinking about operating on their babies."

"Yeah, navy blue is respectable and conservative, and it's not as boring on-screen as black. I think it'll be good."

"Okay, navy blue it is," I say. "I'll go get a bunch of tops, but do you think you can help me pick out the best-looking one?"

"Sure—what are friends for?"

I go to the mall where I used to work as a security guard, and I purchase six navy blue tops with a range of feminine to masculine cuts. I'm not sure how I'll feel about my gender expression when the day of the interview arrives, and my experience has been that my level of femininity or masculinity can change at a moment's notice, so I figure I might as well be prepared with some options.

When I get home, I call Diana and invite her over to check them out.

"Okay, let's see 'em!" Diana says when she arrives.

I lay them out across my bed.

"That's it?" Diana asks.

"Yeah—why?" I ask.

"Well, they're all the same," Diana says.

She's sitting in the big, comfy armchair that faces my bed and the ornate, nonfunctional fireplace in my room.

"No they're not!" I reply.

"Hida, they look almost identical," she says.

"No, look—this one's got a V-neck, and this one's got a round neck, and this one's got a maroon stripe…"

"Where?" Diana asks, bending over to take a closer look at the shirt.

"Right here!" I say, pointing to the small stripe on the side of the collar.

"Oh my god—that's so tiny I can barely see it!"

"Well, it's there. And this one's kind of girly, with the boatneck…"

It's a close-fitting, long-sleeved shirt with a neckline that reveals my prominent collarbones, which I've always been told are sexy in a feminine way.

"*That's* girly?" Diana asks, suppressing a giggle.

"Yeah, look at it. It's a girl's cut. It's from the women's department."

"Yeah, maybe the *masculine lesbian* women's department…" she says, laughing openly now.

"Okay, look—do you wanna help me or not?" I ask, starting to get frustrated.

I fling myself down on the bed, across the tops, and look up. The high ceilings make the room feel palatial; it comforts me.

"I do, I *do*," she says, starting to full-on crack up. "It's just that all these tops look almost identical to me…"

She's laughing so hard she has to stop, and even though I'm frustrated, as I look at the tops more closely I start laughing, too, because I can see her point. It feels great to laugh, actually, after being so stressed out about this.

"I kind of see what you mean," I finally say once I've regained my composure, "but you know, it's not like one of the options was ever going to be super frilly or anything! I said I want to feel like myself, remember?"

"Yeah," she says, reeling herself in. "Okay, try them on and I'll tell you which one I like best."

Twenty minutes later we've decided on the one with the small maroon stripe.

Manhattan, New York
April 2001

I had wanted to hang out with Angie, whom I rarely get to see because she's practicing medicine in New York now. I thought it would be a good way to relax before the interview, but my flight was delayed and it's already ten by the time I get dropped off at my hotel.

The hotel is nice, a small boutique place on the Upper West Side. It feels more like a very large home than a hotel, which I like. There's no one in the small, sophisticated lobby when I check in, which I also like. I feel the need to go into deep meditative mode to prepare for this. The less stimulation the better.

The room is small too—narrow, but with tall windows at the end that make it seem bigger. Within it are expensive-looking modern furnishings and I spot gorgeous metallic-colored sheets on the bed. *Ah, I made it*, I think, throwing myself down on them. I'll be seeing my mom and telling her about this, but not until after it's over.

I need to call Angie from the room phone to tell her I can't make it, but I switch on the TV and go to the bathroom first. When I walk back in, I see a bunch of punk rock-looking folks on the screen.

"Crowds have started to gather to pay homage to the lead singer of the musical group that many consider the best punk band of all time," the reporter is saying.

Huh?

"Joey Ramone passed away early this morning at the age of…"

Oh my god, Joey Ramone? I'm surprised to feel tears welling up.

Like so many people I grew up with, I love the Ramones. They're from Queens, which gave all us Queens kids something to be proud of, and I loved them so much in high school that they actually became one of the few American bands that my mother could recognize. She liked them too and would bop her head to songs like "Sheena Is a Punk Rocker" and "Rock 'n' Roll High School" when I played them.

Around the time I left Wesleyan, Beth had talked me into seeing Iggy Pop, another punk rock idol of mine, with her. It was one of the only things I'd been able to drag my depressed ass to that whole winter. And not only was Iggy incredible, but on my way to the bar I stopped for a few seconds, and when I looked up, I saw Joey, leaning against a post, looking even cooler in person and even taller than I'd imagined.

I couldn't help but stare for a moment, and as I did, he looked down in my direction. He was wearing those round rose-colored sunglasses he often had on, so I couldn't tell if he was actually looking right at me, but it felt like he was, and I know it might sound a little silly, but it was a special moment for me. It felt like having his energy so close to mine was a gift to help me get through that hideous time. And I guess it's not such a strange idea when you think about how people will travel far and wide to see spiritual gurus whom they admire, and benefit from being in their presence.

I admired Joey. He was weird-looking and weird-sounding, but his creativity and his spirit were so strong that they burst onto the world stage, forever searing a mark of rebellion onto our cookie-cutter society. He showed everyone that you don't have to fit into the mainstream mold to shine and soar.

"People are gathering for a memorial service being held at the legendary punk club CBGB…"

I call Angie.

"Hey! What took you so long? I've been waiting," she says.

"I know, I'm sorry—my flight got delayed, and I would've called sooner but the car was there waiting the minute I got out of the gate. I just got to the hotel."

"Oh, okay."

"Hey, did you hear about Joey Ramone?" I ask.

"Yeah. It sucks, right? It's been on the news for a while."

"I guess I missed it because I was on the flight. I hear they're holding a memorial service down at CBGB's pretty soon."

"What—you wanna go?" she asks.

"Yeah, kind of. I mean, it's Joey Ramone."

"Well, I'll go down there with you if you want," she offers.

I pause for a moment.

"Let me think about it," I say. "I *really* want to, but I worry that we might get caught up down there, and I'm getting picked up early tomorrow morning."

"Hmm, yeah, it's a tough call. This interview's important," she says.

"Yeah, tell me about it. I'm so nervous."

"Well, just think about it and let me know. I'll be up for a bit, and I'd be down to go."

We hang up, and I am torn. On one hand, it feels a little like fate that I should happen to be here and *able* to go to the memorial, since I'd regularly be three thousand miles away. On the other, this interview means a great deal to me, and it's why I'm here. I want to do the best job possible, and that might require getting a very good rest.

I close my eyes and meditate. I went to my first meditation retreat in 1994 with my martial arts school, and I've been what you could call a "moderate meditator" ever since, doing it mainly when I need clarity. It's not long before the answer becomes clear. I should stay at the hotel and go to bed.

I give Angie another ring to let her know.

"Okay, I'm a little disappointed 'cuz I wanted to see you, but I get it, and I want you to do well," she says sympathetically.

"Thanks, girl. I love you," I say.

"I love you too. Go get 'em tomorrow. I know you'll do a great job!"

I feel so lucky and grateful for the friends this life has given me. And for having had the opportunity to experience Joey's music and presence.

I wake up the next morning before my alarm, with plenty of time to shower and be ready and checked out when the car comes at eight thirty. I'll be going to my mom's home in Queens later, so I need to stay at the hotel only one night.

She and my dad have been separated since 1996—about five years now—and she's managed to do so well in her career in real estate that she was able to buy her own house in Bayside, Queens, a nicer neighborhood than the one I grew up in.

I'm proud of her.

When I arrive at the studio, I meet Alice, the producer, who is as wonderful in person as she's been on the phone. She seems to understand how vulnerable I might be in an interview like this, and she does her best to prepare me and make every step along the way as comfortable as possible.

The interview is being shot in the rented-out suite of a different hotel. They have plenty of food and a private room that I can relax in when Alice and I are done. The film crew is setting everything up in the main room. They have to check the angle and the lighting on me from time to time, but after a while, they don't need me anymore and there's still about fifteen minutes left before Lynn Sherr, the woman who is interviewing me, shows up.

I go into the private room and check my hair in the mirror. I notice that my heart is racing, so I decide to meditate.

I close my eyes and breathe deeply, knowing it will help. It does. I think about what it is that I really want to say and convey. My thoughts start to race and jumble when I do, but the Universe, that force that I feel connected to, has never steered me wrong. So I decide to just ask it to help me.

Universe, I say quietly as I look in the mirror, *please help me give the best interview that I possibly can. Please use me to convey the message that will best help intersex people all over the world and best reach the thousands of people who will watch this show. I thank you in advance for doing so, knowing that everything is happening just as it should. Thank you.*

I feel calm, and in a minute I hear them asking for me. I go out and meet Lynn Sherr, who is very nice, and I do the interview. When it's over, Lynn and the film crew tell me I did a fantastic job. We have lunch and then go to Riverside Park to shoot the B-roll footage.

Afterward, Alice takes me out to dinner, which is when I learn she's a Buddhist. I tell her about the prayer I did before filming, knowing she'll understand.

"Well, they showed me a few clips of your interview," she says, smiling, "and I think the Universe heard you loud and clear."

"Hi, Hida Patricia!" my mom says an hour later, pulling me into a hug.

Although we have our differences, my mom is a sweet woman. Despite her lack of acceptance around my being a lesbian and so many other things, I can't help but love her. Deeply.

She makes us some tea and we sit down to talk. I consider telling her about *20/20* right then, but it's a little late and she's tired. So I decide to wait until tomorrow.

The next day, I wake up happy about the day before, but with round two of nerves. I know it'll only get worse the longer I wait, so I make the decision to tell her right after breakfast.

"So, Mom, you might be wondering why I'm here, huh?" I ask her.

"You told me it's for work, right?"

"Yeah." I take a deep breath. "I'm nervous to tell you about this, but you may find out anyway if I don't, so here it goes. You know how I've mentioned a few times that I'm doing some activism?"

"Yes, about gay things, right?"

"Uh, not exactly. I've been saying that's what it is because I thought it would be easier for you to understand," I confess.

"Well, what is it then?" she asks.

"I've been doing activism about being intersex, and that's why I'm here. I did an interview for the show *20/20*."

"*20/20*? The one with Barbara Walters?" she asks, looking surprised.

"Yeah."

"Oh, she's very good. What did you talk about?"

"About being intersex."

I can tell that the word *intersex* must have slipped by her the first time I said it.

"Intersex? What is that?"

I give her the briefest, simplest explanation I can.

"Oh, okay, but why are you talking about that?"

"Because *I'm* intersex, Mom."

My mother pauses, looking confused.

"What?"

"I'm intersex," I repeat.

"Oh my god, what are you talking about, Hida Patricia?" she says, starting to laugh.

"I'm intersex, Mom. I have a big clit."

She looks at me quizzically.

"You know, the clitoris?"

I try to pronounce it the way I imagine it might sound in Spanish.

"Cleetorees," I say, gesturing toward mine. "The part that women have."

"Oh yes, okay. But what do you mean? *Women* have that, right?"

"Yeah, but mine is larger than normal," I say.

"What do you mean? I don't remember that..."

"I don't know how often you changed my diaper, Mom, because you were working, but you must know what I'm talking about?"

"No!" she exclaims. "You're normal, Hida Patricia. You're a beautiful girl!"

"Thanks, Mom," I say, smiling, "but beautiful or not, I have a really large clitoris. So large that I'm considered intersex."

"Hida Patricia, I know you have always liked being different, but do you think I would not know about this? I'm your mother."

I find it odd that she's having this reaction to my news, given who she is. But I have heard the weirdest stories of denial from this community.

"Look, Mom, I don't know how or why you missed this, but if you need me to show you," I say, a little surprised that I'm saying it, "I will."

My mother locks eyes with me intently. My proposition is kind of a challenge, and even though she has always been extremely shy about nudity—her own or mine—she hates being told, or feeling like, she can't do something.

"Okay, fine—let's go," she says. "Show me, because I know you are my daughter and you are a girl, so I don't know what you are talking about."

We go to the bathroom upstairs. It's large, and for whatever reason, it seems like the appropriate place to do this. I have to admit that even though she's my mother, this feels unnatural, especially because I was not raised to be nude around others, including her.

"Okay," I say, undoing the top button of my jeans, "here you go. Take a look."

I pull down my jeans and she crouches down to get a good look. Seconds pass in silence.

Man, is this awkward, I think to myself.

"Well, do you see?" I finally ask her.

More silence. She stands up straight and looks at me with an expression I've never seen before. On anyone. It's a little surprised, but kind, and... something else I can't place. It's almost amused, but not in the regular way, like with nostalgia or something. A memory perhaps? It's difficult to tell.

"I mean, I don't know how many clitorises you've seen," I say, "but I think you can tell that this is not what they usually look like, right?"

"Yes, Hida Patricia. You're right," is all that she says. Then, "I'll meet you downstairs, okay?"

I head down the stairs to join her a few minutes later.

"So, Hida Patricia, I believe you now, but that doesn't matter that you are like that. Why do you have to talk about it?"

I can tell she's a little mortified, and I am not the least bit surprised. Sometimes I am too. So I tell her all about intersex genital mutilation, or IGM, which is what I've recently begun calling the nonconsensual genital surgeries that are inflicted upon intersex people. I tell her all about what I've seen. She listens intently, taking it all in.

When I'm done, she says, "I see, Hida Patricia. Yes, that's terrible. But it didn't happen to you. We didn't do that to you, and you are beautiful and normal, so why do you have to talk about it on TV? It's so personal... so private."

"I know, Mom. But the problem is that nobody talks about it. Nobody knows that we're here, and that's what makes it easy for people to keep doing it."

"But Hida Patricia, you could get fired!"

"No, Mom, it's cool in San Francisco," I assure her.

"Yes, but Hida Patricia, you don't know—"

"Yes, Mom, I do. It's okay."

"But somebody could hurt you!"

I can tell she's starting to get a little upset.

"Mom, look, it's going to be okay. Nobody's going to hurt me—I promise."

"I just don't know why you have to talk about these things in public.

You know people don't always like people who are different, Hida Patricia!"

I clasp her hands in mine.

"I know, Mom, I know. But I want to help make these terrible things stop."

"I know; you were always like that, since you were little. You were always fighting with your father when he bothered me," she says, smiling at me, her love shining bright in her eyes. "But Hida Patricia, who is going to help *you*? These people aren't paying you to help them, right?"

"No. It's not like that…"

"So you have to take care of yourself. I know that it's bad, what is happening, and that you want to help, but you can't help everybody."

"I know, Mom, but I *can* actually help with this. And there are not that many people who can, because a lot of intersex people have been affected by IGM, so there are very few people who can say that we're fine just how we are."

I pause.

"See, other people are not talking about it," my mother says. "You have to think about yourself first. You're not in law school anymore. You need to make money because money is more important than this stuff, Hida Patricia. This is not a career…"

"But it is more important to me than a career, Mom," I say.

"How can you say that? Are you dreaming? You have to live in the real world!"

I try to think of a context that I can possibly explain this in that will make sense to her.

"Okay, Mom, remember when we were growing up and we used to see things on TV sometimes about Martin Luther King, and you used to say what a good man he was?"

"Yes," she says.

"And remember how you used to say how much he helped his people, black people?"

"Yes."

"Well, he gave up his career to do that," I say.

"Yes, but that's different. Black people were getting hurt—killed sometimes even."

"Yeah, but my people are getting hurt too. Every day. Doctors are cutting up their bodies when they're babies and leaving them mutilated in a way that they can never enjoy sex. They often become depressed, and some of them have even killed themselves."

"Yes, but why do you have to be the one to do this? You're not rich, Hida Patricia. You need help too!"

"I know I'm not rich," I say, laughing, "but Martin Luther King didn't have to do it, and I don't think he was rich either. I mean, there was no reason why, of all the black people out there, *he* had to be the one to do it, right?"

Judging by the look on her face, I think she may finally be understanding me.

"So it's not really about that. It's not about *having* to do it; it's just about wanting to do it. It's just about it being important to you. And if it hadn't been important to him, he would have had his career, but the black community would have never had his help—the help that you used to tell us was so good. So which one was more important in the end?"

I pause for a moment to let my words sink in.

"I'm not saying I'm Martin Luther King, but this cause is very important to me too. My people are being hurt, badly, and to me it's more important to try to stop the hurt rather than focus on having a great career—even money. I know not everyone feels this way—I guess maybe most people don't feel this way—but I do. Do you understand, Mom?"

"Yes, Hida Patricia, I do," she says.

And I can tell she means it.

LAST WORDS FROM MONTMARTRE

Qiu Miaojin (1969–1995)

Born in Changhua County in western Taiwan, Qiu studied at the National Taiwan University before moving to Paris where she studied with philosopher Hélène Cixous. Qiu's first novel was published in 1994, when there was a media frenzy in Taiwan targeting lesbian communities resulting in a number of suicides. Her final novel, *Last Words From Montmartre* comprises 20 letters that can be read in any order, a homage to her fascination with non-linear structures of avant-garde cinema. Qiu took her own life at twenty-six.

LETTER FOURTEEN
May 31
(We have nothing to fear but insincerity.)

The mouth stands for sincerity. The nose stands for generosity. The eyebrows stand for integrity. The eyes stand for sexual prowess....
   I stroke her face lightly, every feature, murmuring to her how beautiful she is to me. Yes, it's her. The image that flashes through my mind is of a bird flying past drifting clouds; the illusion is what floats to the surface of the water when you stare into it. Is that what I saw among the hovering clouds? Or is it what I've seen in my heart? An image I dreamed of her? Or is the flowing water itself an illusion?
   Yes, she is a simple woman. I can't describe Xu's physical appearance, how her beauty is engraved in my heart.... I think a sculptor must

carve the way his lover looks in his mind by imagining, that he must find a temporal focus as solid as marble in order to chisel out a permanent image in the shifting sands. This is how it is, right?

I met Xu in September 1992 and in December I boarded a plane to Paris; our chance meeting became a honeymoon. I first lived in a small village, and the following September I moved to Paris for graduate school. That June we took an oath and maintained a perfect relationship and Xu resolved to be the rock supporting my vague ideas about studying abroad, illuminating the path of my lonely self-pursuit with her radiance. More than three hundred letters kindled my love's glowing resplendence. This love, this grace, how can I deceive myself that there is someone as beautiful waiting for me; how can I ignore my heart and tell myself that I could love someone else; how could I pretend not to have seen the outline of my life as she tailored it and say that I could belong to someone else and say that this isn't how "love" is, it's something other, it's somewhere else....

June 1994, Xu flew to Paris and we realized our idealistic dream of a loving union, until February 1995 when I accompanied her back to Taiwan and our union disintegrated with each passing day.... You could say that the one before my eyes was no longer a "her" I recognized, and when she returned to France to live, her final promise to me, she had already left her body and I had already lost a Xu who loved me 100 percent. I've often thought that she returned to Paris not to love me but to torture me. The more she tried to treat me well, the more she lashed out. Our relationship crumbled. After she started being unfaithful to me in August, I fell into a state of insanity, destroying myself bit by bit, tearing myself down, twice planned to die so I could escape from the gory narcoleptic nightmare that was my life.... And she grew colder and colder, more frightening, committing more serious acts of unfaithfulness.... I was unable to stop myself from hurting her.... The deepest feelings in me had been gutted, and it was as if I was confronting my most ferocious enemy.... She too seemed nearly destroyed, terrified that I'd crossed the point of no return....

In March 1995 I returned to France to continue my studies. To persuade me to leave Taiwan, Xu promised we'd work together to revive our love and try to recover and that she would wait for me with hope.... I was too vulnerable and too fragile, and couldn't imagine that she was no longer the "she" I had trusted and respected, though in fact that "she" with integrity had already been destroyed by my own hand.... (Yes, destroyed by me, a month before she came to France I had already destroyed the deepest part of her that she had opened to me, and when I realized she didn't want to care for my heart and didn't want to return to France—and that she herself couldn't acknowledge this—I turned away and flung her love root and branch down to the ground, and I resolved to go live alone in France, to stop waiting for her, and in despair I locked myself in my little apartment, pulled out my phone cord, and blocked her out.... By then her heart was broken, and the spirit of her love had flown away.... Before a month had passed she rushed to Paris to get me back, to save our relationship. Oh, it was a she that wasn't even recognizable to herself, for she really did not want to leave home!)

Until the day before I "died" for her, I still believed in her integrity, her sincerity, and I still trusted her.... On March 30, ten days after leaving Taiwan, she was sleeping in someone else's bed.... In the telephone booth I died in the blink of an eye, experiencing in one moment the entire cumulative effect of the violence and murder of half a year of her unfaithfulness. Yes, I died... true death. Happening. Death. Death. Happening.

Crazy screaming uncontrollably, striking the glass and the metal frame of the phone booth uncontrollably, blood streaming from my numb head.... I howled at her through the receiver, "Tonight I'm going to die!"... A police car was parked nearby and four officers wanted to take me away, but I insisted on finishing my call.... In the midst of this turmoil I heard Xu crying that she would leave the other person's place immediately and go home and call me right away, each lie she told putting my life even more in jeopardy.... Beyond the lies there were only more lies…. Two policemen pulled me from the telephone booth and I resisted them, trying to pick up the receiver again…. I was taken to the police station; my brain felt like it had exploded and I just sat there catatonic on the floor, feeling as if there were many pairs of feet treading on my body, which felt severe pain yet was numb…. I forget how I managed to stand up and march out of the police station, or how I walked home. I've forgotten everything except the deep spiritual scars. I felt my spirit pushing me to go home quietly, go home and sit near the phone to wait for Xu's call…. I arrived home and my whole body felt swollen with a dislocating ache and my vital organs felt as if they'd been squeezed, and I vomited continuously…. In the darkness of early dawn as I sat next to the telephone in the living room a voice exploded into my ear: "You're really going to die!"

I thought about the portrait of van Gogh, after he had cut off his ear, with the bandages wrapped on his head, and I thought about "Apollinaire's head bandaged in white" that Osamu loved so much.

"Someone lives with an unfaithful 'woman.' He kills the 'woman,' or the 'woman' kills him. This is an inevitability."

—Angelopoulos, *Reconstruction*

Translated by Ari Larissa Heinrich

LETTER FROM A TRANS MAN TO THE SEXUAL *ANCIEN RÉGIME*

Paul B. Preciado

Paul B. Preciado (1970–) Preciado is a Spanish philosopher who studied with Jacques Derrida on a Fulbright scholarship. His interests include pornography, architecture and gender identity. He writes academic literature about the influence of architecture on sexual norms, while his more personal work reflects on his experiences with hormone therapy. Elsewhere, he has worked as a curator and a teacher.

Ladies, gentlemen, and others,

In the midst of the crossfire around the politics of sexual harassment, I would like to take the stand as smuggler between two worlds, the world 'of men' and the world 'of women' (these two worlds that could very well not exist but that some people try to keep separate by a kind of Berlin Wall of gender), I want to give you news from the position of 'found object' or rather 'lost subject' during the crossing.

I am not speaking here as a man who belongs to the dominant class, to whom the masculine gender was assigned at birth, and who was brought up as a member of the governing class, of those to whom the right is granted or rather from whom it is demanded (and this is an interesting analytical key) that they exercise masculine sovereignty. I am not speaking, either, as a woman, given the fact that I have voluntarily and intentionally abandoned this form of political and social embodiment. I am expressing myself here as a trans man. Thus I am not claiming, in any way, to represent any collective whatsoever. I am not speaking, nor can I speak, as heterosexual, or as homosexual, although I know and inhabit both positions, since when someone is trans, these categories become obsolete. I am speaking as a gender defector, a fugitive from sexuality, as a dissident (sometimes awkward, since I lack the pre-established codes) of the sex-gender binary regime. As a self-guinea pig of sexual politics who is carrying out the experiment – not yet thematized – of living on each side of the wall and who, by dint of crossing it daily, is beginning to be tired, ladies and gentlemen, of the recalcitrant rigidity of codes and desires that the heteropatriarchal regime imposes.

Let me tell you, from the other side of the wall, that the thing is much worse than my experience as a lesbian woman allowed me to imagine. Ever since I have been living as-if-I-were-a-man in the world of men (aware of embodying a political fiction), I have been able to verify that the dominant (masculine, heterosexual) class will not abandon its privileges just because we send out some tweets or let out a few cries. Ever since the upheavals of the sexual and anti-colonial revolution of the past century, heteropatriarchs have embarked on a project of counter-reform – to which now the 'feminine' voices who wish to continue to be 'importuned/disturbed' are joining. This will be the thousand-year war – the longest of wars, knowing it affects the politics of reproduction and the processes through which a human body is constituted as a sovereign subject. In fact, this will be the most important of wars, because what is at stake is neither territory nor city but the body itself, pleasure, and life.

What characterizes the position of men in our techno-patriarchal and hetero-centric societies is that masculine sovereignty is defined by the legitimate use of techniques of violence (against women, against children, against non-white men and women, against animals, against the planet as a whole). We could say, reading Weber with Butler, that masculinity is to society what the State is to the nation: the holder and legitimate user of violence. This violence is expressed socially in the form of domination, economically in the form of privilege, sexually in the form of aggression and rape. On the contrary, within this political epistemology, feminine sovereignty is linked to the capacity of women to give birth. Women are sexually and socially subjugated. Only mothers are sovereign. Within this regime, masculinity is defined necro-politically (by men's right to put to death) while femininity is defined bio-politically (by women's obligation to give life). One could say of necro-bio-political heterosexuality that it is something like the idealized eroticization of the mating of Robocop and Alien, thinking that with a little luck, one of the two will find his footing...

Heterosexuality is not just, as Wittig demonstrates, a technology of government: it is also a politics of desire. The specificity of this libidinal regime is that it is embodied as a process of seduction and romantic dependence between apparently 'free' sexual agents. The positions of Robocop and Alien are not chosen individually, and are not conscious. Necro-bio-political heterosexuality is a government practice that is not imposed by those who govern (men) on the governed (women) but rather an epistemology fixing the definitions and respective positions of men and women via internal regulation. This government practice does not take the form of a law, but of an unwritten norm, a transaction of gestures and codes that have the effect of establishing in the practice of sexuality a division between what can and cannot be done. This form of sexual servitude rests on an aesthetic of seduction, a stylization of desire and a historically constructed and codified domination eroticizing the difference of power and perpetuating it. This politics of desire is what keeps the ancien sex-gender régime alive, despite all the legal processes of democratization and empowerment of women. This necro-bio-political heterosexual regime is as degrading and destructive as bondage and slavery were in the time of the Enlightenment.

The process of denouncing violence and making it visible that we are currently experiencing is part of a sexual revolution, which is as unstoppable as it is slow and sinuous. Queer feminism made epistemological transformation the condition of possibility of social change. It called binary epistemology and the naturalization of genders into question by asserting that there is an irreducible multiplicity of sexes, genders and sexualities. We understand today that libidinal transformation is as important as epistemological transformation: we must modify desire. We must learn to desire sexual freedom.

For years, queer culture was a laboratory of invention for new aesthetics of dissident sexualities, confronting techniques of subjectivation and the desire of hegemonic necro-bio-political heterosexuality. Many of us long ago abandoned the aesthetic of Robocop-Alien sexuality. We learned from butch-femme cultures and BDSM, with Joan Nestle, Pat Califia and Gayle Rubin, with Annie Sprinkle and Beth Stephens, with Guillaume Dustan and Virginie Despentes, that sexuality is a political theatre in which desire, not anatomy, writes the script. It is possible, within the theatrical fiction of sexuality, to desire licking shoe soles, to want to be penetrated in every orifice, or to hunt your lover in a forest as if he were sexual prey. However, two differential elements separate queer aesthetics from that of the hetero-norm of the ancien régime: consent and the non-naturalization of sexual positions. The equivalence of bodies and the redistribution of power.

As a trans man, I disidentify with the dominant masculinity and its necro-bio-political definition. What is most urgent is not to defend what we are (men or women) but to reject it, to disidentify ourselves from the political coercion which forces us to desire the norm and reproduce it. Our political praxis is to disobey the norms of gender and sexuality. I was a lesbian for the majority of my life, then trans these last five years; I am as far from your aesthetic of heterosexuality as a Buddhist monk levitating in Lhasa is from a Carrefour supermarket. Your aesthetic of the sexual ancien régime does not make me come. It doesn't excite me to 'importune' anyone. It doesn't interest me to get out of my sexual misery by placing my hand on the ass of a woman on the metro. I feel no kind of desire for the erotic-sexual kitsch you propose: guys who take advantage of their position of power to get laid and touch asses. The grotesque, wounding aesthetic of necro-political heterosexuality turns my stomach. An aesthetic that re-naturalizes sexual differences and situates men in the position of the aggressor and women in that of victim (painfully grateful or joyfully importuned).

If it is possible to assert that in queer and trans culture we fuck better and more, it's on the one hand because we have extracted sexuality from the realm of reproduction, and on the other, more importantly, because we have tried to free ourselves from the domination of gender. I am not saying that queer and transfeminist culture escapes all forms of violence. There is no sexuality without a shadowy side. But it is not necessary for shadow (inequality and violence) to prevail and determine all sexuality.

Representatives of the sexual ancien régime, get to grips with your shadowy side and have fun with it, and let us bury our dead. Enjoy your aesthetic of domination, but don't try to make your style a law. And let us fuck with our own politics of desire, without man or woman, without penis or vagina, without axe or gun.

Arles, 15 January 2018

Translated by Charlotte Mandell

HANDLE WITH BEAR

Lawrence Schimel (1971–)

Schimel is a multilingual writer and translator, working predominantly with the science fiction genre in graphic novels, children's books and adult fiction. He finds that queer norms differ between nations and believes that literary translation can facilitate cross-cultural education and empowerment. He was born in New York and studied at Yale University, but has lived in Madrid for the last twenty years.

"It looks ridiculous," I told him, looking up at his head as we stood at the crosswalk at Gran Via, waiting for the light to change.

"You need to relax and get into the Holiday Spirit," Aiden replied.

"But Christmas is over already!" I complained. Which was technically true: Christmas Day had passed two days ago. Not that you would notice here in Spain, where the holiday was still in full swing. From what Nacho had told us last night, Christmas was a drawn-out affair here, which lasted until 6 January, known as the *Día de Reyes*, the Day of the Kings. It actually made a lot more sense to me, giving gifts on Reyes, which is when the Three Wise Men did actually show up bearing their gifts, rather than on Christmas Day itself. But then, I couldn't imagine England practically shutting down for nearly two weeks of festivities and jollity; a demonstration of the difference between our Protestant work ethic and a Catholic country like Spain.

"When in Rome, do as the Romans do," Aiden said, unflappable in his good humor, as we joined the surge of pedestrians crossing the street.

"First of all, we're in Chueca, not in Italy," I grumbled. Chueca was the "gay neighborhood" of Madrid, which we'd just entered by crossing the street. It wasn't the source of my bad mood; on the contrary: with any luck, coming here would help me find someone to help perk me up.

I was somewhat jealous that Graham had abandoned us again, to go off to Nacho's place and have sex. Not that I wouldn't have done the same thing in his position. What I resented, if I was honest with myself, was not being in the position to abandon my mates.

"Second of all," I continued, "did you notice how only the heterosexuals engage in this sort of frivolity?"

To my dismay, just then, two incredibly hot studs wearing matching silver wigs, their arms around each other, turned the corner onto Calle Hortaleza and started walking toward us. Both Aiden and I watched them in reverent silence, and as one we both turned to watch them until they disappeared from sight, turning right when they reached Gran Via.

"It's still inappropriate for a bears' bar," I insisted, a mix of embarrassment to be seen with him wearing that and all the free-floating general cussedness I was feeling. "Neither deer in general, nor reindeer in particular, have a place in the fauna of the bear subculture."

"Then I'll stand out. Since I don't speak the language, I have to do something to give me an advantage if I hope to hook up." And with that, Aiden pushed through the doors into Hot.

As I followed him inside, I was just glad he hadn't changed into his kilt as well when we stopped at the hostel to drop off our afternoon's purchases.

It had been something of a lark to come to Spain for our holidays. I forget if it was Graham or Aiden who'd broached the idea one day at lunch but, whoever it was, it quickly took hold as the plan for New Year. Graham had heard wonderful things about Madrid's club scene, and all of us enjoyed a bit of fantasizing about Spanish men.

The thing is, Graham had been a bit more proactive about it than the rest of us. He'd moved all his online profiles to Madrid weeks ago, so even before we landed at Barajas airport his dance card was more or less full. Although the first guy he met with, Nacho, seemed to be turning into one of those holiday romances, given that Graham had stood up the second guy on his dance card to spend a second night with Nacho, and from the way things were shaping up, he'd spend tonight with him as well. It felt almost as if Graham were spending his holiday with Nacho instead of with us, which was fine, I was happy for him, even if I was jealous. And Graham's beau was turning into somewhat of a boon for us as well, since Nacho had become our local guide. He was off from his job until after Reyes, so the times he wasn't having sex with Graham he was happy enough to take us out and show us the local nightlife, or other touristy things like shopping at the Christmas market in Plaza Mayor this afternoon, where Aiden bought that stupid moose-head hat.

Nacho had been the one to recommend that we come here, to Hot, which he said was one of the few places that had some sort of scene this early (early by Spain's standards: it was 8 p.m.) with its two-for-one drinks during happy hour. And there definitely was a lively scene: the place was pretty packed, with sexy hirsute men of all ages and sizes. I hurried to slip into the brief wake created by Aiden, some men shifting back to give him room as he headed straight to the bar while others took a step back to get a better look at all of him. By the time I caught up with him, he had already ordered a beer for both of us. *Cerveza* was one of the first words Nacho had taught us, and even I could count to *dos*.

"*Gracias*," I said, as Aiden handed me a bottle of the local brew: Mahou. He had unzipped his jacket, but he hadn't taken off that damned hat, and it looked like he planned to wear it the entire evening. And nothing I could say or do seemed likely to have any effect on his decision.

I couldn't explain why, but it seemed that Aiden's good spirits only left me feeling even more Scrooge-like. Maybe it was the whole holidays atmosphere, with its relentless good cheer and the constant insipid carols, not to mention years of childhood frustrations: years of getting "appropriate" boy presents instead of the ones I truly wanted, awkward gatherings of the extended family clan, the usual stuff a shrink could have a field day with if I wasn't so averse to the idea of paying for the privilege of lying on a couch and spilling my guts to some stranger. I tended more towards self-medication, I reflected, taking another sip of my beer. Weren't trips abroad just another way to drown one's sorrows? Or at any rate, to distract one from them? (With the hope that on one's return everything didn't seem even bleaker by comparison; it is my theory that this explains why so many people show holiday snapshots for months after they get home, as if that could let them recapture or drag out the holiday feeling a bit longer.)

"So here we are, three friends in Madrid over the holidays," I grumbled, highlighting Graham's absence.

"Lighten up," Aiden said. "You're on holiday. Try to enjoy yourself a bit. Live it up!" He spread his arms above his head in a wide, camp gesture, before letting them fall back to his side. "Besides, this is precisely what friendship is about: giving your mates space to do their thing without going all jealous. That's why they're friends and not boyfriends."

I opened my mouth to reply with some biting and bitter retort, but Aiden's comment (and no doubt the beer on an empty stomach) set me thinking. I already knew I wasn't jealous of Graham, not in a sexual way: it's not that I wanted to be having sex with him and resented Nacho for having sex with him instead, or even the reverse, that I wanted to have sex with Nacho (although I wouldn't have minded that) and resented Graham, competitively, for getting to do so. If I was jealous of anything, maybe it was Graham's sudden independence, whereas I was feeling almost nostalgic for our friendship, for things to be as they had been before, for nothing to change.

Friendship was such a curious thing, really; it was so much harder to understand than sexual attraction. That, at least, made perfect sense; even if I didn't share a particular kink or fetish I could more or less understand the basic concept, or accept that it floated someone else's boat even if it left mine high and dry. And that attraction could be there, even if it wasn't mutual, even if it was never acted on.

But friendships were another matter, much more tenuous and inexplicable. Sometimes they happened by pure chance, rather than any shared interest. In our case, it was almost from proximity more than anything else: we all worked in the same office for TNT in Lount. Which could in theory have fit some gay-fantasy scenario (the hunky delivery man in his uniform) except we all worked in the back offices instead of making the rounds in our distinctive orange vans delivering packages. Graham and Aiden were both team leaders and I was a resource manager, something boring but necessary to keep everything flowing properly. But what did we really share beyond our jobs and our sexuality? The three of us had hit it off somehow, for some unknown reason. It's not that we were the only gays at the office; TNT had a special gay diversity group, on an international level, and while Lount was not a hotspot of gay life, there were at least a dozen other homos who were out of the closet in our office. So why only us three and not those others, who were just office acquaintances? They didn't have the intimacy we all did, and not just the three of us: we three were also part of a sort of clique within our little TNT world with a few (straight) women and even one or two straight men. We knew all about each other's lives because we were together all day at the office, using lunches and smoke breaks as a chance to gossip. Not to mention keeping up on all the gossip through Facebook and email.

Would we all still be friends when we moved on to other employers? Or was our friendship merely a convenience? Like regulars at our local, comforting because they were known and unchanging.

Carmen was still part of the group, even though she'd just gotten promoted to the head office in Amsterdam and now spent three weeks a month traveling between TNT centers. We just didn't see her as often. Of course, she still worked for TNT, so there was still that team-spirit bond. If she'd moved to some other company, would we all (understandably, naturally) just drift apart over time?

Here we were in another country (the others all had spouses and/ or kids to deal with, so only we three single gay men had decided to spend Christmas together abroad) and already the ties that bound us were beginning to fray. Or were they really? I asked myself. What was so different about the three of us heading in to Birmingham (Lount, after all, didn't offer much in the way of a nightlife, gay or otherwise) one weekend, and one of us abandoning the other two because he'd pulled?

The difference being that here I didn't speak the language and, as a result, I was clinging too hard to the world I knew: my two mates who were here in Madrid with me, or even just the memory of our group, lost in my head like this, thinking drunkenly about all of us and the mystery of our friendship. I determined to try to live in the now, to have a good time, even if it felt almost like a threat or an obligation: I would enjoy myself, whether I wanted to or not.

"I think we should go over there and talk to those two guys," Aiden said, indicating two very young Spaniards. They were both gesticulating wildly and yet standing very close together; I couldn't tell if it was because of the press of other bodies around them or if it was something to do with their being Spanish.

"They look like they're barely old enough to drink," I said, already breaking my determination to enjoy myself. "I prefer men to boys."

"Well, I think they're kind of cute. And I think they might be interested. At least in me. But there's two of them, so I'm willing to share."

"Was your beer much stronger than mine or is this just wishful thinking?"

"They're talking about my hat."

"How can you hear what they're talking about from across the bar?"

"They're signing," Aiden said, as if it were self-evident. And as I watched them, I realized it should have been obvious that they were deaf, and they were not gesticulating to accentuate their conversation but rather conversing entirely with their hands.

"I can't believe this. You don't speak Spanish but you can understand Spanish Sign Language?"

"My niece is deaf. The whole family learned British Sign Language so she wouldn't feel left out when we got together for holidays and what-not. I don't think it's so very different from signed Spanish."

And without waiting for my consent, he started heading across the room. Once again, I was pulled along in his wake. This time, though, I felt like we were a couple of some sort, instead of just friends: coupled together by both being strangers in a strange land. A moment ago, we had both been equals in our outsider status, but now Aiden had discovered that he could indeed communicate with these deaf Spaniards, for he was chattering away with them, it seemed, from how fast their hands were flying. It was fascinating to watch, and not merely because all of a sudden this friend I thought I knew so well seemed a completely alien being to me. Not that being able to speak sign language was the same as suddenly sprouting tentacles or something (although he did have those stupid antlers sticking off the top of his head), but it did feel almost like there were some new dimension to him, or rather, it underscored how even though we might feel like we knew everything about one another there was still all these hidden depths we didn't know anything about. Things that weren't necessarily secrets, it's not like Aiden actively kept his knowledge of sign language or his deaf niece from me (and presumably the rest of us): it had just never come up before. But I was still left somewhat blindsided by the surprise, not the least because I was now excluded from their chatting.

So I drank faster than I probably should have. Aiden gave me the drinks ticket and I pushed my way back to the bar to get our free second beers. While I was waiting, I looked back at the three of them, and for a moment I felt disoriented, as if I had gone back in time a few moments only now I was all alone, and Aiden had crossed over to become one of them. As if he had gone native somehow, whereas I was still a foreign visitor. I think it had to do with language, with being able to communicate, whereas all I could do was watch. Watch and think, although since my thoughts were becoming so somber and morbid I tried to just watch.

There were two of them, and they were both enough alike to make it hard to tell them apart at a quick glance. Not once you really looked at them, but in that cursory way that often makes people lump racial or ethnic groups together by broad obvious features instead of individual traits or personalities. Both boys were white without being too pale, with dark hair and dark eyes, and they were both dwarfed beside Aiden although they were probably 170 cm in height. Though it was a bear bar they both looked quite slender, even under the many layers of winter clothing. They were both in their very early twenties, though one of them had a sparse beard that only made him look even younger than his clean-shaven companion. They both radiated that youthful fresh-faced energy and earnest intensity. Or maybe it was because they were deaf, I realized, that they looked at everything so carefully, so strongly, so fully, because they were absorbing only through their eyes what we would take in through our eyes and ears. It was something we took for granted so easily, those of us with all our senses, even if in raucous and noisy environs like this bar the absolute quiet of being deaf might be a welcome relief. But that was just being cheap and facile, I told myself, since there would be lots of other times when I would strain desperately to hear something, if I were to suddenly lose my own hearing.

Even after the bartender gave me the two beers, I watched them from afar, trying to discern what differences I could see from here, before approaching and seeing up close the other differences. Aiden had his back to me as he chatted with them, so to start with I dubbed them Left and Right in my head. Because they both were looking primarily at him, glancing between his face and his hands, as his fingers moved through the words he was trying to say. (For all that Aiden offered to share, he was quite obviously the center of attention for both of them.) Right was the one with the attempt at a beard, something it would take him a few more years to grow into. Not to mention his assurance. Left seemed to be the much more dominant of the two, gesticulating (I mean talking) more (more often, more fluidly), grabbing Right by the shoulder to get his attention, or one of them would touch Aiden for the same reason. At first I thought he was just being pushy, but as I watched them I realized personal space must be so different for them, casual touching a necessary part of the conversation process.

I thought of Graham and Nacho, no doubt also touching right now, having sex or maybe in a post-coital tangle, and I felt even more isolated and alone, in that way that you can only feel when surrounded by other people at a bar where no one pays you any attention.

So it felt almost a like relief to go back to them, which was strange, since I hardly knew the two of them; even Aiden barely knew them, although he at least could talk to them. But they had taken on a sort of singular identity, this threesome, and my friend was part of it and yet also still my friend. I stood beside them, waiting and watching, not wanting to interrupt, but Right noticed me, and touched Aiden's shoulder, and he turned his head to look at me, with those goofy antlers on his head, and said, "Thanks, mate," as he reached out for his beer, and it was sort of a shock to hear him talk again; I had been thinking of him as part of their group almost more than mine.

He turned back to the deaf boys so I watched the crowd a bit and then watched them. I wondered if it was considered rude to watch a signed conversation if you weren't involved, if it was like eavesdropping. Up close, I could see that Left's face was more narrow than Right's, with a pointed chin that made him look dainty or elfin. Left also had a piercing under his lip, a little metal stud that caught the light from time to time. Right had stronger features: a squarer jaw, sharper cheekbones. I didn't really know Spain well enough to identify its regions, but I found myself wondering if maybe he was Basque or from some other northern region.

He has nice eyes, I thought, before I realized that I could see them so clearly because he was looking back at me, and not at the conversation. I glanced away, my face turning red to have been caught staring at him, and I saw that the conversation had been derailed. Or perhaps it had evolved to a new level: Aiden and Left were kissing.

There is something contagious about being in the presence of sex. It's probably biological. I think that's what makes so many heterosexual men so uncomfortable about seeing gays: confronting the fact that they recognize the desire before them as something they, too, share, even if it's just a glimmering, a little tiny tickle.

And the kissing going on between Aiden and Left was definitely sex, even though they were both fully dressed and in public.

I was suddenly nervous. Not because I was turned on by watching my friend make out with a boy he had just picked up, but because now Right was also excluded, and that left him and me alone. Alone in that way two people can be together in a crowded bar where their mates have just hooked up with one another.

It was an awkward situation under the best of circumstances, but to top it off, I didn't know how to talk to a deaf person.

I looked at Right again, and he was definitely watching me and not the two of them, not the bar in general: that intense look I had noticed earlier.

I opened my mouth to say something, to explain that I didn't know what to say or how to say it. Of course, almost immediately, I realized my instincts were all wrong, I couldn't just speak, I had to try to convey what I wanted to say through non-verbal means. Unless maybe he could read lips? Although that would only work if I could speak Spanish.

Right looked at me for a while longer with those intense dark eyes, and then he said aloud, in accented but passable English, "So you're Eric."

I was flabbergasted. Not so much that he knew my name (obviously Aiden must have told him) but by the fact that he could speak. I had just assumed that because they were deaf, they must be mute as well. And it turns out that he could not only speak, but speak English as well.

"Yes," I said, beaming at him. I could feel words bubbling up in me, all the conversation I had swallowed with my beer, feeling isolated and alone, while lost in my thoughts. I hated myself for feeling so relieved, but I began to feel sympathy and understanding for that kind of British traveler I had always disdained before (more for how it smacked of colonialism than for fear of recognizing myself in him, how little had I known myself before!) who suddenly become bosom buddies with any stranger merely because they could speak the Queen's English.

I realized I had answered vocally again without thinking. Maybe Right could read lips, I thought. Or maybe I had made the assumption he was deaf, when he was merely someone who could also speak in sign, like Aiden.

"And you are?" I asked aloud. "Aiden didn't have a chance to introduce us before, and it looks like he's otherwise indisposed right now."

Right smiled. "I'm Javi," he said. And he leaned toward me.

How forward they are in this country, I thought, closing my eyes before he could kiss my lips. But he merely kissed one cheek, and I remembered the local custom and quickly offered the other cheek for a second kiss. Only two here, as far as I recalled; I could never keep straight in which countries it was three, or which side to start on.

"Pleased to meet you," I said automatically, each of us falling back on the ritual pleasantries to smooth out the awkwardness of the situation. "And I am glad you can not just speak, but you speak English as well."

"Did you think I was deaf?" he asked. It would no doubt take me a while to think of him by his name, Javi, instead of as Right.

"At first I just assumed… and since Aiden didn't say anything otherwise."

He laughed. "I only learned it recently. I am an interpreter. Spanish Sign Language is now officially recognized as a language in Spain. Just like Catalan or Basque. But there are few people who know how to speak it. So when I lost my job, I started to study it. And now I work as an interpreter between deaf people and hearing people. And there is always work."

"That's a job that I had never stopped to think about before," I said.

"The world is always changing," he said. And as if to underscore his point, he pulled an iPhone from his pocket. "Excuse me," he said, and answered the phone, rattling off a stream of Spanish I couldn't understand at all.

I was amazed at how smoothly he moved from one mode of conversation to another, slipping between languages and media: from hand signals to high-tech gadgets.

"Sorry," he explained to me when he was done with the conversation. "Friend having a fight with another friend."

"It's OK," I replied.

Then he grabbed Left's shoulder, interrupting the kiss. A flurry of signing followed. Aiden grinned at me and winked. He was still wearing his antlers, even with all that tongue-wrestling. I didn't know if I was getting into the holiday spirit at last or if I was simply on my way to getting drunk and didn't care any more.

"Just one minute," Javi said, tapping away at the touchpad screen to write a message of some sort.

"No worries," I replied. "Why don't I get us another round?"

Aiden and Left were at it again, so rather than wait for a reply I made my way back to the bar and ordered and paid for two beers, then right away gave in the ticket for two more.

But when I got back with the drinks, Aiden was zipping up his coat. "Miguel has invited me back to his place," he explained. "In case I don't go back to the hotel tonight, I'll see you two tomorrow morning some time. I'll send you an email. Have fun."

Suddenly, Left swooped in and gave me a kiss on either cheek, though we hadn't even been introduced yet. Miguel, that was his name.

And with that Aiden and Miguel were gone.

I was still holding the four beer bottles, two in each hand. "Thanks," Javi said, as he took two of them from me. He put one on a sort of shelf behind him and drank from the other.

"*De nada*," I replied. I figured I might as well show off my few words of tourist Spanish. Besides, I was feeling dizzy by how fast things changed: now it was just me and Javi, who because he spoke English, felt more like a friend than someone I had known for less than half an hour in a bar.

And even though Aiden and Miguel had left, there was still a sexualized zing lingering in the air. Or maybe it was because we knew they were on their way to Miguel's place to have sex. But I felt now that when Javi looked at me, sex was more of a possibility between us than it had been before, even though he was still so young, still so fresh, and I tended to like men who were the opposite, a bit rugged, and in general older than I am.

"Everything OK with your friend?" I asked, thinking it was a neutral topic of conversation.

"Yeah, I sent an email to another friend who said she could stay there."

"You're probably too young to realize it," I said, although as soon as it was out of my mouth I knew how pompous that sounded; good thing I wasn't trying to pick him up, I thought. "But this whole email thing has really changed the world. When I was young, I used to have a pen pal. I don't know if you even know what that is: I used to write letters to a girl my age who lived in Johannesburg. We would send letters back and forth every week."

"Did you ever meet her?" Javi asked.

"No, we never did. I wonder what happened to her."

"You could probably look her up on the internet." He pulled his iPhone out of his pocket again and offered it to me.

"No, no. Thank you. I may try and find her. I hadn't thought of her in years, but I don't need to do it right now." I took a sip of my beer, feeling pensive again. "I know I must sound like a drunken old queen, but back then, communication was something special. It wasn't something we took for granted the way we do with emails or SMS, something just dashed off."

"I bet you're not as much of a dinosaur as you pretend to be. How old are you?" Javi asked.

"It's not just a question of age," I said, avoiding the answer. "The world has changed. And the whole gay world has changed, too. How people meet: these days, back in England, it's all on the Internet, it's like shopping by numbers. It's all so... de-humanized in some way. Like, what happened to real letters? Now we send little electronic blips of emails and SMS and tweets. Sometimes I feel like everything is in some secret code. And I only speak the old language. I can only speak one language, English. I don't even speak a second language, like you do."

'There's always sex," Javi said, suddenly tugging my hand and pulling me away from the wall, out into the middle of the room.

"What?" I said, my mind trying to make sense of what he'd said even as my body followed him.

"Sex. As a means of communication," Javi said.

He was now standing at the entrance to what Nacho had told us was the dark room.

"Come with me," he said. "I'll tell you a story."

I wondered, for a moment, how we had come to this. I was on the brink of sex with a boy I would never ordinarily look twice at.

Was this the sexual freedom that happened only when one was far from home?

What could this boy see in me?

Was this because I was a foreigner, something exotic?

Was this just a pity fuck because our friends had abandoned us and he was bored and why not pass the time together in a search for mutual pleasure?

Had this sexual tension always been there, between us, even if I didn't recognize it before? Maybe it had been dormant in me, something that was only set into motion by Aiden and Miguel, like ripples after the splash of their sexual charge?

If Miguel lived nearby, they might be having sex by now. But in a bed. Which is how I thought it would happen for me, if it were to happen on the trip. Not in a back room in a bears' bar, with a wisp of a boy who wasn't even a cub.

At the same time, I had to live my own life, my own story. I was being offered sex just when I had been feeling left out, both my mates having managed to hook up with guys they had chosen.

And even if this wasn't the guy I might have chosen, maybe this was one of those unexpected plot twists. Or maybe I was just drunk enough to be thinking all of this.

I could listen to how someone else told the story. Or I could maybe tell a story or two myself.

I reached out and took Javi's hand, and followed him into the back room.

THE WOUNDED MAN

Abdellah Taïa (1973–)

Based in France and writing in French, Taïa is from Morocco, where homosexuality remains illegal. His books focus on the paradox of identity as a gay citizen in a country where homosexuality does not officially exist. Though he has distanced himself from Morocco, where he feels insecure, he has not renounced Islam, and finds inspiration in queer-friendly periods of Islamic history.

We had broken fast about two hours earlier. It was dark now. And Hay Salain was abnormally quiet. It was as though the whole population of this working-class district of Salé except our family had suddenly moved to the far side of the river Bou Regreg, close to Rabat Beach. It felt as though something extraordinary was about to happen, something that might engulf the country, the earth and all those still here below. A squall bringing with it hope, rain and a new year. Or perhaps the apocalypse: the end, right now.

My mother, M'Barka, was sleeping soundly.

Ramadan was hard on her. But despite the exhaustion of fasting, every day she insisted on preparing sweet treats, crêpes, *harira* of course, a soup she preferred sour, with lots of tomatoes and lemon juice. There was a time when my sisters would have helped her to make every day of the sacred month a spiritual and gastronomic feast, an endless ritual. Now, the house was deserted. Three floors empty of people. Everyone had left, moved to some other place, some other town, some other country, another world, living among strangers, people I would never know, people I would never truly accept. Now there was only my mother, my little brother Mustapha, whom we saw very little of, and me at home. Now M'Barka was constantly afraid that she would be left alone. 'Loneliness,' she told me over and over, 'is a slow and agonising poison'. This made me terribly sad. Though I couldn't quite understand her pain, when I heard her say such things, it made me want to cry. Every day she begged me not to hang around in the city after my lectures at Rabat University, begged me to get home early, before it got dark, to take the bus and come back and occupy the house, keep her company, do everyday things with her, brighten her day by my simple presence, amuse her, cheer her, warm her, re-fashion our family before nightfall.

Late at night, when we were about to be separated again, she would beg me not to go up to my room, beg me to stay by her side until she fell asleep. Sleep was death. Ever since my father's sudden death a year earlier, my mother suffered from terrible fears, from crippling panic. And so she clung to me. M'Barka slept on a bed in the living room, dominated by the imposing television. She who had always hated 'that contraption', as she called it, had finally found in it a friend to keep her company through the day, a machine that produced sounds that would comfort her a little, though not always.

Recently, thanks to the satellite dish – now that they had finally become affordable – we could get French channels, which particularly interested me. I watched *Arte* whenever I could. It made me feel like someone, like some hip intellectual student interested in things other people found boring or challenging. I felt proud. Alone in the living room, I gave myself airs.

This was the role I was playing that night, having wolfed down the delicious Ramadan treats mother had prepared. I turned on the television. There was a film on *Arte*. A film that had started without me. Locked in the toilets of a train station, Jean-Hugues Anglade was crying his heart out. He, too, obviously felt abandoned. He was, also, obviously struggling with something, with loneliness maybe. I felt an immediate empathy for him (for the actor and the role he was playing). Through my extensive knowledge of cinema, I managed in less than a minute to identify this film I had never seen before. It was Patrice Chéreau's *The Wounded Man*. A French film made in 1984. A cult film. Banned.

My mother was sound asleep. This film was showing and there was nothing anyone in Morocco could do to stop it or interrupt it to deliver some religious or moral homily to the young hero, an outcast, his hair a little too long, who loved men, who loved a man.

I was confronted by a dilemma. Confronted by my desires. I was determined to watch this film to the end, even as fear gripped my guts. Constantly on the alert. My mother, sleeping in the bed just behind me, might wake at any moment and catch me in the act. Then she would know my secret, my only secret, the other part of me, the object of my affection. She would have hysterics. There would be a scandal. I would be ashamed, I wouldn't know what to do or what to say.

My stomach hurt. I had eaten too much when I broke my fast and the meal sat heavily on my stomach I was aroused by the passion that suffused the film, that haunted Jean-Hugues Anglade and the other characters. They lived only for this, for sex, for love, for danger. You feel attracted to a man, flirt with him, pick him up, cajole him, buy him, you play with him, rape him, dump him, little by little tear him to pieces. I was fascinated, hypnotised by these images. And I wanted to do what these characters did. I wanted to be one of them. An outcast. I wanted to love as they did. Love another man. Alone. Savage. I wanted to touch myself. Caress myself. Lick myself. Bite myself. Let myself be drawn to a strong man and give myself to him.

My stomach grew bloated. My penis grew hard. And I did not know what to do because I was still terrified, in spite of this desire that streamed from the screen, bathing me, turning my world upside down, driving me insane.

My mother was snoring, her breathing regular, her snoring sometimes loud, sometimes soft. Now and then it stopped. When it did, I immediately changed channels. I couldn't help but interpret each silence as a sign that she was about to wake up, come round, discover me watching this forbidden film. After an interminable minute waiting, watching her intently to make sure her eyes were really closed, that she was still far from me and the images I was watching, I would feel somewhat reassured and would turn back to *The Wounded Man* and his story. And immediately I would feel the same passion, the same primal fear.

Jean-Hugues Anglade was in love with a tall, handsome, dark-haired man, I think. A bit like Gérard Depardieu in the early '80s. A masculine, sensitive, tough, ruthless man. A king. A dictator. A pimp.

Anglade had fallen for this man the moment he first set eyes on him. His world henceforth would revolve around this man; he would forget everyone else. No one else could matter to him as much as this man. Almost immediately, he abandons everything to follow him – his former life, his family. He finds himself following the man, stalking him through streets, train stations, car parks, trying clumsily to seduce him so he might spend a moment with this, with his body. So that he might be loved by him, but in vain. Anglade's passion is absolute. It could not but be heartbreaking and tragic.

Patrice Chéreau's film, tumultuous and brutal as it overwhelmed me that night and as I remember it still, is extreme in its presentation of love, extreme in the power sex exerts over all bodies. The film is a litany of punches, arguments, chases, trafficking of all sorts, tears, orgies, blood, sperm, sordidness, obsessions and death. It is the tale of a bleeding young man, doomed in advance, hurtling inexorably towards a crime of love.

I've forgotten his first name. I was him, loving and frustrated as he was. Ready, like him, to abandon everything for a dream, for a strong man, for this rare feeling, this exceptional creature. And yet still petrified. In a desperate search for the unique object of desire. The beloved. What Americans call 'The One'.

One man and no other. A man older than I was so I could learn from him, relive a certain past with him as part of an unacknowledged couple. A *faqih*, a master, a baker, a man of God who prays five times a day, a visionary, a parent, an uncle, a cousin...

The film played on, its power, its despair, its religion burning themselves on to my eyes, into my mind. Without realising it, I was already a convert, a master, an adept of this way of living, of seeing, of straying, the jostling bodies, the surge of pleasure before you go insane, more insane. Here before me was the forbidden, touching my scrawny now suddenly courageous body. Behind me, too, was the forbidden.

My penis grew harder. My heart grew darker. My eyes grew redder. I was happy and sad. Thrilled yet frozen as though whipped by a wind from the north, from Tangiers. There were moments when I wanted to shake my mother awake, have her see these images, connect her to this film which so moved, so overwhelmed her well-brought-up son. And I wanted to go to her, press myself to her, climb on to her lap, place my hand on her belly, feel her breath on my back, on my neck, smell her scent in my nostrils, on my skin. Go back to the source, the first door, to my first opening on to the world, on to life, on to light. And there, in that place where it all began, that first threshold, carve out a space, a seat, a hole, and weep, all the while watching this wounded man, this young man, this brother bewildered by the searing intensity of love, weep, cry for him, go with him in my tears. Gently take his eyes into my mouth, lick them slowly one by one then finally drink the faintly salted water that streamed from them, trickled over his cheeks, his skin.

I identified with him. I was dreaming. I was fantasising. I wasn't thinking. Not any more. I was in pain. Pain in my eyes, my thighs, my knees, my penis.

When I came to myself again, the wounded man was still on the *via crucis* of love. This man's fate – *mektoub* – was being played out here, in our home, this house without a father, in our almost empty living mom, in our privacy, our silence, our darkness.

I had thought I was sophisticated. Now, watching Patrice Chéreau's film for the first time, I realised I was still a naïve film fan watching films, all films, the way I had before. Before: when, at childhood's end, programmed by others, the religion of Indian movies and kung-fu films entered me for ever. I rediscovered myself. In dark, crowded cinemas surrounded by prostitutes and wicked boys, I drank in these images, and these films delivered me from the bounds of my country and connected me to an art which was gradually to become my reason for living, for looking beyond, looking above. Soaring up above the world, seeing myself naked and coming back down to earth prepared to do battle.

Now I was at war. In revolt. A few days before the sacred night of Laylat al-Qadr.

My mother's music stopped suddenly. No sound came from her mouth, no wheeze, no snore, no breath. Was she holding her breath? Was she dead, had she gone, fearless and unafraid, to join my father? Was she awake? Was she, like me, watching *The Wounded Man*? Did she understand the meaning of these strange images from another world, from hell? Would she suddenly get to her feet, scream, shout at me with the voice she used on her bad days, pull my hair, punish me, pinch me, curse me? Castrate me there and then?

My heart hammered in my chest, I turned to look at her. Her eyes were open but she was staring at the ceiling. She was still dreaming, still caught up in the images of a dream that was hers alone. A little reassured, I switched channels and, in a small voice filled with respect, asked her if she needed anything. Her reply came immediately, as though she had prepared it long ago, while still asleep. 'A glass of water, *habibi*!' I rushed to the kitchen to get her one. She was very thirsty, she had come back from a long journey. She asked for a second glass. 'Another glass, *habibi*, or I'll die… May God ble—' I didn't need to be told twice. I all but ran back into the kitchen, overjoyed at the blessings she was heaping on me, as always, blessings that were always the same, that spoke of paradise as something certain, not imagined.

Her thirst quenched, M'Barka returned to her sleep, her dreams. But just before she closed her eyes again, she gave me a blessing that stunned me even more: 'Watch, my son… watch television if you want… You're not bothering me… watch whatever you like…'

I turned down the volume and waited for the sound of my mother snoring before turning back to *The Wounded Man* and its bruised hero. By now, he had come to the end of his tether, he was tired of this unrequited love, of the humiliations, tired of wandering, yet still hopelessly in love. The road to his crime – to the first and last time he would possess the body of the beloved – was almost at an end. Only death, only murder could give this young man's tragic story, his sublime love, a meaning, a goal, a structure.

Naked, pressed against the man he loved, he was suffocating him with his bare hands, suffocating him even as he made love to him. He was giving himself completely to this man, his body, his heart, his mind, his skin, his blood, his breath. He was giving his life in taking the life of the man who, to the end, had refused to commune with him in this embrace, in this religion of emotion.

It was a tragedy.

Love, like life, which in miraculous moments brings light and passion, is a tragedy. I knew this intuitively. I was twenty years old. *The Wounded Man* reminded me of the fact once more, once and for all, I had been warned. It was up to me to decide. Give up? Never.

The credits rolled. Hervé Guibert's name, the writer who had co-written the screenplay with Patrice Chéreau, appeared. I had forgotten Guibert: this film, this story, they are his, too. His life. His way of life. A life I had discovered and loved in his books. He had been dead four or five years now. Tears streamed from my eyes. Finally. For what? For whom? I did not know precisely how to answer, how to answer myself. For Hervé Guibert, whom I knew intimately through his books? For the hero of the film who had become a murderer, a brother, a friend, myself? For my father, who had passed away too soon, before he could see me become a book, a written record? For my mother, who was slipping back into childhood fears? For life, which, deep down, in spite of the pleasures of Ramadan, was sad and terribly lonely?

Even now I do not know. Even now, I weep when I think about that moment, the end of the film, Hervé Guibert, me... and my mother screaming in silence. I weep for all of us.

The following morning I woke up late. I had only one thought. To go and see my favourite cousin Chouaïb, who I was a little in love with, seduce him, corrupt him, press myself against him, persuade him to break fast with me before dark, break fast together, both of us thinking sexual thoughts. Then climb the hill in Bettana, his neighbourhood, from where, next to the old cemetery, we could see the far bank of the river Bou Regreg, Rabat, the Tour Hassan, the Kasbah of the Udayas, the public beach where poor people went. Smoke some kif together. Lay my head in his lap. Close my eyes. Then, calmly and reverently, tell him about the film I had seen the night before and gently, openly, tempt him into sin, into transgression.

Sin deliberately.

God would be watching us.

We would go on. To the end. To the sea. To the heavens.

Cursed. One day I would be cursed in love like *The Wounded Man.* But while I wait, with Chouaïb in my heart, my cousin with his faint moustache, a wicked boy, his sturdy body holding me, I go almost every day towards the lights of the cinema, eyes tight shut.

Translated by Frank Wynne

THE BREVITY OF CIGARETTES

John Better Armella (1978–)

is known for his intimate interviews with leading Latin American artists and intellectuals and for his association with the evasive drag legend Pedro Lemebel. Documenting the Colombian underground, his poetry is salacious and raw. It is both serious and camp. He calls out grave social injustices with savage, sarcastic, petulant humour. He may be found writing as his alter-ego, China White.

> *I may be a black sheep, but my hooves are made of gold.*
> —P. B. Jones (while under the influence)

Whether it's a transvestite taking a drag on her damp *Pielroja* on some corner of barrio Santa Fe, a middle manager asking with feigned dignity, "Marlboro, please," or a precocious little girl smoking her punk brother's butts in secret, cigarettes possess the brevity necessary to tell a story, not in the style of Jim Jarmusch, where they accompany an espresso, and the black-and-white screen accentuates a bitter encounter between Tom Waits and Iggy Pop. Instead, this is a strange and even brief story, the story of someone who asks, *Do you smoke?*, a question that conceals a dark motive.

Once upon a time there was a hotel in the center of Bogotá; but also a public library and a museum, which I frequented in the early days after my arrival in a city that resembled an architect's mockup: a lawn and glass on one side and, on the other, an alley infested with the urine and feces of a multitude that survives beneath air ducts and in the skid-row rooms of the metropolis.

"Do you smoke?" says the guy who's been following me since I left the Museum of Modern Art, where I saw a precarious exhibit of David Hockney. A slight nod of my head accepting his invitation is all it takes, and next I'm sitting in one of those downtown cafés with immense panoramic windows, through which the urban pastiche can be seen on parade, at once severe and solicitous. Where are they going? I wonder.

When one talks to a stranger, one always begins with a lie:

"My name is Alejandro... Yes, I just arrived in the city... No, I don't know anyone... House? No, *amigo*, a hotel a few blocks from here... Umm... it's called *La Cuna de Venus*... How much do I pay? Fifteen thousand pesos a day."

The La Normanda café is one of the places downtown where you can talk and, more importantly, smoke without worry after the passage of the smoking ban in public spaces. I feel very comfortable, and the guy is nice; he's dressed in a nice suit, without loose threads or obvious signs of repair, with an attractive copper tie and gold cufflinks; his face is healthy; and he looks like he just had a hot shower. He's around forty years old; he says he works for important people, that his car is parked nearby, that he likes coming downtown, the people, blah blah blah, that he likes to make friends, blah blah blah, that he's been looking for I don't know what for years, blah blah blah.

"Well, *amigo*, I've got what you've been looking for," I tell him. My comment solicits a brief smile that allows me to catch a glimpse of his teeth, long and pointed, slightly stained but not unattractive.

"A drink?" he asks.

The taste of vodka in this climate is always welcome, even more as it begins to get dark and the hills become covered in a thick gauze, a frozen curtain that descends on Bogotá's streets, which causes them to seem sadder than usual.

After a couple of drinks, I start to enjoy the conversation more, to the point of sharing certain confidences. W is a really fascinating guy, with a keen sense of humor. On the other side of the glass, we watch a strange-looking character walk quickly by, a has-been of Colombian boxing, a black man dressed in a leather jacket that hangs slightly below his waist, faded jeans, and an umbrella that hovers strangely above him.

"That guy had the world in his hands," W comments, "and there's nothing more dangerous than a boxer with the world in his hands. At any minute, he might start punching you, until there's nothing left."

"You have to punch something in this life," I say.

"Tell me, Alejandro, when did you arrive in Bogotá?"

"June 9, 2004," my answer comes, like I'm an automaton, as if repeating a sentence that's been recorded a thousand times on tape, as if reciting my full name or my ID number or my date of birth. I think that a person shouldn't keep an exact record of anything, except perhaps a fond memory from childhood or adolescence. But the act of recalling X date, being able to reproduce it with such exactness to the point of revealing its most intimate details, the methodical description of the day, the weather, the names of buildings seen, cold voices spoken through intercoms that say "We're sorry, we can't help you," "Go away, please, or we'll call the police," "Mr. Hat has left on a trip this very afternoon, leave your name, and I'll give him your message," makes us feel safe.

All those voices and images are proof that something happened, that the tape hasn't been erased, that something deep down went *bang!*, and its echo still reverberates, that life branded you with an iron like livestock so that you never forget, and my brand says: "09-June-2004."

"Is anything wrong? Would you like another cigarette, Alejandro?" W says.

As I listen to him talk, hearing the tone of concern in his voice, the way he offers to light my cigarette, as if saying, "Warm up a little," makes me wonder whether I'd met him by accident that day, if maybe… No! Bogotá had already prepared an unforgettable welcome, but now's not the time to tell that story; I'll need a whole pack of really strong cigarettes, longs, so I can blow puffs of black smoke, like a fireplace where you burn letters and photos of someone you truly hate, and my hate has a name, the name of a respectable *señor* of Colombian literature, a son-of-a-bitch who abandoned me to the jaws of a city that wasn't able to swallow me completely, a city that bestowed on me the dark credentials necessary to write a book that I will call: "THE DIRTY MR. HAT."

"Love, you said you were going to tell me a story, and you've barely said a word since we got here," W says.

The motels in Bogotá, at least the ones downtown, are filthy rat holes. Through the room's tiny window, I can see Seventh Street clearly, packed as usual. It's funny, but among the mass of people, I'm able to distinguish a pair of familiar faces. Unlike other people I've bumped into on a rainy afternoon, W is the only one I've told that I write. He's a sensitive sort of guy, who lacks the smell of wet rags that men in Bogotá have, tightfisted sonsabitches who spend all day on the prowl, moving from one side of downtown to the other, catching whatever they can for a few coins.

"Why did you want to come to this place? We could have gone somewhere nicer," W says.

With the same regularity I used to frequent museums, churches, or parks, my curiosity has led me to every kind of dive: bathhouses, massage parlors, discos, and the infamous and not-so-pleasant bookstores in the city's core, rooms that reek of disinfectant, small booths that play porn videos where someone services you for twenty thousand pesos: damp labyrinths as dark as a wolf's mouth, temples of fast sex in a fast, merciless city. And in that terrycloth darkness, the crouched murmur of a presence: some fag panting like an out-of-breath animal whispers "Come 'ere"; that's what the bookstores are for, to "go" when someone says "come," without exchanging names, saying absolutely nothing, because within seconds your mouth is being pumped by his package at a pulsating rhythm. "*Ay, amor*, but I want to see your face," but why a face in a place like this, in a city like this, because ever since you arrived in Bogotá your name has been Efraín, Alejandro, Fernando, and you've never bothered to say thank you when they hand you a twenty-thousand-peso bill, and you muster the nerve to swipe the last bill from their pocket.

"Come over here to me, Alejandro," W motions, patting the bed.

Fifteen minutes later:

"You haven't said anything, was I that bad?"

"You did fine, W, don't worry, I was just thinking," I said, rubbing a wet semen spot on the sheet.

"What were you thinking about?"

"About the time I was in prison, a disgusting shithole called the URI. I'm wondering if you would have gone to look for me, if you would have taken me something to eat, if suddenly..."

Within minutes W has dressed rather nervously and says goodbye, claiming he has a pending matter. I could see him, through the room's tiny window, walking up the street, more at ease. I suppose I shouldn't have mentioned the jail thing, but it was too late—it was really too late! So I went downstairs and rang the exit buzzer. The woman in charge of the motel, a husky woman whose face is wrapped in a thick wool scarf, says to me in a muffled voice:

"Your friend paid the room until tomorrow at noon, but just until noon." As I opened the gate, she continued to mumble something I didn't understand.

"That's okay," I said, "I'm just going for cigarettes. I'll be right back."

But I wasn't.

2009

Translated by George Bert Henson

PRIVATE PARTS: ANTI-BODIES

Nicholas Wong (1979–)

Born and educated in Hong Kong, Nicholas Wong chooses to write poetry in English – a second language he refers to as "alternative native." His collection *Crevasse* won the 2016 Lamda Literary Award. According to Rigoberto González, Crevasse "inhabits the fiery crossroads that connect sexuality, masculinity, language, and race—a radical space that challenges the stubbornly trite assumptions about queer and Asian identities." Wong is assistant poetry editor for *Drunken Boat*.

Born as a suckling machine, hooked
to nipples on malevolent male
chests, where hair grows like black grass
in barren deserts. Inside me a groove
deepens, which I have mistaken
for love. My therapist says *Be alone, the gap will
heal*. As if *alone* were a persona.
To be alone is to be someone else, to reject
paired objects: chopsticks, socks,
movie sequels. My nose, my heart
breathing and beating in solo are the world's
bravest singletons, I should learn from them.
Is this how hermits become hermits? When pity
pinches their organs, they cut
open their bowels with a sword to see

what solitude looks like. It looks like
the mouth of their caves, the lips
I have kissed, slightly parted like the cowboy's
in a cigarette ad. Or a honeysuckle,
blossoming, anthers curling
upward, petals pitifully apart.

FIG. 370. HUNCHBACK DUE TO TUBERCULOSIS OF THE SPINE

Jacek Dehnel (1980–)

Poet, author, screenwriter and translator Dehnel has an unusual style. He writes about trinkets, mementos and decaying works of poor-quality art. Many critics dislike his triviality and floridity. He claims that the avant-garde is now accepted more readily than the traditional, but that there is wisdom and beauty in history. He married in London in 2018, but continues to campaign for marriage equality in Poland.

Peaceful, so peaceful, he sits completely still,
frail, collected, and to the left below
a large gray placard with "Diseases of the bones,"
beside "Two sequestrums, TB of the thigh,"
"Curvature of spine from atrophy of discs,"
and "Elephantine compression."
                                          The painter's care
(and photographer's before) caught even
the smallest details: upholstery hobnails,
plush nap, varnished gloss on the stool's round legs,
fine whorl of his ear, the close-cropped hair,
and above all, swollen contour of his hump,
exquisite defect, deformity's degree.

FIG. 370. HUNCHBACK DUE TO TUBERCULOSIS OF THE SPINE

Sadness and hunchbacks look alike in Graz, Berlin,
Vienna, Drohobycz, and Kiev, so I don't know
where he posed, frozen, in some city studio,
disrobed for the photograph, implored
to fix his sight on a minuscule point
in the niche.
                    Life's vigor, that roiling stream,
which, swollen with spring melt, wrests reedy clods,
loose gravel, forking willows from the banks
and carts them, snarled, to the sea, to the sea
—it winds down another path, a different one,
which cuts him off. You see it clearly
not in the gruesome hump and fragile knees
but that solitary hand, suspended free before
him in the morning light, there between
the legs of the stool: helpless and wan,
painted in haste, since of no use.
From that limp palm, this teen's life unspools:
an almshouse death, an old age begging coins
at church fronts in Vienna or Berlin,
years without lovers or money, in beds
sufficiently narrow, with unremitting pain
in varied joints, his youth in hospitals,
and the stifled light of the studio at dawn
when he rises from the stool and behind the screen
dons trousers, shirt, and overcoat, then thanks
Herr Doktor, Herr Photographer before
bowing politely and heading to the door.

Warsaw, 28 June 2004

Translated by Karen Kovacik

THE PENNY DROPS

AKA I'm Coming Out 2

Juno Dawson (1981–)

Originally from West Yorkshire, Dawson moved to Brighton to start work as an entertainment journalist and PSHE schoolteacher. She began writing books about puberty and gender fluidity for the people of her students' generation, while she herself began a gender transition process. In 2017, she wrote her first novel for adults, *The Gender Games*. She serves as School Role Model for UK charity Stonewall.

I owe my new life to a young woman called Charley. I don't think she'll mind me mentioning her by name. When I met her, she was fourteen years old and in one of my writing groups for gifted young people. She is also trans and had started secondary school as a girl.

This was not, I hasten to add, the school from *Glee*. This was a real, hard core, South London state school. They had stabbings (one, quite inventively, with the pointy end of an afro comb) and gangs and all that jazz. I can only imagine the kind of bravery it took for her to rock up on her first day at a new school in a skirt.

Yes, people talked behind her back, but I guess that's preferable to hurling abuse (or afro combs) at her face. What was interesting was how – three years in – most people had stopped caring. With access to testosterone blockers, Charley would never go through 'boy puberty', meaning she looked and sounded like any other teenage girl and had a wonderful support network of lovely friends.

I was spellbound by the zero fucks Charley seemed to give. Her stresses were about her controlled art exam and poetry, not her gender. She was so, so comfortable. I couldn't help but wonder how my life would have been different if I'd had the knowledge (and access to drugs) that her generation have.

But it was too late. My body *did* go through boy puberty, so I was stuck with it, right?

Wrong. And that was where it began.

The coming out process was slow and laboured, but only because transitioning is a fuzzy-edged, ephemeral beast. Unlike my late-night Dean Cain sexuality revelation, my gender identity took a little longer to solidify. In fact, I can't pinpoint the precise moment I started to think I might be trans.

Gender is *learned* behaviour and *trans*gender is no different. Much as restaurants started to introduce gluten-free options to their menu, a third option was becoming widely available on the gender buffet: male, female, trans.

The media – more powerful than ever – was responsible for this new awareness. Since Nadia Almada won *Big Brother* in 2004, we have seen Laverne Cox, Isis King (*America's Next Top Model*), Chaz Bono, Candis Cayne, Carmen Carrera, Andreja Pejić, Paris Lees and fictional characters Hayley Cropper (*Coronation Street*) and Jason Costello (*Hollyoaks*) on the telly. Conchita Wurst – who fits the brief of performative transgender – won Eurovision. All of these things happened *before* Caitlyn Jenner came out as transgender.

Isis King was living in a homeless shelter in New York when she appeared in the background of a photoshoot on *America's Next Top Model* in 2008. She was spotted by producers and competed in the show's eleventh season. 'I didn't really have any role models,' Isis says. 'I saw *Paris Is Burning* so I'd seen Octavia St Laurent and fell in love with her confidence and poise. Other than seeing that, there were really no girls on TV that I saw myself in. My mom was always my role model.'

Making history as a trans woman on the youth-oriented CW network didn't enter King's head at the time. 'I just wanted to win and have a better life than living in the shelter. I didn't realise the magnitude of the impact it would have. In a way I'm glad, because I would have put more pressure on my twenty-two-year-old self. Not being aware also allowed me to be more authentic, which I believe resonated with many more people.'

King's appearance on *ANTM* was seven years prior to Caitlyn Jenner's *Vanity Fair* cover and five years ahead of Andreja Pejić's coming-out. Awareness was *not* where it is now. 'It was hard across the board,' King tells me. 'The industry wasn't really ready to accept a trans model back then. I had my fair share of amazing experiences but it was an uphill battle. It still is.'

I watched Isis from the other side of the world – a trans woman around my age, who looked absolutely gorgeous. Vitally, she was widely accepted as 'one of the girls' by the majority of other contenders. Whether she knew it or not, Isis was a beacon. 'I heard from kids all around the world. It has not stopped in almost a decade! All age groups, but now the little kids are like *I was in elementary school and saw you...* man I'm getting old, but I love it.'

Isis is philosophical about her participation in this social sea change. She shrugs it off when I ask if she was aware of making a difference. 'I dreamed of the change, and I'm honoured that my story, even if it's a crumb, has helped that progression.' And then the big question: Which comes first: media representation or a shift in public opinion? It's a chicken-or-egg mystery. 'Now we live in a world of social media and quick turnaround, I think it used to be mass media [representation] first, but I believe now it's 50/50, because sometimes the media is very controlled and the only knowledge or footage might start from a Facebook live video that goes viral.'

She's right, of course. Prior to broadband, only the gatekeepers of the mass media controlled who I could and couldn't see in TV and film. Now, the mistress of my own media consumption, I could seek out my own role models.

Before I had only known what being transgender was, but now I had *seen* it. Now I *recognised* it. Importantly, I had also now seen trans women around my age. April Ashley and Caroline Cossey – both trans icons – were so much older than me that it was difficult to align their experience to mine.

It seemed that real-life girls, like Charley, and celebrity ones were living their trans lives quite happily. And, just maybe, so could I. Unlike the last time round, this time I wasn't immediately scared. I was a grown-up, I had relative security and a wonderful network of friends. As such, I was able to vocalise my concerns free from worry.

Transition – contrary to popular tabloid opinion – doesn't start by lopping your genitals off. It starts with a questioning process.

The first person I spoke to was my dear friend Sam. This was late 2013, and we were in a Thai restaurant near Clapham Common. I was eating beef massaman curry (as you do). I had, to an extent, summoned her from Camden, as I wanted to talk through my turmoil. 'I wanted to talk to you about something quite serious,' I told her.

'Is it that you're a woman?' she said, sort of half kidding, I think.

'Well…' I began, and it went from there.

Sam has been at my side through various phases (there was a period in 2005 where I dressed like a tweedy country gent à la Guy Ritchie, for example), so – perhaps fairly – she did question my commitment to transitioning. At the time, I was in the relationship with Erik too, so I wasn't sure if it was fair to carry that on while questioning my gender.

Questioning, in my mind, is absolutely part of any transition, so it was where my gender transition began. It starts with opening your mind – just a peep hole – to the possibility that facts about yourself you have previously held true might not be. It's as much about letting go as it is letting something in.

This is not to be sniffed at. For about fifteen years I had truly believed I was a gay man, and been resigned to living as one. If that wasn't true, it was a real ground-shaker. Nothing would be the same ever again.

And so I did nothing.

At various times since I started transitioning, the climb from the bottom of Kilimanjaro just seemed too daunting. At Basecamp One, looking up, it's fucking terrifying. It's easier to just go home. In my case, although I strongly suspected I should have always been a woman, it was much, MUCH easier to just 'make do' as a gay man.

In fact, I threw myself into 'making do'. My last year as a man was the one where I really went for it. As mentioned, I worked out, I drank gallons of protein shakes, I grew a huge beard, I took full and lively advantage of London's gay scene. I took that trip to Ibiza and had sex with the whole fucking island. It was fun. I was MASCULINE TO THE MAX. I broke up with my boyfriend anyway, but not for wholly trans-adjacent reasons.

Even after speaking to Sam, I very much decided that living out my years as a gay man was infinitely preferable to changing every last element of my being: my name, my body, my career, my family, my friends… It seemed to me that transitioning would be a hugely destructive act.

But sometimes you have to burn everything down. Forest fires, as destructive as they seem, have been used and controlled for hundreds of years. They clear away excess grasses and shrubs and they stimulate the germination of more desirable trees. Sometimes you have to destroy everything for something better to take its place.

I benched the idea for much of the next year, but *something* shifted over the winter of 2014. The idea had been a-brewing for the best part of twelve months. Nothing especially eventful happened on New Year's Eve 2014 – I went to my friend's club night in Vauxhall – but on New Year's Day I was more resolute than I had been in a long time. Perhaps there really is something about January and resolution. Whatever the reason, I went to meet my friend Louis at a greasy spoon. He was chomping his way through a fry-up, but I was way too hungover, so sipped on a peppermint tea between emergency trips to the toilet.

I told him I was *definitely* a woman. I told him I *might* transition. The hard part, I felt, was in getting from A to B. What was interesting is how *surprised* those first few people were. With the exception of the protein-shake years, I've always worn my feminine side close to the surface: I was the sixth Spice Girl, I was Cherry Filth. I think when a man embraces femininity, as a culture, we spring to 'gay' rather than any indicator of him being non-binary, genderqueer or trans, which perhaps shows where we are in terms of failing to understand the difference between sexuality and gender.

Louis, as Sam had been, was lovely and understanding, but both admitted this was something of which they had no experience. In fact, Louis was the final nail in the coffin. I told him that I assumed that *all* gay boys had spent their entire childhood wanting to be women. Immediately, without missing a single beat, Louis (a gay man) said he had never once even *thought* about what life would be like if he was a girl.

Oh. Shit.

Having *never* been comfortable with Gender's lurking presence, I guess it figures that I'd never had that sense of Gender security Louis had. It radiated from him in an insouciant shrug of his shoulder. He was a boy, then he was a man. Oh god, how I wish it had been that easy for me.

But it wasn't, so what's the fucking point in booing about it.

Again, feeling very resolutiony, I found a therapist who specialised in sexuality and gender matters. For the first time in my life, I had more on my plate than I felt I could deal with solo, and my friends admitted it was well outside of their sphere of knowledge.

The first few sessions with Therapist Dean didn't go *quite* as expected in that he did a very good job of talking me out of it. His methods wouldn't suit everyone (which is why it's best to talk to a few people before settling on a therapist – I didn't only meet with Dean) but he spoke of the realities of transitioning and it hit me like a ton of bricks.

'You'll never be a woman,' he told me.

WAY HARSH, TAI.

My thinking has always been fairly dichotic – all or nothing – so being told I would never be biologically female was enough to make me file the idea away, possibly permanently.

Instead, the first few months of therapy focused on my lingering feelings of dissatisfaction and inability to feel the full gamut of emotions. It seemed, after much talking, that my hideous time at school had rendered me, for want of a better phrase, dead inside.

It sounds so obvious, but we had to spend a lot of time going through what different emotions look and feel like, given that I was only really experiencing anger fully. If you've seen Pixar's *Inside Out*, you'll know how the inside of my head was functioning. The little red one was firmly in control. Sadness and Joy were often ignored entirely.

The former issue was as important. I've had sexified boyfriends, career success, a nice flat, enough money to survive on, friends and family, but I've *never* felt entirely satisfied. Is this a terrible symptom of modern aspirational living (which instils an understanding that there's *always* something you should be wanting), or is it that I've been living in the wrong gender my whole life?

Dean's point, as strong as it might sound, was this: What if I transitioned and still didn't feel satisfied? How would *that* feel? It was so important that I didn't view transitioning as a way to fix all the wrongs in both my head and life. Transitioning, I believe, will right my gender, but possibly nothing else. Obviously, I hope there are knock-on benefits of living in the right gender (how could there not be?) but there are no guarantees. It's not a magic wand that will fix all my woes.

What Dean was trying to do was get me to understand the realities of transitioning. Instead of hoping I'd simply wake up a woman – and be readily accepted as such – he needed to make me realise I was getting the full deluxe trans package, with all its hardships. I will be a woman – I am a woman – but I will also always be trans. That has its own pride and its own pitfalls.

Whatever we discussed, and although I oscillated between male and female, the desire to live as a woman wasn't going away. At the *Attitude* Pride Awards in 2015, I mingled with the great and good of the LGBT community, but was especially impressed with (award recipient) RAF search and rescue officer Ayla Holdom, whose transition hit the (very mean) headlines because she just so happened to work alongside Prince William.

What was especially cool – although quite unfortunate for her – was that she couldn't actually attend the awards, as she had to work. She sent a video thanking *Attitude* for the award, but her mother and sister were there to pick up the award in person. As with Charley, it was inspiring to see a normal trans woman just living her life. It was especially encouraging to see her family's unwavering support, making me wonder if my family could survive a transition too.

It was time to shit or get off the pot. Absolutely by accident and not being overly dramatic, I went to the doctor's on my birthday in 2015. Yeah, I know. I'd like to take this opportunity to thank my lovely, wonderful and not-uneasy-on-the-eye GP, Dr Clark.

I had been warned by the NHS website that my GP might not know what 'a transgender' was, so I might like to print out a forty-two-page PDF explaining them to him. Given that Dr Clark had 'read my book review in *Attitude*' (if that's not the best euphemism for being gay, I don't know what is), I hoped I'd be OK.

As it was, Dr Clark was brilliant. We sat and talked for about half an hour (sorry patients in the waiting room, your bunions had to wait) and came up with a plan. As waiting lists in London were beyond horrific (two years? I don't think so), he agreed at once to refer me to Northampton Gender Identity Clinic, where the wait list, although still long, wasn't *that* long.

I consider myself very lucky to have a GP who totally got what was going on – he'd even done training at a GIC. Not every trans person is so fortunate. I guess it's a bit like therapists; had the first GP been shit, I'd have found a better one.

The referral, to me, signalled the point of no return. It's never felt like the wrong decision either. Some anti-trans voices, and the media, are fucking obsessed by the tiny minority of trans people who go through a so-called 'detransition'. I don't see that happening for me, although so what if it did? I think gender is fluid. One person's shifting identity is hardly rock-solid evidence that being transgender is harmful or somehow not-a-thing. There are no official figures on this subgroup, but Dr Stuart

Lorimer – a gender clinician based in London – has had fifteen out of over 4000 patients cease hormone treatment or socially revert to their original gender... that's 0.4 per cent.

It was time to come out to everyone. Bit by bit, I told my friends as and when I saw them. I told my publisher and the publications I write for. It was also time to tell my family – which we already covered.

Now, I don't for one second consider myself famous. Even *within* the world of children's publishing, I don't really think authors get true fame. J.K. Rowling is an obvious exception, but, to be honest, if Stephen King or Jonathan Franzen strolled into the coffee shop where I'm writing this, I doubt I'd notice. Nonetheless, I knew I'd have to come out 'publically', as it were, to my readers and other 'interested parties'.

Initially, there was a half-arsed plan to make an announcement at the *Attitude* Awards in October 2015 but it a) didn't pan out and b) would have been a bit naff, in hindsight. They were giving April Ashley a lifetime achievement award and me 'coming out' would have definitely hijacked her big moment. However, at that event – by which time I was pretty much 'out' to anyone who cared to ask – I spoke to the very excellent journalist Patrick Strudwick, and he suggested I could tell my story to him for Buzzfeed. Patrick is a fantastic writer who cares deeply about LGBTQ rights and representation, and I knew he'd handle the story with great sensitivity.

He came round to my flat shortly after I'd relocated back to Brighton and we talked for the best part of two hours. I said everything I wanted to say and I'm still really proud of what Patrick and I achieved with that interview.

The article went live while I was the Deptcon YA convention in Dublin. This timing worked out well – I felt sufficiently removed from the situation, a little like I was in hiding. I needn't have worried; the response was nothing but wonderful. My Twitter and Facebook feeds lit up with warm and supportive messages from all over the world.

Initially, I decided to stick with 'James' and 'he' until I was 100 per cent on a name. Also, at the time – and with Gender closer than he'd been in years – I still very much felt I looked and dressed 'like a man' and didn't want people calling me 'she' when I hadn't yet made a single change to any area of my life. That was my personal preference.

By curious coincidence, Germaine Greer had picked that very day to vent her spleen (again) about trans women, so I found myself drawn into that furore, along with austerity chef Jack Monroe, who also came out as trans non-binary on that day. Weird... there must have been something in the water that week.

What was especially wonderful was, later that day, I appeared on a panel about writing teen horror with bestselling authors Derek Landy (*Skulduggery Pleasant* series) and Darren Shan (*Demonata* series). Brilliantly, news of my transition wasn't even mentioned and I was just allowed to discuss my expertise – teen fiction – which is the way it should be for all experts: male, female, trans or cis.

That day was wonderfully freeing. To be honest, I was rapidly losing track of who knew 'my secret' and who didn't. Having everything out in the open, and being able to strap the Buzzfeed interview to the top of my Twitter page, meant I didn't have to keep saying the same thing over and over – it was there for everyone to see.

That night I got possibly the drunkest I've ever, ever been in my life. I celebrated by vomiting all over Dublin and having sex in a nightclub toilet. The next morning was spent projectile vomiting in the disabled loos at Dublin airport before I had to visit the sexual health clinic the following Monday for a course of precautionary PEP. It's odd to me that I'd sabotage such a glorious day by getting blackout drunk and fucking in a toilet stall.

Like I said, the only thing that changes is your gender.

SIX WOMEN I'M NOT

Cat Fitzpatrick (1982–)

The founder of the Trans Poets Workshop, Cat Fitzpatrick is currently the Director of the Women's and Gender Studies program at Rutgers University. Her poetry collection *Glamourpuss* was nominated for a Pushcart prize. She is currently working on a verse novel about trans women in Brooklyn making terrible choices. A topic, she insists, she knows a fair bit about.

meditations on having sex with straight men who don't know you're trans whilst pretending to be a literary character

LAVINIA

I thought I'd never talk again: It seemed
I lost my speech when I received these scars.
They threatened to disclose so much about
My past but I kept dumb. Well if I'd talked
I would have only cursed myself: 'Your fault,
You bitch, it's all your fault' or 'Hide your shame
From view, you heavy hairy flesh-and-bone,
Your skin shows up the truth, you'll always be
A man' or such. Self-hatred for self-love,
And what's the good in that? At nights I kept
The tears and ululations down. But now,
Enough. Nobody made me anything,
And if you'd kiss me then you'd find I have
A tongue that's getting ready for to speak.

GRENDEL'S MOTHER

If I've been set apart, then where's the mark?
I mean, ok. I've got this love-bite on
My neck, but he has no idea, I think.
We're by the water watching sunset leave,
And holding hands. I guess I'm holding back.
You might call that a choice, but if I left
(I will leave, I won't call) and swum into
The sea, out past the fires on the oil
Refineries and underneath the waves,
Down to a secret place, to wait, afraid,
Until some hero came to kill or kiss
Me, then I'd accept our curse. I may not stay
With him, but when I'm done I'll go and get
Another drink, and try to keep my head.

EVE

Bittersweet? Oh, I'm sorry. Talk to me,
All ignorance, about the things we'll do.
What should I say? I've tried to tell myself
That there's no harm in it, and sure as hell
I wish I'd some desire for him to fall
In with, but here, as elsewhere, when I should
Be lips to lips, bright eyes, I find I feel
Ashamed to own my nakedness, to bear
His look. My vagina's almost a work
Of art I should be proud. Oh, innocence,
The things that you don't know! He wonders why
I taste so sweet Sweetness, that's lubricant,
And not my nature. Wonder why I'm bitter?
Bite the apple. I never asked for this.

HELEN'S GHOST

As if I come from long ago, or far
Away, self-consciously, I dress and do
My face and show myself, so eager that
I grasp at every little touch I get.
What carnal substance can I conjure up?
Am I enchanting? Can I haunt your dreams?
Some secret knowledge this: Will you screw me?
Of course he will. And so the bargain goes:
He calls me up, I come; I take a risk
On my appearance, unbecoming flesh
Mixed up with spirit; I catch onto his breath,
Return his kiss, as if his lust might then
Inspire or quicken me, as if somehow
He'd draw me a new body on his lips.

CRISEYDE

Bite me! Bite me! Pull my hair. Hold me
Against the bed, and let me struggle, and
Then stop! and then softly again: just trail
Your lips and fingers, take some time with me.
I can perform positions till the sun
Comes up on us. I have rehearsed this show.
Next we'll lie down, the curtains drawn,
And then he'll fall asleep. And then I'll go.
Faithless? He courted me. I have to leave
Behind my shame, that past in which I have
No place, and learn to get by as I can.
I made no promises to him and told
The lies I needed to, no more. I'm not
Untrue. And all I'm taking is my time.

PENELOPE

Here, in between of sleep and waking up.
Feet first, I find my room all full of day:
I've washed up on my bed, and now the sun
Is drying off my dreams, warm sheets for sand,
On what I see is that familiar shore
Where I've been drawing out my threads, these years,
Spinning my stories and unpicking them.
These years, weaving a body out of words,
Unravelling it again, as if my life
Were just material, as if I'd get
It right sometime. What if some man came back
And took my hand and said 'it's me'? I am
Not her. We none of us can be like them.
None of these stories do us any good.

THEY KEEP KILLING US
Sergio Loo (1982–2014)

Born in Mexico City, Loo was a prolific and influential queer poet and writer in Latinx literature. From his early twenties, he published a number of collections of poetry, creating a unique style that is challenging, fragmentary and unsettling. His last book, *Operation on a Malignant Body*, was a prose-poetry exploration of living with cancer, that eventually killed him at the age of thirty-one.

They stuck photocopies in the urinals again and again we covered them in our names. Sheets of paper advising what to do if you hook up with someone in the club: always use a condom, introduce your hook-up for the night to someone you know, tell people where you're going to be. But the thing is, we don't listen, we really do just think with our asses, scrawling our email addresses and phone numbers all over the pieces of paper along with our names and specifications: 'I'll suck you off', 'Hung', 'Goes all night', 'For bondage and threesomes'. They're killing us. It's no joke and the worst part is we enjoy falling as if we're wounded little swallows with our tight trousers and our cold, shining eyes like disco balls in an empty nightclub. Last week, for instance, there was another murder in the papers. Someone hooked up with a guy, here in the Vaquero according to some people, though others say it was right in the Calle de Cuba, in front of the police car on patrol or the hotdog stand, and he was found stabbed to death a few blocks away near the Plaza Garibaldi. Horrible. Other people say it happened in the Marrakech Salón – the Marra – and that the victim was one of those art-school kids who think they're so alternative because they drink guava-flavoured pulque in La Risa on Mesones and then head to the Marra or La Purisima or Bellas Hartas to dance electro-cumbias. That he made art using PowerPoint. That I'd slept with him. It's not true: he was a sculptor and he rented a tiny room in an old building on the Calle República de Brasil where there was barely enough space for his sculptures – all of which were of cocks – and a microwave and a mattress. He was an artist on the mattress too. I don't remember his name but I remember he had really good weed. *Really* good. Apparently it was him in the papers last week. His five minutes of fame. A photo of what turned out to be his last and, in spite of all the blood, his most brilliant performance, clearly influenced by the work of Teresa Margolles. But anyway, that weed he had was seriously good. I would have gone out with him just for that and the things he could do with his tongue. They say the guy who went off with him that night, the murderer, is right over there, the one with the beer in his hand and the little beard. But I don't believe it. I think that guy with the beard is the ex of an ex of one of my friends. Well, not a friend exactly, but we were sleeping together for a while. And he's so inoffensive and boring we suspect he's probably straight. Because we're not like that. We have a sixth sense that leads us into trouble, into sleeping with the son of the most homophobic and murderous politician around or at the very least hooking up with the blind beggar in the metro. I even think they're wrong about the victim, that it wasn't the tongue-and-PowerPoint artist but someone else, anyone else, like it was last month as well. That one had been in the Oasis, pistachio-green leather boots, checked shirt, stonewashed blue jeans so tight you could see everything: a little cowboy. He lost his sombrero dancing with a transvestite with muscles as hard as his own hard feelings. But everyone's forgotten about him by now, he's yesterday's gossip. Or maybe not. Or maybe you need three people to get killed one after the other before they stick up more photocopied notices about staying safe that none of us read. Because, they remind us, HIV is always a danger, because discrimination is always a danger, because murderers come here, to the Calle República de Cuba, looking for us, crazy idiots that we are who'll hook up with anyone. And what can we do? They whisper pretty things in our ears, grab us down there, two lopsided smiles, a beer – a lager, a pale ale – and then they slit our throat. The fag-killer was a regular in the 33 and the Oasis and nobody even realised. The thing is, all we cared about was dancing on the bar, stripping on the bar to win a bucket of beers courtesy of the barman, hooking up with the barman with the nice ass. Taking a photo with the barman with the nice ass and posting it on Facebook. But it never used to be like that. The oldest regulars in El Vaquero, the ones who are part of the furniture by now and equally destroyed, say that no, it never used to be like that. You never used to get homophobic crime. The bars weren't as obvious as they are now. The Butter, for example, the one on the corner of Lázaro Cárdenas and Salto del Agua, was all painted grey and the only clue to what it contained was a butter-fly on the doorbell. You rang and they let you in. They wouldn't let just anyone in, though. First they'd make sure you were part of the scene. They said *the scene* back then, not *gay*. They looked for signs in your eyes, you made your gaze all deep and tender, halfway between Elizabeth Taylor and a wounded animal. It happened quickly, there were no people strutting around in the street saying darling this, darling that. You went in quick-smart so nobody saw. You put your make-up on and got changed inside. And then you changed back on the way out. Because any bastard might come after you, or worse, the police could catch you and blackmail you. Either you gave them some cash or they threw you in the cells for being a poof. Or they took your diary so they could call everyone in your family and say you'd like them to talk to you like a lady in future, darling this darling that, that you painted your face when you went out, that you liked sucking cock. That you had AIDS. Homo-phobia didn't exist back then. The word hadn't even been invented. There were only crimes of passion. Unless you were Juan Gabriel or a transvestite superstar like Francis García singing at the Blanquita theatre, your death would be reported in the entertainment section. Or along with all the other blood-spattered corpses in the sensationalist crime rags. The body of another nancy-boy stabbed to death, and from behind, what a treat, and there was never any doubt about the conclusion: his lover, who was almost certainly married, had killed him because he'd slept with someone else, the little slut. Because fags will be fags, devious and twisted like the black eyeliner that runs down our cheeks when we cry. So they never bothered investigating. That's how they covered everything up. That's how they killed us. They said we killed each other because we were gay and gays cheat and lie. It was our destiny and their titillating entertainment in the headlines the next day. Case closed. Nothing more to say. But now we're part of the city's 'diverse' fauna, protected and tolerated by the government like little animals at risk of extinction, arriving every night like baby dodos, hopping idiotically along the Calle de Cuba as soon as the organ-grinders have stowed their instruments and gone home to bed. En route to the Vaquero with checked shirt, snakeskin boots and moustache, the thick, lustrous moustache of a serious hunk; to the Marra in a bright-coloured T-shirt, over-the-top hair and sunglasses you'd be more likely to see on the beach or the cover of an 80s teen magazine. Retro-style or cyberdog. Or even better, even cooler, a jock, a metrojock, showing off muscular arms, plucked eyebrows and highlights. Tight white T-shirt, braces and trousers slipping down over your ass. We're theirs for the taking, every weekend and on paydays it's even worse. We might as well go out in wedding dresses, but the thing is, what else can we do, we're beht, we're buggers – we want to party. Because it's not the free-for-all it used to be. Now everyone turns up with their mates. Or they're after a sweaty-palmed boyfriend they can take to the cinema and all that. We come here to dance or get taken away by the next fag-killer. Because if you just want to fuck it's easier to use Manhunt or bear.com (motherf...! Now all the fat men are bears and as sought-after as caviar, those god-damn hairy delicious princesses). But to fuck, plain fuck, in real life, the bathhouses are your only option. The Mina, by the Hidalgo metro. Or the Sol, by Guerrero. And what was the one behind the Teresa cinema? Oh, the pornos they used to show in the Teresa, good times... I remember one where everyone was a caveman, like the Flintstones only with eight-inch dicks. The women shouting and shouting, yabadabadoo and us hopping from one seat to the next. You'd spot someone by themselves and make your move but then they weren't by themselves and instead had someone kneeling in who knows what space, merrily sucking away. I never saw the famous art deco façade. The only artistic thing I saw there was the performance of the woman who sold little bags of rancid popcorn in the corridor, as happy as if she were in the House of Disney cinema, the one that's now the church of San Judas. But those days are gone. A lot of people died after getting infected. There was the Savoy cinema, too. But anyway, back then the best thing to do was hang around the ticket booth, acting like you couldn't make up your mind whether to go in, like you were too embarrassed or you'd already seen this one or something. That way you'd hook up in no time with the next guy to arrive. That way you didn't have to shell out for a ticket and maybe you just went straight to the Mina bathhouse instead. Because the Mina is the Mina. There are other baths nearby but I don't remember which. And there's a hotel along 5 de Mayo where it's dirt cheap and you don't even get keys, you just open the door. And you can't lock it. I've never heard of anyone being killed on the way out. Not in the Alameda park either, where you only have to linger a few moments for someone to appear, and someone else after that. Though to be honest they're always the same ones, and seriously old-school: past-it grandpas and rentboys. Then, once you're there, the best thing is to go to the handicrafts market by Balderas and hook up with some tourists. Or try your luck in the Hidalgo metro. Although if you hook up with someone in the metro you'll still end up in the Mina. All roads lead to the Mina. Or the Finisterre, on the Calle San Rafael, but that's a bit further away. And you'll need to come all the way back, too. Because you need to find your soulmate this payday Friday. Because you need to make sure the PowerPoint artist wasn't actually killed. Because you need to ask him if he'd like to do it again or at least give you the number of his dealer. Because you need to write your phone number on the photocopied sheets of warnings, along with your email address and the fact you want to hook up, for whatever, because we'd rather be dead, rather be rejected, rather even be murdered than be bored.

Translated by Annie McDermott

BINARY

Zhang Yueran (1982–)

Born in 1982, Zhang Yueran (张悦然) is widely considered one of China's most influential young writers. She began writing at the age of fourteen, and was quickly recognised with awards and prizes. She studied English at Shandong University. To date, she has published two collections of short stories and three acclaimed novels.

Translator's Note: Chinese gay slang for 'top' and 'bottom' is '一号' and '零号' respectively, that is 'number 1' and 'number 0'. If you're not sure how this works, look at the shape of the numerals.—Jeremy Tiang

This is how it works: 0 moves to 1, and 1 moves back to 0. An endless cycle.

0.

In April I returned to the town of B, to Mountain Lake Road. Before coming back, I'd been living in the middle of a dank forest, writing my novel with a pen like a twig. I saw no one. Sleep was the only visitor to come between me and my writing. Each time it afflicted me, I fell into a spiral of dreams that deposited me on Mountain Lake Road, yes, that wide road in the town of B. Huge cars rushed by as I stood on the pavement, wondering what I'd come to see.

These weren't particularly bad, as nightmares go, but I invariably woke from them unable to remember how I'd planned to end my novel. I had to revise it from the beginning and see where it led, but before I could get there, the dream came again, like a typhoon, and I'd wake to find another startled morning with my ending blown away.

Naturally, I developed a great interest in Mountain Lake Road, a place I was unfamiliar with. It seemed to hold some kind of symbolic meaning for me, but I couldn't even remember what it looked like. So it made sense to return to B, where I might finally be able to finish my novel.

Facing this strange road with its speeding cars, I felt at a loss. Even though I took every precaution, the first time I crossed the road, I was hit by a car coming from the west.

It was a long time before I regained consciousness and climbed up from where I was sprawled on the side of the road. Just then, Sange appeared, darting across the road. He was wearing an ultra-tight pair of jeans, and over that a mid-length dress in red and grey checks. His hair was permed, and the cigarette in his hand emitted little sparks. The morning haze in this polluted northern city made me cough. How's this for the ending of a novel, I thought to myself. But perhaps this was our destined ending anyway – Sange had been missing for a long time, but the minute I came back to Mountain Lake Road, there he was.

Can this encounter be dealt with so simply, I wondered, or should I write a few more lines? For example, I ran over, my mouth slightly open, my breath visible in pure white bursts, and we talked about the past. What did we do? Sit? Lie down? At the time we were in the middle of the road, where the traffic policeman stands during the day, spitting clouds, fog streaming from our mouths, dabbing at our nostalgic tears. Or maybe I stayed where I was, the same pride I'd had since I was a little girl preventing me from going forward, glaring at this incomparable lover on his street corner. His dress was a copy of one I'd owned long ago, though I gleefully noted that his buttocks were too flat to give it a good shape. As he walked past a stern old lady sweeping the street, she stared at this boy with his parasol skirt and flame-coloured hair, waiting for him to get close enough so she could lash out at him with her broom.

Mountain Lake Road opens into a crossroads. I continued north while my lover went south.

1.

I continued north after seeing Sange. Mountain Lake Road is the widest in the city, lined by neat rows of trees. In the early morning, with the north wind blowing, each car that zoomed past seemed to slap me across the face. I soldiered along the red-brick pavement, not thinking for the moment what my destination might be.

In fact, all the while I was deliberating whether I should stop. I no longer remembered what was in the north, and seeing Sange had made my broken heart take precedence over my desire to keep going. Leaning forward as I was at a sixty-degree angle, I no longer resembled a young girl.

Finally, I came to a halt. I was not a serious walker, and hadn't brought a water bottle, or tent, or torchlight, or tampons, or any phone numbers. All I had on me was my novel. I'd promised my novel I would finish writing it before the end of April. It didn't like the wind, and the nights after April were too full of emotion. My novel feared being ruined – turned into an essay or even a love letter, weeping blood-tears. I decided to sit down where I was and finish it. My notebook was the colour of night, a background of balloons with a sweet cartoon cat resting on them. When I was fifteen, I'd fought with Sange and he'd flung my book to the floor. The cat lost its colourful head, leaving only the stump of its neck with a brown bow-tie around it. The headless cat had been with me for five years now, the pages once used to scribble notes to Sange, where even now some of his scrawled love letters were wedged, was now where my novel lived.

My novel would end on this northern morning. Two people meet, but they don't fight, nor do they embrace. Everyone is wearing comfortable shoes. They walk past each other, and then a new year begins, and everyone oversleeps, forgetting many things.

But the minute I sat down to write, Little Kou appeared beside me in a shiny new black sports car.

My memories of Little Kou are all to do with colour. When we were in high school, Little Kou liked to sit in the front row, painting her nails. She enjoyed changing their colour to suit the occasion – the same shade as copper sulphate for chemistry lab, bright blood red when we had to dissect a pigeon for biology. Once I saw her on her way to a piano lesson, her nails alternately black and white. I'd heard she'd died in a car accident, and her funeral was like a flower garden, our classmates sent chrysanthemums in so many different colours. I was far away from B at the time, and all I could think of was what colour her nails were at the time of her death.

I'd never been close to Little Kou, but her fascination with colour endeared her to me. When she stuck her head out of her car to call to me, I was glad to find she hadn't died after all, and stuffed the novel back into my bag before standing to welcome her.

She said, 'I'm getting married today.'

I replied, 'You can't be, you're younger than me. You're not old enough.'

She ignored this, and continued, 'And you're invited.'

I hesitated, noticing that her fingernails were clear today – a magical transparent colour. When she touched me, I felt nothing, as if her nails didn't exist. They reminded me that I'd missed her, and so I said, 'Why not? I'll come. Where is it?'

'Mountain Lake Road.'

0.

I walked south along Mountain Lake Road, Little Kou ahead of me, leading the way.

Back at the crossroads, I glimpsed Sange through a gap in the speeding traffic. I almost cried out in surprise – I'd been gone at least an hour, and he was still here, walking north this time. His jeans were very tight, not because he was fat – in fact, he'd lost a lot of weight – but because he always picked jeans even skinnier than he was. The skirt flared out around his legs like a morning glory, and his cheeks puffed as he dragged on his cigarette, like a bagpipe player.

Little Kou stood on my left, her weightless hand clutching mine. She said, 'There's Sange.'

'Right,' I said.

'He's wearing a skirt. He's a homosexual.'

'I guess.'

'Is that why you split up with him?'

'Yes.'

She laughed at this, and turned to me. 'You know, when you were still together with him, I liked him too.'

I looked closely at her. Her invisible nails were lightly digging into my flesh now.

She continued, 'Once, I hid behind a tree right at the back of the schoolyard to eavesdrop on the two of you. The wind was puffing out your clothes. I saw him put his hands into your blouse.'

I could feel my face change. 'Are you still getting married?'

'Of course,' she said, her laughter brightening.

Sange had changed direction, crossing the road towards us, his face pale, moving as silently as a snowman.

As he reached me, I realised Little Kou had disappeared. perhaps she'd ducked into a nearby alleyway to get married, although I'd never seen any streets branch off Mountain Lake Road. My hand, in fact my whole arm, smelled strongly of nail polish. And Sange's scent was like an octopus, its tentacles reaching for me as I took a step towards him. I coughed a few times before raising my head to face this encounter.

Neither of us could help being agitated. We'd separated with many years of emotion behind us. I wanted to hug him, but discovered that Little Kou's nail polish had somehow superglued my arm to my body. When I tried to reach for him, all I managed was to wobble like a penguin. Awkwardly, not knowing what to do or say, I blurted out, 'Did you see where Little Kou went?'

He nodded. 'They've remodelled that cemetery. Little Kou's grave was moved to Twelfth Month Mountain. I'll take you to see it another day.'

Then we stood where we were, not even trying to prolong the conversation.

A peculiarity of the town of B is the great difference between dawn and early morning. At five minutes to seven, mist shrouded Sange's face, blurring the moment. At seven o'clock, the air cleared, and his features surged towards me. I felt a burst of panic.

But perhaps the difference was really in myself. They've done studies to show that the heart beats faster in the morning. My heart felt like it wanted to leap from my chest. I guess Sange must have felt the same way, because we blushed at the same moment, and said goodbye.

Then I turned to the north, and he turned south. I didn't dare turn back as the thud of his leather shoes receded, but thought I could detect a girl's footsteps joining his, a familiar sound, accompanied by a familiar scent. Even without looking, I knew he was with Little Kou.

1.

A little after seven, sunrise hit Mountain Lake Road. I continued north. You don't see many knights these days, but there he was, on a big horse, a white thoroughbred. He was in shining armour, brighter than the sunlight. I stood still, waiting for him to pass, but instead he halted in front of me.

He wore no cologne, and his eyes were wider than my lover Sange's. His breath was a man's, and his body rippled with boundless strength, the waves of an ocean I had yet to explore.

I've never been able to understand men like this, tall and rough. I was in love with Sange, a delicate boy. He used to polish my nails and braid my hair.

The knight asked me how to get to Twelfth Month Mountain, but seemed in no rush to get there. He dismounted, and held his horse as we talked. I told him I was a traveller, and I'd only be in B long enough to finish my novel. He said he wanted to go west to find the silk road, but first he'd have to exchange his horse for a camel. I thought the wide skies and sandstorms of the west would set off his fine profile, and nodded to show I approved.

We began talking about love. I told him about Sange, but couldn't go too far into my description, otherwise I'd have to explain how I resisted men like the knight.

'You've known him since you were seven?'

'Yes,' I replied.

'That explains why he's a homosexual. A lady academic has written that when a little boy's best friend is a girl, he'll prefer boys when he grows up.'

'Is that how it works?' I was sad to learn this. It seemed this was an irretrievable fact, decided for me many years ago.

'You see, he understands you, a girl, too well. He knows every part of you. And so women have lost their mystery for him.'

This knight was far cleverer than I'd taken him for at first. He was ready to go now. Abruptly, he said, 'Come to the west with me. I'm still interested in girls.'

His frankness moved me, and I agreed. 'But first,' I added, 'Take me back down Mountain Lake Road. I have to say goodbye to Sange.'

0.

The knight set me down, and left me to walk over on my own. I felt I'd let him down in some way. 'You can water your horse or something,' I offered.

'I'll be here. Do what you have to.'

I walked south. Sange appeared again, heading north. It was about nine in the morning. He'd been here several hours now, still in his dress, mincing like a crane.

We met in the same place, the middle of the road. I brought him to one side and we sat on the pavement. We chatted by way of goodbye. I showed him my novel, still missing its ending. He placed the book on his knees and read it earnestly, reciting aloud sentences that pleased him. I interrupted to say he'd picked my favourite bits. I told him a knight was waiting to take me away, and he seemed surprised. We talked about our innocence, that we were still virgins. He asked if I regretted being with someone like him.

'A little. I became a Believer later, and these sorts of affairs are a stain on the soul.'

Sange and I had never talked like this, saying everything we had to say. He even apologised for ruining the cat's head on my notebook. We faced into the north wind and talked until sunset. The sun was tipping over the horizon before we finally ran out of conversation. We were drained. I stood to go, and he kissed me. I hugged the yielding body of my lover.

As I walked away, he called out, 'I hope you finish your novel soon.' My heart filled with warmth as I left, walking north.

1.

I couldn't find the knight. Perhaps I'd taken too long, and he'd met another damsel. I had no regrets. It was thanks to him I'd been able to go back and tell Sange everything I needed to. This was important to me. I'd be able to finish my novel with a grand reunion, and then start a new life.

I reached for my novel to continue writing, only to find it had vanished. I must have left it on the pavement on Mountain Lake Road. That thought made my body turn, and head once again to the crossroads.

0.

It was darkest night now. There were fewer cars, although the remaining ones were flying past. I was almost hit a few times, but somehow managed to avoid them.

I never get tired of saying this: I saw Sange again. Night-time is so cold in the north, but my lover wasn't even wearing a jacket, just that dress with its many clashing lines. He slowly drifted down the road. I stood opposite, wondering what to say. These constant encounters were damaging our relationship. I refused to cross. And there was Little Kou, standing with him, her clear nails glinting like the lights of hell, the smell of varnish suffocating me. I took a deep breath and turned, fleeing towards the north, abandoning my notebook.

Mountain Lake Road is surrounded by tall trees, close to Twelfth Month Hill. At night, forest creatures emit unimaginable noises. I sprinted through the dark. There were no street lights, only the starry glow of passing cars.

At the end of the Mountain Lake, before it turned into another road, I stopped for breath and saw the knight standing there. He seemed sad. I said, 'You're still here, good, let's go.'

Against the night sky, he seemed desolate as a shadow puppet. 'Heading west was just a beautiful dream. I can't go. You can't either. Those who die on Mountain Lake Road are doomed to wander it forever, their spirits unable to leave.'

I looked at him in shock. My foot, already off the ground ready to take a step away from Mountain Lake Road, slowly drifted back to earth. The rumble of cars started up as dawn arrived, and the knight led his horse back down the road, just like always.

Translated by Jeremy Tiang

SELECTED POEMS

Keith Jarrett (1984–)

Born in London, Jarrett made his poetry debut in 2005 – like many of his generation – in Poetry Slams. He is a former UK Poetry Slam Champion and won the International Slam Championship in Rio in 2014. His play, *Safest Spot in Town*, was performed at the Old Vic and on BBC Four in 2017. His first full-length collection of poems *Selah* was published in 2017. Jarrett performs in both English and Spanish, and his poems addresses issues of identity, race and sexuality.

A GAY POEM

They asked me if I had a gay poem
So I said "Straight up, no!
"My poems don't meander between straight lines
My poems don't mince their words
Or bend
Or make queer little observations"

They asked me if I had a gay poem
So I answered honestly
That, no, I didn't have any gay poetry
And even if, unthinkably, I did
What would it say about me?

I mean, even presenting the question
Puts me in a precarious position

And how would I even begin to broach the subject
With my own creation?

Like… "Excuse me, poem, are you gay?
Have you grown up contrarily to what I wanted you to say?
I most certainly didn't write you that way
Was it something I said, something I did that turned you?
Maybe I should have peppered your verses
With sport, girls and beer
Maybe as your author I deserted you…
Or did another writer turn you queer?"

Ok, let's say, hypothetically, that this poem is gay
Maybe it's just a confused poem that needs straightening out
Maybe I could insert verses from Leviticus
Speak over it in tongues
Douse it in holy water
Recite it the Qu'ran
Give it a beat, beat, beat
Boom box blasting out in the street
"Batty poem fi dead, batty poem fi dead
Rip up chi chi poem inna shred"

They asked me if I had a gay poem
And I answered "No"
But the truth is I didn't know
Until one of my very own poems stepped up
And tapped me on the shoulder
It said, "Look here Dad/Author
I'm now that much bolder
And I'm not confused
And not alternative
And even though the words I choose to marry with

Make me different
It don't make me any less eloquent

"I don't need to be overly elegant
So maybe that's why I stepped under your gaydar
But why are you so afraid to embrace it?
Face it! It's just another part of me
You can't erase it

"The more you try to label me with your twisted synonyms
The more you say you hate the sinner
And despise the sin
The more you try to clip my words
And stifle my expression
The more I know it's you, not me,
Whose morality should be called into question"

They asked me to read out a poem
They said, "Choose one of your strongest
One of your best
Choose a poem that don't stand for any foolishness"
And they asked me if I had a gay poem...
So I said
Yes.

EMERGING FROM MATTER

Psalms 22:14: 'I am poured out like water, and all my bones are out
of joint: my heart is like wax; it is melted in the midst of my bowels.'

I   GIVE THANKS

For the following, as listed:
fragment of a god (unnamed);
fragment of a frieze;
a sketch of a figure of a head from a frieze;
a horse head, chariot-less;
a complex rendering of a myth, in parts:
(let's say: a lapith, wrestling
a drunken centaur rapist at a wedding);
a youthful Hercules with a bow and lion skin
(plump cheeks held up by a ledge,
spreading through centuries of retelling);
a south-facing foot from a metope;
a cacophony of numbered limbs,
laid out like xylophone bones;
a row of ancient stones, speaking in the tension
of their bodies twisting.

Listen.

II   GIVE THANKS

to he who has fashioned the man with the key,
with loose-jointed arms,

give thanks for the man of vague
gestures, a vogue dancer
in the midst of gods, satyrs
and other miscellaneous torsos

Give thanks to the palimpsestuous
renderings of the artist Rodin, part-prophet part-crazed–

Praise be to the transcendent treasures
from which he unearths new songs!
Skin scraped clean of their original cultural meanings
by time's savage ravaging
These time-torn fragments now repositioned to face
    Bloomsbury
Praise be to the paint-peeled, colour-erased sculptures
The deities never-before intended for eye-level
now banished to the ground, and made to stand among men
The men and beasts designed to decorate each frieze
now sketched and sketched again
Hear them speak:

I turn towards the temple and smile (says one)
I turn towards Rome and spit (says one)
I turn towards home and [run/yearn] (says one)

III · GIVE THANKS

For this cluttering of torsos:
Torso of the failing man with broken nose
Torso of the slave in warrior pose
Torso of the messenger god
Torso of the river god, the winged thing,

the censored sex
the vexed, the impotent
torso of the indignant revisionist
torso of the broken taxonomist
torso with swiping fingers,
the Tindr dater,
placed in impossible positions
torso of the Brexit negotiator
in limbless limbo
Torso of the fast-fading empire
Of diminishing stature
Torso of the white marble fragility
Torso of the toxic masculinity
Caressing its hollow shoulder joints
Weeping translucent tears

IV   GIVE THANKS

Give thanks now
To this head borne out of stone
Thought emerging from matter
Becoming Thought alone
An idea truncated.
A rough-hewn block
Into which all protégés, all lovers sink
She is drowning, not daydreaming
In her Parisian studio
Clawing, rasping and returning
She is a body learning to entomb itself.

I, too, have made gods of men, she says
I, too, have carved hell's gates with marble kisses, she says

I negotiate artist and muse and mistress
she says.

She turns towards the artist she loves
She turns towards her home and laughs
She turns away from her image and runs.

V   GIVE THANKS   epilogue

All life is fragmentary. Limbless, we rise
Headless we rove
Cased in clay and found in bronze
Distressed stone makes blood of our song
We become sketches of gods

UNDERSKIRTS

Kirsty Logan (1984–)

Logan is a Scottish author of fantasy and magical realism, known for her thoroughly and elaborately designed worlds. She often employs fairytale conventions to explore themes of modern sexuality: for example, the dual or non-binary natures of mythological creatures; or coming of age in incomprehensible worlds. She is also active as a speaker, blogger, literary editor and mentor.

GIRL #1

She found me with my hands around chickens, fingers stretched wide, thumbs over beaks. My skirt, mud-weighed, tugged at my ankles as I dipped low. Silly to curtsey while armed with birds, I knew, but it had to be done. If I'd let go they'd've flown at her, chuttering through her red hair. And what a sight that would've been! The lady, still horsed, with her legs one on either side and her skirt hitching up to show a handspan of stocking. And her horse as white as cuckoo flowers, with its little red haunch-spot not quite hidden by the bridle. I kept my thumbs tight over those dangerous beaks.

So there I was, tangle-skirted and chicken-full, and I'll never know what she saw in me then. Enough, any case, to offer coins to my father – bags full of glinting, enough to make his moustache disappear into the folds of his lips. For my mother, it was the title. Lady's Maid. Fine fetters for the youngest of eight, last to leave. No word from my siblings for years, long gone as they were – the last we saw was the hellfire from their heels across the tops of the hills. And my betrothed, he of the thick knuckles and pale gold hair? The transparent boy who tumbled me across hay, who licked at my earlobes and stickied my palms? I forgot him within a day.

I'll never know what My Lady saw in me, but I know what I saw in her. She was a mirror. Mud-weighed and birdhanded as I was, she still knew me. She knew the things I had been thinking, down deep between my lacings, under the wooden heels of my shoes. The words I shaped with straw before kicking away: she knew them. We were tied as sisters, cousins, lovers. This link between us is a red silk ribbon, a fine silver chain, a length of daisies punched together. It's the loveliest thing I ever saw.

THE HOUSEKEEPER

I'll not be taking part in mistress's activities, oh no. She brings the girls up to the house and that is as it is, but I'll have none of it. She's a fancy lady, no doubt. But even fancy ladies don't need a dozen handmaids, and them changing every few weeks to a new crop of girls. It's to the end that I can't even remember their names, not a one, not a single one. Just a *you there* will suffice for that sort of girl, to my mind.

Such harlotry in their little looks! Mouths round and red like quims, and their bodices low as anything. The mistress must pick out the stitches before she gives the girls the dresses, mark you. No proper dressmaker would make a lady look such a pinchcock.

The first maid was fine enough – mistress did need help with her dressing and suchlike, and her red cheeks and brown hair looked regular enough to fit in at the house. For a while she tied mistress's corsets and arranged mistress's hair, and I kept firm out of their way. Plenty to keep me busy kitchen-side. But I couldn't pretend I didn't see what mistress was about. Tip-tapping through the back corridors where she'd no business to be, flipping up skirts and losing her rings inside girls. Mistress parading those wagtails thinking it was like to tempt me, thinking I was like to be kept feverish at nights with thinking of their ways, that I was like to be some dirty tom. And me with my eyes on the floor like I'm meant! They'll go to the devil, the lot of them. I've got two eyes; how long can I pretend I don't see?

THE LADY

Oh, how I have loved. My days are flaxen and holy with love. My nights are viscous, lucid, spilling over. My finger pads hum. The roots of my hair feel gold-dipped; the meat of my eyes is speckled with gold; gold dust blows across my cheeks. The girls, the girls, and their love. No need for sleep when their saliva is sustenance. Their sweet country cunts and their kiss.

I find them, I whisper of my home, and they're up on my horse before the daisies close. The look in their eyes is clean as dawn. Their fingers in my mouth taste of buttermilk. My castle is a mother, is a lover. Once upon a time, I say, and they follow my hooves inside the walls, and I close the door up tight behind them.

My enchantments keep them for a turn of the sun or a phase of the moon, and then they find the chink in the walls and slip out faster than smoke. I know they look back. I see the light glint off their eyes.

Some do stay; one or two starbellied and honeyfed girls. I tuck them under my swan wing and tickle them close, close enough to share heat. They love love as I do. They see the straight line of my jaw along the length of their thighs and they see how it fits, the geometry of bodies. They have wondered for so long why nothing ever fits, why the knobs of their spines press hard on chairbacks and why they can't lie parallel in bed, and then there I am. I know how to fill the gaps in a girl.

THE DINNER GUEST

She wanted us to know. She's proud of it, I'm sure. The strumpet. The slippering little… but let me tell you. You will see.

Two dozen guests for dinner and it was out with the partridge tongues and the songbird hearts in cages of ribs, along with wine sweet enough to pickle kittens. How the ladies cooed! Codswallop, I say. But the ladies like their food to sing.

Three courses in and we were a maid down. I knew because she was a comely thing, applecheeked and applebreasted, with a glint in her eye like she well knew the parts of a man. I'd been devouring her charms between sips of the lamb-blood soup, and then – gone! For moments I frowned my way around the room, as surely even the most coddled maid would never dare abandon her post mid-meal. And then my eye's wanderings noticed how the lady of the house shifted in her seat! No soup ever caused such moans from a throat, and yet the lady was purring like a pussycat. Seated opposite the lady, I had an artist's perspective; full frontal, so to speak, perfect for observing that actress's change in expression. Shifting my feet under the table, I knew the shape of a body; even through the soles of my shoes I could feel it was that applerumped maid. And the lady moaned, and the lady wriggled; and all the other ladies peered into their soup and began moaning around their spoons.

Such soup, they cried! Such flavours! Bravo!

All the ladies were shifting and groaning, rocking in their seats like they had pigs rutting away at them. You'd have thought it was the greatest soup ever to have been swallowed.

By the bottom of their bowls, the lady was smiling wider than a dagger's blade. The maid was back in her place, her lips plump and wet as a rose after the rain.

And so you see! That grinning tart put on quite a show for me. I know it was for me, because all that ladies do is for the eyes of gentlemen. And I do look forward to seeing more of that lady.

GIRL #6

I stayed for a year. I was not the only one – it was three to a bed in My

Lady's chamber – but still I stayed. I don't know what I was searching for. I don't know if I found it.

Living in that house was like living inside a painting – one of those lush, dark oil paintings: a still life of overripe fruit, a severed boar's head, and a cat toying with a pitted wheel of cheese. Everywhere I went, I was sure people could smell the sweetsalt fleshness on my fingers. Men in the street stopped to stare, stopped to lick their lips, though I was shoulder-to-ankle in my cloak. Her scent went that deep: right under my flesh, all the way to the marrow. For months after I left, I would still catch the breeze of her when I angled my body just the right way. There were creases and edges of me that I just could not get to, and that is where she hid: too far down to scrub out.

My parents knew, somehow. They could smell the shreds My Lady left in me. I went back to the muck of the kitchen and the heat of the stables, but there was no good to be found. Everything was overlaid and underpinned with her. My dresses would not fit: they were too tight, too low, however much fabric I added on. My scarf would not cover my hair, and tendrils slipped out to frame my rosy cheeks. My mouth felt always swollen, always reddened.

I married – a cutout man, all hands and knees – and I stood wide-eyed as a nun in my white dress, calm as can be, like ice would stay cool in my palms. I imagined My Lady when I vowed, thought of how she would glitter and cackle to see her bedfellow in snow-coloured chiffon. I thought my vows would topple her, but she clambered up on them. She strung each word and wore them as a necklace, warming them like pearls.

I never knew what hate and love meant before My Lady.

THE LORD

What makes a woman is a performance of duty, and my wife has long been womanised. I saw well enough to that. From the day I flung her across my pommel to the band of gold, to the hanging of the bloodied sheet to the clockwork of the household, she is a daughter of Eve through and through. Each duty is performed admirably: she whips servants with a firm wrist, she wears her dresses better than a mannequin, and she moans louder than the priciest whore. Her mask will never slip. I do not need to see her to know that.

I dress for her dinners, do I not?

I pay gold for her trousseau, do I not?

I let her take on whichever little maidens she likes, do I not?

That is what makes me a man. I do what needs to be done. I do it fast and I do it well, and no rabbit was ever safe from my arrows.

That is her desire: a man as straight and solid as a wall for her to lean on. A woman's world is the size of the distance from the bedroom to the kitchen. What is she without me? She is unmanned, an empty case. A woman is an actress, and the only thing keeping her on stage is the width of her smile.

I am born a man. I do not need to perform.

THE DAUGHTER

Yes, I told. My father deserved to know. He's a devil with a clefted chin, but he still needed to know about my mother's wickedness because it just was not right. It was not holy. The path to glory is not paved with swooning girls, and no one ever found grace between two legs. So I told and I told and afterwards I glowed for days.

God knew about my mother's sins and my father is the God of this house, so he should have known too. It was my duty, that is all, and it did not matter about my own scuttering feelings or how many times I caught the flash of bare shoulders through the keyhole because it was not about that. It was about staying good. It was about grace, and keeping my own white heels straight on the shining path to heaven. My mother's own feet were no good for that path, after her grubbing in the dirt like that, ingraining those maids onto her flesh. Such things cannot be cleansed and there are no dirty feet in heaven. There is no jealousy in heaven and there was no jealousy in my heart over those girls. They were welcome to my mother. She was a pitcher full of filth with her mouth full of blood and I did not want her attention. I did not want it.

My glow was not from the deed of my telling, understand. It was from the knowledge of God, deep inside me the knowing of all His glory, His radiance warming me through the dark of night. It was grace shining out of me.

THE FRIEND

I attended their house for dinner, the same as a dozen other lords and ladies. I expected an elegant meal – rabbit tongues, perhaps, or eels' eyes – and wine in five different colours. The lady served all my expectations, and her conversation was characteristically delightful – all scandals and intrigues with veiled names. She laughed and touched my hand at all the right moments and, like a fool, I was charmed. Me, in a gown with patched underskirts, and my jewellery only paste – I was the one the lady wanted! No man ever seduced with such confidence. Her smile was as warm as fresh-baked bread, but her eyes were sharp at the corners.

I did not expect to become entangled in her activities. But I tell you; no one could have resisted the lady. After dinner the gentlemen slumped off for cigars and brandy, and the ladies fluttered to the sitting room for champagne. It was not usual for ladies to have so many drinks – it does go to one's head, and as every lady is told, there is not much in her head to absorb all that alcohol. It sloshes about in the space. That must be why I was fooled as I was – it must be!

One by one, the gentlemen visited our sitting room and held out their hands for their ladies. One by one, the ladies flitted out. The room was sotted with champagne and the walls were undulating – I swear they were, the lady is a magician! – and then it was just me and the lady, and then the sitting room became the lady's chambers. The girls' hands were soft as the insides of furs. Their laughter was church bells and their kisses; oh, their kisses. I had never known it could be such a way.

Our discarded skirts were piled high as a church steeple and our throats hummed with lust and we felt honey flow from our bodies, and finally the lady sat at the peak of a tangle of girl-limbs and surveyed her kingdom, when in walked the Lord.

THE GIRLS' MOTHERS

We knew. From the start, we knew. But we knew too what our girls were. This world is a cold and rutted place for those with brows raised above the horizon.

A handful of shiny circles and these girls are tied to any neat-shoed lady, like or not – but we liked it fine, shame to confess. We liked the words of this Lady and the promise of ever after. The love of a mother for her child is stronger than tides, but we know that the best way for a child is to put one foot in front of the other. Half of a woman is given away each time we split ourselves with child, until all we cradle at night is a scrap of soul. The Lady was a shining road, flat and straight enough for our girls, and she would lead them into the dawn. Our girls had always had itching feet, after all. So we took the coins and we took the promises, but they did not fill the space our girls left.

At nights we pushed with all our breath to hear the thoughts of our girls, but even the harness of daughter to mother can be severed if the walls are thick enough. The Lady's walls were thicker than muscle, and we could not break through. We made believe that our girls smiled like they always had strawberries in their cheeks, and that their shoes were silky as a pigeon's neck feathers. We were not the stepmothers from fairy tales. We did what we thought was best.

We knew what the Lady was, but we liked her shipwreck-quick smile and the shine on her shoes. We liked her white horse with its one red spot. That horse was just like our girls, we knew, and no amount of whitewash can cover that red dot.

THE ABBOT

It is easy to understand why a lady would wish to escape. We all tire of this earthly plain before long. The way out is grace, and glory exists inside all of us.

The entry into heaven cannot be rushed, and for the lady it will be as slow as she needs it to be. The duty of an anchoress is no easy one, we know that well enough. The contemplation of the grave is perhaps the most difficult, but the lady has as much time as God has granted her. She is young yet, and there will be many years for her to appreciate the gifts of her enclosure. She will find peace in solitude, I am sure.

Her husband has assured me that the lady has craved bare walls and silenced voices for many a year. The lady is fortunate indeed that her husband is willing to sacrifice his wife for her own good. It cannot be easy for him to run a household of women alone, but he is a good man to think only of his dear wife, and I am sure that God will reward him.

The lady's enclosure begins this evening, and I must prepare. The road to heaven is a pebbled one, and she will need a firm hand to steer her through. The contemplation of darkness will help her better than the touch of a hand ever could. Of this, I am sure.

THE LADY

My skin hums with it. My flaxenbelly and my moonsmoke, and there are holes, there are holes in me through which the love escapes. The men are men and they are hard, there are no summits to them, nothing to climb up or slip down. My fingers fit into the gaps between the bricks. The moon is the size of my eye. The buttermilk and the daisies, the redness inside cheeks and within the holiest of holies, within the edges of a girl, and this is grace, and this is glory.

FORGET THE GIRLS

Alma Mathijsen (1984–)

Born in Amsterdam and educated at the Gerrit Rietveld Academie, Mathijsen published her first collection of short stories at the age of twenty-two, in which she imagines having sex with twelve Dutch public figures. She describes her approach to writing as fluid, intuitive and fast. Much of her work explores the divides between platonic and romantic love within female relationships.

My darling Kay,
Seven years ago I fell in love with a woman who didn't want to exist.
I remember everything.
I remember the party where everyone flung off their tops and you stripped off your trousers.
I remember dancing in the supermarket underneath the speakers.
I remember the two of us breaking into the Beer Bikes depot and puncturing at least one tyre in every beer cart.
I remember stealing pickled herrings at the Mayor's cocktail party so we could set them free in the canal.
I remember the soirees at my publisher's and you hiding all the glasses in the hedge, one after another, to make the caterers pull their hair out in despair at the end of the party.
I remember the North Sea and you dragging me by my feet down to the bottom.
I remember the breakfast buffet in the Winter Garden at the

Krasnapolsky where we could get drinks at six o'clock in the morning when all the clubs had shut.

I remember that we never ran out of words, that there was always more we wanted to tell each other.

I remember burying myself in your shoulder.

I remember the floor of Café Tabac.

I remember lots more parties, and I remember how you always asked if it was okay for us to leave together.

I remember that it was okay.

I remember how the two of us stopped going out.

I remember us turning down invitations because we were bigger and better than any celebration of anything whatsoever.

I remember my flat in Slotervaart, the lift that took forever to reach my floor and that we didn't give a damn.

I remember the woman next door banging on the wall when we were working out a speech at four o'clock in the morning on why Sylvia Plath's suicide clearly had nothing at all to do with Ted Hughes.

I remember bottles of wine.

I remember cardboard boxes of wine.

I remember five confetti-coloured donuts wrapped in supermarket plastic.

I remember midnight pizzas.

I remember delivery men at our door and their puzzlement.

I remember watching fireworks from the balcony; the sky above Amsterdam was lit in a thousand colours.

I remember the explosions, still ringing in my ears years later.

I remember your thigh pressed gently against me when we sat beside each other.

I remember that we never kissed.

I remember that I never saw you naked.

I remember, hazily, other people asking what was going on.

I remember saying that friendship can be just as authentic as romantic love.

I remember blank expressions and how I changed the subject, talking about something insignificant instead.

I remember Lenie de Zwaan and how much we loved her.

I remember us listening for the sixth time to a radio documentary so we could hear her say that friendship should have exactly the same status as marriage.

I remember how you wanted to make tea but let the kettle whistle away in the kitchen so you could keep on listening to her.

I remember you bringing me fruit, and frying steak for me in the evenings.

I remember the bright yellow walls of the hospital.

I remember every smudge on the wall of the psychiatric unit.

I remember the worried expression in Dr. Zadeki's eyes, as if all his patients were flitting past him every moment.

I remember you sitting with me.

I remember sitting with you on a café terrace in the city centre and the number of rugs you tucked around my legs, though it was late summer.

I remember us gazing at girls with ribbons in their hair, how they laughed at the night which hadn't yet started.

I remember feeling jealous.

I remember you noticing.

I remember going quiet.

I remember you looking at me, you were so concerned, so genuinely concerned about me.

I remember feeling lacerated by Amsterdam, how it made think of times I could no longer have.

I remember how the others slowly drifted away.

I remember you staying.

I remember you saying that the city didn't belong to us anymore.

I remember us leaving.

I remember us driving into Voorhorst again, for the first time since we were girls – strange little Voorhorst.

I remember how everything looked the same and totally different.

I remember that the trees were taller.

I remember that my parents' house on the village square had turned brown.

I remember the smell of tobacco in the walls, every kind of brown from top to bottom.

I remember you setting to work with gallons of white paint.

I remember you painting everything white, the floors, the furniture, and how I could only be an onlooker because I couldn't bend down.

I remember how I lost the knack of writing, how the urge to write gradually left me.

I remember the top-of-the-range IKEA bed with pocket springs.

I remember expensive sheets and soap flakes.

I remember Toni Braxton.

I remember us only listening to music from the past.

I remember how the world of today vanished, a little more each day.

I remember us closing the curtains.

I remember you sandwiching a marshmallow between two cookies, as they do in America.

I remember that when I told you I was cold you had a fireplace built so we could have a proper fire.

I remember that neither of us ever managed to light a fire that burned longer than five minutes.

I remember how we just gave up on the idea and instead gazed at blazing balls of newsprint.

I remember shopping bags full of everything we wanted.

I remember sitting in the kitchen for hours and you dumping the fourth piece of burnt chicken in the trashcan.

I remember that I didn't miss Amsterdam.

I remember that I didn't miss anything.

I remember how I slowly sank away in our house on the square.

I remember us forgetting appointments in the city, sometimes accidentally, but mostly on purpose.

I remember having my phone contract cancelled, you ringing Vodafone on your own phone, them asking you why, and you saying we didn't need to be so accessible anymore.

I remember my laptop, folded shut in the corner of the bedroom; the curtains were my horizon now.

I remember the way you looked at me, your mouth slightly smiling.

I remember the feeling of pressure behind my eyes.

I remember feeling scared of the pain, always asking myself if it would get worse and if I'd be able to bear it.

I remember you letting me be scared without you yourself being scared, that you lay down beside me to count the cracks in the ceiling.

I remember my world getting smaller.

I remember wanting to go out of doors to feel the wind on my face and how you opened the balcony doors then shut them again after five minutes because that was better for my health.

I remember that the skin behind my ear started to twitch, for hours at a time sometimes.

I remember you putting warm facecloths on my neck when the glands were swollen.

I remember you bringing supper upstairs on a wooden tray.

I remember gradually forgetting what the living room looked like, where the television was exactly, and the precise shade of beige of the sofa.

I remember every single smudge on our bedroom wall, every single mosquito and its particular death.

I remember that lying down started to feel uncomfortable and twisting and turning from my left side onto my back then onto my right, then in the middle of the night having to get up and stand straight.

I remember you standing in the dark by my bedside, looking at me.

I remember you saying I shouldn't have to suffer so much pain.

I remember putting all my hope in you.

I remember eating apple puree flavoured with cinnamon.

I remember that the next day I was less conscious of the throbbing pain in my lower back.

I remember being able to tell a story without having to shift position halfway through.

I remember the pain gradually ebbing away and being replaced by sleep; I could doze for days under the blankets in our white room.

I remember not really knowing what I was doing with my time, and forgetting that Wednesday was long past.

I remember not being able to eat the fat on a cutlet.

I remember you bringing the television upstairs and then taking it downstairs again the next day because I hadn't watched it.

I remember books giving me a headache – they felt like a hand gripping the back of my brain, always tighter and tighter.

I remember not remembering any of my dreams; I used to write them down sometimes, before, as a source of inspiration, but now I always woke up feeling blank.

I remember my body not doing what I demanded, the leg that just lay there, motionless, no matter how many signals I sent down to it.

I remember you sitting on the bed with a deep frown on your face.

I remember us doing exercises every morning afterwards and how you twisted and turned each joint at least twenty times over.

I remember having to lean on your shoulder to walk around the room.

I remember the cups of tea, the sugar pretzels that very often now I just left aside, and the little pots of full fat yoghurt.

I remember that the yoghurt had a brackish aftertaste, which you said was because it was an organic farm product made by traditional methods.

I remember feeling dizzy whenever I sat up in bed and that there was a tingling sensation which only stopped after some minutes if I made myself concentrate on a fixed point on the wall.

I remember when I was still really very young how people on television would talk about good days and bad days; when I was

a child I thought these days were predetermined, and it was only
when I myself became ill that I realized that the worst thing is not
knowing when the bad days will come.

I remember that I had both: good days and bad days.

I remember the two of us together on the bed.

I remember that those moments made it easier for me to bear the
constant lethargy.

I remember you brushing my hair, and how you concealed from me
the strands of hair that had fallen out; you didn't want me to see
them, and I didn't want you to see that I'd seen them, so I said
nothing and let you carry on brushing.

I remember that I stopped having my periods and you said I should
find it a relief, but that wasn't what I felt and I knew you'd noticed.

I remember how you held my head the night it all became too much
for me.

I remember apparitions.

I remember feeling nauseous all the time and not feeling any better
after throwing up.

I remember a world where everything was white and a person kept
coming into view, someone with a shape like mine, and how that
person kept fading in and out of view, and how this person was
clean at first and then started bleeding, and how this person was
all covered in blood when they left the scene, and then it started all
over again.

I remember that you had to hold me tight.

I remember how long I was scared.

I remember that I couldn't imagine me ever calming down again.

I remember not even wanting to calm down.

I remember wanting it all to be over.

I remember wanting it all to be over and done with, and with you too.

I remember that being the point when I did calm down.

I remember that you kept grasping my head, how my neck relaxed in
your hands.

I remember the lump in my throat every time I had to swallow.

I remember seeing myself: lying there, in that big bed, my arms limp, my legs thick with blood, my face drained and pallid.

I remember that there was no way I could carry on like that.

I remember not saying anything.

I remember missing the pain: given the choice between apathy and pain, I'd have chosen pain, because then at least there would have been a spark of life in me, some fighting spirit.

I remember the word 'quicksand' and how often my thoughts turned to it.

I remember looking for a way out.

I remember being conscious of the heart in my ribcage, a heart, by the way, that at this very moment deeply resists all these words, squirming inside a body which is trying to take better care of itself.

I remember yet more yoghurt.

I remember never feeling awake.

I remember you staying at home, although I hadn't asked you to do so, and how you used to wash me on the bedroom floor.

I remember feeling terribly guilty because I'd never be able to look after you.

I remember how that ate me up.

I remember trying to guess at your motives – if I said it aloud I knew I would destroy something, yet I still kept thinking it over, why you stayed.

I remember taking refuge in my imagination as I did in the past when I was bored, then I could build worlds in my head through which I navigated exactly as I wanted.

I remember when you weren't there I sometimes managed to stay in my own world for hours; I'd found a temporary exit, a way out that could perhaps become a bridge.

I remember a small groove in the ceiling, a light dent where the tip of my little finger would fit precisely.

I remember one morning when the light shone differently into the room, whiter than usual, and you didn't sit on the edge of my bed but fed me standing.

I remember fleeing even further into my own universe that morning.

I remember seeing your lips move, seeing your eyes screaming, but I couldn't hear you.

I remember your hands gripping tightly onto my arms and how I was slowly ebbing away.

I remember that you had to force the spoon through my lips, more and more often.

I remember this, although I don't remember it well; I can see your fingers in front of my eyes and feel the metal on my mouth, the rest is whiteness.

I remember two options, which I suddenly saw clearly; I could either let myself be slowly erased so I could get lost inside you, creep into you, hollow you out and fill you up, melt away and circulate through your veins and arteries, stay with you until you turn to clay, or I could imagine a way out for myself and believe in it so completely that it would become real.

I remember that I chose the second option and I'm so sorry.

I remember that I slowly had to work myself loose.

I remember that each day I imagined another piece of my world.

I remember that in the past I had never had any problem imagining myself as separate to you and that the moment I let that thought enter my mind the possibility truly existed.

I remember that I did think of a way out.

I remember that I could move my big toe.

I remember that I could stay awake for a few hours at a time.

I remember feeling pleasure when I stroked the edge of the sheets with my fingertips.

I remember asking you to open the curtains; you asked me if I was sure.

I remember not understanding what you meant and seeing the fear in your eyes as you nervously pushed the curtains open.

I remember not wanting you to feel afraid and at the same time not
    wanting you to feel you were smothering me, which you were.
I remember the pillows you propped behind my back every afternoon,
    every glass of lemonade, every piece of meat.
I remember each time you washed between my toes with a flannel.
I will remember for ever that my heart is breaking, because I know
    things are better now.
I want you to know this.

Iris

Translated by Antoinette Fawcett

THE AVENGING WHIP

Max Lobe (1986–)

Born in Douala, Cameroon, Lobe moved to Switzerland at the age of eighteen, to study in communication and politics Lugano. Raised on the African literature of Ahamadou Kourouma and Alain Mabanckou, his first novel, *39 Rue de Berne*, won the 2014 Prix du Roman des Romands. This was followed by *La Trinité bantoue* and *Confidences*, Lobes writing often focus on issues such as illegal immigration, sexual identities in traditional societies and postcolonial theory. In Lobe's native Cameroon homosexuality is still illegal and penalised by five years in prison.

The weather's so hot at the moment that I can't be assed to do anything. I spend all day vegging out in front of the TV, watching shows aimed at the unemployed, even though I have a real job. And when I'm not staring at the box and doing my eyes in… well, I sleep, I eat. I sleep some more and I eat some more. In other words, I do fuck all.

When I opened the mailbox this morning, I realized that I was making a serious mistake. The bills for the things that rule our life here brought me down to earth with a bump. True, I've been able to put enough away, my job pays well. But as my mother often says: "Money's nothing! It comes and it goes." That's why you always have to keep your assets topped up. So, this morning, I decided to go back to work after several weeks of bumming around.

I'm seeing a "client" this evening. We arranged to meet in front of the Gare Cornavin. He said he'd come by and pick me up there at the station.

So I'm off for a little jog to get myself into shape, because in my profession, looks matter—as they do in most professions, come to think of it. Yes, looks matter. Of course they never tell you that you weren't hired because you're ugly, or because of your big fat belly. But success doesn't just rely on looks. You also need a little something between the ears. And me, I haven't got anything. In any case, not enough. Back home in Bantu country, I finished the equivalent of compulsory schooling here. Then, as a result of life's ups and downs, I pitched up here, kind of by chance.

Then I thought long and hard about what I could do, seeing as I have no qualifications, nothing. I wanted bucks. Big bucks. And fast! No way was I going to be a tough guy and get a job as a bouncer in a club. Honestly, it's a waste of time. No way was I going to fuck my back up doing cleaning, either. Anyway, cleaning's a job for old women! A guy like me, two hundred and twenty pounds and six foot four... dusting furniture? No thank you.

I reckoned there were three options open to me:

1) Bank robber—this is Switzerland, and honestly, there's no shortage of banks.

2) Drug dealer — they say you can make a good living, even if you only sell tiny, tiny little amounts.

3) Rent boy—apparently Nyambè has given me all the assets for that.

Of the three options, the first two seemed too risky. The day you get caught "you go to jail for the rest of your life!" as my poor little grandmother back home in the Bantu village used to say. And seeing as I don't want to be in prison for life, the third option sounded the most sensible. Healthier. And honestly, even Nyambè won't hold it against me.

It's eight p.m. when I rock up super-cool at the Gare Cornavin. I'm togged out like a businessman going to a client meeting. Bow tie and dinner suit that fits me like a glove. It even looks as if it has been sewn and ironed onto me. I'm holding a medium-sized black leather bag in my left hand. In the other, a cigarette. I wait for my client. He's a little late. Just a little. Like three or five minutes.

A Mercedes convertible with tinted windows pulls up in front of me.

The window on the passenger side winds down and I cop a look at my client. An attractive man, the wrong side of fifty. Graying hair and unshaven. He's wearing a shirt that's as blue as the sky this summer. I get into the car and I'm impressed by his watch. Impressed… well, kinda. But even so! I've never seen a client with such an expensive-looking watch. But I curb my thoughts. You're here to work and earn your dough. Who gives a fuck about the rest?

"Are you OK?" the guy asks.

"Yup."

"How long have you been doing this?"

"Forever," I reply coolly.

He carries on driving. He doesn't speak again. In my line of business, people don't talk much. They just do.

His place is huge. He must be a powerful guy. Like really powerful. Some Geneva big shot.

We're all settled in the lounge. He goes over to the bar and shows me a bottle of whisky. I shake my head. He looks at me questioningly.

"I'm doing Ramadan," I say.

"Are you a Muslim?"

Are you a Muslim?!

"Yes," I lie, adding, "I don't smoke and I don't drink."

"What a funny Muslim you are!"

"…"

"Orange juice? Water?"

"Water, please."

"Here's a glass of water. With this heat…"

He dips his lips in his glass of whisky, then blows out the smoke from his cigar. He stares at me. He seems to be under the spell of my good looks. I'm a pro and I have a radar for things like that. I look around me. This is the lap of luxury. But I'm not overawed. In my line of work, I'm lucky I only meet European fat cats.

I pick up the black leather bag containing all my gear.

"Where can I get changed?"

"Over there, there's a bedroom to your left."

"What about the bathroom?"

"There's a bathroom in there."

I stride toward the bedroom where I'm about to swap my dinner jacket for a black vinyl jumpsuit. For this client, I went to the trouble of slipping on a pair of mini-shorts, to wow him with my powerful thighs, worthy of a real Bantu.

When I come out of the bedroom, the sound of my boots makes the gentleman jump. "Wheeew!" he gives a low whistle.

I spread out my kit on the coffee table: three types of plaited leather whip, two straps, dildos, a rope, handcuffs, a gag ball, and a gag with bit and bridle. Within minutes I take my client to a whole other universe. I switch off the lights. I light red and black candles. I remove his clothes. I handcuff his hands behind his back. I bind his ankles tight together with my rope. I gag him with the bit and put him on the leash.

Now he's kneeling in front of me, his face as red as a beetroot. Slowly, I unzip my vinyl shorts and display the gift Nyambè has given me that is most intimidating: my cock. The guy's eyes widen. I laugh. I laugh softly. Then suddenly I roar with laughter like the bad guys in cartoons. I let my hand hover over the table, pretending to hesitate over which whip to use. Then hup, no more time-wasting. I pick the toughest whip. I go and stand behind my client. I strike the floor with my whip, he shudders. He seems scared. Ooh, the bad boy! I laugh louder. I stamp on his back with my boots and force him down further toward the floor. He complies. That's what he pays me for: to obey me. Right! Now let the fun begin. No more time to lose. "Time is money," my heart tells me.

I thrash his back hard with my whip. Ouch! This must be doing him good. He tries to yell, but he can't, he's gagged. I pull on the bridle and raise his head slightly. No, not like that. I stamp on him a bit more. There! Like that. Good position. Excellent position, even. That way he'll feel the sting of my whip on his white skin better. And thwack! A good thwack-thwack of the whip! His flesh turns red. The blood rises to the surface. I love that. I laugh. Another thwack, and deep inside me my spirit starts talking. And thwack! That's for my ancestors, slaves for hundreds of years. And thwack! Harder! That's for my grandparents in the Bantu forests, oppressed by colonization. And thwack! Yes! That's for all your multinationals that come and raid Bantu country. And thwack! Harder! Thwack! Let's say that it's for the debt we'll never be able to pay. I bring the avenging whip down on him over and over again. My client torpedoes. The pain does him good. While my revenge comes down all the harder. Yeah, my revenge is rooted in my guts. And thwack! Another more powerful crack of the whip. That's for the borders you close to stop us from coming here, to your country, the white people's country.

My client rolls over. He lies on his back. That means he's beginning to feel the pain. Too much pain. He can't stand the pain any more. But no, boy. No! I'm master here. I'm the one who tells you what to do, get it? That's what you pay me for. So let me get on with my job. I jerk the leash violently. I put him back in his place. I have a final crack of the whip to deal him. And thwack! That last crack really is very powerful. This one's... Let's say it's for all the racism we suffer in your country. Oh, I'm really getting off on this! It gives me a hard-on. Now I'm going to gently remove the gag, giving him a couple of hard slaps. I'm going to fuck his ass and he can scream all he wants. Too bad if his classy Geneva neighbors call the cops. I don't give a fuck. I'm just doing my job.

He yowled like a dying animal for half an hour. I spat on him a number of times. He licked my sweat. With my big, hard hands, I flogged him. He loved that. So did I, of course.

After a very long session, I took a nice relaxing shower. I put my dinner suit back on as elegantly as I could. When I came out of the shower, I found him lying there, exhausted. I smiled at him. "You are a god," he said. "Thank you," I mumbled. He held out an envelope. "Here, this is for you." I looked inside. Fifteen one thousand Swiss franc notes. What a nice surprise! He's given me a five thousand bonus. I'll be able to send more to my family back home in Bantu country. I'm over the moon.

I gave him my business card again, like any real professional, in the event that...

"See you soon," I said, heading for the door.

"Yes. There's a taxi waiting for you outside."

Translated by Roz Schwartz

SELECTED POEMS
Andrew McMillan (1988–)

Born in Barnsley, South Yorkshire, McMillan cites 2008 as the pivotal year in his life: he broke up with his first boyfriend; the Great Recession hit his hometown; and he committed himself to writing poetry. His debut, *physical* (2015), was the first poetry collection to win The Guardian First Book Award. It also garnered numerous other awards and, in 2019, was voted as one of the top 25 poetry books of the past 25 years by the Booksellers Association. His second collection, *playtime*, won the inaugural Polari Prize.

SCREEN

at the beginning I asked you
to let me watch you watching porn I think
I needed to see you existing
entirely without me your face lost

in concentration on another's
rhythm to know if we could work I knew
that you would end up loving me too
much I thought you needed other idols

months later I saw him the actor
from that film we watched unmissable
petals of the neck tattoo he seemed
to look at me as though he knew I'd seen

him naked his body a deep well
of things I would not ask a living soul
to do I wanted to shout *stranger I*
have seen your skin and you are beautiful

he was standing at the train station
more vulnerable than I remembered
much smaller too I imagined him
heavy with the hope of other men

taking someone home the look on his face
when he realised how timid
he was without direction how
ordinary the unlit curves

of his shoulders were I imagined him
stopping mid kiss pulling back mumbling
this just isn't going how I wanted
this just isn't going to work

IF IT WASN'T FOR THE NIGHTS

I tour my foreign voice
through the tin roofed halls of semi rural provinces
I barely understand the lines
but the crowd goes mad and claps
of thunder thrum the valley where I sleep
and my lonelyhaircut cellist eyes the bar between us
and I gargle salt and sleep alone
and back across the border the man I love is curled
to someone else and they don't speak a word
and outside a precious bird doesn't comprehend
the language of its wings
and frost hums on the weathervane

if it wasn't for the nights Steffan I'd come home

A GIFT

for the ones I never touched for the ones
who wanted to watch films who wanted
to talk who wanted silence and said I
talked too much for the one I saw
weeks after laughing for the one who served
me coffee and didn't recognise my hands
for the optimistic ones who write

their names on toilet walls the ones
I never called for the ones I called
who didn't answer who left our love
suspended from the ceiling hooks
of that meatmarket city for the ones
who left and settled down the ones who wanted
knowledge were curious who gained something

from each encounter used each other
who took what they needed for everyone
they hurt who felt burned out the ones who
didn't realise everyone was burning
the ones who never slept who died nightly
the ones who said they'd kill for it for all of them
a gift we were young we only had our bodies

I MET A GIRL NAMED BAT WHO MET JEFFREY PALMER

Imogen Binnie (1990–)

Born and raised in New Jersey, Binnie's early writing appeared in her zines *The Fact That It's Funny Doesn't Make It A Joke* and *Stereotype Threat*. Her novel *Nevada*, a fierce, furious take-no-prisoners tale of a New York trans punk was shortlisted for Lambda Award in 2014.

We could have the Jeffrey Palmer conversation, but it would be a waste of time. Here's how it would go: I'd want to talk about what he wrote, what he took from Alan Watts and what he rejected, how he was almost on the same page as his contemporary Eckhart Tolle, but where the fissures were and why—why they used such different language. I'd want to talk about his correspondence with Ken Wilber. If you were still with me, I might show you the tattoo on my bicep from a letter he wrote to Wilber when Wilber was already ignoring him: *quantification is both an over- and under-simplification of something so simple and complex as the self.* If you were keeping up, I might explain that as much as I find Palmer's work to be true and effective, I don't know if he really understood what Ken Wilber was doing—but you wouldn't be following me.

I could tell you about what Palmer thought about Daniel Quinn, Noah Levine, Sun Tzu, Yogananda—Rhonda Byrne. I'd want to tell you about how the beauty of Palmer's writing is how self-evident it is, how little interpretability there is, that that is the point. But your eyes would already have glazed over. You wouldn't want to hear about his influences, who he influenced, or why.

Completely disinterested in content or context, you'd be like "Man, webcam meditations, though. It just seems like such a silly waste of time. I sure couldn't ever waste so much time on that." And I'd be like, I know. You and everybody else. That's not interesting, that's what everybody who only knows him from that stupid *Vice* article from two years ago says.

So when I want to talk about Palmer, I do it on the internet. It's retro but I post on two message boards: a discussion board about his work and a board for trans women under thirty. Last December—almost a year ago now, when I was fucking that boy Charles, when my hair was red and I used to wear that awful green eyeshadow—there was a little convergence where a conversation about Palmer came up on the message board for trans women. And like most times you hear his name, it came up as a joke; in a thread about philosophy somebody was like "Jeffrey Palmer, LULZ." I didn't want to out myself as someone who actually appreciates his writing—someone who actually does the work everybody else thinks is so funny—so I just neutrally mentioned that I'd read some of him. And this girl Bat was like, "Oh, I met that weirdo once!"

Obviously you can't just be like, "OMFG YOU MET JEFFREY PALMER: SWOON." You'd just get kicked off the internet, or worse. I think I posted something like, "Oh cool." Still neutral, like neither endorsing him nor disowning him. But I threw up a little.

I checked out her profile and she was in New York, too. I threw up some more, but I didn't really do anything, because while I did want to hear more, I was nervous that I would've sounded at best kind of uncool and at worst like a wingnut cultist if I'd asked directly, and I couldn't bring myself to ask about him in a mocking way.

I didn't do anything about it for a couple days. I remember almost writing private messages to her a couple times, but feeling embarrassed at my phrasing, or at seeming all eager, or at caring at all. So I went to work. I chopped wood, carried water. When I had shifts at the coffee shop at night, I did my webcam meditations in the morning, and when I worked in the morning, I did them at night. I was feeling really uncentered, though, and I couldn't get it out of my head that there was a girl in this town—a girl I could meet—who'd met Palmer.

Then one night I let Charles sleep over because he'd said he'd make me coffee in the morning, which was a change of pace. I'm the one who spends all day every day making coffee, and it had made me laugh. I mean, I liked Charles okay, but we were definitely not in love. For one thing, he didn't really have a sense of humor, but more importantly he kind of dismissed my affection for the oughties—he thought the Animal Collective poster over my bed, my primary instance of décor, was just a picture of some ugly blobs, and he wouldn't even listen to the playlists I made for him—but I was fucking him because he was hot and didn't have weird shit around my body, not because we were emotionally compatible. He was an unimposing guy, only a little taller than me, but he was so lean. He had these small, muscular shoulders, and when he fucked me, he would lose himself so completely that I'd lose track of my body, too. He's the only person I've ever had sex like that with.

I mean, when we weren't fucking, he would talk about computer things, and his new headphones, the album he had apparently been working on for a long time, bands from now, all this stuff I didn't care about. I tried to be interested but the interest wasn't there. We would have made a terrible couple.

So anyway I remember very clearly that night he stayed at my house, we slept all tangled up, and then I woke up that morning with the idea firmly in place that I was going to e-mail this girl. I kicked him out without letting him make coffee. I wasn't mean. He was very sweet, and he even kissed me goodbye. I made myself a coffee, sat at the computer, and wrote a super direct message:

Hey, I actually am kind of interested in Jeffrey Palmer, what was he like?

She didn't respond for almost a month. This was back when I was wearing that Strokes shirt every day. That month disappeared into Brooklyn, and then I got a short e-mail from her. She was like:

yeah totes, I dunno, what do you wanna know?

—Bat

She signed the e-mail, "Bat."

This is how I imagine Brooklyn in 2008: there was an American Apparel on every corner. This was before American Apparel became the big store at the end of every mall in America, back when it was still cool—before Dov Charney became governor of California and sold the company to Target.

Everybody was wearing American Apparel, tight skinny jeans and tank tops that were sort of oversized, so they draped across tiny rib cages like ancient Roman tunics almost. Everybody was in their early or mid-twenties. Bedford Avenue was always so crowded with people of all races and both genders that there were people walking in the street, slowing down traffic, even in the middle of the night. It was like a 24-hour 4th of July barbecue. Everyone was holding a can of Pabst with beads of water dripping down the sides and everyone was tall, very thin, and had long hair, even the boys. The girls' hair was longer though. Some people would be wearing headbands.

Sexually it was a total free-for-all: boys kissing boys, girls kissing boys, girls kissing girls, boys kissing boys and girls at the same time, bodies squirming together along the sidewalk like the sweatiest gay disco in the seventies. Total humidity.

Everyone was a graphic designer and everyone was in a band and every band made dreamy, swoony music with lots of reverb and echo and vague distortion. You'd go see them at the Trash Bar or Southpaw or the McCarren Park Pool or go into Manhattan and see them at CBGB's.

You'd make out with your boyfriend, who was the singer of the second-to-last band of the night, in the men's bathroom. They'd just have performed and he'd be sweaty, his hair damp, the hollow under his clavicles, and he'd reach his arm around and pull you close and grab your ass and your breath might catch and you'd feel his cock, hard in his tight jeans, so maybe you'd suck him off, right there, even though there was no lock on the door.

Everybody had those iPods that were like four inches long and two inches deep. Most people had the little white earbuds but some people— your boyfriend—would have big, oversized headphones that kept out the world around them. Sometimes he'd wear oversized, slouchy hoodies.

So on any night of the week, since everybody freelanced, everybody would stay up all night doing coke at somebody's beautiful converted loft either in Williamsburg or out in Bushwick somewhere, making out or watching Wes Anderson movies or listening to the new Ariel Pink album or talking about Jonathan Safran Foer or Dave Eggers' new book and smoking cigarettes and talking, sprawled across black leather couches.

The boys all had permanent stubble that was usually just long enough to be soft, but sometimes it was short and rough and it scraped your face when you kissed them.

Everyone was a spaced-out kind of happy, and everyone had enough money, and everyone was pretty, and everyone read books, and all the boys had such thick eyelashes that they looked like they were wearing mascara, and all the girls were the kind of tough that boys can't even be.

After I got Bat's e-mail, I did some math. Palmer died in 2011, so if she met him, she must've been at least fifteen or sixteen in 2010, right? Maybe younger but probably not. So that would make her, like, thirty-five or forty right now. She was probably older. It didn't matter. I was just already thinking, I am going to meet this woman.

The main reason I was already thinking I wanted to meet her was that she had met Palmer, and I wanted to pump her for everything I could get about him. But another reason is that Jeffrey Palmer lived out his last two decades in Brooklyn. He was one of the original gentrifiers, back in the early nineties, who came to Brooklyn from Manhattan, back when people still wanted to live in Manhattan. I didn't think somebody who was in her thirties or older would be posting on that message board—and come to think of it, nobody over thirty even should have been posting there, which was my first hint that maybe Bat wasn't one hundred percent together, although maybe she'd been posting there since she was under thirty and got grandfathered in—which meant that most likely she'd met Palmer in Brooklyn in the early oughties. Which in turn meant that she'd probably lived in Brooklyn back then, and it seems like everybody else who was there then has either gotten old and boring and gotten over all the androgyny and danger, or else they've moved away and don't talk about it.

I wanted to hear firsthand what it was like in halcyon Camelot.

The more I thought about it, the more I threw up. I got all twisted up with nerves over talking about Palmer, and about meeting an internet person in real life, and even about owning up to my obsession with that time period. I shook it off, though, and sent her exactly the message I wanted to send her:

Can I interview you about him? Is it okay if I record it?

If I record it.

I should know by now that it's never as bad as you think it's going to be to out yourself—as anything—but I was surprised that I felt relief on sending it. It was out of my hands. Letting go of it, pushing back against attachment, erasing—of course it was a relief.

I drink a lot of coffee, but I usually just either drink it at work for free or steal it from work and bring it home. I can't afford to go out to other coffee shops; it's why Charles and I didn't go on dates. I couldn't afford my half. I mean, I still can't, I still live in the apartment I was living in then. I'm making a little more an hour at the coffee shop than I was back then, so I'm still just scraping by. But I live in Brooklyn.

You know my life story: when I was little, my parents let me wear girl clothes all I wanted. Even to school. At school, by first grade, I was getting enough shit from other kids that I stopped and convinced myself I was over it. Toward the end of high school I admitted to myself and then to everyone else that I wasn't over it at all and started wearing girl clothes again. Changed my name. Got on hormones. Moved to New York. It's the same life story you've heard from a million trans women. It's pretty much everybody's story, although I guess some of us don't move here. The only real difference in my story is that for a long time I was super resentful about the years I'd spent trying to be a boy—I was drinking a lot, having bad-news sex with jerks, doing too much coke, whatever, 'til at twenty I found Palmer's book *The Ephemeral Now* on the kitchen table of a boy whose name I don't even remember. I took it, read it, and started letting things go.

So I feel like I owe Palmer pretty much whatever agency I have in my own life. I would've stayed in that town, married and childless, 'til I died, if I hadn't learned to let go of the resentment I had toward a bunch of five-year-olds I'd been in first grade with, the twelve-year-olds (boys and girls, both kinds of lunch tables) who ostracized me so effectively in junior high, and all the boys in high school I had desperate, secret crushes on.

I'm not mad at being broke. I'm not mad at being trans. I'm not mad at pretty much anything, and it's not because I actively try not to be mad—it's because I actively try to own, confront, and let go of that anger. It's not complicated.

So that's why I decided to spend eight dollars on a coffee at the Verb with this girl I'd met on the internet. Nobody really knows much about Palmer, because his writings were all published posthumously, and I doubted I'd ever have another chance like this.

In retrospect, of course, there are reasons he kept his personal life so personal, and the fact that I wanted so badly to know more about him only shows how far I still had to go in terms of spiritual growth. I'm not mad at my younger self about it, though.

*

I met her at the Verb, that café on Bedford Avenue in Williamsburg that's been around since forever, right next to the Ikea. It feels true that it's been there for decades: the wood's all old and dark and chipped, and even though I know that lightbulbs go out instead of just getting dimmer, it feels like the lightbulbs haven't been changed in forty years. When I walked in, Interpol was playing on the speakers in the corners of the room, and I was like, why do I work at the stupid coffee shop by my house instead of here? It would probably start to feel like hokey nostalgia-town eventually, but still. I bought a coffee, got a table, and started recording sound.

When she walked in the door, I knew this was the woman I was here to see. She looked normal enough, just tired. Her hair was long and dark and cut in these very shaggy layers, limp enough that it might as well not have been a haircut at all, the way it hung. She was wearing an old white tank top, skinny jeans, these cowboy boots that looked ancient, and a short suede jacket; basically, she looked like me on a good day, when I'm really into my outfit, feeling like I've got a modern version of a Cat Power thing going on, except instead of 28 and vegan, if I was sixty and didn't really take care of myself. Which made me feel tired.

"Buy me a coffee, doll?" she asked, walking straight up to my table and sitting down.

"Uh, sure," I said, immediately off-balance because I'd budgeted for one coffee, and the eight bucks for hers was going to come out of next week's food money.

Once in a lifetime opportunity, I remember telling myself. Let it go.

So I bought her a coffee, which she immediately started drinking, even though it was way too hot. I was like, are you so skinny because you don't eat? Do you think coffee is food? But I had that feeling like I was in the presence of such an unknown quantity that I didn't want to say anything to make her freak out or hate me or leave and not tell me about Palmer, so I just tried to be cool.

*

I know I shouldn't have recorded it. Or, at worst, I should have listened to the recording once when I got home, meditated on it, and deleted everything. But I didn't. I still have it.

"So hey," she said. "You're like, a JP nut, right?"

"Kinda," I said. "I guess."

"That's cool," she said. "I remember after he died, when kids were first starting to read him, I was like, that fuckin weirdo? Seriously? but I guess people get something from it or whatever, so I shouldn't talk shit."

"Why do you think he was a weirdo?"

"Oh my god, that fucker lived in this VHS tape castle in his own private kingdom of like... Wait okay."

You can't hear it on the tape, but I swear to god here she drank the entire cup of coffee. I still couldn't even sip mine because it was too hot. I remember thinking, this is a weird conversation, and being kind of bummed out that she hadn't introduced herself, that we hadn't hit it off—that I already knew on some level that she wasn't going to tell me anything that would mean anything to me, spiritually.

I already knew that this was a mistake, that I shouldn't have been recording.

"Okay," she said. "So around like 2008 I was friends with that guy Pete Malkowitz?"

She paused for me to acknowledge that I knew who Pete Malkowitz was, but I had no idea.

"He was in that band The Fourth Joke?"

Blank look.

"They had a song on one of the *Twilight* prequels' soundtracks," she said, moving on. "That was their big moment. Pete knew everybody at all the clubs and he'd get us into shows for free, so we'd go see bands like every night back when he was still around. Anyway Pete was friends with this girl Melissa and one night he was like, you've gotta meet Melissa, so while I was at Pete's place off Manhattan and like Metropolitan one night, this girl Melissa buzzes up and he lets her in and I'm like, fuck you Pete, you just want me to meet this bitch 'cause she's trans too? But he's like whatever man, he's so fucked up on I don't even know what that you can't even be mad at him.

"So this girl comes in, and she's nice, kinda shy, doesn't want any coke, doesn't want any weed, just kinda hangs out and drinks—y'know not a small amount of beer—and then, like, hours later we find out that Pete went up to the roof and fell asleep, but we didn't know that right then. Suddenly it's just the two of us in the room.

"I'm like, so how do you know Pete, and I don't even remember what she said. Who cares? We start talking, and all she wants to talk about is trans stuff, and I was kinda skeezy at the time, I was kinda like whatever, like maybe I'm gonna play it off like maybe I'm not trans, but eventually it gets boring just listening to her stutter and hesitate and not say anything, and all I've been able to think of the whole time is like, if you get to pick your own name, why pick something so fucking boring like Melissa? I mean why not pick something cool?"

"Like Bat," I say. On the recording I sound bewildered; I think by this point I've parsed most of it out, but at the time you can hear in my voice how alien the dynamic she's describing is to me.

"So I ask her and she's like, I don't know, somebody told me that you have to pick something incongruous so nobody will think twice about it. I snorted and hit the fucking bong, I was like, whatever. I remember I was healing this—" She showed me a big faded blob of ink on her forearm. "—and I was trying not to scratch it, I was like, whatever, darlin'. Then the night kind of blurs and then I guess that's how we became friends."

"Uh-huh," I said.

"So yeah anyway turns out my first impression was wrong, she was actually pretty cool, she let me crash on her couch for a couple months after I got fired from Capone's. She was really funny, too, you just had to drag it out of her. Uh, she died. But maybe like a month after that night at Pete's—he died too, actually—I was at her place and she was like, I've got to go pick up this coat or something I left at my friend's house, I'll be back in an hour or two. But I was like, Whatever, I'm not doing anything and I've got an unlimited Metrocard I found—I don't know how long it's good for, but I might as well take advantage. I'll come.

"I guess in retrospect she didn't really want me to come but back in the day I could be kinda pushy and like, god knows how she knew Pete, and I didn't know any other friends she had, but I figured I was being a good friend if I came along. I was prioritizing that shit, being a good friend. So like, I went with her way the fuck out to like Mapleton, or Dyker Heights or some shit, where you can smell the ocean, and this guy lived in a house. Like a detached house, not an apartment, he had the whole thing."

183 93rd Street.

"So we go in, and she's like, I'll be right out, like she expects me to wait outside, but it was early in the spring and I'm kind of chilly so I'm like nah, I'll come in, and inside the house, like the whole place—from top to bottom—every wall is like a bookcase full of VHS tapes. It's seriously like something out of an early scene in a David Cronenberg movie, where it's not totally freaky yet, just kind of weird you know? Just like setting the mood?"

"Sure," I said.

"So okay like whatever, the only thing in this house is VHS tapes, there's no couches or tables or fucking room on the walls to hang anything. I pick one up but Melissa slaps my hand and I'm like, Okay, sorry, and we go up the rickety stairs right inside the front door—they've been painted white so many times you can feel your feet sticking to them, like inside an old church or something—up to the second floor where it turns out he's in this bedroom, on the bed, filming himself, talking into one of those old-timey camcorders."

He was doing webcam meditations.

"I'm like, This whole house is a dusty pile of old tapes when the whole world runs on Netflix and DVD's and shit, and you're filming yourself with a video camera from 1984 the size of a fucking dog? I don't say anything, though. Melissa's like Hey, and dude turns the camera to her, keeps filming, he's like, hey, all pimply face and fat belly and shit."

Which matches the couple of pictures of him that we've got. At this point I'm basically salivating and hanging on every vulgar word she says.

"He's like, Hey, your jacket's under the bed, which makes sense that it would have to be hidden because it's not a fucking VHS tape and obviously all that's allowed in his house is VHS tapes and VHS recorders and, like, this guy himself. So she gets her jacket out from under the bed. He doesn't even get out of his bed; he's wearing this old black t-shirt with a hole at the seam of one sleeve, he looks pretty gross actually. Like his hair's all greasy and he's kind of pimply. Melissa's like, Thanks, she digs her jacket out, and we go downstairs and leave."

"That's it?" I ask.

"Yeah, pretty much," Bat says. "Well I mean, y'know, I found out about his shit later. After he died and they started publishing his books and stuff Melissa was like, Dude, Bat, remember that guy? You met him once, and I was like Who, Video McCamcorder? She was like, Yeah, and explained about how his work was actually kind of important, and how he was recording on videotapes 'cause they were analogue so they couldn't get leaked the way an album or a movie does, and how he took a magnet to them right before he died, fuckin' dumbass."

"Why was he a dumbass?" You can hear defensiveness in my voice.

"I dunno, man," she says, leaning back, away from my microphone. "I mean for one thing, videotapes, they're not fuckin' digital. You can't erase something analogue with a fucking magnet, even a huge fucking giant magnet like the one homeboy used. Some deep thinker, doesn't know the difference between analogue and digital. Plus: spilling your guts, watching yourself spill your guts, then erasing it? Wingnut shit, man. I don't even get what his quote-unquote philosophy was supposed to be—that all things pass? Big fucking insight."

The conversation pretty much ends here because I got too pissed off to keep being nice to her. I asked if she'd ever read him, and she said she hadn't, and I was like so where the fuck do you get off talking shit about shit you don't know shit about, and then it pretty much goes downhill. We're not friends. Who cares.

*

Because this is what Brooklyn is like now: it sucks.

After that conversation, I remember riding home thinking about it. Thinking: of course you should let this go. And I mean, I knew Palmer wasn't the most physically attractive guy, that's one of the first things he had to figure out a way to work through, to overcome, to accept and leave behind. He wrote about it. It was hard to hear about it from somebody else, though, especially in such indelicate terms. And to hear the house he inherited from his mother, where he did his most vital work, where he had the epiphany about furniture and clothing and clutter and people and emotions and clearing out clarity, to hear it described in such stark terms… by the time I got home I'd of course integrated it into an opportunity to let an idol go, to kill a Buddha, but I was still throwing up a little in anticipation of doing a webcam meditation about it. Maybe a long one. Maybe an important one.

I was thinking about Bat, too, though. How did a person get like that? I could sort of understand the relationship between her and Melissa— like, this was back when trans people were supposed to go "deep stealth" and it was awkward to know another trans person and nobody ever mentored anybody else and being trans was totally stigmatized and people called each other "GG's" and "t-girls" and "trannies" and "auto-gynephiliacs." But why be so obnoxious?

Cocaine?

I've done my share of cocaine, and it didn't stop me from looking for a piece of serenity. And why was she so judgmental? Was it leftover pain from transitioning back in the Stone Age when you still had to get a psychologist to write a letter that said you weren't crazy, even though they all thought you *were* crazy, and then you had to carry that letter with you everywhere? I know that back in the day you even had to pay for hormones, so only rich trans people even got to transition.

I don't know, man, I still don't. I try to have empathy but seriously: fuck those damaged goods. No room for that in my life, even if it's in a context of respecting elders. Fuck a pointlessly moochy and judgmental elder.

The first thing I did when I got home, though, was look up VHS tapes. Turns out Bat was wrong: they occupied this weird grey area between analogue and digital. Like the information they communicated was digital in that it was zeroes and ones, but the tape, the medium itself, degraded from magnetic contact with the VHS player every time they were read. They communicated their digital information in an analogue way. So knowing she was wrong about something, I didn't want to believe anything Bat said. But everything else was spot on: the description of 183 93rd, the quantity of videos, the attention to his video recorder instead of the people in the room with him; these all fit with what we know about Palmer. She wasn't making it up.

I sat down at my desk, turned on my computer, turned on the video recorder, and I started talking. I explained about how meeting Bat had been an impulse I understood from the beginning to be selfish and counterproductive, but as a human being with flaws I hadn't been able to resist. I talked about how she probably *had* met Palmer, and how she was probably a jerk the whole time; that being trans, or having met Palmer, or having lived in Brooklyn in 2008, or having probably seen all the best bands—none of this made her anything other than herself. And who she was wasn't me, and who she was didn't have anything to teach me.

I digressed: of course there was something for her to teach me. There was a lot to learn from her about idolatry and euphemisms and hero worship and how age doesn't necessarily do anything good to you. I talked about how maybe Jeffrey Palmer wasn't attractive but that didn't matter. I remember talking about how Charles actually was attractive, one of those thoughts that bubbles up and then you let it go. I finished by talking about how in a macro sense of course none of this mattered, and in a micro sense it was all an opportunity to learn and grow and strengthen and let go.

I watched the video once and then erased it. Then Charles came over.

CRIMSON

Niviaq Korneliussen (1990–)

Korneliussen is one of very few Greenlandic authors to have found a readership beyond her island nation of 56,000 people. She translates her own novels into Danish, which are then translated abroad. They feature rapid, choppy narratives about queer adolescence. Awkward, surreal metaphorical intrusions are a trademark of her style.

The sunlight through the window has made everything hot and I kick my duvet off my sweaty body. I smell my hangover breath, which reminds me of yesterday's awful events and I feel a strong urge to take a bath. The memory of the sausage man makes me nauseous and I remember my legendary throwing-up act and laugh, which actually makes me cough something up. I hurry out into the kitchen and chug an entire bottle of Coke and do everything I can to keep it down. Last night has really taken its toll. I sit down on the sofa and crunch some leftover crisps while I wonder why Arnaq still hasn't come home. It's a shame that she drinks so much all the time since she lost her job. My little brother is best friends with her, and I really hope she won't be a bad influence. Arnaq's a woman, an *arnaq* – the very word for woman – with a mind of her own, who's never boring and here I am, waiting for her to come home with new stories. I have a wish. I want Arnaq to have hooked up with another woman, to turn up with a gay morning-after story. But of course, Arnaq's a woman with a mind of her own, and sometimes I envy her laid-back lifestyle. If Arnaq, who can easily hook up with another *arnaq*, has hooked up with a man, then I can't be bothered to hear about it. I'm suddenly dying to know. I yearn for excitement.

Just as I'm losing patience, I hear somebody trying to open the door and I hurry over. A rather intoxicated Arnaq enters the room as if she's fucking royalty and I laugh at her.

'What's up, Arnaq? Did you sleep at all?'

'The night is still young. I'll sleep when I die!' she says cheekily, stripping off her coat.

'Where've you been?' I ask, hopefully.

'Not telling!'

'Did you go home with someone?'

I follow her into the living room.

She sits down on the sofa and refuses to say anything. Gives me a playful smile.

'Woman? Man?'

'Does that matter?' she asks, slightly irritated.

I know that she doesn't like to be quizzed like this but I'm too curious to give up.

'No, it's irrelevant. I just want to know because you tell such great stories.'

'What about you? Did you bring Kristian home with you? You should be the first one to spill,' she says.

'Who's Kristian?'

'Oh, come on! Were you that drunk? Kristian!'

The sausage man's name is Kristian, apparently. If I'm going to get her story. I'll have to tell her about my horror show.

'I brought him home with me,' I say with a laugh.

'Honestly? Here? Surely you know, don't you, that I had a thing with him? Yep, that manwhore!'

She roars with laughter.

'He remembered. He totally knew this was your place. He said so.'

'Shit, how embarrassing!' she says and begins to laugh uncontrollably.

'What about you? Who did you hook up with?' I ask.

'You can't tell anybody else!'

'Who would I tell? I promise I won't.'

'Inaluk.'

'Inaluk who?' I ask.

'Inaluk Inaluk.'

'*Inaluk?*' Now this is a surprise.

She nods.

'Is she gay? I thought she had a guy?'

'Please don't tell anybody!'

'I'll keep quiet. Don't worry.'

'I think it was the first time she was with a woman,' she says, slightly embarrassed.

'Oof. Was she bad?'

'No, but she was a bit hesitant.'

'How do women do it?' I ask Arnaq, without thinking.

'Can't you figure it out? God, you have no imagination!'

She gets up from the sofa and walks over to her room.

'Arnaq… I was just asking.'

'Then come here. You can't know until you've tried it! LET'S SCREW!' she jokes from her room.

What would it be like, how would she react, if I did come, what would it be like to try with her, what might it do to our friendship, what would she look like naked, would she not look sexy, how would she kiss, how would she screw, what would it be like, how could I go in there? I couldn't. I wouldn't dream of it. My thoughts make no sense. I'm simply tired of sausages. Believe me, I've tried all sorts of sausages. Cocktail sausages, frankfurters, red, brown, yellowish, big, small, sausages… you name it. I'm sick of them. I'm off sausages. I want to take a bath, scrub my body clean so that the stench of sausage can vanish without leaving a trace in the water pipes.

Plan:

No more sausage.

*

Friday once again. It's a strange week for me. I haven't been to classes and I need to get out a bit. I decide to switch off the computer although I keep thinking of stuff I've found on the Internet. Romantic attraction, sexual attraction or sexual behaviour between members of the same sex or gender. Google knows everything. But I still haven't found the answer. Doubt, ignorance and confusion make me restless. But even so, I don't want to go back to my comfort zone. My comfort zone is gone. I've recovered from that fucking travesty last Friday, and Arnaq and I have decided to deal with our restlessness. Hope has returned from the dead, popping up like the devil. All I need is to see her briefly. Because I need to get to grips with my desperate brain.

'What have you bought?' I ask Arnaq as she walks in.

'A bottle of vodka and some mixers,' she answers in a breezy voice.

'A whole bottle? That'll kill us!'

'What did you get?' she says.

'Four beers.'

'Four beers? I'll teach you how to party!' she laughs. Maybe she thinks she should be proud of herself for always being shitfaced. I know I don't want to get drunk and I will prove it. She's fucking well not going to drag *me* down with her.

'Four shots of vodka!' I shout through a crowd of people to the bartender.

'Four?' asks Arnaq happily.

'It's on me!'

Because I haven't seen hope yet. I want to escape that horrible disappointment. I want to get shitfaced! I want to party till I'm invincible! But things are looking up as my favourite song comes on in the bar: 'Crimson and Clover' by Joan Jett and the Blackhearts.

'Arnaq, where will the after-party be when it closes?'

She isn't listening to me. Maybe she's fucking delirious.

Fucking delirious.

'Fia! Did I tell you I was crazy about a woman? Do you remember that?'

I nod.

'Don't look now! There's a woman with short hair right behind you. It's *her*!'

I turn my head slowly. Am excited to see a lesbian but immediately disappointed at what I see. Apart from her beautiful face, she has the body of a man. Without the sausage.

'Wouldn't it just be the same as being with a man?' I ask her jokingly.

'Oh fuck, but she's so sweet! I'd marry her if she didn't have a girlfriend.'

'Has she got a girlfriend?' I ask.

'Ugh, yes. She's here. She's coming over,' she says, surprised.

I turn my head calmly so that nobody notices. Sara. Then I grind to a halt. I'm now running on hope.

I admit it: for the first time in my life I'm feeling something very powerful. I don't think I can escape it. I'm about to enter new territory and I'm horrified. I'm about to cross the line but I can't stop. What is it I feel? Lust. How do you say lust in Greenlandic? It's risky. It's *very* risky. I just can't stop until I get what I want, I don't *want* to give up. It's *that* taboo. My body's struggling to survive, and I'm fighting to breathe because I'm being smothered. I can feel my lungs fighting to keep up. I want her. I'll go mad if I don't have her. Lust. My pulse rises. My blood begins to flow again. After three years, arisen from the dead, ascended into heaven. Or down? I don't give a shit. I've come alive! Jesus, welcome back to life!

'Hi,' says Sara, brushing my back with her hand. Suddenly I can't figure out what to say and give her a broad smile instead. I want so much to kiss her that I can hardly control myself. 'Crimson and Clover' is still playing in the background, giving us the perfect soundtrack.

'Are things okay with you?' I think she asks me.

'Yes, I'm fine. How about you?'

Am positively surprised at my answer and feel safe.

'Fine, thanks,' she answers. 'Nice meeting you the other day.'

'Same here. It's nice to see you,' I hear my heart say.

She smiles and seems charmed by my reply but then straightens her back when she sees Arnaq next to me.

'We were on our way home. See you again soon,' she says.

No, fuck no, please don't leave me, stay by my side, don't go away. Let me touch you, let me kiss you, let me take you home to my place, no fucking way, no, don't disappear, you'll smash me into a million pieces if you disappear, you'll knock me down just when I've finally stood up, you're killing me now that I've come alive again, please, oh God please, don't leave me again.

'Where are you off to?' I hear myself say, but the person I'm talking to doesn't hear me. She's left me. My survival instinct kicks in. Need to survive. I feel the need. The need to survive. I turn towards Arnaq.

'Fia, did you hook up with Sara?' she asks me, covering her mouth.

I remain silent as she begins to stare at me and I can no longer keep my secret.

'No, we haven't been together...'

'Since when have you been attracted to women? Wh-what's going on?' she stutters and laughs.

I feel the need. 'How about we get out of here?'

She gives me a confused look. I look her in the eye. She's no longer confused. She's turned on. Feels the need too.

Through a crowd of people, making a beeline for a taxi, towards Qinngorput, a new area of Nuuk, our hands touching, my heart's racing, it hurts, sexual attraction, animal behaviour, survival, silence on the way in, awkward opening the door, have you brought your keys, she passes me, touching my body with hers. She's willing, she's hot, thinks I'm hot too, don't know what I am but I am drunk, 'Let's go to my room,' she says gently, puts me down on her bed, can hardly, don't know how I'm to begin, thank goodness for Arnaq, she calls the shots, strips off in front of me, her stomach, bra, thighs, new sight, dark sensation, my body says it's right, my brain's in doubt, she's coming closer, climbs on top of me, 'Do you really want to?' she asks, 'Is it okay?' I ask, she comes closer, her breathing is getting heavier, what I see is beautiful, fragile, want to touch but am unable to, tremble, she's my friend, don't want my friend but her body, I want another woman, but I replace her with Arnaq, an *arnaq,* my thoughts are moving fast, time stands still, her lips touch, first my neck then my lips, she has no beard, doesn't sting, she's soft, lovely, but she's Arnaq and not Sara, but that's okay because she's an *arnaq,* a woman, everything moves inside me, remember now that this is how it feels down below, it tickles, I look up at Arnaq, can hardly believe, 'Are you wet?' she asks, I say 'Yes' and ask her whether it's okay, 'It's okay, you just follow me,' she says, can no longer recognise the Arnaq I know, kiss Arnaq, the hot girl, kiss the holy *arnaq* again, the holy woman, our hands take off clothes, our bodies, our skin, touch each other, her hand brushes, reaches where, the next thing is what I fear, but I move my hand, am able to because it's not Peter, reach the place, discover that it's not a sausage, I confirm because it's not a sausage, I confirm that I like it, have found my answer.

I wake up relieved that Arnaq isn't there and hurry into my bedroom. I don't know what to feel about last night's revelation. Strange that it was Arnaq. Yet not strange that it was a woman.

I'm scared of last night's revelation. My dream of getting out of my comfort zone has been fulfilled, and I have no idea what to do. Last night answered many of my questions, and my heart aches in a way I've never known before. I confirm what I can't get out of my mind. I'll have to tell Sara. I'm suffering. But I'd rather feel pain than not feel anything. I take a piece of paper and start writing; what I feel, the things I want to do to her, how sweet she is… The words come to me from the song – our song – 'Crimson and Clover'.

*

Sara. One woman. Two weeks of fantasies. Thousands of unspoken words. Millions of questions. Thoughts and emotions that rush towards infinity. Hours slowing down. My numb self can feel again. My fantasies become stronger. I no longer doubt my existence. Only I haven't seen her again. The spring night is bright, quiet. Now and then some drunk people pass by. Have been lying in my bed for hours and I don't think I can fall asleep. All of this has blown me wide open and I have to tell somebody. I begin to long for my little brother. I ignore the time and give him a call as he's always supportive.

'Hi,' he says.

He's with a crowd of people by the sound of it.

'Hi, am I disturbing you?' I ask him in a voice that is loud but a bit croaky because I haven't spoken all day.

'No, wait a moment. I'll go outside.'

'That's okay. I'll call you back tomorrow.'

'No, I've just gone out. Are you okay?' he says. It's quieter now.

'I'm fine. I just miss you.'

Just listening to his voice makes me almost burst into tears.

'I miss you too. It's good to hear from you. I really want to see you.'

'What are you doing?'

'We're at an after-party. My friend invited me yesterday evening, and we went into town.'

'Hope it's fun.'

Don't know what else to do so I start to say goodbye.

'Come and join me,' he says enthusiastically. 'I'll pay for the taxi.'

Find the thought of drinking off-putting but accept the invitation so that I can get out. I'll only fester if I stay here.

I arrive in a taxi and see that my brother's waiting to pay my fare. The strange feeling inside me fades as I give him a hug, and I'm ready to tell him what's happened. It's about time. The first step. My life will change, I can feel it. We enter one of the many blocks of flats, and on the staircase I already smell cigarette smoke and hear music and laughter. I feel awkward because I'm not drunk but am comfortable with my brother, who's standing next to me. We walk towards the living room and pass some drunken people. We meet a crowd of young people sitting on sofas, and I look around for someone I might recognise.

It really *was* love at first sight. I'm now absolutely sure that she sees me. It's true that I've met Love. I see that she knows it too when her eyes meet mine. I acknowledge that she has also acknowledged it when she walks over to me and gives me a smile. I fetch the paper out of my pocket and give it to her. Because words can't explain or describe. I give her my heart. She reads it, looks me straight in the eye, moves away from me, and my heart stops. Sara, you've won my heart... And she picks up a guitar. We look at one another among dancing bodies. Sara; my heart... Sara, my heart.

She sings. Our song. Which is precisely when my heart begins again. Beats once more. It was *meant* to be. It was meant to be you. It was meant to be me and you. She walks over to me, and my world is totally silent. I only look at her, and the sensation within me is infinite. She takes hold of me and escorts me out of the door, and I don't resist. The spring night is invigorating. Nature has quietly come to life again, and that's all I hear. There's something beautiful in front of me. From Greenland to infinity, and back again... What a day to be alive. She reads the note I have been carrying around for two weeks. The spring night gives me life, and Sara kisses me. What a day to realise I'm not dead. Love has rescued me. And I realise that this is my coming-out story.

'Crimson and Clover,' she says.
    'Over and over,' I reply.

Translated by Anna Halager

ACKNOWLEDGEMENTS

I would like to express my sincere thanks to:

Roz Kaveney for her advice, for our meandering conversations, her flashes of brilliance and her extraordinary humanity.

Sam Wells for his invaluable help in a number of aspects of this book.

Lawrence Schimel for so many suggestions, recommendations and submissions that they could have made an anthology in their own right.

I am grateful to my editor Clare Gordon for her encouragement, her support and her patience, and to my agent Matthew Marland for seeing the book into safe harbour.

Above all I would like to thank those readers/writers/editors whose suggestions, advice and dire warnings crucially informed my reading and shaped the present anthology. Among them, I owe particular thanks to translators who led me to discover queer writers and poets from a host of different countries and cultures and from many different eras – without their contribution, my reading, and this book would have been inestimably poorer.

My thanks to: Ravi Mirchandani, George Henson, Andy Houwen, Mara Gerety, Peter Bush, Roz Schwartz, Aron Aji, Sophie Hughes, Carolina Orloff, Nichola Smalley, Jeffrey Zuckerman, Ulla Lauridsen, James

Kates, Jamie Richards, Rebecca DeWald, Mark Weiss, Shabnam Nadiya, Ruth Ahmedzai Kemp, Diane Arnson Svarlien, Charlotte Whittle, Sophie Rebecca Lewis, Geoff Brock, Carol O'Sullivan, Dennis Dybeck, Gerry Dunn, Jennifer Feeley, Tsipi Keller, Tony Chambers, Brian Bergstrom, Jeremy Tiang, Rosalind Harvey, Corine Tachtiris, Ed Moreno, Hilah Kohen, Shengchi Hsu, Johanna Bishop, Sean Bye, Annie McDermott, Eric M.B. Becker, Antoinette Fawcett, Milena Deleva, Adriana X Jacobs, David Auerbach, Katherine Young, Samantha Pious, Laurel Ann Taylor, Katherine Adams, Camilla Lu Chen and Mattho Mandersloot.

EXTENDED COPYRIGHT